# Global DifFusion

Magical Fusion

Book 4

Jonathan Brooks

Cover Design: Yvonne Less, Art 4 Artists
Edited by: Ellen Klowden

Copyright ©2024 Jonathan Brooks

All rights reserved. No part of this publication may be reproduced, distributed, or transmitted in any form or by any means, including photocopying, recording, or other electronic or mechanical methods, without the prior written permission of the publisher.

The following is a work of fiction. Any names, characters, businesses, corporations, places, and events are products of the author's imagination or used in a fictitious manner. Any resemblance to any actual persons, places, or events is purely coincidental.

Cover Design Copyright ©2024 Yvonne Less, Art 4 Artists

# Acknowledgements

I would like to thank all my Patrons on Patreon who are supporting me through my writing endeavors, while also giving me valuable feedback on my works-in-progress!

In addition, I want to thank everyone on Royal Road and my beta-readers for helping me make this the best book it can be!

**Aaron Wiley**
**Brett Siegel**
**Grant Harrell**
**James Boyles**
**Kelly Linzey**

# Table of Contents

Acknowledgements ... 3
Recap ... 6
Chapter 1 ... 10
Chapter 2 ... 16
Chapter 3 ... 22
Chapter 4 ... 29
Chapter 5 ... 36
Chapter 6 ... 43
Chapter 7 ... 51
Chapter 8 ... 59
Chapter 9 ... 66
Chapter 10 ... 72
Chapter 11 ... 80
Chapter 12 ... 87
Chapter 13 ... 95
Chapter 14 ... 102
Chapter 15 ... 110
Chapter 16 ... 118
Chapter 17 ... 126
Chapter 18 ... 132
Chapter 19 ... 140
Chapter 20 ... 146
Chapter 21 ... 155
Chapter 22 ... 161
Chapter 23 ... 169
Chapter 24 ... 176
Chapter 25 ... 182
Chapter 26 ... 188
Chapter 27 ... 197
Chapter 28 ... 205
Chapter 29 ... 212
Chapter 30 ... 219
Chapter 31 ... 227
Chapter 32 ... 234
Chapter 33 ... 242
Chapter 34 ... 250
Chapter 35 ... 257
Chapter 36 ... 266
Chapter 37 ... 273
Chapter 38 ... 281

| | |
|---|---|
| Chapter 39 | 288 |
| Chapter 40 | 295 |
| Chapter 41 | 302 |
| Chapter 42 | 309 |
| Chapter 43 | 317 |
| Chapter 44 | 324 |
| Chapter 45 | 331 |
| Chapter 46 | 337 |
| Chapter 47 | 343 |
| Chapter 48 | 353 |
| Chapter 49 | 361 |
| Chapter 50 | 369 |
| Chapter 51 | 380 |
| Chapter 52 | 387 |
| Chapter 53 | 394 |
| Chapter 54 | 406 |
| Chapter 55 | 415 |
| Chapter 56 | 422 |
| Chapter 57 | 429 |
| Chapter 58 | 437 |
| Chapter 59 | 444 |
| Chapter 60 | 450 |
| Chapter 61 | 457 |
| Epilogue | 464 |
| Final Stats | 472 |
| Author's Note | 476 |
| Books by Jonathan Brooks | 478 |

# Recap

Larek Holsten had his entire world turned upside-down when he was accused of trying to kill the Headman's daughter, but that was only the start of his new life. After witnessing a Scission attack on a nearby town, the former Logger was discovered to have the potential to wield a magic he never wanted; as a result of this discovery, he was ordered to attend Crystalview Academy upon the threat of death if he didn't comply.

Along his journey to the Academy, the sheltered teenager learned more about the world than he ever knew existed – though not all of it was good. The prejudice that the common people held toward his height weighed upon him, even though he knew it wasn't something he could do anything about. This prejudice continued after he arrived at Crystalview, though it wasn't quite as intense as he feared; it helped that he learned a little about *why* everyone born in the Kingdom reacted to him the way they did – even if it wasn't fair. Unfortunately, that was the least of his problems.

What he had to worry about instead was his own inability to cast a spell, thanks to his initial efforts that literally blew up in his face. On the other hand, he also discovered that the accidental permanence to his spell patterns was actually beneficial when it came to creating Fusions. Not only that, some strange fluke gave Larek incredibly high starting stats that far outstripped anything a normal Fusionist – even a Grandmaster – could apply toward the formation of Fusions, and his instinctual understanding of their creation put him head-and-shoulders above everyone else.

But Larek also had a secret that he didn't dare to share with anyone. In a world where those with magical potential only became Mages or Martials, who were those with ability to manipulate Stama internally, the former Logger had the ability to become *both*. This came to a head when the Academy was attacked from inside the city and Larek was forced to unlock a Martial Battle Art in the heat of the fight, though he had no control over the process.

Unfortunately, after the battle against the Scissions, his *Fusions* Professor was found to have been killed, and Larek was jointly blamed for the explosion of hundreds of *Healing Surge* Fusions on the roof of the Academy along with the now-deceased Professor, as well as the temporary comas that many of the Mages suffered as a result of using these healing Fusions that Larek created. As a punishment, the Dean of Crystalview decided to send him away to Copperleaf Academy far to the south, along with his friends and a group of first-years that were left without a place to stay as a result of the explosion.

Escorted south by a caravan run by Merchants, Larek and the other transfer students were attacked by Bog Goblins, which eventually led to the Fusionist revealing some of his abilities and even his Status to multiple people – his friends included. After finally hitching a ride on the SIC Transportation Network, which was comprised of giant carriages pulled by equally large Canniks, Larek was able to experiment a little more with his Fusions by creating some physical stat boosts for the Martial trainee graduates that were accompanying them on their journey.

Overall, traveling south was largely uneventful besides allowing Larek to expand his capabilities as a Fusionist, but his introduction to Copperleaf Academy certainly was not. To his good fortune, his studies included an *Advanced Fusions* class with Grandmaster Fusionist Shinpai, who agreed to teach him after learning about Larek's obscenely high Pattern Cohesion and Mana regeneration rates, as well as his ability to make extremely strong and near-permanent Fusions.

Unfortunately, the ecstatic student Fusionist had caught the eye of multiple parties due to completely different reasons. First, his height was noticed by a particular Noble named Ricardo, who ended up capturing and torturing him in order to discover if something catastrophic called "The Culmination" was occurring. During that interrogation, Larek also learned that he was likely something called a half-breed, which was a half-human and half-Gergasi or half-"Great One" – the race of giants that used Dominion magic to enslave the people of the Kingdom, and were still enslaving the Nobles to that day.

Healing and then freeing himself through the use of Fusions, Larek ensured Ricardo and his two Martial trainee helpers couldn't spread the news about his origins and also protected his family from harm by eliminating all three of them and hiding the bodies. That wasn't the only complication to his existence at Copperleaf Academy, however.

Through helping an injured Martial trainee one day, Larek accidentally revealed that he had a Fusion that could heal people – and those in charge of Fort Pinevalley wanted it. Unfortunately, sharing that kind of thing would also likely reveal his dual nature as both a Mage and a Martial, but the choice was taken out of his hands as he was essentially forced to compete in the upcoming Skirmish.

To prepare for the set of competitions that pitted teams of Mages and Martials against each other, Larek created some powerful defensive Fusions for his team to use. Penelope, the blue-haired

Martial trainee that had caused the Fort to start looking into Larek more than he cared for, was their team leader. Other members were two other Martials named Bartholomew and Vivienne, as well as a fifth-year Mage student, Kimble. Nedira joined the team that was expected to fail spectacularly because they barely had any time to practice together, but they managed to pull off wins through the competition because of Larek's powerful contributions.

After his team was accused of cheating with Larek's Fusions, it was revealed by Dean Lorraine to the entirety of the Academy and Fort that Larek was a Fusion prodigy, a person who was able to create Fusions better than anyone else in the world.

This revelation, along with their win at the Skirmish, led to Larek becoming quite famous at Copperleaf Academy. With that fame came new dangers along with new responsibilities, and Larek was tasked with creating Fusion after Fusion for the SIC, as directed by Grandmaster Fusionist Shinpai and by the Dean. Despite everything he was creating, he was never able to figure out how to improve his Skills to the point where he could make Advanced Fusions.

While experimenting with some new ideas, Larek figured out how to create a healing Fusion that would work for non-Martials as well as a brand-new Skill that had never been seen before: *Focused Division*. Because learning this new Skill could help with spellcasting, he was tasked to help teach the faculty of the Academy; unfortunately, his Dominion magic ended up being used to impart the information to the faculty, almost killing him in the process.

Shortly after starting the new school year, the Academy and Fort was visited by a Gergasi, who demanded of the Dean and the Vice General to bring his child to him. Discovering that this Lord Vilnesh was his father, Larek and his companions were led by Shinpai to an escape tunnel after the Dean and Vice General were killed. With a significant amount of money from his created Fusions and instructions to go to Silverledge Academy and Fort Ironwall, they fled as quickly as possible while staying out of sight, fighting monsters as they made their way through the countryside. After their first major battle, Larek unlocked the ability to absorb Aetheric Force, which could be used to increase his maximum Skill levels.

Saving a group of SIC members, Larek and his companions accompanied them to the overcrowded town of Whittleton, which had seen an influx of refugees fleeing the appearance of monsters all over the Kingdom. Having seen and heard about the powerful Fusions that Larek had created for his friends, the Major in charge of the local SIC force believed that they would be better utilized by her forces and arranged for them to be taken from Larek and his group, potentially even turning them in as deserters. In an attempt to appease them, Larek made Fusions for the entire SIC force, but that apparently wasn't enough, as the group of companions was ambushed when leaving the town.

Having foreknowledge of the ambush, the Fusionist turned the tables on them and forced them to leave without anyone getting hurt. Just when they were departing, something appeared nearby that immediately put everyone on alert; the appearance of an Aperture, what could almost be called a permanent Scission, was a great cause for concern.

Nearly killing himself and everyone else who went to destroy, and inevitably close, the Aperture, Larek and his companions were unprepared when another Gergasi appeared out of the sky. Chinli, the Gergasi, promised to spare his friends (who had their memory wiped of all knowledge of Larek) if the Fusionist agreed to come along without a fight, and with great reluctance, he agreed. Unfortunately, along their flight back to the Enclave, they were attacked by Warped Void Hunters, and during the battle, Larek was pulled into a void; when he could perceive the world again, he found himself transported to an entirely different land.

During his struggle to free himself from the lake where he fell, Larek finally unlocked his Martial side, going so far as to have obtained the *Stama Subjugation* Skill – though he still didn't have any idea how to properly use it. Finding his way to a nearby town, he quickly learned that he was not in the Kingdom of Androthe anymore, but was instead somewhere called the Sealance Empire, which was apparently a long way from home.

Now, Larek has to find a way back to the Kingdom, sooner rather than later, so he can rejoin his companions…

…and possibly save the world while he's at it.

# Chapter 1

"I'm really not comfortable with this," Larek whispered to the Protector sneaking through the underbrush next to him. They, of course, were much more adept at maneuvering through the familiar – to them – terrain without making noise when compared to the tall Fusionist, but he had to admit that he was a lot better at watching where he put his own feet than he used to be. Whether it was due to watching Vivienne glide through just about any environment like a shadow or through his own awareness of his lack of subtlety in movement, Larek was *slowly* improving.

Fortunately, their prey wasn't a hyper-alert horde of monsters that could hear him trampling his way through the brush from a mile away. Unfortunately, the reason they weren't hunting monsters was because their targets were... people. Not just random people on the street, because that would be ridiculous; no, these were people that apparently *deserved* to be hunted down and killed, based on their heinous actions. It wasn't the reason or reasons that these "bandits" hiding in the strange forest near the town of Enderflow needed to be killed that bothered him, though.

It was the whole killing people part that he wasn't comfortable with.

Granted, he had killed people before – namely Ricardo and the two Martial trainees who had captured and basically tortured him for their own pleasure – but he could argue with himself that it was self-defense. The fact that it was self-defense *after* he had already escaped was irrelevant to him; their knowledge of him as a half-breed Gergasi had been too dangerous to let them go free, as it could harm him even further than the physical injuries that they had inflicted upon him. Revenge for how they treated him played a small part in his actions, as well, but it had primarily been about ensuring his own future safety.

At least, that had been his own internal justification at the time that their deaths occurred. It had been before he had been discovered by the Dean and his *Fusions* Professor, who figured out his secret with seeming ease, so it seemed reasonable at the time. It was only later that he considered if it was even necessary, as he was sure that the powerful Dean would've been able to do something about the three who had captured and hurt him. But then he remembered what they did to him and his roommates... and decided that even if he knew about everything that happened afterwards, he would still do it all again. As callous as it might seem, he concluded that they *deserved* what was done to them.

Just as these so-called "bandits" apparently deserved what was coming to them. Thieves and murderers was what he was told they were, accosting travelers and caravans that traveled from elsewhere in the Empire of Sealance to and from the town of Enderflow. While he didn't have the best relationship with caravans and the Merchants that led them, these bandits were taking all of their goods and killing everyone accompanying the wagons. Or so it was assumed, as there was no trace of any bodies left after the caravans were ambushed and the people were never seen again. It was only after a single caravan guard managed to escape and get word to the Protectors in Enderflow that knowledge of where these ambushes were taking place was even discovered.

All of which led to Larek creeping through the forest filled with odd trees as part of a force of over two dozen Protectors from town.

"It doesn't matter if you're comfortable with this or not, Martial Larek," the woman behind the helmet hissed back at him in an annoyed whisper. Protector Ashlynn had essentially been his prison guard since he arrived at Enderflow nearly a week prior, despite the fact that he wasn't... exactly... a prisoner. "This is what you have to do to work off your obligation."

Obligation. Otherwise known as the punishment he had to endure for injuring an Ectorian; more specifically, breaking the wrist and lower arm of an Ectorian named Gwest, who made the unfortunate mistake of thinking Larek was dead and attempted to take the Fusionist's belongings. It was an accident on both sides, as Larek could certainly imagine his semi-conscious body appearing to be deceased at the time, while his own reaction had probably been a bit more violent than absolutely needed in order to demonstrate that he still lived.

Healing Gwest with the aid of the *Healing Surge* Fusion on his robe – once Larek was able to shove a heaping of exotic foods down his throat to recover his energy – had gone a long way to absolving his obligation toward the rag-wearing scavenger, but he soon found that it hadn't been quite enough. That turned out to be because the Ectorians, one of the two races living in the Empire, were fiercely protected, and anyone caught harming one of them was prosecuted severely.

He still wasn't exactly sure of the relationship between the rag-wearing, lighter-skinned Ectorians with their strange way of speech and the darker-skinned Brolencians, who made up the rest of the population and who generally seemed to be in charge of everything in town. At first, he thought it might be some sort of servant or even a slave type situation, which immediately put him on edge thinking about the Gergasi back in the Kingdom, but that didn't seem to be the case once he investigated further. Instead, the people in charge treated the Ectorians like some sort of hard-working little brothers that needed to be protected from anyone or anything that might choose to do them harm.

Regardless of their social relationship, the end result was that Larek was still to be punished for what he had done, despite his best efforts to try to eliminate the problem with his healing. It certainly helped to reduce what they were calling his "obligation" from 5 years of hard labor to only a month of service with the Protectors in Enderflow, so he guessed that it was better than nothing.

For the first few days, there wasn't much for Larek to do other than rest in the same building he had been brought to when he first arrived, where he ate even more to aid in his recovery; thankfully, he wasn't required to pay for the food he consumed because of his obligatory service with the Protectors, though with the amount he ate he was sure they would've preferred to charge him. The lack of pressing business was interrupted when the caravan guard appeared and relayed the information on the "bandits" nearby, and he finally got called up to fulfill his obligation.

"I'm well aware, but I'm just not as comfortable killing other people as I am monsters," Larek replied. That was the biggest hangup he had concerning his role in accompanying the Protectors on their search for the bandits; it was the fact that they didn't do anything to *him*, *his friends*, or *his family* that prevented him from being alright with their deaths — especially since he might be the one who dealt that fate to them.

*Then again, why is it fine for me to kill monsters? Is it because they are more likely to attack and kill innocent people due to their nature, so it's the job of the SIC to stop them? If that's the case, then how are these bandits different from the monsters back in the Kingdom? Based on the information I've been given regarding their activities, I'd be helping the people of the Empire by ensuring they are no longer a threat.*

For some reason, this justification for their deaths still didn't sit well with him. He could understand the necessity, as the only other option was perhaps to imprison them for a lengthy amount of time, but it felt wrong. Perhaps he was a hypocrite because these bandits didn't directly affect *him*, but Larek couldn't see it any other way—

Having not really paid attention to where he was going, as he was watching his feet more than the area around him, he was momentarily startled when a hand closed around his right arm and held him in place.  Stopping his movement, he looked over curiously at Protector Ashlynn, but other than her leather glove-covered hand on his arm, she wasn't paying attention to him.  Rather, her helmeted face was peering ahead.

As soon as Larek obtained a glimpse of a large clearing ahead and heard the voices that he'd somehow ignored until that point, including the screams of those who were suffering incredibly painful tortures at the hands of these so-called bandits, all his reservations about killing these people faded away.

It didn't matter that he didn't personally know her or was not directly affected by the way one woman was stripped bare, had a rag shoved into her mouth, and then was whipped to within an inch of her life before a metal collar was slipped over her neck; it mattered naught that he had no specific knowledge of the man who had his feet smashed into masses of flesh and bone to prevent him from running away; and it certainly made no difference if, before he came there, he wasn't even aware of the two small children that were—

Feeling a sudden upwelling inside of his chest as he watched the gruesome scene underway along the clearing, all that Larek could now focus on were the dirty, sadistic men – and women – wearing a variety of dark brown and green clothing that was likely designed to help blend them into the strange forest.  They needed to be stopped, no matter what.

"Here's the plan—" Larek heard the beginnings of the whisper next to him, but he was already gone.  With his best friend in his hand eager to spill blood, the enraged Fusionist took off toward the clearing without a whit of tactics in his movements, as the only thing he could think of was killing these heinous people.

As he felt his strength suddenly increase substantially in a moment, he vaguely realized he had activated his *Furious Rampage* Battle Art without conscious thought.  He was too enraged to analyze how he did it, or even how the Stama in his chest reacted to his use of the Art, but that wasn't exactly what was important to him at the moment.  What was important was closing the distance between himself and the first of the bandits, who was in the process of committing unspeakable acts on children.

He felt another surge of energy flare through his chest and do something to his body, but he was too riled up to comprehend what it was.  His feet, which had already been pounding along the ground with incredible speed as they utilized his Agility of 83, felt as if they might fall off as his pace increased.  He was running so fast, in fact, that as he approached his target, the man seemed to move in slow motion.  Eyes turned toward him a fraction of a second before his axe came around in a sweep as he passed by the despicable man; Larek was both pleased and unsatisfied as the blade of his best friend passed completely through the arms and upper torso of the bandit, sheering lengthwise through what was essentially his shoulders.

He was pleased because he had managed to bisect the deplorable man, shearing through his clothing, his upper arm bones, his upper ribcage, and his spine all in one blow – and he barely felt any resistance. The sensation was patently unlike killing monsters back in the Kingdom, as he realized that most of them had at least some sort of natural resistance to damage that this bandit did not.

Larek was also unsatisfied for two reasons. The first one was something he aimed to rectify soon: This was just the first of his targets, and his *Furious Rampage* demanded more. Already moving toward the next horrid person in his sights, who was still perceptually moving as if they were trying to fight through an extremely dense gelatin, he knew the demand would be satisfied soon.

The second reason he was unsatisfied was because he had been aiming for the man's neck in order to decapitate him.

His aim was off because he wasn't used to the sudden burst of speed, as well as being unused to fully utilizing his Martial stats in general. Even as he barreled toward his next target, he could feel himself starting to lose control, and not because of his *Furious Rampage* – which was starting to mess with his focus as everything gained a red tint in his vision. He could feel himself slipping away, similar to what had happened back at Crystalview when he first unlocked the Battle Art. He was holding on to his focus as much as he could, but he was starting to lose control – which was the last thing he needed when he could barely handle his body with all his stats how they were. It hadn't seemed to be a problem before, but with his Strength stat doubled and his Body stat reduced by 30% due to *Furious Rampage*, as well as what he did to increase his speed, it was feeling all out of sorts.

His balance was so off that when he went to turn toward his new target, he stumbled slightly, meaning that when he finally reached the scraggly bearded man holding a whip, he smashed right into him instead of chopping him in half like he had intended. The impact of his chest against the head of the bandit was so great that he felt a rib snap in the process – but the other man got it so much worse. Not only did the bandit's neck snap instantly, but his head caved in and then half-exploded outward in a spray of disgusting blood, skull fragments, and brain matter that covered the front of Larek's robe.

The unexpected impact caused Larek to lose his balance completely, and he fell into a jumble of arms and legs as he became entangled in the corpse of the man he just killed. It was at that point that he felt whatever speed increase he had just used wear off, and by the time he picked himself up, time seemed to return to normal. Two arrows suddenly impacted him as he focused in on his next target, punching into his robe but not breaking through because of the *Multi-Resistance Cloth +9* Fusion on it, though it also made him belatedly realize that he hadn't activated his *Repelling Barrier*.

When he tried to focus on it in order to activate it, something interfered – as if it didn't want him to turn the Fusion on. The complete failure to activate his Fusion brought his working mind up short as the *Furious Rampage* took over control, until Larek was left as a spectator of his own body as it tore across the clearing toward one of the archers that had deigned to fire upon him. They attempted to run, but they were no match for his normal speed, even without whatever he had done earlier. As he witnessed himself strike out at the bow-wielding bandit and cut through her chest, he could only observe in horror as the initial strike was apparently not enough. A follow-up flurry of chops completely dismembered the woman, leaving her in a dozen different pieces scattered along the blood-soaked ground.

His awareness of everything after that was disjointed, even as he felt his body starting to break down slightly from the Battle Art for some reason, as if it was harming him physically. The brief flashes of awareness were disturbing as he continued to rampage against the bandits, even as the occasional attack by an arrow or sword-strike hit against his exposed skin. Eventually, the bandits, apparently seeing that he was unstoppable, started to flee – but he was too fast. Larek hunted them all down one by one, his *Furious Rampage* activating several times over the 5 minutes it took to clear the bandit encampment – all of which Larek had no control over in the slightest. Finally, with the last one dead, the fury and rage that had infused his body drained out like a hole being opened in the bottom of a bathtub, and a weakness that had been building for a while slammed into his body and mind, knocking him out cold.

# Chapter 2

"I don't care what kind of obligation he has toward Enderflow, Magistrate. He's too dangerous to work with."

"Be that as it may, he got the job done, didn't he?"

"Well, yes, but there's a difference between 'getting the job done' and what *he* did. Not only did he not follow orders, which put the prisoners in danger, but he didn't leave any of the bandits alive to tell us if they were working alone or if they had contacts elsewhere. From our preliminary investigation, there is a fairly good chance that the victims from previous caravans had been trafficked somewhere; unfortunately, we have no leads as to where they went."

Larek drowsily awakened to the conversation he was hearing in the background, and it was only when he was fully conscious that he comprehended what was being said. Memories of his "righteous" rampage against the despicable bandits flowed through his mind as he kept his eyes closed, and he mentally shrunk back as he remembered bits and pieces of what he ended up doing to those people. While he still felt as though they deserved it for what they were doing to their victims, the conversation made him aware that he had messed up. And messed up *badly*.

Not only had he put the victims in danger by acting out as he did, as the bandits could've killed their victims when they saw him coming, but he also killed any of them that may have been able to shed light on their illicit activities. It hadn't occurred to him at the time that what they were doing to their victims wasn't unique, and that they had been selling people to what he could only assume were slavers of some kind. He'd heard that those who dealt in slavery existed in some of the fringe nations and empires of the world, but hadn't thought he'd ever come face-to-face with it; the forced magical slavery imposed upon the Nobles of the Kingdom was more than enough interaction with the horrible practice as it was.

"Be that as it may, if we forgive his obligation, it will set a precedent we can ill afford, Protector Ashlynn. He must serve out the rest of his service with the Protectors... though you can certainly choose *how* he will participate." There was a momentary silence as the voice that Larek recognized as the one who had questioned him when he first arrived in Enderflow shuffled around for a moment. "Regardless, he's still your responsibility, so do what you can to keep him in line, for just a short while longer."

Larek heard footsteps walking away, followed by another set coming closer.

"You can stop pretending, Martial Larek; I can tell that you're awake."

Hearing Protector Ashlynn's tired-sounding voice, he opened his eyes to find himself lying in a familiar-feeling bed in a room he recognized as the one he had been staying in since he arrived at Enderflow. How he ended up there, he had no idea, though he could only assume he had been carried back from the bandits' camp and thrown in his room when he proved to be unconscious.

Turning his head, he saw the Protector – and she appeared just as tired as she sounded. Dark circles under her eyes, a frown that looked permanently etched onto her face, and what appeared to be old blood still covering a part of her leg armor that hadn't been cleaned up led to an entire package that screamed exhaustion and impatience. With a sigh, she gazed at him with dead-looking eyes.

"I take it you heard my conversation with the Magistrate?" she asked, and he nodded. "I meant it when I said that you're too dangerous to work with. Sure, you're strong – there's no denying that – but you're undisciplined, reckless, and somehow this is the worst of all, *untrained*. We watched you essentially charge into the clearing with apparently no brain in that head of yours, throwing yourself all over the place with no sign of any skill or even a plan. I don't know how they do things in the Kingdom, but as far as I can tell, you don't have even the slightest bit of training. By all that is holy, how you haven't died yet, I'm truly perplexed."

Larek struggled to sit up, the weakness in his body just as present as the last time he inadvertently used his Battle Art, though he wasn't quite as hungry as he expected.

"I apologize for my behavior," he began as soon as he was able to sit up. Looking down, he was happy to see that he was still wearing his robe, though his axe was currently leaning up against the wall out of reach. "I've yet to formally begin my training as a Martial and haven't developed any... control. I wasn't aware that such a thing would happen, however, or I would've warned you. It was seeing what they were doing to those people that set me off—"

"I take it that you've never seen anything similar before?" the Protector suddenly asked, interrupting him.

He shook his head.

"Unfortunately, it happens from time to time with us being so far to the western portion of the Empire," she explained. "This portion of the Empire was only claimed from the wilds a few decades ago, when slavery was more prevalent than it is now. It wasn't exactly lawful, as it isn't now, but in the wilds... Well, 'anything goes' is a common saying when speaking about unclaimed lands. This isn't the first bandit group that we've uncovered continuing the practice, though its methods were a bit more... *extreme* than what we've seen before."

For such a thing to be so common that it didn't seem to faze the woman was unconscionable to the Fusionist, but then again, his own Kingdom had a slavery problem – even if most of the people didn't know about it. Regardless, he had done what he could to at least stop what was happening with that current group of bandits, even if he had gone about it in completely the wrong way.

"Again, I apologize for my actions; it won't happen again."

"You bet it won't, because I'm not taking you out ever again. You may have to complete your obligation to the town, but I'm not going to put my people at risk if you suddenly lose control like that in the future. As far as I'm concerned, as soon as your time is up, I want you gone before the day is out."

She spoke a bit harsher than he would've wished, but he couldn't deny that it was probably for the best. If Larek was faced with another situation like what had just happened, he wasn't sure if he'd be able to prevent the same thing occurring again.

"Then what do you want me to do?" he asked.

She just waved at him still in the bed. "Nothing, for now. Rest up since you were unconscious when we dragged you back in here – which was no easy feat, by the way – so I assume whatever it was you did back there had some adverse effects."

"How long was I out, by the way?"

Protector Ashlynn thought about it for a second or two. "From the point when you collapsed to when you woke up, I'd say that it was approximately 12 hours. The wounds you had sustained during your chaotic frenzy of poor decisions seemed to be healed before we even secured the caravan victims, so you don't have to worry about having been bedridden for days."

That reminded him. "What about, uh, how are the victims? Do they need further healing?" While he didn't have any *Graduated Parahealing* Fusions on him, he still had the *Healing Surge* one on his robe that would help with some of the injuries. Anything too bad would likely end up with them in a coma, but at least they would be better.

"Most of them weren't too bad, compared to what you saw that set you off; either they were being saved from being tortured because they were to be used for something else or they just hadn't been selected yet. As for the others, they have already been seen to and will require extensive recuperation. Most of the damage, unfortunately, is to their minds because of the terrible ordeal they went through."

Wanting to be useful, considering that he had messed up his role in the attack against the bandits, he offered to heal who he could. "But my method of healing the worst of the injuries might end up putting them into a temporary coma," he warned.

"You can do that?" the Protector asked, a look of skepticism on her face. She had seen him heal Gwest, but his broken wrist and lower arm had been a relatively clean break compared to what he saw happening in the bandit's clearing.

"I can. There are limitations and risks, but it will speed up their recovery time immensely, nonetheless."

"Then I'll see about you getting to visit them when you have the chance. Rest up first, as most of them aren't going anywhere, and I'll see you later."

His minder left quickly after that, *hopefully to get some sleep*, he couldn't help but think. Larek felt bad about his uncontrolled actions and how they had likely caused even more problems, but there wasn't any way to change the past; he could only strive to prevent the same from happening in the future and to make up for what he did however he could. That included healing those who had suffered from the bandits' vile ministrations – but Larek needed to rest up and eat some more before he did something like that.

It was only after he got up, feeling a weakness in his body that felt like he had been wrung out to dry, and got something to eat that he started to feel a little bit more normal. With that normality came the ability to think about what had actually happened. Not his actions, specifically, though that was a symptom of what was worrying him; instead, he was finally able to acknowledge that his statement of losing control was completely accurate.

It was as if his rage had taken on a life of its own, and it somehow consciously (or perhaps unconsciously) tapped into his Stama to activate his Battle Art. Even thinking back on the event, he was unable to pinpoint exactly *what* or *how* it was all accomplished, and even now he had no idea how to activate *Furious Rampage* again even if he wanted to. Controlling his Stama was a completely foreign subject to him, and while he had unlocked *Stama Subjugation* after falling into the lake nearby, he still didn't have the smallest inkling of how to even touch the roiling energy inside his chest.

And he had tried, too, during the first few days in Enderflow, while he was initially recovering. Without much else to do, he had done everything he could to take control of the Stama inside his body, up to and including what Penelope had mentioned about "subjugating" the energy and bending it to his will. Nothing seemed to work; it was there, just out of reach, similar to how it was before he unlocked the Skill; unlocking it seemed not to have made any difference in how he perceived the resource inside of him.

As it was, unless he was able to figure it out on his own, he was going to need instruction on exactly how to go about controlling and subjugating his Stama for use in Battle Arts. It was too dangerous to let it go for long, as it was much too powerful to be unrestrained; the proof of that was how it didn't seem to allow him to turn on his *Repelling Barrier* during the fight with the Bandits. Instead of Larek controlling his *Stama*, his Stama was controlling *him* – which was a frightening feeling, to say the least.

Who knew what it would do next?

When he got back to his temporary room inside the barracks after eating his fill once again, the Fusionist laid himself back on his bed and finally looked at his notifications from the battle against the bandits.

*New Battle Art Learned!*
**Consuming Speed**
*Effect: Triple Agility stat while reducing Body stat by 60%*
*Duration: 20 seconds*
*Base Stama Cost: 300*

**Axe Handling** *has reached Level 84!*

**Long-Distance Running** *has reached Level 11!*

As he had half-expected, Larek had learned another Battle Art, *Consuming Speed*. At first, it seemed beneficial, as it tripled his Agility stat – which was probably what made the bandits seem to be moving in slow motion, as he was moving so fast in comparison. But its detriment was a reduction of his Body stat by 60%, which was not the best situation; when he added in the 30% reduction of his Body stat due to *Furious Rampage*, at one point he had a whopping, and potentially dangerous, 90% reduction in his Body stat.

He could've died if the bandits had been just a little bit quicker or hit him a little bit harder while he had the new Battle Art activated. Without his *Repelling Barrier* being active, the safety of his body had been in jeopardy – and he had no control over anything to prevent his death. If he hadn't gotten lucky and killed them all before they could effectively fight back, there was a very good chance he would've died.

Using those Battle Arts in combination again would be the last thing he wanted to do.

Apart from the new Battle Art, the only Skills that had increased were his *Axe Handling* Skill and for some reason his *Long-Distance Running* Skill; he could only assume the latter was because he was sprinting at his targets with the use of his new Battle Art and that made a difference somehow. There was no increase in any of his Mage Skills because he hadn't done anything lately, with his Pattern Cohesion so messed up, and the Martial Skills that would've been utilized during the battle – Pain Immunity and Body Regeneration – were already at their maximum Level. In his uncontrolled state, he didn't even try and dodge any attacks sent against him, and he didn't throw anything, so those two Skills didn't progress any further; the same went for his Blunt Weapon and Bladed Weapon Expertise Skills, as his axe was still apparently considered a tool and not a weapon.

What surprised him, but probably shouldn't have, was that despite using Stama during the fight, his *Stama Subjugation* Skill didn't budge even an inch. He supposed this was because there was no "subjugation" going on, unless one counted "Larek Subjugation" rather than Stama – because that was how it felt.

The Fusionist supposed that he should've used some of his banked Aetheric Force to increase the maximum Skill level for Body Regeneration before he went out and fought the bandits, as it likely would've been useful, but he had been saving it all for when his Pattern Cohesion had fully recovered. He'd been planning on waiting until he could actually create Fusions again, but if he was going to head back out with the Protectors from Enderflow, it would undoubtedly be beneficial if he was able to raise a Skill level during that time. He should probably also use the AP he earned from his last increase in personal Level, but again he had been saving it until he was fully recovered.

Exhaustion overcame Larek as he considered what to do, until he eventually decided to leave his eyes closed for a little bit. Before he knew it, he was awakened by sounds outside of his room, causing him to get up and stretch, feeling much better for some reason. It was only when he left the room and looked outside that he realized that he had inadvertently slept through the night.

Energized from the sleep, he went in search of more food – and to find out where the injured people they had rescued from the clutches of the heinous men he had slain were being held.

# Chapter 3

Healing the physical injuries of the bandits' victims was easy enough for Larek to accomplish, though they at first shrank away from him when he arrived at where the wounded were being held. At first, he thought it was his height that made them wary of his presence, but he realized he was still wearing his ring with the *Perceptive Misdirection* Fusion on it. Even if he hadn't been wearing it, no one had mentioned his height as something disconcerting – not even those who had physically carried him back to town when he was unconscious. They would've undoubtedly noticed that he was taller than what their visual perception told them, but none of them seemed fazed in the least.

No, they shied away from him for a couple of reasons that were in no way related to his physical characteristics. The first, and most impactful to Larek, was that most of them had – at least in part – witnessed his deadly rampage against the bandits. Such brutality and wanton destruction imparted upon those who had hurt them so badly was disturbing even to those who had suffered, and they acted as if they expected him to lose control like that again at any time. While that wasn't likely to happen, they didn't know that, so it made them wary of his presence.

The second reason was that, in addition to their physical injuries, they had also suffered severe mental trauma related to what was done to them. As a result, the victims shied away from *everyone*, not just Larek; he wasn't sure whether he felt better or worse upon seeing some of the injured acting the same way with some of the healers trying to help them. Regardless, this mental and emotional trauma was something that, unfortunately, he couldn't heal with a Fusion. Having dealt with something similar, if not exactly the same, when he was captured and tortured by Ricardo, the Fusionist knew that only time would help to heal those types of wounds.

That the caravan victims were thankful for their healing wasn't immediately obvious because of their mental states, especially as two of them slipped into a temporary coma due to the extent of their horrific injuries, but he could see a little bit of hope shine in their eyes when their bodies were put back together. It made him feel as if he had at least partially made up for his mistakes earlier, but he was also glad to eventually leave the multitude of rooms, located in an expansive one-story building in the middle of Enderflow, where the victims were being treated. Seeing them healed of their physical injuries only seemed to highlight their battered mental states; given that he couldn't do anything to help in that regard – only make it worse with his presence – Larek found that he'd rather make himself scarce.

His service to the town wasn't impacted by his offer to heal the victims, as no time was taken off, though from his interactions with Protector Ashlynn from that point on he found that it at least seemed to mitigate a portion of his rampaging mistake. As much as he wanted to leave the town and make his way back to the Kingdom, he was actually thankful that he was forced to stay in the relatively quiet town so that he could recuperate fully from everything that had happened to him.

Fortunately, there were no more reports of bandits or missing people, which meant that Larek didn't have to go out and kill anyone else. Not that they would've brought him along, as the overheard conversation was proof enough that they didn't trust him not to lose control, but he was glad that he didn't have to worry about being forced into that position once again. Unfortunately, the lack of reports or other information about the bandits' contacts also meant that the Protectors were no closer to learning where previous victims might have been sent. Larek felt horrible that his actions led to this lack of information, but there wasn't really anything he could do to help; in fact, he was told in no uncertain terms that his help was *not needed* for such an investigation.

Instead, his obligation of service to the town of Enderflow shifted to one of simple guard and patrol duty in and around the town. It was highly boring work, as he basically wandered around looking for anything suspicious or that might prove a threat. The only time over the first week that he saw action was when a giant alligator emerged from the distant river and somehow managed to sneak into the fields where the Ectorians toiled away. No one was seriously hurt as they fled the large beast, though one of the Ectorians sprained their ankle when they ran away from the danger the alligator posed. That was easy enough to heal with his Fusion afterwards – almost as easy as killing the alligator with his axe, as the beast was fairly slow on land and its durable skin couldn't withstand the sharpness of his bladed tool. It was less of a fight and more of an execution as he was able to slip around the snap of its jaws and separate its head from the rest of its body with a single strike.

It turned out that gator tasted a little bit like chicken, as he found out after the beast's corpse was butchered and cooked up later that night.

Besides that one brief activity, two weeks after arriving in the town half-starved and relatively weak saw Larek fairly well-recovered; it wasn't just his physical body that had recovered, but his Pattern

Cohesion, as well. When he gazed internally at his pattern, no longer was it torn and ragged to the point where a light flexing of his Pattern Cohesion would cause it to break apart like wet paper. In its place was a strong, healthy internal pattern that was – if anything – *better* than it had been before; it was as if the damage that he had done to it and had healed over the last few weeks of non-activity had made it more durable and resilient. When he finally decided that he was as healed as he was going to get, he took the time away from his patrolling duties to finally create another Fusion.

Because he hadn't tried anything in weeks in fear that he would damage himself further, Larek started small. Just a simple *Strengthen Stone +1* Fusion on a palm-sized rock he picked up outside.

It was at that point that the powerful Fusionist discovered that something was wrong.

"What's going on?" he muttered to himself, after he finished the simple Basic Fusion. It had been created easily and quickly, settling itself into the rock in his hand without any problem and it appeared perfect – but it wasn't the Fusion that was the problem. It had been formed as flawlessly as his usual creations and was as strong as anything he'd made before; if anything, the Pattern Cohesion imbued into the Fusion was stronger and more permanent-feeling than before, which he could only attribute to his strengthened Pattern Cohesion. He felt that if his creations hadn't been at the point where they would last for a lifetime or longer, then it was quite possible that his new Fusions would. In addition, some of the Fusions – such as the ones he'd put on staves with offensive abilities – would suffer much, much less from repeated usage, meaning that they might be able to be activated more frequently. He suspected that the formations wouldn't be at the point where they would *never* break if stressed too much, but they had nevertheless made a significant jump in resiliency.

So, if the Fusion was even better than before, then what was the problem?

In short, it was his Mana regeneration.

Having not used any Mana since he arrived in the Empire of Sealance, he hadn't noticed anything different with it. Now that he had finally used some to fill his Fusion, which was only a small amount for this particular Fusion (approximately 14 Mana), he noticed that his Mana didn't refill in a blink of an eye like it did before. In fact, to completely refill the 14 Mana he utilized, it took a little under 2 seconds.

Granted, such a regeneration rate would've been absolutely fantastic for any other Mage in the Kingdom, but for Larek it was *shockingly* slow. To one who was used to refilling *thousands* of Mana in a second or less, this reduction was of significant importance to him and would hinder his Fusion-making capabilities. He relied on his tremendous regeneration rate to create the powerful Fusions within minutes, completely blowing away the Fusion Times that were associated with the Fusions he had access to. Over 100 hours for a Fusion was something he could do in minutes – or at least he could *before*; now, with his much-slower Mana regeneration, he'd be lucky to get something like that done in less than a full day.

Just to check if it was a fluke, he created a *Multi-Resistance Cloth +2* Fusion on his bed sheet he was comfortably sitting on, using 475 Mana to fill it up. It completed just as expected… and his Mana regenerated at the much-reduced rate as he feared.

Having his fear confirmed, Larek was at a loss to explain what had happened to cause such a change. It wasn't a small difference, either, as it was extremely detrimental to his ability to create Fusions.

He thought at first that it had been caused by his Martial "awakening" as he gained access to his Stama, but for some reason that didn't feel right. Some intuition told him that far from being a hindrance to his Mana regeneration, it should've actually enhanced it somehow, as his body was in harmony now with the energy within it. He then thought that it was a result of his stronger Pattern Cohesion or his recent usage of his Battle Arts, but neither of those seemed plausible, either.

It wasn't until he finally started to spend his accumulated Advancement Points and Aetheric Force that he discovered what he thought might be the reason.

To start, he used his 20 AP and split it evenly between Intellect and Acuity, adding 10 to each, in an effort to give himself a bigger Mana pool and to hopefully increase his Mana regeneration. His maximum Mana went up to 1,600 after his Intellect rose to 80 and was doubled by his *Intellect Boost +10* Fusion – an increase of 200 Mana. As far as his Mana regeneration… he didn't see any difference when testing it out with additional Fusions.

With the 5,424 AF he had access to use on increasing his maximum Skill Levels, he increased his *Fusion*, *Pattern Formation*, and *Mana Control* Skills to a maximum of 37, brought *Multi-effect Fusion Focus* up to 20 from 17, and spent some to gradually bring *Pattern Recognition*, *Spellcasting Focus*, and *Magical Detection* up to a maximum of 21.

**Mage Skills:**
**Multi-effect Fusion Focus Level 17/20 (200 AF)**

**Pattern Recognition Level 20/21 (210 AF)**
**Magical Detection Level 20/21 (210 AF)**
**Spellcasting Focus Level 20/21 (210 AF)**
**Focused Division Level 31/31 (310 AF)**
**Mana Control Level 32/37 (370 AF)**
**Fusion Level 33/37 (370 AF)**
**Pattern Formation Level 33/37 (370 AF)**

It was the most Aetheric Force he'd used all at once, and it incapacitated him for a few minutes while it went to work adjusting his Skill maximums; but once it was done, he sat up in bed and looked around to see that the world had slightly changed.

***Magical Detection** has reached Level 21!*

In reality, it wasn't the world that had changed; it was his perception of it. That perception of the world was now inhabited by a vision of very faint wisps of multi-colored strands of light that were just on the edge of visibility. He discovered that if he concentrated on them hard enough, he could make them out well enough, though they were sparse in number; despite their sparseness, they were easy enough to see floating around everywhere. When he wasn't thinking about seeing them, though, they disappeared into the background.

Confused at what these insubstantial strands of light were, he dismissed them as he experimented with another simple Fusion to see if anything had changed with his increase in Skill maximums. Unfortunately, nothing seemed to be different with his Mana regeneration, as it was the same slow rate as it was before, but he thought he discovered what the multi-colored light was.

Mana. Or at least the equivalent of Mana, just floating around everywhere.

When he spent his Mana, he watched as these light strands gravitated toward his body, where they disappeared as they were absorbed into his skin. More of the floating Mana streamed in from outside of his room at the same density as his room held before, no more and no less, as it was replenished both in the space and into his body. He found that if he actively moved toward the incoming strands of light, his Mana regeneration ticked up slightly – but it was barely noticeable, and he only discovered it because he was monitoring it closely.

In addition to being absorbed by his body, there was also a steady stream of light flowing into his permanent Fusions as they absorbed the ambient Mana from the environment to keep them running. Thankfully, they didn't seem to be too affected by the low density of the light strands around the room, though he was sure that if he had another few sets of the ones that were covering his robe and his axe, they would quickly begin to "starve" from a lack of Mana.

What did he learn from all of this? Well, he learned that he could now see free-floating Mana in the air, and that his body absorbed it in order to replenish what he spent, as well as powering Fusions. As for why he hadn't seen it before? Well, he could only assume that the density in the Kingdom was so great, being in close proximity to the large breach and additionally the presence of Scissions and now Apertures, that it was virtually indistinguishable from anything else. It was only here in a land quite far away from the origin of Mana – which he learned hadn't really been present before The Transition a thousand years ago – that it was sparse enough to make out the multi-colored strands individually.

That, in turn, led to Larek's problem. Without the same density of Mana floating around the area, his Mana regeneration suffered. There simply wasn't enough of it nearby to fill him up quickly, so he was limited to his current rate.

The only solution was to get back to the Kingdom, or at least in closer proximity to the area, to replenish his Mana at his accustomed rate. Unfortunately for him, he was still a couple of weeks away from leaving Enderflow due to his service obligation, so getting back would have to wait a little longer.

His plans were derailed a little bit by these revelations, as he had been intending to remake his staff and to replace his current Martial stat Fusions with stronger ones now that his body could handle it, but those required a lot of Mana to complete and more ambient Mana that was absorbed from the environment to maintain. He had also been thinking of volunteering to add some Fusions to the Protectors' equipment as he thought it would give him something to do in his time off, making their weapons sharper and armor more durable, but now he was rethinking that whole plan.

First, he didn't want to inadvertently cause the people of Enderflow to want more and more of his Fusions for their people, trapping Larek in place just like the Dean and Shinpai had used him to create Fusions for the SIC. Granted, he was eventually "paid" for his work, but he was also worked so hard that he'd needed to take a break to restore his internal pattern after how much he had done for them.

Secondly, he was still technically incognito as a "Martial" from the Kingdom without any magical skills other than what he used with his

Stama. He didn't want to reveal that he could create Fusions, as they might then ask if he could cast spells in defense of the town; when he would tell them that he couldn't, he wasn't sure how they would react. Would they think he was lying? Would they know that it was "impossible" for a person to be both a Martial and a Mage? Was capture and exploitation a possibility? He didn't know the answers to those questions, of course, and also didn't want to find out.

Lastly, if he was going to spend his slowly regenerating Mana on anything, it would be for his own benefit, as the more Fusions around the area, the lower the Mana density would be. Without the ability to create large amounts of powerful Fusions by the handful, he had to be more selective regarding what he did end up making. As for what that entailed, he decided to do something he'd been wanting to do for a while, but never seemed to have the time as something more pressing was always taking his attention.

In other words, Larek was going to clean up his Fusions list.

There were now so many Fusions on the list that it was hard to keep track of them, but with the recent increases in his Skills above 30, he now realized there was a solution to it all as long as he had the time to apply himself to the effort.

With that goal in mind, Larek spent the next few weeks of his service obligation to the town of Enderflow making dozens of small Fusions in the privacy of his room.

# Chapter 4

*Congratulations!*
*You have learned **5** Fusions of a similar type for a particular Stat Boost and now understand the fundamental elements of that Fusion!*
*As a result, all <u>Agility Boost</u> Fusions will now be combined into a singular Fusion. The only functional difference will be related to Magnitude.*

<u>**Fusions Lost:**</u>
**Fusion – Agility Boost +1**
**Fusion – Agility Boost +2**
**Fusion – Agility Boost +3**
**Fusion – Agility Boost +7**
**Fusion – Agility Boost +10**

<u>**Fusion Gained:**</u>
**Fusion – Agility Boost**

*In addition, all <u>Agility Boost</u> Fusions have slightly reduced Mana Cost and Pattern Cohesion requirements, as well as a reduction in Fusion Time.*

***-5% Mana Cost***
***-5% Pattern Cohesion***
***-5% Fusion Time***

*Congratulations!*
*You have learned **5** Fusions of a similar type for a particular Effect and now understand the fundamental elements of that Fusion!*
*As a result, all <u>Camouflage Sphere</u> Fusions….*

  The progress he made in consolidating his different Fusions into a more manageable list was actually a lot faster than he expected considering his low Mana regeneration rate. The reason for this was that many of those he had created before were a higher Magnitude, and so he was able to create the lower Magnitudes with less of a Mana Cost and was able to fulfill the requirements to consolidate them all together. Thankfully, everything that wasn't related to materials only required 5 of that certain type of Fusion in order to consolidate; for things such as *Multi-Resistance Cloth, Leather,* and *Wood*, it required 10

– but that was easy enough to accomplish with a few low-Magnitude additions to the list.

At one point in his endeavors, as he was finishing up the last of the material Fusions, which was made easier as he added silver, gold, and platinum (from his coinage) in addition to cloth, leather, glass, wood, stone, iron, and steel to the materials he was creating them on, he received another notification that made him even more pleased that his efforts were beneficial for more than just cleaning up his Fusion list.

**Congratulations!**
*You have consolidated **10** different materials as part of your Fusions and now understand the fundamental natures of those different materials! As a result, Fusions on these materials...*

*Cloth*
*Leather*
*Glass*
*Wood*
*Stone*
*Iron*
*Silver*
*Gold*
*Steel*
*Platinum*

*...will no longer require the material(s) as part of the Effect designation to be effective, as they will be automatically included in the process.*

<u>Fusions Lost:</u>
Fusion – Graduated Illumination Strong Glass
Fusion – Graduated Illumination Strong Iron
Fusion – Graduated Illumination Strong Silver
Fusion – Graduated Illumination Strong Stone
Fusion – Graduated Illumination Strong Wood
Fusion – Illuminate Iron
Fusion – Illuminate Steel
Fusion – Illuminate Stone
Fusion – Illuminate Wood
Fusion – Multi-Resistance Cloth
Fusion – Multi-Resistance Leather
Fusion – Multi-Resistance Wood
Fusion – Red and White Illuminate Cloth

Fusion – Red and White Illuminate Iron
Fusion – Red and White Illuminate Stone
Fusion – Red and White Illuminate Wood
Fusion – Sharpen Iron Edge
Fusion – Sharpen Steel Edge
Fusion – Sharpen Stone Edge
Fusion – Sharpen Wood Edge
Fusion – Strengthen and Sharpen Iron Edge
Fusion – Strengthen and Sharpen Steel Edge
Fusion – Strengthen and Sharpen Wood Edge
Fusion – Strengthen Iron
Fusion – Strengthen Leather
Fusion – Strengthen Steel
Fusion – Strengthen Stone
Fusion – Strengthen Wood
Fusion – Strengthen Steel and Wood

*Fusions Gained:*
Fusion – Graduated Illumination Strong
Fusion – Illuminate
Fusion – Multi-Resistance
Fusion – Red and White Illuminate
Fusion – Sharpen Edge
Fusion – Strengthen and Sharpen Edge
Fusion – Strengthen

  Not only did this reduce his Fusion list even further, but there was a portion of the notification that he paid special attention to regarding the material or *materials* used in the Fusion. When he experimented shortly afterwards using a *Strengthen +1* Fusion on a spear he "borrowed" from the Protectors of Enderflow, he found that he now didn't have to designate what materials it affected in the Effect portion of the formation as long as the Fusion was in proximity to the connected materials. In this instance, he placed the Fusion on the wooden shaft of the spear just below its steel blade, and while the formation wasn't technically touching the steel in any way, it was close enough to be included in the Effect, nonetheless. Further experiments showed that the further the Fusion was away from the secondary material – such as when he placed the Fusion further down the shaft – it required a higher Magnitude in order to "reach" the other material.
  What this advancement ultimately meant was that he wouldn't have to worry about separating all the different materials on any

objects he added Fusions to, including armor and other weapons. He found that he could also mentally exclude a material if needed, as *Strengthening* leather on armor that was half steel wouldn't be beneficial; if he added a *Multi-Resistance* Effect into the same *Strengthen* Fusion designed for steel and included both steel and leather in the *Multi-Resistance* Fusion, then he could essentially cover an entire article of armor in a single Fusion – something that he wasn't capable of doing before this.

It was an amazing change to his repertoire of Fusions, and he could only imagine the possibilities in the future...

...if only his Mana regeneration could keep up with what he could imagine doing with this newly acquired material function.

Nevertheless, only a day before his service obligation to the town was up, Larek managed to finish his Fusion consolidation. He looked at the list and was happy with what he saw.

**Mage Abilities:**
**Spell – Bark Skin**
**Spell – Binding Roots**
**Spell – Fireball**
**Spell – Furrow**
**Spell – Ice Spike**
**Spell – Lesser Restoration**
**Spell – Light Bending**
**Spell – Light Orb**
**Spell – Localized Anesthesia**
**Spell – Minor Mending**
**Spell – Rapid Plant Growth**
**Spell – Repelling Gust**
**Spell – Static Illusion**
**Spell – Stone Fist**
**Spell – Wall of Thorns**
**Spell – Water Jet**
**Spell – Wind Barrier**
**Fusion – Acuity Boost**
**Fusion – Agility Boost**
**Fusion – Area Chill**
**Fusion – Body Boost**
**Fusion – Camouflage Sphere**
**Fusion – Extreme Heat**
**Fusion – Flaming Ball**
**Fusion – Flying Stone**

- Fusion – Graduated Illumination Strong
- Fusion – Graduated Parahealing
- Fusion – Healing Surge
- Fusion – Icy Spike
- Fusion – Illuminate
- Fusion – Illusionary Image
- Fusion – Intellect Boost
- Fusion – Intellect and Acuity Boost
- Fusion – Muffle Sound
- Fusion – Muffling Air Deflection Barrier
- Fusion – Multi-Resistance
- Fusion – Paralytic Light
- Fusion – Paralytic Touch
- Fusion – Personal Air Deflection Barrier
- Fusion – Pneuma Boost
- Fusion – Red and White Illuminate
- Fusion – Repelling Barrier
- Fusion – Repelling Gust of Air
- Fusion – Sharpen Edge
- Fusion – Space Heater
- Fusion – Spellcasting Focus Boost
- Fusion – Strength Boost
- Fusion – Strength and Body Boost
- Fusion – Strengthen and Sharpen Edge
- Fusion – Strengthen
- Fusion – Temperature Regulator
- Fusion – Tree Skin
- Fusion – Water Stream

Not only was he able to clean up his list, but his frequent creation of Fusions – while none of them were particularly powerful because of his Mana limitations – also managed to increase his related Skills to their current maximums.

***Multi-effect Fusion Focus*** *has reached Level 20!*

***Pattern Recognition*** *has reached Level 21!*

***Spellcasting Focus*** *has reached Level 21!*

***Mana Control*** *has reached Level 37!*

***Pattern Formation** has reached Level 37!*

***Fusion** has reached Level 37!*

    The Skill increases also netted him another personal Level, which gave him an additional 18 AP to spend – which he immediately shoved into Intellect, giving him a total of 98 Intellect. When it was doubled by his existing boost Fusion, he had a total of 196 with a maximum Mana pool of 1,960. This wouldn't have been a large increase to Larek when his regeneration was still incredibly fast, but now the additional 360 Mana in his pool made a huge difference in creating slightly stronger Fusions. That didn't mean he'd be making anything over a Magnitude 3 or 4 anytime soon, unless he wanted to wait hours for his Mana to regenerate, but a higher starting Mana pool was always beneficial to get the job done much faster.
    Overall, his efforts were well worth the time he put into them, and he was looking forward to working his way back to the Kingdom soon. Not only did he want to acquire more *Aetheric Force*, but being unable to create the Fusions he wanted to because of the low ambient Mana density was quite annoying. In addition, while he could've made himself another mage staff with offensive Fusions on it, though with a lower Magnitude than the one he left back in the Kingdom when he was captured by Chinli, actually carrying it with him or using it would be a mistake if anyone saw him. That would likely reveal that he had made it, which was something he wanted to avoid at the moment.
    Strangely enough, during the last few days of cleaning up his Fusions list, Larek also noted that his Mana regeneration was gradually starting to increase in speed. It was barely noticeable at first, and he initially thought he was mistaken when his pool refilled a few seconds before he had estimated it would. By the time he finished with the list, what had normally taken just over 4 minutes to refill his new Mana pool of 1,960 at his regeneration rate, now took only half that time; at about 16 Mana per second now as opposed to 8 Mana, that was a significant increase. His first assumption was that his Acuity was finally helping to speed things up with his regeneration, but that was only until he looked around with a focus on the air in his room and noticed that the Mana density had also increased.
    *That's great! If this keeps up, I'll be back to normal in no time—*
    He interrupted that happy thought as he realized what that meant. If the Mana density was increasing in the area, then that was likely to mean that it was increasing *everywhere*. And if it was increasing everywhere, then the ambient Mana pouring out of the

Kingdom was increasing significantly as a result. Moreover, if it was increasing as fast as it seemed to be, then that could only mean one thing—

Larek was suddenly knocked flat on his back in his bed when an invisible shockwave of force spread through his room and beyond. As he sat back up and tried to make sense of what had just happened, he noticed that the ambient Mana density jumped yet again; it wasn't to the point where it was close to the Kingdom's density, but it appeared to be slowly getting there.

More than that, however, he heard screaming coming from all over the town, but it was impossible to determine exactly what they were yelling about, because his focus was on something else entirely.

Somewhere on the very edge of his perception to the east of the town of Enderflow, the impossibility of a Scission appearing in the Empire of Sealance had just occurred.

# Chapter 5

*Did I cause this to happen? Is my presence here a catalyst for that Scission to appear?*

Larek didn't know, but the sounds of screaming coming from somewhere in the barracks caused him to run out of his assigned bedroom, only to emerge into a chaotic mess once he reached the main leisure space for the Protectors where they hung out between patrols. A third of the figures inside the room were on the ground or collapsed partway in chairs or draped over tables, screaming their heads off in what appeared to be pain – though there were no visible wounds that the Fusionist could see. Most of the remaining Protectors appeared dazed, as if they were unaware of what was going on, though there were a few who were attempting to figure out what was going on with their comrades.

Stopping as soon as he saw the chaos, Larek witnessed something that gave him a clue as to what was happening. The Protectors that were already screaming suddenly convulsed uncontrollably for a few seconds before their screams ramped up yet again. At the same time, Larek inadvertently focused on the environment and the Mana that floated around the space. As he halfway expected, the density of the multicolored strands of light was more than it was even a day ago; with the appearance of a Scission nearby, it seemed plausible.

What he *wasn't* expecting was that the light strands floating around suddenly streamed toward the screaming individuals, where they disappeared into their bodies, absorbed just like Larek absorbed them to replenish his Mana. Because he was watching, he also noted that on about half of those convulsing, the light changed subtly as it entered them, and he had the distinct feeling, when he saw how it transformed, that he was looking at Stama in its raw form.

*Are these strands of light not Mana, but something that encompasses both Mana **and** Stama?*

Larek didn't have time to ponder it further than that as the screaming abruptly stopped, leaving a deafening silence that was interrupted a few seconds later by the pained moaning of those that had been affected. While no one else present likely knew what exactly happened to them, the Fusionist vividly remembered the process in which his Mage half had been awakened back at Crystalview Academy. He could only assume that this was what had happened to them, and those who had Stama injected into them had their Martial side "cracked open" – as Penelope would say; he couldn't say for sure that was what happened, given that his own Martial awakening was quite a bit different, but it seemed plausible.

But that just begged a bevy of questions. How did this happen? Why these people? Was it in response to the Scission appearing? Are they now Mages and Martials?

With no answer ready at his fingertips, Larek noticed the familiar face of Protector Ashlynn among those that had suffered the abrupt awakening; she was slowly picking herself up off the floor, appearing unsteady as she got to her feet with a stunned expression on her face. The moment he took a step in her direction to see if he could gain any answers from her, a notification appeared in front of him that caused him to stop.

*Warning!*

*Corruption saturation has surpassed the second threshold!*

*At this stage, the Corruption has now diffused to every corner of the world, though it only has a tenuous foothold in most locations. While the Guardians continue to assist in maintaining the original breach, they have proven to be unable to halt the upwelling of Corruption that is constantly being infused into this world.*

*Since the appearance of the first Aperture 1,468 days ago, the advancement of the Corruption has not been curbed, though great gains were made in pushing back its diffusion. Unfortunately, this has proven to be unsustainable, and drastic measures were instituted by the Guardians.*

*As a result of passing the second threshold of Corruption throughout the world, a great working was unleashed that has unlocked the potential to be a Mage or Martial in millions of people all over the world. In addition, a small portion of necessary knowledge was imparted to the newly awakened individuals with potential, giving them the tools to curb the advancement of the Corruption on a global scale.*

*No longer will the Guardians be alone in their valiant efforts against the dangers that threaten the entire world. It is now your duty to go forth and fight the physical manifestations of Corruption that even now are emerging from Scissions in the fabric of reality.*

*Do not panic, and do not wait to protect your lands! The danger that these physical manifestations of Corruption will create a permanent Aperture leading to the world of Corruption is real, and preventing that from happening should be your first priority.*

*While Scissions are **temporary** portals into the world of the Corruption, Apertures are **permanent** connections between the two worlds. These permanent connections are established when the Corrupted Aetheric Force present in their physical manifestations....*

The notification went on to repeat the earlier notification he received back in the Kingdom referring to Apertures, which he thought was strange given that he already knew about it. When he got to the end, which also ended with the phrase, "Good luck and good hunting!", he quickly reread it all to make sure he was understanding what he had read. There were three main points that he focused on, each of them stranger than the next.

First and foremost, the notification mentioned that it had been 1,468 days since the first Aperture had appeared, which he mentally calculated to be just over 4 years. That was impossible, however, as he had only been in Enderflow for about a month, and the Aperture appeared – and was temporarily closed – less than a day before he arrived. So, either his previous notification about locating and closing the *first* Aperture was a lie, as there had been at least one that had appeared around 4 years before, or...

...he had somehow lost time and it was actually 4 years later from when he was transported to the Empire of Sealance.

Unfortunately, the latter reason would also explain how things had gotten bad enough that the Corruption was spreading all over the world rather than concentrating on only the Kingdom – *in only a month*. If it had indeed been around *4 years* since the first Aperture, then he could see how it might have gotten that bad if the SIC back home wasn't able to get a handle on the situation in a quick enough manner. For it to have progressed this much in a matter of years was still very troubling, nonetheless; he couldn't imagine how bad it was back home for the Corruption to spill over to the rest of the world.

And that world was completely unprepared for what was happening to them.

The second thing that caught his attention was mention that a small portion of "necessary knowledge" was imparted to those who had been affected by an awakening. While unsure of what exactly this meant, Larek could only assume that each person was given a rudimentary understanding of what they could do with their newly granted power; given that there were no Mage Academies or Martial training Forts nearby to help them learn how to cast spells or how to apply their Stama for Battle Arts, he supposed this made sense. *How exactly this knowledge was imparted to them was a mystery*, though the Fusionist supposed it was similar to how he had gained access to certain Mage Skills immediately after his awakening in the Academy, though on a greater scale.

He also thought it was patently unfair, as Larek had needed to learn everything from scratch at the Academy, and it seemed as though the basics were being taught to these people for absolutely nothing. He could certainly use a course on Stama manipulation and the usage of Battle Arts, as he was fairly certain that he hadn't been imparted any new knowledge on those processes within the last few minutes.

Lastly, he noticed that the notification didn't seem as *personalized* toward him or even toward the Gergasi "Guardians". Instead, as he closed the notification from his view and looked around the room, it quickly became clear that *everyone* received a notification, not just himself or those who had been magically awakened. Whether or not the content was the same was something he'd have to find out, but he suspected it was similar if not identical.

"What is going on?"

"How did this happen?"

"This isn't real, is it?"

Larek heard variations of these questions as he made his way over to Protector Ashlynn, his main point of contact within the organization of the Protectors. He hadn't seen much of her after the bandit incident a few weeks before, but while he knew a few of the other Protectors by sight, Ashlynn was the only one he had spoken with for more than a minute or two.

"You. What do you know about this?"

She had seen him coming and locked onto his tall figure immediately, firing off her question with a demand in her voice that he hadn't heard since he was first taken into custody just after arriving in town. "Not much, unfortunately," he admitted, coming to a stop in front of the woman. "I can only assume that the SIC inside the Kingdom were unable to contain the Apertures that were opening up everywhere, and this is the result."

"So, you're saying that it's *your people's* fault? And what did that notification mean about Scissions and 'physical manifestations'?"

He shook his head. "No, it's not their fault; if anything, it's the so-called 'Guardians' that caused the problem in the first place."

"Guardians? I saw that mentioned in the notification; who, exactly, are they?"

The Fusionist debated on how much to share about the Gergasi and the slavery of the Nobility in the Kingdom, as well as the origins of the breach, the Scissions, and the monsters that emerged from them. As he hesitated, his peripheral vision showed that many of those that had been affected by their magical awakening had recovered enough and had gotten over enough of their initial shock to hear Ashlynn ask Larek the question. When he didn't answer right away, there was a movement toward him that he immediately identified as threatening, so he held up his hands to stop them.

"Hold on, I'll tell you all you want to know, but there's something more important that you need to deal with before it becomes a problem," he said quickly, which stopped them in their tracks. "Do you all feel something coming from *that* direction?" he asked, pointing toward where he felt the Scission in the far distance. "That's a Scission, and it's in the process of unleashing monsters into this world. If you all saw the notification about Apertures, then you need to kill them before they can establish a permanent connection to the world of the Corruption."

"Monsters? Those are just old wives' tales, aren't they?"

Larek chuckled at the question from one of the Protectors, a man he didn't know by name but had seen around, as the naiveté in the question sounded like Larek did more than a year ago before he left home. *Or is that more like 5 years ago if I'm right about the time difference? I still need to find out if that is accurate or not.*

"Unfortunately, no. The monsters that are about to emerge from the Scission are the 'physical manifestations' that the notification referenced, and it is imperative that you stop them before they can establish a permanent Aperture. I don't personally know how long it will take for these monsters to get one up and running, but I would err on the side of caution. In other words, there's no time to waste."

Some of the Protectors still seemed skeptical, while the shock of everything that had happened over the last minute or so continued to affect the others, at least according to their faces. Protector Ashlynn just looked thoughtful, along with a bunch of others, and glancing at those who appeared lost in thought, he realized that most of them were those who had gone through a magical awakening.

"What is all this nonsense on my Status? Strength, Body, and Agility? And what is Stama—oh. Ohhhhh. I see." Ashlynn's eyes focused on Larek. "Is this what it means to be a Martial like you? With the use of Stama and these Battle Arts?"

He hesitated again before answering. "Sort of? I had just begun my training, and I wasn't given any knowledge of how Stama is used or how to properly use Battle Arts. I can only assume by the notification that *you* did?"

She nodded slowly, her eyes unfocused again. "In a manner of speaking. I have a pair of Battle Arts listed on my Status and I *think* I can probably activate them with some practice manipulating my Stama." Her eyes locked onto his abruptly. "But you say that we're limited on time?"

"Yes! You need to kill those monsters as quickly as you can—"

"What do you mean, 'You'? You're still under your service obligation, so you're coming with us."

Now Larek was confused. "But I didn't think you wanted me to participate in anything like this after the last time things didn't work out so well. Was I wrong?"

"You aren't wrong, but this is different," she said impatiently. "I want you with us to help to identify these monsters and this 'Scission', and I'm not letting you out of my sight until you answer more of my questions. If this is a threat to the town of Enderflow and the Empire of Sealance, then it's imperative that you share with us everything you know."

That sounded fair enough to Larek, and since he had finished his Fusion consolidation, he didn't really have anything else to do. Besides, the opportunity to kill more monsters wasn't something that he could easily pass up, especially if it provided him with more Aetheric Force to use toward his Skills. Glancing at his ring that held the *Perceptive Misdirection* Fusion on it that Shinpai had created, he realized that it probably only had another few weeks before it faded away completely; before that happened, or at least before he returned to the Kingdom, he needed to be able to replicate it. In order to do that, he was fairly certain he needed to have his *Fusion* and *Pattern Formation* Skills both at Level 40; the creation of Advanced Fusions was tantalizingly close, but to get there required more Aetheric Force.

That meant killing monsters.

Fortunately, he wouldn't be doing it alone, as at Ashlynn's words, the entire group of Protectors started to move, gearing up for a fight as they strapped discarded armor to their bodies and picked up their stored spears. Within a minute, they were ready to go and started marching out of the door and into the street, with Larek following behind along with Protector Ashlynn – where they discovered that it wasn't just the Protectors that had undergone a harrowing magical awakening. When he added in the panicked mutterings and screams of the rest of the town's population, things were even more chaotic than what he walked into coming out of his bedroom in the barracks.

Thankfully, Larek didn't have to deal with any of it, as Protector Ashlynn took immediate charge of the situation, contacting those in charge of the town and breaking off a third of the Protectors to restore at least a semblance of order. The rest of them headed off toward the stables to get mounted up, though Larek refrained from taking a horse to ride. They were a bit too small to handle his actual size and weight, and he could run faster and for longer than a mount, anyway.

"Are you sure you don't want one?" Ashlynn asked, strapping on her helmet as she settled herself on her horse.

He shook his head. "No. Now that you're a Martial, you'll find that your stats will enable you to run faster and longer distances than ever before."

Rather than look skeptical, a thoughtful expression crossed her face before she ordered the Protectors to move out. Larek loped alongside Ashlynn, who took to the front of their formation of 27 Protectors behind her, in 9 rows 3 riders wide, finding it good to stretch his legs after so long being confined to the town or his bedroom creating Fusions.

Just as they were leaving town and angling toward where everyone could feel the Scission in the distance, the power coming from it abruptly spiked... and then shut off just as quickly.

"They've emerged," he explained at the familiar Protector's questioning glance. "As long as we head in that direction, we should run into them."

With only a nod in response, she flicked the reins in her hands to urge her horse to move faster, which meant that Larek had to speed up as well. Before long, they were galloping along the dirt road heading in the general direction of where the Scission used to be, with Larek wondering the entire time what exactly they would find when they got there.

# Chapter 6

"I guess this is what the notification meant by the Corruption only gaining a 'foothold' over the rest of the world," Larek muttered as he looked out over the semi-flooded plain in front of him.

The journey toward the location where the Scission had appeared didn't take all that long once they left Enderflow, though they did have to cross a small stream in their path. Thankfully, there were a few large rocks interspersed over one section of the stream that allowed Larek to jump across the 20-foot-wide tributary of water without getting more than slightly wet, so it was no hindrance in the least. When they crested a small hill that looked over a semi-flooded plain filled with short grasses and a few scattered trees dotting the landscape here and there, they discovered the results of the Scission almost immediately. Or to be more accurate, the monsters that emerged found *them* and hopped their way over to the riders as soon as they were spotted.

"What are these… *things*?" Protector Ashlynn asked him once they all dismounted and readied to defend themselves from attack. They were going to have to wait another minute or so, because while the monsters were only about 100 feet away, they moved rather slowly due to a lack of lower appendages.

"They're **Wilde Mushdooms**."

"Mushdooms? Like… mushrooms with a hint of wild doom to them?" The question caused a few chuckles to emerge from the assembled group of Protectors, but they quieted quickly after that as their professionalism kicked in.

Larek shrugged. "I didn't name them; I only learned about them in the few classes I was able to take at the A—Fort. Don't let the silly name fool you; they can be a pain if they manage to bite you, as you'll suffer from a venom that can kill a full-grown person if enough of it is injected into the body."

The Fusionist was overstating the danger quite a bit, however, as Wilde Mushdooms were quite weak, even in comparison to most of the other monsters that appeared out of Category 1-type Scissions. He had learned about them as part of his *Monster Knowledge* classes in conjunction with his *Scissions* classes; the majority of his knowledge of monsters was limited to those of the weakest variety, but thankfully they were also the most common. As for these Mushdooms, they were generally thought to be one of the easiest monsters to encounter. Granted, they historically appeared with a few other waves of plant- or fungi-based monsters that were slightly more difficult and were considered just fodder at best or an annoyance at worst. In this case, as had been similar back in the Kingdom before the Aperture appeared, there didn't seem to be any other monsters that came with them through the Scission.

There were over 1,000 of them, however, which only slightly increased their danger to Larek and the Protectors. Even outnumbered a little over 34 to 1, he didn't think they would have much problem killing the Mushdooms; in fact, Larek thought he would probably be fine all by himself, even if he didn't have his protective robe.

"Any other information you know about them?" Ashlynn asked tersely as she gripped her spear tighter, visibly taking his warning seriously.

"Well, as you can see, they're very slow and can only move by bending their stalks and hopping forward. Their caps open like a large jaw, and they use them to try and bite their victims using hardened and sharpened points inside their mouths to pierce bare skin, where they would then inject a fungal venom into the victim's body. As far as weaknesses go, they are highly susceptible to fire, and their physical bodies are extremely weak, vulnerable to just about any type of melee attack." Larek was proud of himself for remembering that much about them, as he hadn't been the most dutiful student when it came to learning about monsters – unlike his roommate, Verne, who seemed to soak up all that knowledge like a sponge.

"Do they have hearts or... something like that?"

That wasn't something he knew, unfortunately, and he admitted as much. "I'm not sure. My studies only mentioned that they are extremely weak and not something to be worried about overly much. I assume that if enough damage is done to them, they'll die just like any other monster."

Raising her voice as the Mushdooms continued to close the distance between them, she shouted, "Crescent staggered formation 1!" At her command, the Protectors arranged themselves in two staggered lines in a crescent or half-moon shape, with the back line slightly behind and in between the front line. The formation didn't make any sense to Larek, even as he took his position on the right end of the formation and Ashlynn moved to the left of the lines.

It wasn't until the 3-foot-tall mass of Mushdooms finally hopped close enough to the Protectors that he saw it in action. With their spears in position, the front line of Protectors stabbed out at their targets, piercing completely through the caps of the lead mushroom monsters, before their weapons were violently pulled out to the side, ripping apart even more of their caps in the process. From that one attack, it was plain to see that the attacks were more than enough to kill the Mushdooms, proving just how squishy and vulnerable their soft bodies were. It was also obvious that the Protectors were quite skilled in using their spears, as their strikes were precise and well-timed, with a minimum of wasted movement. Larek supposed that made sense given that their expertise in wielding the weapons was likely due to a General Skill related to their profession, just like his own Axe Handling Skill was so high.

As soon as the front line removed their weapons from the corpses of the Mushdooms they killed, they took a step backwards just as the back line stepped forward. This maneuver allowed the front line to recover from their initial strike while the back line moved forward to stab at the next Mushdoom that hopped forward attempting to take advantage of the first line's occupation with the dead monster. This didn't work so well for the Mushdooms, it turned out, because they were immediately skewered by the back line which was now out front. From there, the cycle repeated itself as the front line stepped forward again, allowing the back line to recover as they stepped back, and so on from there.

He could see that it certainly worked well for them, though he had trouble figuring out where the formation came from in the first place. Since they didn't have monsters in the Empire before this, what would they use this particular strategy for? His wandering thoughts were interrupted as the swarming Mushdooms finally got close enough to encompass the entire formation from side to side; that also meant that they were close enough to register that *Larek* was nearby – and as if by some unspoken command, they shifted toward the Fusionist as a group.

"What are they doing? Are they targeting you?" Ashlynn shouted her question even as she proceeded to kill another Mushdoom that was turning away from her to start hopping toward Larek.

"Uh, yeah, I guess they really don't like people from the Kingdom of Androthe!" he shouted back, his reasoning the best he could come up with for the moment. He really didn't want to explain his background, either now or later, and he thought it seemed plausible enough.

She didn't question it any further than that as she called out different formations for the Protectors to shift to as the monsters started to ignore them in favor of attacking Larek. As for him, he was quickly inundated by masses of hopping fungi and couldn't concentrate on anything but swinging his axe into them. His sweeping strikes sometimes hit 3 or 4 at a time, and because they were so much shorter than him, his attacks cut into their caps at an angle, which chopped a large portion of their front side off of them.  Most of his strikes managed to kill them in one hit, though if he wasn't lucky enough for that, he at least cut through a sufficient portion of their cap that they were essentially defanged.

He eventually used his feet to kick, squish, or otherwise demolish the Mushdooms that got close to him and wasn't able to slice apart with his axe.  There was no real strategy to his defense, just swinging his axe and kicking out and hoping to hit something, though he was aware enough of his surroundings to move away from the piles of mushroom pieces that began to hinder his movement, allowing him to get a better position and to keep the monsters from surrounding him.

Not that he was in much danger, considering that the few times one of the Mushdooms managed to reach him and bite at his legs, they couldn't penetrate his robe.  He barely felt the "bites," as it was, other than a slight pressure on his leg and one time on his knee, but if they somehow found a way to reach his face he might be in trouble.

A few chaotic minutes of fighting was all it took for him to finish off those that surrounded him, while the Protectors took advantage of their distraction to tear through them from behind.  Their destruction was so quick that he wasn't even winded from his exertion and was completely unhurt; even better, none of the Protectors were injured or were even close to being injured in the monster assault.

Silence fell over the slaughtered corpses of the Mushdooms as the last one fell beneath his axeblade, before there were a few cheers from the Protectors that were quickly taken up by the others.  Even Protector Ashlynn appeared happy with their victory, if her guarded smile was any indication, though she was generally more reserved most of the time.

Larek didn't rejoice, however, even as he felt the Corrupted Aetheric Force from the slain monsters enter his body.  By the time it was purified, he would discover that he had received a total of 261 AF from killing the same number of Wilde Mushdooms – which was more than welcome for only a few minutes of work.  But that wasn't what made him refrain from joining in on the victory celebration.

It was just too easy.

Naturally, 1,000 of the Wilde Mushdooms would've been a severe issue for any nearby villages or towns that weren't expecting their appearance, and an Aperture that was able to constantly create them if left alone would eventually become a problem to the local area, but this seemed like a weak introduction to the dangers that Scissions and their monsters could represent. He might've been a little jaded when he compared this attack with what he experienced in the Kingdom, but that didn't change the fact that it felt... wrong, somehow. Or not wrong, per se; instead, it was almost like it was incomplete, like something else was supposed to happen.

"That was much easier than I expected, Larek. I thought these monsters would be much more difficult," Protector Ashlynn said, startling him from the thoughts in his mind.

"They usually are," he admitted. "I think that the Corruption, which flows through a large breach in the world inside the Kingdom, hasn't had a chance to fully saturate the entire world, so you're going to see the weakest of monsters here to begin with. I suppose that's a good thing, though, as you're going to need to practice your new abilities as Mages and Martials in order to fight anything stronger. You might be brave and experts in wielding those spears of yours, but what happens when your strikes can't penetrate the flesh of a powerful monster, or you fight something that is immune to physical damage? You're going to need to learn how to use Battle Arts and spells in order to defend yourselves effectively when the really powerful monsters appear."

Her jovial attitude disappeared as he spoke, and she nodded slowly at his words. "This was one of the weakest monsters that can come out of Scissions?" she asked.

"One of the weakest, if not *the* weakest one. If what I surmise is true, then anything else you face will be slightly stronger than these Mushdooms, though probably not a lot stronger for a little while. I can't guarantee that, though, so you're going to need to learn how to fight stronger monsters—"

Larek cut himself off as he felt something in the distance. Looking at Ashlynn, he could see that she felt it, too.

*I was right. This isn't done yet.*

Off to the south was yet another strong feeling of a Scission, though it felt different. He quickly identified the feeling as the same one he had felt when faced with the Aperture in the Kingdom, and could only assume this was the same.

"Another Scission? Already?" she asked, startled.

But the Fusionist shook his head. "No, that feels like an Aperture. It must've released its monsters while we weren't in range to feel it, and now they've had enough time to create an Aperture."

Larek did some mental calculations in his head. If the Scission had appeared around the same time that the one that spit out the Wilde Mushdooms had, then it took less than a half hour before the beginnings of an Aperture were formed.

That was... worrisome. If it happened that fast with *all* monsters, then it was no wonder that the Kingdom couldn't keep up with the Apertures that were opening everywhere. If the length of time before an Aperture was formed depended on the strength of the monster, on the other hand, then they would have a better chance to kill the stronger monsters before that happened; if this was the case, then something must've happened back in the Kingdom that prevented them from reaching these stronger monsters in time.

Regardless, that didn't help him or the people of the Sealance Empire at the moment, other than to demonstrate that it was inevitable that the Apertures would appear no matter how fast they attempted to react to the opening of new Scissions.

"Let's go close it, then—"

Again, he shook his head. "Not yet. You have to let it form completely first; otherwise, you won't be able to temporarily close it." Having learned from his first experience as well as the information his notification on Apertures provided him, he knew it was best for them to wait a little bit. "But we can at least make our way there and see what we're up against."

Taking their time, an hour saw them looking at a small forest of the same trees that had surrounded the lake he had landed in a month ago – or at least they *had* been the same trees before the Aperture changed them. Now they had been transformed into something that looked unreal, as if someone had painted over a section of the forest with colors that appeared to mimic the right shades of leaves and bark on the trees but was just wrong enough that it almost hurt his eyes to look at them.

After waiting a few more minutes, the first of the monsters that inhabited this transformed forest appeared, and it was nothing like what he expected.

"A **Gooper Fairy**," Larek named it as soon as he saw it. Another physically weak monster, the Gooper Fairy was only a foot tall and looked vaguely humanoid in shape, but its face appeared as though all the dark green skin it possessed had been partially melted off. Fangs an inch long completed the visage, though the pair of diaphanous wings on its back seemed oddly out of place on the frightening-looking monster.

Where the Fairy became deadly was its usage of some sort of strange magic that allowed it to fling out 6-inch balls of multi-colored acidic "goop" that could cling to most surfaces like an extremely sticky adhesive, which hindered movement while the acid ate through most materials. The rate at which it ate through depended on the material;

steel was nearly impervious, while with skin and flesh it was unfortunately quite fast.

Larek told Protector Ashlynn everything he knew about the Gooper Fairy, with a warning that the best defense against them was to kill them from afar. He couldn't remember how far or how fast they could fling their balls of goop, but it was a good bet that anything within 10 to 15 feet was vulnerable.

When one of the Protectors approached and tried to stab the Fairy, he nearly had his face melted off when a ball of goop nearly hit him in the face; he was only saved from such a fate when he rolled out of the way, but by that time he was out of position and was forced to run as another goop ball was sent in his direction only a few seconds after the first.

Larek quickly moved forward and tossed his axe end over end, his practice with it while Logging giving him a bit of accuracy, and his sharp tool sliced completely through the Fairy in a spray of green blood as it fell to the ground. The Fusionist retrieved his axe while also receiving a total of 2 AF from the kill, but was nearly hit by a ball of goop as another Fairy fluttered nearby. Running out of the oddly colored forest, he was glad to see that the monster stopped at the boundary rather than giving chase, as he didn't want to fling his best friend again and risk it getting lost.

"We'll come back with some long-range weaponry and clear this place out," Protector Ashlynn said. "Bows and arrows aren't exactly our preferred weapons of choice, but we do know how to use them," she explained after seeing Larek's confused expression.

As they started to head back to Enderflow to obtain the long-range weaponry they needed to clear out the Gooper Fairy Aperture, Larek and the others felt yet another Aperture open to the northwest. Turning toward the woman, who now appeared shaken at so many threats being nearby, he could only shrug. "I guess this is your new normal. At least your patrols won't be as boring as they were before."

"I'll take boring any day over whatever this is."

He couldn't blame her, as this was extremely unexpected for all of them. One thing they had going for them was that they already had trained fighters that could help them clear out most of these Apertures with a minimum of difficulty. They also had a multitude of people that had been magically awakened throughout the town that they would eventually need to rely on to help when things got worse and the monsters got stronger, but hopefully they had some time before that happened.

His presence was also a benefit as he was able to give them a little more context on what was happening, which he did while they journeyed back toward the town. He went over the history of the Kingdom as he knew it, the Gergasi and their "Guardian/Great One" monikers, the enslavement of the Nobles, and the origin of the breach the Gergasi opened that had ended up putting everyone in the world in danger. The only thing he left out was his own origin and his dual Mage/Martial status, as he didn't feel that was important.

Why wasn't it important? Because he had no intention of staying in Enderflow any longer than necessary. With the way things were going in the Empire of Sealance, he was eager to get back home and find out if he had indeed somehow lost 4 full years of time inside the void-like thing that had transported him thousands of miles away. He still needed to learn how to use his Stama and Battle Arts, and while he thought he might be able to learn a little from Ashlynn and the rest of the people who had acquired Martial status in Enderflow, he was worried that they would attempt to force him to stay somehow so that they could milk him for even more knowledge of the dangers they were going to face from the nearby Apertures and the monsters they created.

He refused to be used or taken advantage of again like that. He'd have fulfilled his service obligation in one more day; once that was done, he was gone and on his way back to the Kingdom.

If there was even a Kingdom to go back to, of course.

# Chapter 7

Larek spent the rest of that day and the next moving from Aperture to Aperture around the area, either participating in killing hundreds of different monsters or simply providing information to the Protectors so that they could finish the job – especially against targets that required a long-range solution. During the fights, not only did Larek earn an additional 1,240 AF, which brought him up to 1,655 AF to spend on upping his Skills' maximums, but he also managed to increase two of his Martial Skills *and* two of his General Skills in the process.

**Dodge** *has reached Level 11!*

**Throwing** *has reached Level 6!*

**Long-Distance Running** *has reached Level 12!*

**Axe Handling** *has reached Level 86!*

It was progress of sorts, at least, and he was happy enough to have the opportunity to improve himself before he left the town of Enderflow. He also increased his maximum Skill in *Fusion* to 40 and his *Pattern Formation* to 38 in anticipation of Leveling them up as he traveled, getting him one step closer to being able to make Advanced Fusions.

On the morning that his obligation to the town was fulfilled, what he had half-expected to happen came true when he was confronted by Protector Ashlynn as he was packing up his stuff in anticipation of going shopping through Enderflow's marketplace for traveling supplies.

"Please don't go, Larek," she abruptly requested. She didn't beg, as that wasn't exactly something he could ever picture her doing, but it was close. "We need your expertise and advice to help keep us protected. We haven't even cleared whatever is to the northwest—"

"I'm sorry, Protector Ashlynn, but I must go," he interrupted her before she could plead further. He genuinely felt bad for their situation, especially as he got to know at least the Protectors of the town, but this wasn't his responsibility, and he frankly didn't want to be there anymore. "I need to get back to my own lands. With all that has happened here, I'm worried about what I'll find back home."

He hadn't really shared much of his situation back in the Kingdom with the woman (or anyone else for that matter) because he didn't want to have to lie, but he was telling the truth about being worried. Not only did the presence of Scissions and Apertures in a land that had never had them before hint that something catastrophic had potentially happened, but the possibility that he had lost *years* of time was also of great concern. Thoughts of his family that he had buried inside his mind due to being unable to help them floated back to the surface. *They probably think I'm dead, having not heard from or about me in at least 5 years. And how have they been handling these Apertures which are likely scattered all over the Kingdom by this point? Are they even **alive**, for that matter?*

Thoughts of his friends who were forced to forget him and move onto Silverledge Academy and Fort Ironwall were also at the forefront of his thoughts, though he didn't worry about them quite as much. They, at least by this point, could protect themselves from the monsters around the Kingdom in one way or another; his family, not so much.

"I... I understand. Are you sure there's no way to convince you to stay another couple of days?"

Larek shook his head. "No, I've been away long enough. And from what I've learned, I have a long way to travel before I get back. I've already spent too much time here as it is, though it was necessary to recover and to fulfill my obligation to the town."

Ashlynn slowly nodded as he walked past her, ready to finish preparing for his journey. As he passed by, she laid her hand on his arm to stop him. She looked up into his eyes, which was strange because he had the feeling that she could actually *see* his actual eyes and not the twisting of her perception that his ring produced.

"Stay safe out there, Larek," she said softly, before her voice changed to something a little harsher. "And promise me that you'll figure out how to use your Stama and Battle Arts before you hurt yourself or someone else."

That took him back a little bit, as he hadn't actually admitted that he was having issues with both those things. He opened his mouth to respond, but he wasn't sure what to say as he was so surprised.

"Don't look so shocked. This whole 'Martial' thing involving Stama and Battle Arts might be new to me, but I know enough to understand that you have absolutely no training in how to use either of them. *Neither do I*, of course, but the rudimentary knowledge of *how* to use them is up here somehow," she said, pointing to her head with her other hand.

*So unfair. I wonder if I stayed a few days, she might be able to train me how to—*

"Unfortunately, I'm fairly certain I don't know enough to teach you how to use it properly," she said sadly. "Until I actually use it properly for the first time, it's more of an instinctual knowledge rather than something I can put into words to help you. Give me a few months and I might be able to—but no. I can't ask you to stay that long when you need to get home." She took her hand away from his arm, nodding again as if making a decision. "You better go if you're going to make good time on the roads," she continued, her voice back to the no-nonsense tone he was used to from her. "You have that copy of the Sealance Empire map I gave you?"

"I do." It was in his pack, and it turned out that the Empire was as big or even bigger than the Kingdom, though it was hard to tell because a third of it was actually islands out in the ocean. If he were to travel a little more west, he would eventually hit the ocean, something that he resolved to see for himself sometime because that much water seemed impossible to him. Unfortunately, backtracking just to see some sights wasn't something he wanted to waste time on right now, considering that he was told a normal traveler crossing the Empire from his location to the border of Lowenthal, the lands east of the Empire and a place he'd have to cross in order to get to the Kingdom, would take them at least 5 months.

Crossing Lowenthal would take at least another 2 months before he even got to the border of the Kingdom of Androthe, which meant 7 months of travel – a significant chunk of time all by itself. Of course, with his ability to move quickly and his exceptional endurance, thanks to his Martial stat, which meant he wouldn't tire out even after hours of running, he could cut that time by at least 80% if he pushed himself. But then he had to take into account finding places to sleep at night, because he would eventually get tired, as well as restocking his traveling supplies.

And none of that even took into account the fact that the lands were now likely infested with Scissions, Apertures, and the monsters that those two things brought forth. He wanted to continue improving his Skills so he could create Advanced Fusions, which meant stopping to kill as many monsters as safely as possible along the way for their Aetheric Force.

As a result, he couldn't easily put a timeframe on when he would get back to the Kingdom, let alone finding his parents, traveling to Fort Ironwall, and discovering where his friends ended up. A thought about Nedira and how she would react to seeing him again after so long was interrupted by the knowledge that she wouldn't know him because of what Chinli had done, but the desire to see her again burned strongly in his heart for some reason.

"Very well. Good luck, and I hope you make it back to your home swiftly and safely." With that last announcement, she left his room with her back held straight and stiff – but that was how she usually appeared, so he didn't think anything of it. He paused for a few seconds before starting on his way, leaving the barracks as quickly as possible before he was stopped again; even doing that, he noticed the disappointed looks on some of the Protectors' faces in the gathering room, but he ignored them as well as he could. They would be fine without him, especially as he heard the night before about plans for those who had undergone the magical awakening throughout the rest of the town being trained to fight the monsters, so soon enough they would have more than enough help to go around.

Once he exited the Protectors' barracks, he swiftly made his way down the street toward his destination. The one benefit of his patrols over the last month was a familiarity with the town layout and the location of different shops and services. The overall composition of businesses was remarkably similar to the ones he'd seen or heard of in the Kingdom, though he personally didn't have a lot of experience with visiting them. Still, they were familiar enough to him that he knew where he needed to go, and he had traveled just enough to know what he needed to get, so planning his shopping trip was relatively simple.

Thankfully, while the monetary system in the Sealance Empire utilized oddly shaped coins with marks on them that were completely different from the ones Larek possessed from the Kingdom, his were still accepted as valid currency – though with a slightly unfavorable exchange rate. That didn't matter all that much to him, however, as he was fairly certain he had more than enough to last him years even if he was ripped off.

His first stop was the Tailor, a man named Johan who ran a shop filled to the brim with bolts of cloth with different shades and textures, as well as a hefty quantity of already-crafted shirts, pants, socks, and underthings on racks and shelves. Almost all of it was made of lightweight material that was perfect for the environment, which he found was hot and humid – at least in comparison to what he was used to. That was definitely something he needed, as his robe was created using a thick, wool-like fabric that held in the heat more than he liked; if it wasn't for his Body stat being so high and able to adapt to the higher temperature, he was sure he would've overheated the first day he was in Enderflow.

Unfortunately, none of the already-crafted clothing would work for Larek given his size. While the people he'd seen in the Empire were, in general, slightly taller than those from the Kingdom, there was a large difference between an average height of 5 foot 5 inches and his own 7 feet. Which was why he had visited the Tailor a few days before to commission a set of clothing that would fit him, having thought ahead toward his departure at the end of his month's obligation to the town. He remembered the issue that they had back in Whittleton regarding clothing being available for him, and since he had the luxury of time, he took advantage of it to have something custom made.

To have it done accurately, however, he'd deliberately taken off his *Perceptive Misdirection* ring before entering the shop so that his measurements could be taken. While Johan the Tailor had originally been slightly taken aback at Larek's height, his professionalism kicked in immediately and he had thrown himself into measuring the Fusionist with a fervor that was surprising. "'Tis a challenge, m'boy!" the Tailor had said at the time when he saw the bemused expression on Larek's face. "Might be I get a few Skill Levels in *Tailoring* for this!"

He supposed that Johan's enthusiasm made sense, as he knew how difficult it was to raise a Level past a certain point, especially in General Skills. Profession Skills fell into that category, and while Larek's Level 86 in Axe Handling was a bit of an outlier with how quickly it Leveled, he was aware that most other people would be lucky to see something of that Level before they died of old age.

When he walked into the Tailoring shop, with his ring deactivated, he expected Johan to be behind the counter as he had been before, but that didn't turn out to be the case. Instead, the Tailor was standing in the middle of his shop with an intense look of concentration on his face as he waved his hands around in front of him. Larek paused at the strange activity for a few seconds before he focused on looking at the man with a little more focus on the Mana density in the air. In no time at all, it became obvious that Johan was attempting to control his Mana by bringing it outside of his body as there were stirrings in the strands of light around him, but he wasn't having much luck as of yet.

*Even the Tailor went through a magical awakening?*

"Oh, drat—ah! Larek! You're back!" Johan shouted excitedly as he caught sight of the Fusionist. "Can you believe that I was lucky enough to be chosen for the duty of protecting the world? Me? What do I know about flinging spells around? Well, other than what's now inexplicably in my head, of course."

Somehow, the man was even more excited than he had been when facing the prospect of gaining a few Levels in his *Tailoring* Skill. Larek smiled at the enthusiasm and briefly considered offering some advice, but he held off, not wanting to reveal his status as a Martial *and* a Mage. That, and he was about to leave and didn't want to get roped into helping any of the residents of the town with their newfound abilities, as he had places to go and monsters to kill.

"That's amazing, Johan! I'm sure you'll figure it out at some point." He only paused a second before asking, "Did you happen to get my clothes made?"

His enthusiasm wasn't extinguished in the least over the change in subject as the Tailor nodded and rushed behind his counter. Before long, he was pulling out two full sets of clothing, one of them made of lightweight material that was flowy and would fit in quite well with the local population. The second was made of thicker material that was almost on par with his robe; it would be hot in the current environment, but he figured it would be a good backup in case he needed it, and would be necessary once he got closer to the Kingdom. They wouldn't look so out of place back home, and he felt as if he needed to have it created now because he wasn't sure if he'd be staying anywhere in the future long enough to have it done.

"Here you go, young man! I even managed to Level *Tailoring* twice during the process because they were so different from anything I've made before." He looked ecstatic at that fact, and Larek couldn't blame him; two Levels in a General Skill in such a short time was almost unheard of.

For anyone but Larek, of course.

"I'm even throwing in this extra bag I had lying around because you helped me advance my Skill, so that you don't have to try and stuff it into that one you're already carrying around. You should be able to easily attach it to your other pack, so that you don't have to worry about multiple straps crossing over your body."

Thankful for the gift, Larek immediately figured out how to tie it to his existing sack attached to his back, and was able to settle it easily with the extra clothing inside. He was itching to get out of his robe, but until he had time to add some Fusions to his new articles of clothing, he wanted to keep his Boosts and defenses in place.

"This is excellent work, Johan. How much do I owe you?"

The Tailor only thought about it for a second before he answered. "I believe the remaining balance is 1 silver and 2 copper, but if you give me a silver I'll call it even." Larek had already paid half up front for the work, and while he only received 85 silver instead of the

100 that he would normally get for the gold piece because of the unfavorable exchange rate, it still let him know that he would be flush with funds for a long while yet.  During his patrols, he had peeked at the prices of food and other supplies that he would soon be loading up with and determined that he probably wouldn't be spending more than 10 silver for everything, and that included a simple tent and a bedroll, which were the biggest expenses.

That would leave him with the equivalent of a little under 25,000 silver coins due to the pair of platinum coins he possessed, even with the unfavorable exchange rate.  He figured that was more than enough to get him home.

His work creating Fusions for the SIC was finally paying off in a tangible way that he was able to experience personally.  Granted, his companions back in Whittleton had gone on a shopping spree with some of the coinage that he had gained from his work, but he didn't really comprehend how much they spent or what things cost.  The economic situation might be a little bit different in the Empire as opposed to the Kingdom, but if they were anywhere near similar, then he was finally understanding why Bartholomew had boggled at the amount, saying that what they carried away from Copperleaf had been more than his father's Duchy collected in taxes every year.

"Thank you again for the work!"  Johan smiled happily as he accepted the silver coin, which was in local currency, as Larek had a small amount of it for easier purchases around town.

"I appreciate how fast you got it done.  Good luck with the whole saving the world thing, Johan," the Fusionist called back to the Tailor as he left, who was already starting to experiment with his Mana once again.  As he left the shop, he slipped the ring back on his finger to camouflage his height from the rest of the townsfolk, before shaking his head at the thought of the Tailor being a Mage.  It wasn't just him, he knew, as dozens or perhaps hundreds of others in Enderflow had also undergone the change a couple of days ago, and he could only shudder in apprehension as every single one of them would be experimenting with something that they only partially understood.  He was sure that more than one mistake would end up costing lives in the long run, but that was inevitable even back in the Kingdom if the students and trainees of the Academies and Forts weren't careful.

For his next stop, there was a general store of sorts where he picked up a bedroll and tent, as well as a nice, sturdy walking stick that he was planning on turning into a Mage's staff to replace the one he left back in the Kingdom.  After that, he loaded up with many travel rations and food that would keep for at least a few days and packed them into his bag, stuffing it full to near bursting. With all his preparations completed, Larek pulled out his map to confirm that he knew where he was going, before stashing it away and heading out the road that led to the northeast, where it would eventually join with a major artery leading through the middle of the Empire and was the swiftest route to his eventual destination.

As he left the town of Enderflow behind, he felt as if a great weight had been lifted off his back. While he wasn't required to help them anymore, there was still a moral obligation that rattled around in his mind to help these people learn what they needed to survive the influx of monsters covering their land. However, given that Larek considered himself just barely able to make sense of everything as it was, he didn't think it was either necessary or a good idea.

It would be like the blind leading the blind.

# Chapter 8

It was mid-morning by the time he left Enderflow, and it was only just past noon when he encountered his first monster that attacked him as he was resting for a few minutes. He'd been running at a pace where his *Long-Distance Running* Skill kicked in to help reduce the energy needed to maintain that speed, while his Martial stats provided the extra oomph to allow him to keep that pace for hours before needing to rest. After a few hours, he found that while his endurance was high enough to not become tired from all the running he was doing, his body needed food to supply it with energy in order to do it. As such, he stopped around noon when the sun was high in the sky to move off the road and into a small copse of trees nearby that provided some shade.

His journey thus far had been uneventful even as his strides ticked up the miles in between him and the town of Enderflow. The landscape had generally been similar to what was around the town, with half-flooded fields and distant rivers and bunching of trees near what he assumed were lakes, though he couldn't see them from his perspective. In the far distance, what appeared to be some shorter mountains poked up into the skyline, while relatively closer than that was a veritable forest of trees similar to the copses seen around the local area. They were too far away to tell for sure, but they appeared to be a bit larger than the ones he was taking shade under while he consumed some of the freshest food he had purchased a short time ago.

He was in the middle of chewing a strip of some sort of dried meat that had a fishy – but not unpleasant – taste to it when a rustle above him alerted him to the danger a second too late. Larek was taking a step backward in response to the sound as he looked up, but something suddenly scraped something sharp across his face before impacting his chest. The weight behind the blow was insignificant and only made him stagger back slightly, but the attack against his face was bad enough that it made up for it.

As his survival instincts kicked in, he looked to see on the ground near him what appeared to be a 4-foot-long beast of some kind, shaped like a lithe ferret but at least three times as large. A brief glance at the bloody claws – on what he recognized as a **Tree Weasel** – proved that it had been the one that had attacked him. More than that, the fact that he could only see out of one eye meant that the sharp claws had likely sliced through the other with startling effectiveness. Even as he snatched his axe from his holder – which he had transferred outside of his robe for easier access – he felt a brief flash of pain from the wounds to his face, though it was quickly suppressed due to his *Pain Immunity* Skill. What was more worrying to him was the fact that he was down an eye, and a memory of Barrowford where he had his face ripped apart by a flying skeleton bird was enough to send a surge of panicked energy through his limbs.

As such, when the Weasel gathered itself on the ground to jump at his face again, his body reacted jerkily to interpose the axe in front of his body with the blade facing forward, directly in line with its upward jump. He nearly lost control of his tool when he felt the impact of the monster's head against the unnatural sharpness of the blade, but he managed to keep it steady as the beast essentially killed itself as it was cut in half, splashing its bloody pieces all over his robe. The blood wouldn't stain, fortunately, as the Multi-Resistance Fusion on it helped to repel the substance, but that wasn't really his concern at the moment.

As soon as he saw that the Tree Weasel was dead, Larek took a better grip on his axe as he looked up to see if there were any other surprises there for him, just in time to have a second Tree Weasel descend on him from his peripheral vision. Better prepared, he steadily held his axe again and shoved the blade in front of the Weasel's downward arc, and the monster obligingly cut itself in half as it impacted his Logging tool.

A quick glance around with his good eye, of which his vision was turning red as blood leaked into it from his other wounds, showed that he was safe for the moment, or at least he couldn't see any other Tree Weasels preparing to attack him. He activated his *Healing Surge* Fusion and stiffened as it kicked up his natural Body Regeneration to heal the wounds on his face; no more than 10 seconds later, he nearly threw up his recent meal when he felt and *heard* his eye reform in his socket, as it sounded like a wet plop that was more than a little disturbing. Fortunately, he managed to keep it all inside as his healing finished, leaving him hungry and covered in drying blood where it had spilled out of the rips in his face.

With one hand on his axe and the other reaching into his pack to get more food, he kept his eyes roaming over the nearby trees and his ears open to the sound of any rustling that might give away another ambush. After a few minutes of chewing through more of the meat he had previously been consuming, as well as a few hard biscuits that were buttery flavored if dry, he felt quite a bit better. A few sips of water from a waxed leather canteen he had purchased at the general store along with his bedroll and tent washed it all down, and he felt ready to go again.

Except he didn't move back to the road. Instead, he went to go find more of the annoying Weasels, which he could only assume were nearby. There was a faint feeling of an Aperture somewhere close by, though he had missed it while he was running and later trying to replenish his energy. He resolved to keep his senses active while he ran in the future, as he wanted to make sure he didn't miss any others so that he could kill their monsters and accumulate Aetheric Force. While that was *a* motivation for Larek to move through the forest, which now that he took a better look at he realized was subtly different in shape than he would normally expect, it wasn't the *only* motivation.

Revenge upon those that hurt him and took his sight away again, even if only temporarily, took precedence. *No one gets away with making me bleed my own blood.*

It didn't take long before he found his first victim, especially as it came right for him. Until it jumped off the trunk of the tree it was hiding on, the Tree Weasel's fur coloring made it difficult to see; but now that he was aware of the danger and alert, the monster didn't stand a chance as he swung his axe at the target, bisecting it with a single slice through its body. Half of it impacted against his robe, but it wasn't with enough force to hurt him in the slightest. Just as from the other Weasels he killed initially, Larek saw that he received a single AF as a result of its death, which wasn't a lot when all was said and done – but that didn't matter as much to him as taking out his frustration of nearly being blinded again on his weasely victims.

Larek continued slaughtering his way through the small copse of trees, looking up the entire time to find the Tree Weasels as they descended upon him in ambush, until he realized he could feel the Aperture nearby.

Looking around his immediate area, he found it easily enough behind another tree, and it was just as small as he expected, given his recent experience with it.

His previous knowledge of Apertures had been limited by his exposure to only a single one back in the Kingdom, along with the notification that explained their origins. What he hadn't realized until he had participated in the temporary closing of the ones near Enderflow was that they varied in size substantially, based on the monsters that emerged from them. For the Tree Weasels, that meant that the sphere of the Aperture was only 2 feet in width, which was just wide enough for the lengthy monsters to slip out.

Their smaller size also meant that they required less force to temporarily close them. The Apertures were physical in a sense, as they could be attacked and damaged, but they couldn't be permanently "killed"; instead, what he and the other Protectors from Enderflow had done was strike the sphere with their weapons until it shrunk in size to the point where it appeared, for lack of a better word, dormant. No new monsters would emerge until it was active again, but as for any monsters that were left in the Aperture's territory that hadn't been killed before the sphere was temporarily closed?

They would immediately attack whoever was trying to close the Aperture, racing in from wherever they roamed around the territory. They had learned that the hard way when they accidentally left a few dozen monsters alive when they attacked the Aperture, only to have to scramble to defend themselves when they were abruptly assaulted by a swarm of monsters. After that, they made sure to clear out the roaming monsters throughout the territory first, which was much easier because they tended to only move solitarily or in small groups, rather than a full horde of them like during a Scission.

Now, though, he was counting on his attack against the Aperture to bring all of the darn Weasels to him. He didn't really want to spend another half-hour wandering around and clearing the rest of them out, as he still wanted to make some distance on his journey that day.

Striking out with his axe at the relatively small, floating sphere located in the middle of the copse of trees, he immediately saw it begin to reduce in size and determined that a few more blows would likely close it. At the same time, he was also aware of sounds coming from all around him as the trees seemed to come alive. A quick glance around his location revealed that the normally hard-to-spot Weasels were streaming in from all over the Aperture's territory, bouncing from tree to tree in an effort to defend their connection to the world of Corruption. Larek readied himself for the inevitable attack as he raised his axe…

…only to spin around and slice through two different trees in quick succession behind him, causing them to quickly start to topple over. He moved to another one a few steps away and did the same thing, slicing easily through the trunk of the tree with a single blow since their trunk diameter was relatively small – not anywhere near the thickness of the Rushwood trees he was used to back in the Kingdom.

The falling trees were easy enough to avoid, but the point in taking them down wasn't just for fun, but to provide fewer options for the approach of the incoming Tree Weasels and to give him some room to maneuver. The trees crashed down just as the first of the monsters arrived near the location of the Aperture, and Larek leapt backwards as it attempted to jump nearly 20 feet to land on him, only to find that it had missed him and landed short on the ground below. The Fusionist was quick to take advantage of this as he swept his axe in a downward trajectory and lopped off its head; using the momentum of his swing, he brought it up just in time to catch another Weasel that flung itself at him only to miss him by a few feet, and it was cut in half before it even had a chance to land on the ground.

Now that he had some room to move, Larek maneuvered himself into the middle of the clearing he had created as he watched the enraged-looking monsters have to jump down off their trees and make their way over the ground toward him rather than try and land on him from above. It quickly became clear that the Weasels were quite a bit less agile while on the ground as compared to hanging off the side of a tree, and while a few of them managed to jump and impact his body, none of them got anywhere close to his face. Their claws attempted to shred through his robe, but the *Multi-Resistance* Fusion on it stopped even their naturally sharp implements from cutting through it.

Larek lost count after the first few dozen were killed, and it was only when no more attempted to attack him that he relaxed and looked around him, seeing that more than 60 of them had streamed toward his location. Other than a scratch on the back of his hand that bled profusely until he stopped it with a pulse of his *Healing Surge* Fusion, he was unharmed.

*That was much easier than hunting them all down myself. A bit more dangerous, granted, but easier and faster for sure.*

In fact, the only thing in danger had been his packs, as they weren't protected by any Fusions; but fortunately, none of the Weasels managed to strike out at them on his back, either because they couldn't reach or they didn't consider it a priority. He resolved in the future to ensure his belongings were stowed away before he did something like this again.

That thought made him pause for a moment before he started moving toward the Aperture. *I'm doing this again? I thought I might just be killing whatever monsters I ran across, but this is something completely different. Should I be closing these Apertures wherever I go, even if it isn't my responsibility?*

The short answer and the long answer to that were complicated. The short answer was no, because he knew that the Sealance Empire would have to figure it all out, and closing these Apertures wasn't something he needed to do. The longer answer was that it wasn't about any type of responsibility that closing these Apertures was a good idea, as it was simply a means to an end. Sure, he could kill whatever monsters he came across on his travels and even occasionally take some time to hunt down a few more here and there; doing so would inevitably get him enough AF, by the time he arrived in the Kingdom, to achieve his goals of making Advanced Fusions, but it wouldn't necessarily be quick. From his experience thus far, the monsters that emerged from the permanent Apertures were relatively weak and not very numerous when compared to Scissions – as long as their territories were small, as the larger the territory, the more monsters there would be inside of it.

Therefore, he could only count on receiving 1 or possibly 2 AF per monster when he killed them, and accumulating enough to raise his maximum Skill Levels would take months if he only confronted those that were nearby on his journey. But if he deliberately sought out the Apertures and brought all of the monsters to him…

He considered this approach for a few minutes as he killed a Tree Weasel that emerged from the Aperture after a few minutes or so as it regained its previous size. It was something that he hadn't seen before, because the Protectors had closed the Apertures they encountered almost immediately once the monsters were cleared, so it was slightly fascinating how the entire process worked. Apparently, if the sphere was damaged without being closed right away, it would eventually recover its previous size as it "healed" the damage done to it; he'd seen this happen back at the Trizard Aperture – when they were working to try and destroy it before they knew what it was, of course – but that was a completely different situation because it "healed" itself rapidly due to its initial activation. What he saw now was what he could only assume was the normal method of its activity, along with it sending out more Weasels to replenish those that had been killed by Larek.

He had an idea to sit there and kill every Weasel as soon as it emerged, thereby gaining another point of Aetheric Force every few minutes or so for very little effort. Putting this plan into effect to see if it would work, he stood there waiting for another one to appear, but it wasn't until nearly 30 minutes later that the next one came out and immediately attacked him – and almost instantly died as it was cut in half by Larek's axe.

*Hmm… if they come out every 30 minutes or so, then that means approximately 48 Tree Weasels every day. Based on how many there were when I got here, which turns out to be a total of 82 according to how many AF I've received thus far, then it would take a little under two days for it to fill up again. From what the original notification said about*

*Apertures, it was only once they reached that point that they would begin to spread their territory and send even more monsters out to inhabit their newly expanded territory. How fast that occurred is something I don't know, but I'm sure those back in the Kingdom would have a better idea.*

*Regardless, I can't just wait around for a day and accumulate less than 50 AF for the trouble. I think my original idea to venture out and close all of the Apertures I encounter is probably the quickest – if not the safest – route to earning enough AF while still maintaining a steady pace.*

With that conclusion having been reached, Larek approached the Aperture again and slashed at it a few more times, watching as it shrunk down to something the size of his fist. It was completely inert with only a very tiny sense to his *Magical Detection* Skill that indicated that it was even there, and any other attempts to attack it with his axe ended with his tool simply rebounding off with absolutely no effect.

With the Aperture now temporarily closed, Larek slid the axe back into its holder on his waist, before leaving the clearing he had made in the copse of trees, the bisected corpses of the Weasels he had slaughtered scattered all over the ground. He briefly considered whether there was anything on them that might be useful, such as meat that he could cook for extra sustenance, but he dismissed it out of hand. He still had plenty of foodstuffs in his pack, and enough money to last him for years of buying even more on his journey, though he didn't expect it to take nearly that long. As for the rest of the Weasel bodies, he didn't really think there was anything valuable in them, other than perhaps their claws. However, knowing that he had a long journey to go and not a lot of room in his packs to carry much, he left them alone for now; besides, he wasn't exactly knowledgeable about harvesting such items for use in something else.

That was definitely something he thought he needed to work on in the future, however, especially if he was going to continue killing monsters at the incredible rate he had planned.

Stopping by where he first entered the copse of trees, Larek picked up his walking stick from where he had let it drop after being ambushed and wounded. Using it to guide his way back to the road, he broke into a run as he continued his journey back to the Kingdom.

# Chapter 9

Now that he was actively searching for existing Apertures to close, Larek began to concentrate on the feelings they gave off from a distance. They were quite different in intensity compared to Scissions and newly forming Apertures, as they were more of the annoying buzzing of a fly in your periphery rather than the sense of a gigantic threat bearing down on you. He had been ignoring the few that he sensed nearby up to that point, because they weren't exactly his priority, but now that his plans had slightly changed, he paid attention to them.

The first one that he faintly sensed after the Tree Weasels was far off the road to the south; he judged it to be approximately 2 miles in that direction, which was a bit of a detour if he was being honest with himself. He decided to skip it for now as he wanted to see if there was anything closer to his path, because he didn't want to spend hours going out of his way to reach these kinds of distant Apertures unless he had no other choice.

Thankfully, a few hours and many miles of running after he left the copse with the Weasels, he finally sensed one that was only a half-mile or so off the road to the north. Looking in that direction as he got closer, the territory that had been claimed by the Aperture was fairly obvious because the gradually drying plains leading up to the larger forest in the distance were covered in snow. Remembering back in the Kingdom and the **Snow Spiders** he and his companions had encountered after leaving Copperleaf Academy, he thought that they might be a slight problem if they managed to surround him, but he thought that he could probably take them out without too much trouble, regardless.

It wasn't Snow Spiders that inhabited the territory around the Aperture, however, but **Arctic Yetilings**. Unlike some of the much larger Yeti monsters that he had learned about, which were 10-foot-tall bipedal monstrosities that had the strength in their blue-skinned fists to smash a Mage flat and had an easy time hiding in snowy environments due to their shaggy white hair covering the rest of their bodies, the Arctic Yetilings were *much* smaller. At only 3 feet tall, they were easily able to lie down in the foot of snow that covered the area around the Aperture, camouflaging them from Larek's sight entirely well enough that his first sight of one of them was when he accidentally stepped on one and it immediately attempted to bite his leg off at the knee.

Unfortunately for the little white-haired monster, whose strength was much less than the grown-up version, its bite had absolutely no chance of getting through his robe. Having already taken his axe out when he entered the snow-laden territory, Larek immediately swung down and cut off its head, the Yetilings' blue blood splashing brightly against the backdrop of pristine white snow. Disturbed at how completely it had been hidden from view, Larek realized that this was exactly what the plan he had concocted was for, as he immediately strode toward the floating sphere easily seen in the middle of the snowy plain.

He was ambushed twice before he arrived at the Aperture, which he easily fended off with a few simple swipes at the ambushing monsters, in each of which he immediately smacked one with his bladed tool. Immediately, the snow throughout the territory – which stretched to encompass a circular area that was at least 300 feet in diameter – burst upwards in dozens of spots, sending particles of snow flying in a cloud that obscured his view a little bit. Soon enough, the sight of at least a hundred of the little Yetilings barreling through the snow as if it wasn't even there met his eyes, and it was all he could do to prevent being overwhelmed within the first few seconds.

They might've been small, but they moved through the snow like a fish through water. As a result, when the initial wave hit him from all sides, he was forced to fight off nearly 20 of them in short order, and his swings were a blur of frantic chopping and slashing as he attempted to keep them away from him.

Things got worse when he discovered that the hairy monsters weren't just mindless beasts bent on his destruction, as one of them picked up a fellow Yetiling and *tossed* it toward Larek from approximately 10 feet away. The Yetiling flew through the air on a collision course with his face, and Larek narrowly managed to get his axe handle up to block it before impact. The white-haired monster attached itself to the shaft of his tool and held on, dragging it down before ripping it out of his hand with a strength he hadn't seen in them before that.

Thankfully, it had no chance to utilize the axe against him as it fell to the snow below right on top of the extremely sharp blade, which cut through most of its body and severed its spine in the process. Unfortunately, it was now covering his major means of defense against the onslaught of Yetilings, and he didn't have the time or opportunity to bend down and pick it back up. As a result, the former Logger was forced to turn to his fists and feet as he punched yet another Yetiling flying through the air at him after being tossed by its comrade. He felt the bones in his hand creak a little as the skeleton of the monster was harder than he expected, as if it was made from ice rather than bone. Nevertheless, his awkward punch was more than enough to cave in a good portion of the Yetiling's chest, which incapacitated it, if not killed it outright.

Kicks, slaps, and punches were all he could manage to muster against the rest of the monsters as they attempted to pile onto him to drag him down to their level, but he refused to let them win. Showing absolutely no skill whatsoever, he eventually used his elbows, knees, and even his forehead to smash into the scrambling, biting bodies around him, suffering cuts and bruises over his hands and face as he responded to the onslaught. At one point, he was fairly certain he broke his left wrist when he attempted to punch one of the Yetilings in the face, only to hit it at what he quickly learned was the wrong angle. Thankfully, a quick usage of his *Healing Surge* Fusion was enough to help set it back in place and heal it up as he used his other limbs to inflict damage.

As much as they might have helped, at no point did Larek feel like any of his Battle Arts were going to activate – which was a worry that he had put a little thought into. Engaging one of the Martial abilities had the risk of pushing him too hard, which could be detrimental if he were to pass out; at the same time, he couldn't feel a single thing in his body that hinted at how he might be able to utilize his Stama. He had a theory that it was only able to be controlled while he was in combat, but that theory didn't seem easy to prove one way or another.

As quickly as it started, the fight was over, leaving the Fusionist with bloody knuckles and an ankle that felt strained after an awkward kick earlier, but another use of his healing Fusion was enough to patch up any of his injuries. Before he indulged in a small feast to replenish his body's natural energies from the healing and exertion, he kicked the corpse of the Yetiling that had ripped his best friend from his hands and picked up the axe from the snow. Looking it over, it didn't look any worse for wear, so he quickly moved to the Aperture and closed it with a few simple swings. At the same time, he felt the accumulated Corrupted Aetheric Force enter his body and start the conversion process into Aetheric Force for him to use.

In total, Larek received 112 AF from the slaughter of the Yetilings, which tracked with his assumption that they were worth 1 AF apiece. It wasn't a large amount, but it pushed his previous total of 229 AF to 341 AF. That wasn't enough to increase the maximum Skill Level of Pattern Formation to 39 yet, but it was close. Conversely, he could also put it toward something that required fewer AF to upgrade, but he held off on spending it for now.

Another surprise met him when he checked his notifications and found one that he had ignored while in the heat of battle.

***Unarmed Fighting*** *has been unlocked!*
***Unarmed Fighting*** *has reached Level 1!*
***Unarmed Fighting*** *has reached Level 2!*

The unexpected Skill appeared under his Martial Skills in his Status, which was a welcome surprise. He had thought that only weapon expertise Skills would be part of the Martial category, but he was proven wrong; then again, he didn't really have a good understanding of what kinds of Skills Martials had access to, and he wished he had asked the Martial trainees with whom he had traveled after leaving Copperleaf more questions than he did. At the time, he had been focused on Stama and his lack of control, and such things like other Skills that might be available hadn't occurred to him.

With the Aperture now closed, Larek quickly exited the area and picked up his staff from where he had left it before entering the territory, then grabbed more food from his pack. Snacking on some dried meat and a few biscuits as he walked back to the road, he gradually realized that he would have to leave his packs out of the territory around the Apertures he worked to close, as half of the biscuits he pulled out had been crushed during the melee. The next fight might end up doing damage to the actual material, and he was hesitant to add any Fusions on them in case he had to store a Fusion or two inside.

He was also going to need to stop for more food supplies more frequently if he continued to require as much healing as he was seeming to need during these fights to close the Apertures. Thankfully, he had the money for it, but then there was the issue of being overwhelmed like he had been today, when he lost his grip on his axe. As interesting as it was to unlock a Skill for *Unarmed Fighting*, he had no desire to use his body to inflict damage on monsters unless he was forced to do that.

It was at that point in his contemplation about it that he realized he had gone through both the fight with the Tree Weasels and that with the Arctic Yetilings without activating his *Repelling Barrier*. He smacked himself in the forehead while he berated himself for such a stupid mistake, kicking a rock on the road in frustration. The only excuse he could think of was that he had taken to keeping it off while with the Protectors as he didn't want more questions about it than he could easily answer, and he didn't want to risk someone envious of its protection attempting to steal his robe from him.

But now that he didn't have to worry about anyone seeing him, he should've been using it any time he went into a fight. That he hadn't realized it until then said something about his state of mind, as the only two things he could think about were getting back to the Kingdom to see how his friends and family were faring and to develop his Skills along the way. Rather than being more cautious now that he was alone and traveling through what was essentially a dangerous foreign land, his combat preparedness had taken an unfortunate dive. Whether it was the newfound feeling of freedom he felt from all the expectations that were weighing him down back home or his self-assured confidence that he had nothing to fear from any of the weak monsters he encountered, he needed to change his mindset – and change it fast. Otherwise, he would make a mistake and end up dying in the middle of what was essentially nowhere for no reason other than his own incompetence.

He had the tools to succeed, after all, but he needed to use them in order to survive.

Thinking about the Fusions that had protected him so well back in the Kingdom, he realized that he needed to quickly replace some of them before he took any more risks. With that in mind and with the daylight slowly dying in the sky, Larek sped up his running and began to ignore the few instances of Apertures he could sense along the way. His goal was the forest ahead, where he hoped to find shelter of some kind so that he could get some Fusion work done where he wasn't sitting in the middle of a field or on the open road. Ideally, the next town would work even better, as he could rent a room in an inn like they had back in Whittleton, but according to the map Larek had copied from Protector Ashlynn, he'd have to travel at least a few hours after night fell in order to reach it. Instead, he was going to have to find something else to shelter himself before it got dark, because journeying through a dark forest at night when there might be monsters around wasn't exactly the smartest idea.

He had to start doing the smart thing eventually if he didn't want to end up dead. He'd gotten lucky to have survived as long as he had, but eventually his luck would run out if he didn't take an active role in making the correct decisions. Being on his own was harder than he thought it would be, but he couldn't help but think it was actually the best thing that could've happened to him.

Naturally, Larek didn't appreciate being deposited halfway across the continent while potentially missing a few years of time, but this was also an opportunity to prove to himself that he was more than just someone that could make Fusions. When he first discovered the ability, it was all he wanted to do, and the obsession to create more and more had consumed him. After learning how to focus and apply that obsession toward the greater good, which had felt rewarding if a bit hollow at the same time, he had begun to wonder if there was more that he could be doing with his life. He still had no desire to confront the Gergasi or figure out a way to close the breach permanently like the Dean had wanted him to do, as that seemed impossible and so far above his abilities that it was more of a nightmarish obstacle rather than a future goal, but he also felt a drive to help people.

Or, at least, help people that he knew and cared about.

In order to do that, he had already planned to increase his abilities with Fusions, but he had already learned that creating Fusions wasn't enough. He had to learn how to use them properly in a fight against monsters, which meant that he needed to learn how to fight.

And what better classroom was there to learn how to fight than confronting the weaker monsters infesting the Sealance Empire? Well, Fort Ironwall was likely better in many ways, in addition to teaching him about Battle Arts and manipulating Stama, but it was half a world away at this point. Just like using whatever material was on hand to make Fusions, Larek was going to use this current environment to hone what few skills he had in fighting to ensure he wasn't just a one-trick mule when he got back to the Kingdom and went looking for his parents and friends.

If he couldn't attend an Academy or a Fort to train himself at the moment, he would use the rest of the world to instruct him. It would take a lot of trial-and-error, patience, and dedication to studying what he was doing right and wrong when it came to fighting monsters. Thankfully, he had more than enough practice staying hyper-focused on any task he dedicated himself to, whether it was Fusions or something else.

He just had to hope he didn't make any more mistakes and die before he learned his lessons.

# Chapter 10

"What can I do for you, stranger?"

Larek smiled at the Innkeeper behind the bar, who had interrupted his incessant wiping of the bartop with a rag that had seen better days at the big man's appearance. Despite its current state, the rag had obviously been effective enough to show a shine on the surface of the bar that seemed unnatural, and the Fusionist realized that something had been applied to the rag that caused it to look that way. He assumed it was some sort of waxy stain, but he'd never seen wood shine the way it did – at least not in the Kingdom.

"A hearty meal and a room for the night, if I could."

The Innkeeper hesitated for a few seconds before replying. "I have a room available, but I don't think you'll fit on the bed," he answered with a chuckle.

Larek kept his smile, showing that the prospect of a too-small bed didn't bother him. "Not a problem; I've been sleeping wherever I could for the last week or so, and just being inside somewhere safe is a luxury I can't afford to be picky about."

His statement stirred some interest among a few of the customers nearby sitting at the bar, nursing drinks. A quick glance at them with an application of his *Magical Detection* Skill showed that there was a hint of *something* around them; he hadn't seen many people on his journey since leaving Enderflow, given that the town – which was more like a village – that was supposed to be inside the forest to the northeast of Enderflow had been completely abandoned when he arrived. At first, he thought that they might have been attacked by monsters coming out of Scissions or Apertures, but there was no sign of distress throughout the village, which was slightly bigger than Rushwood back home. The buildings had been closed up and everything had been removed at some point over the last month, leaving very little behind.

It had been a mystery until he discovered an Aperture further up the road as he kept going, though fortunately he didn't see any sign that the people had been completely stopped by it. There were a few little pieces of evidence indicating a battle against what he could only assume were monsters of some sort, as there were a few pools of long-dried blood and broken weapons, but there were no corpses of people nearby. That there were no corpses of monsters either was explained by the fact that the Aperture had **Spiny Earthworms** that wandered its territory, which had been altered enough that there were odd-looking hills in between the trees of the forest that surrounded it. Granted, the Spiny Earthworms weren't exactly *visible* to be seen wandering around, as they moved through the ground beneath his feet instead, but that wasn't really the point.

The reason there were no monster corpses around was that when Larek killed the 8-foot-long and 2-foot-wide fleshy worms, which had 3-inch-long spines along their entire outer surface, they tended to dissolve back into the earth beneath them and disappear. They were relatively slow, fortunately, and the Fusionist was able to easily avoid what was essentially a constricting attack where they wrapped themselves around a victim and ripped them apart with their spines. Despite the fact that they liked to emerge from beneath their targets and wrap them up before they could react, they weren't subtle about their movements, and it was a simple matter for Larek to jump a few feet away when they emerged and then chop them up with his axe.

Or with an application of the newly created Mage's staff with a *Flaming Ball +7* or *Icy Spike +7* Fusion on it that he had made the night before. It had taken him hours of concentration, which was nerve-wracking given that he was in a tent in an unfamiliar forest while there were monsters roaming about somewhere, but fortunately nothing disturbed him throughout the night. He had made sure to find a relatively protected section of the forest where the land gave way on one side and there was a large fallen tree on the other, as well as ensuring that the closest Apertures he could sense were miles away – but it had still been quite dangerous to do it without someone to watch his back. That was one of the biggest drawbacks of traveling alone, he found, as there was no one to keep watch for monsters or other threats while he worked and later slept, but he had some ideas about that, which he wanted to work on once he got settled into his room in the Inn he was visiting.

Thankfully, no one remarked on anything but his height and general appearance when he entered the town of Lakebellow an hour prior as the sun was beginning to set; he thought it was because had spent another night along the road adding Fusions to his lighter-weight clothing he'd acquired in Enderflow from Johan the Tailor... *or should it be Tailor-Mage now?* Regardless, he was able to add the Fusions he needed to the flowy dark brown pants and loose white shirt, which allowed him to fit in much better than he had back in Enderflow with his robe. It was obvious from his physical appearance that he wasn't a native of the Empire, but at least he didn't stand out as much anymore.

Other than his new Mage's staff and clothing, Larek hadn't been able to create any Fusions because he was becoming exhausted by the days' activities. Not only was he actively moving down his planned route as quickly as he could, but now that he had a long-range weapon to better help him take down some of the more-annoying monsters found at the Apertures, he was spending more time fighting – and healing from the wounds that were inflicted upon his body. It wasn't nearly as bad as it was before he remembered to activate his *Repelling Barrier*, but being surrounded by too many targets for the barrier to handle was still an issue. So was being attacked by something that could pass right through his Barrier, such as the wingbeat attacks by the **Bladed Sparrows**.

He only vaguely remembered them from his classes at the Academy, but what he remembered most about them was their ability to flap their wings powerfully and send out a crescent of nearly invisible, hardened and sharpened air as a long-range attack – which he was privileged to experience first-hand. His *Barrier* did absolutely nothing to stop what was essentially a blade of air coming at him from multiple directions once they swarmed him; it reminded him of how ineffective they were when confronting the Lightning Buzzards back in the Kingdom, and how it seemed as though many of the airborne monsters he had to fight were able to counter his protections with seemingly no effort. The only saving grace was that the air blades themselves were rather small and could barely cut through the top layers of his skin, making them bleed but not too terribly. This was mainly due to the fact that his Body stat now numbered 150 with the new *Body Boost +10* Fusion he had placed on his new clothing, along with the other two Martial stats with the same Magnitude.

The upgrade from a Magnitude 1 *Boost* was incredible, to say the least, as he was now stronger, faster, and had a more robust frame than before – though he had trouble adjusting to the new changes. He still couldn't move quickly for more than a few seconds because it was just too disorienting, but the way he was able to move fast at certain times while fighting monsters had netted him another pair of Levels in his *Dodge* Skill, bringing it to Level 13. When he really applied his increased stats, however, he discovered that he used much more physical energy than before even for simple tasks, which left him exhausted by the end of the day even after consuming more of his dwindling supply of food.

In addition, while he could *feel* the changes wrought by the increased stats, that didn't mean he had the knowledge to use them. Even though he was faster, stronger, and had a more durable body, that didn't automatically mean he was better in a fight against the monsters he fought. He was thankful that many of them were fairly unimaginative in their assault upon him and rarely tried to dodge his attacks, because when they did, he had trouble targeting them. He'd unbalanced himself with an extra-strong swing more than once, nearly falling on his face in the process, but he'd fortunately been able to correct himself before he landed on the very same monsters he'd been trying to kill.

It was a bit frustrating, because he had somehow expected that having higher Martial stats would automatically allow him to know how to utilize them properly. Unlike his Mage stats, which were more mental in comparison and were easy to adapt to, it was a challenge adjusting to the changes in his physical characteristics. After some experiments during his breaks and doing some mental calculations, thanks to his Intellect, he estimated that each point in his Strength stat equated to a 5% increase in his actual physical strength. Therefore, if he was able to lift 100 pounds before he got a Strength stat, he could lift 105 pounds with a stat of 1. That meant that at 150 Strength – which was what he had now thanks to his *Boost* – he could lift 850 pounds, or translate that into 850 pounds of force with a swing of his axe.

Needless to say, that was too much most of the time, and while he could use that type of swing to fell trees all day, fighting monsters was completely different.

He estimated the same increase to his speed via his Agility, around 5% faster with each point in it, but again it was difficult to balance out his speed and strength properly when fighting. It was somehow easier when he didn't have as high of stats, and it got to the point where he was considering putting the Boost back down to +1 or +2 rather than +10, but he was reluctant to do that because he was very slowly becoming used to the changes well enough that it would throw him off if he were to lose that momentum now.

It was either that, or he was too stubborn and willing to put up with the awkwardness he felt when trying to accustom himself to his newly boosted stats. He was sure that the Forts that trained Martials back in the Kingdom were able to teach their trainees how to incorporate their new strength and speed so that it was normal for them, but he unfortunately didn't have that luxury. Most of the time, he didn't even try to apply them during a fight, which worked out well enough for him that he was able to survive the hordes of monsters he encountered on his journey.

All of which led him to the town of Lakebellow after traveling for approximately 6 days and temporarily closing a total of 15 Apertures. He now had enough AF from those confrontations to increase his *Pattern Formation* Skill maximum to 40, as well as enough left over to bump his *Pattern Recognition* up to Level 25. He wanted to be able to learn the Fusion for the *Perceptive Misdirection* Fusion on his ring as soon as possible, as the pattern was quickly fading and likely wouldn't last for more than a few more days at this rate. While he had a fairly good mental picture of it, after having seen it every day for the last month and a half, he hadn't actually learned the Fusion yet; he was hoping that when he got to Level 40 in both *Fusion* and *Pattern Formation*, his *Pattern Recognition* would be high enough to finally learn it.

"You were traveling outside? By yourself?" one of the bar patrons asked, having overheard his conversation with the Innkeeper.

Larek simply nodded.

"Where did you come from?"

He had no reason to lie or keep the knowledge a secret, so he answered, "Enderflow."

The man hummed something and seemed to be doing some mental calculations. "That's an incredibly long way to travel, stranger, especially in times such as these. You must have been on the road for weeks to make it here, and while I see that you're in one piece, the journey must've been difficult. Did you lose your party on the way here? Better yet, where are you from?"

*I'm not sure I like all these questions, mainly because I don't know where he's going with them.* "It was certainly a difficult journey, which is why I'd love something to eat and to get some rest in a real bed for once – even if I don't fit in it!" he said, chuckling. "As for where I'm from, it's a long way from here and I'm just passing through on my way back home." He turned away from the customer at the bar who had asked him the questions and refocused back on the Innkeeper. "So, how's about I get that meal and the room—"

"Delwin says there's something about your clothes that's putting off a strong magical vibe, stranger," the patron who had asked him the earlier questions said, standing up off the stool on which he had been sitting. Behind him, three others dressed similarly and almost appearing as if they were brothers, also stood up with a squeal of stool legs against the wood floor. Still with his *Magical Detection* Skill hard at work, Larek noticed that two of them appeared to have a bit of Mana passing through them periodically, which he could only assume meant that they were Mages; one of them in particular was looking at his clothing – or more specifically, the Fusions on it – like a starving wolf looked at a lost sheep.

*Well, that's just great. Now what do I do?*

Larek might not have been the best judge of character, nor was he adept at reading some social situations, but he could still tell where this was going. He stiffened a little as the man took a step forward, his hand instinctively reaching for his axe, but he stopped when the Innkeeper spoke.

"Alwhin, what have I told you about harassing my customers? You'd better knock it off right now or I'll be contacting Protector Bundy to make sure you remember this time."

The man, Alwhin, stopped his advance and looked disgusted at the Innkeeper before turning his greedy eyes back on Larek. He didn't say anything as he picked up the tankard he had been drinking, drained the rest of it in one smooth gulp, and then slammed it back down on the bar. The Fusionist could see the Innkeeper flinch as his bartop was slightly dented from the action, which told Larek that the man had flexed some of his Strength stat to inflict the damage. That he was a Martial wasn't in doubt by that point, but how much he had advanced upon what he started with was difficult to tell.

Wiping some foam off his mouth, Alwhin stared Larek right in the eyes and said, "I'll be seeing you around, then." As he left, for the first time the Fusionist noticed that the man had what appeared to be an iron mace in a leather holster attached to his hip. It was relatively crude in appearance, as it appeared to have been crafted in a hurry, as the spikes coming out of the metal ball on the end of a wood-and-iron stick were placed haphazardly and were of differing lengths and thicknesses. He supposed that such weaponry wasn't very common in the Sealance Empire considering that they had Protectors to help defend them from most threats. Naturally, that would likely change in the near future as the new Martials around the Empire found their feet and decided on a favorite weapon, and this example was probably just the first example of that happening.

He also noticed that one of the others, also a Martial by the feel of the magical disturbance around him, had two knives in their sheaths strapped to his belt, while the two Mages were carrying around on their hips what he could only describe as long, wooden clubs. He wasn't sure how effective they would be against monsters, but against most non-Martial citizens of the Empire...

Well, the uses behind them became obvious at that point. They weren't designed for monsters, but for other people. Larek wasn't sure what that made these individuals; were they thieves? Simple bullies?

It really didn't matter since he wasn't planning on staying around more than just that night and was expecting to leave early in the morning. If he was lucky, he'd never see them again.

If he did see them again, they wouldn't like his response. Unlike the SIC back at Whittleton, where he at least *understood* their motivations concerning stealing his group's Fusions, these people had no need of them other than greed. At the moment, the Empire of Sealance was more than capable of handling the influx of Apertures and monsters with just their Protectors if it came down to it, as was proven when he accompanied the ones from Enderflow – so they didn't need anything he might provide.

And if Larek was being honest with himself, if he hadn't been fed up with bullies by this point in his life, he certainly was now. He'd already determined not to be taken advantage of earlier when people asked for help; he was darn sure not going to allow someone to take his stuff just because they wanted it.

"I'll take my meal up in my room, if you don't mind," he told the Innkeeper once the quartet of thugs left the Inn. As he looked around the rest of the common room, there were gatherings of other people here and there who had their heads close together as if they were speaking about something secret, but Larek didn't bother to apply his *Listening* Skill to hear what was being said. There was really no need, as most of them were casting glances his way while they spoke, so he could guess what the subject of their conversations was. Fortunately, he didn't get a vibe from them that made him think they were similar to those who just left; he figured it was simply just gossip.

*I really need to figure out this* **Perceptive Misdirection** *Fusion soon, because I want to make some changes to it. I still stand out too much here, even if they think I'm shorter than my real height.*

"Not a problem. I'll have Cynthia bring it up to you in a few minutes," the Innkeeper said, placing a heavy iron key with a cloth loop around it with the number 6 stitched into it onto the bar top. He held his hand over it as he said, "That'll be 2 silver for both the meal and the room."

Rather than wondering if that was a good price or not, as his only experience with an actual Inn had been in Whittleton and they had been outrageously extorted, he pulled two of the local currency out of his pocket where he had placed a handful of coins before he arrived, just to have it handy without having to pull it out of his pack, and then slid them on the bar. The Innkeeper snatched them up quickly and pulled his hand away from the key, saying, "Thank you. And I'm sorry about Alwhin and his brothers bothering you."

Larek just shrugged.

"A word of fair warning, traveler," the man went on, "you should watch your back if you're planning on leaving tomorrow. They know better than to mess with you while you're in my Inn or in town, but as soon as you're outside of the town proper it's a bit lawless out there with the whole end-of-the-world announcement more than a week ago. Good-for-nothings like Alwhin and his siblings have used their newfound power to make a menace of themselves more than usual." He leaned closer and dropped his voice, as if he didn't want to be overheard. "There's even talk that they've been ambushing some of the volunteer groups who've gone out to start closing these Aperture things, though no one could prove that. Lakebellow's Protectors have written their disappearances off as unfortunate accidents as they've fought some of these monsters out there, but I don't buy it, I tell you." He then gave Larek a wink.

The Fusionist was speechless for a moment. "Uh, why are you telling me this?" He didn't want to know anything about these people, as he was planning on leaving in the morning and never coming back.

The Innkeeper appeared taken aback. "Oh, well, you know, I just wanted to warn you in case they confronted you—"

"Thank you; I appreciate the warning," Larek said, his exhaustion from the last few days catching up with him and his stomach growling in protest from being ignored. "I'll head up now if you don't mind, and I'll look forward to my meal." With that said, he grabbed the key and headed toward the left of the bar where a flight of stairs lead upwards. It didn't take long for him to make his way down the hallway in which he found himself at the top of the stairway and to find his room for the night. It took even less time for him to make his way inside, plop himself on the too-small bed, and begin to relax as he felt safe and secure for the first time since he left Enderflow.

A few minutes later, a young woman knocked on his door and delivered a wooden tray filled with a bowl of stew next to a large bowl of rice, along with an entire loaf of still-steaming bread. While he hadn't asked for such a large bounty when he requested a meal, he appreciated that they hadn't skimped in the least.

As he dug in and devoured the food like he hadn't eaten in days, he began to plan out what he was going to work on before he got some sleep for the night.

# Chapter 11

After finishing his meal, Larek moved the small table and chairs next to the locked wooden door for extra insurance against someone getting inside. Despite the assurances that Alwhin wouldn't do something to Larek in the Inn, he had learned to be cautious on his solo journey over the last week. The window looking out into the town of Lakebellow was shut and was small enough that any adult would have trouble fitting through it, and with it being on the second floor of the Inn, he wasn't too worried about anyone getting in that way.

Only then could Larek fully relax as he took off his packs and pulled a few things out that he placed on his bed. They were just simple rocks and a few pieces of wood he had carved out of a tree that morning in anticipation of his creations that night, and they would work as a medium for his Fusions well enough. Theoretically, he had arrived in town early enough that he could've bought something more refined to use, but he was too exhausted from his exertions to stop on the way to the Inn. Thankfully, the town was laid out similarly to Enderflow and possessed almost an identical mix of shops, so it was easy enough to find his destination.

Sitting cross-legged on his bed as he got comfortable, Larek closed his eyes for a moment as he settled himself, pushing away all of the memories of killing monsters and dealing with greedy people who wanted to steal his things or use him for their own ends. Instead, he focused on what was unabashedly his passion, the obsession that he thought about every day.

*It's time to make some more Fusions.*

According to Shinpai, Larek needed to push either his *Fusion* and/or his *Pattern Formation* Skills up to 40 to be able to make Advanced Fusions. In order to do so, he felt as if he needed to do something new; something that would take all that he'd done so far and push the envelope of what he could achieve with Intermediate Fusions. While he had a lot of ideas of things to create when he could finally utilize Advanced Fusions, the limitations of his current bottleneck made it difficult to envision what might push him that last little bit. Fortunately for him, he'd already been considering it while he fought the monsters and closed the Apertures on his way to Lakebellow.

Conveniently, the two main types of Fusions he was considering would help him on his journey as he continued to encounter monsters and acquire Aetheric Force from them – because he wasn't going to stop even when he achieved Level 40 in his most important Skills. As for those Fusions, Larek had decided on his solo journey that not only did he need to start learning how to fight a little better so that he wasn't so awkward in a battle against monsters, but to integrate his specialties into his fighting style. It was one thing to learn how to move better and have his maneuvers flow better in the heat of battle, but if he didn't utilize his other knowledge then he wouldn't be fully utilizing everything he could to keep himself alive – such as when he had forgotten to turn his *Repelling Barrier* on earlier on in his journey.

In other words, he was going to lean into what he was good at and use Fusions to absolutely devastate the weaker monsters he'd been encountering thus far. He already did this in part with his staff and the offensive Fusions that it utilized, but there was so much more that he knew that he could do with them that he'd shied away from thinking about until now. Memories of the deaths of Ricardo and his two Martial trainees had weighed on his conscience since the incident and had been adversely affecting his thoughts in that direction. It wasn't their deaths that had weighed on his conscience, however, because he already knew that they deserved it; it was the fact that he had created something specifically to harm other people which had influenced his thinking.

In general, he was a fairly easy-going person, or at least he liked to think so, and that also applied to his thoughts about other people; he didn't want to hurt anyone, and while he'd had thoughts about not helping some of the common people in the Kingdom because of how they treated him, he hadn't seriously thought about hurting them himself. His experiences in the world had gradually shifted his attitude toward other people as he started to see what people would do when they thought they had a chance to get away with it – or if they thought what they were doing was right. As Larek's viewpoint changed, so did his reluctance in developing Fusions that were designed to inflict as much damage as possible. While he had originally been all about healing and defensive Fusions, only adapting certain spell effects toward inflicting harm when it came to eliminating Ricardo and his cronies, the Fusionist was now leaning toward more offensive Fusions – and he had the perfect ideas for his current situation.

The first Fusion he had in mind was a variation of the *Paralytic Light* Fusion. While he could certainly use the *Paralytic Light* Fusion, which had been so effective against the SIC near Whittleton, to help protect him from the hordes of monsters that swarmed him after damaging an Aperture, simply paralyzing them so that he could pick them off one by one wasn't as effective or as damaging as it could be. The first reason it wouldn't be entirely effective was that non-biological monsters – of which there were quite a few that he had encountered in his journeys – wouldn't be paralyzed by the Effect. Examples of this included the Dirt Golems he fought back in the Kingdom and even the Wilde Mushdooms he'd fought with the Protectors from Enderflow – neither of those would be affected in the least by the *Paralytic Light* Fusion.

    Secondly, even if the monsters he fought had biological forms and were paralyzed, he would have to fire on them from afar with his offensive Mage's staff, since it would affect him if he got too close. While this was a potential solution for staying safe from harm, it also wasn't exactly a way to get better at fighting – which was something he needed to accomplish if he wanted to survive when he got back to the Kingdom. The monsters in the Empire might be weak and therefore a good way to train his fighting skills, but if he just sat back while they were paralyzed before killing them from afar, he wouldn't be improving at all.

    Lastly, if he was confined to long-range attacks only, if the monsters were either immune or highly resistant to the Effects he had on his staff, then those attacks would be essentially useless. At that point, he would have to wait for the activated fields of *Paralytic Light* to deactivate or risk being paralyzed in addition to the monsters, and then he would have to fight the monsters with his axe like he had been doing before.

    Granted, the Fusion he had created for use against the SIC in Whittleton was still something that could be effective, and he would likely create some of them once he was done with his other projects.

    As for those other projects, what he wanted to do was either inflict direct damage to the monsters using a Fusion that he didn't have to manually target, such as the ones on his staff, or to make them weaker so that they would be more vulnerable once they reached him. Right now, he essentially just swung his axe at whatever got close to him or attempted to shoot them from afar with his staff, which typically worked well enough against the monsters he encountered here. Even with an occasional dodge or a flung axe here and there, even his limited knowledge of fighting styles told him that his fighting style was basic and unimaginative. It worked, for now; what he was worried about was when it wouldn't be enough in the future.

    Remembering the Martial trainees back at Fort Pinevalley, as well as his companions that fled Copperleaf with him, the way they moved allowed for them to attack strategically without having to suffer being hit at the same time. Even Bartholomew, with his heavier armor, used his shield to protect himself from being hit; and even then, the trainee didn't typically block a blow straight-on but attempted to deflect it to the side so that he didn't have to cope with the full force of the attack. Penelope moved fluidly through a multitude of stances that kept her moving and away from where the monsters would typically attack her, using the length and width of her large sword to keep the advantage of distance and utilize it for her protection. While Vivienne's fighting strategy wasn't as flashy, she'd used her Agility to amazing effect to move in, strike, and then move away before the monsters even knew she was there. The way she was able to seemingly disappear from plain sight also helped, of course, but that was an effect of a Battle Art and only tangentially part of her style.

What Larek needed to do was find what kind of fighting style worked the best for *him*, as his current style wasn't cutting it. He already had a good idea of what that was going to be based on his experiences once he was solo, as he was able to identify – at least partially – his strengths and weaknesses in a battle. His main weakness was, of course, a lack of knowledge of fighting with melee weapons and movement in a fight; while he thought he could improve these with experience and time, he didn't think he'd be able to be as impressive a fighter as Bartholomew, Penelope, and Vivienne without some formal training at a Martial Fort – along with learning how to incorporate Battle Arts.

Which meant adapting his strengths, which were focused upon Fusions. By creating something that would balance out his lack of fighting knowledge, he could actually start to learn how to handle himself in an assault against monsters, rather than flailing around with his axe and hoping his Strength and Agility would always be enough to carry the day.

All of this led to his designs for offensive Fusions based on *Paralytic Light*. Instead of an area that would simply hold a monster in place, he was hoping to design a Fusion that would actually harm them in some way. The thought of creating some sort of burning square of flames was tempting, but given how likely that would be to start a fire in the surrounding area if he used it, it wasn't something he thought would be safe. So, instead of fire, he focused on three different Effects that he thought might work much better – and would be worlds safer.

The first was based on a combination of the *Binding Roots* and *Wall of Thorns* spells that he'd learned from Nedira. The first spell simply brought roots up out of the ground to ensnare and temporarily trap a monster so that they could be safely killed; the second created a wall of roots with thorns that would minorly injure anything that ran up against it. It was more of a defensive spell, as the injuries from the thorns were minor, and it wasn't considered a very damaging effect.

But since they both featured roots as a major element, Larek thought he could combine them – and use his expertise in making Fusions to increase the damage that was done by the thorns by an order of *Magnitude*.

The Fusion used a similar basic idea behind the *Paralytic Light* Fusion to achieve similar Reactive and Activatable activation effects, though instead of physical pressure upon the ground it relied on any physical movement for the Reactive portion.  When it was activated, the target would be wrapped up in roots that burst from the ground, which tightened around anything within its range, and then ripped to shreds by the thorns attached to the roots.

*New Fusion Learned!*
**Binding Thorns +1**
*Activation Method: Reactive, Activatable*
*Effect(s): Creates binding roots that emerge from the ground to ensnare victims within range*
*Effect(s): Creates sharp thorns that inflict damage upon any ensnared victims*
*Magnitude: Covers a 1-foot by 1-foot by 1-foot cubic area*
*Input: Physical movement detection of over 1 mph, phrase recognition*
*Variable 1: If no movement is detected, deactivates after 5 minutes*
*Variable 2: Upon any physical movement Input detection, creates binding roots with thorns from the ground that ensnare all physical movement Input origins*
*Variable 3: Upon initial mental Activatable activation, activates detection of physical movement Inputs after 5 seconds*
*Variable 4: If the spoken phrase, "Deactivate Binding Thorns", is detected within range, deactivates after 5 seconds*
*Mana Cost: 90*
*Pattern Cohesion: 4*
*Fusion Time: 30 minutes*

**Fusion** has reached Level 39!

Starting out with the lowest Magnitude possible at +1, just to see if it would work, Larek was pleased to see that it had, indeed, been successful.  It only required holding onto the Fusion on the stone he had placed it upon to know that all of the various Inputs and Variables were working exactly as they should.  He was tempted to try it out in his room, but was worried that it would harm the Inn – which he figured wouldn't go over so well with the Innkeeper.

The biggest difference between the creation of *Binding Thorns* and *Paralytic Light* was the addition of the Phrase Recognition Input to turn it off if it was needed. This was mainly so that if he was accidentally caught in his own Fusion that he would be able to extricate himself, as well as to gather up the Fusion once he was done with it if it hadn't deactivated already.

All told, it was a complicated array of connections he had to create to ensure it operated the way he wanted it to. Connecting the Reactive Activation Method to the binding thorn Effect, the physical movement Input, the phrase recognition Input, and the Variable concerning physical movement (which was similar to how his *Repelling Barriers* detected movement, though the threshold was anything moving over 1 mph) was easy enough; but then separating the other Variables so that they connected to the Activatable Activation Method *and then* connected to the Reactive Activation Method to turn it off required a unique use of a Diverter so that the one superseded the other. It was complicated, but as he'd had some time to think about it on his journey, he had most of it worked out before he even started.

In all, it was a 3-by-4 grid that contained a single Mana Cost, Magnitude, and binding thorn Effect, along with an Activatable and Reactive Activation Method, a quartet of Variables, a pair of Inputs, and the specially used Diverter that was the *real* power behind its success. Instead of it being used between two different Effects depending upon various Inputs and Variables, Larek had to mentally change its purpose so that it essentially acted as a "shut-off" switch that would allow it to override both Activation Methods so that it would shut down entirely. It was actually an adaptation of the Override symbol that was used in Advanced Fusions which he'd learned but wasn't able to utilize because of the block that was still upon him from not reaching Level 40 in some of his Skills – but he was one Level closer to that as *Fusion* increased to 39 after his successful creation.

Of course, a Magnitude 1 *Binding Thorns* wouldn't help all that much other than as a minor distraction, given its small area of effect and weaker thorns; in this state, it wasn't much better than the *Wall of Thorns* spell that he knew. Only when he increased the Magnitude much higher would it be of use to him.

Before he did that, as he estimated that it would take at least 20 minutes with the current state of the ambient Mana in the environment and subsequently his Mana Regeneration, Larek moved on to the next Fusion now that he had successfully created the base of *Binding Thorns*.

Once he reached his goal of hitting Level 40 in his two Skills, then he would go back and start producing viable Fusions for the resumption of his journey home.

# Chapter 12

Keeping with the same theme of Fusions as *Binding Thorns*, his next creation was a combination of his *Area Chill* Fusion and the *Ice Spike* spell. Instead of binding a monster with roots, the new Fusion caused an area to become extremely cold in a flash, with the moisture in the air and any moisture within a monster crystalizing into ice – or at least that was the theory. Whether or not it would actually play out like that, especially any moisture in a monster's body, was still up in the air until he tried it out; at the least, if it didn't harm the monsters caught in its Effect outright, he thought that it would cripple their speed so that they couldn't move as fast.

*New Fusion Learned!*
**Frozen Zone +1**
*Activation Method: Reactive, Activatable*
*Effect(s): Creates a zone of super-chilled air that crystalizes the available moisture into ice*
*Magnitude: Covers a 1-foot by 1-foot by 1-foot cubic area*
*Input: Physical movement detection of over 1 mph, phrase recognition*
*Variable 1: If no movement is detected, deactivates after 5 minutes*
*Variable 2: Upon any physical movement Input detection, creates a freezing zone that crystalizes all available moisture into ice*
*Variable 3: Upon initial mental Activatable activation, activates detection of physical movement Inputs after 5 seconds*
*Variable 4: If the spoken phrase, "Deactivate Frozen Zone", is detected within range, deactivates after 5 seconds*
*Mana Cost: 95*
*Pattern Cohesion: 4*
*Fusion Time: 31 minutes*

**Pattern Formation** has reached Level 39!

Even with a brief test, which had him briefly passing his hand through the small cubic area of effect to trigger the *Frozen Zone* Fusion, he wasn't able to see if it froze the blood in his hand if he kept it in there for a while. While it became quite cold, as would be expected, he thought that it *might* eventually give him frostbite on his fingertips if he held his hand within it for a while. As it was only Magnitude 1, he didn't expect anything much different than that, and he was reluctant to "test" anything stronger with his body as he wasn't precisely sure what would happen. Would it freeze all the blood in his hand and cause it to explode once the ice crystals grew? Would it then move on to the rest of his body and kill him? Without being entirely sure of the outcome, he couldn't countenance testing it with himself or even inside the Inn where it might actually freeze all the moisture in the wooden floors and cause them to crack and fall apart.

Along with his new *Frozen Zone* Fusion, Larek had increased his *Pattern Formation* Skill up to 39, inching it one step closer to his goal. Again putting aside the need to make his new Fusion with a higher Magnitude for use against monsters, Larek designed his final Fusion that was meant to target monsters moving along the ground toward him. This next one he was making was a bit more specialized, and he wasn't entirely sure it would actually work, but he figured it couldn't hurt to try. The reason he wasn't sure it would operate the way he thought it might was that he didn't really know if magical healing worked on monsters.

That's right – magical healing. More specifically, an area of effect *Healing Surge*-type of healing effect, rapidly applied at an extremely high Magnitude.

It might sound counterintuitive, but Larek still remembered creating the Fusion back at Crystalview and how quickly the Magnitude 5 version both healed him and made him extremely hungry and weak after only about 20 seconds of use. When he factored in that he also had the *Body Regeneration* Skill that the Fusion tapped into, it should've been obvious back then that it was entirely too much healing for an average Mage or normal person. When he switched to a Magnitude 3 version that he ended up mass producing – and was still the norm for what he used today for Martial-bound Fusions – the results of its use still sent heavily injured individuals without *Body Regeneration* into a temporary coma.

But what if a monster was exposed to a more-powerful version of the same effect? That was what he wanted to find out.

Adapting the *Healing Surge* Effect was easy enough to do with his new Fusion format, as he knew it so well by that point that it required very little effort on his part to make the necessary changes so that it affected a whole area rather than by touch. Unfortunately, the change in delivery method also increased the cost significantly, both in terms of Mana and Pattern Cohesion.

*New Fusion Learned!*
**Healing Shelter +1**
*Activation Method: Reactive, Activatable*

*Effect(s):* Creates an area that sends a steady healing pulse through nearby organisms, repairing wounds and non-fatal injuries
*Magnitude:* 1,000% increase in natural health regeneration rate
*Magnitude:* Covers a 1-foot by 1-foot by 1-foot cubic area
*Input:* Physical movement detection of over 1 mph, phrase recognition
*Variable 1:* If no movement is detected, deactivates after 5 minutes
*Variable 2:* Upon any physical movement Input detection, creates a steady healing pulse through all nearby physical movement Input origins
*Variable 3:* Upon initial mental Activatable activation, activates detection of physical movement Inputs after 5 seconds
*Variable 4:* If the spoken phrase, "Deactivate Healing Shelter", is detected within range, deactivates after 5 seconds
*Mana Cost:* 800
*Pattern Cohesion:* 10
*Fusion Time:* 1.75 hours

**Pattern Formation** *has reached Level 40!*

With the completion of his new Fusion, Larek gained Level 40 in his *Pattern Formation* Skill and… nothing monumental happened. He felt like his understanding of Fusion patterns was strengthened a little, but other than that, there was none of the sudden revelation he had been expecting. Slightly disappointed, but figuring it was because his *Fusion* Skill needed to get to the same Level, he turned his attention back to his new creation and the differences he immediately noticed in its cost compared to *Healing Surge.*

First, at Magnitude 1, the *Surge* only cost 550 Mana compared to the *Shelter's* 800; that wasn't very significant at the current Magnitude, but at Magnitude 5 the difference between 55,000 Mana and 80,000 Mana was fairly wide – and the gulf only expanded at higher Magnitudes. Second, the Pattern Cohesion had increased from 7 to 10, which again wasn't that big of a deal, considering that he had over 27,000 Pattern Cohesion, but at the Magnitudes he was planning for this Fusion, it made a huge difference. Lastly, the Fusion Time increased – but that didn't matter one whit to him.

At Magnitude 10, which was what he had been planning on using for this particular Fusion, he estimated that it would cost a total of 2,000,000 Mana and 4,600 Pattern Cohesion – amounts he'd never used in a Fusion before – but, he figured, it was less than a fifth of his total Pattern Cohesion so it should be fine. At his current Mana Regeneration Rate, which was very slowly improving as more and more Apertures opened all over the Sealance Empire, he estimated that he regenerated approximately his entire Mana pool of 1,960 in 30 minutes. If that was the case, then a Magnitude 10 *Healing Shelter* Fusion would require over 8 hours of focus and feeding all his regenerating Mana into the formation to fill it up.

Even a *Healing Shelter +7* Fusion – which was what he eventually decided to try first rather than *+10* – would require 480,000 Mana and 2 hours of work to complete. The 2,400 Pattern Cohesion required was still significant, but not nearly as much as the Mana Cost. Resolving to make that later along with his other new creations at higher Magnitudes, Larek moved on.

*Three down; one more to go.*

For the final Fusion he wanted to create to aid him on his journey, he desired a counter against monsters that weren't going to be greatly affected by the ones he had already designed. In short, he was tired of being ambushed by Tree Weasels who attacked by landing on his head or airborne monsters such as the Bladed Sparrows who could send air-based attacks at him from a distance which weren't blocked by his *Repelling Barrier*. This was something that he had actually thought about the most since it was what had hurt him the most on his solo travels, and he was fairly certain he had designed something he thought might work – for most of it, at least. He still wasn't sure how to negate certain types of damage, such as the lightning bolts sent out by a Lightning Buzzard, for instance, but his idea would hopefully cover almost everything else.

Essentially, his idea was to repurpose the ideas behind his *Repelling Barrier* and the offensive spells used on his Mage's staff and combine them to make something so much deadlier and more versatile. If it worked the way he hoped, then it could revolutionize the way he approached combat with monsters and would be useful for more than just the intended purpose of defending himself from attack from above.

First, he envisioned the *Repelling Gust* Effect used in his *Barrier* as more of a large, stationary hollow half-sphere that was 8 feet wide, 4 feet high, and a full foot thick. In addition, instead of it covering his body, it was to be projected from the tip of a flat length of wood, which was a foot long, 2 inches wide, and a half-inch thick. Rather than being sent out like a projectile like his offensive Fusions on his staff, it instead moved upwards until it was 6 feet away from the tip, where it would remain stationary.

This half-sphere, dome-like construct of blowing wind wouldn't be nearly enough to stop things like a Bladed Sparrow's air blade attack, especially if it was designed only to turn on when it encountered a physical object. That was why Larek altered its behavior so that instead of blowing powerful gusts of air in a certain direction, he had it moving constantly inside a contained area, similar to what he had done with his other new creations. Rather than a cube-shaped zone, the constantly blowing gusts were held in the three-dimensional shape of the thick dome he designed, forming a maelstrom of wind that could rip monsters apart if the Magnitude was high enough.

Even a constantly swirling dome of wind blasts wouldn't necessarily be enough to stop most things, especially some types of attacks that could slip through the air-based defense without too much trouble, or even heavier monsters that might only be tossed away in one direction or another upon contact with the dome. Therefore, he needed something else that had some physicality to it – and the ability to do some serious damage.

That's where an application of the *Flying Stone* Fusion Effect came into play. By creating a number of sharp "Flying Stones" inside of the dome that were flung around in the contained, chaotic tornado of powerful gusts, it added a way to essentially chew through anything that passed through the dome.

The difficulty came in ensuring that the stones didn't escape the dome or just pulverize each other when they were pushed through the hollow half-sphere, which was only solved by organizing the gusts of wind in such a way that they formed a specific pattern. It appeared to be entirely random where these gusts blew, but instead it was a carefully choreographed series of interlaced routes that the stones would follow, narrowly missing each other as they passed by. It required widening the gust placement a little bit in order to get it to work, as there was still a possibility that the stones would interact with each other, but he hoped it wasn't noticeable. In addition, he also had to add an Input that would detect if a stone were attempting to escape the dome, which would institute another short gust of air to set it back on its path.

Once he had the design in the forefront of his mind, he began the process of creating the next evolution in his defensively offensive Fusions. The complexity of the dual Effects was so great that it took him an extra few minutes to ensure it was all correct, and as it snapped into place on the piece of wood he had carved out, Larek was hit with a number of notifications that physically shocked both his body and his mind.

*New Fusion Learned!*
**Stone Shredder Dome +1**
*Activation Method(s): Activatable*

*Effect(s): Creates a contained dome of rapidly moving gusts of air in a predetermined pattern*
*Effect(s): Forms sharp shards of stone that are moved around by the rapidly moving gusts of air*
*Input(s): Directional orientation, stone perimeter detection*
*Magnitude: 100% of base gust strength, 10% stone shard size*
*Mana Cost: 950*
*Pattern Cohesion: 9*
*Fusion Time: 2 hours*

**Fusion** *has reached Level 40!*

*You have reached Level 23 and have 19 available AP to distribute!*

**Congratulations!**
*You have unlocked the* **Advanced Fusionist** *Specialization!*

*Requirements:*
**Mana Control** *Skill of* 25
**Pattern Formation** *Skill of* 30
**Fusion Skill** *of* 40
*Knowledge of at least* 20 *different types of Fusions*

*The* **Advanced Fusionist** *Specialization also provides these benefits:*

*10% reduction in Mana Cost for all Fusions*
*10% reduction in Pattern Cohesion requirements for all Fusions*
*10% reduction in Fusion Time for all Fusions*

*Warning! The Specializations* Fusionist *and* Advanced Fusionist *are mutually exclusive!*
*Do you wish to accept the* Advanced Fusionist *Specialization to replace* Fusioni—

**Congratulations!**
*You have unlocked the* **Master Fusionist** *Specialization!*

*Requirements:*
**Mana Control** *Skill of* 30
**Pattern Formation** *Skill of* 40
**Fusion Skill** *of* 40
*Knowledge of at least* 30 *different types of Fusions*

The **Master Fusionist** Specialization also provides these benefits:

15% reduction in Mana Cost for all Fusions
15% reduction in Pattern Cohesion requirements for all Fusions
15% reduction in Fusion Time for all Fusions

Warning! The Specializations Fusionist, Advanced Fusionist, and Master Fusionist are mutually exclusive!
Do you wish to accept the Master Fusionist Specialization to replace Fusioni—

**Congratulations, Guardian!**
Due to your unique nature, you have unlocked the **Combat Fusionist** Specialization!

Requirements:
**Mana Control** Skill of 30
**Pattern Formation** Skill of 40
**Fusion Skill** of 40
**Pain Immunity** Skill evolution
**Body Regeneration** Skill of 30
Intellect of at least 75
Acuity of at least 75
Pneuma of at least 75
Strength of at least 75
Body of at least 75
Agility of at least 75
Knowledge of at least 35 different types of Fusions
Unlocked at least 2 different Weapon Expertise Skills
Access to at least a combined 15 Spells and Battle Arts

The **Combat Fusionist** Specialization also provides these benefits:

15% reduction in Mana Cost for all Fusions
15% reduction in Pattern Cohesion requirements for all Fusions
15% reduction in Fusion Time for all Fusions
10% reduction in Mana Cost for all cast Spells
10% increase in the magnitude of all cast Spells
10% increase in the range of all cast Spells
10% reduction in Stama cost for all Battle Arts
10% increase in effectiveness of all Battle Arts

*10% increase in duration of all Battle Arts*

*Warning! The Specializations <u>Fusionist</u>, <u>Advanced Fusionist</u>, and <u>Master Fusionist</u> have been overridden by <u>Combat Fusionist</u>!*
*<u>Combat Fusionist</u> Specialization automatically accepted!*

    All of these notifications made Larek's body shake as one unlocked Specialization after another slammed into his mind, until it felt as if he was going to pass out from the strain. Unfortunately for him, this was just the start of his agony as all of the memories of his learning back in Copperleaf swam to the surface to bombard his thoughts with knowledge of how to create Advanced Fusions. All of the lessons with Shinpai that were thrust upon him in an effort to push him past "The Precipice" came flooding back, filling him with information that was more than a bit overwhelming. It was as if he had learned it all, but it was kept from him because he didn't have permission to use it; now that he had passed the threshold necessary for that permission, it was all just shoved back into his mind with no regard to what else was happening.

    By the time it finished, he was thankfully still conscious – but only just barely. The influx of information and the addition of new possibilities for Fusions crowded his mind, but it was all overshadowed by his exhaustion rearing its ugly head, causing him to lay himself down in his bed and close his eyes.

    He wouldn't wake up until morning.

# Chapter 13

Waking up with the morning sunlight streaming through the slats in the window was a new experience for Larek, as he was used to waking up either before dawn or just as dawn was breaking. As a result, he was momentarily confused and thought himself back in Enderflow in the Protectors' barracks, but then the last week's journey and the night before all came flooding back into his mind and he abruptly sat up, a slight panic in his actions. There was a momentary pain in his head at his movement, and he held his hands up to his temples to massage the pain away; after a few seconds, the pain faded as if it had never been there.

"What—?" he spoke out loud, his voice a little raspy and his throat dry. "What was all that?"

Pulling up his Status, he was again reminded that he had unlocked a new Specialization the night before; in fact, he didn't just unlock one Specialization, but *three*. Of course, "Advanced Fusionist" and "Master Fusionist" weren't even available anymore, as – if he remembered correctly – his new Combat Fusionist Specialization overrode the others.

**Larek Holsten**

**Combat Fusionist**
**Healer**
**Level 23**
**Advancement Points (AP): 0/19**
**Available AP to Distribute: 19**
**Available Aetheric Force (AF): 341**

**Stama: 830/830**
**Mana: 1960/1960**

**Strength: 75 [150] (+)**
**Body: 75 [150] (+)**
**Agility: 75 [150] (+)**
**Intellect: 98 [196] (+)**
**Acuity: 114 [228] (+)**
**Pneuma: 1,350 [2,700]**
**Pattern Cohesion: 27,000/27,000**

Remembering back to what the new Combat Fusionist Specialization provided as far as benefits, he had to admit that it was certainly better for most people – but the additional 10% reductions and increases to Spells and Battle Arts were completely useless to him. In effect, there was no real difference for Larek between a Master Fusionist and a Combat Fusionist, but that was fine with him. The extra 10% reduction in Mana Cost and Pattern Cohesion that it provided over his normal Fusionist Specialization was already a bonus, and he would take what he could get.

What he was more excited about was the knowledge of Advanced Fusions that he had obtained in Copperleaf Academy thanks to Grandmaster Fusionist Shinpai had essentially been "unlocked" and was finally ready to be used. One of the biggest advantages of Advanced Fusions over the Intermediate Fusions he had been stuck with was that there was a much higher limit to the number of Effects that a Fusion could possess – all the way up to 6 different Effects. That still sounded slightly restrictive, but it was also *triple* the number he could use with Intermediate Fusions, so it was a bonus.

In addition to an increase in the number Effects an Advanced Fusion could have as part of the Formation, there was also *no limit* to the size of the formation. It could be as simple as a 3-by-3 grid with three different Effects, or a 100-by-100 grid with hundreds of Inputs, Variables, and other components to make it as complicated as the Fusionist wanted. Of course, there were still categories that Advanced Fusions fell under, named identically to Intermediate Fusions: Simple, Lesser, Minor, Major, and Supreme. They had different thresholds, of course, as a Simple Advanced Fusion had, by necessity, a total of 3 Effects while a Supreme typically contained 6 Effects, though in reality it could contain any number between 3 and 6 Effects if it was complicated enough – such as the 100-by-100 grid mentioned before.

At the moment, his mind balked a little at having to focus enough to create any of the higher classifications of Advanced Fusions, such as Major and Supreme, at least until he had some practice with the easier ones. Unfortunately, his impromptu early bedtime the night before put him behind on what he had planned for the day, so he was going to have to wait to experiment until a later time. Besides, now that he knew he could create them, he would have to parse through all of his knowledge and ensure he was familiar enough with the new components, such as the aforementioned **Override**, to use them correctly in a Fusion. More than that, his journey to that point had been consumed with plans of what he could still make using only

Intermediate Fusions, and he was now kicking himself that he hadn't thought about what would happen once he got to this point.

Then again, it wasn't like he didn't have some ideas, but having an idea and planning out exactly how the Fusion formation was going to be laid out and assembled coherently were two different things. With many of the limitations now lifted, there was so much more he thought he could do – but that would also require some careful planning.

More than just creating Advanced Fusions, there was a loosening of the restriction on *learning* new Advanced Fusions – and he had the feeling that he would be able to also learn stronger spells once he saw them used. He discovered this when he looked down at his hand and glimpsed the ring Shinpai had given him, and he almost instantly learned the *Perceptive Misdirection* Fusion – his first Advanced Fusion.

*New Fusion Learned!*
**Perceptive Misdirection +1**
*Activation Method(s): Permanent*
*Effect(s): Identifies the origin of observers of user using a pulsing wave of Mana*
*Effect(s): Conceals the pulsing wave of Mana by using a void carrier*
*Effect(s): Alters the perception of observers by non-invasive mental manipulation based on distance, making the observer believe user is 1 foot shorter than actual height*
*Input(s): Observer orientation, observer distance*
*Magnitude: Affects observers in a 100-foot diameter*
*Variable 1: Observer distance between 1 inch and 3 inches*
*Variable 2: Observer distance between 3.1 inches and 6 inches*
*Variable 3: Observer distance between 6.1 inches and 12 inches*
*Variable 4: Observer distance between 12.1 inches and 2 feet*
*Variable 5: Observer distance between 2.1 feet and 3 feet*
*Variable 6: Observer distance between 3.1 feet and 4 feet*
*Variable 7: Observer distance between 4.1 feet and 6 feet*
*Variable 8: Observer distance between 6.1 feet and 9 feet*
*Variable 9: Observer distance between 9.1 feet and 15 feet*
*Variable 10: Observer distance between 15.1 feet and 25 feet*
*Variable 11: Observer distance between 25.1 feet and 40 feet*
*Variable 12: Observer distance between 40.1 feet and 70 feet*
*Variable 13: Observer distance between 70.1 feet and 100 feet*
*Mana Cost: 1,500*
*Pattern Cohesion: 55*
*Fusion Time: 3 hours*

Larek thought that the *Perceptive Misdirection* Fusion was oddly created, as it seemed to heavily feature a large amount of Variables based on detecting the distance of any observers. Since he had been focused on trying to learn the Fusion for so long, he intuitively knew that the reason for these distance Variables was because it was necessary to alter what was being seen by the observer depending on how far away they were; as they got closer or farther away, their perception of his height would have to change slightly to compensate. As a result, someone close to him would obviously need to have a different view of him than someone 100 feet away.

He thought that there should probably be a better way to do it, but he'd have to think about it – and soon. Especially since he didn't think the current Fusion on his ring would last much longer.

There were a few other things that were interesting about the Fusion he had just learned. The first was that the Mana Cost was substantially higher for a Magnitude 1 Fusion than he'd seen before at 1,500 Mana. The only reason that Larek could think of to explain that was due to the number of Effects that were in play, and the Magnitude had less to do with how successful the mental manipulation of someone's perception was and was instead limited to the distance at which they were affected.

Secondly, the Pattern Cohesion was also much higher at 55 for a Magnitude 1 Fusion, which meant that only those with a 56 or higher in their Pneuma stat would be able to create it – which wasn't too many Mages, considering that most students in the Academy would only have 78 stat points to distribute by the time they hit Level 10. Higher Level Fusionists would have no problem with this, of course, and especially those with the Advanced Fusionist Specialization, which would decrease these costs by 10%.

Larek also noticed that the Fusion Time was substantially longer than normal, but he ignored that because it didn't really matter to him. Instead, he focused on the one thing that was a lot more interesting, and it was part of one of the Effects. It wasn't the last Effect, which – as he understood it – was what essentially manipulated someone's perception based upon observer distance. While he didn't understand the underlying principles behind this like he would with a spell he had learned, he thought he understood it well enough to muddle through when it came to reproducing a similar Effect. He'd seen it in action enough that he had a front-row seat to see how well it worked, after all.

Nor was it the first Effect, which used a pulse of Mana to identify observers within the area the Fusion affected. He could see how this might be done with his own Mana, as there was certainly a feeling when he controlled it outside of his body and how it interacted with other objects, though using it to "identify observers" as the Fusion called it was probably beyond his abilities if he were to try it on his own. With practice and a reason to do it, he thought he might get the hang of it, but he didn't really have any reason to experiment right now.

That left the second Effect, which somehow hid this pulse of Mana so that it wasn't obvious that it was being used. It apparently worked well enough that even with Larek's new perception of the floating strands of Mana around the environment, he couldn't detect anything coming from the ring and the Fusion set upon it. The steady influx of ambient Mana into the ring to keep it working was visible, but he saw absolutely nothing coming out to indicate that it was using pulses of Mana to essentially look around up to 100 feet away.

It was the phrase, "void carrier", that intrigued and – if Larek was being honest with himself – frightened him. Having been swallowed by some sort of void ball back in the Kingdom when Chinli had been fighting Warped Void Hunters, which transported him not only across the continent but potentially a few years into the future, anything to do with "the void" or voids in general was a bit unsettling. Yet, despite the way his logical mind wanted nothing to do with anything related to voids, there was a part of him that was connected to the idea somehow.

This was made even stranger when he mentally dug into the Effect mentioning the void carriers and he intuitively understood more about the obscure subject than he did both of the other Effects combined. In simplest terms, what the void carrier was designed to do was create a tiny pocket of mass-less void space that enveloped each of the Mana pulses as they spread out from the Fusion. They acted like an extremely thin bubble that completely camouflaged the presence of the Mana inside, while still allowing the Mana to fully observe the world around it.

As for what exactly "void" meant? Well, it was an invisible, endless, empty expanse that was adjacent to his current reality, but normally interacted with that reality in no visible way; only by opening up a connection to it, such as the Effect that wrapped the Mana pulses, was it even tangentially observable in the simplest terms. It was also, at least he suspected, connected to what the Gergasi had done in opening the breach, though he couldn't tell for certain what exactly was done without seeing it himself. That was an eventuality that he didn't want to consider, however, as it would mean getting a little too close to the so-called Great Ones for his comfort.

Regardless of what he thought he knew about it, the void wasn't something he wanted to deal with right now, considering that he had other things to do. His priority that day was to create some higher-Magnitude versions of the Fusions he had created the day before, along with some *Paralyzing Light* Fusions to go along with them, and he figured that would take a few hours of work at the minimum – mainly due to waiting for his Mana to regenerate. After that was done, he needed to load up on more supplies and potentially change out more of his Kingdom coinage for Sealance Empire coinage while he had the chance.

Then, if he was lucky, he would be on the road again in the early afternoon, which would allow him to make at least a little progress before he had to stop for the night. He was cognizant of the need to keep moving no matter what, as he still had a long distance to travel before he got back to the Kingdom. While he knew that he shouldn't feel that way, he had a sense that he had abandoned his friends and family in their time of need and was driven to get back to them as soon as possible.

Rather than get out of bed, since he was already comfortable, Larek spent the next six hours creating stronger offensive Fusions of his new creations. Before he started, he spent his 19 accumulated AP on his Intellect stat, increasing it to a base of 117; with his *Intellect Boost*, it was boosted up to 234. Now with 2,340 Mana as his maximum, he got to work.

For *Binding Thorns* and *Frozen Zone*, he created versions that had a Magnitude of 10 – which ended up costing him a little over 190,000 Mana (which he was able to regenerate in about 50 minutes) and approximately 4,400 Pattern Cohesion each. *Healing Shelter* was one for which he was unable to create a Magnitude 10 version, as it would've cost him 1.7 million Mana – far too expensive and time-consuming at the moment. He compromised with a Magnitude 8 version for 680,000 Mana, which took him under 3 hours of mind-numbingly boring focus to be able to afford the Mana cost, and the Pattern Cohesion was just under 5,000 – still leaving him more than 13,000 Pattern Cohesion for his last Fusion: the *Stone Shredder Dome*.

The *Stone Shredder Dome* was even more expensive in terms of Mana than the *Healing Shelter*, at 950 Mana as the *Dome's* base in comparison to 800 for the *Shelter's*, so he had to make another compromise so that he wasn't creating one all day. At Magnitude 6, he was able to create the +6 Fusion in just under an hour with his regeneration rate, and while it wasn't exactly ideal, it would be a good enough test to see if it even worked like he expected. If it passed the test, he could always make a stronger one in the future if he could find a place safe enough to craft the Fusion for a few hours.

With the sun outside indicating that it was just after noon, and with his stomach rumbling for food, Larek packed his new Fusions away and headed out, grabbing lunch from the Innkeeper along the way. From there, it was just a matter of finishing up his restock of food supplies for the next leg of his journey, which went much swifter than he hoped. With bulging packs of supplies and the new Fusions in his pocket, in anticipation of the Apertures he would test them on in the future, he set off down the road leading out of Lakebellow toward the east.

# Chapter 14

"Where *is* he?"

Alwhin reached back and smacked his brother in the side of the head without looking, while also shout-whispering, *"For the last time, shut up!"*

Corwhin mumbled something that he couldn't hear, which Alwhin supposed was a good thing for all of them hiding behind the stand of trees about a mile outside of the town of Lakebellow and 150 feet from the main road leading east. They couldn't afford to make much noise, and beating his brother for talking back to him would undoubtedly be loud.

*"Bro, I think we missed him,"* Balwin whispered softly by his side, with a low enough voice that it wouldn't carry. Alwhin was glad that at least his oldest younger brother was smart enough to know better compared to Corwhin, but Corwhin had always been a bit strange even for the Gharen family. Fortunately, the youngest – Delwin – made up for Corwhin's oddness with a good head on his shoulders and was the smartest of them... next to Alwhin, of course. Being the oldest meant he was in charge, and his father always told him that being the leader meant that you needed to be the smartest and strongest of the entire group. Hence, since he was the leader, he was naturally the smartest and strongest of them all.

It was unfortunate that their younger sister, Elwina, hadn't been transformed during the changes more than a week ago, because having an inside source of information in town would come in handy right now. They had been waiting hidden in the brush all morning, and he was starting to sweat from the heat of the day, but they had seen no sign of the stranger they had encountered the night before in the Aledeck Inn. Given what information he gained from eavesdropping on the conversation with that annoying Innkeeper, as well as his own questions, he was 100% positive that the man would be leaving earlier in the morning to resume his journey to wherever he called home – because he certainly wasn't from around the Empire.

Yet, there had been no sign of him, despite them arriving in their ambush spot before dawn. He normally hated getting up before the sun, but if Delwin was correct about the worth of the magical clothing the stranger was wearing, then it would be worth it. Not that he had any knowledge of where he could find a buyer for it, as magic was still a relatively new addition to the Empire with the sudden changes – with people suddenly becoming Mages and Martials while

Scissions and Apertures appeared all over the land. His own family was blessed when all but one of his siblings had undergone the change, though as far as he was concerned, it was all that was owed to them and more.

Alwhin had become a Martial and was already Level 6 along with his brothers, with crazy Corwhin being another Martial – though they had completely different ideas of how to fight. Corwhin was more of a "throw myself directly into danger without thought of the consequences" type of person and loved to cut things up with his knives, while Alwhin was more deliberate and waited for the right time to strike with the mace he had crafted in the family forge. It balanced out, though, especially as they had fought hundreds of monsters over the last week in order to increase their Skills and achieve Level 6. They hadn't actually closed any of the Apertures, of course, because that wasn't their responsibility and it was too difficult to get that close to them without being overwhelmed, but they also recognized the advantages they could get from fighting the monsters.

**Alwhin Gharen**

**Level 6**
**Advancement Points (AP) : 2/10**
**Available AP to Distribute: 0**

**Stama: 100/100**

**Strength: 19**
**Body: 10**
**Agility: 10**

**Battle Arts:**
**Empowered Strike**
**Fleetfoot**
**Shield Taunt**

**Martial Skills:**
**Stama Subjugation Level 1**
**Pain Resistance Level 4**
**Throwing Level 5**
**Body Regeneration Level 6**
**Bladed Weapon Expertise Level 7**
**Dodge Level 9**

## Blunt Weapon Expertise Level 11

For one, their Skills increased in Level insanely fast when fighting monsters rather than just practicing on their own, which was what led them to do it in the first place when they encountered an ugly, green-skinned bipedal monster out in the forest one day. It had been extremely easy to kill, especially when they ganged up on it, and that had led to their first Skill increases since the change. Even Balwin and Delwin, who were Mages instead of Martials, had somehow increased their *Magical Detection* Skills just by beating the ugly monster to death, which had made them want to practice and learn how to fling around powerful spells.

Unfortunately, such a thing was apparently difficult and took a long time to get right, though Delwin had figured out how to cast a *Fireball* the day before – and had nearly burned down their house in the process. Balwin was getting close to that point, but hadn't figured it out yet; as for Alwhin being able to use the Battle Arts that were available to Martials, they were a bit unreliable, and he wasn't able to initiate them as easily as he knew he should. But his stats alone meant that he was still strong enough with his club to handle this foreigner passing through town.

Alwhin didn't even blink an eye about killing and robbing the poor bastard, because he – and his brothers – had done the same with a few others who had ventured out of Lakebellow to kill monsters. At first, they were simply going to charge the small groups a fee for being allowed to hunt monsters out in the Scarwood Forest where his family had their cabin (and which was therefore their home territory), but when the first group resisted, Alwhin and his brothers were forced to kill them.

Amazingly enough, their Skills increased just as well when killing *people* as they did with monsters – if not even better. Now, they were taking the opportunity to ambush and kill nearly anyone entering and leaving Lakebellow, though they had to ensure they did it far away from town to stay out of sight of the Protectors; the former town guards had taken it upon themselves to be the main fighting force against the monsters and Apertures and tended to wander around the countryside more than usual, but it was easy enough to estimate their routes. Unfortunately for those townsfolk who decided to risk helping out with that objective in order to improve their newfound powers, they weren't as disciplined or skilled as the Protectors, which meant that they were practically helpless against the Gharen brothers.

Now, with whatever this stranger possessed, if they didn't sell it to buy better weapons and armor, then it was possible that Alwhin might even be able to use it himself. That, of course, depended upon what it actually did, but with how much magic was swirling around it that Delwin could see, he figured it was at least somewhat powerful.

The thought that it might make the stranger so strong that he would be able to resist their ambush never crossed his mind. It was simply unfathomable, especially considering that he and his brothers were likely the highest Level and therefore the strongest individuals in Lakebellow, if one were to discount the Protectors, who were constantly fighting and were undoubtedly slightly higher in Level. But none of them were here to help the stranger, as most of them were out to the west closing yet another Aperture.

"*We couldn't have missed him,*" Alwhin responded with an irritable whisper. "*We've been watching the road all day, and we would've seen him. The only possibilities are that he left **before** we even arrived, or he's leaving later.*" He could only hope that it was the second reason, as he hated wasting his time, but he couldn't help but start to doubt the stranger was even coming. It was foolish to set out on the next leg of your travels so late in the day as the dark would bring about a heightened danger of being ambushed by monsters, but who knew what kinds of stupid thoughts these foreign strangers had? That he had survived a potential journey from Enderflow was probably due to complete luck if that was the case.

They waited in relative silence for another hour before Alwhin decided to call it quits for the day. He figured that he would have to go back into town and find out what happened to the stranger, before making plans to ambush him when he finally left – because he was *certain* that the man hadn't left before them. He also wouldn't be heading back toward the southwest, given that he had just come from there, and this was the only other road leading away from town.

*So, why isn't he here?*

He had no explanation, but he'd had enough and had wasted too much time. He'd make that stranger pay for doing this to him; while he couldn't be killed *twice*, there was always the possibility of torture. Perhaps if the man was restrained and then Delwin began burning the foreigner's body parts with his *Fireball* spell—

"Bro, I think that's him coming—"

Interrupted in his thoughts about torturing the stranger, Alwhin looked toward the road to see a figure toward the west, which was getting larger at a slightly alarming rate. *How fast is he moving? How is that possible?*

Despite the strange sight of what he was quickly able to identify as their intended mark racing down the road with incredible speed, Alwhin was irritated enough with having had to wait so long that he gestured for the others to get ready to move. It was going to be impossible to ambush the man using superior speed, so they were going to have to stop him with their strength and prevent him from being able to escape.

When the man was within 150 feet of their location, he began to reduce the speed of his running for some reason, but rather than be curious about why there was a change, Alwhin could only be happy that they wouldn't have to go chasing this fool down. By the time the stranger was nearly even with them, he was only moving at what could be considered a light jog, and the elder sibling gave the signal to his brothers to attack.

Gripping the handle of his mace in his hand as he stood up where he'd been crouching behind a bush, Alwhin took off toward the man who had stopped and was watching them emerge from the forest with confusion followed by what appeared to be irritation. *Is he irritated that he's being attacked? I'm going to smash that look off his face and enjoy doing it.*

"Really? Why are you doing this? You should be fighting the monsters and closing Apertures, not attacking people along the road like a common bandit."

Being called a common bandit, an insult to someone like himself, made Alwhin stumble a little in his run, but the man's tone of voice was so dismissive that it made him breathe heavily as a film of pure rage filtered over his vision. All he could think of by that point was popping the stranger's head like an overripe melon with his weapon, and there was nothing the foreigner could do to stop him. He and his brothers were powerful enough that nothing could stand in their way—

As Alwhin felt the heat of a *Fireball* shoot past him toward the man, the stranger sighed and said, "Well, I guess this means I can test out my new creations; not quite what I had intended, but I'm tired of all this." As he spoke, he waved his hand and what looked like three rocks shot out in an arc toward him and his crazy brother Corwhin. Something about those rocks screamed danger to him, and even in his enraged state he knew it wasn't a good idea to be touched by them. His Martial brother amazingly thought the same thing and dove to the side with him, landing in the grass alongside the road with a roll.

Springing to his feet, he noticed that the man had completely underestimated his throws and they had instead landed far short of

Alwhin and his brother, and he chuckled at how inept the foreigner was. "You missed," he snorted out with a short laugh.

"Did I?"

Staring impassively at the two brothers, along with Balwin rushing up behind them, the man just stood there as the *Fireball* that Delwin had cast hit him in the chest. He didn't even try to avoid it for some reason, and Alwhin expected him to suddenly catch flame from the impact – but that wasn't what happened. Instead, the ball of flames seemed to bounce off his clothes, leaving only a minor scorch mark where it hit. As it hit the ground, the fireball fizzled out a second later, proving to be completely ineffective against the foreigner. Bells of alarm rang through his head at the sight, but aside from staring at the stranger for a few seconds at the sight of the fireball bouncing off the man's shirt, his brother had apparently decided that this was the time to attack – and Alwhin couldn't let him go in alone. It was at about that time that Balwin also caught up with them and kept going on his run, so the three of them rushed forward in a spread-out line, coming at the foreigner from slightly different angles. It wasn't as good as attacking from completely opposite sides, but it should be more than enough to kill the man before he could do anything else.

Another *Fireball* was cast by Delwin at the same time, who targeted the man's head; his aim was spot-on as it rushed right toward the impassive expression on the man's annoying face, only to be blocked by a bare raised arm, which took the spell entirely this time. Unfortunately, the entire arm didn't light on fire as a result, but Alwhin could see that there was some definite discoloration along the man's skin as he was badly burned. That was more than enough for him, though, as the distraction was all that the other brothers needed to rush in and finish him off.

Alwhin was probably within 20 feet and closing fast when he felt something catch his foot, causing him to trip and fall to his knees, catching himself with his hands as his mace was knocked out of his right to tumble away from him. He didn't get a chance to look back at what tripped him as a mass of brown tree roots burst out from the ground around him and wrapped around his lower legs and arms. He used his prodigious strength to pull and rip them apart, but another root that snaked around his neck threw him into a panic – especially as he felt something sharp pricking into his skin where the roots were touching. In his panic he flailed around, ripping apart a few of the roots in the process and even managed to loosen the one around his neck, but the roots only seemed to multiply and wrap themselves around him even further.

"Help!" he tried to shout, but the root around his neck made it come out a bit garbled to the point where it was more of a gurgle than a comprehensible word. Looking to his left where Corwhin should be, he found his brother frozen, mid-run, like a statue in a hazy cloud of what appeared to be small ice crystals. Even as he watched, still attempting to free himself from the roots, the skin all over his brother's hands and face suddenly burst asunder as reddish crystals emerged from *inside his body*, before he toppled over with a *thud* and the sound of ice cracking.

*What? What happened to him? What did that man do to my brother?!*

His anger at seeing the death of his brother by some magical means he didn't understand pushed back the mounting fear Alwhin was experiencing as he redoubled his efforts to free himself, only for his hands to become sliced up and slippery with his own blood as thorns on the roots made them harmful to handle.

Managing to turn his head to the other side to look for help from Balwin, it was just in time to watch his brother stagger to his knees in a full-on collapse. The skin on Balwin's face and arms appeared sallow and thin, and any of the fat that he'd had — which wasn't much — had disappeared, leaving his brother looking like a corpse rather than something living. Soon enough, after a few more seconds of watching, the latter observation came true as Balwin fell to the side, his skeletal frame erasing most of the features that made his brother who he was and making him seem like a stranger. It was almost as if all the life had been sucked out of him or consumed in some unknown manner.

"Hold on, Alwhin! I'll burn them off of you!"

The voice of his only remaining brother startled him, as he was staring in horror at Balwin's desiccated corpse, before he felt an impact followed by a wash of heat that started burning at his legs.

"You stupid idiot! You're going to burn me alive!" was what he wanted to shout, but yet another root had wrapped around his neck, cutting off not only his breathing but his circulation. As he screamed internally at the fire burning him from below, his eyes widened in shock as the thorns all over the roots wrapped around his body and his limbs suddenly stabbed into him, digging into his flesh with ease. The next moment, the agony of being ripped apart as the roots wrapping him up tightened and shredded his skin and muscles overshadowed the heat of the fire burning through both the roots and his legs.

As his throat was slit and he swiftly bled out from hundreds of bodily wounds, Alwhin's last sight as he lifted his head in defiance was the still-impassive face of the stranger staring off into the distance. He knew exactly what he was looking at, and his last thought was of his last living brother.

*Run, Delwin, run! You can't beat—*

Alwhin Gharen wasn't able to finish the thought as he slipped into the eternal darkness of death.

# Chapter 15

Larek mentally sighed as he aimed his staff and launched a stone from the *Flying Stone* Fusion on the end, watching as impassively as he could as it slammed into the back of the fleeing Mage. The force of the impact was enough to pass through the man's clothing, flesh, and bones to come out the other side, leaving a gaping hole where a good portion of his spine used to be, and the would-be bandit and murderer collapsed and rolled a few times as his momentum kept him moving once he lost control of his body. It wasn't a perfect shot, as he was hoping to make it a clean and quick death, but it was good enough that he doubted the man would live for much longer.

*Why? Why did they have to attack me? This felt less like I was defending myself and more like an execution.*

Perhaps it *was* an execution, as it seemed to Larek that this type of thing was common to these individuals. Their behavior, coupled with the unasked-for warning the Innkeeper gave to him the night before, made that obvious enough. The fact that one of them, the one he had just punched a hole through, had managed to figure out how to cast a spell after a little more than a week since becoming a Mage was a surprise – and would've made them even more dangerous to the local population if they continued to rob and potentially kill people along the road.

Yet, despite the fact that he would classify these individuals as "bad people", Larek couldn't help but be saddened by what he had done. Oh, he knew it was necessary, especially as he was defending himself and warned them to stop what they were doing, but that didn't mean he liked doing it or didn't wonder if there was another way it could've been resolved. His experience with such things told him that there likely was no other way it could've ended unless he was willing to sacrifice himself, which wasn't going to happen.

It was killing the running Mage that bothered him the most, because it felt wrong to kill someone like that when they were just trying to escape. Unfortunately, similar to the reason he had killed Ricardo and the two Martial trainees, he couldn't allow any of them to live to attack him again when he least expected it. The last thing he needed was to camp somewhere that night and be ambushed while he was focused on a Fusion. While his Repelling Barrier would stop most things, it was already proven that it didn't work against balls of flames as they didn't have the physicality to trigger the defense. He ended up simply letting the *Multi-Resistance* Fusion on his clothes handle the spell, and while he was burned slightly by both impacts, his body was more than capable of preventing anything more than superficial damage – which was practically gone already as his *Body Regeneration* kicked in even without using his *Healing Surge* Fusion.

It was going to take something more powerful than that to hurt him at this stage; his defensive Fusions combined with his Body stat made him difficult to harm with weak attacks like that. A higher *quantity* of weaker attacks could hurt him, but a few weak fireballs? He'd suffered much worse than that and survived.

Turning toward the victims of his testing, his stomach felt a little ill when he looked at them. In the case of Alwhin, the individual who had accosted him at the Inn and who seemed to be the leader of this little group, he was actually the least nauseating to look at. After being wrapped up in roots via the *Binding Thorns +10* Fusion, which it was good to see actually held him after he wasn't able to rip them all apart with his relatively high Strength stat, his body was absolutely shredded along with his neck. The blood loss was what actually killed him, as evidenced by the spreading pool of red that was soaking into the ground around his corpse. Once he stopped moving, the roots disappeared, and the stone holding the Fusion remained in place as the only evidence of what had killed the man. It was technically still active and waiting to detect any physical movement, but he could deactivate it with a verbal command at any time.

Overall, the Fusion had been a success; a disturbing sight when used on a person, but a success, nonetheless.

The same went for his *Frozen Zone +10* Fusion – both the success and the disturbing sight. Instead of shredding with thorns, the extreme cold of the area created by his Fusion had literally frozen all of the moisture in the man's body, causing it to crystallize and seemingly to clump together to the point where a large hunk of it pushed itself out of his body. Watching impassively as this happened was one of the hardest things he'd ever had to do, as it made him extremely uncomfortable seeing what looked like bloody growths pop out all over the would-be bandit's corpse – because that was essentially what he was by that time, after having been completely frozen at that point. He wondered if it would act the same if he were to place his hand inside the *Frozen Zone*, or if his high Body stat would negate some of the effect. It worked to stop a lot of the burning caused by fireballs, so it was entirely possible that it would stop the freezing cold as well.

This Fusion, too, had deactivated after there was no movement detected, but the evidence of its use was much more obvious. Any moisture that had been in the grass or even the dirt underneath it had caused the vegetation to erupt in ice crystals similar to the blood from the corpse, killing the plant life as it burst apart from the sudden freezing.  There would be a dead patch in the spot the Fusion covered for a little while, but the dead vegetation, as well as the moisture from when the ice melted, would help to restore it to life in a month or two.

The most disturbing Fusion he had used, however, was *Healing Shelter +8*.  The fact that it worked was good to see, but the result frankly frightened him.  He had known that the *Healing Surge +5* Fusion was powerful and should only be used in short bursts even with someone with the *Body Regeneration* Skill, but it appeared as though a +8 version of that Effect was not only a few steps more powerful, but almost exponentially more powerful.  The reason for that, he discovered while he watched it work, was because the healing energy that infused the attacking man had reverberated around the contained area of effect, enhancing itself in the process.  It was strange to look at, though he had to force himself to look away from it to see what had happened to the man.

It appeared as though all of the life force had been sucked out of him, though in reality it was his own body that essentially consumed itself to fuel the healing that it was attempting to accomplish.  Seeing this, more than anything else, hinted at how dangerous his *Healing Surge* Fusion really was, and if he had actually created something stronger than the +3 version back in the day for all of the Fusions he distributed, it was entirely possible that the temporary comas some Mages had fallen into would've been permanent – or it might've even killed them outright.

As much as he hated how his learning had come to an end at Crystalview, he could better understand why Dean Wilburt was so adamant to remove Larek from the Academy.  That still didn't make what was done to him right, but comprehension of how lucky it was that no one that had used his *Healing Surge +3* Fusion had died was certainly at the forefront of his mind now.

The man that had been caught in the *Shelter* Fusion was now just a heap of bones with paper-thin skin covering his entire body.  In all honesty, he wasn't even sure if the healing Effect had stopped even after he had technically died, as he looked worse than when he finally stopped moving, but the Fusion had eventually deactivated due to lack of physical movement.  Still, it was a heck of a way to go, and if he ever had to defend himself against another person, he would think twice about using it in this way again.  Granted, if he were attacked by a Martial member of the SIC or a Gergasi, they would likely have the *Body Regeneration* Skill and therefore have a bit of resistance to the Effect for a short time, but a Mage or a normal person would suffer just as this individual had.

In a choice between life and death, he knew he would use it if he had to, but only if there were no other options. Against monsters, however, there would be no hesitation; that was, of course, if it even worked against them. His experiment didn't really prove that it was a viable Fusion to use against his main targets, so it would require further testing.

"Deactivate Binding Thorns!"
"Deactivate Frozen Zone!"
"Deactivate Healing Shelter!"

With his commands spoken out loud, he could visually see the areas of ambience around each of the Fusions disappear, leaving the stones the Fusions were on comparatively inert. They would stay that way until he activated them again, and he started to move toward the closest one in order to pick it back up and store it in his pocket for reuse in the future.

It was at that point that something felt a little off, almost as if something was constricting his breathing – but that wasn't it, either. Wary of another attack, he looked around to see if he saw something, or even sensed it like he had the original ambush as a disturbance in the Mana floating through the air—

*The Mana!*

Switching on his *Magical Detection* Skill, he looked for the strands of light that indicated the Mana in the air, and was astonished when he saw that it was *almost completely gone* from the area. Looking further afield, he could see more of it gradually drifting in, but the difference between where he was standing and an area a few hundred feet away was dramatic. It was like looking at a pond that was full of nearly clear water with only a few blurry sections where you couldn't see down to the bottom and a dirty pond that was visibly murky.

Staring down at his clothes, he immediately identified that the strange feeling he was experiencing was due to a lack of ambient Mana in the area. His *Boost* Fusions were having trouble getting enough ambient Mana to provide the full amount, and a look at his Status saw the percentage increase in his stats fluctuating oddly. A quick jog out of the area led him to where the Mana was flowing in to fill the void that was created, likely by his Fusions as they drew in a lot of ambient Mana to power them, and he almost immediately felt the influx of ambient Mana on his clothing Fusions stabilize.

"Well, this could be a bit of a problem," he mumbled out loud, thinking about what had happened.

Larek had originally thought that he could make enough of these offensive Fusions to completely surround him when he attacked an Aperture, but that didn't seem like it would be feasible in the lower-Mana environment of the Sealance Empire. In the Kingdom, he didn't anticipate any potential problems because the Mana density was so high, but his Fusions were literally stripping almost all of the Mana out of the area when all of them were active at the same time. Based on what he had seen of the ambient Mana situation – or lack of Mana, as it was – he could only assume that the offensive Fusions were already at the point of shutting down from lack of Mana by the time they were done finishing off the three men. An attack by dozens or potentially more than a hundred different monsters would take much longer to defeat, and depleting the ambient Mana so that his own defensive Fusions were starved of it was a bad idea in the heat of battle.

"I'd certainly say so. Murder isn't taken lightly here in Lakebellow."

The voice came out of nowhere and startled Larek as he stared at his clothing Fusions in an effort to see if they had been harmed by the reduction in ambient Mana. Fortunately, from what he could see, they appeared perfectly fine; unfortunately, he had bigger problems than checking his existing Fusions as he looked up to see a large group of what could only be Protectors. At their head, mounted on a horse along with the two-dozen other riders, was a large man that gave off the vibe of a Martial, and one that was a bit stronger than the ones he had just killed. Not quite on par with a third-year Martial trainee yet, he didn't believe, but lack of training in using Stama and Battle Arts could be shored up with experience and skill. This man appeared to have both of the latter, as his hair was peppered with grey and his stance and very presence screamed confidence and capability; Larek thought that the man's *Leadership* Skill must've been quite high.

The Protectors with him weren't quite as intimidating as the leader, but he could also sense that around half of them were also Martials and Mages, at least according to how the Mana in the air interacted with them. It was very similar to the Protector breakdown of those that had been changed in Enderflow, which he briefly considered interesting to note – before his mind caught up with the words the man said and his mention of *murder*.

Larek quickly shook his head. "Not murder, Protector. Self-defense," he responded.

"Ah. So, you were just defending yourself when you shot Delwin in the back with what I can only assume is a spell of some kind?" the lead Protector asked, sounding genuinely curious, but Larek could tell that he was anything but curious. He was looking for a reason to charge the Combat Fusionist with murder.

But Larek was confident in his own actions. "Oh? You're on a first-name basis with the bandits around here? I wasn't aware that the Protectors in Lakebellow were so familiar with those that preyed on the weak and defenseless."

*That* brought a thundercloud of anger across the leader's face, while simultaneously causing the other Protectors to shift in their saddles. "Of course not; the Gharen family aren't bandits, just a bunch of troublemakers."

"Are you sure of that? It seems to me that waiting in ambush for someone to pass by on the road and immediately attacking them without any type of dialogue constitutes banditry to me. When I assisted the Protectors in Enderflow with taking down a group of bandits that had been attacking caravans, they didn't hesitate to end every bandit there." Larek was twisting the truth there a bit, since it had been *him* that didn't hesitate to kill every bandit as he lost control of his actions for a while, but he was confident that none of them would've lived much past giving up their slavery contacts even if he hadn't done anything.

"You—" The now-flustered Protector stumbled over his words a little. "You worked with the Protectors in Enderflow? Who did you work with?"

It was a probing question, as Larek could tell that he wasn't exactly believed, and he answered it as honestly as he could. "I worked directly with Protector Ashlynn. She also became a Martial when the change happened, along with about half of the other Protectors, and I participated in temporarily closing quite a few Apertures before I departed." That was all true this time.

"I... see. Still, that doesn't excuse what you did to the Gharen brothers, and especially Delwin who was running away—"

Larek was tired of all the accusations of wrongdoing, whether because of his actions or because of his appearance back in the Kingdom. Cutting the man off, he asked, "Was I supposed to let them kill me? Was I not supposed to use all of the weapons in my arsenal to defend myself? Would it have been better to simply use my axe to kill them in clear self-defense? Should I have let a bandit roam free and possibly gather reinforcements to attack me again?"

"Like I said, the Gharen brothers aren't—*weren't* bandits. They were simply no-good troublemakers—"

"Who likely turned to banditry and murder once they got a taste of the power that the change brought with it. Even I, who was just passing through Lakebellow, heard rumors of people going missing outside of town; blame was put on the Apertures and the monsters around the area, but it's obvious now that this wasn't entirely the case. I can only assume that you and the other Protectors have been too busy handling the local Apertures to investigate these disappearances in detail, but fortunately for you and the rest of the people of Lakebellow, the source of these disappearances encountered someone who could take care of the problem for you. If anything, you should be thanking me for making your part of the Empire just a little safer during these dangerous times." That last part was probably a bit too much, but he was fed up with these people, and anger tinted his words a little. The notification that he had increased his *Speaking* Skill was a surprise, though.

**Speaking** *has reached Level 17!*

"Thank you? No, I don't think so. They might have been participating in illicit activities, but that doesn't give you the right to murder them out of hand. There will be an investigation into this, and if your claim of self-defense holds up, then you'll be free to—"

"Uh, no, that doesn't work for me. I need to get back home as quickly as I can, and any major delay like that is completely unacceptable. I'll be leaving now while you figure out how to deal with this on your own."

"HALT!" the Protector leader shouted. "If you take a single step away from here, you'll have as good as admitted to guilt in this matter. I'll personally chase you down and hold you accountable for whatever crimes you've committed in the Empire—"

Rather than argue anymore, Larek turned on his speed by utilizing every bit of his high Agility stat, as he ran toward his Fusions still on the ground near the corpses. The Combat Fusionist heard shouted commands and the sound of hooves striking the dirt of the road, but he ignored all that as he quickly scooped up the stones and ran down the road at full speed. He could maintain a pace that was faster than a horse for a few hours if necessary, though he would be quite famished by the time he stopped to take a break, which was exactly what he did.

The sounds of pursuit rapidly faded behind him until, only an hour later, he looked behind himself briefly to see no sign of the Protectors. He had lost them, at least temporarily, so it was safe for a moment to eat something while he slowed to a walk. During the walk, he felt an Aperture slightly to the northeast, but he ignored it in favor of putting some distance between himself and the Protectors of Lakebellow. He wasn't sure if the leader was bluffing about chasing him down, as he couldn't imagine a Protector abandoning their responsibility of protecting their town or city just to follow a potential criminal – but he wasn't going to take any chances.

As soon as he was done eating and took a long swig of refreshing liquid from his water bottle, Larek took off running yet again.

# Chapter 16

Larek didn't stop fully running until just before dark hours later. He took minor breaks to walk and eat some food to replenish his energy, but that was the extent of any slowdown in his travels. He hesitated to call it "flight", as if he was fleeing from being held accountable for some crime, but it sure felt a little like that when he came upon a small village and decided to run around it rather than going through it. He didn't want to be seen or remembered by its residents in case the Protector did indeed come through looking for him. When he had thoughts about abandoning the road completely and cutting across the countryside so as to avoid any chance of being noticed, he knew that guilt at what he had done had climbed up inside of him to affect his way of thinking.

It wasn't guilt about killing those men, however. It was guilt about how he had treated the Protectors and ran rather than waste his time explaining or proving that he was in the right. He was also well aware that it was stupid and irrational to feel guilty over something where he was in no way in the wrong, other than perhaps being rude to the Protectors, but he felt it anyway. It wasn't strong enough to convince him to turn around and seek out the Protector leader in order to explain the situation a little better, thankfully.

He had a Kingdom to get back to, after all, and the sooner, the better.

Navigating his way off the road to a spot that was far away from any Apertures he sensed in the distance, he made a cold camp in the middle of a jumble of rocks situated in a large field of grass. The light of the moon above was enough to see by, at least, and he pulled out his map to check on his progress. Tracing his route and remembering what he'd been seeing throughout the day, he knew that he was swiftly approaching a small mountain range; it was more of a long line of high hills than mountains, but compared to the majority of the relatively flat terrain he had been passing through, it was certainly mountainous in proportion.

He'd left behind the large forests that had comprised the last half of his journey, and he was presented with large plains of grass that filled the land until they butted up against the range of hills in the distance. This also meant that the presence of towns and cities was going to increase over what he'd encountered thus far, which had been beneficial when he had first been planning out his route back to the Kingdom, but which now held an element of danger to it as he was not quite on the good side of the Protectors of the Empire right now. He had no way to know if they could quickly share information between towns and cities, but he had at least greatly outpaced a normal horse by the point he stopped for the night, so the danger of him being sought after by other towns and cities from that quarter was reduced. Still, stopping in any inhabited areas was something he'd have to do sparingly in order to somewhat mitigate the risk of being identified.

It was extremely disappointing, but he'd make do somehow. At the least, he could probably get in and out quickly after purchasing any supplies he needed, while staying at another Inn was likely out of the question as it would be too dangerous.

Rather than risk making any other Fusions that night, Larek attempted to get some sleep but had a hard time falling asleep. His paranoia of being found in the middle of the night by the Protector leader – while extremely unlikely because of the distance the Combat Fusionist had traveled – kept him awake until the early hours of the morning when his exhausted body finally succumbed to sleep. He woke shortly after dawn as the light battered his closed eyelids, and while he was tired from not getting nearly enough sleep, his body and mind quickly rejuvenated themselves once he ate something and packed up to leave.

An abrupt decision based on his thoughts of the evening before made him turn away from the route that led back to the road. Instead, he simply headed east and started running. The absence of the road would play havoc on his sense of where he was in the Empire, but given that he still had a long way to go, he figured that if he continued to ensure that he was always heading east he would eventually get to his destination. Plus, with how wide open the current landscape was, he was fairly confident that if it was necessary that he find a town or city to visit, he'd be able to see it from a long way off.

The first thing he noticed, being away from the road, was that the prevalence of Apertures was *much* higher the further away from signs of civilization he was. It took only 30 minutes of running before he came across his first one, and although he had decided to skip all of the ones he had sensed the day before, his lead on any pursuit was great enough by that point that he didn't want to pass up any more chances to gain Aetheric Force – and another opportunity to test out his Fusions. He would have to be selective about which of them he used, given what had happened the day before during the ambush, but it would still be worth any time he spent testing them.

When he found the area where his senses were telling him the Aperture was located, it didn't take long to identify it at the bottom of a slight incline in the landscape. The grasses that had covered the land where the Aperture's territory was now situated had all been burnt away, replaced with an ashy landscape dotted with 20-foot-tall protrusions of what appeared to be hole-filled volcanic rock. Streams of lava seemed to bubble up from underground, twisting and turning in their pathway before ending up in a pool at least 20 feet across. There was nothing living, just a barren hellscape – which made it appropriate that there were demons present as the monsters.

From a distance, Larek could spot small-winged **Demonic Imps** flapping in and out of the holes of the various lumps of volcanic rock, as if they were constantly patrolling their homes. These Imps were approximately 3 feet in height with spindly arms and legs, a pair of leathery wings, a hairless, deep-red-colored skin covering their bodies, eyes that lit up as if with an inner fire, and were holding what appeared to be some sort of three-pronged pitchfork made of some black-colored material. According to his class on *Monster Knowledge* at Copperleaf, these types of demons were simple and not very difficult to kill, as they had very little in the way of defense and a few Mages or Martial archers could hit them out of the air and most likely kill them with one spell or arrow. Their danger only lay in the fact that they spent almost all of their time in the air and attacked their victims from above; otherwise, they were fairly weak.

Or so he had learned. Then again, that knowledge was based on defending the wall of a town or city, not for individuals or groups to go out and kill the Imps that spawned from Apertures. Despite that lack of full knowledge of what they were capable of when a solo individual went up against them, Larek wasn't going to let that stop him – just like it hadn't stopped him from killing the monsters near all the other Apertures he'd closed on his journey thus far.

With a ground-eating lope that brought him to the edge of the barren hellscape, the Combat Fusionist stopped just outside of its limits as he eyed the demons flying at least 10 feet above his height at the nearest holey pillar of volcanic rock. Up close, they did indeed appear relatively weak, so without any other hesitation, he stepped over the threshold over into the Aperture's territory.

The five Imps immediately targeted him because he wasn't attempting to be stealthy, flapping their wings to bring them close to his location. Ensuring his *Repelling Barrier* was active, Larek waited for them to attack... and waited... and waited. Even though there was only 50 feet or so separating him from the flock? Gaggle? Clutch? Swarm? He wasn't sure what a group of demons was called, though he was sure there was a term for it. Regardless, the group of Imps could certainly fly, but they were abnormally slow. It took a good 20 seconds for them to travel the distance and descend to just over his head, where they attempted to stab at him with their black pitchforks, their mouths open with sharp, bloody teeth showing and a disturbing hiss coming from their throats.

Rather than let his Repelling Barrier block the hits, Larek brought his axe up to deflect the pitiful attacks, knocking two of the weapons out of the hands of the Imps, before stretching his arms up to start cutting them in two. That was what he *tried* to do, but the ones he swiped at suddenly disappeared in a flash of dark flames and reappeared a few feet to the left. It reminded him of the teleporting Warped Void Hunters Chinli had fought back in the Kingdom, though he could tell that this was less manipulating the void to move a certain distance away and more of some sort of innate ability that had to do with the hellfire that flashed in the location he struck. It was also instantaneous, as if he was simply dispelling an illusion which caused the real one to appear.

*So, these are a little more difficult than was taught. I wonder if it's because these things are usually killed from a distance and this hellfire teleportation was never used.*

Whatever the reason, the Imps were attacking again as soon as they reappeared, including the ones that had had their pitchfork knocked away by Larek's axe. One of the unarmed Imps managed to sneak past his axe's defense, moving much faster than it had been a moment before, as if the pitchfork had actually been slowing it down. Unfortunately for the demonic monster, its outstretched claws aiming for his neck were shattered – along with the rest of its body – as it was violently sent crashing into the ground because of his *Repelling Barrier*, killing it near-instantly. The others were repelled by his counterattacks and backed off a foot or two, or in the case of the other unarmed Imp, it disappeared again in a flash of hellfire, appearing again a few feet to the left.

It only took Larek's mind a second to realize that each of the Imps moved exactly the same distance to the left, no matter where they were or what kind of attack was used against them. As such, a simple strategy was born as he surprised the Imps by squatting down slightly before jumping straight toward one of them. He swung his axe crossways at it while moving slightly to allow the pitchfork to strike past his side; as predicted, it flashed away again in a burst of hellfire, but Larek carried through with his attack, the axe head swinging toward his left.

A split-second after, it reappeared... right in the path of the sharp-edged tool. His axe sheared through its real body, easily cutting off half of its wings, severing its spine, and destroying the other half of its wings in the process.

Now that he was familiar with how to kill these things, he was suddenly hopping to and fro as he swiped large arcs of his axe through the air, absolutely devastating the Imps that were surrounding him. Fortunately, they weren't intelligent enough to counter his simple strategy, and therefore were unable to adapt to his technique, all of their lives ending within seconds.

Overall, they were relatively easy to kill once he understood how they attacked. Looking around the Aperture's territory, though, he realized that there were *hundreds* of Imps around dozens of the tall volcanic rock pillars. In fact, in his eagerness to start accumulating more Aetheric Force, he had missed that the barren hellscape was at least 50% larger and had more monsters than any of the other ones he'd closed. The only reason for that being the case was if this was one of the *first* Apertures to open in the Empire and no one had encountered and closed it yet.

Unless he wanted to spend the next hour or two moving all over the territory to kill them all, he'd have to attack the Aperture and have them all come to him. With so many of them, more than he'd ever killed by himself, he wasn't sure he could survive if they all attacked at once.

Fortunately, he had one final Fusion to test out, and this was the perfect opportunity. He hadn't used it on the first group since he didn't want to deplete the ambient Mana quite yet, but he had no qualms about using it as soon as he was in position near the Aperture.

He had to kill another two groups, one consisting of 5 and the other consisting of 6 Imps, as he sprinted toward the center of the territory. There were 3 other groups following him at that point, but as they were slow, he had plenty of time to prepare himself.

Pulling out his *Stone Shredder Dome +6* that was on a small length of wood, he placed it in his shirt's front pocket so that its tip was pointing up. Taking a deep breath to settle himself, he reached out with his axe to tap its edge against the Aperture. Immediately, he heard hissing coming from all over the territory; the rest of the Imps were on their way.

He wasn't sure if the apparent speed increase he noticed was a benefit or not; on the one hand, he didn't have to wait as long for them to arrive; on the other hand, if they were faster, they would be able to attack that much quicker.

When the closest of the swarming Imps were only about 15 feet away from him, while still at least 10 feet above his head, Larek activated his new Fusion. As *Stone Shredder Dome +6* was activated, the first thing that the Combat Fusionist noticed was the outrageous noise that the new Fusion created above his head. The sound of rapidly rushing air was certainly not silent; while contained in a dome-like shape, it was like a tornado's swirling winds were caught within the maelstrom of sharp stones. Even the sound of the stones that had been created with the activation of the Fusion made noise, a high-pitched whistling sound that was difficult to listen to for long periods of time.

While annoying and a little overwhelming to him, the noise was apparently infuriating to the Imps. One listen to the horrific sound was enough for them to start flapping their wings in a frenzy, with the closest ones dive-bombing the dome as soon as they were close enough. The change in their attack pattern was slightly worrying at first, but was soon proved to be a boon as they charged straight into the Effects of the Fusion...

...and were violently ripped apart.

Limbs and mangled pitchforks were sent flying off in all directions as the sharp stones and the strong, fast-moving bursts of air tore them apart and tossed them about. The impact with the stones inside the dome caused some of the sharp stones to be dislodged from their path; the cacophony increased as stones smashed against stones, pulverizing them into much smaller pieces, and before long it was a nearly deafening grinding and cracking of stones in the air above him as any semblance of order was lost.

*Hmm... I guess I didn't think about that.*

The effectiveness of the offensively slanted defensive dome was only minorly affected, however. Even as more and more of the Imps literally dove down in an attempt to attack or even pass through the deadly Fusion, the smaller – and yet still sharp – stones were more likely to pulverize their bodies rather than rip off limbs, but that didn't mean that they were any less effective. Instead of body parts being flung everywhere, it was soon raining broken Imp bodies all over the place as they were smashed to mush by what was essentially high-speed sharpened gravel.

Larek lost count after nearly 200 of the Imps essentially killed themselves on the dome above his head, but he could see that there were at least another 100 of them left to go. He'd also been monitoring the ambient Mana density and saw that it had been dropping rapidly, which was a little worrisome. Granted, the Fusion had been going for nearly 10 minutes by that point, because the influx of Imps was fairly steady, giving him no time to turn it off to conserve the available Mana. It still took some time for the furthest to reach him from the edge of the territory even at their increased speed.

Just when he thought it was getting to the point where the ambient Mana density would start to become a problem for the other Fusions on his clothes, axe, and staff, Larek deactivated the dome in between groups. He immediately raised his staff and shot a sharp *Flying Stone* projectile at the nearest Imp, which impaled it with such force that it was essentially ripped in half. Flipping it around, he attempted to do the same to another Imp with a *Flaming Ball*, but the projectile essentially broke apart without doing any damage to the flying demon.

*Ah. Immune to fire; I guess that makes sense.*

Regardless, he flipped the staff back over and shot another stone projectile, killing another Imp in the process, before firing another one off a second later. His newly enhanced Fusions were a lot stronger than the ones he used before he arrived in the Empire, and instead of having to wait 5 seconds, he estimated that he only had to wait a second or 2 between activations to ensure it didn't start to deteriorate.

By that point, the Imps were too close to hit from long-range, as evidenced by one last shot that caused the Imp to activate its hellfire teleport ability. It seemed that if they were within about 10 to 12 feet of his person, they had access to the ability; further away, it didn't seem to work for some reason.

Dropping his staff on the ground, Larek gripped his axe with both hands and got to work. The next 5 minutes was a bit hectic as he jumped around, slicing through hellfire and the actual incoming demons as they descended to attack him, but at no point was he in any real danger. There weren't enough of them by that point to surround him and attack from multiple directions at once, and the strikes that did get through were met with his *Repelling Barrier*. Despite that, Larek was happy when it was finally done, as he had learned something from the fight despite the lack of danger.

The combination of his own Martial prowess with the usage of Fusions was more powerful than he had hoped. While it wasn't a perfect system, mainly because he had to watch the ambient Mana consumption, it was nonetheless a viable *fusion* of strategies going forward. In the future, he knew that he would have to continue to improve his physical combat skills, but he was well on the way there already. Without anyone to teach him what he should be concentrating on, he would likely be slow to advance his skills in that regard; but until he got there, his Fusions would protect him and hopefully even eliminate all of the danger that came with being attacked by a horde of monsters.

As his body absorbed over 300 Aetheric Force, joining the 16 he had accumulated earlier as he made his way toward the center of the Aperture's territory, he smacked the floating sphere a few times to close it. At the same time, his peripheral vision caught a change coming over the outer limits of the territory as it began to shrink, not stopping until it returned to what Larek supposed was its original size.

*I wonder....*

After seeing that the territory had grown at some point, likely because there was no one nearby to keep it from expanding, Larek had an idea for his new Fusions. Looking at the Aperture, he wondered if he could create a Fusion similar to *Frozen Zone* that would constantly do damage to anything inside of its area and then activate it right under the Aperture. If he made it a bit weaker so as not to drain the ambient Mana too far, it might work to keep the Aperture closed almost indefinitely, as it would kill anything that came out and then damage the opening enough that it closed again.

However, as he stepped closer to the Aperture to peer around its immediate area, he felt a bit of fluctuation in the Fusions on his clothing. Peering at them more intently before looking at the Mana density nearby, his *Magical Detection* Skill was showing him something strange. The strands of light that he recognized as Mana were seemingly frozen in place around the Aperture, before resuming their movement around 10 to 15 feet away; when he got too close to the Aperture, his Fusions were having difficulty absorbing the ambient Mana from the environment. It wasn't completely cut off, but he estimated that only about 10% of the Mana that the Fusions he was using normally absorbed was entering them. He hadn't really noticed before because he was usually a bit away from the Aperture while he fought its monsters, but now that he was paying attention, it was more than obvious.

What that meant was an immediate abandonment of any Fusion that could keep an Aperture under control. That didn't mean that a solution might never be created, but it was a problem that he didn't think he could solve right now. Regardless, he had done what he wanted to do by closing the Aperture, which was more than good with him.

Regaining his staff from the ground where he had dropped it, the ecstatic Combat Fusionist left the barren hellscape – which was now also empty of any monsters – and took off at a run, looking for the next Aperture to close on his journey back home.

# Chapter 17

"I'm just passing through and resupplying, Protector."

The armored woman looked at him with a strange expression on her face, but eventually waved him by, free to enter the city of Swiftwater through the gates. At least, he thought it was Swiftwater according to where he thought he was on the now-worn map in his pack, but he had avoided most towns and villages on his travels east to the point where he wasn't *entirely* sure where he was. It would've helped if there was some sort of sign on the outside of the walled city, the first that he'd seen thus far in the Sealance Empire – both the first city and the first habitation that actually had walls defending it. It wasn't even something new due to the recent appearances of monsters and Apertures, as he could see the weathered stone worn smooth in a few places where the traffic rubbed up against it.

His assumption was proven correct soon after entering the busy city as he saw a sign over a permanent market stall located near the entrance that said, "Swiftwater Delicatessen". He'd seen the same sort of stalls in the few towns he was forced to visit over the last month as he restocked his food supplies, and it sold fresh meats and some breads – none of which he typically bought, as he concentrated on foods that would last a while and had a high protein and fat content to replenish his energy.

It was for that reason that he stopped by this city, as he was completely out of food that wasn't just straight meat that he'd butchered from certain monsters he'd killed on his journey. At first, he had done it to simply supplement his diet by having fresh meat, even if it was of questionable quality when he attempted to cook it on a spit over a fire; he had barely been able to choke down his first attempt, as it was quite bad. That attempt had also raised his *Cooking* Skill to Level 2, which made subsequent meals progressively better as he eventually brought it all the way up to Level 7. The one thing he had wished for during his cooking attempts was some sort of spices or seasoning to flavor the meat better, which was another thing he was hoping to purchase while in the city.

Along with more supplies, his other goal was to find a way across the river that was blocking his progress. Swiftwater was apparently named for the wide, fast-moving river that ran alongside the city, and it certainly lived up to that moniker. He'd stepped into the edge of the river in an attempt to see if he could simply swim across, but he'd had his feet nearly swept out from underneath him by the swiftly flowing water. Looking closer at the flow of the river, he had the impression that there were strange undercurrents moving around throughout its entire width which might end up pulling him under if he wasn't careful. He was strong and had more than enough stamina to swim all the way across, even though it was nearly 2 miles wide, but who knew where he would end up as he was washed downstream or sent into its depths by the fast-moving currents.

It was possible that there were narrower places along the river that would be easier to cross, but his map didn't have that kind of detail. All he knew was that there had to be *someplace* to cross, as the Sealance Empire didn't simply end where the north- and south-oriented river appeared. The map indicated that it originated far to the north, which he estimated to be at least 1,000 miles or more away, but that seemed quite restrictive to movement through the Empire if that was the only option. He figured that they had to have some sort of ferry system like he'd seen in the Kingdom, and the docks in the city that he had spotted from afar seemed as if they would have exactly what he needed.

As it was still before noon, Larek figured he would be able to get into the city, pick up his supplies as quickly as he could, and then hit the docks to find some way to cross before night fell. He'd slept in plenty of strange places over the last month, so he was confident he could find somewhere to wait out the darkness once he got to the other side.

He didn't want to stay in the city of Swiftwater too long just in case his description had been spread around by the Protector back in Lakebellow, especially since he no longer had his *Perceptive Misdirection* Fusion on the ring Shinpai had given him. It had long since faded, and his 7-foot frame was visible to everyone, and while the Protector leader had seen the "shorter" version of him a month ago, his height still made him the center of attention whenever he passed through a town. Of course, he didn't stick around long enough to find out if he was actively being hunted, but he was still planning on acting like he was.

He also hadn't found a chance to create any more Fusions since he left Lakebellow, including a replacement for the *Perceptive Misdirection* Fusion. While it should've been easy to accomplish at least a simple replacement, as it wouldn't take much effort, every time he began to settle down and focus on the process, his paranoia about being discovered by those searching for him disrupted his state of mind, making it virtually impossible. For some reason, at least after the first few nights, it didn't affect his sleep as much, but anything related to creating another Fusion filled him with enough anxiety that he could barely think straight. At some point, he knew that he would have to get over it and find someplace extremely secure and safe so that he could focus on Fusions again, but that place hadn't been found quite yet.

It took over an hour to find all the shops he needed to refill his supplies, as it took an extra detour to find someone selling spices and meat seasonings, but he managed to finish his errands in a relatively short time, nonetheless. Once he was satisfied with his purchases and his packs were full once again, he set off for the docks to see about finding his way across the river.

This was where he discovered some devastating news.

"No one's getting across anytime soon."

It hadn't taken long for him to find what appeared to be the person in charge – or at least *a* person in charge – near the docks, which consisted of a dozen long, curved piers with extremely thick stone pilings to keep them stable. The curving of the piers was odd, because the only ones he'd seen in his life had been straight as they jutted out into a river. It wasn't until he really took a look at them that he noticed how they were constructed in a way to help redirect the extreme flow of the rushing water in between the relatively calm spaces in between the piers. With the speed at which the water moved, it would be impossible to dock a ferry or a boat without it crashing into everything. The curving was simply to add some stability to the entire structure, sort of like how an arched bridge worked – or that was his assumption.

The problem he noticed immediately upon arriving at the docks was there weren't *any* boats or anything resembling a ferry ready to carry him across. Along the waterfront were a half-dozen larger buildings with wide doorways practically overflowing with wooden crates and other merchandise that made him think of the caravans he'd traveled with in the past. In front of what Larek could only assume were warehouses holding caravan goods were dozens of men and women lounging under some impromptu awnings created with what appeared to be canvas tacked to the warehouses' outer walls and connected to stacks of crates assembled outside, appearing bored and listless as they lethargically played some sort of game involving dice.

As for the rest of the dock area, it was practically deserted. From what he remembered of the docks around Peratin before he was ferried across with his classmates on their journey to Copperleaf Academy, the docks had been a frantic madhouse of activity that was both overwhelming and confusing at the same time – but this was none of that. There was an Inn along the dock that appeared a bit dilapidated, and it was where Larek could hear some activity in the form of laughter and the sound of some sort of stringed instrument playing, but that was about it.

The only person he saw that appeared to have some answers was sitting at a covered booth just inside the dock area, his chin in his hand as he stared out over the river with a vacant expression on his face. When Larek approached, the man barely acknowledged that he saw him, but roused from his stupor when the Combat Fusionist asked him about getting across. That was when he laughed once a little sadly and told Larek that no one was getting across anytime soon.

"Why? Isn't there some sort of ferry to bring people across?" he asked the man.

"Of course there is," the man snapped, seemingly irritated by the question. "We actually have five of them that depart daily, drop off whatever shipments and travelers are aboard at Riverbend, and then are portaged north to Blackferry. From there, they load up with any shipments and travelers wanting to move toward Swiftwater, and then arrive back here where they are dropped off.

"At least, that's what is *supposed* to happen. Unfortunately, something happened to the ferries during the portage a few days ago, and we've been stuck without a way across ever since." The man put his chin back in his hand and started to drift away again, but Larek brought him back with more questions.

"Is there another way across? Is there a portion of the Swiftwater that is able to be forded by an individual? What about by a small raft or boat?" While he'd never crafted a raft or boat before, he could probably figure it out well enough if he didn't have any other choice. Especially if it was just a one-time use thing and would only have to hold together long enough to get him to the other side.

Unfortunately, the man was shaking his head. "Up near the source of the Swiftwater, I've heard the speed is a bit slower, but that's a long journey – especially in these times. As far as I know, the river doesn't narrow enough at any point to allow for easy fording, and the current near the middle is so strong that any attempts at creating a bridge have failed. It's that same reason that rafts and smaller boats can't handle a crossing, as they don't have enough weight to prevent themselves from being pulled under by the current. Our ferries are the only reliable means of crossing the Swiftwater, and it's been like that for hundreds of years."

*Well, crud. This is definitely going to affect my travel speed.*
"Can you build more ferries?"

The dockmaster, or that was who Larek assumed he was, chuckled. "Who, me? Not a chance. We actually had two full-time

Shipbuilders assigned to Swiftwater to help with maintenance and replacing any portions of the ferries that were wearing out, but the damn fools went and got themselves killed."

"How did they die?"

The dockmaster snorted. "How else, nowadays? The two of them became Mages and joined a group of young hotheads that were going out to kill monsters and close these Aperture thingies. Haven't heard from the entire group in at least a week, so no one expects that they'll be back."

Again, it seemed as though the consequences of the change that went through the Empire – and the rest of the world, assumedly – had gone and messed up his plan to get home to the Kingdom. First, it was creating a problem with some no-good layabouts turning bandit and forcing Larek to kill them, and now the only people able to create new ferries had gotten themselves killed when they went out to kill monsters.

"Is there anyone on the other side of the river that would be able to build some new ferries?"

The man shrugged. "Maybe? From what I knew before the whole change happened here, there were three or four Shipbuilders in both cities on the other side, but I'm not sure if they're even there anymore. We haven't had *any* contact with either Riverbend or Blackferry since the ferries never came back, so it's entirely possible that something happened to the people there, as well. Even if they are all alive and well, it will still take about a month to get a brand-new ferry built, so like I said before:

"No one's getting across anytime soon."

Thanking the dockmaster for the information, Larek left the docks with a last backwards glance at the swiftly flowing river. No ferries being present to bring him across the river was obviously a huge obstacle toward his goal of returning to the Kingdom, because it seemed as though he was stuck for at least a month – or more.

*How long would it take to go around the river?* The map he had acquired from Enderflow and Protector Ashlynn wasn't exactly to scale, but he estimated that he could probably reach it within a month of constant travel, but then he would be quite a bit farther north than he wanted to be and would require weeks of travel to get back on track.

No matter how he looked at it, there was a delay – but did there have to be? Could he find a way to reach the other side without a ferry? The idea of a raft or small boat was supposedly out as a means to get himself across, based on what the dockmaster said, and while what the man said wasn't necessarily entirely accurate, Larek wasn't sure if he wanted to take the chance. If his vessel was caught by the river and pulled under or damaged in some way, then reaching the other side alive would be that much more difficult.

Regardless, unless a ferry arrived in the next hour, he wouldn't be getting across that day. Which meant that he either had to leave the city and find somewhere to camp, or stay in the city. The first was easy enough, but the latter appealed to him since it had been a month since he had stayed somewhere warm and safe. Or at least gave the impression of being safe, because the longer he stayed somewhere, the more risk he ran of being recognized if his description had been spread around.

It was a hard decision, even though he knew that one of them was the smartest – if not the most convenient – choice. By the time he found his steps bringing him through the city in search of an Inn, he realized that both his body and his mind had already decided. Staying in the city was apparently what he was going to do.

There were a surprisingly large number of Inns in the city, but he supposed it made sense because this was a major trading stop. Apparently, if anything or anyone wanted to get across the river, they had to go through here – though it sounded stupid to Larek that they didn't have any other alternatives if something like the current situation happened.

Each Inn he went into was completely full, however, as the Merchants and their people who were waiting to get their goods across had booked them all up. A total of 7 large Inns had absolutely no rooms for him to stay in, which was disappointing, because it meant that he would have to leave the city and stay outside somewhere.

Shrugging in disappointment, he left the last Inn and started to head toward the city entrance, but was stopped when a voice called out to him from an alleyway next to the Inn.

"Hey there, big boy; you need somewhere to rest your head tonight?"

# Chapter 18

Larek turned his attention to the woman speaking to him from the alleyway, and the first thing that he noticed was that she appeared to be quite poor, as she barely had enough clothing to cover herself decently.  The clothing she did have was dirty and torn with holes in places that made him wonder why she even bothered wearing it in the first place, as it appeared so threadbare that he could see through most of it if the sun hit it just right.  She also appeared to be slightly older than he was, though it was difficult to tell as her face was partially hidden in the shadows of the alley.

"You know of an Inn that has a vacancy?" he asked, fighting relief at the thought of there being somewhere he could stay that night.  He didn't know if it was true, however, so he didn't want to get his hopes up too much.

The woman chuckled and replied, "Oh, it's not an Inn like the Workhorse here."  She waved at the building beside her.  "It's more of a place where we—and those that like a little… privacy—can find a little alone time.  What do you say, big boy?"

That sounded like exactly what he needed, but he wasn't naïve enough to not know that certain things – like privacy – came at a price.  This woman wouldn't be asking him if he wanted a place to stay out of the goodness of her heart, so she must want something from him.  "What's the catch?  How much would this privacy and 'alone time' cost me?"

The smile she flashed his way was barely visible in the shadows of the alley, but he definitely saw it.  "For the entire night, my large friend… 50 silver pieces."

*50 silver pieces?  That's quite a hefty increase from what I paid for my last room, but I guess that beggars can't be choosers.  There's nowhere else to stay, so I guess it's this or camp outside again.*

If he had been low on funds, he probably would've refused the offer already, but he was still flush with coins due to sleeping outdoors – and he was really getting tired of his tent and sleeping roll.  If this place really had the privacy and safe space he craved, for at least a night, then it would be well worth it.

The only problem was that he didn't want to bring trouble down on this woman.  Sure, she was taking advantage of his predicament by overcharging him for a room, but she seemed nice enough and likely needed the money to buy new clothes since the clothes she did have really needed to be replaced.

Moving closer to her so as to keep his voice down, he said, "This is something that I could definitely use. I must warn you that I *might* have some Protectors from another town looking for me, and I don't want to bring you any trouble."

At his statement, he could see her smile grow even wider. "Oh, that's not a problem. However, we'd have to charge you double to ensure our safety, but I can guarantee that no one would be able to find you where we're going."

"A full gold? If you can guarantee that no one will find me, then I can agree to that." He paused for a second before he dropped his voice and told her in a threatening whisper, "But if you or anyone else who might be with you tries to screw me over, no one will be able to identify your bodies when I'm done with you." He was thinking of the *Healing Shelter +8* Fusion on the stone in his pocket when he said that, which certainly made that bandit back in Lakebellow unrecognizable.

Larek didn't necessarily *want* to threaten death if she or someone she knew attempted to cross him, but he knew that it was a definite possibility. He didn't know her, and since he was beginning to believe that she was associated with some sort of criminal element there in Swiftwater based on her mention of privacy, it didn't hurt to warn her beforehand. While his moral judgment balked at dealing with whoever these criminals were, he semi-justified it because *he* was technically a wanted person – even if he hadn't done anything wrong.

Expecting her to be taken aback at his threat, she just chuckled with a deep, husky laugh while she continued to smile. "Ooh, I *like* that; I actually believe you'd do it, too. The others won't know what to make of you, but I think this could be quite beneficial for all of us."

Larek didn't know what to say to that, mainly because her words didn't make a whole lot of sense to him.

"Is there a discount if I pay up front for a longer period of time?" he asked, turning his mind away from who these people might be and focusing on his goal. "I'm trying to get across the Swiftwater as quickly as possible, but I was told it could be a month or longer."

"I'm sure we can work *something* out," she said with a visible wink, before beckoning him to follow. Looking around the street outside of the Inn, he didn't see anyone watching him, so he quickly moved to shadow the woman as she hurried down the alley.

From the dark alley, she led him across a street filled with what appeared to be residences, before slipping through a relatively narrow gap between two buildings. Larek had to take his pack off in order to fit through the gap, but it was easy enough since he wasn't so wide. Another sprint across a handful of mostly empty streets and small openings in between different structures – one of which was a stable – was followed up with entering a large storage facility through a side door. The entire time, the woman didn't say a thing to him, and he didn't ask any questions, as it was all he could do to keep up with her despite him having a high Agility stat and she didn't seem to have any stats at all.

It turned out that the storage facility, which was surprisingly not full like the warehouses he saw near the docks, wasn't their eventual destination as they moved toward the back where they passed through a wooden doorway into a much smaller room located in the rear. As soon as he was through, the woman closed and locked the door with a key she seemed to magically pull from somewhere, and then gestured for him to move out of the way. He took a step to the left to remove himself from where he was standing, and then the woman pushed something on the wall that made a faint *click*. The confused Combat Fusionist didn't know what it was she did until she moved to the far wall, which was made entirely from stone blocks, gripped the edge of a block with both hands, and then *pulled* it toward her. Instead of it being a useless exercise in futility, it turned out that the stone block was attached to a larger doorway that slid open without a sound and with seeming ease, as she didn't appear to be straining to move it.

He would've been absolutely shocked if he hadn't seen something similar in the Dean's office back at Copperleaf Academy, where Shinpai had opened a portion of the wall. As it was back then, there was no hint of magic in the way it moved, so he could only assume it was all mechanical in nature.

She didn't wait to enter once the stone block door was wide enough for both of them to fit, and he quickly joined her inside what appeared to be a stone tunnel that ended with stairs heading straight down – at least that was where it appeared to go from his vantage point. It was difficult to tell since he'd had to duck down as the ceiling was a good foot and a half shorter than he was, which caused him to feel like he was nearly doubled over in order to fit.

As soon as they were inside, the woman immediately closed the door behind them and they were plunged into near complete darkness. There were a few cracks or holes in the door that allowed some of the light from the storage facility to filter through, which allowed him to see her struggling with what appeared to be flint and steel as she attempted to light a torch.

He heard her muttering under her breath. "That lazy Sam should've kept this ready to go earlier, but *nooo~ooo*, that was apparently too much to ask." At one point, she dropped the piece of steel, and it bounced on the stone floor, creating a sharp echo that reverberated down the hallway and likely down the stairs. The woman who brought him there froze in place, visibly listening intently. "And now they don't even have anyone watching the entrance," she muttered irritably.

"Here," he said, handing her a stone. Right before she reflexively took it, he activated the Basic *Illuminate +1* Fusion on it, something that he'd created in less than a minute during his travels to help him navigate his way through the land at night and to explore small cave systems to ensure it was safe for him to find a place to get some sleep. This Fusion was the only thing he'd been able to create because it took essentially no time at all; anything that took some real thought or concentration was too much for his anxiety to handle.

The light the *Illuminate* Fusion gave off wasn't very bright, but he also had needed it not to blind him in low-light situations or announce his presence to anyone or any*thing* within half a mile; inside the dark tunnel, it was nearly blinding in the extreme darkness. The woman nearly dropped the illuminated stone as it activated, but somehow managed to juggle it in her hand as she shoved the torch back into the iron-ringed holder he could now see on the wall.

"What—? Never mind, I'll ask you later. Let's go." She held the stone in her hand as if it was a snake that was getting ready to bite her, but she didn't hesitate to use it to lead the way down the tunnel and then down the stairs, which she took dangerously quickly in his opinion, but it was also obvious that a long familiarity with the route allowed her to take it with ease. Walking down the steps bent over was a little more difficult for Larek, but he managed to keep up with her.

He was thankful that neither of them fell, as the stairs went straight down at least 150 feet without any switchbacks or handholds; if either of them had tripped, there wouldn't have been anything to stop them from bouncing all the way down. With his body being so strong now, he doubted he would be too seriously injured, but the woman couldn't boast the same.

Eventually they came to the bottom of the stone steps, and there was a definite temperature difference that even Larek could feel, and he couldn't believe that the woman wasn't shivering with how barely covered she was. *Oh, wait, she is.* Her teeth were just starting to chatter as she practically ran toward the end of another long hallway, where a thick wooden door bound with what appeared to be iron bands presented itself to them. The woman immediately knocked on it with a seemingly random sequence of knocks, and while she cursed under her breath – which he could see since it was so cold – there was the sound of a few bolts being pulled back from the other side of the door.

The glow of firelight could be seen peeking around the wooden door as it opened, though it was washed out a little bit by the *Illuminate* Fusion in the woman's hand. The next thing that Larek sensed was a blast of warm air that escaped from whatever was on the other side, and he realized that *this* was why the woman who had escorted him there had practically flown down the steps. The outer stone tunnels were cold, but there was a warm sanctuary just through the door.

"Finally! Let me in – I'm freezing out here!"

The woman pushed her way inside, past the figure that had opened the door. It only took Larek half a second to realize that the figure was another woman, though in comparison to his escort, she was almost entirely covered up – though her clothing almost perfectly conformed to her body, like a second skin. He couldn't see her face clearly because she was silhouetted by the firelight behind her and the other woman had taken his *Illuminate* Fusion, but he had the impression that she was suspicious of him.

His impression was only confirmed by the way she planted herself across the threshold and pulled two knives from somewhere behind her back, brandishing them in his direction. "An' 'oo mi' ya be?"

It took him a half-second to mentally translate the thickly accented question, which was essentially, "And who might you be?". "I'm just a temporary lodger, looking for someplace quiet and private for a little bit," he answered. "That nice lady who brought me here said that this was a place where I wouldn't have to worry about being found by… others." He gestured to his escort, who he could see inside a larger room as she wrapped what appeared to be a large wolf fur coat around her shoulders. He couldn't see the fire that warmed up the room, but he could feel the heat from it and hear it crackling somewhere, but other than that, the rest of the space was a mystery until he was inside.

"'Dis troo, May?" the woman blocking the door asked over her shoulder, though Larek could tell that she never took her eyes off of him.

"Yes, yes, let him in, Yvette. He's going to be staying with us for a while."

There was a grunt a half-second before the knives pointed in his direction disappeared behind Yvette's back, before she swiftly moved away from the doorway. Taking that as an invitation to enter, Larek walked inside and stopped as soon as he found that he was able to stand at his normal height without hitting the ceiling, which was at least 10 feet above his head.

Looking around the room, he was surprised how warm and inviting it appeared compared to the bare, cold stone on the route there. Long tapestries hung from near the ceiling to cover the walls in a riot of different colors, some with various scenes stitched into them while others were simply interesting designs. In between the tapestries were oil lamps similar in construction to the ones he'd seen in the Whittleton Inn, which helped to illuminate the large room, which was at least 150 feet wide, though only about half that deep. In the middle was a large fire with an iron chimney poised above it that directed the smoke up and out of the room, though where it went after it passed through the ceiling was a mystery.

On the right side of the room was a massive wooden table with a dozen legs interspersed through its length to hold it up, along with a few dozen high-back chairs pushed underneath it. On top of the table were a half-dozen candelabra with half-melted candles still in them, though they weren't lit at the moment. Other than that, it was clear of anything else.

Along the back wall of the room, directly across from him, were a number of closed wooden doors leading to who knew where, all of them painted in a different color, from red, green, yellow, and to even a strange metallic copper color that reflected the firelight.

Lastly, to his left was an arrangement of different comfortable-looking chairs and couches, along with some small side tables that were just far enough away from the central fire to not be *too* hot – though in his own opinion, the heat was already stifling. It was from that section of seating arrangements that Larek realized there had been a quiet murmur of voices which cut off upon his entrance; the source of those voices quickly became clear to him, as it was easy to see in the well-lit room.

They were all women. A few of them were dressed just as sparingly as his escort, a few wore garb similar to the woman who had been blocking the door – which he discovered was a blend of cloth and leather as he got a chance to see the outfits better – while the majority of them wore what he would classify as "normal" attire, or at least normal in the sense of what was worn in the Sealance Empire.

He looked closer to see if he was mistaken about them all being women, but unless they were wearing a really good disguise, he didn't see any men. What he did see, and found strange, was that all of the women were what he would consider attractive, though he supposed that attractiveness was subjective. Even the older women – and in this case, older meant that they were in their 30's or early 40's – were good looking, which was a little intimidating when they all turned toward him simultaneously, stopping their conversations to stare at him.

"Uh..." he said, unsure of what to do now that he was supposedly at the destination his escort promised.

"Right through here, big boy. We've got a bunch of spare rooms ever since... well, never mind, it's not important." The woman who had brought him there had taken off her wolf fur coat and hung it back on a rack near the entrance, before beckoning to him to follow her once again. She led him toward the blue door on the back wall of the room, with Larek conscious of everyone still staring at him. It was more than a little uncomfortable, and he breathed a sigh of relief as they walked through the blue-painted wooden door, leaving them behind. He was also grateful to see that the hallway they entered was at least 8 feet tall, meaning that he didn't have to worry about hitting his head.

"It's right at the end of this hallway here. Your room isn't luxurious, but hopefully it should serve you well enough. There's a brazier in every room to keep the chill off, though it takes a little bit once it gets going to be comfortable. Meals are served every morning and every evening in the dining room section of the common area, which you likely noticed on your way in. Your payment will cover meals and lodging, along with complete privacy. We hold our privacy in high regard, if that isn't clear by now."

She stopped by another door at the end of the hallway and opened it quickly, showing him what was inside. It wasn't luxurious, as she had already admitted, but it was certainly spacious; the 30-foot-by-30-foot room held a bed large enough for even his own frame – or at least most of it – as well as a simple wooden desk and chair, along with a wardrobe where he could put his things. Not that he was planning on letting his stuff out of his sight for long, as his suspicions about the woman and the people hidden in this secret underground facility being criminals of some sort looked fairly accurate.

Regardless, unless they turned out to all be murderers, he didn't really care as much as he supposed he should. All he was worried about was having a secure place to sleep, the privacy and safety to create Fusions, and the anonymity to avoid the Protectors that may or may not still be on his trail. This place had all of that, as he eyed the locks on the extremely sturdy door on his way into the room, and he wasn't about to back out now.

"Speaking of privacy, I wanted to ask you a few things. If it is none of my business, just tell me so and you don't have to answer," Larek said, turning to the woman who still held the stone with the

*Illuminate* Fusion in her hand. "What is this place? Who are you people? And are there any men here, or only women?"

Instead of answering right away or telling him it was none of his business, she sighed and said, "That's a long story, and not one I'm going to tell right now when I'm freezing my toes off." Looking at him, she continued. "Since you're staying here, I suppose you can be told a little about us, but first we need to settle with your payment. It's a single gold for this first night, and if everything works out, we'll talk about a longer term and how much that will cost. Oh, and here." She held out the glowing stone in her hand toward him. "Thank you for letting me borrow, uh, whatever this is."

"Keep it. I've got more," he said, shrugging. It was true, though, as he had a handful of them in his pockets.

"I can't do that – this must have cost a fortune! Besides, we're already extor—charging you an extravagant amount to stay here, so it wouldn't be right."

He wasn't going to argue with her, so he took the glowing stone and deactivated the Fusion on it before putting it back in his pocket. Thankfully, there was an oil lamp directly outside of his doorway on the opposite wall, letting in light, which helped him reach into his pack and pull out a single gold coin, which he then placed in the woman's hands. Was her name May?

"It's Maybelle, actually," she corrected when he asked, making the gold coin disappear... somewhere. "Yvette doesn't speak very well, but I suppose that helps in her line of work. Now, why don't we go back out and I'll introduce you to everyone."

Strangely enough, the prospect of facing all of those stares again was even more intimidating than facing an entire horde of monsters.

# Chapter 19

"You can leave your bags here, if you want."

Larek hesitated for a moment before he shrugged them off his shoulders and dropped them on the floor in the middle of the room. As he walked out, he threw the stone that held his *Healing Shelter +8* Fusion on top of the packs, to the arched eyebrow of Maybelle. "Just in case anyone thinks to start looking through them," he explained as they walked out the door, closing it behind him. "I have some important things in there, and while I'm appreciative of this opportunity to stay here, I don't necessarily trust you enough to leave my valuables unguarded."

The woman didn't seem offended by his honest explanation, though she seemed skeptical, nonetheless. "With a rock? Won't it just make light?"

He stopped his walk, causing Maybelle to stop as well. "No, it will horrifically kill anyone who gets within a certain distance," he said earnestly, wanting to convey the danger to her in case she – or someone else in this underground refuge – took their curiosity a bit too far. "I don't want anyone to die needlessly, so please warn anyone who might be inclined to investigate my things without my permission."

Now there was a reaction, as the woman shivered slightly as she stared into his eyes, and it wasn't from the cold; the fear in them was plain to see, and the reaction wasn't exactly what he was going for when he warned her. He turned away, not wanting to scare her more than he already had, but satisfied that he got his point across. Maybelle began to say something, but out of the corner of his eye he saw her nod once before continuing on toward the door at the end of the hallway.

*I guess the last month alone has changed me more than I thought.*

His paranoia of being discovered and the extreme caution he took to protect himself while on his own had made him wary of almost everything, and that seemed to affect his social interactions with other people. He had been slightly concerned that he'd regressed to his former awkward state when it came to talking to others, but it seemed to have morphed into something that was tinged by his distrust and the hyper-focused state of awareness he'd had to operate under while traveling in the untamed landscape of the Sealance Empire.

It wasn't necessarily a bad thing, but it probably wouldn't make him many friends.

Thankfully for Larek, his return to the large, warm common room wasn't met with stares from everyone inside, though there were certainly some. The still slightly shaken Maybelle led him toward and past the large central fire and toward where all of the women were seated in various states of comfort. Most of them seemed to drape themselves over the furniture as if extremely relaxed, settling into the soft cushions until they looked like they were being consumed by some sort of upholstery monster. The only ones who were sitting upright and rigid, especially as they saw him coming, were the ones that were dressed similarly to Yvette, and they seemed on edge and ready to either fight or flee at the slightest provocation.

Maybelle cleared her throat as she stepped into the middle of the gathering, with Larek in tow. "Ahem. I'm sure you're wondering about this young man with me, and what he's even doing here. In short, he's staying with us for at least the night with a very generous donation to our society, and he may even be willing to stay for a slightly extended time for an additional payme—*donation*."

"Why did you bring him here, Maybelle?" came the question in a stern voice from a slightly older woman than the rest of the group, wearing an ankle-length brown dress made of lightweight fabric and a loosely flowing white top – similar to many outfits he'd seen most of the people in the Empire wear. "You have rooms all over the city to ply your trade; why bring him back to the Sanctum?" She spoke with a definite feeling of authority, and Larek could only assume that this *Society? Donation? Sanctum?* He was beginning to get some answers, but they just led to additional questions.

"I apologize for my admittedly rash decision, Seandra, but this seemed like a rare opportunity. He was looking to avoid attention from a certain type of person, and was willing to, uh, donate a significant amount in order to secure the privacy that the society enjoys. Knowing that we need—"

"We'll be *fine*, Maybelle, whatever you think you know," the older woman said, cutting the semi-clothed woman off. Maybelle shrunk back, clearly chastised, and Larek realized that bringing him to their "Sanctum" was something she probably shouldn't have done. Turning her gaze toward him, Seandra attempted to turn the weight of her authority on *Larek*, but it didn't really affect him as much as it would have even a year ago. Having faced Chinli, a Gergasi who used Dominion Magic to exert her control over people, this was nothing.

"So, who are you, and what exactly are you running from?"

Knowing that it probably didn't matter if he gave his name, Larek did just that – but didn't elaborate on why he was hiding from

Protectors. He still didn't trust these people completely, and giving them that kind of information could be dangerous.

"Let's just say that I ran afoul of a misunderstanding with some Protectors, and it would be best if I stay far away from their attention. They're just doing their jobs, after all, and I would hate to have to kill them over some insignificant misunderstanding."

There were some murmurs from the assembled women at that, but nothing clear enough that Larek could make it out. "Fair enough, Larek. I must ask one question, though, considering that you're talking about killing Protectors." She paused for a second before asking, "Did you kill any Protectors before this? If so, then we'll give you your donation back and ask that you leave; we don't need that kind of attention knocking on our door."

He shook his head. "No, I haven't hurt or killed any Protectors. In fact, I have great respect for most of them, and even assisted some in the past. It is a shame that this whole situation came to be, but I have a goal to get home and I can't let anything – or any*one* – stop me."

"That is good to hear, at least. Where is 'home', if I might ask?"

Again, that wasn't that big of a secret, especially if anyone had seen someone from the Kingdom of Androthe before; while he wasn't exactly similar in height and was different in a couple of his natural features, he would be recognizable. So, he told her, and she nodded without asking any other probing questions such as why he was even in the Empire and how he got there. He was thankful for that, as he really didn't want to have to get into all of that.

"You're certainly a long way from home. I can see why you need someplace to stay while you wait for transportation over the Swiftwater. It is a sore point for all of us who live here, but especially to the *Underworld Society*." She said the last of that with emphasis, clearly expecting him to react, but she looked confused when he didn't show any sign of recognition. Suddenly uncomfortable herself, she shifted in her chair as she went on. "Anyway, I assume you have questions about why the Society is here and about our current state of personnel?"

He did, but the more she spoke, the less he realized he wanted to know. Their private business was their private business, just like his was his own.

Larek shrugged. "Sort of? It's more that I want to know if I can trust you by this point, and that you aren't a group of women that go around the city cutting the throats of innocent people or enslaving them against their will. If you can confirm that you're not doing either of those things, which I oppose wholeheartedly, I don't really care what you do."

She spoke slowly, clearly confused. "No, we don't do anything like that. You've never heard of the Underworld Society? Or just the Underworld? Or just 'the Society'? We have branches all over the world, including in the Kingdom of Androthe."

He shook his head. He had absolutely no idea what she was talking about.

"Hmm... well, we're an organization of members who, to put it delicately, take a less than lawful route to our endeavors, but we never deal with killing any innocent people or slavery."

Larek nodded, indicating that the explanation was good enough for him. It was as he expected, with how secretive they seemed and their living quarters underground. While it might have been a lie that they weren't killing innocent people or enslaving them, he didn't think so. The people he saw didn't really seem the type, though the shifty appearance of the covered individuals told him that they were no strangers to killing people, but he doubted that their targets were innocent.

His assertion that he was satisfied with her explanation was apparently lost upon the older woman, as she began to go into a little more detail. As he listened, he began to put together that this was an international organization of criminals, dealing with everything from thievery, shady merchant practices, smuggling of illegal goods, extortion, assassination (of non-innocents), and even the regulation of carnal entrepreneurs. That last made his eyes go wide as the implication of Maybelle being one of these "carnal entrepreneurs" and the way she had propositioned him on the street hit him, and he saw the woman in a new light. He looked over at her with understanding of the way she was dressed, pity in his gaze, but she didn't seem ashamed of her profession in the least. The way Seandra talked about it, there was a sense of pride of being one of these individuals, though it was honestly beyond his understanding.

"...as for why there are only women here, it's because of *the change*. Every single male member of the Underworld Society in Swiftwater acquired the ability to become a Mage or Martial, and they left one day to hunt down these Apertures in order to get stronger – only to never return after their third expedition. We've been stuck picking up the pieces after they disappeared, and with trade over the Swiftwater being cut off, many of our sources of income have been stifled. Therefore, your donation has come at an opportune time for us."

*Why is she telling me this? I thought she just reprimanded Maybelle for mentioning—wait. Is this my Dominion Magic reacting to her and making her tell me things?*

If that was true, then he was still completely unaware of it happening or what to do to control it. He thought that he might be able to feel it now that he'd been exposed to it up close via Chinli, but that didn't seem to be the case. Then again, Seandra might simply be oversharing for some reason, but he didn't think that was likely at this point; based on the information he'd been told, these people operated in secrecy and wouldn't really appreciate their private matters being exposed. This was further confirmed as he surreptitiously glanced around at the other people around the room, who were looking at the speaker for the Underworld Society as if she was crazy.

"I understand," he finally said after a few seconds of silence. "I can certainly make more... *donations* to your society in appreciation for being allowed to stay here. Otherwise, I figure that if I stay out of your way, then you'll stay out of mine; I value privacy just as much as you all do, so I think this temporary accommodation will be beneficial to all of us."

"That is good to hear and is perfectly acceptable," Seandra said, clapping her hands once, which was loud in the suddenly quiet room. "I will certainly inform you of any information I gain on the resumption of ferry transportation, as it is vital to all of us. In the meantime, dinner is being served, and it would be my honor to have you join us."

The fact that the woman was speaking strangely and acting weird wasn't lost on the rest of the assembled women of the Underworld Society, but none of them contradicted Seandra directly. Still, his *Listening* Skill picked up a lot of confused comments and questions murmured as everyone got up to move toward the other side of the room, where the table was already set for a meal. Sitting down at a spot he was directed to at one end of the table, he watched as platters of grilled seafood, large bowls of leafy greens, and plates of breads and cheeses were brought out and placed on the table by even more women. These ones were dressed similarly to the majority of the other Society members, so he couldn't tell if they were actual members or simply employed by them.

Larek really didn't want to talk more to the other diners at the table, and he was fortunately saved from speaking with Seandra as she sat all the way at the head of the table. None of the women near him seemed inclined to start a conversation, either, contenting themselves with throwing furtive glances in his direction, which he ignored as he dug into the food with enthusiasm. It had been a while since he'd eaten something that wasn't already prepared or had been cooked by himself, and the quality of the grilled fish that he scarfed up just went to show how poor his own *Cooking* Skill was in comparison.

When he was done, having eaten at least three times the amount as the next diner, he excused himself and headed back to his room. No one followed him with anything but their eyes as he left, and he got back to where he would be staying without incident. Once he opened the door, he half-expected there to be someone dead on the floor who decided to test their luck at getting to his packs, but the room was completely empty. After deactivating the *Healing Shelter* Fusion on the stone with a verbal command, he activated one of the *Illuminate* Fusions in his pocket for light, closed and locked the visible deadbolt on the door, and then picked his packs up and deposited them on his bed, along with himself.

As soon as he sat down, all the stress of the day seemed to hit him with a flare of exhaustion, and all he wanted to do was sleep in the comfortable bed by that point. It was more than that, though, as there was a noticeable drain on his physical and mental energy that he couldn't explain right away, but when he thought about inadvertently using his Dominion magic earlier, he considered that this might be a side effect.

Whatever it was, he did his best to shrug it off as he had some things that he wanted to do that night before it was too late. He'd love to bathe and wash off the filth of his travels, but he didn't have the physical drive to get up out of the bed for much of anything by that point. Instead, he unpacked a few of his things from his bags, setting them out in front of him as he sat cross-legged on the bed and closed his eyes.

Even doing that made him even more tired, but he pushed it away as he centered himself and focused on the concentration needed for creating a Fusion. At first, it seemed as though his anxiety and paranoia had disappeared, now that he found himself someplace relatively safe, but it wasn't entirely gone until he got up with a groan and placed the *Healing Shelter* stone on the floor relatively near the door, so that it would cover anyone or anything that might try to get inside – deadbolt or not. It was something he would have to think about better in the future, but for now, he hoped it would be good enough.

Fortunately, when he sat back down on his bed and attempted to focus once again, it worked. With a tired smile to himself, Larek opened his Status and really looked at it for the first time in weeks.

# Chapter 20

The first thing Larek noticed about his Status was that it had changed a lot... and yet, it hadn't changed significantly in the areas where he really wanted it to change. That was, at least in part, because he hadn't been able to sit down and create any Fusions, but it was also due to not applying any of his Aetheric Force toward increasing the maximum Level of his Skills. Granted, he'd had more than enough time to do this while he was traveling, but he never felt that it was necessary since he wasn't going to be able to work on improving them. The thought was always, "Tomorrow I'll do it, because I'll have time to really think about and work on it," but that tomorrow simply turned into the next day, and then the next.

Now, though, he was finally able to slow down and look at all of it calmly and with focus.

**Larek Holsten**

**Combat Fusionist**
**Healer**
**Level 23**
**Advancement Points (AP): 6/19**
**Available AP to Distribute: 0**
**Available Aetheric Force (AF): 13,547**

**Stama: 1500/1500**
**Mana: 2340/2340**

**Strength: 75 [150] (+)**
**Body: 75 [150] (+)**
**Agility: 75 [150] (+)**
**Intellect: 117 [234] (+)**
**Acuity: 114 [228] (+)**
**Pneuma: 1,350 [2,700]**
**Pattern Cohesion: 27,000/27,000**

**Mage Abilities:**
Spell – Bark Skin
Spell – Binding Roots
Spell – Fireball
Spell – Furrow

Spell – Ice Spike
Spell – Lesser Restoration
Spell – Light Bending
Spell – Light Orb
Spell – Localized Anesthesia
Spell – Minor Mending
Spell – Rapid Plant Growth
Spell – Repelling Gust
Spell – Static Illusion
Spell – Stone Fist
Spell – Wall of Thorns
Spell – Water Jet
Spell – Wind Barrier
Fusion – Acuity Boost
Fusion – Agility Boost
Fusion – Area Chill
Fusion – Binding Thorns +1
Fusion – Binding Thorns +10
Fusion – Body Boost
Fusion – Camouflage Sphere
Fusion – Extreme Heat
Fusion – Flaming Ball
Fusion – Flying Stone
Fusion – Frozen Zone +1
Fusion – Frozen Zone +10
Fusion – Graduated Illumination Strong
Fusion – Graduated Parahealing
Fusion – Healing Shelter +1
Fusion – Healing Shelter +8
Fusion – Healing Surge
Fusion – Icy Spike
Fusion – Illuminate
Fusion – Illusionary Image
Fusion – Intellect Boost
Fusion – Intellect and Acuity Boost
Fusion – Muffle Sound
Fusion – Muffling Air Deflection Barrier
Fusion – Multi-Resistance
Fusion – Paralytic Light
Fusion – Paralytic Touch
Fusion – Perceptive Misdirection +1
Fusion – Personal Air Deflection Barrier

Fusion – Pneuma Boost
Fusion – Red and White Illuminate
Fusion – Repelling Barrier
Fusion – Repelling Gust of Air
Fusion – Sharpen Edge
Fusion – Space Heater
Fusion – Spellcasting Focus Boost
Fusion – Stone Shredder Dome +1
Fusion – Stone Shredder Dome +6
Fusion – Strength Boost
Fusion – Strength and Body Boost
Fusion – Strengthen and Sharpen Edge
Fusion – Strengthen
Fusion – Temperature Regulator
Fusion – Tree Skin
Fusion – Water Stream

**Martial Abilities:**
Battle Art – Furious Rampage
Battle Art – Consuming Speed

**Mage Skills:**
Multi-effect Fusion Focus Level 20/20 (200 AF)
Pattern Recognition Level 21/21 (210 AF)
Magical Detection Level 21/21 (210 AF)
Spellcasting Focus Level 21/21 (210 AF)
Focused Division Level 31/31 (310 AF)
Mana Control Level 37/37 (370 AF)
Fusion Level 40/40 (400 AF)
Pattern Formation Level 40/40 (400 AF)

**Martial Skills:**
Stama Subjugation Level 1/20 (200 AF)
Blunt Weapon Expertise Level 1/20 (200 AF)
Unarmed Fighting Level 2/20 (200 AF)
Bladed Weapon Expertise Level 2/20 (200 AF)
Throwing Level 8/20 (200 AF)
Dodge Level 17/20 (200 AF)
Pain Immunity Level 20/20 (N/A)
Body Regeneration Level 30/30 (300 AF)

**General Skills:**

**Cooking Level 7**
**Bargaining Level 8**
**Beast Control Level 9**
**Leadership Level 11**
**Writing Level 11**
**Long-Distance Running Level 18**
**Saw Handling Level 15**
**Speaking Level 17**
**Reading Level 17**
**Listening Level 43**
**Axe Handling Level 89**

The biggest changes that had been wrought by his journey were the increases in his General and Martial Skills. The aforementioned *Cooking* Skill had increased all the way to Level 7, which made his impromptu meals of cooked meat more palatable as its Level went up. *Bargaining* had also increased at some point to 8 when he was negotiating for food at a village or town – but he could barely remember when or where it had happened. *Long-Distance Running* had risen to 18 from all the running he'd been doing, which – along with his Martial stats – meant that he could run longer and farther than ever, before he became extraordinarily tired. *Listening* rose to 43 simply from his paranoia and listening for any signs of pursuit or danger, as well as utilizing his hearing when he was confronting an Aperture and its monsters. The last of his General Skills to increase was *Axe Handling*, which had gone up to a whopping Level 89!

As for Martial Skills, the only two he'd increased had been *Throwing* to Level 8 – up 2 Levels – and *Dodge*, which had gone up to Level 17 from Level 13. Such increases in *Axe Handling* and *Dodge* were due to a lot of practice using his axe and concentrating on moving around his chosen battlefield rather than simply standing still and hitting anything that got close to him. With the application of one of his offensive Fusions – and occasionally two of them simultaneously – to help watch his back, he had spent some deliberate time working on being cognizant of the monsters around him, which had been made easier when he discovered that he could detect the Corrupted Aetheric Force inside of them.

It was a faint feeling, especially in such weak monsters, but it was enough to give him a warning if one of them was close enough to attack him. Most of the time, he wasn't able to react fast enough to deflect an attack or kill the monster who was trying to kill him, but as the weeks went on, he was getting much better at anticipating their assaults.

That being said, he was fairly certain that he was still poorly executing his rather inept fighting style; it was better than before, but if it wasn't for his Fusions, he would've been seriously hurt or possibly killed multiple times during his journey. As it was, he still suffered from numerous wounds originating from attacks that made it through his defenses, though none of them were too serious – only annoying and requiring more energy from his body to heal.

The worst of his wounds was when Larek had encountered an Aperture with **Snowflake Pixies** – over 150 of them, in fact. He had begun his attack on the Aperture by doing what he normally did when finding a new one: reconnaissance. The lightly frost-covered field of grass had been relatively unassuming at first, as the area hadn't changed much from the presence of the opening into another world like some he'd seen, as the small amount of frost present wasn't too different from the normal space around the area. At first, he didn't see anything through the edges of the frost-covered grass, and there was nothing flying above it; the only thing that had been a bit strange was that the air had a charged aspect to it, and it appeared as though there were snowflakes drifting along lazily everywhere.

After nearly a half-hour spent looking for whatever the monster of the Aperture was without success, prowling through the grass in almost every section of it waiting to be attacked, he decided to simply smack the Aperture and make all the monsters come out of hiding to attack him.

It worked… a little too well.

Needless to say, Larek wasn't prepared for 150 winged figures no larger than a foot tall to suddenly appear out of the drifting snowflakes all around the area and swoop toward him with incredible speed, seeming to almost teleport with how fast they were. While he'd been in a few tight spots before this one, this particular fight nearly ended him right then and there. Why? Because his defensive Fusions didn't work the way he hoped.

First, he didn't even bother setting up his *Frozen Zone* Fusion, as while it *might* work against a monster that came from an environment that caused frost to cover the area around the Aperture, he wasn't going to count on it. Second, the *Binding Thorns* he set up behind himself before smacking the Aperture was entirely useless, as the Snowflake Pixies flew just above the roots' maximum reach. He had been expecting something that was hiding in the grass or underground; he'd found *Binding Thorns* worked just as well underground as above.

This, unfortunately, didn't seem to be the case, hence why that particular offensive Fusion was effectively useless.

That's when he quickly activated and threw out *Healing Shelter*, which missed many of them because they were close enough to attack him already – but it wouldn't have mattered even if he had placed it out before the fight started. It turned out that the Snowflake Pixies, contrary to what he remembered about them in class, were small, winged humanoids made entirely of nearly frozen water and ice. The structure of their bodies was ice while the nearly frozen water flowed through them like blood; that particular tidbit of information didn't matter all that much, other than the fact that they didn't heal in the same way as a living being – so *Healing Shelter* was also useless.

They also didn't necessarily attack from above, as they liked to swoop down and launch a cloud of extremely tiny, sharp-edged ice particles that looked like fluffy snowflakes in the light, but were actually quite harmful – especially when inhaled. Passing right through his *Repelling Barrier* because they were too small and insubstantial to be detected, the ice particles practically shredded his mouth and lungs, and even his eyes were temporarily blinded as they were pierced by the deadly cloud. He remembered collapsing on the ground as he couldn't breathe anything but blood as he received a blast from dozens of the Pixies simultaneously; thinking about it later, he thought that he might've been able to handle a dozen or so at the same time, but the concentration of ice cloud attacks seemed to feed upon each other as they practically tore all of his more sensitive and vulnerable flesh apart.

Thankfully, the Snowflake Pixies weren't very smart and began to bodily attack him one at a time while he quickly recovered through the use of his *Healing Surge*. He wasn't sure what they were trying accomplish, perhaps to try and stab him with their sharp, icicle-like arms, but they essentially shattered once they got too close to him; while their attacks might have passed through his *Barrier*, the Pixies themselves certainly didn't – and they turned out to be quite fragile when blasted by a gust of wind.

For those that weren't able to attack him by the time he recovered, Larek took his *Stone Shredder Dome* and held it out in front of him as he got to his feet, which helped not only to block further ice particle clouds by dispersing them within the maelstrom of death inside the dome, but he was also able to rip them physically apart as he spun in a circle. He ended up draining a bit of the ambient Mana in the area after the use of so many powerful Fusions and had to flee as soon as he finished closing the Aperture – but he survived, which was the important part.

*Barely* survived, because it had been a close thing when he genuinely thought he was going to die; when he couldn't breathe or see and his insides felt like they were on fire, he thought that was the end. Fortunately, his *Pain Immunity* kicked in and allowed him to think about how to get himself out of the situation he was in as he activated his healing. If it hadn't been for a combination of his Skills and his healing, defensive, and offensive Fusions, he wouldn't have made it. He didn't even want to think about if the ambient Mana had been depleted before he had healed himself.

Apart from that grievous injury, everything else had been fairly superficial – and beneficial to slowly teach him how to move to avoid anything worse. He'd even taken to turning off his *Repelling Barrier* when he felt he was in a situation where it was beneficial to have the threat of being hurt to spur on his efforts to improve, which he thought was working at least a little bit. The fact that his *Dodge* Skill increased by 4 Levels was proof enough that he was getting better at avoiding the hits that he normally would've had to suffer; not all of them, of course, but his adapted movements had improved his fighting ability more than he thought they would. Larek was sure that he was missing something vital that he probably would've learned had he gone to Fort Ironwall, because he didn't think he matched the smooth prowess of the Martial trainees he'd observed.

Either that, or it could be that they were somehow utilizing their Stama to aid in their movements, which meant that he was out of luck because he hadn't been able to even touch it quite yet, so the *Stama Subjugation* Skill had been stuck at Level 1. There also hadn't been any hint of his Battle Arts taking over at any time, which he thought might be because he had a tight rein on his emotions – so he'd call that a win, as he wanted to avoid that as much as possible.

Apart from those changes, he also had 13,547 Aetheric Force available to use to increase his maximum Skill levels – which was such an incredible number that he was at a loss for where to use it at first. Doing some mental calculations, he eventually worked out how he wanted to distribute them. At first, he thought about going all-in on *Fusion* and *Pattern Formation*, but then he realized that every single Mage Skill he had was important to the Fusion process – even Spellcasting Focus, as it helped to focus his knowledge of the spells he knew to different Fusion Effects.

With that in mind, he more evenly distributed the Aetheric Force throughout his Mage Skills, bringing *Multi-effect Fusion Focus*, *Pattern Recognition*, *Magical Detection*, and *Spellcasting Focus* to a maximum of Level 25, while *Focused Division* – his recently acquired

Skill he discovered back at Copperleaf Academy – was brought to a maximum of Level 35. As for *Fusion* and *Pattern Formation*, they were increased 5 times to a maximum of Level 45 – along with *Mana Control*, which had lagged behind at Level 37 previously.

In addition to his Mage Skills, Larek also turned his attention to one of his Martial Skills: *Body Regeneration*. Having used it frequently on his travels, he thought that it would be beneficial to be able to increase its Level further; he was fairly sure it would increase the speed at which his body healed from wounds, which would only improve the effects of his *Healing Surge* Fusion.

Over the next few minutes, he started feeding the Aetheric Force he had accumulated into his Skills, feeling as each of them had their maximum Level increased. No more than 15 minutes later, he was done and ready to begin making a few Fusions before he went to sleep for the night.

**Available Aetheric Force (AF): 77**

**Mage Skills:**
Multi-effect Fusion Focus Level 20/25 (250 AF)
Pattern Recognition Level 21/25 (250 AF)
Magical Detection Level 21/25 (250 AF)
Spellcasting Focus Level 21/25 (250 AF)
Focused Division Level 31/35 (350 AF)
Mana Control Level 37/45 (450 AF)
Fusion Level 40/45 (450 AF)
Pattern Formation Level 40/45 (450 AF)

**Martial Skills:**
Stama Subjugation Level 1/20 (200 AF)
Blunt Weapon Expertise Level 1/20 (200 AF)
Unarmed Fighting Level 2/20 (200 AF)
Bladed Weapon Expertise Level 2/20 (200 AF)
Throwing Level 8/20 (200 AF)
Dodge Level 17/20 (200 AF)
Pain Immunity Level 20/20 (N/A)
Body Regeneration Level 30/33 (330 AF)

Rubbing his hands together, which were slightly cold due to not lighting the brazier in the corner of the room, he thought that the chill in the stone-covered, underground room was the perfect Fusion to start with.

*Alright, one **Space Heater** coming up....*

# Chapter 21

The effect of the slightly altered *Space Heater +2* Fusion was felt almost immediately upon activating it upon a separate stone and placing it in the corner of the room.

**Space Heater +2**
Activation Method(s): Reactive
Effect: Heats the temperature around a designated space
Input(s): Presence of people
Variable(s): Presence of 1 or more people, presence of 0 people
Magnitude: Envelops a space up to 5,000 cubic feet, increases 20 degrees in temperature
Mana Cost: 500
Pattern Cohesion: 15
Fusion Time: 75 minutes

Originally, the Variable in the Fusion required 3 or more people, as he had designed it for use against Ricardo and the two Martial trainees back in Copperleaf, but now he only needed it to activate when he was around. While he could certainly handle the cold environment that was his underground room, as the chill didn't affect him due to his higher Body stat, he could still *feel* the cold even if it wasn't necessarily unpleasant. The 20-degree jump in temperature that the Fusion produced was a little much, though it wasn't nearly at the same level as the sweltering heat that came from the fire in the Underworld Society's common room.

It was just on the edge of being comfortable, and he thought that he could do better. There was actually a Fusion he had that was perfect for this, *Temperature Regulator*, but it was designed for a single person and required a physical touch to activate. The one that he would likely use was the Magnitude 3 version, which regulated the temperature to a 70-degree base value, with up to a 30-degree difference.

**Temperature Regulator +3**
Activation Method(s): Reactive
Effect: Cools or heats the temperature around a designated space
Input(s): Physical touch, temperature measurement
Variable(s): Ambient temperature + or – 5 degrees difference of 70-degree base value

*Magnitude: Envelops one person, 30-degree difference*
*Mana Cost: 7,500*
*Pattern Cohesion: 60*
*Fusion Time: 10 hours*

    He hadn't even considered it, however, because there was no way he could add yet another Fusion to his clothes or any other accessory. It wasn't that he didn't have *room* to place it, but the area of ambience produced by the Fusion would interfere with the balance of the existing Fusions. There was a little leeway, of course, but unless he began wearing hats or helmets of some kind, there was no space left – and he wasn't exactly a hat-wearing type of person.

    But if he could combine the two Effects into one, then he could create a *Space Heater* that would automatically regulate the temperature in a larger area, rather than just around a single person. Even that wasn't exactly a challenge, as he thought it was pretty easy to get that working in a Fusion correctly; all it would take was altering the Magnitude to the appropriate area and to incorporate the correct Inputs and Variables. But he wanted more than that, and he thought that it was about time to start flexing his ability to create Advanced Fusions.

    The problem with the *Temperature Regulator* was that comfort was subjective to whoever was experiencing it. For Larek, 70 degrees was the perfect temperature for relaxing because it wasn't too hot or too cold; it was a temperature that he could sit in for hours creating Fusions and be perfectly fine. However, if he was exerting himself, such as practicing his footwork in his room – which he was planning on doing while he stayed in this underground facility, so as to keep up with the training he'd engaged in against monsters over the last month – 70 degrees would be a little warm. He was sure that there were times when he became extensively chilly, such as testing out a new *Frozen Zone* Fusion or the like, and he would then want to warm up with an even higher-temperature environment.

    While he was technically creating this Fusion for himself while he was staying underground, he was also thinking of giving this type of Fusion to others – such as Nedira when he saw her again. He distinctly remembered that the Naturalist was constantly complaining about the cold, even when the temperature was pleasant, so 70 degrees wasn't ideal for her; he thought that if she were to be able to pick the ideal temperature, she would say it was 80 degrees – which, to Larek before he had improved his Body stat, would've been a bit too hot. Not overwhelming and on the verge of wanting to melt, but it certainly wouldn't have been comfortable to him. Based on the way the women in the Underworld Society seemed to like being roasted in the common room, he could only assume that they were similar in their preferences.

So, obviously he needed a Fusion that could be altered to whatever temperature was deemed ideal. Larek thought that this might be possible with different spoken phrase Inputs used in Variables attached to other temperature measurement Inputs, which would then trigger different Magnitudes of the heating or cooling Effect. It would be fairly easy to add a dozen Variables dictating specific temperature ranges, which could then be activated with a spoken phrase such as, "Temperature 70", "Temperature 75", and so on.

But even that would only be conceptually considered an Advanced Fusion, due to how many Variables and Inputs he would need; it was technically only an Intermediate Fusion because there were only two Effects instead of the required three. There was also the problem that if more than one person was near the heating and cooling Effects of the Fusion, such as if Nedira had it in a room and someone came to visit, then the visitor would have to put up with suffering from an oppressive heat that the Naturalist considered comfortable.

Sure, it was fairly customizable by having different ranges of temperature, but how often did people agree on things like comfortable temperatures? Then there was the added complication that anyone using it would need direction on the correct phrases to use to change the temperature, so if Nedira forgot what she needed to say to alter the temperature, then she'd be stuck with whatever it was on at the time.

If Larek wanted to create Advanced Fusions, then he had to figure out how to solve this problem while also adding another Effect to qualify. Only in this way would he advance his Skills, because even though he had raised their maximum Level, he had to challenge himself with something appropriate.

Thinking about a solution, he finally stumbled upon the *Perceptive Misdirection* Fusion he'd learned from the ring that Shinpai had created for him. The Fusion had disappeared some time ago from the accessory, of course, and one of his goals that night was to replace and improve upon it so that he could move about Swiftwater with a bit more impunity than he currently enjoyed. It was what he was planning on working on next, but there was something about the Fusion that he thought he could utilize in his new creation. In short, he was intrigued by the Effect that stated that it "alters the perception of observers by non-invasive mental manipulation".

Larek had studied the formation for the Fusion for a while before he actually learned it, and during that time he had gotten a feel for what the Effect – which looked like the side view of a head – actually did. Each Effect in a Fusion had a sense of purpose *fused* into it, which was what made it accomplish what was intended; as Grandmaster Fusionist Shinpai had told him at one point, it wasn't the *symbol* that mattered, but the *intent*. That was what made Fusions more difficult to create than spells, or so he understood, because that intent had to be focused upon during its formation so that the Effect was what was intended. Spells simply followed the spell pattern and accomplished their task immediately, though through *Spellcasting Focus* it could be altered before and during its execution.

All that was to say that the Combat Fusionist had studied that particular *intent* of the Effect and discovered that the description of it didn't exactly explain what he *felt* from it. Yes, it altered the perception of observers by non-invasive mental manipulation as described, but the method behind that wasn't exactly explained until he delved deeper into it. What it *actually* did was constantly assess the mental image of Larek – or whoever was wearing the Fusion – coming from any observers, and then it initiated a feedback loop where it altered that mental image to what it was designed to show. In other words, it somehow read and interpreted the thoughts of any observers and then produced the appropriate image alterations based upon the listed Variables focused on subjective distance.

The more he evaluated the Fusion, the more he determined that the Variables were simply unnecessary as long as the intent behind the mental image alteration Effect was comprehensive enough to cover all of those Variables. He wondered why it had been done that way in the first place, as it made the entire thing overly complicated, but after considering it for a while, he realized that by including all of the distances into separate Variables, it actually made it easier for the Fusionist creating the Fusion.

That sounded counterintuitive on the surface, because wouldn't more segments in the formation cause it to become more difficult? One would think so, but by having every single component clearly separated out, the Fusionist would be able to mentally group them together as a comprehensive whole, as each one only took a small amount of focus to keep them from falling apart during Fusion creation. On the other hand, the focus required to juggle every single distance extrapolation into the Effect was impossible for a Fusionist to handle... or at least every Fusionist other than Larek. He thought it would certainly be a challenge, but one that the hyper-focused state he fell into during Fusion creation was more than capable of handling.

While he wanted to try recreating the *Perceptive Misdirection* Fusion with those changes later, Larek wanted to see if he could adapt it to his current problem. Having a fairly good idea of how the mind-reading and feedback aspects of that particular Effect worked, it wasn't long until he thought he had a solution – and it was one that he thought was a good way to experiment with Advanced Fusions like he hadn't been able to before.

In essence, what he needed was some way to change the temperature in a space that was dependent upon what those within range mentally considered to be the most comfortable temperature. This mind-reading Effect helped to determine that, giving Feedback to the Fusion to raise or lower the temperature – but he also needed it to affect each person individually. By combining the single-person focus of *Temperature Regulator* and the broader area of *Space Heater*, the Fusion should be able to determine the correct temperatures for everyone within a certain area and change the temperature of each person's individual space to whatever they thought was the best temperature for them at that time.

Creating different temperatures within an area would likely be an extreme draw on the nearby ambient Mana, but he thought he solved that by only heating or cooling each person rather than the entire space. The wild fluctuations of Mana flowing through the formation would also stress the Fusion's formation, and while Larek's formations were abnormally strong, even they would be worn down by constantly changing temperatures of those being affected. To solve this, he had to utilize a number of Amplifiers to compensate for a larger draw of Mana moving through the formation, Diverters to handle a number of different Magnitude components, and brand-new **Regulators**, which did what the name implied: They regulated the amount of Mana flowing through the heating and cooling Effects based on fluctuations of extreme Mana draw.

The Regulators didn't *prevent* the Effects from triggering, only slowed them down if it was necessary. What that meant was that if there were just one or two people inside the space, the amount of ambient Mana drawn in was fairly stable, especially if their temperature fluctuations weren't wild; in this case, the temperature changes would be almost instant for those experiencing the Effects. Add another dozen people, however, all with different ideal temperatures, and the Regulators would step in to regulate the flow of Mana moving through the formation to prevent strain. In a practical sense, the people would experience the change in temperature at a slower rate until it eventually stabilized on what they desired.

He also had to put a new **Limiter** in the Fusion, which put a limit on the amount of ambient Mana the Fusion could draw from the environment to power itself.  While most Fusions did this automatically because they could only draw Mana dependent on Magnitude, this particular Fusion could use *large* amounts of ambient Mana to power multiple Magnitudes and Effects, and if he didn't have a Limiter, it could collapse upon itself if too much was suddenly drawn in.  He didn't want to imagine the destruction it could cause if it were to fall apart and explode with millions of Mana inside of it if 100 or more people suddenly entered its field of effect and there was no Limiter on the Mana Cost components.  With the Limiter, the changes in temperature would be limited to what he thought the ambient Mana in the Sealance Empire could handle on a constant basis without depleting it all; he was making it for his room, after all, and depleting all the ambient Mana around him would be a poor idea if he wanted his other Fusions to keep functioning.  The Limiter could be mentally adjusted to different limits during the actual Fusion creation, at least, so he could change it later once he made one for Nedira.

As for what the Limiter would actually do if 100 or more people entered its area of effect?  With a reduced load of Ambient Mana coming in, the result would be that each person would experience a weaker temperature change than would be normal, so if someone was practically freezing, they would become warmer but might not reach the ideal temperature for them.  It was a trade-off, but he thought it would work well enough – and would prevent anyone from dying because it wouldn't overload and fall apart.

It took him another half-hour to completely form the mental image of the formation in his mind, taking extra special care to focus on the mind-reading and feedback Effects.  Once he thought he had it ready, he began to assemble the formation and centered it over yet another rock he'd pulled out of his pack earlier, this one approximately the size of his hand and mostly flat and generally square-shaped.  It took him over an hour of concentration to fully complete the Fusion, pushing his regenerating Mana into it as quickly as he could while using his hyper-focused state to hold everything together.  There were a few moments when he felt his concentration starting to slip because there was so much that needed to be held together, but when he finally let it go to *click* into place on the stone, he breathed a sigh of satisfied relief before he was inundated with notifications.

# Chapter 22

Thankfully, Larek wasn't knocked flat on his back like usual when he was bombarded by notifications of Skill Level-ups and unlocking new Fusions, but it was still a heady feeling and slightly uncomfortable – which was also accompanied by the fact that he used around a quarter of his Pattern Cohesion for the Fusion. The feeling passed quickly, and he was able to concentrate on looking at what he had achieved with his new Advanced Fusion, *Automatic Strong Temperature Adjustment*.

New Fusion Learned!
**Automatic Strong Temperature Adjustment +10**
Activation Method(s): Permanent, Reactive
Effect(s): Identifies the origin of individuals using a pulsing wave of Mana
Effect(s): Conceals the pulsing wave of Mana by using a void carrier
Effect(s): Determines the ideal temperature for identified individuals by non-invasive mental manipulation based on preference
Effect(s): Cools the air temperature around individuals
Effect(s): Heats the air temperature around individuals
Effect(s): Strengthens stone
Input(s): Individual ideal temperature preferences
Magnitude(s): Envelops individuals in a 100-foot diameter
Magnitude(s): Changes temperature up to a 60-degree difference from ambient temperature
Magnitude(s): 500% increased durability
Variable 1: Number of individuals within designated space
Regulator(s): Dependent upon Variable 1 and utilized Limiter capacity
Limiter(s): 100 Mana/s
Mana Cost: 250,000
Pattern Cohesion: 5,750
Fusion Time: 273 hours

**Multi-effect Fusion Focus** has reached Level 21!
**Multi-effect Fusion Focus** has reached Level 22!

**Pattern Recognition** has reached Level 22!

**Spellcasting Focus** has reached Level 22!
**Spellcasting Focus** has reached Level 23!

***Mana Control** has reached Level 38!*
***Mana Control** has reached Level 39!*

***Fusion** has reached Level 41!*

***Pattern Formation** has reached Level 41!*

That single Fusion managed to increase most of his Mage Skills a total of 9 Levels, which was incredible. More than that, he could feel that the complete Fusion would do exactly what he wanted, including the mental feedback portion of it, which was something brand-new for him and he hadn't been entirely sure it would work. Activating it on his bed after deactivating the *Space Heater*, his new creation was proven to work exactly as he intended, and he experimented with thinking about changing the temperature around him so that it was cold enough to see his breath, to hot enough that he was on the verge of sweating. His stats wouldn't allow that to happen without being in an area that was even hotter, but he could at least feel the heat even if it didn't affect him like that.

Looking over the new Fusion, he noticed that there were a few additions he hadn't seen before written out as it was. The first was the Limiter, which he had simply applied to his understanding of the local capacity for using ambient Mana, but it seemed to have converted to an actual number: 100 Mana/s. There was some tolerance to that, of course, since he was also thinking about his existing Fusions at the time and the draw of ambient Mana they demanded, so the actual limit against the ambient Mana in the Sealance Empire was probably around 400 to 500 Mana/s before it started to drain too much.

Then there was the Regulator, which was dependent upon the Variable concerning the number of individuals present, as well as the amount of ambient Mana being drawn in, as notated by what was being utilized by the Limiter and the Mana Cost component of the Fusion. Since there was no way for it to evaluate each instance of the Fusion and search for if there were too many fluctuations, it instead simply based how much regulation of Mana flow was needed depending on how many individuals were present, which was a factor of how much Mana was being drawn in.

In all, this Fusion had 6 different Effects, the most he'd ever put together before, and copied two of the same Effects as *Perceptive Misdirection* as it searched for individuals, but the mental manipulation Effect was limited to simply evaluating the preferred temperature and giving the Fusion feedback. The next two were the most important, as they were what cooled or heated the air around the individuals depending on their preference. The last Effect was almost an afterthought, but having the stone he placed the Fusion on break at some point, releasing the Mana inside of it, would be bad; therefore, he added a Magnitude 5 *Strengthen Stone* Effect to ensure that didn't casually happen.

With the number of Effects, multiple Mana Costs to handle those different Effects, a total of 10 Magnitudes to handle extreme fluctuations in temperature, and the other components needed to make it work, the Fusion ended up being a 6-by-6 grid, for a total of 36 different components – by far the largest one he'd ever created. Looking at all the lines of the Fusion, he noticed that more than a few of them weren't as perfect as he usually liked to create, as they were thinner in places or not as straight as normal, but there was nothing he saw that would compromise the efficacy of the Fusion. He put the inconsistencies down to the fact that this was his first real attempt at a powerful and complicated Advanced Fusion like this and was likely a result of losing his concentration a few times during the process, but after his Skill Level increases, he felt that next time he would have an easier time of it.

More than all of that, his ability to alter an unfamiliar Effect that he'd never actually *used* in a Fusion before gave him some other ideas for experiments, as well as knowing that he had just discovered something about mental feedback that would be *immensely* useful going forward. For instance, spoken phrases to activate or deactivate a Fusion? That was a thing of the past, as he was fairly certain he could simply have the Fusion turn on or off with a *mental* command at a distance.

There were already plenty of Fusions that relied on a mental nudge to activate and deactivate them at a touch, so why not at a distance? The sheer potential for that kind of accessibility was enormous, and he began reconstructing almost all of his offensive Fusions for this new function – as well as thinking of even more that could be just as, or even more, effective than the ones he already had. There were defensive Fusions that could benefit from it as well, though he'd have to think about how exactly to utilize them, especially for ones that worked with a Reactive Activation Method, such as his *Repelling Barrier*.

But before he did anything else, there was one other thing he needed to accomplish before he went to sleep. In short, he needed better protection against anyone who might wish to cause him harm.

The *Healing Shelter* Fusion he had set up in his room near the door was all well and good, but it didn't protect him from everything – for the same reason he hadn't used it extensively while traveling to help guard him from the environment when he made camp for the night. There were flaws in it that would allow non-biological monsters to pass through it unharmed, and there were a few instances where he'd used it before that a monster had passed through its area of effect entirely too fast to be severely harmed by it.

There was one instance where he was fighting around an Aperture that was protected by **Spring Serpents**, which were 6-foot-long snakes with a flared hood of skin around their head that made them look almost like a dinner plate on the end of a stick. What gave them their name, however, and what he had observed killing a few of them when he ventured toward the Aperture, was that they could coil their bodies tightly into a pile like a tightly wound spring, before releasing the coil and launching themselves at great speed in an arcing horizontal direction. When he hit the Aperture and the Serpents converged on his location, they had demonstrated this by essentially propelling themselves at him from over 30 feet away at incredible speed, their 3-inch-long fangs dripping a greenish venom that acted more like a strong acid against his skin.

Larek had prepared for the fight by placing down a *Healing Shelter*, as they were biological and would succumb to the extreme healing of the Fusion, but they sprang through it so quickly that they were only marginally affected by the time they reached the other side of the area of effect. At that point, he'd had to use his *Stone Shredder Dome* in a panic to start chewing through the onslaught of springing monsters, as *Frozen Zone* also wouldn't have enough time to properly freeze them before they passed through, and the same went for *Binding Thorns*.

He ended up killing them fairly easily after that, suffering only a few bites and injuries from their acidic venom, as his *Repelling Barrier* was enough to knock most of them down once they got close, only to be finished off with a clean axe strike that cut off their oversized heads. What he learned from that was yet another flaw in his Fusions, and that also applied to his current situation in his underground room.

If someone were able to open up his door and attack him from the hallway while he was sleeping, such as with a projectile weapon of some kind, his *Healing Shelter* would do absolutely nothing. Of course, Larek never slept without his *Repelling Barrier* active and ready to stop anything from hitting him like that, but the defensive Fusion wasn't perfect either. What if they threw in a bag of a substance that filled the air with a potent, poisonous gas?  Neither Fusion would detect it, and therefore they would not protect against it, and he could die in his sleep if he breathed it in and his *Body Regeneration* wasn't able to keep up while he was unconscious.

There were a myriad of ways that Larek could think of that someone with ill intent could exploit to kill him while he slept or was in the middle of making Fusions, but there was no way he could find a way to defend against them all.  What he could do was formulate a way to eliminate or lessen the flaws in his current protection.  If he was careful about it, his new Fusion would be useful not only for his room down in the Underworld Society's secret hideaway, but also while he resumed traveling on the other side of the Swiftwater.

The problem was that he'd already exhausted most of his ideas for defensive Fusions during his preparation for the Skirmish at Copperleaf Academy.  There were only a certain number of spells he knew from which he could draw inspiration for defensive purposes, and the Effects that he'd developed from other ideas weren't exactly suited to keeping him perfectly safe from any harm.

But he didn't need a perfect defense, because he was doubtful that any such thing existed.  There would always be something that he hadn't thought of to protect against, and it was a fallacy to think that there wouldn't be someone or something smarter or stronger than him that could navigate its way through his defenses.  What he needed was something that would get him through the majority of situations he could think of and shore up his weaknesses, leaving him to deal with anything else that might arise in the future.

The first element of that defense was something he hadn't included in his arsenal when he created his new staff, and later regretted it: *Camouflage Sphere*.  He'd been only thinking about the offensive properties of the staff at the time, and the idea that he'd be going after Apertures and their monsters, so who needed to be hidden?  It was only after what happened outside of Lakebellow and being chased by the Protectors that he wished he had placed it back on the staff, but he was unable to do the Fusion for it while he traveled.

But now he had the chance to fix that, though not necessarily as part of his staff; he had other ideas of what to put on his long-range offensive weapon that might make it even more useful in a fight.

Being hidden from sight was only the first step in the defense, because by itself the Fusion didn't necessarily "protect" him from anything but prying eyes.  Monsters that relied on hunting by smell or sound could still detect him even if he wasn't visible, and if some person *knew* he was there, then it didn't stop them from approaching the

*Sphere* and entering it to find him.  Therefore, he needed a physical aspect to his defense that would prevent that from happening.

He immediately thought of his Stone Shredder Dome, as it did a good job of keeping things from passing through it, but if he used something like that, the sound of it being activated would be like a signal fire to those looking for him – because it was far from silent.  The rushing of the air, as well as the whistle of the rocks as they flew through the *Dome*, was actually quite loud, and using it to try and stay hidden and safe was the last thing he wanted.

Instead of a violent dome of hardened air and stones, Larek thought about something he had created back at Copperleaf while preparing for the Skirmish.  The *Muffling Air Deflection Barrier* Fusion had been used to deaden the sound of his teammates practicing from reaching him while he worked on Fusions as well as preventing stray projectiles from hitting him.

**Muffling Air Deflection Barrier +6**
*Activation Method(s): Activatable, Reactive*
*Effect(s): Muffles sound coming from outside variable space; creates a stationary barrier of hardened air around a variable space*
*Input(s): Sound waves impacting perimeter of variable space, external object at speed*
*Variable(s): 8 X 10 X 8 foot space, speed detection over 10 miles per hour, speed detection over 80 miles per hour*
*Magnitude: 100% reduction in sound, 300 damage resistance*
*Mana Cost: 130,000*
*Pattern Cohesion: 500*
*Fusion Time: 179 hours*

This was certainly an option, as he could turn the muffling effect around and keep any sounds from escaping the area around him instead of from reaching him, though he wasn't sure if he could allow external sounds to reach him while inside.  The hardened air was certainly enough to prevent most attacks against it, unless it was swarmed or hit by something powerful, but he could also increase the Magnitude and make it able to withstand even more damage.

There were two problems with it as far as he could see.  The first was the same one that he'd been struggling with ever since coming to the Sealance Empire, in that keeping even a lower-Magnitude version active for hours on end would consume quite a bit of ambient Mana to keep it running.  The second problem tied into the first, as it would draw even more Mana once the Reactive portion of the Fusion detected a projectile at speed, stopping it before it could pass through. That wasn't a big deal, but the wall of hardened air wasn't present at all times, only when it was needed to prevent a projectile from passing through – which meant that someone could walk right through it with only a little resistance from the muffling Effect.

So, what he needed to figure out was how to reduce the draw of ambient Mana, incorporate a camouflage aspect to the *Muffling Air Deflection Barrier*, and figure out a way that something wouldn't be able to reach him just by walking up to him. The solution, at least for the latter problem but which also helped with the others, was an adaptation of what he used in his *Paralytic Light* Fusions, as "light" was already a component of the *Camouflage Sphere* because it bent the light to disguise what was inside the sphere.

In effect, the Fusion he designed started with a camouflaging dome of bent light in a 20-foot radius around its origin, followed by a barrier of dense air that muffled any sound from escaping, which was consequently much easier – and required less ambient Mana to maintain – than blocking sounds from outside of the dome. As for the protective barrier of hardened air, he utilized the outer dome of bent light camouflaging what was inside as a trigger, as anything that disturbed the light would cause it to activate. By keeping the thickness of the camouflaging light rather thin, as he didn't intend to use it while on the move, it cut the cost of ambient Mana needed to maintain it – which he hoped solved that problem, as well.

**Secure Hideaway +10**
*Activation Method(s): Activatable, Reactive*
*Effect(s): Muffles sound and prevents it from escaping designated space*
*Effect(s): Creates a stationary barrier of hardened air around a variable space*
*Effect(s): Bends light in a dome shape around Fusion location, camouflaging everything living inside from outside visual detection*
*Effect(s): Using non-invasive mental manipulation, activates or deactivates Activatable Activation Method upon detection of mental phrasing by specific individual*
*Effect(s): Strengthens wood*
*Input(s): Sound waves impacting inside perimeter of variable space*
*Input(s): Ambient light detection*
*Input(s): Bent light disturbance detection*
*Input(s): Individual-specific mental phrasing*
*Variable(s): Light fluctuations of up to 5,000 lumens*

*Variable(s): Mental phrasing of "Activate Secure Hideaway" or "Deactivate Secure Hideaway" by Larek Holsten*
*Magnitude(s): 20-foot radius dome, 100% reduction in escaping sound, 500 damage resistance, 500% increase in wood durability*
*Mana Cost: 187,500*
*Pattern Cohesion: 5,175*
*Fusion Time: 287 hours*

**Multi-effect Fusion Focus** *has reached Level 23!*

**Pattern Recognition** *has reached Level 23!*

**Spellcasting Focus** *has reached Level 24!*

**Mana Control** *has reached Level 40!*

**Fusion** *has reached Level 42!*

**Pattern Formation** *has reached Level 42!*

    This Fusion only took him about 45 minutes to finish on the block of wood he had carved before he came to the city, but it was yet another successful experiment! With another 6 Skill Level increases, bringing him to a personal Level of 24 and 19 more AP to spend – which he held off on spending for the moment – he was quickly becoming more and more proficient in creating Advanced Fusions. A perusal of his work showed that it was slightly better than his first Advanced Fusion, but still not perfect; it was nonetheless evidence that he would continue to improve.

    Verbally deactivating the *Healing Shelter* Fusion that had previously been there to protect him, he placed his newest Fusion on the floor of his room so that it enveloped both his bed and the edge of the doorway, and then settled down to sleep, relaxing fully in confidence for his safety for the first time since leaving home.

# Chapter 23

Waking up in the morning, or at least he assumed it was morning because he was underground without any way to see the sun, Larek felt amazing. He stretched and yawned loudly, feeling better and more relaxed than he remembered being in a long, long time. For the first time since he was little, there was absolutely nothing that he *had* to do that day, thanks to not being able to travel over the Swiftwater river without assistance. His overarching journey home was still a priority, but he was stuck there until a solution was found, and consequently he had nothing pressing to do.

Taking his time getting out of bed, he looked again at the Fusions he made the night before, seeing that both the *Automatic Strong Temperature Adjustment +10* and *Secure Hideaway +10* were still functioning normally and were only drawing a minimal amount of ambient Mana into their Mana Costs components. Since it was just him nearby, the *Temperature Adjustment* didn't need to absorb too much ambient Mana, and until something broke the light surrounding his *Hideaway* dome, it was only camouflaging a stationary location and muffling any sounds from escaping. It turned out that having it stationary was a huge saver of Mana compared to when it had to assess the directional observation of other people when he was moving with *Camouflage Sphere*, which helped to keep from draining the local ambient Mana.

That was obvious even when he shifted his perception to look at the strands of light that marked the nearby Mana, which hadn't changed in density much during his travels. It appeared to be handling the usage of Mana from all his Fusions just fine as it was constantly being replaced, though he had to take care in the future if he was to stay in that underground area not to add too much more of it in his room.

*Which reminds me, I need to discuss what I'm paying – or donating to – this Underworld Society for the privilege of staying here longer.*

Once he was fully awake and ready to start moving, he mentally deactivated both Fusions as he headed for the door to exit his room, his stomach grumbling a little in hunger. He opened the door and was momentarily taken aback as he saw Maybelle standing there with her hand raised as if to knock on his door. She squeaked in surprise and stumbled backwards, but Larek moved quickly to grab her arm before she could fall and let her head impact the stone wall behind her. He could heal her with a Fusion if she hurt herself in that way, but he would prefer not to have to.

As soon as she was steady, though still with a frightened look on her face, he apologized. "Didn't mean to startle you, Maybelle. Are you alright?"

She held her hand to her chest as she closed her eyes to regulate her breathing, and he couldn't help but see that she was still wearing – or not wearing, as it was – the bare minimum of clothing that he could tell nearly left her shivering from the cold in the hallway. When her breathing was regular once again, she opened her eyes and looked up at Larek. "Yes, I'm alright now – but you gave me a fright, opening the door like that! Were you waiting to scare me or something?"

He shook his head. "No, I was just leaving to find the bathing room and to get some breakfast. Have I missed it already by sleeping in? I have to admit that it's harder than usual to tell what time of day it is down here."

"Bathing room? Oh, my dear, I think I forgot to mention it last night." She sounded genuinely apologetic, but then she smiled strangely at him. "But I can show you where it is, and even give you a little *assistance* if you'd like?" Then she winked at him.

Having found out what it was she did for a living the night before, Larek could formulate a guess as to what she meant by that. However, he had no interest in that right now, as thoughts of a bath and then food were paramount in his mind. "I appreciate the offer, but I'll have to decline. I do want to talk about payment or whatever is needed for staying here longer. I know I discussed it somewhat with Seandra last night, but I'd really like to lock that down as soon as possible."

Maybelle appeared disappointed in his rejection of her "services", but she responded to his statement quickly enough that he nearly missed it. "Seandra also wanted to talk about it after breakfast, so you should get your answer then. Come, I'll show you the bathing room and leave you to it."

He nodded and began to follow her, but turned back for a moment and mentally directed his *Secure Hideaway* to reactivate; the Effect was nearly instant, as he felt and saw the Fusion activate with a barely noticeable ripple over the dome of bent light creating the camouflage, and he knew his stuff would be safe while he was gone. Bathing, on the other hand, was going to be a little tricky because he still had memories of Vivienne catching him while he was vulnerable in the bathtub, and he wasn't going to let that happen again.

Larek almost went back to grab his *Hideaway* for use in the bath, but he left it where it was because it was much more important to protect his things at the moment. He could handle himself for a few minutes in the tub, after all.

Thankfully, the bathing room was able to be locked and was only for private use, as it wasn't large enough to be shared with more than one or two people at a time. While in the tub, Larek spent the entire time watching the door and the room itself, looking for anyone trying to sneak up on him, but there really wasn't any place for people to hide. His paranoia reared its ugly head while he got himself really clean for the first time since he left the town of Enderflow, but he managed to make it through his bath quickly and with a minimum of fuss.

Breakfast, on the other hand, was much more relaxed as far as being paranoid went, as he was fully clothed and armed with Fusions that were able to protect him if anything dangerous arose. He scarfed down the eggs and what appeared to be odd-tasting fish sausages, and ate nearly half a loaf of bread before he was done; the food did wonders to replenish his body after a month of travel, continuing what dinner had started the night before.

"So, what are you looking to donate to the Society? And how long were you planning on enjoying our hospitality?" Seandra asked as soon as he was finished eating, though she and all the rest of the women nearby weren't even halfway done with their meals. He was surprised to see that there were only about a quarter of the women that were there during dinner the previous night, though he supposed that they were out and about town doing... whatever it was they did. From what he understood from the Underworld Society's leader's explanation, most of their work was legitimate, so he supposed that many of them were involved in relatively normal professions.

Larek cleared his throat, unsure if he should try and bargain for a lower donation or just provide something that he thought would be more than acceptable. From the older woman's tone of voice and how she sat in her chair at the large table, she seemed to have recovered most of her composure and authority that had likely been affected by his Dominion magic, and she seemed all business now without a hint of give to it.

"Well, I was thinking that I would stay here until travel over the Swiftwater has been reinstated. How about a donation of—"

"500 gold pieces," Seandra interrupted him, her firm voice startling him a bit at how harsh it sounded. "That's the only worthy donation that will allow you to stay here any longer than today."

*Whoa. What just happened?*

The other women around the table also appeared to be taken aback at the sudden demand, so he knew it wasn't just *him* being shocked by the high number. "Uh... Can I ask why it should be that high an amount?"

"Because we've had word of Protectors conducting a search for you already this morning, and your presence here puts us *all* in danger," she said matter-of-factly, though that fact didn't seem to have been shared with everyone since they appeared surprised.

*They tracked me here already? How? Do they have some sort of long-range communication system that I'm unaware of?*

Larek was suddenly glad that he hadn't spent more than an hour or so in any villages or towns along his trek through the Empire, because it was quite possible that the Protectors might have caught up to him before this point. Still, it was strangely a relief to know that they were still hunting him, knowing that his paranoia hadn't been for nothing. He was also glad that he hadn't been able to find a vacancy in any of the local Inns, as he would've been located quite quickly.

The only problem now was that he wasn't sure if he had 500 gold coins to give to these people. Thinking about his remaining bag of coins in his pack, he thought that if he were to exchange everything for local currency, including his platinum coins, he might have around 300 or so. Even if he was somehow able to scrounge up 500 gold coins, he knew that he was being taken advantage of by this Underworld Society because he required someplace to stay that was private and relatively safe from being found by the Protectors. It would also leave him at their mercy if they were to demand an even greater "donation" in the future if they thought they could squeeze it out of him. In short, he had no other choice but to pay if he didn't want to risk himself in the wild lands of the Empire with all the monsters lurking about, or attempt to stay in the city where those in authority could easily find him.

Or so they thought.

He shrugged. "I see. Well then, I guess I'll be leaving. Thank you for your hospitality," he told Seandra, moving to rise out of his seat.

"Wait," the older woman said quickly, as if worried that he was leaving, but it felt rehearsed to Larek. "If you don't have the funds to fulfill the donation requirements, then perhaps we can negotiate a deal. If you volunteer to work for us for—"

"Oh, I have enough to fulfill the donation requirements, but extortion is where I draw the line," he responded, getting to his feet and finding himself towering over Seandra and the other women seated around her. While the leader of this branch of the Underworld Society matched his gaze without flinching, the others withdrew, and a few of them flinched when he glanced at them. "I was ready to make a good-faith donation to your Society for a full gold every day that I was planning on staying here, but that apparently wasn't good enough for you.

"Based on what you told me last night, this type of thing is a normal enterprise for your Society to engage in, but to have it directed toward someone enjoying your hospitality is in very poor taste. Therefore, I'll be leaving once I get my things and hopefully I'll never see you again. Because if I do, then I'll remember this conversation and take action to ensure that you don't try and take advantage of me again. Good day."

**Speaking** *has reached Level 18!*

Seandra looked shocked and angry at his statement, as if she couldn't believe he was talking to her like that. It seemed as though not only did his Dominion magic wear off, but it had turned her against him – as if her mind knew what had happened and was rebelling.

*Hmm... I wonder if that's what happened in the Kingdom? With all the common people having their dominating enslavement broken, were their emotion-filled reactions to Dominion magic and the Gergasi so powerful that it was even passed down as a hereditary trait?*

It certainly made a lot of sense if that was the case, as he was now able to see it in person as it happened to him. The fallout from the use of his Dominion magic was yet another reason why he wanted to get control of it – if only so that he could control when it was used; if he had his way, the times he planned on using it would be... *never.*

As he turned away from the table, he caught Seandra moving her hand just above the table in a strange gesture. It didn't take more than a step away from the remains of his breakfast to find out what it was for, as a half-dozen figures in tight, dark-colored leathers surrounded him. He recognized them from the night before as the "assassins" mentioned in the Society's activities, and one of them was even Yvette, the first person other than Maybelle that he'd met when he arrived. All of them had their faces covered with a dark cloth that only left their eyes exposed, but he could see both confusion and determination in their gazes, as if they weren't sure exactly why they were being called upon to stop him from leaving, but would obey their orders, nonetheless.

He glanced around the room to see if Maybelle had an explanation for this, as she seemed to want to be genuinely helpful, but she was nowhere to be seen. Crossing his arms over his chest with a heavy sigh, he turned around to look at Seandra, who had a smug look on her face.

"We can't allow you to leave just yet, Larek. You see, you have something that we need and as soon as we get it, you can go."

"And what is that?"

"More of those magical lights you showed Maybelle. She told us about them, and it sounds like they are Fusions from your homeland. While most people in the Sealance Empire have heard about their supposed wondrousness before, there are very few that have actually *seen* them in person to know that they are entirely real. One of those people who have seen and held one in their hand is *me*, so I have the unique ability to recognize something valuable when I hear of it.

"In short, I want all of these lights you possess, as well as any other Fusions you may have. Once I have them, as well as a sizable donation from you – don't worry, we won't leave you with nothing – you'll be free to go. How does that sound? Quite simple, right?'

He shook his head, though she misinterpreted the gesture. "No? I assure you that this is the best solution, as we can simply take what we want from your corpse if we have to, but I doubt it will come to that, correct? You seem the sensible sort, Larek."

"You *really* don't want to do this, Seandra. Please call them off and let me go on my way, and I'll forget this ever happened."

Larek was starting to get a little angry from yet another person trying to take advantage of him and attempting to steal his Fusions, but he held that anger down as he didn't want his Battle Arts to suddenly activate – and he wasn't sure if he could stop them from slaughtering everyone in the room. If it wasn't obvious at first, the reactions of the other people around the table to Seandra's threat and ultimatum showed that while they were part of the Society, they weren't exactly behind this attempt to steal from him. That being said, not a single one of them voiced their concern that they were taking this too far, as they simply sat there, looking meekly at their leader.

"Just... let you go? As simple as that, right? No, I don't think so. I'm the one with all the power here, so—" As she was talking, Larek caught her looking off to his left, no more than a glance, but if that wasn't a signal to attack him, then he was blind. Rather than react, he simply ensured that his *Repelling Barrier* was still active from when he had turned it on earlier, and stood there.

The Combat Fusionist didn't see or even hear the strike aimed for the back of his neck, which was impressive all by itself. It would've been even more impressive if it had actually hit him, but the knife the assassin was wielding was violently flung to the ground in a powerful gust of wind, and the speed at which it happened snapped the wrist of the woman while it sent her tumbling to the floor. There was a grunt of pain from her as she rolled quite acrobatically with the sudden downward force, and he could see her spring up to her feet out of the corner of his eye, holding her broken wrist against her chest.

    Silence descended upon the common room, broken only by the harsh breathing of the injured assassin, before pandemonium broke out as a multitude of reactions to the event took place.

# Chapter 24

"Get him!" Seandra screamed, pointing at him even as she knocked the chair she was sitting in over on its back as she abruptly stood up. Panicked screams erupted from the other women around the table as they scrambled to back away from the sudden violence that had erupted.

Shaking his head as he pulled his best friend from the holster on his side, Larek held his axe out in front of him crossways as he was suddenly mobbed by veiled assassins from all sides. The half-dozen that he had seen before were joined by twice the amount that seemed to come from nowhere, though it was quite possible that they were hiding just out of view, which just complicated matters.

Even as four more of the knife-wielding women stabbed at him and were thrown around by his *Repelling Barrier*, another pair of knives bypassed the protection of the Fusion as it hit the limit on the number of active gusts and pierced his back. Or at least they tried to pierce his back, but his shirt was strong enough with its *Multi-Resistance* Fusion to prevent them from cutting through the fabric. The impact of both weapons hitting him was still strong enough to knock him slightly forward and temporarily hurt before his *Pain Immunity* Skill kicked in and he caught his balance.

If the assassin had been surprised at the ineffective attack, she didn't show it, as she adjusted her next strike to hit the back of his unprotected neck. As she stabbed forward, the *Barrier* finally reactivated now that it had the opportunity, sending her and her knives slamming into the ground as she was caught by the powerful gust. She hit the stone floor hard enough that he wouldn't be surprised if she was seriously injured, but he didn't have a second to evaluate if she was going to be an ongoing threat or not.

Because every other assassin was still attacking him, and it was time to go on the offensive. He had tried to warn them and negotiate his way out of the situation, but once that failed, he knew there was no other choice. It was either kill or be killed, and he didn't feel like dying anytime soon.

Applying his Strength and Agility stats, which he'd had a bit of practice with in short bursts during his fights with monsters over the last month, Larek swung his axe around in a sideways sweep, catching another of the assassins behind him as she tried to stab him in the back. He tried not to dwell on the sight of its blade cutting through the leather of her outfit before slicing entirely through her upper torso and out through the other side. Even as her top half fell to the floor on top of her legs, she attempted to attack him on the way down, stabbing at him with her knives – but they triggered the Effect of the *Repelling Barrier*, causing the free-falling half of the woman to abruptly spin vertically in the air, flinging the lifeblood coming out of her severed torso everywhere, including at Larek.

The blood was moving at such speed and had a physicality to it that triggered his Barrier once again, sending it shooting down into the floor to splash disturbingly all over the stone. The assassins saw that as well and, thinking quickly and evaluating the situation with a speed that was astonishing to him, suddenly sprinted to the table and begun chucking plates, forks, and cups at him with incredible aim, which triggered the *Barrier* over and over. As he applied his Agility to rush toward them, they started including sharp throwing knives that they pulled from somewhere along their bodies – and for the first time Larek was injured.

One throwing knife lodged itself in his lower left arm, which wasn't covered by his shirt, which he immediately pulled out and tossed back at the nearest veiled figure, but the throw was clumsy because he wasn't used to throwing knives; it was actually caught and returned by her the next second. Another one somehow slipped through a gap between his shirt and his pants that only appeared as he was moving and lifting up his axe to help block the onslaught of items being thrown at him, which caused him to grunt in discomfort as it lodged itself into something in his right side. He was about to pull it out, but a third knife spun as it flew toward his face, and it was only his quick movement throwing himself backwards that saved it from piercing through his eye and into his brain. Unfortunately, the movement still allowed it to slice at the edge of his throat, cutting through his firm flesh to open up the main artery in his neck.

It wasn't an overly serious wound, but he could immediately feel the blood pumping out of it; if he wasn't careful, he'd bleed out before he had a chance to heal it, but he knew that he needed to remove the knife in his side before he activated his *Healing Surge* Fusion. Needing his hands free in order to do that, he cocked his arm back and launched his axe at the nearest assassin, which caused the knife in his side to tear at his inside further with the movement.

The Logging tool flew swiftly through the air and impacted the upper right shoulder of the assassin he was throwing it at, despite her attempting to dodge. The blade cut entirely through the leather, flesh, and bone, literally disarming her even as it ricocheted and deflected upwards on its flight, where it finally lodged itself in the stone wall above the easy reach of the assassins.  As he pulled the knife out of his side and tossed it to the floor, Larek initiated his healing Fusion and felt his wounds repair themselves rapidly – but he was far from being out of danger.

**Throwing** *has reached Level 9!*

As he rushed the assassins with his superior speed, he managed to catch one before she could escape his path, and he slammed his fist into her chest with such force that he felt her ribcage practically shatter as she was propelled backwards into the far wall, where her head smacked against the stone with a hollow sound, and she fell bonelessly to the floor.

Unfortunately for Larek, he still hadn't perfected his ability to control his speed and wasted valuable time stopping himself so that he could reorient toward one of the other assassins.  In essence, he was like a bull that could charge ahead but had difficulty turning, and it was something he was working on during his fights with monsters, but hadn't had as much progress as he'd like.

It also turned out that the intelligence of his opponent was a major obstacle, because when he targeted the nearest assassin, she immediately flipped backwards in an acrobatic tumble, making her impossible to pin down.  The others began moving rapidly around, already recognizing that he was faster than them, but only in short bursts.  It was extremely frustrating and was just one of the things he had wished he had been able to improve during his month-long journey, because it was quickly becoming a problem.

Fighting people was so much harder than fighting monsters.

Then, in just the few seconds since the fight started, Seandra had corralled the screaming women that had been around the table and convinced them to join in on killing Larek.  They weren't assassins, of course, but they saw how effective throwing things at him was, so they took over the barrage of table items even as the assassins continued moving around and tossing knives at him.

"ENOUGH!" he shouted, pulling a handful of items from his pockets at the same time.  Tossing one of the rocks in his hand at the assembled women across the table that were throwing things at him, he threw the other two toward the assassins, before pulling out a length of wood that he held in his hand and activated.  The *Stone Shredder Dome* flickered into existence, and he swung it around himself, blocking the projectiles sent his way while also keeping the approaching assassins back – and right where he wanted them.

As the rocks he threw rolled to a stop, he prepared for them to fully activate in a few seconds, which would either begin to freeze, constrict, or overload them with healing, ending the fight. He hadn't seen which ones he threw where, but as Seandra and the other women around the table began to scream as roots suddenly burst out of the stone floor and wrapped themselves around their limbs, he quickly found out.

Unbeknownst to him, activating and throwing that one first was a mistake, as the assassins were apparently incredibly quick-witted as well as being swift. One of them, seeing that what he threw out earlier was killing the others, turned her attention to the stone that landed near her feet. Reversing her grip on her knife, which had a sturdy metal spike on the pommel, she knelt down and smashed at the stone. Larek caught the action as she slammed it down the first time, and watched as it withstood the blow – but just barely. The problem was that he hadn't strengthened the stone when he had made the Fusion originally, as it was only an Intermediate and therefore he was unable to add that Effect, but it was a fairly strong stone, and he hadn't had any problems with it needing reinforcement – until now.

Oh, no.

Even as he watched the actual Fusion activate, which proved to be his *Healing Shelter*, the threat of imminent death and the rising anger at these people who were going to die for absolutely no reason triggered something inside of him in his panic. Faster than a blink of his eye, his Stama rushed through his entire body, activating what he quickly discovered was his *Consuming Speed* Battle Art.

The world seemed to slow to a crawl around him, as he focused on the assassin getting ready to strike his *Healing Shelter* Fusion again. Even as he saw the spike on the pommel of the knife descending onto the stone, he saw some fluctuations in the Fusion formation and realized that the first blow – while it hadn't shattered the stone – had damaged it enough that it was already falling apart. The second blow would just speed up the process that was already happening.

From what he could tell, there was no stopping what was about to happen… so he didn't try. Instead, he used his incredible speed granted him by his Battle Art to run; he nearly ran toward his room because his stuff was there, but he quickly decided that it was folly. Based on the amount of destruction he predicted was about to happen, he didn't think that he'd survive.

But there was one thing he wasn't going to leave behind.

Dropping the *Stone Shredder Dome* so that he'd have both hands free, Larek sped past the slow-moving Assassins and dodged around the thrown objects still in the air, before leaping toward the wall where his axe was lodged. He landed on the vertical surface feet-first even as he gripped the handle of his best friend. Launching himself off the wall as he yanked the tool out of the stone, his substantial Martial stats aided him in launching himself across the room.

Right toward the exit.

The door was closed and locked, but Larek's momentum meant that he smashed into the wood-and-iron door with enough force to cave in a portion of it while cracking the hinges. Injured by the impact as he felt more than a few bones in his upper body snap, he rebounded from the door but landed on his feet. With a powerful kick at the barrier preventing him from leaving, he felt a large portion of the already damaged door splinter, which caused it to slam open and let him out.

Running to step out of the underground sanctuary for the Underworld Society, he felt the moment when the *Healing Shelter* Fusion was shattered, releasing all of the stored Mana inside of it in an instant. The explosive shockwave as the Mana decompressed from its formation flung him out of the common room and down the tunnel he'd traveled down the day before.

He was still airborne when another shockwave went off as another of his Fusions broke, pushing him even faster down the tunnel. Emerging from the tunnel, he was flung at incredible speed at the stone steps in front of him, which he could barely make out in the dim light of the common room behind him. Larek managed to somehow turn his body while mid-air so that he didn't land on the steps head-first, but hitting it side-first was still incredibly painful – especially as a third shockwave blasted him forward even faster.

Dazed by the impact, which had him rebounding back and upwards, the fourth and final shockwave emerged as the last Fusion in the common room detonated, which sent him flying up the stairs at speed. The angle of his ascent was fortunate because he avoided hitting either the ceiling or the steps again, which was incredibly lucky since he couldn't see a single thing in the darkness.

He actually ended up hitting the upper wall near the entrance to the passageway found in the storage building up above. The impact certainly didn't help his broken body, but at least he landed in a place where he wasn't going to suddenly fall back down the stairs.

*That* would've hurt a whole lot more.

As it was, he activated his *Healing Surge* Fusion as quickly as he came to a stop, even as his ears were inundated by incredibly loud crashing noises that he felt indicated that the entire underground complex was collapsing from the damage that had been caused by the exploding Fusions. Laying on his back as his body put itself together, he felt the *Consuming Speed* Battle Art draining from his body, taking most of his strength with it. As the bones inside of his body shifted back into place and the worst of his internal injuries were repaired, Larek deactivated the healing Fusion a second before he slipped into unconsciousness.

# Chapter 25

Larek woke to complete darkness and the heavy feeling of rock dust covering his face, along with the unmistakable exhaustion that came with a lack of food and water for an extended period of time. More than that, his body was worn out, like a dishrag that had been squeezed until all of the water was expelled from it, leaving it dry and brittle. He struggled against the exhaustion and weakness as his mind finally caught up with where he was and how he got there.

*My Battle Art activated again? I still want to know how it did that, but at least it saved my life.*

Larek thought it was strange how he could comfortably move at such extreme speeds caused by his *Consuming Speed* Battle Art, when trying to utilize his Agility stat in a fight was so difficult. It was almost as if the Battle Art brought with it an innate knowledge of how to utilize it effectively, which he wished would translate to normal use of his stats, but that didn't seem to be the case. When it wasn't active, he could remember himself moving with such grace and accuracy in his movements, but he couldn't remember *how* he had done it or extrapolate the processes from his memories.

Regardless, that was neither here nor there right then, because there were other issues that Larek needed to address at the moment. Obtaining food to replenish his energy was just one of them, and it might not even be the most pressing. Sitting up was a chore in and of itself, but so was breathing; he coughed a few times as he inhaled the dust-filled air, and while the dust might have been the cause, he thought that the air felt thinner than normal. The memory of the incredible explosions caused by his detonating Fusions filled his mind, along with the horrible thought of being buried alive in the underground refuge.

Looking down at himself, the only things he could see were the Fusions on his clothes as they absorbed the ambient Mana in the environment, which seemed to be fluctuating a bit – *likely caused by the Mana-fueled explosions, I bet.* To his right, he could make out the Fusions on his axe where he had dropped it after passing out some time ago, and he was amazed that he had managed to hold onto it in his flight. He was even more amazed that the shockwaves that had propelled him on said flight hadn't destabilized the Fusions he was currently looking at, as that would've resulted in his death at that point if they were to explode.

Unfortunately, neither the strands of light he saw as ambient Mana nor the Fusions on his possessions actually shed visible light into the environment, so he was essentially blind to his current circumstances. Reaching into his pants pockets, he found that they were empty; he belatedly realized that he had left all his *Illuminate* stones with his pack and all his other possessions, which were most likely buried under literal tons of rock at that point. Regret hammered at his psyche over the loss of his stuff, as much or more than the loss of lives that had occurred down below. He hadn't intended to hurt anyone when he woke up that morning—*is it still the same day?*—but things had escalated so quickly that he was left with his head spinning from the sudden brutal fight and subsequent explosions.

His first priority was to determine how much trouble he was in and to extricate himself from his current location. After he was free, he could look for sustenance to replenish his energy, and only then could he figure out what to do in the future, now that all of his possessions except the clothes on his back and his axe were gone – including all of his coinage. That also included his transfer letter from Copperleaf to Fort Ironwall, which was important, but that was far down on his list of priorities right now.

Feeling around himself, Larek detected a heavy coating of dust all along the stone floor he found himself sitting upon, which made sense if a portion of the underground area had collapsed. Not finding anything directly around the area that he might be able to use for a Fusion, he instead grabbed his axe and carved out a small slab of stone from the floor before he got to work.

Thankfully, the *Illuminate +1* Fusion only took 20 seconds to complete because it was such an easy, Basic Fusion to create that it was barely any effort. It only took that long because he had trouble concentrating with how hungry and weak he was, but it was slowly getting better the longer he was awake and actively doing something.

"I'm so screwed."

Instead of echoing through a long stone stairway below him, his voice was deadened by the presence of collapsed stone all around him, leaving the Combat Fusionist in a pocket of space approximately 40 feet long and as wide as the staircase itself. When he turned his attention toward the exit, using the newly created illuminated slab of stone, he saw that the tunnel that led to the secret doorway in the storage facility had collapsed similarly to the majority of the stairway, leaving him completely trapped with no way out. He thought that he might be able to dig his way out eventually, but he was also worried that trying to shift the dirt-and-stone-filled tunnel leading to his escape might cause even more of it to collapse. Looking at the space that contained him and noticing that there were cracks all around its stone shell, he didn't think it would take much abuse before it collapsed upon him.

What it also showed, and matched what he felt, was that he was slowly running out of air. The shortness of his breath was the first indication, but with both ends sealed up, there was no way for new air to get into the space.

So, either he did nothing and suffocated to death, or he attempted to dig himself out and risked the rest of it collapsing down on him. While he would, of course, choose the latter option, even standing up and moving around at that point was a challenge because of how weak he was; he couldn't fathom digging even a portion of the collapsed tunnel out in his current state of exhaustion.

That was why Larek thought he was screwed, because he couldn't see a way out of his predicament. He was low on physical energy, and even if he wasn't, it was almost guaranteed that the rest of the complex would collapse while he was digging himself out. Ready to simply give up in despair, he laid back down on the stone floor, staring at the ceiling in hopelessness. As if to emphasize his fears, a trickle of dirt somehow squeezed itself out of a crack in the stone, nearly landing on his face before he jerked it aside at the last moment.

It was watching the tiny stream of dirt fall inside the cavity that had him sitting up in shock. *Hold on – I think I have an idea!*

Quickly slicing another slab of stone out of the floor with his axe, he trimmed it down until it was more of a foot-long, rectangular rod that he could easily hold in his hand and point in a direction he desired. Then, setting it in front of him, he devised a hastily put-together Fusion on the fly, based around a spell he had recently – at least relatively recently – learned from Nedira when they were escaping from Copperleaf: *Furrow*.

**Furrow**
*Magnitude: 3 cubic feet of dirt*
*Base Elemental Damage: 0*
*Base Elemental Effect (Dirt Manipulation): Gently moves a certain amount of dirt in the desired direction*
*Restrictions: Rocks greater than 3 cubic inches cannot be shifted*
*Base Mana Cost: 15*
*Base Pattern Cohesion: 2*

*Furrow* was designed for moving quantities of dirt for assistance in farming, or so the Naturalist had explained, but it was also able to shift rocks – though the spell had a limit to the size of the rocks that could be moved. Fortunately, Larek had learned that his Fusions could bypass these kinds of limitations if he ensured the Magnitude was high enough, but there was only one way to find out.

To help with moving the larger stones, he also tapped into the knowledge of how his *Flying Stone* Fusion worked to propel the stones that were formed. In this case, he didn't need to create any stones because they were already there; what he needed was the propelling portion of the Fusion, and he quickly created an Effect that would do that with *much* larger stones.

Once he thought he had something that might work for what he needed, Larek fell into his hyper-focused state without even double or triple-checking his formation, as he had the feeling that he didn't have time to waste. The formation came together with his Pattern Cohesion quickly, and Larek began to shove all of his Mana into it as soon as possible. He ignored his impatience as his Mana regenerated, slightly faster than normal for some reason, as he kept all of the different components in the Fusion together firmly in his mind.

Larek lost track of the time as he continued to pour Mana into the Fusion, and it never seemed to be enough to fill it up. He belatedly realized that he probably should've limited the Magnitude to 10 instead of the 12 he went with for this Fusion, but he wasn't sure if a +10 Fusion would be enough; he only had one shot at this, and if it didn't work, he was as good as dead.

Larek acknowledged and then ignored the cracks he could hear popping through the sanctuary where he sat that was rapidly becoming unsafe, even as more trickles of dirt fell inside and piled up all around him. His hyper-focused state was the only thing that saved him from losing control of his Fusion when one of the streams of dirt suddenly fell directly on the back of his neck, falling down his shirt to bunch up a bit before spilling to the floor.

Just when he thought he would never finish the Fusion before everything collapsed around him, Larek felt the formation suck in the last little bit of Mana and *snap* into place on the end of the rectangular stone rod.

**Earth Mover +12**
*Activation Method(s): Activatable*
*Effect(s): Propels large quantities of dirt in the desired direction*
*Effect(s): Propels large quantities of stone in the desired direction*
*Effect(s): Strengthens stone*
*Input(s): Dirt detection, stone detection*

*Magnitude(s): Propels up to 12,000 cubic feet of targeted area, 120 feet away from Fusion origin, with 120,000 pounds of force*
*Magnitude(s): 400% increased durability*
*Variable(s): Directional orientation, material recognition*
*Mana Cost: 540,000*
*Pattern Cohesion: 13,300*
*Fusion Time: 424 hours*

**Multi-effect Fusion Focus** *has reached Level 24!*

**Pattern Recognition** *has reached Level 24!*

**Spellcasting Focus** *has reached Level 25!*

**Mana Control** *has reached Level 41!*
**Mana Control** *has reached Level 42!*

**Fusion** *has reached Level 43!*

**Pattern Formation** *has reached Level 44!*

As soon as Larek snapped out of his hyper-focused state, he sucked in a great breath as if coming up for air from diving into a lake, only to find that the air was now so thin that he could barely get any into his lungs. The dust that was inhaled was minimal, as most of it had settled by that point, but that didn't matter if he couldn't even catch his breath.

Without a moment to spare for attention to his notifications, he grabbed the stone rod and held it up while pointing it at the collapsed exit. With a mental prayer that his formation could handle such an Effect without breaking down while he held it in his hand, he activated his new *Earth Mover +12* Fusion...

...and nothing happened.

Worried that he had done something wrong, he shifted his perspective to look at the Fusion closer, only to see that all of the ambient Mana around him was being sucked into the formation at an alarming rate. With the amount of Mana flowing into it, the Fusion practically glowed with intensity, and before he could worry that it was going to explode, the Mana was suddenly converted into the Effect he had designed.

The collapsed exit in front of him shifted slightly at first, before it was blasted straight ahead with an eardrum-shattering screech of ripping rock. In less than two seconds after it finally started the process, there was a perfectly round tunnel bored straight through the debris and out to the storage facility beyond. The Fusion didn't affect the wood used in its construction, but the stone foundations were ripped apart and joined the rest of the dirt and stone torn from the new tunnel, wrecking whatever was left outside – which didn't seem to be a lot. A quick glance showed that it wasn't just the tunnel that had collapsed because of the explosions earlier, because it was more than likely that the entire building had come down at some point.

All of that happened within a few seconds, which was more than enough time for the ceiling above Larek to suddenly give out as the pressure from the exit area weakened whatever was holding it up. Aware that it was already weak, and with an infusion of fresh air from the hole he had just bored outside, he rapidly lifted the rod above his head while it continued to work, blasting out a wide trough of earth up and out of his location in an arc, before sending everything above him shooting straight into the air. Saved from his refuge collapsing on him prematurely, and with the open sky now above him, Larek felt the *Earth Mover* deactivate as it ran out of easy-to-absorb ambient Mana.

*Uh, oh.*

Still looking up, he realized that the propelled stone and dirt that went straight up had reached the apex of its flight and was now descending again. Without the Fusion to propel it away again, most of it was going to land right on top of him.

With a burst of energy born of fear, Larek snatched up his axe and scrambled toward the exit, falling a few times as he tripped over the uneven foundation, before he found himself inside what was left of the wrecked storage facility. He finally did slip and fall when the ground shook underneath him, timed with the blast of dirt and stone falling back to the ground from its flight.

His panic-born energy hadn't run out quite yet, so he picked himself up and out through the hole he had made with his Fusion, climbing over fallen wooden beams from the collapsed building the further he went, before stumbling into the street – and right into the presence of a group of mounted Protectors aiming their spears at him.

# Chapter 26

Larek finished eating the second surprisingly delicious fish sandwich he had been given as prisoner fare before washing it down with the large stone pitcher of water, not even bothering to use the cup that had been provided along with it. He sat back on his undersized bed and laid himself down, his legs dangling over the end at the knees, and put his hands behind his head as he felt himself drifting off to sleep once again.

The same routine had been going on for the last two days after he was imprisoned by the Swiftwater Protectors upon his escape from the Underworld Society's destroyed underground sanctuary – and he didn't mind it in the least. At the time, he didn't have the energy to avoid being captured by them and therefore didn't even put up a fight. They even had to literally drag him back to their barracks and the cell they threw him in, because he was too weak to walk at that point. A meal shortly after arriving had him feeling better immediately, as well as a long nap afterwards, and every time he woke up, he had another meal waiting for him inside his cell enclosed by steel bars, slipped in through a small opening near the floor. Not once did he actually see any of the Protectors who had captured him, though he could hear them moving throughout the barracks and speaking with each other occasionally.

He was just fine with that, though, because he didn't have the energy to talk with them – though that was rapidly changing as his body and mind recovered from his recent near-death experience.

When he woke up later, he stretched and sat up, looking around for more food but not seeing any ready for him. Determining the amount of time that passed while he napped was nearly impossible, but he thought that this last one had only been an hour or two, so no additional meal made sense.

Straightening his clothing as he got up, which the Protectors thankfully left on him rather than stripping it away from him like they did his axe, he sat on the edge of the bed and finally paid attention to his cell for the first time since arriving. Every other time he had been awake, he had been shoving his face full of food, and recovering from his ordeal was more important to him than where he was.

It was a fairly small cell, though it thankfully had 8-foot-tall ceilings to go with the 100-square-foot space, and there was a tiny side table where he placed his food tray and pitcher, his too-short bed, and a chamber pot in the corner – which he hadn't needed to use, as his body converted every single thing he ingested into energy without any waste. Three of the walls were a thick, dense stone while the last was a wall of steel bars that were set 4 inches apart from each other, along with a locked gate and the aforementioned gap along the bottom that was used for pushing in food deliveries.

Outside of the cell, he could barely see that he was on one side of a hallway that had a series of oil lamps burning that marginally illuminated the entire place, and he thought there were other cells on either side of him – both of which were empty. In fact, he was fairly sure he was completely alone in this part of the barracks, as he heard absolutely nothing other than some Protectors moving around outside of a door on one end of the hallway.

Now that he had most of his energy back after eating and getting plenty of rest, right now was the perfect opportunity to escape... if that was what he wanted to do, of course. Which it was, but not before he found out where his best friend was being held; after all, there was no way he was going to leave the axe behind after saving it from being buried underneath the remains of the Underworld Society's Sanctuary.

But before he did attempt to escape, a quick test of the bars of his cell showing that he could bend them easily enough if he had enough time to do it without making too much noise, he had to figure out what to do after he was successful.

What were his overarching goals? To get home to the Kingdom, find his family and friends, and figure out what went wrong there that caused such a mess with the rest of the world. The latter goal was secondary to the first two, because while he cared about it, he wasn't sure if there was anything he could or even *wanted* to do to reverse what had already happened.

To achieve those goals, his first step at this point was to cross the Swiftwater, and to do that without killing himself in the process, he needed a way across – a way that would eventually be provided by the return of ferries at some point. He wasn't the only one that needed transportation, of course, but the presence of the merchants waiting to move their goods across the river ensured that it would *eventually* happen, even if Larek didn't know when.

It was already going to be difficult negotiating his way onto a ferry without arousing suspicion, but it would be nearly impossible to do it if he escaped from the Protectors and they were constantly searching for him in the city, knowing that he was there. He had a bit of anonymity before because those searching for him didn't know exactly where he would be, but at this point they were more than aware he was in the city and likely stuck looking for a way across the Swiftwater along with everyone else.

There was always the option of going north and making his way *around* the river, but that would add even more months of travel to his journey; at this point, this wasn't that big of a deal because it would help to distance himself from the Protectors searching for him, but there was now another problem.

He had lost all of his money inside the collapsed Underworld Society complex. His staff, his extra clothes, his bedroll, his transfer letter, and his actual packs were also gone, but he could always create or purchase more of those things – other than the letter – if he had money, which he didn't. Therefore, if he did decide to go north, he'd have to go with absolutely nothing but his clothes and his axe – because he was planning on getting it back – so supplies would be difficult to get. Journeying without already prepared rations of food was extremely risky, even if he was able to supplement them with meat from killed monsters; there only had to be a day or two of no edible monsters before he would begin to starve.

He could steal from a shop or two in the city, or perhaps swipe some things from one of the packed warehouses near the docks, but he would only do that as a last resort. Unless someone personally did something to him, he was loathe to hurt them if there was another alternative; he'd already killed dozens more people in the Empire of Sealance than he thought he would have to, and while their deaths were either justified or accidents, they still weighed on his conscience. Stealing from innocent merchants would only compound the guilt, but he would do it if he didn't have any other choice.

So, what option did that leave? There really was only one for the moment, which was to wait and see what the Protectors had planned for him. If they simply chose to imprison him for a month or so, then he had absolutely no problem serving the sentence if they continued feeding him during the day and allowing him to rest. But if it was something more serious? That was entirely possible, as he didn't know whatever the law was in the Sealance Empire; he knew that violence against Ectorians and Protectors was punished severely, but he didn't know what exactly they were charging him with. Was it simply the deaths of the four men back by Lakebellow? Or did they consider him the prime suspect in the Underworld Society's destruction?

Regardless of what they were going to charge him with, he needed to prepare for the eventuality of breaking out from imprisonment if things went sideways. To do that, he needed Fusions; thankfully, he had materials at hand to help with that.

A few hours later, as Larek sat on his bed and finished yet another Fusion that was added to the growing pile underneath his bed sheet, there was finally a visitor to the cell block – and it wasn't someone bringing his next meal.

"Stand up. It's time," the Protector stated formally, his helmet covering his face. Behind him were another half-dozen Protectors crowded into the hallway, all standing at attention with their spears held straight up. A cursory glance at them indicated that none of the Protectors behind the one that spoke had undergone the change to become a Mage or a Martial, but the same couldn't be said about whom he assumed was the leader. *Definitely a Martial.*

"Time for what?" he asked, surreptitiously slipping the completed Fusions from under his bed sheet into his pocket. They would rattle around a little when he moved, but there wasn't any helping that; to lessen the number of them in his pocket, he kept a specific one palmed into his hand – just in case it was needed immediately. "You haven't even told me why you brought me here, and there's been no one to ask."

"Silence. Follow me. Try anything suspicious and we won't hesitate to kill you where you stand." The orders sounded very familiar, and Larek was reminded of his initial confrontation back in Enderflow with Protector Ashlynn – though in that case he was *technically* in the wrong because he had inadvertently injured an Ectorian. He was curious as to what they were going to accuse him of at this point.

Rather than argue, since it didn't seem as though this Protector was willing to explain anything, he simply walked out of the gate in the cell once they unlocked it, having to duck through the opening to fit, as it was made for shorter people. The Martial Protector led the way down the hallway with two of the other Protectors walking backward and pointing their spears at him, while the other four were behind him doing the same thing. It was a bit ineffective when they had to fit through the door, as it only allowed one person through at a time, but they managed it well enough by taking turns and ensuring he was guarded at all times.

Larek didn't really care what they did, because he was busy looking around the large room they emerged into that reminded him of the barracks back in Enderflow – though on a much grander scale. This one had stone columns throughout it supporting the roof, and there were a few desks in one corner, tables and chairs filling about a third of it on the opposite end, and what appeared to be a large training area in the center that was occupied by a few Protectors training – in more than just their spears. He saw the application of Stama in use with

Battle Arts as two Protectors dueled each other, both of them still wielding spears, though one of them was wearing a small buckler along one of their arms.

As Larek watched, the one not wearing the buckler suddenly jumped at least 10 feet into the air before descending upon his opponent, who blocked the blunt tip of the spear stabbing at him with his buckler. He was nearly knocked off his feet, and probably would've been if it hadn't been for a flare of Stama in his feet that let him shift them quickly to a more balanced position, and he counterattacked as soon as he was stable. The descending jumper was just straightening from where he landed in a crouch and barely deflected the attack with the frantic raising of the spear's haft, which meant he was unprepared when a Stama-powered Battle Art infused his opponent's foot again as he was kicked in the stomach. The man went flying out of the space allocated for the fight and the duel was called in favor of the buckler-wearing Protector.

*They've already figured it out? I wish it was that easy for me. Perhaps I can learn from—*

A not-so-gentle prod from behind shook him from his thoughts as he had slowed his walk to watch the fight. Larek hadn't activated his *Repelling Barrier* quite yet because he didn't want it known that he had it ahead of time, because if he needed to quickly escape, he figured it would be best kept as a surprise.

Thankfully, the spear to his back didn't do more than poke him as it couldn't cut through his clothing or break through his tough skin, but he got the message. Hurrying to catch up with the Protector leading the way to wherever Larek was supposed to be headed, he found that he was directed to a door along the back of the much larger room. After having experience with the inside of a Protector headquarters, he was fairly certain that this was an interrogation room of sorts.

He wasn't sure if that was a good sign or not.

Larek soon found himself in a chair across from three Protectors of some importance, if their age and bearing had anything to do with it. They had all recently undergone the change, as well, including one that was a Mage – which was more than a bit worrying. Mages could sense his Fusions, after all, and he had *a lot* on him.

The Mage, an older woman with just a touch of grey in her hair, looked at him intently, spotting the Fusions immediately, and he could tell that she was just about to say something when the man in the middle cut her off before she could begin.

"When they told me they caught an agent of the Underworld Society fleeing their little hidey-hole, I wasn't expecting someone from…

the Kingdom of Androthe? Is that where you're from? Are you simply an agent checking in on the branch here in Swiftwater, or are you here for something else?" The voice of the Martial Protector in charge was deep and powerful, almost as much as Larek's before he began to regulate it when he spent more time with people.

Those questions were certainly not what Larek had been expecting to be asked, and he stared at the man for a few seconds trying to comprehend what was going on.

"Not speaking, huh? Typical of your kind. I'm assuming that you have absolutely no idea what caused the collapse of the Sunwares Distribution Facility on Vardo Street? Or what caused half of Hardaway Park a few blocks away to sink into the ground? Or better yet, what caused a massive expulsion of earth to fly up from the ground and demolish half of the mayor's house a half-mile away?" The man pounded on the table in anger, nearly cracking the wood, before he continued. "You're lucky that there were no deaths from whatever this was, though there were plenty of injuries and *thousands* of golds' worth of property damage. If someone innocent had died because of this, then we'd be having a much different conversation."

*No one innocent died? That's a relief... but that also means that he doesn't care that the people in the Underworld Society were killed. Or does he even know? With everything collapsed on top of them, as well as there likely being very little trace of them left after experiencing the explosions point-blank, it's quite possible that he's ignorant of exactly what happened down there.*

"What can you tell us about what happened?" the man next to the Protector's leader asked, sitting forward with a friendly look on his face and in the tone of his voice. "We would really like to know some details, especially if we have to be worried about this happening again. It would certainly go a long way to reducing whatever punishment is in store for your involvement with the Underworld Society."

*Ah. I see. One of them is gruff and harsh, while the other is trying to be nice in order to draw out information – and to entice me with a reduced punishment if I share what I know instead of simply demanding it. Clever... but what is the other Protector here for?*

That's when his *Magical Detection* Skill perceived a hint of something surrounding him in a cloud, and he recognized it immediately as a truth-detecting spell. He'd only seen it a few times, but there was a feeling to it that was unmistakable. It appeared a bit unstable, as if it was ready to fall apart at a touch, but that was understandable if this woman was only a Mage for a bit more than a month.

*A new Mage and she already knows how to cast spells – and has access to a truth spell? How is that in any way fair?* He wished he had been able to see her cast it so that he could learn it, but she had obviously done it just before he arrived.

Fortunately, knowing that he had a truth spell around him, he could take advantage of that to prove his innocence. "I am in no way affiliated with the Underworld Society. In fact, I only learned about the Society the night before." There was little chance that he could get away with complete ignorance, given that he was found emerging from their hideout, but he could at least distance himself from them.

All of them appeared surprised at his answer, especially when the Mage nodded at his response. "Then what were you doing there? And do you know what happened?"

He only hesitated a moment before he answered. "I was looking for someplace to stay while I waited for the ferries to be built, because I need to get across the Swiftwater. All the Inns in the city were filled up, and I was *propositioned* by a nice lady who told me she had a place where I could stay. It was extremely expensive, at a full gold piece for the night, but I didn't really have any other choice other than staying outside of the city or sleeping on the street." He wouldn't have slept on the street, but that it was an option was at least the truth.

They just stared at him until he continued. "As for what happened, well, the women of the Underworld Society learned the hard way that they couldn't extort me and unfortunately paid the price."

There was complete silence in the room, before the man in charge barked, "What?"

Larek turned his attention toward the woman, who seemed to shrink back slightly at his gaze. "All that happened in their Sanctuary was entirely their fault, though I must take responsibility for being the ultimate cause of their destruction. I apologize that such a thing caused so much damage, but I'm glad to hear that no one else was killed." He winked at the Mage. "And that is the *truth*."

The spell around him fell apart a second later as the woman lost her concentration at his words. "But... how... what... where?" The unfortunate Mage Protector could barely get her words out.

"When and why?" he asked with a smile, completing her list of questions. "No idea. I was knocked out for a while so I couldn't tell you when, and I can only assume that greed was the reason why, but it could be something else." *Like my Dominion magic being used on Seandra.*

"So... you admit that you were the ultimate *source* of so much damage, but not the one who *caused* it?" the lead Protector asked, trying to regain control of the interrogation.

"In essence... yes. It was never my intention to harm anyone when I came here, as I was hoping to simply pass through."

"Then that means that you're at least partially liable for the damages – by your own admission. The mayor is breathing down my neck to find the ones responsible for this, and if what you say is true, then those *directly* responsible for it – or so you say – are dead. That means it falls upon you to pay for the damages."

Larek knew that this was absolutely ridiculous, as he technically hadn't been the one to actually create the explosions, and they only happened because the Underworld Society was trying to manipulate him... sort of what these people were likely trying to do as well. However, he didn't think it would be prudent to blast his way out at the moment, because he didn't feel any malicious intent from them. In addition, he did feel slightly responsible for what happened, though not nearly on the scale they seemed to indicate. *Regardless, they're trying to take advantage of me, exploiting my honesty like the Society was attempting to exploit my need to stay away from the Protectors.*

In the end, it all came down to whether or not he thought some sort of restitution was warranted; if the answer to that was that it really *wasn't*, ignoring it could cause some problems. He was fairly confident he could still escape and make a run for it if necessary, but that would just leave him in a rough position without any supplies. It was doable, of course, but he'd rather not have to worry about being chased anymore – which was something he needed to ask about at some point, since these Protectors hadn't mentioned that they were already looking for him.

That thought worried him: that they were simply keeping him there until someone from Lakebellow could identify him to the Protectors there; but for some reason, he didn't think this was the case. While he wasn't *the best* at reading people, he didn't see any signs of them knowing who he was or that he was already wanted by the Protectors from another town. *Was Seandra lying? Was that just a ploy to get me to capitulate to her demands?* He had no way of knowing without more information, but that wasn't something he was going to ask about at this point so as not to call attention to it.

Regardless, that only tangentially affected what was currently going on. Now he had to decide if he felt responsible enough for the damage that was caused by his exploding Fusions. His first instinct was to completely deny any responsibility that would cause him to be "punished" for it, because it wasn't technically him that caused it. Then again, none of it would've happened if it hadn't been for his Fusions, just like the explosion that occurred on the roof of Crystalview Academy. Overall, he felt just responsible enough to want to make up for his part in the damage in Swiftwater, though it really depended on what they asked from him.

Larek knew that they were trying to take advantage of him and the situation, but he also needed a place to stay while he waited for transportation over the Swiftwater river. Of course, if the tradeoff for not being chased around anymore was too much for him, he could always leave – with or without permission.

He finally responded with a shake of his head. "Depending on what you're asking, any type of payment for damages is going to be a bit hard, as all my things were buried with the remains of the Society – including all my money."

The Mage rushed back into the conversation before the lead Martial Protector could respond. "But there must be *something* you can contribute that might be of equal value." She pointed toward his shirt. "Such as what in the name of the Emperor is *that* in your clothes? Do you know how that was made? Can it be taught?"

*Ah… hmm. Maybe? Well, I **know** I can probably teach her, and others, how to make Fusions by this point, but do I want to risk my Dominion magic acting up again? That didn't work out so well the last time – as evidenced by the deaths of those in the Underworld Society. On the other hand, I don't have a lot of choice here; either I run, or I try and teach Fusions to people who just became Mages a little over a month ago.*

"Perhaps. If this is what it takes to make up for the damages I had a *very small* part in causing, let's talk about it."

# Chapter 27

"No, you have to make the Pattern Cohesion you're using for the formation more permanent than what you use for spell patterns, as it needs to fuse into the material you're using as a medium," he told the frustrated Mage for the tenth time. "Otherwise, it's going to simply fall apart like that every single time; you're fortunate that it hasn't permanently harmed you when it has fallen apart, but it's only a matter of time."

"Argh! How is it that the others learned so quickly, but this feels impossible to me?!"

Larek sighed, a headache forming that he attempted to massage away but couldn't physically touch it. He knew that he would have to stop soon or the use of his Dominion magic in his teaching would start to thoroughly drain his energy. Fortunately, he'd gotten across to the Mage Protector that had negotiated this form of "payment" to compensate for the damages his Fusions caused that he had to take frequent breaks and could only teach so long every day. After two weeks of teaching the new Mages of Swiftwater, only on a 1-on-1 basis to reduce the strain of any Dominion magic being used, he was beginning to recognize when he was starting to push himself too far.

"Unfortunately, as I've explained before, people have different abilities when it comes to their new status as Mages." Gesturing to the young man, he asked, "You said you're quite adept at casting your new spells?"

"Of course," the Mage, Jaundry, replied haughtily. "I was able to cast a spell faster than anyone else in Swiftwater, and I've already achieved Level 9 from all my Skill increases. Which is why this should be *simple*, because everything else was so easy."

The Combat Fusionist had to admit that gaining Level 9 in less than two months since the change happened was impressive, but it also helped to prove his point.

"That's exactly what I've been trying to tell you," Larek explained. "You're *really* proficient at casting spells, which is where your specialty lies. This doesn't mean that you're suited to making Fusions, though I'm sure with your abilities that you'll be able to pick it up at some point in the future, with enough practice and time."

"Or you're just *teaching* it wrong," the man accused, but Larek held up his hand for him to stop before he went any further.

"No, I'm teaching it just like I taught the others, and they picked it up fine." He pointed to himself. "You know what *I'm* really proficient in? Fusions, as you no doubt can see. You know what I'm absolutely horrible at? Casting spells. I would bet that you, even after just barely being able to put together a spell pattern, are better at casting a single spell than I will *ever* be. I'm envious that you're able to do something that seems so easy for you to accomplish, but for me is impossibly hard. Does that sound familiar?"

Jaundry was silent for a few seconds as he stared at Larek. "You really can't cast spells?"

"Not well or effectively. For me, they are essentially useless." *Except for blowing up Scissions, I guess. Still, all that I told him was technically true.*

"Hmph. Well. I suppose I can't be the best at *everything*," the haughty mage said, most of the frustration having leaked out of his tone. "I'll keep practicing what you taught me, though, because I feel like I'm close."

"You should definitely do that," Larek said as the other Mage rose to leave. "Back in the Kingdom, most Mages could make a few Basic Fusions, but very few are proficient enough to go further than that. The lack of proficiency doesn't make them any less, because they are much more proficient in other areas – just like those with specific Specializations are better at one thing or another. Being a Fusionist probably isn't where your path lies, but you can certainly learn to do a few of them eventually, if you put in the time to practice. Or, and this might be a better idea, concentrate on your spellcasting, as you don't seem the kind of person that wants to sit still for hours on end creating Fusions."

"Ha! You're right about that," the other Mage chuckled. "Even sitting here with you for an hour was almost too much for me. Thanks, Larek. See you around."

With that departing line, Jaundry left the small room where the two of them had been sitting on the floor on some comfortable pillows – just like he remembered back at Copperleaf Academy. It was a smaller room than the one where he learned about Intermediate and Advanced Fusions with Grandmaster Fusionist Shinpai, but it served just as well because it was private and quiet.

A minute or so after the other Mage left, Larek got up and left the room as well, hunger causing his stomach to grumble. Knowing that he had around 2 hours before his next "student" would come for instruction, he went to the Protector barracks' mess hall, where he picked up lunch and set into it with abandon.

Near the end of his meal, Mage Protector Zinnia sat down across from him. Larek looked up at the older woman, the same one with whom he had negotiated trading his teaching for payment for damages to Swiftwater.

"Larek. How are you?"

He shrugged. "Fine."

"That's good to hear." She sat there looking at him while he finished up, not saying anything else – which was strange in and of itself. While he hadn't gotten to know the Protectors very well, Zinnia was his primary contact with those located in Swiftwater, just like Ashlynn had been back in Enderflow. As a result, she had spoken to him at least a few times every day, and that wasn't even including the first day when he taught her how to make Fusions. Like Jaundry, she wasn't adept at creating the formations necessary to be a very effective Fusionist, though she did eventually catch on after a few days of practice.

Even that was astonishingly fast when compared to the efforts of the Mage students back in the Kingdom, who required months or years of practice and effort to produce their first Fusion, though it usually took less time after that to improve upon their work if they were suited to being a Fusionist. Zinnia would never be a Fusionist, but she wasn't too concerned about that; she was more of a big-picture kind of person, he quickly discovered, as she expanded his teaching of Fusions not only to herself and other Protectors, but *every* new Mage in Swiftwater.

Larek, of course, wouldn't be expected to teach each and every one of them, considering that there were a few hundred of them in the city. Instead, he was expected to teach around 5% to 10% of them, so that the knowledge was out there and could be disseminated to the rest of the population, as well as being distributed to other towns and cities. She didn't believe in hoarding this type of information like some would, and she felt it was better for the Empire if more people knew about it.

He was leaving that to her and the other Mages of the Empire, because as soon as transportation was available to get over the rushing river, he'd be gone with his "payment" already discharged by that point. Larek thought that the idea of spreading the knowledge was a good thing, however, because it could only benefit the people in their fight against the Apertures, so it made him feel proud, having a small hand in making that happen.

What was even more remarkable about the whole thing was that around half of the 20 Mages to whom he had taught Fusions had picked up the process extremely fast, while the rest – such as those like Mage Protector Zinnia – eventually understood enough to be able to make Basic Fusions like the majority of the Mages back in the Kingdom.

But with 9 of the 20 he'd taught picking it up so quickly, to the point where they were able to create a Basic Fusion within an hour, Larek wondered how much of that success was due to natural ability and how much was due to his Dominion magic.

That was because, for the first time, he could *feel* it at work when he began teaching someone Fusions. It was so subtle that if he hadn't been looking for it, he wouldn't have even noticed it; but when there was a noticeable discharge of energy from the area around his head, making him slightly weaker for a brief moment, he immediately knew what it was. Following that, the attention that his students paid to him seemed to intensify, and they picked up his instructions rapidly at that point with very few questions. Those things were the only pieces of evidence that anything was actually going on, but it was enough to let him know that it was working.

Not that he *intended* for it to work, as he still wanted nothing to do with Dominion magic, but he had no control over it. He couldn't activate or deactivate it like he would a Fusion; it just seemed to work on its own, though nearing the end of the two weeks, he was beginning to have an inkling of how he might affect it when it *did* work. It all boiled down to his subconscious desires bleeding into the magic, which dictated how it was applied to his target.

For his Fusion students, the only thing his subconscious was thinking about was the hope that they would pick up the process quickly so that he could move on to someone else – and that was it. He didn't want anything from them in return, no obedience or anything like that, so it was fairly simple, subtle, and straightforward. It was also what the students desired from him, so it wasn't noticeable to them, and therefore, they didn't rebel against it.

Thinking about his interaction with Seandra and the Underworld Society, he realized that he had probably been subconsciously thinking about wanting to know more information on the Society and what they did, to ensure he was indeed safe down there – which was how he got Seandra to spill most of what she knew. It was also certainly not what the Underworld Society leader wanted to reveal to him, so she rebelled against the subtle Dominion magic used against her, which was likely what drove her to do what she tried to do to Larek.

As for his other inadvertent uses of Dominion magic in the past, they all followed similar veins. The Professors to whom he attempted to teach the *Focused Division* Skill had the same desire for it, but he thought that there were just too many of them for it to be effective – as well as straining his body when he overused the magic. For Penelope and his other bodyguards assigned to him at Crystalview, Larek must have triggered some sort of need to be protected during the Skirmish, which translated to a desire in them to protect him from everything and everyone.

Then, of course, there were his friends: Verne, Norde, and Nedira. He could only assume that his Dominion magic latched onto his desire for friendship and to have at least one person not looking at him like a freak of nature. He believed that his magic could only safely affect what was already there inside of a person, which made him more confident that Nedira and the others really did care for him as a friend – and perhaps more than that, in the case of the beautiful Naturalist. If that inclination hadn't been there, then they probably would've had a reaction such as Seandra did, though perhaps not so *explosive*.

Overall, while this delay in returning to the Kingdom chafed at him, he couldn't deny that it was doing him some good. Traveling for a month through the Empire while paranoid about being found by Protectors had worn him down more than he cared to admit, and having the opportunity to rest and relax was beneficial to his mental well-being. More than that, learning about his Dominion magic, while he still hated it on general principle, helped him think about the future and how he might be able to control it better than he did right now – which was essentially having no control at all. At the least, he understood it better than ever, even if that understanding was left without any way to stop it from activating in the first place.

As Larek swallowed his last bite of lunch, he looked at Zinnia still sitting across the table, staring at him. "What is it? Can I help you with something? More questions about Fusions?" he finally asked.

The Mage Protector jerked as if he had startled her, even though she had been staring at him. After a few seconds, she seemed to collect herself enough to respond.

"Not... exactly. You've done a wonderful job teaching the people already, and I can tell that what you've done will be more valuable than any monetary remuneration that you might have provided – as much as the mayor would disagree," she chuckled for a few seconds, before a more serious look fell over her face.

*Uh, oh. Does this mean they heard something from the Protectors in Lakebellow?*

He'd surreptitiously asked Zinnia a short time ago about anyone else looking for him, and while she seemed surprised at the question, he could tell that the first time she heard about Larek was when he had been found after the Society's underground hideaway collapsed. He concluded at that point that Seandra had been lying about the

Protectors already looking for him, though that didn't mean that they never would be.

"No, it's something else." *Here it comes....* "We finally heard from Riverbend – on the opposite side of the Swiftwater – and finally learned what happened over there to the ferries." *Oh... what? Not what I was expecting.*

"What happened?" he asked, unsure if he wanted to hear the answer.

"It seems as though an Aperture no one had detected opened close to the route where the ferries were ported upriver from Riverbend to Blackferry, and they were ambushed by the monsters in the area. We had suspected that this was the case, as it would certainly explain why nothing ever came back over, but the problems only got worse from there.  When the group didn't arrive at Blackferry, a few groups of Mages and Martials were sent to investigate, only to find the site of the ambush with everyone dead – and the ferries were found to be heavily damaged but largely intact.

"That was when they, for some inexplicable reason, decided to send all of their Shipbuilders from both Blackferry and Riverbend to see if the ferries could be repaired and reused." She paused and shook her head. "Any guess as to what happened?"

"Please don't tell me that every single Shipbuilder was killed."

"Then I won't tell you that," she replied, a sad smile on her face. "Because one of them survived, but he ended up having his left leg and right arm bitten off by whatever monsters ambushed by the others, and he was only saved when the rest of his group managed to escape."

"And I'm assuming that a one-armed and one-legged Shipbuilder isn't so great at building ships."

"You would assume correctly.  They apparently have a single apprentice Shipbuilder with them that is whole, but she is comparatively slow and doesn't know everything.  That wouldn't matter too much if they had been able to recover the damaged ferries, but they were nearly demolished in the fight that killed or wounded the rest of the Shipbuilders."

Larek was quick to see where she was going with this. "So, what you're saying is that there likely won't be any ferries coming in the next few weeks?" Zinnia nodded. "How long do you think it will be, then?"

"From what I've learned, we have two Shipbuilders coming here to Swiftwater from Galestrom in the northwest, but they won't be here for another two months or so.  There's another one coming from the capital to Blackferry, but that will probably be about six weeks. *Then* they have to build a ferry, which could take another month. Best guess? At least ten more weeks before we see the first ferry able to make the route across, and that's assuming that the ones coming here can quickly finish the partly constructed one on the dock here."

*I probably could've traveled to the north and gone around the river by the time a ferry is likely to be back here up and running,* he thought morosely.

"If you're hoping that I'll stay here longer to teach more Mages about Fusions, we had an agreement that it would only be until the first ferry arrived or a month passed," he warned her, thinking that he saw where this was going. He had no intention of doing more than he promised, and he thought that if he left as soon as he was able, he might even be able to beat any new ferries arriving by going north and around the Swiftwater. *I might even take off early if I feel as though my obligation is satisfied.*

She held her hands up placatingly. "No, no, nothing like that. We stand by our agreement, and we have no intention of demanding or even asking you to stay beyond that," she assured him. "Instead, I have a different question for you."

Somewhat mollified by her statement but now wary of what she was about to ask, he prompted her to go on.

She hesitated for a few seconds before blurting out, "Are there any Fusions that you could create that might help us get across the Swiftwater?"

Surprised for the second time in only the last few minutes, Larek was taken aback at the unexpected question. He immediately wanted to respond with a "No," because if he could create something like that, then he wouldn't have been stuck there in Swiftwater in the first place. But when he thought about it for more than a few seconds, he decided that he might as well give it a try. If it didn't work, he could always leave when his time was up.

While he thought about it, Zinnia hurried on with even more. "We wouldn't have you do it for free or as part of the payment to the city for the previous damages, of course. If you can figure out how to get some sort of trade up and running again, you'll definitely be paid for it."

The Mage Protector seemed desperate for some reason. When he asked her about it, she explained, "Things are getting bad out there in the city. Civil unrest is on the rise, with the lack of trade across the Swiftwater leaving hundreds of those working for the Merchants without anything to do, and they are starting to blame the citizens of the city for the problem – who are already suffering from the lack of trade. When we add in the Apertures appearing, monsters roaming around, and the sudden destruction of different areas of the city from below, it's only a matter of time before something sets the disgruntled people in Swiftwater off in a way we might not be able to easily contain.

"While trade and the management of the docks isn't really our responsibility as Protectors, the well-being of the city certainly is. I can tell you that if something isn't done soon, there might not be much of a city left by the time the ferries are completed – if they're completed at all. With travel precarious between different portions of the Empire right now, who knows if the Shipbuilders will even make it here?

"Your aid isn't necessarily a last resort, as efforts are already underway to try and find a way across to restart trade, but they will take time and will undoubtedly be less effective without a Shipbuilder nearby. Therefore, I'm asking to see if you know of anything that might be of help – because we're becoming desperate here." The pleading in her voice was almost heartbreaking in its sincerity, but that wasn't what swayed him.

It was the thought of a challenge to his abilities with Fusions – and the thought of getting across the river much faster than anticipated.

# Chapter 28

"This is what we have to work with?" Larek asked, looking at what essentially appeared to be the skeleton of a partially built ferry. "Partially built" was a bit of a stretch, however, as it was essentially just the sad-looking frame of a boat sitting in the dry dock in Swiftwater.

"Yep, that's her," the thickly bearded Dock Foreman confirmed, waving toward the wood and iron frame.

"Her?" he asked.

"Absolutely; our ferries all tend to have a temperamental personality, and what could be more temperamental than a woman!" he responded, slapping his knee before he bent over in laughter. He stopped quickly when he caught the look Mage Protector Zinnia threw at him, and Larek simply ignored what was apparently a joke that he didn't quite understand.

"And there are no apprentice Shipbuilders here to continue the work?" the Combat Fusionist asked.

"Nope. Nor are there any within the city with the knowhow to complete construction of the ferry, as such Shipbuilder secrets aren't widely shared," the Foreman answered, his demeanor a bit more subdued under the harsh gaze of the Protector.

"Secrets? About how to build these ferries? Why would that be a secret?"

The man rubbed the back of his head as he considered Larek's questions. "Well, I don't rightly know *why*, but I do know that they do something to their ferries that allows them to travel the Swiftwater without breaking up, while also making them lighter for portage on the other side. What that is, though, I – nor anyone else in Swiftwater – don't rightly know." The Dock Foreman sniffed loudly before turning his head as if he was going to spit on the ground, but a look at the Protector made him swallow whatever he was going to expectorate.

"Uh, well, anyway, let me or anyone else on the dock know if we can help with anything, and we'll be sure to rush on over," the man continued, raising a cloth to wipe the sweat off his brow despite the cool morning. Without another word, he turned on his heel and took off, disappearing out of the large dry dock building within seconds.

Putting the Foreman from his mind, Larek looked again at the skeleton-like frame of the partially built ferry, comparing it to the very basic drawing he was provided of what it was generally supposed to look like when it was done. Only by squinting at it could he see that it was even the same boat, and it was quite a bit different from the ones he had ridden on in the Kingdom.

The first thing he noticed about the ferry was that it was a bit narrower than he expected: approximately 25 feet wide; the ferries in the Kingdom were at least twice the width, if not wider. This was balanced by the fact that it was *long*, somewhere around 100 feet long, as opposed to the Kingdom's almost square-shaped 60-foot-long ferries. The second thing he noticed about the one in the picture and the dry dock was that its keel was tapered to a sharp point, rather than being relatively flat-bottomed, compared to what he'd seen before, which didn't make a whole lot of sense to him considering that they had to portage it on the other side – and a flat-bottomed boat would likely be a whole lot better for that kind of thing.

There were a bunch of smaller differences that he could see, though what caught his attention was the steering oar along the back which was made out of what appeared to be iron. It wasn't present on the partially built frame, but it was remarked upon in the picture he was looking at, and he couldn't help but think that if it was completely made out of iron it would be *extremely* heavy. It was contained in a heavy-duty iron and wood frame along the rear of the boat, and he wondered if the entire ferry would tip over backwards from all the weight on it.

Then again, he wasn't a Shipbuilder, so what did he know?

Practically nothing, that's what. All he knew about ferries was limited to riding on a few of them back in the Kingdom, and other than a passing interest in what they looked like while he was on them, he'd had other things on his mind at the time which didn't allow him to dig deeper into how they worked. He did know that the ones he rode upon used guide ropes strung across the river and poles to propel them by pushing off from the riverbed, but that was about it. He could see some poles in the drawing, but they were shorter and looked more for pushing away from a dock rather than used to push off from the bottom of the river. Besides, he was told that the river was quite deep, which was another thing that made it dangerous in addition to its speed, so it probably wouldn't have worked anyway.

"There's no way I can figure out how the Shipbuilders constructed this thing and had it work, Zinnia." Looking at the drawing and the skeleton frame one more time, he shook his head. "I'm not a builder of any kind, though I do know my wood a little from my previous profession. That being said, this is completely different from what I know of ferries back in the Kingdom of Androthe, and I wouldn't even know where to start with this."

"You can't help?"

Rolling up the drawing, as it wasn't doing him any good, he responded. "I didn't say that. I said I can't finish this ferry the way it was designed, because I don't have the knowledge to do that. But that doesn't mean I can't do *anything*. I think I'm going to have to rework this whole thing by designing something simpler, perhaps a more flat-bottomed boat?" he mused.

"Uh, well, I can't say that I'm an expert on these things," the Protector said, gesturing to the wooden frame, "but I think the problem with flat-bottomed boats was that they are too hard to control in the Swiftwater, as they have a tendency to spin uncontrollably and even flip over completely. At least, that's what I've been told – but I'm not all that knowledgeable about it, either."

"That strong, huh?"

She nodded. "Oh, yes. Every year there are at least a few daring souls who think they've got it figured out and go out onto the water unprepared, never to be heard from again. That's the only reason I know as much as I do, though I'm sure there's a lot more that I don't know."

*Hmm.... This is harder than I thought.*

The more he looked at what he had to work with, and compared it to what he little he knew of navigating through the water (which was next to nothing), the more he began to think that this project was impossible. His Fusions couldn't put together a boat, after all, especially if he didn't understand how it worked; a simpler boat could probably be achieved with the help of some of the dock workers who had nothing to do, but it likely wouldn't get across the river in one piece – nor with everyone and everything still safe upon it.

That was when he started to think about *how* they would even get across in the first place without being swept downstream. The Kingdom's ferries only had to navigate much slower, shallower rivers, where using guide ropes and poling were easy enough. Here in the Empire, at least on the Swiftwater, they seemed to utilize a different keel shape and a rudder, which he assumed allowed it to cut across the river without capsizing or being uncontrollably swept downstream, though they still didn't go *straight* across – hence why there were two towns on the other side, and then they had to portage the ferries upriver in order to come back.

*Could I do something like that?* He knew at once that such a thing wasn't likely with his lack of knowledge and experience in such things, and that he wouldn't even know where to start. Even if he did, he could spend months trying to get something like that to work, even with the aid of Fusions, because it was so foreign to him that it almost hurt his head just thinking about it.

*What other ways could I use to get the boat across in one piece?*

Larek immediately thought about the types of Effects based on spells that he knew. The first one he considered was something like the *Water Stream* Fusion, which shot out a stream of water with incredible force, allowing it to cut through most softer materials like they were paper. Could that be used to propel a boat forward? No, that wouldn't work, because there was no opposing force on the area where the Fusion originated. For instance, when he added the *Water Stream* Fusion to a staff, it didn't push the staff with *any* of the force that shot out the stream of water; otherwise, it would've likely tried to rip itself from his hands whenever he used it.

The same went for Effects included in Fusions such as *Repelling Barrier*; the gusts of air that were formed might be powerful, but they didn't push back on anything with equal force.

*What about freezing a portion of the river with something like* **Frozen Zone** *and sliding across the ice?* That was a good thought, but he realized that the water was so fast-moving that the ice would simply be carried downstream even faster than a boat would be. In addition, freezing that much water in such a large area needed for the ferry would be difficult and extremely Mana-intensive; he could imagine making a Fusion that could do it, but it would work for all of 30 seconds before all of the ambient Mana was sucked out of the environment.

The same problem arose when he thought about somehow floating the entire boat on a cushion of air, created by forming a larger and slightly less forceful *Repelling Barrier* along its keel, but having the gusts blowing up into the boat instead of down into the water. He *thought* it might work to lift the ferry, but it would also require so much Mana as to make it impossible to use for more than a minute or so before the ambient Mana was drained away.

*But what if I made it smaller? Such as one that would fit just... me?*

As he considered how he would put something like that together, he became more and more excited over the prospect of creating some sort of personal flying contraption that would allow him to hover straight over the river without any problems at all. There were some problems he needed to solve, such as propulsion, balance, and steering, but he thought that it might eventually be possible.

He mentally shelved the idea after a minute or so of thinking about it, because he had something else he needed to do first. While getting to the opposite side of the river was his ultimate goal, he needed something from the people of Swiftwater just as they needed him. He wouldn't get far without supplies, and to get those supplies, he needed to earn them. *Besides, by doing this, I might be able to figure out the problems with my personal flying craft along the way.*

Turning his attention back to the prospective ferry, Larek was drawing a blank on what else he could do. That was until he remembered the river near Rushwood and how they pushed their finished logs into the water, where they floated downstream to the sawmill. It wasn't how they floated or even the process of directing the logs into the mill, however; instead, it was how the sawmill operated through the use of a water wheel to rotate the saw they used for cutting and shaping the logs they processed for use elsewhere. He remembered seeing it, the time he had visited with his father, amazed at how something as simple as a wheel using the power of water flowing through it could do something like that.

Larek, of course, had absolutely no knowledge of the inner workings of such a process, and while he thought about somehow harnessing the power of the rushing Swiftwater to power some sort of internal propulsion system, he scrapped that idea quickly. Instead, he wanted to use the water wheel itself for propulsion, sort of like when he was swimming and using his hands to pull himself along the water.

How would it be powered? Fusions, of course. More specifically, a strong *Repelling Gust of Air* Fusion that would push downward on the wheel, which would then in turn propel the ferry forward. Simple enough – or so he thought.

With the help of Zinnia, along with some paper and a stick of charcoal she brought with her, he began to sketch out his idea. His first inclination was to put one waterwheel on each side of the ferry, which was sized to be more aligned to the dimensions he knew about from the Kingdom, but he quickly disregarded that idea as he thought that the whole thing would be just too wide at that point, as the wheels would have to be large in order to move through the water easily.

That was when he considered moving it to the back of the ferry, which seemed to flow much better, as it would be *pushing* it from the back rather than essentially *pulling* it from the sides. Then came the problem with steering, as he had no idea how you were supposed to steer something so large without the large rudder he saw on the drawing of the normal ferries. The trick to the rudder system was beyond his comprehension, especially as it had to be easily moved through what were likely to be extremely strong forces of swiftly flowing water pushing against it, and while Larek thought that *he* would be strong enough to control it, he wasn't sure if anyone else could.

Therefore, he thought about his previous plan to have a wheel on either side of the ferry for steering – and he suddenly had an inspiration that made those side wheels obsolete. He had been thinking of the water wheel as a relatively thin wheel on the backside providing propulsion, but what if he made it much wider, such as nearly half the size of the ferry's width – and then put two of them side-by-side, so that if the boat wanted to turn, only one of the wheels would have to be activated?

Then came the wheel itself, as the more he thought about the water wheel from the sawmill, the more he realized that it was designed to catch the water rushing through it rather than pushing against it. Redesigning it was a matter of thinking about how he swam through the water; when he had the fingers in his hands pushed up against each other, he created much more surface area to push against the water than if he had his fingers spread apart. Cupping his hands also helped, as it allowed him to really dig into the water and push himself forward, though it was more the surface area that counted, especially when he added his arms into the process.

As a result, Larek changed his original plan for a relatively closed water wheel with smaller pockets designed to catch the water to one with larger sheets of wood that would *dig* into the water with a lot more surface area. These long sheets of wood would be arranged like the spokes of a wagon wheel, allowing the greatest amount of water to be pushed away, sending the boat forward.

"That's like nothing I've ever seen before," Zinnia remarked as she looked over his shoulder at the drawing when he was finished – or as finished as he could be without going into the smaller details. "How is that even supposed to work?"

Cleaning his charcoal-stained fingers on a rag he found inside the dry dock, Larek shrugged. "I'm not rightly sure yet, but if I can get the Fusions for them right, I'm sure we'll figure it out. Do you think we can have the dock workers start on construction of the body of this ferry? It's relatively straightforward, or at least I hope it is."

"Sure, I'll talk to the Dock Foreman in just a moment. Do you want to talk to a Cartwright about this... wheel?"

"Cartwright? Oh, like the ones that make wagon wheels?"

"Yes, precisely. I don't think the dock workers would be suited to something as intricate as that, as it seems important."

Larek nodded, knowing that it was probably the most important part of the boat, other than the Fusions he was going to add. "I can do that. Is the city covering the materials and labor for all of this?" he asked.

"They are – or at least they will once I talk to the mayor," she admitted. "I hadn't broached the subject with anyone yet, as I wasn't sure if you would even be able to do anything, but if you think this will work...?"

"It should – or at least I'll figure out something that does. I have a good feeling about this plan, though."

"Good enough for me; it's better than anything that anyone has thought of so far, so we might as well take our chances."

It wasn't exactly a shining vote of confidence, but then again, Larek wasn't altogether confident in his idea, either. Before he did anything else, he supposed that he should make a smaller model of what he had planned, just to ensure that his Fusion ideas were solid before beginning on the larger one.

With that in mind, he broke off from Zinnia and went looking for this Cartwright she mentioned earlier.

# Chapter 29

Larek placed the relatively tiny model ferry boat into the water at the docks, and he winced when the swift-flowing water caused the wooden construction to beat itself against the stone of the dock. Fortunately, the *Strengthen* Fusion that covered the entire model was strong and effective enough to prevent it from breaking apart into dozens of pieces.

Not that it was a whole lot to look at, as it was basically a watertight box of wood with an upward-angled front end and a set of two simple wooden wheels, which had slats like paddles on them that were connected to a few pieces of wood which acted as a frame to hold them. The wheels were attached to the frame and a central axle – which was essentially a wooden dowel – running through the middle of each paddle wheel. The two wheels were separated by a simple piece of string wound around the axle in the middle, and the axle itself was greased up with the same grease they used on cart axles and wheels. All in all, it was approximately 2 feet long and about a foot and a half wide, but it was exactly what he needed to test his idea.

On the upper portion of the back side of the box were two slightly different Fusions on the wood itself, each placed so that they would target one or the other paddle wheels they were in front of. It was these Fusions that would determine whether this idea was viable or not.

*New Fusion learned!*
**Left Gust of Air +4**
*Activation Method(s): Activatable*
*Effect: Forcefully pushes away nearby targets with a strong, continuous directional gust of air*
*Effect(s): Using non-invasive mental manipulation, activates or deactivates Activatable Activation Method upon detection of mental phrasing by individual in proximity*
*Input(s): Mental phrasing*
*Variable(s): Mental phrasing of "Left one", "Left two", "Left three", "Left four", or "Left stop"*
*Variable(s): Directional orientation*
*Magnitude(s): 100%-400% of base gust strength, mental detection up to 40 feet*
*Mana Cost: 19,000*
*Pattern Cohesion: 200*

Fusion Time: 21 hours

New Fusion learned!
**Right Gust of Air +4**
Activation Method(s): Activatable
Effect: Forcefully pushes away nearby targets with a strong, continuous directional gust of air
Effect(s): Using non-invasive mental manipulation, activates or deactivates Activatable Activation Method upon detection of mental phrasing by individual in proximity
Input(s): Mental phrasing
Variable(s): Mental phrasing of "Right one", "Right two", "Right three", "Right four", or "Right stop"
Variable(s): Directional orientation
Magnitude(s): 100%-400% of base gust strength, mental detection up to 40 feet
Mana Cost: 19,000
Pattern Cohesion: 200
Fusion Time: 21 hours

  The two different Fusions were necessary because he found that if he only had the one, it was impossible to have a mental component to activate them because they would both hear the command at the same time – meaning that it was impossible to activate one and not the other, so turning was out of the question. It wasn't that big of a deal, at least, because all it really required was a different mental phrasing from "Left" to "Right", which was easy enough to accomplish.
  He also added the ability to change the Magnitude of the air blowing onto the paddles, as it wouldn't always be necessary to move at a single speed; he could only imagine the disaster that would come from one of these ferries trying to dock when it was moving at full speed.
  Thinking about that, Larek smacked himself in the forehead because he just realized he didn't include any way for the boat to reverse. *I'll add that on to the final boat if this proves to work here.* He thought it would be easy enough to add on to the existing Fusions with a "Reverse left one" command linked to a separate directional orientation Variable, so that it would switch from aiming down to aiming straight ahead, which would cause the wheel to rotate the opposite way. *Phew! There's a lot more to consider about these things than I expected.*

Thankfully, he'd been able to get this basic model of his proposed ferry the same day he had come up with the idea, especially after talking to the Cartwright – who seemed eager for work after trade in the city essentially dried up with nothing coming in or going out. The cart maker was more than eager to try his hand at something unique, especially as it potentially had the ability to restart the trade system, and he got to work on the model for as much his own sake as for Larek's. After seeing it on a smaller scale, Carven the Cartwright was able to extrapolate what was needed for the larger scale – though he had some concerns.

"Based on what you seem to need, I don't think it will hold up too well under what you propose," the Cartwright informed him while working on the model. "The stresses to the wood from turning through the water will rip it and the framing apart without something like iron or steel braces and connections."

"That was also a concern of mine, considering how much iron seemed to be involved in the previous ferries," Larek admitted. "I think that my Fusions will be able to strengthen the wood to the point where it will be just as strong as iron or steel."

He wouldn't necessarily be able to *Strengthen* the entire ferry when it was done, as that would likely absorb too much ambient Mana from the environment on a constant basis, but Larek thought that the entire wheel system was more than doable.

"Suit yourself. Don't blame me if it cracks and splinters within minutes, however."

"I won't. And thank you for your help."

Carven chuckled. "If it gets things moving around here, I'm happy to help – for a price, of course."

"Of course. Mage Protector Zinnia mentioned that she would be handling that, so I'll have her talk to you."

"Fine with me. I'm not going to charge for this model, as it's kind of fun to see if I can even make something like this and it doesn't require too many materials. The larger ones, however, are going to cost you."

Now it was time to see if the cost would be worth it or not. As he watched the model bob in the water and bang against the dock, he started to think about the mental commands he needed before he was interrupted.

"Is it working? Or is it broken?" Zinnia asked from her vantage point near him.

"I haven't started it yet, but that's what I'm working on now."

Without further ado, Larek thought "Left one," and "Right one," in rapid succession – and the paddle wheels immediately started to turn as he saw the ambient Mana being absorbed by each Fusion. It was barely a trickle, as the Magnitude being utilized was only at 1, but it was more than enough to start the model moving through the water.

"It's working! It's quite slow, though," the Protector said, bending down to watch it better.

She had a point, as it was just barely moving upstream due to the speed of the water flowing against it. If it were any slower, it wouldn't be going anywhere. Larek mentally ordered the air to increase to Magnitude 2 with "Left two," and "Right two," and he finally saw it begin to move forward with a bit more speed. It was still only at a casual walking speed, but it was enough to show progress.

"That's a little more like it," Zinnia began to say, but cut off when Larek increased the Magnitude of both paddles to 3 – and it took off at what was a good running speed for most people.

"That's... impressive, to say the least. I never thought anything could fight past the current of the Swiftwater like that, but I guess I was wrong."

Larek acknowledged her statement with a nod, but his concentration was on the model boat. Before it got out of range of his mental commands, which was currently set to a 40-foot radius from the model due to the strength of the highest Magnitude, he tested its turning by reducing the right paddle wheel down to Magnitude 1 while the other was still at 3. It wasn't an abrupt right turn, but it was still fast enough that he struggled with his mental commands as it turned and then headed straight back toward him with incredible speed which was aided by the current. He ordered both wheels to stop before the model would have smashed itself into the stone dock, and he was just barely able to have the left wheel turn on again for long enough to rotate it so it was facing back upstream. He turned it off again once it was facing the right direction, letting it bump against the dock, before mentally commanding both wheels to start at Magnitude 4.

There was an immediate *crack* that resounded over the water as the wheels began to spin at a blur, but before he could see what happened, the model practically jumped out of the water at an angle, before splashing down at an angle, with its front portion underwater. The wheels, which appeared damaged somehow but were moving too fast for him to see what exactly was broken, were submerged in the process, pushing the boat forward into the water, where it immediately disappeared as it dove straight down due to the angle of its entry.

Shocked at what just occurred, Larek reacted too late, and the model was out of range of his mental commands in no more than a few seconds; he could still feel it down below in the river, growing further and further away, before it disappeared completely. A few seconds later, there was an abrupt upwelling of water from a point about 150 feet away – outside of the dock, thankfully – the result of an explosion as the Fusions on the wooden model were destroyed.

"What was *that*?" Zinnia asked, her eyes wide as she watched the water that had shot up fall back into the river.

"I guess I overdid it there," Larek said, slightly perturbed. "Note to self: Start slow before ramping up the speed." Turning to Zinnia, he answered her question. "The model likely slammed into the bottom of the riverbed at full speed, which broke it apart despite my *Strengthen* Fusion – which wasn't too strong, as I didn't want to steal away the area of ambience the other Fusions required. When the Mana was released, the result was the explosion underwater you saw."

"Was that... what happened underground with the Underworld Society?"

He nodded. "But the Fusions they broke were much more powerful."

"I see." She paused for a moment. "But we shouldn't have to worry about them exploding on the ferry, should we?"

Shaking his head, he said, "No. I'll make sure the areas around the Fusions are much stronger, so there shouldn't be any problems. It would require the full-scale destruction of the entire boat to cause them to fail, so I wouldn't worry about it."

As he left the docks, happy to see that his idea certainly had merit, he couldn't help but think about when it was scaled up to match what was being built. Would it require too much ambient Mana to maintain the constant gusts of air? Would the frame or wheels crack and break if too much strain was put on them, like what Carven the Cartwright suggested? Would he have to worry about the full-scale version dipping underneath the water and diving straight down?

Those were some of the questions he needed to answer before he tested the larger version, because he couldn't afford to have it crash into the riverbed and break apart like his model. Especially since he'd likely be on board at the time.

Fortunately, over the next few days, as dozens of dock workers arrived at the dry dock to participate in the construction of the very first Fusion-powered paddle boat on the Swiftwater river, he was able to determine the answers to a few of those questions. The first was whether or not using the gusts of air would absorb too much ambient

Mana, and that was as easy as creating a Magnitude 10 version of his new Fusions (with a reverse directional Variation added to it) and testing it out. He actually got his answer faster than it took to create the *+10* version of the Fusion, as it required nearly a *million* Mana to fill it up initially.

What he discovered was that the limit that the Fusion could maintain without actively draining the ambient Mana was a Magnitude 9 gust of air. Considering that he would need a pair of Fusions on the boat, and each of them would be in relatively close proximity, the limit would be around Magnitude 7 for each of them. It would only be possible to maintain that kind of output if the ferry was in motion, moving to areas of greater Mana density; otherwise, even at Magnitude 7, the ambient Mana would drain too quickly.

He also considered that he'd have some *Strengthen* Fusions on the wood of the ferry to prevent it from breaking apart and to handle the strain, but he thought that Magnitude 7 for the air gusts was still appropriate. He had a feeling that the Fusions at that Magnitude would be more than enough to turn the paddle wheels, though just how fast that would be when in the water and with such a large ferry – and loaded with people and goods – was something that would have to be tested later.

The same went for testing the frame of the new ferry and the paddle wheels when used at such a Magnitude, but he was already planning on a Magnitude 12 *Strengthen* Fusion to encompass all of the moving and structurally thinner parts of the design.

Lastly, he questioned whether the front of the boat would at any time dive under the water, and those he talked to who lived and operated around the river said that it was a distinct possibility, especially if the weight of the cargo on board wasn't distributed correctly. To counteract this, he planned on putting a few Reactive *Repelling Gust of Air* Fusions near the front of the ferry, which were essentially inverted forms of the one he'd put on the staves back at Copperleaf when confronting Ricardo, as they targeted the underside of the boat rather than the water. This would essentially push the boat back up at the expense of more ambient Mana, but it would at least prevent the boat from sinking below the waterline.

While thinking about that, he considered if he could've done that from the beginning instead of the entire paddle wheel contraption, by pushing the boat from behind, but he realized that the number of Fusions necessary to propel it through the water would be prohibitive considering the available ambient Mana. In other words, it wouldn't work for long, and he wasn't even sure it would work at all.

But it did give him a little more insight into what might work for his other, more personal, project he had imagined earlier. Unfortunately, he didn't get a chance to dig into that any more over the next few days as he was busy with the construction of the ferry, but once he could step away for a moment or two, he was planning on devoting his full attention to it.

# Chapter 30

It was amazing what could get done when people were motivated to do something, a fact that was obvious when the large 50-foot-wide by 70-foot-long ferry came together in a total of 3 days. The dock workers weren't exactly the most knowledgeable about shipbuilding, though with a little help from Carven the Cartwright, they quickly learned a few tips about how to ensure the entire frame was strong enough to handle the river and the weight it would bear on top of its structure. He also helped to ensure the huge empty portion of the keel was kept watertight to act as additional floatation and elevation for the large, mostly flat section above that held everything secure.

It wasn't pretty, and Larek was fairly certain that there was more to shipbuilding than they had applied during the process, but they had also erred on the side of caution by ensuring that everything was as strong as possible. When they dismantled the existing framing that had been in the dry dock, they essentially incorporated what they saw into the new design, regardless of their knowledge, but it at least *looked* like a boat that would float.

What took the most time was finishing up the paddle wheels and installing them into the rear of the ferry, which required Larek and a few Martial Protectors that had volunteered to help; it was only their combined strength that allowed them to get all the separate pieces into position. Despite only being wood, the wheels were *heavy*.

After those pieces had been installed, the rest of the dock workers completed the finishing touches on top of the ferry – which they knew well enough to complete without his input. Having experience working around ferries for a living, they knew exactly what was needed to ensure the safety of the people – and the goods – that were going to be transported, so he left them to it.

While they worked on that, Larek started the process on the Fusions he would need. In his little free time in between sessions of helping with the boat, he had already created the *Left* and *Right Gust of Air* Fusions with a Magnitude of 7 and an additional Variable with the ability to reverse the direction of the paddle wheels, so he worked on installing them onto the boat itself. On the back of the ferry's body, Larek carved a thin section of the wood off the planks nailed into place, before slotting in the square of wood he had used as material for the *Air Fusions*. With a few gentle taps of his axe head on nails he placed on the corner of the wooden square, it was affixed into place and nearly flush with the rest of the body. He did the same with the other wooden square with the other Fusion, centering it near the other paddle wheel, and he was done.

At that point, it was time to make the large *Strengthen* Fusion that would strengthen the wood and iron used primarily in the rear portion of the ferry. Instead of individual Fusions for each part, which would've taken entirely too long considering how many parts were involved in the paddle wheels alone, he opted to do it all at once. With the way his combined material-based bonuses worked, he could strengthen them all without any issues, as long as they were connected in some way.

The volume of material involved in the Fusion didn't really affect the Magnitude placed into the formation; instead, it affected the required Pattern Cohesion and the Mana Cost – the latter more than the former. To cover something the size of what he planned, he estimated that he was going to need approximately 360,000 Mana and 1,300 Pattern Cohesion for a Magnitude 12 Fusion; he remembered that the table he added that same Magnitude Fusion to back in Copperleaf, when proving his ability with Fusions to the Vice General there, cost him around 120,000 Mana and 950 Pattern Cohesion, so it was a considerable increase but not a crazy amount. If the Fusion had been more complicated, rather than it being a Basic Fusion, it probably would've cost a lot more.

As he sat down on the deck of the ferry where he was going to place the *Strengthen +12* Fusion, he began to construct the formation and sink into his hyper-focused state where he would begin to pump in Mana, but laughter coming from the dock workers behind him broke his concentration. Looking back at them, he could see that they weren't laughing at him or even at anything on the ferry, but were laughing at each other due to some antics of one kind or another that they were engaged in. Despite the fact that they were working hard to finish up the details on the deck, they were clearly happy to be doing *something*; more than that, they were working toward reestablishing the route for their profession, so their mirth and joviality was understandable.

It didn't really help Larek, however, as their movement over the deck was also causing it to shift minutely in the dry dock, eliciting creaks from the newly installed wood to echo through the building. All of that, combined with their voices and sporadic laughter, was distracting, and while he thought he could probably work through it, he had another thought. Well, two thoughts, actually, but he didn't think that asking them to leave while he created the Fusions was a good use of their time.

Instead, he took a mental step back and considered the *Strengthen* Fusion from a different angle. Larek had always placed it on the material he wanted the Effect to improve, which was how it was taught in the Academy and in the books he had read. It also made sense, in a way, because that particular Fusion was related to the material itself, such as a *Strengthen Wood* or *Strengthen Iron* Fusion; with the changes to his application of materials, he was aware that he didn't have to designate the material specifically in the Fusion. He still placed it on the material he was working with and designated what he wanted it to affect, however, even if it was able to strengthen more than one material at a time now. In the case of the *Strengthen* Fusion he was about to place on the deck of the ferry, he would have to include everything he wanted it to strengthen into the Effect component, mentally shoving each individual item into the list of connected things it would affect.

But with his recent exploration into larger area-of-effect Fusions, such as *Frozen Zone* and *Secure Hideaway*, he hadn't really considered whether he could do something like that with the *Strengthen* Fusion. Now that he had a chance to think about it, he realized that it could certainly be done, though he would have to convert it to at least an Intermediate Fusion in order for it to work. But by doing that, would it then become too expensive in terms of Mana Cost and Pattern Cohesion?

There was only one way to find out – but he was going to take it a bit more cautiously than he normally would, especially if he was planning on it eventually being a Magnitude 12 Fusion. Starting with Magnitude 1, he grabbed a loose chunk of wood that had been tossed on the deck at some point during construction and placed it in front of him. Even with the distractions going on behind him, he was easily able to put together a new formation incorporating the *Strengthen* Effect as well as Inputs and Variables related to distance and material composition. It only took a minute or so to make a Magnitude 1 version of his new Fusion idea, and before he knew it, he was holding his effort in his hand.

*New Fusion learned!*
**Strengthen Area +1**
Activation Method: Permanent
Effect: Strengthens designated materials within a designated space
Input(s): Distance detection
Input(s): Material detection
Variable(s): Wood material composition detected

*Variable(s): Iron material composition detected*
*Magnitude(s): 100% increased durability, 10-foot designated diameter range*
*Mana Cost: 60*
*Pattern Cohesion: 3*
*Fusion Time: 28 minutes*

*It worked!*

Or at least he thought it did. Larek could visually see the Effect when he focused on it, and any wood or iron within 10 feet of the piece of wood with the Fusion on it was strengthened. The only way he was able to slightly tell was by taking his axe and making a tiny mark in the decking both in and out of range of the Fusion, and there was a slight difference in how much pressure he had to use to cut through the wood. It was barely noticeable given how sharp his axe's edge was, but since he was looking for it, the difference was clear as day.

Looking at his unlocked Fusion, he did some mental calculations on how much it had changed from something as simple as *Strengthen Wood +1*. The Mana Cost had increased from 15 to 60, the Pattern Cohesion was up to 3 from 1, and the Fusion Time had nearly tripled from 10 to 28. It was definitely more expensive in terms of resources, but he had expected that since this was an Intermediate Fusion now. What he wasn't sure of was if it was worth it over the Basic *Strengthen* Fusion.

When he heard laughter again behind him, he knew that it was more than worth it; there were multiple reasons why, but the one that was most important to him was that the new *Strengthen Area* Fusion would allow him to create the Fusion in peace and quiet and then move it to the ferry when it was finished, installing it just as he had the *Right* and *Left Gusts of Air*.

The only worry was that it would end up being too much of a drain on the ambient Mana along with the propulsion system with the paddles. He frowned when he realized that it probably would be, which meant that he wouldn't be able to use a Magnitude 12 version of *Strengthen Area* like he wanted with the original Fusion; he thought that he *might* be able to get away with a Magnitude 11, but – to be safe – he would settle for a Magnitude 10. That was still quite strong, and with the iron also being strengthened to hold it all together, he hoped it would be enough; the only way he would know was to test it out.

Larek retreated to an office located next to the dry dock where he was able to close the door and block out most of the distractions, which was exactly what he needed to get the new Magnitude 10

*Strengthen Area* Fusion completed. It required a base Mana Cost of 150,000 Mana and 1,725 Pattern Cohesion, which was reduced by his Specialization bonuses, meaning that it took him less than an hour to finish. Once it was done, he brought it back out to the nearly finished ferry boat, installed it right in the center of the deck, and smiled when he saw that the new Magnitude 10 version of the Fusion covered a 100-foot diameter range – which encompassed the entire vessel. Thankfully, the dock workers seemed to have finished installing the rest of the stuff necessary on the deck, because otherwise it would've been difficult for them to manipulate the wood of the deck in any way.

The difference in strength of the wood that comprised the majority of the boat was like night and day compared to how it was before, and when he went to install the forward *Repelling Gusts of Air +10* Reactive Fusions that would help prevent the ferry from submerging, he had difficulty carving into the hull even with his extremely sharp axe. With some effort, he was able to do it, but he nearly had to remove the *Strengthen Area* Fusion to finish it off.

And with those last ones installed on the new ferry, it was done. Being only midday by that point, all the dock workers and the Cartwright that had worked on the project were there, along with a group of Protectors led by the Mage Zinnia.

"Is that it?" she asked, her face both pleased and skeptical at the same time.

Honestly, he couldn't blame her for feeling that way, because the whole thing wasn't pretty, but if it functioned like it was supposed to, then it really didn't matter.

"Yes, that should be it," he acknowledged. A thought hit him a second later. "How… how do we get it into the water?" Considering that the ferry was basically suspended above the floor of the drydock using large stone pillars as anchor points, he wasn't sure what to do from there.

"That's something we know about, at least," the Dock Foreman strode up to him with a pleased look on his face. "We've helped to move every single ferry off of the dry dock and out to the water for the last few hundred years, so it's something we can do. Of course, none of them looked like this, especially with those wheel-thingies on the back. How strong are those parts back there? We don't want to break anything this close to launching it into the river."

When the Foreman described their normal method of moving new ferries into the water, Larek was worried for a moment, but trusted that his *Strengthen Area* Fusion would still be strong enough.

"It should be fine, but take it slow."

Less than an hour later, they were all ready to go. With a powerful heave of the wooden poles that had been slid underneath the large boat, over 200 men – and a few women – lifted the boat off the stone pillars and struggled to move it forward. It only rose a foot or so, but that was enough to completely separate the ferry from the pillars, and it was therefore straightforward enough to shift it toward the large opening in the building. They were coordinated enough that they were able to set it down a few times as they moved it forward to give themselves a break, until the boat was barely teetering on the edge of the pillars, ready to fall downward.

That was what they were waiting for, it turned out, as the outside of the drydock was a ramp lined with large, smoothly trimmed logs held in place by more volunteers. With a last heave, the ones doing the lifting of the boat pushed it over and down onto the ramp, where it hit the first of the logs with a thump and then kept going. Using the logs as a sort of rolling conveyor, it quickly picked up speed as it headed for the swiftly flowing river, which was enclosed in a special dock that was more than capable of keeping it in place once it was freely floating.

Larek winced slightly as the back end of the boat, which held the paddle wheels, scraped along the ground since it was a designed to be a bit low so as to get maximum depth into the water, but not only did the wood not chip or splinter, it didn't even seem to be affected by the impact. Before too long, the wheels spun as they were dragged along the ground, helping to move it faster, and there didn't seem to be any issues with it being damaged.

Before he knew it, the boat hit the water with a splash, punctuated by the Fusions on the front – designed to prevent it from submerging – lifting the front of the ferry up, causing even more pressure upon the back end, but everything still seemed fine. As it entered and was taken by the rushing water, it moved about 20 feet downstream to bump into the stone dock there, bouncing a few times before it settled.

"Well, it didn't sink, at least," Zinnia said with a small smile.

Larek was about to head to the dock and jump on the newly launched ferry, but he hesitated as he looked around. "I was going to test it out by myself, but I thought I'd ask if you or any of the dock workers wanted to come along. It *should* be safe enough, but I also can't guarantee that."

The Mage Protector looked extremely hesitant, but she eventually nodded. "I'd like to come along."

She wasn't the only one, as every single dock worker *and* the Cartwright wanted to come along, and he wasn't going to deny them the opportunity as long as they knew the risks. It seemed no one cared about that as they climbed aboard, wanting to be "part of history" – or so he heard several times stated by a few of the dock workers.

Once everyone was on board, some of them were *entirely* too close to the edge of the ferry for Larek's liking, but at least they held onto the posts and ropes set up around the perimeter for safety. Larek spoke up and cautioned them one more time. "Last chance to depart before tests are underway! Again, this is untested, and I'm unsure of how this will work, so this is your last warning!"

No one moved, though they did start to look impatient by that point.

Chuckling at their enthusiasm, but feeling a bit of it himself, Larek took his position near the back of the ferry boat, where there was something akin to a podium he could stand behind and hold onto while the vessel was in motion. With a deep breath, Larek mentally commanded the *Gust* Fusions to start at Magnitude 1, which was the lowest speed the Fusion was capable of. It went all the way up to Magnitude 7, which was greater than the one he used on his test model, but it was necessary for something of this size.

Sensing and even feeling the Fusions activate, there was no movement in the wheels. Looking closer at them, he could see the magical energy working as it should, but it just wasn't enough to start the process. Upping both wheels to Magnitude 2, he saw them finally begin to turn, though they were very slow. The right side of the boat scraped against the stone dock as the entire boat traveled about a foot in the first few seconds, so Larek quickly adjusted the Magnitudes of the wheels so that the right one started moving at Magnitude 3 while the left was at Magnitude 1. With the wheels already in motion, even the Mag 1 wheel was able to keep turning – albeit very slowly – while the right one sped up considerably.

It wasn't quite enough to get them to turn out of the current pushing them against the dock, so he increased the Magnitude of the right wheel again, bringing it to 4 – and that was when he finally saw some progress, even if it was a slow turn. Upping both wheels another Magnitude, now at 2 for the left and 5 for the right, the ferry finally moved enough away from the dock that they weren't even touching it anymore. There was a resounding cheer from the passengers, and Larek smiled as he aimed the head of the boat toward the opening of the dock area, which led to the open river.

It took some practice coordinating when to stop or slow the wheels so that he didn't overshoot his turn, but Larek eventually got his heading correct and activated both wheels to stay steady at Magnitude

5. Even at that speed, it took approximately 2 minutes for the boat to reach the open river, moving slowly – but it was also succeeding at fighting against the current without being pushed downstream.

The sound of the rushing air along with the slap of the paddles hitting the water was quite loud, but no one seemed to care. With the smile now wide on his face, Larek bumped both wheels up to Magnitude 6, paying special attention to the wheels to see if there was any strain from being blasted with such a powerful gust of air, but they didn't seem to be affected by it. As for the speed of the ferry boat, the difference between Mag 5 and Mag 6 was noticeable, as they really began to move; if he had to judge, he would say that its speed at least tripled, if not more than that.

He could see the pleased looks on the faces of the passengers, including the nervous Mage Protector Zinnia, who was holding onto a nearby rope with a death grip. The dock workers were even slapping each other on the back in congratulations, which he supposed was deserved since they had worked hard to build the boat in such a short time.

But they hadn't even seen the fastest speed yet.

Monitoring the absorption of ambient Mana, he saw that it was still at acceptable levels, especially since they were constantly moving. As if that gave him tacit permission to push it further, he raised both Magnitudes up to 7, the limit, and the boat lurched ahead as the speed of the vessel increased dramatically. The leap from 6 to 7 still didn't put any strain on the wheels and their frame, at least from what he could see, but the speed increased yet again as it doubled. Looking back at the wheels and how they interacted with the water, he saw at once that it wasn't likely to get much faster than that, as they were moving so quickly by that point that the water they were pushing through was unable to refill what was shifted out of the way behind them fast enough. If the wheel turned any faster, it would be trying to push against empty air as the water displaced by the bulk of the ferry couldn't fill the void left in its wake fast enough.

Despite that, they were moving quite quickly, and the passengers stood in awe at how the shoreline passed them by. Larek was also impressed that his idea had actually worked, because he honestly didn't know if it would or not when he first started the project. As he looked over at Zinnia, who still hadn't loosened her grip on the rope she held, she nodded at him as if in confirmation of a job well done.

*Well, I guess that's done... so, what now?*

# Chapter 31

The answer to that question was a bit more complicated than he liked, because he was hoping to be paid for his work and then take the ferry to the other side of the river as soon as possible so that he could resume his journey home. The issues that prevented that from happening arose almost as soon as he returned to the Swiftwater docks after spending another half-hour or so testing the limits of the ferry boat.

"I... don't have your payment yet, but I will soon!" Mage Protector Zinnia admitted to him when he asked her about it. He had parked the new boat, and the workers quickly tied it to the stone dock, using what appeared to be leather pads along the side to prevent damage to the boat as it moved against the stone. Though based on the strength of the wood, Larek thought it was more likely that the *stone* would be damaged than the wood of the boat, but either way it was probably a good idea.

"What do you mean? I thought all of this was already approved." He specifically remembered her saying that she hadn't gotten approval yet until he told her he could actually accomplish what she wanted him to do, but then she indicated shortly afterward that she had received it. It was what led to having help from all the dock workers and the Cartwright, after all, because he remembered overhearing that they were getting paid for their assistance.

*Is she screwing me over?* He began to get angry at being taken advantage of yet again, and he nearly turned to the Fusions on board the boat and erased them right then and there. If they weren't going to pay him for his work, then they simply wouldn't enjoy the benefits of—

"It was! The mayor approved it, but the large payment coming your way has... hit a bit of a snag," she said quickly, holding her hands out as if she could sense the frustration in Larek and his desire to strike out. "The Merchant Guild is refusing to release the funds unless you agree to help build another half dozen of these ferries if this one proved to be successful, and then they would pay you for each and every one. This is completely unacceptable, of course, and the mayor along with the Protectors are already preparing to storm their compound and force them to pay you for—"

Some of his anger drained away as he realized that it wasn't the Protectors – and more specifically, Zinnia – that were withholding payment, but some "Merchant Guild". He started planning his own crusade against them to ask for his money, which he desperately needed for supplies to continue his journey, but he paused as the Mage mentioned something that caught his attention.

Cutting her off before she could say any more, he asked, "How much are we talking about for all of them?"

Zinnia paused, temporarily taken aback at his question. She hesitatingly said, "Uh, for the one you already finished, the payment was a full 15 platinum coins, and a further 15 for each additional ferry boat you completed. It's... an absurd amount of money, of course, but I tried to convey to them that you were in a hurry to get across the river—"

"Would I have to stay for the construction, or would they be fine with just the Fusions? If they are willing to settle for just the Fusions, I'll take 10 platinum for each set of them for the 6 boats, and then they can take their time constructing them to their specifications. I'll leave detailed instructions on how and where my Fusions need to be installed, but almost anyone can do that part."

She was silent for a few seconds as she stared at him, before she slowly nodded. "I'll take that offer to them. I can't see any reason why they'd refuse, however. I should have an answer for you by morning."

As she and a few of the other Protectors that had been there for the test of the ferry boat quickly departed, Larek left the dry dock and returned to his temporary room inside the Protector barracks where he'd been staying since he'd been released from his cell. Since he didn't have any money, it wasn't like he could afford to go anywhere else, and at least the food was free.

After stopping by the mess hall to get either a very late lunch or a very early dinner, he headed up to his room to think about the day – and to prepare for later. He was ecstatic that his plan for the ferry boat had succeeded, but it had also given him a lot of ideas for more Fusions, including one for a personal flight contraption, though there were still some things he needed to work out before he attempted anything like that. Aside from that, he was severely disappointed that yet again someone was trying to take advantage of him by expecting him to capitulate to their demands; it made him so frustrated when he encountered either greedy people who wanted something that wasn't theirs or people who tried to make him provide something in exchange for something else that was already his due.

That was exactly what this "Merchant Guild" was doing by withholding their payment for services rendered, and if they wouldn't negotiate or agree to simply pay him for the work already completed, he would have to find a way to *make them*. He had no desire to hurt anyone, of course, but he also needed the money to pay for supplies for his journey; he would find a way to acquire what he was owed in one way or another.

The potential for even more money was another reason why he asked about payment up front instead of having to wait while the additional boats were constructed, because he had no desire to stay in Swiftwater longer than necessary at that point – which meant leaving within the next day or two at the latest. While he primarily wished to avoid any further conflict with these people, which agreeing to their demand would accomplish, he realized that doing so would essentially take advantage of *them* in return.

How? Because they likely expected creating such Fusions for each boat would take him *days* of work, because that was how long the first one took. What they failed to realize was that it only took that long because he wasn't entirely sure it would work and had to design the Fusion to fit its new purpose, which had, indeed, taken a while to perfect. But now that he knew what he was doing, he thought that he could probably make 6 sets of ferry boat Fusions *that night*.

All thanks to a Skill he'd been neglecting lately: *Focused Division*.

His work over the last few weeks, both with teaching and by recreating the Fusions he'd lost when the Underworld Society hideaway collapsed, had increased most of his Mage Skills to their new maximums.

**Mage Skills:**
**Multi-effect Fusion Focus Level 25/25 (250 AF)**
**Pattern Recognition Level 25/25 (250 AF)**
**Magical Detection Level 23/25 (250 AF)**
**Spellcasting Focus Level 25/25 (250 AF)**
**Focused Division Level 31/35 (350 AF)**
**Mana Control Level 45/45 (450 AF)**
**Fusion Level 45/45 (450 AF)**
**Pattern Formation Level 45/45 (450 AF)**


With most everything now up to the maximum it could be until he was able to accumulate more Aetheric Force, the two remaining Skills he had that weren't at that maximum were *Magical Detection* and *Focused Division*. *Magical Detection* had even gone up by 2 during those few weeks along with almost everything else, giving Larek another personal Level; he was now at Level 25 with an additional 20 AP to spend, which put his total available at 39 AP. He still hadn't figured out where to place them yet, as he was still getting accustomed to his Martial stats, so he decided to hold onto them until he discovered where they would be the most effective.

    Despite all of those improvements, he hadn't even touched *Focused Division* because there was never a need for him to make more than one Fusion at a time. The offensive Fusions that had ended up being destroyed down below the city were ones of which he only desired to have a single one of each of them, as having more was unnecessary at that point in time. He could barely use a pair of them simultaneously without draining all the ambient Mana around, so anything past the first was just extraneous. Perhaps if he was in the Kingdom and didn't have to worry about Mana density levels they would be more useful in multiples, but for now there was no reason to do it.

    But he could certainly create multiple copies of the ferry boat Fusions. Doing so would accomplish two things at once: increasing his *Focused Division* Skill Level and earning an additional 60 platinum. Along with the 15 from the first boat, he thought 75 platinum coins was more than enough to see him all the way back home, so he was willing to put in a few hours of work and take advantage of the Merchant Guild's naivete on how long it would actually take him to accomplish them all. It was easy money by that point, and he wasn't planning on sticking around long after he received his payment. He didn't want them to understand how relatively trivial it was now for him to make copies of already created Fusions, after all.

    If the worst happened and they refused to pay anything at all, he would simply stuff some packs full of food from the mess hall in the Protector barracks and then hijack the ferry to take to the other side. He wouldn't even erase the Fusions on it in a fit of rage like he'd wanted to do earlier, mainly because it wouldn't matter even if he did. He hadn't told anyone how they worked, after all. And until he got paid, the ferry was essentially just a floating piece of wood that was practically useless for anyone who didn't know the correct mental phrases to use.

    He, too, could extort them for payment if they wanted to play games.

    Pulling the stacks of square-shaped wood panels, which he had prepared a few days ago when he was starting the process of making Fusions for the ferry boat he had just finished, over to the bed, Larek sat down and did a count. He needed a total of 5 Fusions per boat: 1 *Right Gust of Air +7*, 1 *Left Gust of Air +7*, 1 *Strengthen Area +10*, and a pair of *Repelling Gust of Air +6* for the front to prevent submerging. In total, if he was to make Fusions for 6 ferry boats, he was going to need 30 boards. Counting them up, he found that he had a total of 40, so it was more than enough for the work he needed to get done.

Getting into a comfortable position, he placed the 6 of the boards arranged in front of him and prepared the *Right Gust of Air +7* Fusion, but he made sure to thicken it enough so that he could use his *Focused Division* Skill to essentially copy it into 5 additional and identical Fusions to place on the other boards. It took less than an hour to gather and infuse enough Mana into the formation, and after approximately 6,000 Pattern Cohesion was consumed in the process, he was able to divide his large Fusion into 6 identical formations before directing them onto the board.

**Focused Division** *has reached Level 32!*

*Excellent! That was easy enough.* Larek had to pause and wait about 20 minutes for his Pattern Cohesion to recover a bit, because he spent a good chunk of it and still had more to do. Once it had nearly filled up completely again, the Combat Fusionist did the same thing for the *Left Gust of Air +7* on another half-dozen wooden boards.

**Focused Division** *has reached Level 33!*

Another wait while his Pattern Cohesion regenerated, and then he was on to the *Repelling Gust of Air +6* Fusions. They were Intermediate Fusions of the Simple Classification, as they only had a single Effect and very few Inputs and Variables. At Skill Level 30 in *Focused Division*, Larek had only been able to create 11 equal copies before they seemed to fall apart during the division process, but he had a feeling that with even the few new Levels in it, he could make at least one more.

Thankfully, he was correct. If he hadn't been, he would've been able to feel it as he was dividing them and would've settled for 11, but he didn't feel any hesitation while he was undergoing the process. By the time he was done, he even thought that he could've done one more, but that might be stretching it.

Of course, once he Leveled up the Skill again, he was confident that 13 was easily within his reach.

**Focused Division** *has reached Level 34!*

He had to wait even longer before tackling the final Fusion, because creating 12 copies consumed nearly half of his Pattern Cohesion. Instead of simply waiting there on his bed, he left his room and ate a late dinner, as he was hungry from all the mental work he had been doing. The break did him good, because by the time he got back, he was essentially ready to go.

This was where his process became a little bit more complicated, because normally his *Strengthen*-type Fusions had Permanent Activation Methods, because it was important for them to be activated all the time. However, if he was going to store these *Strengthen Area* Fusions with the others, then they needed to be changed so that they could be Activatable; otherwise, they would constantly be absorbing the ambient Mana around them, which would also start decaying any nearby Fusions within their area of ambience. When a full *half-dozen* of them were put together, the result would be even more devastating.

Thankfully, the other Fusions he'd created were Reactive and on "standby;" they didn't require much in the way of ambient Mana, so even stacking them together wouldn't harm them. Only if they were activated would they start consuming ambient Mana, so it was fairly safe to store them as a set.

All Larek had to do was change the Activation Method to Activatable from Permanent in the formation, which was easy enough to do, but he also made a mental note to ensure that whoever was responsible for installing them on the boats protected them from anyone inadvertently deactivating the Fusion. If it happened while they were in mid-travel with the paddle wheels in motion, the result could be catastrophic, with the destruction of the boat being the least of the worries they'd have to deal with.

**Focused Division** *has reached Level 35!*

**Magical Detection** *has reached Level 24!*

Another hour later, he was finished and feeling drained, as he had used nearly half of his Pattern Cohesion once again, but the Fusions for the additional 6 ferry boats were done. More than that, he had hit the current maximum Level for his *Focused Division* Skill *and* had increased his *Magical Detection* Skill, which was only a Level away from hitting its maximum of 25. Those increases alone were worth the work he put into the Fusions, but if he was lucky and this "Merchant Guild" agreed to pay him upon delivery of them, then he would be set as far as supplies went for a long, long time.

After separating the stacks of Fusions into 6 distinct piles, all of them ready to go for the next day, Larek finally tucked into bed, dreaming about the Fusion possibilities for the 10 unused wooden boards he had in the room.

# Chapter 32

Stepping off the ferry boat onto the dock at Riverbend, Larek adjusted the over-filled pack to sit comfortably on his back before running his fingers over the special new leather belt he had acquired in Swiftwater. He nodded at the smiling face of the ferry boat captain, who waved at him in return, the enthusiasm of the man infectious enough that there was a spring in the step of the others who disembarked along with the Combat Fusionist, and there was an air of celebration to the whole event.

Trade had resumed along the Swiftwater, which was a momentous occasion for the cities and towns that relied upon it.

For Larek, he was just glad that a way over the fast-flowing river had finally allowed him to cross and resume his journey home. The very faint jingle of coins secured in his pack certainly helped as well, as they would make everything that much easier.

Thinking about earlier that morning, he was greeted at breakfast by Mage Protector Zinnia, who had passed on the good news.

"They've agreed," she had told him. "Though they have some questions. If the answers are satisfactory, they'll pay the full amount of 75 platinum coins upon receipt of the Fusions, and you'll be free to leave."

"What kind of questions do they have?"

She went on to list them from a sheet of paper she pulled out of her pocket, and Larek answered them almost as quickly as she finished. Most of them had to do with how the Fusions worked, which he gave a general idea of but didn't specify the phrasing needed so that they wouldn't screw him over. There was only one that he wasn't sure how to answer truthfully, because he didn't know.

"...alright, that makes sense. Last questions, then: How long will these Fusions last, and will they need to be repaired or replaced at some point?"

"I'm... not actually sure how long they will last, because I haven't seen any of the ones I've created degrade yet. As you remember from my training with you, normal Fusions only last a few months to possibly a year at best, but mine are a lot stronger than that." She nodded, so he went on. "As for needing to be repaired or replaced, as far as I can tell there should be no reason for that. The only thing that could potentially break them down is from rapid overuse as I explained before, so stopping and starting the Fusions at a high ambient Mana draw will begin to degrade the formation over time. Normal use should see them last for decades or longer." That was what he thought, anyway.

"They will be glad to hear that. As soon as you have the Fusions done, let me know and I'll—"

"They're done. I finished them last night, and they're sitting up in my room."

She had been practically speechless at his statement, but after seeing what he could do, she wasn't skeptical.

After that, the morning was a rush as he was brought to the Merchant Guild to hand over the Fusions and accept payment, which went much smoother than he thought it would, considering their demand to create more ferries. He then spent an hour with a half-dozen boat captains employed by the Guild on the completed ferry as he demonstrated and explained how they controlled the vessel; unsurprisingly, they were leaps and bounds better than him in maneuvering the large boat in the water, despite not having controlled anything like the paddle wheels before, let alone mentally commanding the Fusions.

He even got another increase in his *Bargaining* Skill as a result of the transaction.

**Bargaining** *has reached Level 9!*

After that, he went on a shopping spree with his new funds, purchasing supplies that would be needed for traveling through the rest of the Empire, including his new belt. What made it special were the pockets attached to it with simple flaps that kept them closed, but could be tied if it was necessary. He'd already filled a few of them with his different Fusions to make them more accessible, especially in combat, and to keep them separated and easier to pick from rather than in a jumble inside of his pocket. But even with what he'd filled them with, there was still a lot of room for others, which gave him an idea for more Fusions he could create and use now that he had someplace to store and easily access them.

Who knew that a simple leather belt with pockets could be so useful?

His new walking staff-turned-offensive weapon filled with Fusions knocked against the stone of the dock as he moved away from the hustle-and-bustle of the celebratory crowd as crews began to unload the first crates of goods off the boat in weeks. The people of Riverbend noticed him, of course, but they moved out of the way without more than a glance; thanks to the ring he slipped onto his finger as soon as he started moving through the crowd, he was no longer seen as someone 7 feet tall, but was instead under 6 feet – or just a little over the average height of most of the others.

His features didn't even stand out as being different because he was from the Kingdom, because Larek had altered the *Perceptive Misdirection* Fusion he had learned from the ring Shinpai had made for him and made it better. It was something that he had been thinking about since he had learned the Advanced Fusion, but hadn't been able to change anything until he had some time to experiment – which the last few weeks before he had started on the ferry project allowed him to have.

He found that when he increased the Magnitude of the original *Perceptive Misdirection* Fusion past the 1 it had been at before, it allowed him to do more with the non-invasive mental manipulation of any observers than simply making them think he was a foot shorter. Using what he'd learned from the *Automatic Strong Temperature Adjustment* Fusion, in regard to identifying the ideal temperature for an individual based on preference, he was able to tap into the expectations of an observer when they looked at him.

The majority of the time, people didn't *expect* to see someone walking around who obviously came from some other place in the world, especially when 99.9% of the people they interacted with on a daily basis were locals. With that thought going into the Fusion, he altered what observers saw so that he was not only shorter, but also someone they expected to see walking around – which he figured was probably a Brolencian (the majority of people he saw in the Empire), but he didn't dictate *who* they saw, other than it not being someone they were familiar with. He didn't need random people coming up to him and engaging him in conversation as if they had just seen an old friend, after all.

In addition to being a shorter version of someone they expected to see walking around, he was also able to insert a feeling that he was unremarkable and relatively harmless. It required a Magnitude of 5 to accomplish that successfully, as anything of lower Magnitude wouldn't seem to take that Effect properly, and he had experimented with it once back in Swiftwater. It was a strangely liberating feeling being able to walk around the city without anyone really noticing him beyond a glance, because even though he wasn't hated or feared by the general population like he was in the Kingdom, they were still obviously wary of him because of his foreign features and height. When wearing the ring, he found that he could've easily walked out at any time without anyone saying anything to him, skipping out on his obligation to teach the

Mages of the city about Fusions, but at that point he still didn't have any way to safely cross over the river.

As he began to discover how effective this non-invasive mental manipulation could be, he worried about going a bit too far with it. *How much manipulation of their perception is too much? Could I make people who see me think that I'm a friend or a loved one? Or, turning that around, could I make them become intimidated by me and voluntarily give me all their money in exchange for their lives?* The latter thought sickened him, as he wanted nothing to do with something like that, because it sounded entirely too much like Dominion magic for his liking. In fact, the entire Effect of the *Perceptive Misdirection* Fusion felt a bit too manipulative to be comfortable with it beyond what he absolutely needed in order to get around safely. He resolved to keep an eye on its effects on people who observed him, and if it seemed like it was harming them in some way, he would discontinue its use immediately.

Until that happened, though, he would use it to ensure he wasn't bothered walking through a village, town, or city, because if he didn't have to travel across the entire Sealance Empire while avoiding populated areas, he wouldn't. Because his identity was essentially obscured due to the Fusion on his ring, he didn't have to hide anymore.

With most of the hubbub in the town of Riverbend happening near the docks, and rightly so, it didn't take Larek long to navigate his way through the town and out past the last of the buildings there. There were the beginnings of a wall being constructed around the outskirts of the town, as if they were just now responding to the influx of monsters and Apertures throughout the Empire, but it was essentially abandoned at the moment as everyone was located near the docks to see the unusual ferry arrive. The unfinished and unguarded gate proved no hindrance to him as he walked through it, and soon enough he was back on track to getting back home after the lengthy delay.

Running at full speed as soon as he was out of sight of the town, it only took 10 minutes for him to sense the first Aperture nearby, and he immediately switched his course to head toward it. As he approached the obvious edge of the Aperture, he slowed down and came to a stop as he considered what he was looking at. The landscape he was traveling through was rather pretty, with a mountain backdrop in the distance with snow-capped peaks, while around him was a large valley between gentle hills dotted with random tree stands. The knee-high grass he stepped through was waving in the comforting breeze that passed through the valley, and the thousands of multi-colored wildflowers clumped up in various areas gave the whole scene an idyllic quality that was both refreshing and peaceful at the same time.

That was until one came upon the area where the Aperture he sensed was, which seemed like a blight upon the land, as it appeared as though a dome of darkness had fallen from the sky and landed inside the valley. The blackness encompassing the dome was so complete that he couldn't even see inside of it, like it was a solid wall of shadow that didn't allow light to penetrate it.

*What the heck is this?*

While his education in both Academies didn't exactly cover Apertures and the changed environments that were produced, he couldn't think of any type of monster he'd learned about that would create this dome of darkness. Immediately cautious, he dropped his pack just outside of the dome to ensure he didn't lose it, because he was unsure of what would happen when he went inside, before bending down and digging into the dirt beneath his feet. With a jagged stone in his hand, which he quickly cleaned the dirt off, he sat in the grass and began working on a Fusion. A very short time later, he produced a new version of *Illuminate +7*, creating a Reactive Intermediate Fusion with mental phrasing commands and multiple Magnitudes so that the illumination Effect could be increased or decreased at a thought. He also added in a directional detection and orientation Input and Variable so that it didn't simply shine the illumination everywhere, which could blind him, but was instead aimed in a cone-like pattern in a specific direction.

The creation of such a Fusion was coming easier and easier as he was now familiar with mental commands, and the *Illuminate* Fusion was one that he'd already known well enough to make without too much thought. Directing it in a specific direction was adapted from all the work he'd done with his staff-based offensive spells and the air gusts used on the ferries, so it all just kind of came together with a few tweaks here and there.

The new *Directional Illumination +7* Fusion was approximately twice as expensive in terms of Mana Cost and Pattern Cohesion in comparison to the simple *Illuminate +7* Fusion, but that still wasn't very costly. He was able to finish it off in a few minutes, and it was only when he was standing up that he realized that, for the first time since he'd killed those bandits back near Lakebellow, he wasn't concerned about Protectors sneaking up on him. Whether it was his relationship with the Protectors of Swiftwater, his new *Perceptive Misdirection* ring, or because he was more confident in his abilities to avoid their notice, all that mattered to him was that he had finally broken away from his paranoia.

That meant he could finally create Fusions while traveling, even if he wasn't staying in a town or city. With a smile that turned to a frown as soon as he looked at the dome of darkness nearby, he gripped his staff in his right hand while he held the new Fusion on the stone in his left, angled so that the Fusion was pointing ahead of him.

Taking his first tentative steps inside, he mentally activated his new *Directional Illumination* Fusion at Magnitude 1, and a conical beam of light shone out of the stone and impacted the dome without any visible effect. Bumping it up to Mag 2 and then 3, he finally saw some of the darkness recede when the light impacted it, though instead of banishing the shadowy substance, it sort of *diluted* it so that it wasn't as solid-looking. It also didn't reach that far into the dome, only a foot or so, and Larek increased the Magnitude even further. Each successive increase in the light beam's strength further diluted the darkness and allowed him to see farther inside, until Magnitude 7 allowed him to see the farthest of all.

It was hard to even look at, though, because the light – even without shining everywhere – was blindingly bright and was almost as bad as the darkness for obscuring what was ahead of him, so he reduced it back down to 6 and found he could handle it much better, even if it came with reduced visibility.

Cautiously moving inside the dome with the Mag 6 cone of light extended ahead of him, as soon as he passed through the edge of the Aperture's environment, he felt the darkness closing around him like he'd just jumped into a pool of inky blackness. It was oppressive-feeling, like it was trying to push into him even as he waded through it, but he shrugged off the sensation because it wasn't debilitating in the least. Just.. slightly uncomfortable.

His new illumination Fusion was the only thing that made the experience bearable, as it pushed back the darkness wherever he pointed it. The first thing he noticed was that the actual environment hadn't changed compared to outside the dome, though all the grass and wildflowers were dead and crunched under his feet as he moved through it. He could immediately tell that it wasn't due to lack of water or due to a monster killing them, but because they had a complete lack of sunlight due to the oppressive darkness.

It only took him a minute to discover the first of the monsters that inhabited the Aperture, though he didn't really get a good look at it before it disappeared. As soon as his light shone upon the dark splotch that looked like the living shadow of some sort of large, hovering rodent, it screeched briefly before being abruptly cut off, dispersing into a shadowy smoke that evaporated before his eyes. A second later, he acquired a total of 2 Aetheric Force, surprising him at its sudden acquisition.

*I killed it? With the light?*

Given that the environment was dark, and the monster looked like a shadow, he supposed it made sense that light would harm it – and a bright light like the one he had would be even more effective than usual.

Larek ended up killing two more of the strange, shadowy monsters on his way to the actual Aperture, which took him longer than he expected. He hadn't really noticed it from the outside, but the Aperture's territory was *huge*, as if it had been allowed to expand since it was first formed. Given the nature of the monsters inside and the environment itself, he thought it likely that none of the nearby towns or cities had been able to close it before now.

*I guess it's good that I'm here, then.*

Finally reaching the floating sphere that marked the entrance of the Aperture, he bonked it sharply with his staff, and then waited for the onslaught to begin. He didn't have long to wait, as it seemed as though the shadowy rodents could move extremely quickly through the darkness of the environment, and soon enough Larek was swarmed with dozens and then hundreds of the things from all sides.

Using his new Fusion, he swept it in an arc around him, but it couldn't be everywhere at once. Within seconds, even as he took to firing out fiery and stony projectiles from his staff wherever he could (which seemed to have an effect on what he was calling the **Shadow Rats**, though not as much as his light), he experienced what felt like cold scratches all over his legs and back, which passed completely through his *Repelling Barrier* without triggering anything, as well as his clothing as if it wasn't even there.

He could tell that these scratches were only barely breaking the surface of his skin and weren't deep, but there were certainly a lot of them. Thankfully, the attacks lessened as he continued to sweep his light in a circle, killing dozens of the Rats at a time; at one point, he attempted to sweep through one right at the edge of his vision with his staff, but the wooden weapon simply passed through it without seeming to harm the shadowy figure.

It took nearly 10 minutes for the last of the Shadow Rats to disperse into nothing once his light passed through it, and it was at that point that Larek healed himself. His legs and back felt like he had jumped into a thorn bush and rolled around a couple hundred times, as they were covered in shallow scratches that drew a little blood, but nothing serious. He knew that if he'd had a lower Body stat, he'd have suffered *a lot* more; as it was, it was annoying more than anything, as his *Pain Immunity* Skill essentially numbed any pain after the initial scratches.

He was then slammed with a large amount of Aetheric Force that he later saw was worth 524 AF once it was all purified, bringing him to a new total of 603 AF. *Not bad for about 30 minutes of work.*

After smashing the Aperture to temporarily close it, he made his way out of the area, finding that the dome of darkness had shrunk considerably in size, until it was only about a quarter of the area it held when he first went in. As he departed the Aperture's territory, he saw the dead grass and wildflowers outside in the sunlight for the first time, and there was a clear delineation of time expanding away from the dome. The vegetation inside the dome of darkness and right outside of it was the most decayed, showing that it had been dead longer, while near where the edge used to be before he closed the Aperture, it was only "recently" dead.

*Given that it's been about 2 months or so since the change and the Apertures arrived in the Empire, that is a significant amount of growth if it hadn't been closed before this.* He dreaded what it would look like if it was allowed to continue growing for a year or more. *I wonder if that's what happened back in the Kingdom? Were one or more Apertures allowed to grow out of control?*

It was too soon to tell, but he suspected that this was the case, given how quickly things got out of control. If one of the Apertures back home grew larger for multiple years, then that could mean one of their territories might be so large that it was overtaking entire cities in its expansion. It was all the more reason to return to the Kingdom, because the people he cared for were there, and if there was a threat like this happening, then he needed to help stop it in order to keep them safe. If he didn't and it was allowed to continue expanding, then it was only a matter of time before it consumed the entire world, flooding enough Corruption into the environment to kill every living thing.

As much as he didn't desire to be a hero destined to save the world, he couldn't just sit back and watch it burn all around him.

# Chapter 33

The next month and a half of travel was spent making up for his delay, as Larek didn't stop except to rest in between closing Apertures, eating, and sleeping while utilizing his *Secure Hideaway* Fusion to ensure he was relatively safe at night. He only stayed in a town he didn't even know the name of once during the first week, as every other time night arrived he was nowhere near any population centers. As he moved further into the interior of the Sealance Empire, at least according to the new map he acquired back in Swiftwater, the more frequent the villages, towns, and even cities were as he traveled; so after the first week he was almost always near someplace he could stay at an Inn for the night.

His ring, coupled with the local currency he had acquired from his work on the ferry boat Fusions, was enough to let him pass through most places without much of a stir. Restocking his supplies along the way, he made tremendous time and practically ate up the miles with his Agility stat-enhanced speed. He had even made it to the capital, where the Emperor supposedly ruled over the vast reaches of the Empire, but he only stayed for the day before leaving again before he saw anyone he thought might be "important".

Before he knew it, Larek was nearly to the border of the Empire, where he decided to slow down for a day of rest. By the time he made this decision, he found himself in a small town on the edge of a wide and flat plain, where the landscape was more than a bit drier than most of the rest of the Empire he'd observed thus far, and trees were few and far between. Dry dirt underneath his feet was accompanied by spiny plants and scrub bushes, and heat seemed to radiate up from the ground rather than descend from the sun overhead.

Striding into the town, which was encircled by high stone walls that appeared to have been in existence since the town was built, he immediately ran into a problem.

Along his journey, things had been fairly easy and straightforward, even with his quick pace and incessant drive to continue moving as fast as possible while still desiring to accumulate Aetheric Force. Only a few Apertures along the way gave him any bit of trouble, but they were more about access rather than difficulty in killing the monsters there. For instance, one of the Apertures appeared to have manifested in the middle of a cave system in a mountain range he passed through, and it took him a few hours to find a way inside. Another was at the bottom of a lake and had **Toothy Fish** that attempted to bite him with their serrated teeth, but they were fortunately physically weak, and he was able to literally slap them away when they got too close, killing them almost instantly.

There were only two complications he ran into on his journey. The first issue, which arose when the population centers of the Empire became more numerous, was that it became more and more difficult to find an Aperture nearby that hadn't been closed already. It was good to see, in the sense that the Empire seemed to be understanding the danger that they posed and were beginning to get a handle on them, but it also made his own accumulation of Aetheric Force stagnate. That didn't mean that he had been unable to find any, only that he had to go out of his way a few times, delaying his journey a bit, but it was worth the extra trips. In all, he had accumulated just under 25,000 AF, allowing him to vastly increase the maximum Level of his Mage Skills.

Along the way, especially when he was safe and secure at night, he spent some of his time improving these Skills up to their new maximums, though he didn't create anything new – only variations of what he'd already made before. He still had some ideas for new Fusions, but his head wasn't in the right state to work them out while he was constantly on the move, and there hadn't been any need for anything since he'd created the *Directional Illumination* Fusion.

Because he had made so much progress along the way, keeping up with his new maximum Skill Levels, he had also increased his personal Level not just once or twice, but *three* times, bringing him to Level 28 – and he now had 101 AP to spend on his stats, though he didn't know where to put them. All of the battles against Aperture monsters also increased some of his Martial Skills, such as *Unarmed Fighting* by 1 Level, *Throwing* by 1 Level, *Body Regeneration* by 1 Level, and *Dodge* by 2 Levels – but he hadn't figured out how to get the latter past Level 19, where it seemed to hit a wall. A few of his General Skills also increased, including *Axe Handling* to Level 90, but they weren't quite as impactful as the others.

His Status was starting to look pretty impressive, but he knew that he still had a long way to go before he was satisfied that he could protect all of his friends and family. Whether it was powerful monsters that had opened Apertures in the Kingdom or the Gergasi, Larek knew he wasn't exactly ready to go up against either of them.

**Larek Holsten**

**Combat Fusionist**
**Healer**

Level 28
Advancement Points (AP): 19/20
Available AP to Distribute: 101
Available Aetheric Force (AF): 247

Stama: 1500/1500
Mana: 2340/2340

Strength: 75 [150] (+)
Body: 75 [150] (+)
Agility: 75 [150] (+)
Intellect: 117 [234] (+)
Acuity: 114 [228] (+)
Pneuma: 1,350 [2,700]
Pattern Cohesion: 27,000/27,000

Mage Skills:
Pattern Recognition Level 35/35 (350 AF)
Magical Detection Level 35/35 (350 AF)
Spellcasting Focus Level 35/35 (350 AF)
Multi-effect Fusion Focus Level 40/40 (400 AF)
Focused Division Level 45/45 (450 AF)
Mana Control Level 50/50 (500 AF)
Fusion Level 50/50 (500 AF)
Pattern Formation Level 50/50 (500 AF)

Martial Skills:
Stama Subjugation Level 1/20 (200 AF)
Blunt Weapon Expertise Level 1/20 (200 AF)
Bladed Weapon Expertise Level 2/20 (200 AF)
Unarmed Fighting Level 3/20 (200 AF)
Throwing Level 10/20 (200 AF)
Dodge Level 19/20 (200 AF)
Pain Immunity Level 20/20 (N/A)
Body Regeneration Level 32/33 (330 AF)

General Skills:
Cooking Level 8
Bargaining Level 9
Beast Control Level 9
Leadership Level 11
Writing Level 11

Saw Handling Level 15
Reading Level 17
Speaking Level 18
Long-Distance Running Level 20
Listening Level 43
Axe Handling Level 90

Still, it was decent progress for what he had been able to find as far as monsters and their Aetheric Force. He never thought he would be disappointed by not finding enough deadly creatures that were trying to kill him along his journey, but that was strangely the case. It helped that they were all still quite weak, and apart from a few unique challenges that he faced trying to kill them effectively, he was never in any real danger.

It was also why Larek hadn't felt the need to place his available AP into any of his stats quite yet, because there hadn't been anything that felt like it required a boost – though that could change soon. He was slowly but steadily getting used to his increased physical stats that came from his Martial side: Dodging attacks became much easier when he utilized his incredible Agility; what few hits made it through his defenses did less damage to him thanks to his Body finally adjusting; and he was getting better at managing his Strength correctly in combat. He was more than aware that he had a lot of work still to do to improve, because he still had very little talent in a physical fight other than moving fast and hitting hard, but he figured that would come in time.

As he became more accustomed to those stats, he thought he was almost ready to start adding additional AP to them. Another few weeks would probably do it if he kept improving, but he didn't want to add anything until he was comfortable or if it was absolutely necessary.

So, while finding enough monsters to kill to acquire Aetheric Force was probably a *good* problem to have, it was the other issue that came up that was the problem – which was what he encountered when he entered the current town on the border of the Empire.

"Hey! Who are you and why does my head hurt looking at you?"

Larek grumbled under his breath as he looked over at the guard standing next to the gate to the town, a wicked-looking iron mace with a wooden shaft in his hand held threateningly out toward the Combat Fusionist. His other hand was up rubbing his temple as if it pained him, which it probably did.

Why did it pain the guard? Because the man was also a Mage that had skewed his distribution of AP toward his Acuity instead of being more balanced between all three stats. That wasn't normally a *bad* thing, as it would greatly increase their Mana regeneration rate (if they were planning on casting generally weaker spells more frequently), but the imbalance sharpened their mental defenses to the point that his *Perceptive Misdirection* Fusion actually hurt them slightly and made his appearance slightly blurry. The greater the difference between Acuity and the other stats, the worse the pain and blurriness would be – meaning that this Mage on guard at the gate had it skewed quite significantly.

Or at least that was what he had figured out thanks to a friendly Mage Protector he met a few weeks before, who was only slightly pained by looking at Larek. When the Combat Fusionist had tentatively explained what his ring did and why he had it, he was worried that the man would either want to steal it from him or try to and take him into custody, but his worry was unfounded. In exchange for a brief Fusion-teaching session with the older man, Donald, he learned that the Mage was more interested in new knowledge about the wonders of magic and couldn't care less about why he was utilizing such a mentally manipulative Fusion. What eventually came of that was that Donald posited that those who had higher Acuity than the other Mage stats – as the Mage himself did – would be less affected by his ring's Effects, and would attempt to see through the misdirection of their perception, which subsequently caused the pain and blurriness.

While he didn't have any other proof that this was the case, he'd met at least a dozen other Mages – a few Protectors, but most not – who'd experienced pain and blurriness when he was around. Depending on the severity of the side-effects, the responses of those who experienced these maladies ranged from dismissing it as a temporary inconvenience to full-on accusing him of being some sort of monster in disguise sneaking through town and only *they* could see Larek for who he really was. Needless to say, the latter type of response had him fleeing from town sooner than he really liked, so as not to incite a mob wanting his head. It was unfair, but it was also a drawback of his Fusion that he hadn't expected, and he wasn't sure how to eliminate that type of experience in certain Mages.

As a result, he kept the ring and simply hoped that its benefits outweighed the negatives in the long run, and thus far that had proved to be the case. In fact, in the last town, everything had been going well before he triggered a response in a nearby Mage; recognizing what was happening, he quickly fled out of sight through an alleyway, took off his ring and placed it in one of his belt pouches, and then spent the rest of the time without his disguise. Larek received many more cautious looks from the residents, with a few deliberately avoiding him by moving across the street when he passed by, but he was able to finish his business – with slightly higher prices for supplies than he thought was normal – and then left without any problems after that. Unfortunately, it also meant that he camped outside that night instead of staying at an Inn, because he still didn't trust the people there to behave correctly toward him when they knew where he was. It was a minor inconvenience, but necessary in his mind.

But now it seemed as though Larek was already being confronted by someone who was fighting the mental manipulation of his ring's Fusion, and he hadn't even entered the town.

"Uh, well, it's because—" he tried to explain, before he was cut off by the pained Mage guard.

"Monster! It's a monster trying to infiltrate Day's End! Kill it!" the man shouted, and a *Fireball* spell pattern was formed in front of the guard. A second later, it was filled with Mana and the roiling ball of flames was shooting straight toward him. Thankfully, his speed and his practice at dodging attacks lately had improved his reaction time, so Larek was already moving out of the way. As he felt the heat of the *Fireball* pass by him as he stepped out of the way, the Combat Fusionist was immediately cognizant that the projectile wasn't alone as a glowing arrow shot from the top of the wall slammed into the *Repelling Barrier* that Larek had instinctively activated as soon as he knew there was going to be a problem.

The glowing arrow was immediately shunted into the ground, where it exploded in a spray of hard-packed dirt that was kicked up. A few of the clumps managed to make it through his defenses and impacted his lower legs, but he barely felt them as more than firm thumps against his skin. Unfortunately for the guards at the gate, the explosion of dirt – along with a few small-but-sharp stones – was much worse.

The other guard, who was just barely starting to move toward him with her spear raised, had her leather breastplate and part of her face peppered by the shrapnel of the explosion, causing her to fall back in surprise and pain. She wasn't a Martial, so she had no stat-given defense against the force of the explosion, but he didn't think she had been too harmed by it other than a few scratches and likely a few bruises.

The Mage who had cast the *Fireball* spell and flung it at him was a different story. He was only hit by a single shard of stone from the explosion, but that was bad enough as Larek watched it, as if in slow motion, suddenly smash through the Mage's upper cheek before sliding through his eye socket and up into his brain. It didn't penetrate very far, as most of its momentum had been arrested by the impact, but it was more than enough to drop the Mage bonelessly to the ground as his brain was impaled.

Larek thought that he might be able to heal the man if he was able to get to him fast enough, but another glowing arrow from up above – shot by yet another Martial archer on top of the walls – made him dodge to the side and roll out of the way rather than have it explode by his feet again.

By the time he got to his feet, the fate of the guards down below had been noticed – which was when a bell was rung somewhere just inside the gates that he couldn't see from his position, and he could see what appeared to be a few other guards *and* Protectors running toward the gate from inside the town.

*Well, crud. Wasn't expecting **this** when I came to town.*

He went to move toward the fallen Mage who just had his brain impaled by a stone, hoping to heal him before he technically died, but another arrow – not powered by a Battle Art like the others – was interrupted by his Repelling Barrier as he took a step forward. His hesitation at the attack cost the man his life as he looked up to see that some of the Martial Protectors heading toward the gate were *fast* and would arrive before he could do any healing. Having been forced to pay for punching someone back in Enderflow and being partly responsible for the damage done to Swiftwater, Larek had no desire to be punished for something he had absolutely no responsibility for.

This was not his fault, even if his Fusions had played a small part, and he refused to let these people accuse and punish him for something that *they* ultimately caused.

So, Larek took that possibility away as he turned around and ran away. It didn't take more than 30 seconds before he had pulled far enough away from his pursuers because his Agility was probably three times greater than any of theirs, and he cut a path toward the north to take the long way around the town. As he ran, he realized that he felt *slightly* guilty about what happened to the Mage, but not enough to return and turn himself in. He'd been delayed long enough, and it wasn't his fault.

Right? *Yes, it wasn't my fault. I wasn't the one who attacked so recklessly, and if that Mage had simply waited for an explanation, he'd still be alive. Besides, it was one of the Martial archers up on top of those walls that technically killed him, not me.*

He wasn't exactly happy with his justifications, but there was a point where he had to let others take responsibility for their own actions – and this felt like one of those situations. It was almost more disappointing because he was running low on supplies and had hoped to stock up in the town, Day's End if he heard the name correctly, though he knew that he was probably a little more callous than normal with the sudden and unfortunate loss of life that had just occurred.

*Well, hopefully it won't matter. As soon as I pass over the border into Lowenthal, I'll find another town and restock there. Hopefully they'll take the local currency, because I don't really have anything else at this point.*

Stopping and squatting down behind some scrub bushes about 15 minutes later, wanting to avoid being seen at a distance, Larek took out his well-used map and perused it one last time. While Day's End wasn't labeled on the map, the previous town he'd visited had been, which was how he knew he was getting close to the border. The only problem was that the space on the map where Lowenthal was located was pretty much a blank space without any defining features included in it, and then right on the edge of the map was the border with the Kingdom of Androthe. He hadn't really thought to ask what kind of place Lowenthal was, because he figured it would be similar to what he'd been traveling through, but when he looked off to the east all he saw was a vast, featureless expanse that seemed to change colors from the dry greyish-brown dirt from the current environment to a pale yellow punctuated by a few small hills.

*It can't be that different, can it?*

Regardless of whether it was or not, he was about to find out.

# Chapter 34

It was bad – worse than he thought was possible, in fact.

As soon as Larek passed what he assumed was the border of the Sealance Empire, which was designated by a change in the environment rather than by any posted signs or other obvious landmarks, he realized immediately that he was going to have some issues.

That was because Lowenthal was a desert – or at least the portion close to the Empire's land was a desert.

Sand stretched out as far as the eye could see to the east, with dunes breaking up the monotony of absolutely no visible environmental landmarks anywhere; it was simply a vast stretch of nothing as far as he could tell. Based on his map, which was extremely lacking in detail, the sand could stretch for a few miles or the entire length of the country? Nation? Uninhabited area? He wasn't exactly sure, and he again regretted not asking anything about it while he had the chance, thinking that he would be able to pass through it without any trouble.

It wasn't the heat of the desert during the day that was the problem, even though it was *hot*. A quick stop for the production of a *Temperature Regulator* that he was able to keep on his person was enough to alleviate the extreme heat that affected even him with his high Body stat. It wasn't unbearable without the Fusion, only uncomfortable, but if he was going to be traveling through the desert, he might as well be as comfortable as possible.

It also wasn't the brightness of the sunlight, which seemed to reflect off the sand like tiny mirrors if he looked at it the wrong way. It was annoying but not debilitating, and he eventually learned to squint and adjusted to the brightness after a few hours of travel.

The random gusts of hot wind that seemed to come from nowhere, kicking up sand that got inside his clothes and did its best to infiltrate his facial orifices, were also highly annoying, until he pulled out an extra shirt he'd obtained all the way back in Swiftwater from his pack and wrapped it around his head. Leaving only a small space to see through, the protection helped keep sand from entering his ears, nose, mouth, and – for the most part – his eyes, while also helping to reduce the strain of the bright sunlight reflecting off the sand.

All of those added up together were bad enough, but they still didn't cause him too many issues. Solutions to alleviate most of the uncomfortable portions of traveling through a desert were able to be found, including a quick realization that the dry air was making him extremely thirsty. Utilizing a very weak version of his *Water Stream*

Fusion, which was normally designed to be used offensively at higher Magnitudes, Larek was able to use the Fusion on a spare stone he had in his belt to shoot a stream of water into a stone traveling cup he'd been carrying around with him. While more than half of the water splashed out of the *Strengthened* stone cup in the process, wetting the desert temporarily before the water disappeared in the sand, it was still effective enough to provide him with something to drink anytime he wanted.

    Food would eventually become a problem if he didn't find someplace soon to pick up some supplies, but he figured he would be fine for at least a week – especially if he was able to find some more Apertures and monsters that he could butcher and eat along the way.

    No, the main problem he encountered almost immediately upon setting foot in the desert was the sand itself. Loosely packed and almost slippery in consistency, Larek found himself floundering as his feet and legs quickly sank into the sand up to his knees, and it was a struggle to move forward. He attempted to run faster so that he wouldn't give the sand the chance to sink his feet, but it was like trying to run on water most of the time; at a few points, he was able to run nearly 50 feet before his right boot suddenly passed through the top layer of sand and got caught, causing him to trip and nearly fall flat on his face.

    It was a pain to simply walk through the desert, and with safely running essentially out of the question, he could only go so fast. After a few hours, and by the time the sun was starting to set, he thought he had maybe traveled a little over a mile in that time, which was, to say the least, disappointing. He was used to traveling dozens of miles every day due to how fast he could run, even with stopping to kill monsters and close Apertures; his current pace was slow enough that if something didn't change, he estimated that it might take him a year or more to pass through the thousands of miles to where Lowenthal was supposed to be.

    He spent an uncomfortable night in the desert, mainly because whenever he laid himself down in his bedroll, he would begin to sink down; he buried himself in sand a few times before he decided to simply sit up while he tried to sleep, which helped to keep him from being buried but was necessarily uncomfortable. He was also blasted by the cold night winds every once in a while, because he hadn't been able to pitch his tent, as there was nothing for the stakes to hold onto.

    In the morning, which couldn't come too soon in his opinion, Larek trudged back toward the Sealance Empire side of the border with the desert of Lowenthal, spending hours backtracking until he stepped onto solid ground once again. He then emptied his boots of all the sand that had accumulated inside of them, shook his entire body to dislodge the itchy granules that snuck their way inside his clothes, and set up his tent there and then with his *Secure Hideaway* to prevent anyone from seeing him. After a quick meal and then a much-needed nap, he woke up in the afternoon and contemplated what he was going to do now.

What he needed first and foremost was information. At the moment, he had no idea how large the desert was inside of Lowenthal; if it was only 20 miles or so before it changed to something else, he thought that he could traverse it even if it wasn't the most comfortable trip. Possibly a little bit longer if necessary, all the way up to 50 miles, but he couldn't see himself having the mental fortitude to slog through the desert day after day for weeks on end – especially if there was no place to stay and resupply. Which was another tidbit of information he needed, because as far as he'd been able to see in the desert, there had been no sign of any type of habitable land.

If Larek discovered that the desert was even larger than 50 miles in width, he wasn't sure what he'd do. What was even worse, at least as far as his development was concerned, was that he hadn't sensed any Apertures around him while he had traveled through the desert. He was sure they were there somewhere, because it would've been strange had they completely skipped the large desert area when they were all over the Sealance Empire. Even if he did eventually sense them, how difficult would it be to get to them? Going out of his way and heading north or south instead of east would only delay his trip over the sands, and he would have to make a decision as to whether it would be worth it or not.

In the end, there was no help for it: Larek would have to go someplace to learn more about Lowenthal. He thought that he could probably head back to a previous town he'd visited, one in which he hadn't been involved in the killing of a guard, but he also didn't want to have to backtrack almost an entire day if he could help it, as he'd already wasted one going in and out of the desert. As a result, he headed back to the town of Day's End, wanting to try one more time to get through its walls without causing an incident. If he was lucky, there wouldn't be any more people there that would be affected by his *Perceptive Misdirection* Fusion, and everything would be fine. If not... then he'd figure it out from there.

Contrary to his fears, when he arrived at the town he had the fortunate opportunity to insert himself into a small caravan of wagons that was arriving from deeper in the Empire. Walking calmly into the rear of the caravan, his presence only drew a few glances from the caravan guards and a few merchants, but they ignored him as if he was of no consequence. He was slightly nervous as he passed through the gates, but none of the guards – all of whom were Mage and Martial Protectors this time – looked at him twice.

Soon enough, he was inside the remarkably large town and surreptitiously broke off from the caravan to look for supplies and information. He was surprised at how extensive the town was, as it was almost as populous as a small city, given its location on the border and the complete lack of farming being done outside the walls or anywhere within miles of the town. Knowing that this meant all of their food had to be brought in from outside, likely by caravans such as the one he just snuck in with, he couldn't understand why the town existed in the first place.

While he was tempted to stay the night rather than sleep outside again, he knew that the longer he was inside the town, the more likely someone would have the right stat allocation to detect what he was doing to their perception. Instead, he did some shopping through the marketplace there, buying up foodstuffs at a premium rate – further validating his thought that the town of Day's End brought in all of their food supply from elsewhere – so that even if he did have to run, he'd at least be properly supplied.

From there, he was at a bit of a loss for where to go to find out the information he needed about Lowenthal. Normally, he'd visit the Protectors and see if they had any information he could acquire from them, but with his previous visit still visibly setting the few Protectors he saw patrolling the streets on edge, he didn't think it was a good idea. Besides, from his experience with them, he found that it was at least twice as likely for someone to have gone through the whole Mage and Martial change a few months before if they were already a Protector, so the chance of one of them being a Mage that could identify him as the "monster" was much greater.

Instead, he decided to visit an Inn anyway, though not to stay; he'd learned on his travels that people who visited common rooms of inns were people who tended to gossip and share information that Larek had found largely inconsequential, but occasionally he'd heard a little about the road ahead. This was especially true when he stayed in places that catered to merchants, since they tended to travel a lot and therefore had a lot more to say, which he was hoping to find here.

It didn't take long to find out where the caravan with which he had snuck into the city had gone after they had unloaded their wagons, and he made his way into the Inn of Daylight's Trust, which was a strange name – but many of the Inns he'd visited had been oddly named, so he thought nothing much of it. Sitting down at an unoccupied table in the corner, he recognized a handful of the people from the caravan seated at the others, along with many that he figured were on the wagons but hadn't been visible.

Just after a serving woman took his order of whatever dinner they had ready, Larek's hearing detected something that caught his interest. It wasn't an entire conversation that answered all his questions, as much as he would've appreciated that, nor was it something that gave a hint of where he could go to discover what he needed to know – that would be entirely too easy. Instead, as he looked over at what appeared to be a raised platform in the opposite corner of the room, he saw someone bent over a stringed instrument of some kind, plucking the strings while they seemed to be adjusting some knobs along the side.

As he looked closer at the figure, a few things stood out to him. First, the long, green hair looked somewhat familiar for some reason. When he got a better look at the brown-skinned, six-fingered hand that looked like the tips of tree branches, attached to stick-like arms, it finally clicked.

*Verne.*

He was about to get up and shout with joy at being reunited with his roommate when the figure lifted their head and he got a clear look at their face, which had a small scar running down the side. It was obvious that this wasn't Verne. In fact, judging by the shape of their figure under a tight-fitting green dress that matched the color of their hair, this individual was female.

As she began to strum a few chords on the musical instrument she held in front of her, supported by a thin strap that wound over her shoulder and was attached to two points on the instrument, Larek looked for any sort of familiarity in the dark-skinned, tree-like woman, but he couldn't see anything other than her general appearance that reminded him of Verne.

His perusal of her features was interrupted when she began to sing in a language that was completely unfamiliar to him, and yet he could almost sense the meaning behind the words as the song flowed beautifully through the Inn's common room, capturing the attention of everyone inside. Even the Innkeeper behind the bar seemed to be enraptured as he leaned forward on his elbows and watched the woman with a small smile on his face, and all movement came to a halt as the servers stopped what they were doing to listen.

Larek wasn't sure how long he and the others simply sat or stood where they were, listening to the green-haired tree woman, but his hunger sharpened a bit once she stopped, and he twitched a little as if he had suddenly come out of a hyper-focused state. Glancing out the window, he was slightly startled to see that the angle of the sun showed that approximately two hours had passed while he had been entranced with the woman's singing.

*Wow. What in the world was that?*

As the woman twisted to put the instrument behind her back, Larek caught a glimpse of some sort of dark chain around her neck like a necklace, though he had to say that it really didn't suit her either in style or coloring. Not that he was an expert or anything – far from it, actually – but it seemed to him that it was extremely out of place.

"Serena, Serena! Beautiful as usual, my darling," Larek heard coming from one of the tables where the caravan members were seated. An older man with short, dark hair streaked with two front-to-back bands of white hair like the horns on a ram, taller than the rest by at least a few inches – but nowhere near Larek's real height – smiled at the woman, though Larek didn't see any sign of enjoyment or happiness in that smile. Instead, what he thought he saw was greedy pleasure, and it was just barely short of being lecherous.

It was a wonder what Larek could pick up from watching people over the last month when they completely disregarded his presence, which was yet another benefit of his *Perspective Misdirection* Fusion. He was somewhat thankful that his observation of so many people without their attention had been so fruitful in further discerning social interactions, but at this point he wasn't sure if it was beneficial or not.

Mainly because, while he wasn't 100% sure, he was fairly confident that there was some sort of negative relationship between the singer and this merchant. This was nearly confirmed when she seemed to ignore his comment as she looked away. Larek wasn't sure if it was intentional, or she was just trying to look elsewhere, but she ended up looking straight at the Combat Fusionist and almost instantly locked eyes with him.

At that moment, he knew he would have to extricate her from what was obviously some sort of forced situation that she had no way to escape from without his help. Not because she looked similar to his roommate, Verne, or because she had a nice singing voice. No, it was because when she looked at him in the eyes, she looked at his *actual* eyes and not the fake, shorter perception that everyone else saw.

*Great. I don't have time for this. But... well, if she's originally from the Dyran Hearthwood the same as Verne, she might have information that could be beneficial to me. It would be a shame if I let her go when she might know about Lowenthal and the desert and would be willing to share. If she was near home recently, she might even know what's going on in the nearby Kingdom of Androthe, for that matter.*

It was an extra complication that he didn't really need, but he knew that he would have to save her from whatever situation she was in, even if it jeopardized his stay in Day's End. He simply had to figure out what was going on – which was probably the easiest thing in the world, right?

# Chapter 35

As Larek stared back at the woman, the wooden table he was leaning on began to subtly vibrate. Before he could pull away at the sudden motion, there was a feminine voice in his head that sounded suspiciously like the singer from the Dyran Hearthwood.

*"Can you hear me? Oh, please let this work!"*

Larek pulled away from the table in shock, feeling the strange connection disappear once he was no longer touching the surface of it. However, curiosity at what he had just experienced got the better of him as he placed his bare right hand back on top of the tabletop, and he felt the strange vibration occur again.

*"You can hear me! Keep in physical contact with the wood and we can easily communicate… or at least you can hear my thoughts. Unfortunately, unless you have a way with wood like my people, you won't be able to speak back to me."*

Glancing up at the green-haired woman, he could see the intent gaze she sent his way, which was completely at odds with the fairly upbeat tone she was using to speak into his mind. As for how she was doing that, he looked down at her foot and saw that it almost seemed to melt into the wooden floorboards; those floorboards then ran all the way under the wooden legs of his table, then up to the tabletop, and finally to his hand. Larek remembered how Verne had been adept at shaping wood with some sort of natural non-magic ability he possessed; he wondered if speaking through wood was simply the next stage in development of that ability.

He returned a subtle nod that caused the woman to turn away. At first, he thought she hadn't seen it, but then he realized that staring at him for much longer would probably be a poor idea if she was communicating with him through such secretive methods.

A moment later, she was strumming her stringed instrument again, playing a sorrowful-sounding melody, but she didn't sing. Instead, she continued to speak to Larek without looking at him.

*"You may be wondering who I am and why I'm talking to you. First, as you may have heard, my name is Serena Grovewhisperer and I first traveled to the Sealance Empire to establish…"*

As he listened to her story while she played her instrument, many of Larek's questions about the state of the Kingdom and the nearby lands were answered, including what was going on with Lowenthal and the town of Day's End. There were still a few things he needed answers to, but she unknowingly helped him decide what to do just by explaining her plight. Unfortunately for her, she was also under a misconception about who he was and why he was there in the Empire in the first place.

*"...and so when I saw you, my own abilities with mental manipulation through the use of my voice allowed me to pierce the illusion your spell is attempting to insert into my mind. Please save me from this horrid merchant, and help me in my quest! I'll do anything you want..."*

Larek ignored that last part, because it was so desperate-sounding that it made him uncomfortable just to hear. However, he couldn't ignore her plight because she was engaged in something with the merchant that was nearly akin to slavery; that, and she had supplied him with information that he would've been hard-pressed to obtain otherwise – such a boon must be rewarded. Getting her away from the "horrid merchant" wouldn't be that big of a deal, if he was understanding what she had said well enough, but she probably wouldn't appreciate that he was going to abandon her shortly thereafter.

He reluctantly nodded again when she briefly glanced at him, and while she didn't show any outward sign that she saw it, he could hear the happiness in her voice.

*"Oh, thank you so much! We'll be staying in Day's End for two more days while Merchant Paleth conducts his business, but then we'll be gone – so act before that happens, if you would! Now, I better concentrate on what I'm doing or he'll become suspicious – and that's never a pleasant experience for anyone."*

The mind-speaking woman cut all contact with him as the table stopped vibrating and she once again sang beautifully, though Larek listened with only half an ear as his thoughts were on what he'd learned – and what he was going to do about it.

First and foremost, he reviewed what he'd learned about Lowenthal – if indeed it was the truth. He was cognizant that what he was told could be the complete truth or simply a stretching of that truth, all to get him to help her – but he wouldn't blame her for doing such a thing being in such dire straits as she was.

The land of Lowenthal wasn't overly large when compared to the Sealance Empire or the Kingdom of Androthe, but 1,000 miles of desert was still an enormous chunk of area to cross. Unfortunately, that was all that was out there – just vast stretches of sand and the occasional rock formation sticking out of the dunes. But it supposedly wasn't always like that, because there had been a thriving civilization spread throughout the *underground* ruled by a lizard-like race called the Drekkin – at least until the changes that occurred only a few months before. The long underground route was the only viable connection between the Kingdom of Androthe and the Sealance Empire, created with sturdy tunnels that stretched almost the entire distance between each of the larger lands.

Cities filled with hundreds of thousands of these Drekkin once ruled and policed the trade route through their land, though not everything was always amiable between the Empire and Lowenthal. Raids consisting of hundreds of unbloodied, 3-foot-tall Drekkin had plagued the town of Day's End for centuries, hence its high walls and its presence along the border. It was also the only border town situated close to the desert, because it was directly across from where the underground trade route began, and it was positioned to be both a major trading hub for those passing through to and from the Kingdom and a defense against the periodic raids by Drekkin. It was the latter that gave the town its name, in fact, as by "day's end" all the guards and Protectors on the wall had needed to look to the east, because the Drekkin were not fans of the heat for some reason and avoided the sun and daytime as much as possible.

At least, it was that way until the Corruption spread everywhere throughout the world. Something rumbled deep within the desert, shaking the land and collapsing most of the tunnels that had been carved through what most said was actually bedrock beneath the sand. Since then, there hadn't been any sign of any Drekkin, and since the entrance to the underground world was cut off simultaneously with the collapse of tunnels, there was now no way to get back to the Kingdom via that method.

What that essentially meant was that Larek would have to travel up top to pass through Lowenthal, which he already knew was going to be a chore. However, considering his Fusions and the ideas with them that he'd been thinking about for a while, it wouldn't be all bad if he was successful. Delaying a day or two in Day's End would be beneficial in the long run, he thought, and would actually save him time on his journey if he was lucky.

It would also give him time to formulate a plan to free Serena, though he doubted that would go as smoothly as his Fusion projects. A few hours later, as the Inn filled with even more people who arrived to enjoy the melodic stylings of the exotic, tree-like woman, Larek finally got up and asked the Innkeeper for a room.

"Rooms are in short supply because we have multiple merchants staying with us in the hopes that the route east will reopen," the smiling Innkeeper stated. "Not that anyone thinks that will happen anytime soon, but they're all chomping at the bit to be the first to resume trade *if* it occurs. Regardless, what that means for lodging is that the available rooms are going at a premium rate." The man paused, looking Larek up and down. "It's 80 silver a night. I know, that's expensive, but I've got to—"

"Done." Larek cut him off before he could say any more, before slapping a hand down on the bar top and lifting his hand. A pair of gleaming gold pieces shone there, and it was snatched up in the blink of an eye by the other man, whose smile became even wider. "Keep the remainder, if you would, if it'll pay for my meals as well."

The Innkeeper nodded, before handing him a key. "Dinner is already being served, and it'll continue to be fresh until 9 pm tonight. Breakfast starts at 7 am, and lunch is at noon. Enjoy your stay."

A few minutes later, Larek was up in his room and on his bed, digging through his supplies to lay out the planks of wood he'd been lugging around since Swiftwater. He hadn't really had a chance to use them for any big projects, though he'd temporarily utilized them to consolidate his newest Fusions to declutter his Fusion list while traveling, and to help advance his Skills to their new maximums. But now he was looking to create something that would allow him to journey over the desert at a faster rate than simply struggling through the shifting sands on foot.

However, before he could get started with anything other than some preliminary planning, there was a knock on the door followed by it opening. *I... locked that, didn't I?*

He did, of course, lock it, but the answer to what happened appeared a moment later when he saw Serena slip inside before closing the door behind her, a piece of wood in her hands shaped like the key he had used to enter the room in the first place. Not only that, but the wooden bar he had placed across the door had shifted just enough to allow the door to open without hindrance.

*If she hadn't knocked before coming in, I would've taken her for an assassin. It seems as though very few things are safe from someone like her – especially if wood of any sort is nearby.*

"I don't have long; Paleth is entertaining some individuals down below and allowed me a break," she began to say as soon as the door was closed. "Now, how are you going to get me away from him?"

*Wow. She's quite demanding, isn't she?*

"Uh, well, first of all, I need to let you know that I won't be going with you into the Empire—"

"What? But I need your help to search for a spot to plant our new grove, as the one in the Dyran Hearthwood is becoming too dangerous with its proximity to the powerful Apertures opening up in *your* Kingdom. It's my entire purpose for my travels here, and if it hadn't been for my misfortune to be sold into indentured servitude to Merchant Paleth by the caravan I took to get here, I'd already be done! My people are counting on me to do this, and when they come I need to have everything ready—"

"What makes you think they'll actually be able to make it here? You know, considering that travel through Lowenthal is so difficult?"

She barely paused for a breath before she answered. "Oh, I'm sure it will all be fine by the time that happens. What's more important is that you get this iron chain off of me, so I can be free of Paleth and get back to my purpose here!" she practically shouted, before demanding, "How are you going to do that?" as if it was a given that he would drop everything to help her.

"What is that iron chain and why does it matter so much?" Larek asked, confused. He had expected to help her escape from the Merchant at some point over the next couple of days as he figured out how to get to her without being detected, but now she was here talking about the chain around her neck?

"It constrains most of my... other abilities and makes me weak. The caravan I was traveling with turned out to be scoundrels and slipped it over my head while I was asleep before essentially selling me to that Merchant. It's not *technically* slavery, as I have to work like you saw before to pay off my purchase price, but it amounts to the same thing! Now, how are you going to get it off?"

Different thoughts were warring in Larek's head at the moment, as this "indentured servitude" sounded so much like slavery that he instantly hated it. At the same time, the woman's demanding tone was so different from the voice he heard in his head earlier down in the common room that his back was up, and he didn't *feel* like helping her as much.

In the end, it was a combination of things that finally convinced him to help. Her current plight as a quasi-slave, her goal to look for a new grove for her people who had been under attack as the Apertures apparently spread past the borders of the Kingdom in the four years since Larek had been there, and the fact that she had been helpful in providing information to him – even inadvertently – was enough reason despite her attitude.

"Fine, I'll help get it off of you," he finally acquiesced. "But like I said, I'm not going to accompany you."

"We'll talk about that more when you've removed the chain," she mumbled, though there was a glint in her eye that made him instantly wary. "What kind of preparation do you need? There's no opening on the chain links, and its much stronger than normal iron— whoa, what are you doing?"

Larek had stood up and brought his axe to his hand, before advancing toward the woman.

Putting her hands up as if to stop him, Serena's face twisted in fear. "Sure, taking my head off would allow you to slip it off, but it'll still kill me!"

"That's not what I'm doing. Now, stand very still if you would." When she kept backing up, eventually slamming up against the closed door, he added, "Unless you don't want it off?"

Breathing heavily, she put her hands down slowly. "What are you going to do?"

"Exactly what I said. I'm taking that thing off of you. Hold still; I don't think this will hurt, but if it does, I can heal you."

Before she could react, Larek took a quick step forward and chopped his axe at her neck, controlling it expertly with his *Axe Handling* Skill. As the sound of shearing metal followed by a *ping* as the chain snapped met his ears, he discovered that his strike was probably a bit heavy as there was also a dull snap as the impact of the axe blade against the chain snapped what appeared to be her collarbone and sliced into her neck.

A moment of confusion was followed by an inhalation of breath, and Larek knew that she was about to scream. While he didn't really fear the attention that her screaming at the top of her lungs would bring, it would also make her escape that much harder. Therefore, he swiftly put his left hand up to her face and covered her mouth, before placing his axe back in its holder. Once it was securely stored away, he grabbed her left hand with his right before placing it on his chest and activated his *Healing Surge* Fusion.

The screams that he was already muffling with his hand grew louder as she was healed of the damage he had done to her with the strike, before trailing off after a few seconds. Figuring that she was healed, he took his hand away and saw that the woman was staring at him with wide eyes even as her shoulders drooped from the toll the Fusion had taken from her to heal the damage.

She was about to say something, but the both of them looked down at the iron chain that had fallen to the floor as it seemed to shine brightly for a moment before fading away. As she looked back up at him and felt at her collarbone to discover that it had been healed, she smiled at him as the fear disappeared.

"Thank you! Thank you! Thank you!" Larek was suddenly worried that she would jump on him and kiss him all over his face, similar to how Penelope had reacted when he had saved Bartholomew from dying, but she just stood there as she softly clapped and bounced up and down, her exhaustion dissipating after a few seconds. "By the way, what is the name of my savior?"

"It's Larek. Larek Holsten. And you're welcome. Sorry for the damage, but it was the only way I could see to get it off in a hurry, and you should be fine now, if a little weak from the healing. Do you need help getting out of town? I can probably pick you up some supplies for your journey."

She stepped forward and placed her hand back on his chest, not so that she could be healed, but for another reason entirely. "Oh, no, I don't think that will be necessary, *Larek Holsten. You'll be accompanying me on my travels to help protect me while I fulfill my purpose here. But don't worry, a big, strong man like yourself deserves a reward for freeing me from my captors, though I'll make sure that I don't **drain** you too much along the way.*"

As she spoke, her voice shifted from being friendly and thankful to something much more demanding and forceful. There was an incessant prodding at his mind that was highly annoying, as it seemed as though it was trying to influence him somewhat, but it was pathetically ineffective.

Larek shook his head, somewhat sorry to disappoint the woman and her worthy goal. "No, I have my own goals and can't afford the time to accompany you. You're on your own from here on out."

Serena twitched backwards in surprise at his words, before her face and parts of her body started to distort and twist into disturbing shapes. After a few seconds, her face had transformed into a rictus of anger and sharp, angular features, and her voice deepened harshly.

*"You MUST accompany me, or you will DIE. OBEY my commands. My WILL is strong enough to enslave your soul—"*

As the pressure pushed against his mind, stronger and stronger, he found his mind starting to bend. Before too long, he was fairly certain that it would break, but there was nothing he could do. It was only at that point that a feeling he had been ignoring up until that point occurred to him, though it struggled to make itself be heard against the pressure he felt. The faint feeling of Corruption radiated off of the woman trying to force her will upon him, and he suddenly realized that she actually *was* a monster or had at least been changed by one. As if his thought solidified the truth of that, his *Magical Detection* Skill helped him look at the green-haired woman and felt the not-so-subtle influence that had taken over her body.

*Can I free her from it?*

Unfortunately for her and the potential for being saved, she mentioned the word "enslave" and Larek reacted faster than he ever had before. Reaching up with his hands, he gripped her head and twisted with all his strength, snapping her neck with a *\*crunch\** as it rotated in completely the wrong way. Her body fell to the ground instantly as all life left it, and a large cloud of Corrupted Aetheric Force sprang out of it, only to be absorbed a moment later by Larek.

It was a whole lot more than he expected. Later, he would find that it had given him 800 AF once it was purified in his body – an incredible amount, and the most he'd received from any monster so far, including the Trizards back in the Kingdom at the first Aperture.

Looking at the corpse on the floor, he was shocked to see that the woman's outward appearance had reverted back to what it looked like when he first saw her; it also made him feel a little bad for not being able to help her, but he didn't regret what he had done since he had been actively attacked by her. Still, how would he explain the body—

It turned out that he didn't have to worry about that, as the corpse began to break apart into wisps of dark-green and black smoke, as it dissolved into nothingness over the next few minutes. He'd never seen that happen before with a monster, especially one that had a physical form, but he supposed it was a side-effect of whatever he had actually killed. He still didn't know what exactly he had dealt with there, and frankly didn't really *want* to know.

Regardless, it was done, and there wasn't anything he could do about it, other than use the information he'd learned to get across the desert of Lowenthal. There was always a possibility that she was lying about the difficulty of traveling over the land, given that she was somehow being controlled or possessed by a monster, but he didn't think that was the case.

After ensuring that his door was locked once again and hoping that there wasn't another one of these possessing monsters with the ability to get through locked doors roaming about, Larek sat back on the bed and looked at his wooden planks. Before he did anything more, he pulled out a stone from his pouch and activated a *Secure Hideaway* Fusion to help protect him in case something did manage to find its way inside his room.

Once it was up and protecting him, he got to work.

# Chapter 36

Running through the arid landscape outside of Day's End, Larek thought about the night before and had to shake his head at how it all turned out. His willingness to help someone out of a bad situation had nearly blown up in his face like a stray *Fireball*, but at least he got information on Lowenthal and a little about the situation back in the Kingdom out of it. From what Serena had mentioned, the land had become so unsafe that the monsters from the Apertures had spread to other nearby lands. That she was supposedly coming to find a new place for the Dyran Hearthwood was in question, given her nature of being possessed by a monster, but the situation certainly seemed like it was at least mostly true back home.

What confused him the most was why she mistakenly thought he was on the run from the SIC. During the mind-to-mind conversation, Serena had mentioned that she was certain that he had fled from the Kingdom and was hiding out in the Sealance Empire; she said it in a way that made it seem like such a thing was common and so, of course, it made the most sense. But for the SIC members back home to be literally *fleeing* from the Kingdom, commonly enough for it to be known by outsiders, then it had to be quite bad. In addition, it practically *confirmed* that Larek had been stuck in the void for around four years, because otherwise it wouldn't have progressed to this point. All of that still didn't answer the question of *how* it got as bad as it sounded, but it was a start on the information concerning the Kingdom, at least.

In the end, it didn't really matter when or how it happened, but he was now even more desperate to get back as soon as possible to find his family and friends. Which was why he was running essentially out in the middle of nowhere to test his new Fusion to see if it would actually do what he designed it to do. He couldn't safely experiment with it in the town of Day's End, but out here there were no buildings or people that might get hurt if it didn't turn out the way he imagined.

Setting down the wooden square on which he'd created the new Fusion, he stepped back a dozen feet and mentally activated it. With a simple mental command of, "Lift 1", a blast of air shot down into the ground from below the board of wood, kicking up a dust cloud that was blown out in all directions. As the dust blew past him, he held up his arm to protect his face from the cloud, but he took it down as soon as possible to see the results of his test.

It was a good thing that he did, because otherwise he might have missed the wildly flipping square plank a second before it smacked him in the face. Dodging it at the last second by moving his head, Larek whipped his entire body around to watch the flipping wood stabilize a little before shooting off into the distance. It had gone so far at such a speed that it was quickly out of mental command range, and he watched it begin to arc almost straight up into the air. At some point, the wooden plank began to spin again as it flipped out of control, before he saw it stabilize again – but this time it was pointing straight downward toward a pile of sharp, jagged rocks.

"Uh, whoops."

Throwing himself onto the ground while covering his pack, the inevitable happened. Larek turned away from the explosion that occurred when the wooden board rocketed downward at incredible speed before smashing itself to pieces on the rocks below. While there was a Magnitude 8 strengthening Effect in the Fusion to make the wood stronger, even that couldn't withstand such an impact against sharp rocks with momentum aiding it in the endeavor.

Thankfully, the explosion was far enough away from Larek that he was only buffeted by a strong blast of wind and small debris that made it through his *Repelling Barrier* because of the high quantity of it. There wasn't enough of the explosive force to affect his other Fusions, thankfully, but if it was any closer, he didn't like his chances of survival.

Picking himself up, he looked to the crater that had been the pile of sharp rocks, and then around him as he saw chunks of those rocks having been blown up to 200 feet away from the site of the explosion. Breathing a sigh of relief that nothing worse had happened, and also thankful that he hadn't tried this inside the town, Larek reached inside his pack and pulled out an identical Fusion on a similar board of wood.

"Alright, so what did I learn?" he mused as he stared at the Fusion in his hand. "Well, it obviously works, but the material isn't necessarily the correct one due to its weight and... shape? The gusts of air shooting up from below are impossible to stabilize because if it's just a fraction of an inch off, then it sends the whole thing spinning out of control instead of providing simple upward lift. I can try and stabilize it with the three other gusts I have in place at different angles, but I'm not sure if that will be any more successful. Weight might help, though."

While he hadn't exactly been planning on testing it himself yet, Larek didn't see any other solution. If he placed something on top of the wooden plank, it would simply fall off as soon as it lifted in the air if it was tilted even slightly. But if *he* were to stand on top of it, he thought he could adjust his stance and weight enough to keep it stable.

Placing it down on the ground, Larek took a deep breath before he stepped onto the plank of wood. It was only 12 inches wide on each side, so he had to place his feet together to fit, but he managed somehow. Bending his knees to have a better ability to adjust his weight, Larek activated the same mental command as before, and a blast of dust blew out in a ring underneath his feet as he was jerked upward – all of an inch before his upward momentum stopped.

Due to his Agility stat, he was a lot more agile on his feet than he used to be, but even that wasn't enough to make it easy staying on top of the board as it attempted to slide out from underneath him. Every minute adjustment of his weight had the wooden plank shifting slightly as the air gust constantly pushed at it from below, but he eventually got the hang of it enough that it became easier to keep it level. *I'm sure that this would be much easier on something larger.* He regretted not building something that would be better suited to utilizing his new Fusion before he started with his testing, but it was a little late for that right now. When he went back to the town, however, he would look into getting something more appropriate.

Once he had it stabilized, Larek increased the strength of the gust of air Effect from below, using the mental phrase, "Lift 2", and he immediately felt a difference as he rose upwards at a steady pace. That steady pace was only an inch or so every second, but it was still progress – but it also required some additional concentration to keep the board steady. "Lift 3" was used once he was about a foot above the ground, and he suddenly began rising at a much faster speed at about a foot per second.

*I did it! I'm flying!*

Using what he'd learned from creating the ferry boat Fusions, Larek had adapted the ideas to create a Fusion that would allow him to lift off into the air. Of course, he was planning on putting it on some sort of… vessel? He wasn't quite sure about it yet, but just like the ferry boat had utilized the specific Fusions that had been created for it, the Combat Fusionist would have some way to utilize his new creation.

Of course, he wasn't done yet. Included in the Fusion were three other directional gusts of air Effects, located along the rear of the board, the left side, and the right side. Just like turning the different paddle wheels on the ferry, his air gusts would allow him to move forward or turn, depending on which ones he had active.

Once he was approximately 10 feet in the air, he tested out a new mental phrase, "Forward 1" – which was where everything went wrong.

Suddenly thrust forward, Larek was immediately knocked off the small board, despite knowing the thrust was coming. As he fell backwards and plummeted to the ground, he looked up to see the board spinning in crazy flips and rotating in wild circles. Remembering to deactivate it this time, the simple mental phrase, "All Off" was enough to shut down both gusts of air, and the plank followed Larek down to the ground.

Landing awkwardly from 10 feet up wasn't the most comfortable feeling, but his Body stat shrugged off the impact with only a slight twinge in his backside where he hit the ground first. That soon faded as he got up and brushed himself off before retrieving the deactivated Fusion, thankful that it hadn't slammed itself into a bunch of sharp rocks like the last one. Even falling from a mile up wouldn't damage the wood too much – as long as it didn't thrust itself into the ground.

Staring at the Fusion again, he decided that he didn't want to take the risk of hurting himself more than necessary, so when he got back on the wooden plank he limited himself to Magnitude 2 for the "Lift" portion of the experiment. Strangely enough, a few inches over where he had increased the Lift last time, or at about 14 inches off the ground, Larek didn't rise into the air any further. Looking below himself at the packed dirt beneath the overlayer of dust that had been blown off, he thought he understood what was going on. The air gust, when it blew upwards toward the block of wood, kept up the steady stream of air that he was expecting, but it also had to go somewhere after rebounding off the wooden material. From what he could tell from the dust still being picked up, it spread out to the sides and seemed to curl around itself back to the ground in a sort of flattened sphere that had the Fusion at the apex sitting on top of the upper flattened portion.

He wondered why it didn't simply spread out constantly before dispersing. It only took a few seconds of watching it at work to realize that the rebounding air was being pulled in by the Fusion's Effect once it hit the ground and curled in on itself, before being forced back up into the wooden plank in an endless cycle. In other words, the system of recycling rebounding gusts created a cushion of air that the Fusion was riding on top of.

It was at that point where he was bending over and forgetting to pay attention to his balance that he discovered that the cushion seemed to have an unintentional stabilizing effect. As he bent forward to look closer at the recycling air, he half-expected to fall off, but somehow the cushion nudged the block of wood back into the place of equilibrium it preferred on top and flat against the rebounding air. He soon found that there was a limit to the nudging it could do as he bent too far forward and the cushion essentially collapsed, sending him falling forward, and the plank shot away uncontrollably. Thankfully, he was again able to deactivate it before it went too far, and he was able to try again.

Magnitude 3 brought him up to a dozen feet before it stopped, and again the stabilizing effect was felt as an even larger cushion of air was created, though it didn't feel *quite* as stable as the Mag 2 version. Still, he was able to stand on the block of wood without too much trouble by that point, and small shifts of his weight didn't cause it to tip him off or fly off in crazy directions.

Magnitude 4 shot him up over 50 feet in a matter of seconds, and his balance was lost almost immediately upon acceleration. He deactivated the Fusion while still in the air once again, and he fell back to the ground – though this time he landed on his feet with a small *crack* that he could hear and feel in his ankles and knees. They weren't severely damaged by the fall, as he essentially just popped his joints from the impact, and any injury that might have been sustained was quickly soothed by his *Body Regeneration* Skill.

"Well, it looks like Magnitude 3 is the limit – if it's just me on top of that piece of wood, of course. Once I attach it to something, that could change things."

Having established a baseline of strength that he could handle at the moment, he continued his experiments. Limiting himself to Mag 2, he initiated the "Forward" gust of air at Magnitude 1 to see if that would allow him to move.

Prepared for the acceleration this time, he bent his knees as he moved forward at what he would consider a fast walk for a normal person. The gust of air coming from behind to push at the wooden board did something to the cushion of air below, as the air rebounded sporadically since it was facing a much smaller edge than the flatter bottom. As a result, the cushion became slightly lopsided as additional air was pushed into the system, causing him to tilt slightly forward. Larek was also physically pushed against by the rebounding air going up and over the upper side of the board, but it had lost most of its power and couldn't really budge him.

Magnitude 2 Forward gust of air, however, was entirely too much and destabilized everything, causing Larek to fall off again and deactivate the Fusion.

Unperturbed by the failure, he tried again at a Magnitude 3 Lift gust of air, and found that the Forward gust at Mag 1 barely affected the cushion below him. Magnitude 2 Forward gust of air made him tilt a little as he was pushed forward, but he was barely able to hold on – though his speed moving forward had increased to a decent run for a normal person. As soon as he attempted a Mag 3 Forward gust of air, he deactivated the Fusion almost immediately as he was basically pushed off.

    Turning was a challenge as well, as even a Mag 1 gust of air blasting against the corner of the board was enough to move it – and it was a lot more than could be easily controlled. Keeping the blast of air going for a second sent him spinning around in a circle and he was unable to stay balanced. He discovered that if there was some forward momentum, the turning wasn't out of control, though he had to activate and deactivate the right or left gust of air immediately. He thought that he could probably adjust this on his next iteration of the Fusion, because he was already finding things that could be tweaked to improve the whole thing.

    With his semi-successful experimentation done, Larek gathered up his things and stored them back in his pack before taking off for Day's End again. As much as he didn't want to spend more time in the town than he had to, it was also the only source of the materials he'd need to construct some sort of vessel to carry him across the desert; he had no plans to stand on top of a foot-square piece of wood the entire time, after all. In addition, if he was going to be moving across Lowenthal, which according to Serena didn't have any aboveground places for him to stop and resupply, he was going to have to bring everything with him – including as much food as would be needed for the trip. Thankfully, he was able to create water so that he stayed hydrated in the heat and dry air that would affect even Larek with his high Body stat, but food was another thing entirely in the barren desert.

    Which inevitably meant a larger vessel to hold all of those supplies, which would take some time to construct. While Larek had a little experience in creating vessels thanks to his time in Swiftwater and the ferry boat, he was by no means an expert. Instead, he thought that he was going to have to contract someone to help him construct it so that it didn't take days or weeks to finish, because he wanted to leave as soon as possible. And so that it didn't fall apart along the way, as he wasn't exactly confident in his construction abilities.

    He thought about all this as he saw the walls to the town in the distance, and he slowed down before he was within sight of those watching the road heading off to the west. It just wouldn't do to be seen running at a speed that likely no other people in the entire Empire could match – at least, not yet. He was sure they would get there eventually, but for now, such a display was out of place…

...and he still wanted to blend in as much as possible. He didn't need another incident like the ones he'd experienced in Day's End already.

# Chapter 37

Getting back into town was a bit nerve-wracking, as there was no caravan to sneak inside with, but fortunately the guards on duty only gave him a cursory glance before letting him through. Larek was thankful that they didn't have anyone on duty that would be affected by his *Perceptive Misdirection* Fusion, but he was still wary of everyone he passed just in case he ran into someone who would be.

Instead of going back to the Inn right away, Larek spent some time looking for someone who might be able to construct a vessel for him. Almost immediately, the Combat Fusionist discovered his first obstacle: an extreme lack of wood available in Day's End. He supposed it should've made sense that they wouldn't have large quantities of wood in such a dry area, where there were essentially no trees worth noting within miles. Larek had been fooled by the wood that the Inn possessed inside of its walls, but he quickly learned that such a display of material was more about prestige and to fancy-up the place than practicality, because while wood wasn't exactly *expensive* in Day's End, it wasn't common, either.

Instead, most of the material used around the town was either stone or metal-based, as they were much more plentiful with a quarry nearby and ores from under the Lowenthal desert that used to flow out from the area – before all the tunnels collapsed, of course.

Having had luck with a Cartwright in Swiftwater, he sought out the resident member of the profession in Day's End, and while the man was friendly enough, his response to his inquiry about working on a project was met with resistance – but not quite in the way he expected.

"I'd love to do it, but I got nothing to work with!" the man complained, kicking what appeared to be a scrap piece of a spring away from him, which bounced off the wall of the large stone, barn-like workshop. Looking around, there were a few such pieces of scrap, but that was about it; the workshop was relatively bare, otherwise. Along the back wall was a large workbench with a myriad of different tools hung up or slotted somewhere, all of them neatly organized and ready to be used, while what appeared to be a forge was set up in the corner, its fires out because it wasn't being operated at the time, as there were no projects that needed to be worked on.

The Cartwright went on. "I used to be extremely busy every day of the week, as we had caravans and their wagons moving in and out of Lowenthal constantly, and everyone needed their conveyances in tip-top shape! I even had to construct new wagons *weekly* because most caravans treated the ones they had so poorly that eventually they became impossible to repair without replacing everything, so it was easier and cheaper to simply buy a new one. But now, with trade essentially coming to a halt, there's no need for my services!

"As a result of my lack of necessity, there's no more wood coming into the town from outside sources, and almost all of the ores that came out of Lowenthal have been sold off. I believe the last of them were already sold, though they still haven't been taken away yet; supposedly there's a merchant coming to pick the rest of them up, but I haven't really been paying attention too closely to that. They could be here already, for all that I know.

"But to fully answer your question, yes, I *could* build something like that out of very thin sheets of iron with a simple wood framing, but I don't have enough metal for that even if I melted down every piece of scrap here I could get my hands on. There's also no way I can afford the market rates to purchase the ore from the merchant who's picking it up, either."

Larek thought about it for a moment. "If I was able to acquire the ore, would you then be able to do it? If so, how quickly could it be done?"

The Cartwright looked skeptical, but he waved his hand at the empty workshop. "As you can see, *if* you can get that ore to me, I don't have any other projects to occupy my time. Even given that, I believe it would still take me at least two days to complete it fully. Possibly faster if everything goes smoothly. I fortunately have enough wood for the framing and a small platform, but that's about it – the real holdup is the iron. What do you need this for, anyway? It has no wheels, so I don't even know how you expect to move it—"

"I'll see about getting you that ore," Larek said, interrupting the man before he could ask too many questions. He had no desire to explain that he was making something that could be used to fly through the air, because he doubted the Cartwright would believe him. "Hopefully I'll have it for you by tonight."

"Good luck. Those Merchants are tight-fisted suckers, so try not to lose all your money. By the way, you never asked how much I'll charge for this project."

Larek shook his head. "I'm sure you'll charge me a fair price, but we can wait to see if I actually acquire the ore for you. You'll be hearing from me soon."

Before the Cartwright could say anything else, the Combat Fusionist had taken off for the Inn again. He had a fairly good idea who this "Merchant" who had bought up all the rest of the ore was, though he wasn't looking forward to talking to the one who had kept Serena captive. His reluctance wasn't necessarily because he didn't like the fact that the man had someone in indentured servitude, which sounded like slavery, but because he was unsure how much the man actually knew about the woman and the monster she had either become or had been possessed by.

\* \* \*

"Find her! She has to be here somewhere!" Paleth shouted at the two people in front of him, incensed at their incompetence. "I paid a hefty sum to purchase her debt, and I'm not about to let that go to waste!"

His two Caravan Guards, Emilia and Gort, passively stared back at him, weathering his outrage stoically. Sometimes he wished they would cringe and bow subserviently like he thought he deserved from his subordinates, but then again it was their calm and extremely competent natures that led them to be the best Guards that his money could buy. What was even better, their contract was still active for the better part of a year, so while they might have both undergone the change that granted them these magical abilities that many people seemed to have nowadays, they weren't about to break the contract. He thought that they were secretly grateful for it, otherwise they would be encouraged to go fight monsters and close these Apertures that had sprung up all over the Empire.

They'd already had plenty of opportunity to improve themselves by fighting the monsters found along the trade routes, of course, so it wasn't like they were lagging in experience by staying his Caravan Guards. If anything, what Paleth was doing was *even more* important than their work, as he was supplying necessary materials to crafters who were making the weapons needed to combat the monsters and Apertures. That included why they just happened to be in the town of Day's End, where they were picking up the last of the ore that had come from Lowenthal and the Drekkin cities underground. As this was the last of it for who knew how long until the tunnels were reopened – if they ever were – he was going to make a killing when he sold it further into the interior of the Empire.

He was expecting such a glorious payday that he had splurged and bought the debt of the very woman he was now haranguing his guards about. The beautiful Dyran, Serena Grovewhisperer, had accompanied the final caravan out of Lowenthal from the Kingdom of

Androthe and her homeland before the tunnels collapsed, but something had apparently happened to her along the way.

Paleth thought that it was simply old Drekkin superstition, but supposedly they believed that some sort of demon prowled the tunnels around their underground cities, said to possess unwary travelers to make them commit foul deeds. They even developed a special — and valuable — metal that they used to bind the victims that these demons possessed, worn in a chain necklace that restricted their abilities, whatever those might be. It was that chain necklace that first drew him to the green-haired Dyran when he just happened to be in Day's End when her caravan arrived, but it was the story that she had incurred a hefty debt to the Drekkin that allowed him to purchase that debt and have her for his very own. The caravan master had been desperate to get rid of her and make his money back, as he had to pay for whatever crimes she had committed — which he never received details of, but they didn't matter to Paleth — himself, and they both walked away from the exchange happy.

At least, he had been happy until she had up and disappeared the night before. At first, he had planned on simply killing her and disposing of the body... well, not *him*, but his guards would take care of it... so that he could obtain the chain necklace around her neck, but when he discovered that she had such an enchanting singing voice that Innkeepers would *pay* him for access to it in their common rooms, he began using her as an additional way to make money. When her fame spread far enough, he was at the point where he didn't even have to pay for lodging his people, which was more than worth it on their own.

Of course, this all counted toward her debt, but it would be a long time until she paid off the 5 platinum she had cost him to purchase her.

But now she was gone, and the necklace with her. But he *would* find her and make sure she never left his sight again. He'd been too lenient with her, despite the warnings he received from the Merchant he had purchased her from that she was dangerous. He'd never seen it himself, but if she was able to escape so completely from him and his Guards, then there must be some truth to it.

"It is possible that she left Day's End—" Emilia noted, but Paleth immediately shook his head.

"No, that would've been noted. Besides, where would she go? The nearest inhabited town is a few days away on foot, and none of our supplies are missing. She wouldn't leave the town without some way to survive out there, even if she wanted to escape." Looking at them intently and deepening his voice to impart the seriousness he was projecting, he said, "Like I said: Find her. She's in town somewhere. She couldn't have just disappeared."

He would have her back, but if she somehow eluded him, he'd rather just kill her and take the necklace as compensation. It would be a severe disappointment, as he enjoyed not having to pay for lodging lately, but he'd at least be able to recoup what he'd paid for her debt by selling the special chain to the right buyer.

As the two Caravan Guards turned to leave to follow his order to find the woman, Paleth noticed someone coming through the Inn's entrance. The man was fairly nondescript in serviceable, yet slightly dusty clothing seen on nearly 90% of the male population of the Empire, and the Merchant nearly let his gaze slide past him, but when the individual looked his way and started moving toward him, he took another look. *Hmm... there's something strange about him. Is that a woodcutter's axe on his belt and a walking staff in his hand? Also, why does he look familiar? Oh, yes, I think I remember him from the common room the day before. I wonder...?*

"Wait. Have you had a chance to ask this man if he's seen Serena? He was also here yesterday," he told his Guards.

They shook their heads – which was surprising, because they were usually very thorough in whatever they did. To have missed this man in their questioning raised some questions.

Having seen that they were now looking at him, the man faltered slightly in his step as he continued to approach Merchant Paleth, which was slightly suspicious all by itself. When taken with everything else, he locked his fingers together in front of him on the table, giving his Guards the sign that he wanted to question this individual and to capture him if he attempted to run. Gort nodded almost imperceptibly in the corner of Paleth's eye, and the Merchant knew that he had gotten the message across.

"Merchant Paleth?" the man said, his voice much deeper and with a strength behind it that was surprising, and was at odds with his appearance. As a Merchant, he prided himself on being able to read a person or a situation so as to best take advantage of them for the most profit, but everything he was reading now about this man was utterly confusing. When Gort slipped his hand over the handle of his sword attached to his belt, showing that he thought this individual was extremely dangerous, that just added to the mystery.

"Yes, I'm Merchant Paleth. Is there something I can help you with?" Paleth asked with as much earnestness in his voice as possible. If the man was dangerous, he didn't want to have a confrontation here in the Inn, as he could end up getting hurt if there was a fight; that, and he wanted to lure the man in with a false sense of security by having a chat. Conversation was always preferable to a confrontation, as one could learn so much more from the former – and he might get some answers with just a few simple words. Much easier that way.

"Are you the merchant that bought all the rest of the ore from Day's End?"

*That... is not what I was expecting him to say. Wow, I'm really off with my reading of people today; I guess losing Serena has affected me more than I thought.* That being said, it was now obvious who this person was.

"Ah. You're one of those who believe that we're taking advantage of the situation here in Day's End and profiting off your misfortune, aren't you? Or at least you work for someone who believes such a thing? I'm sorry to disappoint you and your employer, but the deal has already been made, and we'll be leaving tomorrow." He paused for a moment as he sat forward, staring at the man for a few seconds with an intense gaze. "You can tell whoever sent you that if I encounter any type of misfortune to my caravan or discover any misdeeds preventing me from taking that ore away from here, that'll be the last mistake they or their families will ever make. Do I make myself clear?"

Sufficiently cowed by his threat, as his ruthlessness was known around these parts, he expected the man to immediately leave – and was surprised yet again.

"Uh, well, that's not why I'm here. I don't work for anyone in particular, and I don't care what you're doing with the ore. However, I *do* want to buy it from you. How much are you expecting to make from it when you take it from here?"

Paleth was tongue-tied for a moment as he comprehended the question, before chuckling at the joke the man just told. "Buy it from me? Ha! Seriously, who sent you? There's not enough money in Day's End to cover how much I'm planning on making from this. Unless you have a rich uncle who lives in the capital that can loan you 15 platinum, then you're—"

Paleth cut himself off as the man whipped the pack that the Merchant hadn't even noticed off his back and began reaching inside of it. Emilia and Gort pulled their swords out and held them out toward the man threateningly, but he didn't even seem to notice as he started pulling out one platinum coin after another, placing them in 3 stacks of 5 coins in the center of the table.

"15 platinum, you said? I was worried for a moment that it would be more," the man said, apparently relieved. Paleth had to calm himself down a little as he saw the wealth so simply placed on the table, which was at least 50% more than he expected to earn from the ore once it was all sold. That wasn't even considering transportation expenses and the overhead involved in the process, along with all the negotiation time it would've taken to secure maximum profit from those he conducted business with.

"Uh, yes, that seems to be in order. Where—?" he started to say, before he had to start again as he temporarily lost control of his voice from the excitement in it. "Where did you want it delivered?"

"The Cartwright here in town. I have a project I need assistance with, and the ore is a necessary component."

*Even better.* "I can have that done as soon as we're done here. Is there anything else I can help you with?" he asked.

"Actually, do you have any extra travel rations? Food that won't spoil for a month or longer? I'm going to need enough for at least 3 people to last that long."

In Merchant mode now, having recovered from the shock of selling the ore at an extremely high profit margin, Paleth thought about what he had available inside his caravans. He certainly did have foodstuffs that were suitable for lengthy periods of time, though he didn't have nearly enough for 3 people to last an entire month. He'd already sold most of what he'd brought with him to the local merchants in Day's End for a low markup, who then sold it to the population for their own profit. If he played it right, he could probably buy some of it back from the local merchants at the markup price and still come out ahead from this man who seemed to be made of money.

"I can have that delivered along with the ore. All it will cost you is… a single platinum," he said, and he sensed his Guards stiffen at his words. They might not be merchants, but even they knew that he was screwing over this man with a price that was enough to feed three people for a *year*, if not longer.

Reaching inside the pack, the man withdrew another coin and placed it on the table. "Done." As Paleth went to reach for it, the man spoke again. "However, I know that you've vastly overcharged me for both the ore and the food, but I'm willing to overlook that if you answer a few questions for me."

*Ah. Sharper than I thought.* "Alright, fair enough. What is it that you wish to know?"

"Was it you who put that chain on Serena Grovewhisperer?"

*Again, not what I expected.* He shook his head, before explaining where she got it and how he obtained her. It wasn't a secret, after all, and it was probably easily enough discovered if the man had simply asked around Day's End since the transaction happened in the town. Paleth thought that he was being tested, so he answered honestly since there was no reason to lie.

"Ah, I thought it might be something like that. Then did you know that she had been possessed by a monster?"

"No, that's just a superst—did you say, 'had been'?"

The man nodded, before pulling something else out of his pack and dropping it on the table. It was a familiar chain made of special Enexro metal supplied by the Drekkin. The last time he had seen it, the unbreakable chain had been around Serena's neck, but now it appeared as though it had been cut cleanly through one of the links – which was an impossibility if what was said about Enexro metal was true. It could be melted down at high temperatures, but it was nearly impossible to cut through without very special and expensive materials.

"Yes. She attempted to attack me by subverting my will and I had to put a stop to it... permanently. Once she was dead, her body dissolved and disappeared once what was possessing her left its host, leaving this behind. I apologize for being the bearer of bad news, but I thought you should know."

For the first time in years, Merchant Paleth was at a loss for words. He wasn't sure what to say, so he simply picked up the chain and let it run through his fingers, identifying right away that it was the same chain; he had momentarily thought it might be a fake since it had been cut cleanly through, but there was no mistaking Enexro metal when you held it in your hand. It had a subtle feel to it, like a hum that couldn't be felt or heard, which made it easily identifiable.

"Well, if that's all, then I'm looking forward to your deliveries. I have more to do today, so I'll leave you to get to it." The man moved to leave, and Paleth's Guards began to prevent him, but the Merchant made a motion with his hand indicating that he should be allowed to depart. While he was disappointed that Serena – *who was a monster, apparently!* – had been taken away from him, he would easily be able to recoup his loss from paying for her debt with the chain he was holding in his hand. In addition, he'd made enough from the transaction with the ore to allow him to not only expand his caravan, but to look into some additional markets.

But first, he had to fulfill his end of the bargain and get some things delivered.

# Chapter 38

Larek bent down underneath the large wood and iron structure, having to crawl in order to fit under where it was suspended upon four large pillars. It was familiar to him from his experience building the ferry boat, though on a much smaller scale. Fortunately, his project had been roughly the same size as a decently sized wagon, so the Cartwright was able to adapt his setup in his workshop to accommodate Larek's strange request.

Slipping the thin sheet of iron carefully into the central slot that had been created for it on his new vehicle's undercarriage, he used a small mallet to bend the edges around the inserted iron plate until it was secure and relatively flush with the rest of the bottom. Crawling back out, he climbed up a stepladder that allowed him to see the other Fusion he had already installed along the rear wall of the vehicle, checking to make sure it hadn't been dislodged from all his banging.

"I still don't know why you would want such thin iron plates," the Cartwright said, shaking his head with his hands on his hips. "I had to reforge them a few times when they bent far enough to crack. Frankly, and this isn't a knock on my own skills, they're flimsy and likely to shatter with a good blow of a large hammer, and they will offer absolutely very little protection if something were to try and pierce through it."

"But it's light, which is the most important feature," Larek replied, looking at the completed Air Skimmer. At least, that was what he was starting to call it in his head; he'd wanted to call it something grand and impressive like "Sky Flyer", but since it didn't actually fly through the sky, but instead skimmed above the surface of the land he traveled over on a cushion of air, he settled on Air Skimmer.

Mentally triggering the *Strengthen Area +8* Fusion he had placed along the inside back wall of the Air Skimmer, he felt and saw it activate as it drew in ambient Mana, before it took Effect. At a strange ringing sound like a bell being struck, the Cartwright took a step back in surprise as the very thin iron plates on the outer shell of the vehicle seemed to shrink the tiniest bit as it formed itself around the internal wooden frame. Not having made anything this large from all iron before, Larek was surprised at the reaction, but it seemed like it was a natural reaction to the iron becoming much stronger and more durable. The wooden frame on the inside was also strengthened, but the effect was more noticeable on the metal for some reason.

"What just happened?"

Chuckling, Larek walked over and tapped on the outer shell of the Air Skimmer with his mallet a few times, and he could sense that the metal had, indeed, strengthened quite a bit. With a much harder smack with a little of his Strength stat applied to it, which caused the Cartwright to inhale sharply, he looked to see if he had damaged the iron sheet. When he looked close enough, he could see a tiny little divot, but that was about it.

"That should do," the Combat Fusionist said, satisfied at what he saw.

"What? How?"

Patting the man on the back gently, all he said in response was, "Magic. Don't worry about it." Looking over at the pile of food supplies that had been dropped off a few days before by the price-gouging Merchant, he began to lift up and load the filled crates and bags into the Air Skimmer. As he was doing it, he looked over at the flabbergasted Cartwright and asked, "How much do I owe you, by the way?"

He really hoped it wasn't more than a few platinum, because while he still had plenty of what he had earned in Swiftwater left over, he knew that he was likely going to need some back in the Kingdom to resupply.

"Huh? Oh, uh, no charge."

"What? Come on, you did all this work and—"

Before Larek could finish, the other man waved toward the giant pile of ore that was now sitting in the corner of his workshop. "I'm pretty sure you said you're leaving this here and that it's mine, so I'd say you pretty much paid for my help multiple times simply from that. Besides, helping you relieved some of my boredom, and it was an interesting challenge. I should be thanking *you*… but I'm still keeping the ore." The Cartwright grinned, shaking his head at the enormous pile of ore.

It was actually a bit more than Larek expected when he acquired it from the Merchant, but he was honestly just happy that it was more than enough to get his project completed. He didn't need the ore and was fine with just leaving it for the Cartwright and the town of Day's End to use – even if it cost more money than he'd ever thought he'd spend on a single thing. Still, what was money used for other than to purchase what one needed? He needed the ore, he had the money to pay for it, and that was the extent of the transaction. Theoretically, he could sell it to the Cartwright or the town for a fraction of what he paid for it, but he didn't need more money right now, especially with the Cartwright charging nothing for his help.

"So, uh, what are you planning on doing with this? Transporting it out of here is going to be more difficult once you fill it up. It might have been relatively light before, but with all those supplies, it's going to be *heavy*."

Larek finished loading the last of the supplies inside the Air Skimmer before he looked at the entire thing one more time. At a total of 10 feet long and 6 feet wide, it essentially looked like a rectangular box with 4-foot-tall sides, though on the front end the wall was angled like a giant wedge to better cut through the air ahead. Extending from the corners of the walls was a sturdy wooden frame that extended 9 feet above the bottom, which supported a thin iron plate that extended out to the sides another 2 feet, designed to keep the hot sun from beating down on everything inside the Air Skimmer.

While Larek could handle direct sunlight – though it wouldn't necessarily be pleasant – his supplies weren't exactly meant to be in the sun for hours on end, day after day. It would still be hot, but they would likely survive that well enough; it was the extreme heat of direct sun that would cause them to spoil much, much faster.

Other than the wedge on top and the roof above his head, the only things other than the basic wood frame and the iron plates were the large wooden floor that covered all but the wedge portion of the Skimmer, along with a simple, 4-foot-tall bar of iron that extended up from the center that had a second, smaller bar on top sitting perpendicular. It was essentially a handlebar that he could hold onto while in motion; it didn't move or do anything else other than give him some stability, but he figured it would definitely be helpful based on his previous experiments.

"Don't worry, I've got more of that 'magic' that'll let me move it. You may want to step back in case this blows out a lot of dust," he warned. After moving essentially out of the workshop, the Cartwright stared in confusion as a blast of air underneath the Skimmer kicked up a bunch of dirt and sawdust from the construction.

After most of it had settled, Larek looked to see that his new floating vessel wasn't exactly floating yet. At Magnitude 1, the upward thrust produced by the gust of air wasn't even enough to lift it off the pillars supporting it from underneath. A moment and an increase in Magnitude later, he finally saw it shift slightly, but it still wasn't enough to lift it. Magnitude 3 finally had an effect... if just barely. He watched as it tried to lift up on one corner but immediately settled back down, and it appeared to be a bit unstable. Shutting off the gust of air, he thought he knew what the stabilization issue was, as he climbed back up the stepladder and shifted some of the supplies around, equalizing the load a little better. His next attempt at Mag 3 showed better stabilization, but it was still barely enough to move upwards.

Finally, at Magnitude 4 he saw the result he was hoping for as it rose a few inches off the 3-foot-high stone pillars, which was more than enough for him to work with. Moving behind it, he gently pushed it forward, and it floated on the cushion of air he was hoping to see, until it was floating just over 3 feet above the surface of the workshop.

It was at that point that he realized he should've warned the Cartwright a little bit more about what to expect, because he was holding his hands over his ears and crouching down where he was located just outside the workshop. While the building was large, it was still an enclosed space, and the sound of air rushing at such speeds, and with it caught in the recycling cushion system, it was *loud*. His own hearing was even affected by it despite his Body stat, but he could ignore it fairly well without becoming debilitated.

*If I redo the Fusions on this, I should probably add some* **Muffle Sound** *effects to it in order to reduce the noise. If I can even fit it in somewhere, of course.*

Slowly lowering the Magnitude from 4 to 3, and then all the way down to 2 before deactivating the Fusion — since Mag 2 or 1 did absolutely nothing to lift the vessel — he moved over to apologize to the Cartwright, though he stopped when the man stood up and looked at the Skimmer with wonder.

"That's amazing! Do you know what this means? We can have flying wagons moving all over the Empire, transporting goods and even people at high speeds! Actually, how fast can it go? Can you make more of these? Will it run out of power? If it does, how far will it go? Can this travel over the desert?—Wait. You're planning on using this to traverse the desert, aren't you? On *top* of the sands? I don't think anyone's done that before, but if it's possible to get to the other side, then you've made something extraordinary! And to think, *I* helped create this!"

"Whoa, whoa, slow down," Larek said, holding his hands out for the frantically excited Cartwright to stop talking. "This is the only one I can make, and it requires a special magic to produce and a special ability to control it. For now, this is a one-of-a-kind mode of transportation, but I'll think about producing more in the future. For now, though, I've got to get going because I'm already behind."

"B-but this is something that you should share with the world—"

"I've no time for the world right now. I have family and friends I have to find and ensure are safe. Please, if you wouldn't mind, move out of the way. Thank you so much for your help, but I really must be going." As the Cartwright had been talking excitedly he had moved to the front of the Air Skimmer, but he quickly jumped out of the way as Larek activated the gusts of air once again. It was quickly loud enough in the workshop that while he saw the Cartwright speaking, he couldn't make out the words. Well, he probably *could* if he really tried, but like he told the man, he'd already wasted enough time.

    Instead of increasing it to Magnitude 4 again, he discovered that Magnitude 3 was strong enough once it was close enough to the ground to create a cushion of air that allowed the Skimmer to lift a full 2 inches. That was all that was required to get it moving, and he pushed it ahead of himself as he was more than tall enough to look over the walls to see where he was going. The Cartwright appeared slightly furious at being ignored, but Larek didn't really care by this point; he'd already concluded his business with the man supposedly to the satisfaction of both of them, and there was no reason to stick around and talk now that the man had seen what his Fusions could do.

    He was tempted to climb aboard the Skimmer and control it from there, but he was still wary of doing such a thing inside the town. Lifting from the ground straight up was one thing, but trying to go forward while turning without any practice was something he'd rather have a lot of space around him to try – which the inside of Day's End didn't have in abundance. Fortunately, as he was forced to nudge the Cartwright out of the way with the front of his new vessel, Larek found that the town streets outside of the workshop were more than wide enough to accommodate what was essentially an 8-foot-wide contraption when he considered the roof overhang width.

    To say that he drew a crowd was an understatement, as the blasts of air keeping the Skimmer floating weren't exactly silent. As he made his way toward the gate, a group of 5 Protectors arrived and followed along, but fortunately they didn't try and stop him as he halfway expected. Fortunately for him – and them, since he didn't want to have to answer any questions and wasn't doing anything wrong – he made it to the gate and passed through without anyone barring his path. He could vaguely hear dozens of people trying to talk to him, likely to ask what this "thing" was that he was pushing and why it was making so much noise, but he didn't concentrate on their voices with enough focus to actually hear them.

    Approximately 100 feet from the town, he looked back at the gates and saw that everyone was still watching him as he deactivated the gusts of air, noticing that the Merchant from whom he'd bought the ore and supplies was watching him, with extreme curiosity and wonder marking his features. He could only assume that he was thinking the same thing as the Cartwright had, but Larek had no inclination to speak to the man any further than he had; buying what he needed and telling the Merchant about Serena while returning the strange chain to him was all the interaction he wanted or needed.

Quickly climbing aboard, he settled himself underneath the roof of the Air Skimmer and held onto the handlebars for stability as he activated the lifting gusts again. As he expected, Mag 1 and 2 did nothing except blow out some dust from below. With his additional weight, even Mag 3 barely got off the ground. Magnitude 4 brought him up a full 2 feet, less than what he'd seen in the workshop, but he supposed that it being less made sense due to the greater load it was designed to push.

He was tempted to push it to Magnitude 5 to test how high he could go, but what he needed more was to get some distance from the town and to practice turning and stopping. With a quick mental phrase, "Forward 1", he felt the gust of air impact the back of the Skimmer and start moving it. At first, he inched along, but after he slowly started to gain momentum, he was moving at a fast walk – much faster than he expected at such a low Magnitude.

He concluded that with more surface area to push, as well as what was essentially a frictionless cushion of air that it was floating upon, it was easier to gain and then maintain a certain speed with a vessel with some weight to it. It also felt relatively stable, so he increased the forward-thrusting gust of air to Mag 2. With a temporary jerk of extra speed and a slight, momentary tilt forward, the Air Skimmer was moving at a decent running speed for a normal person. Magnitude 3 was even faster, as he moved at what he estimated to be about twice the speed of Mag 2; but it was also right on the edge of being too much, as he could feel under his feet that the cushion of air couldn't maintain its structure if he were to go any faster. It was possible that he might be able to do it with a Magnitude 5 gust of air lifting him from below, but he wasn't going to test that while he was already in motion.

Next came turning, which was much easier due to some modifications of the left and right gusts of air he had made. Now, every time he used the mental phrases, "Left Turn" and "Right Turn", the gust of air would only activate for a half-second before deactivating. It required another new component that he hadn't used before, but knew about from his learning of Advanced Fusions: **Interval**. What the Interval did was connect an Activation Method, an Input/Variable set (such as a specific mental phrase), a Magnitude, and an Effect, causing the Effect to only be activated for a specific interval.

In this case, the Activatable Activation Method ran through an Interval set at 0.5 seconds to the mental phrase Input, "Left Turn" Variable, Magnitude 1 component, and the gust of air Effect that was aimed at the forward right side of the Air Skimmer. What it effectively did was only activate the gust of air for a half-second, and it gave just enough of a push that it allowed the vessel to turn without spinning out of control.

In reality, with the Skimmer moving on the cushion of air, it was almost like the equivalent of sliding on ice. As a result, the gust of air on the right side of the vessel simply rotated the entire thing slightly while still maintaining its original heading, and only when the push from the back caught up with the change would it begin moving in the new direction. That made turning in a certain direction to reach a specific destination difficult, unless he planned out his turns far in advance. It was more of a curve than a sharp course correction, but it worked well enough that it would get him to where he was going.

Lastly, he needed to test stopping the Air Skimmer, which nearly resulted in him crashing the entire thing. With a fifth gust of air added to the front of the vessel, designed to help slow it down and stop it, he made a mistake by turning off the forward-thrusting gust of air from behind before turning on the Magnitude 1 gust that blew from the front with the phrase, "Stop 1". Even though there was no active push from behind, the Skimmer still had momentum as it glided along its cushion of air – but it wasn't much. However, upon activation of the stopping gust, it was almost as if the Skimmer had run into a wall, as it stopped so abruptly that the front dipped down and the back came up, nearly flipping the entire thing over. A few of the crates and bags shifted along with the abrupt change in equilibrium, but everything quickly settled back down as it partially stabilized and began to be pushed backwards.

Deactivating everything, he got everything put away back where it should be and tried again, this time slowly decreasing the forward gust of air in Magnitude and maintaining it at Mag 1 before activating the stopping. It was a delicate balance that he had to maintain as it slowed to the point where he could deactivate the rear gust of air, and there was still a slight jolt when the stopping gust took effect, but it wasn't nearly as bad.

With the success of his testing and practice, he eventually turned his new Air Skimmer toward the east and started on his journey home over the long stretch of desert.

# Chapter 39

Hovering 10 feet over the desert on a large air cushion as he initiated Magnitude 5 on his upward-lifting gust Effect, Larek felt the Air Skimmer stabilize before he tested his forward progress with a Magnitude 1 constant air gust. When that seemed just fine, he moved up to Magnitude 2 and then 3, finding that – similar to when he was only about 2 feet off the ground at Magnitude 4 lifting gust – it was right on the edge of being unbalanced from the rear-based thrust. He didn't bother to test anything stronger, either with his lift or his forward momentum, as he was already moving at a decent enough speed at a good height that he didn't think he needed much more than that.

As he traveled east above the sands that seemed to stretch out endlessly in every direction – except the west, where the Sealance Empire he had just left behind was located – Larek finally had a chance to relax. With the wind of his passage through the air doing its best to cool him off under the roof that kept most of the beating sun off him, Larek thought about all he had accomplished over the last few days while he had been waiting for the Air Skimmer to be constructed.

First, of course, was the Fusion that made it all possible, *Multi-Thruster*. It was a strange name that it had been given, but he supposed that it described what it did in the most general terms. By "thrusting" powerful gusts of air at the Air Skimmer, it allowed the vessel to float on an air cushion and move in different directions, all with an application of some mental phrasing to control it.

**Multi-Thruster +6**
*Activation Method(s): Activatable*
*Effect: Forcefully pushes against nearby targets with a strong, continuous directional gust of air*
*Effect: Forcefully pushes against nearby targets with a strong, continuous directional gust of air*
*Effect: Forcefully pushes against nearby targets with a strong, continuous directional gust of air*
*Effect: Forcefully pushes against nearby targets with a strong, continuous directional gust of air*
*Effect: Forcefully pushes against nearby targets with a strong, continuous directional gust of air*
*Effect(s): Using non-invasive mental manipulation, activates or deactivates Activatable Activation Method upon detection of mental phrasing by individual in proximity*

*Input(s):* Mental phrasing
*Variable(s):* Mental phrasing of "Lift 1", "Lift 2", "Lift 3", "Lift 4", "Lift 5", "Lift 6", "Forward 1", "Forward 2", "Forward 3", "Forward 4", "Forward 5", "Forward 6", "Stop 1", "Stop 2", "Stop 3", "Stop 4", "Stop 5", "Stop 6"
*Variable(s):* Mental phrasing of "Right Turn" and "Left Turn"
*Variable(s):* Directional orientations
*Interval(s):* 0.5 seconds, stop
*Magnitude(s):* 100%-600% of base gust strength, mental detection up to 60 feet
*Mana Cost:* 145,000
*Pattern Cohesion:* 500
*Fusion Time:* 77 hours

    Surprisingly, the *Multi-Thruster* Fusion wasn't too expensive in terms of Mana Cost and Pattern Cohesion compared to some that he'd created lately, though that could also be because he only needed a Magnitude 6 variation for what he needed it to do. What made it a lot more complicated was how many different components to the formation there were, in addition to the maximum number of Effects his Advanced Fusion could sustain, which was currently only six. What helped him be able to complete it was that most of the different Effects were similar in execution, being gusts of air, which made it simply a matter of ensuring that each Effect was matched up with the correct Variables and the idea of directional orientation.

    It was also his largest formation to date, as it was a 7-by-7 grid for a total of 49 different sections with 6 Effects, 6 Magnitudes, 6 Mana Costs (to help with powering so many different Effects, which were likely to be used simultaneously), 26 Variables, a pair of Intervals for the turns, an Input for mental phrasing, an Activatable Activation Method, and a single Splitter that was used to aid in the splitting of Mana feeds through the formation when the turns were being utilized.

    He thought that the only reason he had been able to keep all the different components of the formation separate while still in a cohesive whole had been because of his increased Skills that aided him in the process, including *Fusion* and *Pattern Formation* which were at Level 50, along with *Multi-effect Fusion Focus* at Level 40. *Mana Control* at Level 50 had also helped him to separate his Mana flow into the formation as it was split across the 6 Mana Cost components, which was beneficial for the flow of Mana throughout the Fusion and to prevent strain in the future; with so many different Magnitudes and Effects, it was much better to use multiple sources of ambient Mana that were pulled from the environment, rather than a single one where it would all flow through.

Creating the Fusion to his standards had taken a few hours that first night when he got back to Day's End after ensuring that he had the ore and food supply situation taken care of with the Merchant, so that gave Larek time to experiment with some other things. The first was to completely redo the Fusions on his staff and apply what he'd learned over the last few months.

Stripping the staff bare other than the *Strengthen* Fusion that was still operating just fine, he placed a new variation of the different offensive Fusions he'd used on it before that took advantage of mental phrasing, multiple Magnitudes, multiple Effects, and multiple Interval components used in the formation. What he was able to put together was an offensive Fusion similar to before, but able to become weaker or more powerful at a thought by switching the Magnitude of the icy projectile it created.

Why would he need different Magnitudes, when something more powerful – when used against monsters – was almost always the better option? The answer to that was in two parts, and it had to do with the current Mana density of the area and the multiple Intervals he used. First, activating his previous staff Fusion – which had a Magnitude of 7 – was fine for the Mana density around the areas he fought in in the Sealance Empire, but constant use for about 10 minutes would reduce the density quite quickly. If he happened to use one of his other offensive Fusions, such as *Frozen Zone*, he could only activate something like *Icy Spike* on his staff for a minute or two before it would begin to deplete the density too quickly to sustain his attacks.

Which naturally led to wanting to use an Effect that used much less Mana; hence, a lower Magnitude. An *Icy Spike* at Magnitude 1 was obviously weaker and did less damage to a target, as well as flying through the air as a projectile much slower than a higher Magnitude, but it also used a bare fraction of the Mana required to form and launch it when compared to those higher Magnitudes. Larek used a baseline of about 6 ambient Mana used per Magnitude 1 *Icy Spike*, which was only 1 Mana higher than a Mage would use to cast an *Ice Spike* spell. Each subsequent increase in Magnitude increased the amount of ambient Mana needed, generally doubling in cost – though it was more an estimated range than anything set in stone. So, at Magnitude 7, it would cost somewhere between 360 and 400 mana per use of the offensive Fusion, which was substantially higher than the Magnitude 1 Effect.

What that meant was that, even on the low end of that range, the Fusion could produce around 60 Magnitude 1 *Icy Spikes* for the same cost as a single Magnitude 7 projectile. Previously, this wasn't really something he could do, since even if he had a staff with a Magnitude 1 *Icy Spike* Fusion on it, activating it more than once a second was difficult because he'd had to activate it each time with a mental thought. In addition, while his formations were strong, they couldn't handle the stress of the constant activations without being damaged over a length of time, even at Magnitude 1. Thankfully, his Fusions were stronger than they were back in the Kingdom, and by ensuring that the lines in his formations were as perfect as possible, it lessened the risk that they would get stressed and therefore damaged.

Now, along with being able to use the Interval component, he was able to find a way to increase the speed at which the Effect would activate. It turned out that he could make the interval between activations *very* short, so with a wait of only 0.05 seconds between each activation, that meant he could launch 20 icy projectiles per second; when activated, they came out of the end of the staff essentially as a constant stream of ice. Granted, they didn't do a lot of damage and were generally weaker with less impact than a Mage would get out of an equivalent spell, but when there were 20 of them per second... well, quantity occasionally had a quality of its own.

With each increase in Magnitude, there was a separate interval set up that reduced the speed of activation, with Magnitude 2 being 10 per second, Mag 3 at 5 per second, and so on. He added Magnitudes all the way up to 8 into the Fusion, so that if he needed something a little more powerful he would have access to it, but Mag 8 would require almost 10 seconds between each projectile to reduce the chance of depleting the ambient Mana too quickly.

Needless to say, the increase in the effectiveness of his staff made it even more formidable and versatile than it used to be. Not only that, but because he had the ability to add additional Effects like never before, his Fusion wasn't limited to just shooting out sharp ice projectiles. Using mental phrasing made it easy to switch between what was essentially *Icy Spike, Flaming Ball, Flying Stone,* and *Water Stream*. They couldn't be used at the same time, because that wasn't something he was able to figure out without completely destroying the formation during use as multiple streams of Mana pulsing through the grid would tear it apart, but switching between types of elemental projectiles was as easy as a thought.

It also helped that he only needed to add the new *Variable Repeating Elemental Projectile* Fusion, or what he was calling in his head

*VREP* for short, to one end of the staff, as it meant he didn't have to flip it around to launch a different type of projectile. He almost added a *Repelling Gust* Effect as well, but left it off because the Fusion was already complicated enough without adding an additional complication; with 4 different elemental Effects, it was already significantly better than anything he'd had before.

But that wasn't the only Fusion he had worked on while he was waiting for the Air Skimmer to be constructed. Pulling out one of the stones he had in a specific belt pocket, he held it up in front of himself to take a closer look. It was a relatively easy Fusion to make, as it was only a Simple Intermediate Fusion in complexity – but he hoped that it was nevertheless effective.

After the experiences he'd had both in the Kingdom of Androthe and in the Sealance Empire, there were a couple of things that Larek had learned about himself. First and foremost, he couldn't cast spells because his ability to create strong patterns made it impossible for them to disperse after the spell's effect was cast, resulting in it detonating after pulling in too much Mana. Secondly, it was this strong quality to his patterns that allowed him to pump so much Mana into a Fusion formation without it exploding, because it was designed to hold a certain amount of Mana safely. The problem, of course, was that he had to make sure that the Fusion wasn't damaged, or else it would also detonate due to the Mana being violently released from the pattern. He'd seen this with the *Healing Surge* Fusions back at Crystalview, and just recently with the Fusion he'd created on a board of wood, when it smashed at full speed into a pile of sharp rocks.

But what if he could take advantage of this unfortunate tendency to explode when damaged, instead of it being something that he sought to avoid? It was the answer to that question that led him to create his newest Fusion: *Weaken*.

Being very familiar with the *Strengthen* Effect by this point, he began to wonder if he could do the opposite. It turned out to be extremely easy, as he simply took the symbol that normally defined the *Strengthen* Effect of a Fusion and *inverted it* inside its space in the formation. Accompanying that was the idea that instead of making something stronger, it would instead make it a lot weaker, to the point where even a thick bar of steel could be bent and even torn apart with something as simple as someone's fingers – if the Magnitude was high enough, of course.

When he applied this to something like the stone in his hand, the normally hard rock would break apart and even shatter when enough force was applied to it. This sounded counterintuitive to use on any type of material, but that was precisely what he wanted it to do – and to do it quickly.

Using a mental phrase that was able to reach up to 150 feet away, Larek could activate the Fusion on the stone, causing it to be weakened considerably. His idea behind this was very simple; throw one of these rocks at a monster, mentally activate it while it was in flight, and then when it hit something with enough force, the stone would shatter and release the Mana contained in the Fusion formation all at once, creating an explosion. Additionally, to ensure that his mental activation didn't activate *all* of his stones, he also had an Input and Variable set added that required him to have had physical contact with it within the last 5 seconds. To make sure it actually shattered, he raised the Magnitude to 10, meaning that it would be extremely weak and would be affected by just about anything it impacted afterwards, unless it landed on a cloud or a pile of feathers.

Because it was a simple, relatively uncomplicated Effect, it was inexpensive to create. At Magnitude 1, it only cost a total of 15 Mana and 1 Pattern Cohesion, and would take a normal person 10 minutes to fully form the Fusion. At Magnitude 10, it required a total of 37,500 Mana and 575 Pattern Cohesion, and would take about 68 hours for a normal Fusionist to create.

Even that was expensive for a one-time use Fusion like the one he was designing, but that didn't take into effect his *Focused Division* Skill. At Level 45 in the Skill, he discovered that he could create a full *20* copies of the Fusion simultaneously, and although the Pattern Cohesion cost increased with each copy, it was still under 3,000 Pattern Cohesion to create them all at the same time. As a result, he now had 40 copies of the *Weaken* Fusion on a bunch of rocks in his belt pockets, and he was ready to test one of them.

Slowing down the Air Skimmer so that he was only moving at the speed of a fast walk, he chucked the stone in his hand to his right, where it soared through the air in an arc that would take it at least a few hundred feet away. As soon as he saw that it was going generally where he wanted it, he mentally activated the *Weaken* Fusion and watched it as it landed. Within a second of impact, an explosive detonation that created a large eruption of sand occurred, and even at about 300 feet away, he felt a very small shockwave pass through him.

**Throwing** *has reached Level 11!*

The unexpected increase in a Skill aside, he was more surprised at how well his idea had worked. His *Weaken* Fusion had been highly effective, obviously, but now he was wondering if it was *too* effective. He'd have to take caution not to make it explode to close to him, or he could end up hurting himself as much or more than whatever he was aiming at.

    Shrugging with a thought that it was probably a good problem to have, Larek smiled as he imagined his *Weaken* bombs killing monsters from hundreds of feet away.  He was still thinking about his success as he increased the speed of his Skimmer's movement again as he flew over the seemingly unending desert.

    Unfortunately, he was so distracted that he didn't notice the disturbance he had caused in the dunes, as something underneath the sand stirred at the sudden interference in its domain.

# Chapter 40

It was nearly 5 hours into his trip over the desert, as the sun began to approach the horizon toward night, that Larek realized something that made him slowly bring the Air Skimmer to a stop, though he kept it floating above the sand. It wasn't something that he had forgotten, nor did he visually notice something that made him want to pause, and there wasn't a pressing need to stop and eat from his supplies, though he was getting a little thirsty. It wasn't any of those things, but was something that was completely lacking in the land he skimmed over.

Not once in the miles and miles of desert he passed through did he sense a single instance of an Aperture.

At first, he considered that there simply hadn't been any that were near his route through Lowenthal, but that seemed awfully unlikely. When he had been passing through the Empire, he could barely go a mile or two before detecting one, though in the more populated areas it was more difficult because they began to get closed more often, which reduced his sense of them to less than a half-mile. While they were still open, though, he could detect them up to nearly 2 miles away, though at that distance they were relatively faint, and he had to be paying attention to really pinpoint where they were located.

But not once in his current trip over the desert did he sense any Apertures, closed or otherwise. According to the notification that he – along with everyone else – had received back in Enderflow, Scissions and Apertures were supposedly being opened *everywhere*, so it seemed strange that there weren't any in Lowenthal.

Looking at the sand dunes nearby, which didn't appear to have seen any form of life in years, if ever, he had a sudden thought. *Nothing is living on the surface; the Drekkin apparently live underground. Or at least they **lived** underground, as no one back in Day's End seemed to know what happened to them once the tunnels collapsed. What if there are Apertures, but they're far enough underground that I can't sense them?*

He had heard that the tunnels under the sand were deep, near bedrock, at least according to what he'd learned from Serena and a few other people while he stayed there, though the former source was a bit suspect with her being possessed by a monster and all that. Still, he didn't think anyone he got his information from had lied or stretched the truth that far, so it was entirely possible that they actually lived miles under the surface. If the Apertures had opened down there, then that would explain why he didn't sense them at all.

Larek felt slightly disappointed, as he had wanted to continue accumulating Aetheric Force on his trip over the desert, but that didn't seem likely at this point. Even if he had wanted to find a way to dig down to where the Apertures *might* be, he didn't have any way to do that.

*Though, I think I could probably figure out a Fusion that would help with that. Perhaps by utilizing the effect created by the Furrow spell I learned from Nedira—*
*SLAM*

Larek was nearly knocked over as something impacted his Air Skimmer hard enough to shift it both upwards and to the left far enough that it nearly flipped over. He managed to keep his feet as he instinctively gripped the handlebars he had momentarily let go of while he was investigating why he hadn't sensed any Apertures. Once the Skimmer stabilized a few seconds later, he cautiously looked over the right side to where he thought he felt the impact come from.

Thankfully, he saw no damage to his vessel, but as for what had slammed into it, there was no sign.

There seemed to be a disturbance in the sand below, but he couldn't say for sure because the air cushion was moving a lot of it around as it cycled through the system it had created, so it could've been a result of that. He peered over the side and even peeked all around the vessel to see if there was any other sign of what had hit it, but he saw absolutely nothing.

Now wary of there actually being something in the desert, he resolved to keep a better eye out for whatever it might be, because if it had been able to attack him 10 feet above the surface with such a blow and then disappear as if it had never existed, then it was something that might actually be able to harm him. Still, he had no desire to set the Air Skimmer down and investigate at the moment, so he simply reactivated the forward gusts to get him moving again.

Over the next hour, he didn't see anything at all moving along the desert, and if he hadn't *felt* the blow that occurred to the Skimmer, he would've considered that he had imagined it. As the sun began to set, sending the creeping darkness to cover the land, Larek began to look for someplace to settle down for the night so he could eat, drink, and sleep so that he would be refreshed in the morning. Theoretically, he could always keep going and cover more ground, but it was a little harder to navigate in the darkness to ensure he maintained the correct heading and not get turned around. Guiding his way ahead by the stars above wasn't something that he'd ever learned how to do before, so it wasn't something he could rely on to see him pointing the correct way.

Larek finally found a large dune with a relatively level top to it, which he immediately maneuvered his way over and practiced his precise application of the air gusts from his *Multi-Thruster* Fusion. It was as difficult as he thought it would be, and while he hadn't perfected it by the time he set the Air Skimmer down on top of the dune, he had made some progress toward getting there. It sank a few inches but fortunately had enough surface area to keep it from sinking too far, and Larek immediately set up his *Secure Hideaway* before getting himself something to eat. Ideally, he would've preferred to stay in the air while he slept, but the constant use of ambient Mana for prolonged periods of time would deplete the Mana density even at some of the lower Magnitudes, so it wasn't something he could maintain for the entire night – especially when he had *Secure Hideaway* active as well.

And he wasn't going to sacrifice being safe and secure behind his protective Fusion just so that he could stay hovering over the sand the entire night.

After breaking into the food supplies and hydrating himself with the help of a *Water Stream* at Magnitude 1 from the tip of his staff and a simple stone cup, he was ready for sleep. After rearranging some of the supplies in his Air Skimmer so that he would fit, he laid himself down inside the vessel on his side, curving around the handlebar pole in the center. With the help of one of his softer bags as a pillow, he closed his eyes and drifted off to a night of glorious slumber.

Larek woke up as the rising sun was just barely beginning to lighten the world around him, surprised that nothing had disturbed his sleep. Half-expecting to be attacked by something, given his encounter with a mysterious entity the previous day, he was pleased to find that his protective Fusion had obviously worked just as intended and kept everything away from him.

That was until he stood up and looked outside the Air Skimmer, discovering that it wasn't in the same place he had set the vessel down the night before.

"How did I get down here?" he asked aloud, confused at what had happened.

Instead of being on top of a sand dune, he was now at the bottom of one, as if he and the Skimmer had been moved; whether it was the same one he had landed on, he couldn't tell, as they all looked very similar and there was no sign of disturbance on it. There was no indication that he had simply slid down the side of the dune during the night, which he thought was entirely possible since he knew from personal experience that the sand was more viscous than solid. However, that didn't explain why he hadn't even felt the vessel tilt over as it moved down the slope of the dune, which he was sure he would've sensed even while asleep.

A quick look around his vessel's new resting place revealed no signs that anything had approached his location during the night. With no evidence to go on, he shifted his supplies back to where they would be balanced for the upcoming flight, and then lifted off the sand as he initiated his *Multi-Thruster* Fusion. Lifting the vessel in stages, he was nearly at his normal cruising altitude of 10 feet when he caught a flash of something black out of the corner of his eye right before another ***SLAM*** reverberated off the left side of the Air Skimmer. It hit the vessel even harder than before, and the result was worse than before since the cushion of air underneath hadn't fully stabilized the Skimmer, causing it to turn nearly sideways and shoot off to the right – and directly at the sand dune nearby.

One of the food crates slid out, along with one of the bags, before Larek managed to mentally order a reduction in the speed of the upward-thrusting gust of air, which greatly stopped his forward progress before he and the Skimmer impacted the dune at full speed. In fact, it had barely righted itself before slamming into the dune with a *thud* and an explosion of sand, knocking him off his feet and into the interior side of the vessel. Quickly recovering, he got up and took stock of the situation, before being pleased to see that the vessel hadn't seemed to take any physical damage from the hit or the impact, and the rest of his supplies were jumbled but still intact.

As for the crate and bag that had fallen overboard, he almost missed them as he saw the corner of the thin wooden box descend under the sand at a rapid pace, as if something were pulling it down. He was tempted to go after it, since those were some of his supplies, but he wasn't foolhardy enough to jump into danger when something clearly was down there. Soon, even the last hint of the crate was completely gone, and the sand settled where it was as if nothing had happened – just like the times he had been attacked or when his vessel had moved from where it was at the night before.

*Something is going on here, but I'm not sure I want to find out.*

It wasn't anything he'd ever thought about before, but he imagined that being pulled under the sand and suffocating as he was buried under dozens of feet of small granules had to be a bad way to go.

*The sooner I'm out of here, the better.*

Larek decided to begin moving forward as he rose into the air again, hopefully bypassing any risk of being hit again, and it seemed to work. Or at least nothing came out of the sand to attack him.

As he continued on his way through the desert, Larek contemplated what it was that was underneath the endless sand in all directions, but he eventually had to stop because he didn't have nearly enough information to go on. All he knew was that the barren environment wasn't as devoid of life as he had previously thought, though what exactly it was continued to be a mystery. Larek traveled many miles over the next day without anything interrupting his journey, even after he stopped around midday to eat and drink something. At that point, he used a higher Magnitude lifting gust of air to raise him up higher from the ground, though he could tell that it wasn't *quite* as stable as he previously was; what that told him was that trying to move forward while at that height would be a bad idea. Regardless, it afforded him a sense of security for the few minutes he spent gaining nourishment and hydration, which was all he really needed.

When night fell, he again stopped and found a place to set the vessel down, which was in between two large dunes this time in a relatively flat space that had no chance of drifting down somewhere. After setting *Secure Hideaway* up once again, he fell asleep despite being slightly paranoid that something would happen in the darkness.

He was right to worry, as he discovered after he woke in the pre-dawn light. Contrary to what happened the night before, he and the Air Skimmer were now *on top* of a dune with no signs of how it happened. Somehow worse than that, the entire landscape seemed to have changed, as Larek had paid attention the night before to how large the local dunes were and where they were in relation to his vessel, but none of them were even remotely familiar. The only explanation was that he had been transported somewhere else in the desert, but where exactly that was, he had no way of knowing.

Using his technique from the previous morning, he elevated the Air Skimmer from the sand while moving forward, and once again he avoided being hit by something. Whether it was actually effective, or if whatever was underneath the sand was now far away because of the distance he'd traveled the day before, he wasn't sure if he'd ever know.

The next evening, Larek set the Air Skimmer down again, but this time he decided to stay awake through the night. He thought it might be difficult to keep himself active while it was dark and nothing was happening, but it proved to be easy enough because his mind was racing with hyper-focused paranoia, to the point where he doubted he would sleep even if he laid down and closed his eyes.

At a point that he judged to be around midnight, something finally happened that dispelled any feelings of tiredness that he might have felt. It was subtle at first, and even though Larek was paying attention to everything around the area, he nearly missed it. It was only the very soft sound of sand gently rubbing against the shell of his Air Skimmer that alerted him that something was wrong. Standing up from where he had been resting his legs after the day, he looked out at the nearby desert to see something that boggled his mind.

The sand was moving. Not just a little bit, either, but the entirety of what he could see with his eyes was slowly but surely shifting in gentle, undulating waves that he was told that the ocean was like; it delicately pushed his vessel along with it, sometimes with a "wave" of sand pushing him up from below, while other times it rode at the bottom of a valley nearby massive dunes. The speed of the movement wasn't very fast, less than a slow walk for someone like him, but it didn't stop, either.

While there was no sun to easily navigate by, he was fairly certain that it was pulling him to the east – which was where he wanted to go. If it had been pushing him back toward the west, meaning that it was reversing some of the progress he'd made in his travels, he probably would've lifted off the sand to prevent it from working against him. As it was at least somewhat helpful, he let it continue as he stood wide-eyed staring at the sea of sand that was bringing him… somewhere.

Approximately an hour before the pre-dawn light would eventually start illuminating the sky, the movement through the sand began to slow and eventually stopped altogether, leaving him in an area that didn't resemble the place he had settled down at the beginning of the night.

*Mystery somewhat solved, but what should I make of all this? Is this harmful or just a unique quality of the desert I've never heard of before?*

He wasn't sure, but what he did become sure of, as he sat in the darkness of the pre-dawn night, was that something had changed that he hadn't really noticed until he had some time on his hands. In short, as he looked around himself with his *Magical Detection* Skill, it was clear that the Mana density had improved somewhat. It wasn't a huge increase, but it certainly caught his attention since everywhere in the Empire had been relatively similar as far as Mana density went. The only places he found that had *slightly* higher density were around Apertures, especially ones that hadn't been closed at all and were growing large enough to start affecting the density directly – though even those occurrences weren't that great of a difference.

Therefore, the fact that the density around Larek was increasing was due to a couple of potential reasons – or even both. The first was that he was slowly approaching the location of the Kingdom, and the incredible Mana density there was already spreading to nearby lands, at least in part. The second was that there were a bunch of open Apertures nearby that he couldn't detect, but he could at least detect the higher Mana density that they created just by existing.

To do something like that and have Larek detect the change in Mana density at such a distance – since he couldn't yet sense any Apertures – they would likely have to be quite large. Or, it was entirely possible that this was the result of one giant Aperture that was pumping out all the Mana into the desert...

...but that wasn't likely, was it?

# Chapter 41

The next day was just as quiet as the one before, but the night saw another movement of his Air Skimmer. At least, that was what he assumed happened, as he didn't stay awake to watch it happen; he needed sleep after not getting any the day before, and by the end of the day he was practically falling asleep on his feet. He thought that it was strange how exhausted he could get from basically just standing around all day, but it almost felt even worse than if he had been running the entire time.

It was just after deactivating his *Secure Hideout* while he was eating some breakfast in the morning that something finally changed.

It was subtle enough at first that he didn't really register what it was that he sensed, and his mind practically ignored it. That lasted for about a minute before a rumbling that was on the edge of his hearing started to shake his vessel; needless to say, that finally got his full attention. The next moment, out from under the sand – approximately 50 feet away from the Skimmer – came a dark, spherical shape that shot into the air a dozen feet before landing on top of the sand. When it landed, the spherical shape spread out to reveal what it really was, and Larek was able to recognize it from his *Monster Knowledge* class at Copperleaf Academy.

Standing only 3 feet tall, the **Barbed Gator** was just as wide but four times as long at 12 feet – and every inch of it was covered in small-but-sharp barbs that stuck out from its hide. Reptilian in appearance, the four-legged Gator had a massive set of jaws that could nearly fit a 5-foot-tall person into it, and it was able to snap them closed with incredible force. That would be unpleasant for anything that got caught in its mouth, because it had sharp, 3-inch-long teeth that could rend flesh, and once it grabbed ahold of something, it was able to use its powerful back and neck muscles to rend and tear its victims by moving most of its upper body.

Two things about this Barbed Gator stood out to Larek immediately. The first was that this particular monster *was not* what anyone would consider a Category 1-type of monster, which was the only type of monster he had encountered while in the Sealance Empire. Larek could only conclude that if there were monsters, Scissions, and Apertures in the desert environment of Lowenthal, then it was possible that the general strength of them all was higher than the Empire.

The second oddity about the Barbed Gator was the fact that it was in the desert at all. From what he remembered from his classes, the Gator usually appeared in Scissions that had more of a water-based bent to them, along with frogs and lizards as well as crabs and other monsters that were at home near bodies of water. If it was from a Scission, then how was it able to pass through the sand as if it were water? If it was from an Aperture, where was it, and why didn't the environment change to suit it, like almost every other one he'd seen starting in the Kingdom and continuing into the Sealance Empire?

Those things made him think that this Barbed Gator was actually a native of the desert and not a "monster" as he knew them, though it looked extremely out of place and had abilities outside of what he knew about them. Its movement through the sand was one thing, but when it took a single step toward him in the Skimmer, the sand seemed to firm up under its feet and deadly sharp claws, so that it walked on top of it as if it was completely solid ground.

As he brought his staff around to fire at the incoming enemy, Larek realized the rumbling hadn't stopped, as more and more of the Gators burst out of the desert curled up in a strange ball, before splaying their legs apart to land upright on top of the sand. One after another appeared in quick succession, encircling his vessel as if they were working together to surround him. This only enforced his thought that these might be natural beasts instead of monsters, because such strategy coming from relatively unintelligent monsters was practically unheard of.

Regardless of where they came from, it was obvious to Larek that they didn't simply appear so that they could have a pleasant chat with him. With there being so many of them instead of just the one he was planning on killing, he mentally activated his Air Skimmer and pushed the lifting gust of air to Magnitude 3 in order to get him off the ground. Unfortunately, a few precious seconds as the Gators approached were wasted when he realized that the sand underneath the vessel seemed to have hardened around its outer frame, trapping it in place. He thought he *might* be able to break free if he pushed the lifting gust further, but he also didn't want to accidentally rip his only conveyance over the desert apart in the process.

Resolved that he'd need to fight his way out, Larek brought his staff to bear on the first Gator and started to release a barrage of magical projectiles at the one that appeared first. Going with an *Icy Spike* with a Magnitude of 3, which fired out at a rate of 5 per second, the stream of moderately sized icicles flying through the air impacted the head and back of the charging Gator, piercing through an inch or two of flesh. Unfortunately, the barbs worked against Larek as they helped to slow down the projectiles and even shattered a few of them, resulting in much less damage than he expected.

Changing his method of attack on the fly, he instead started launching out *Flaming Balls* at Magnitude 1; 20 fist-sized balls of flame shot out per second, and he was pleased to see that when they hit the barbs covering the Gator, instead of them being deflected or reduced in efficiency, they broke apart and seemed to spread over the barbs, the hide, and the flesh underneath. Concentrating on the head of his target, the heat and flames from his projectiles completely engulfed its upper body, and soon, it couldn't see or move as its eyes were literally melting out of its head. It attempted to dodge away from the stream of fiery death being shot at it, but while a few dozen of the flaming balls missed, it couldn't get away from the majority of his attacks.

It wasn't dead yet, but it was incapacitated enough that it could barely move. So he switched to the next in line, a *Flying Stone* at Magnitude 4, to see what it would do, but that quickly proved to be ineffective. As in, *completely* ineffective, because as soon as the large stone slivers got close to any part of the Gator, the stone was pushed to the side, missing it completely. The only explanation he had for that was that it was using the same ability to pass through sand against the stones that were flying toward it, though how long they could keep that up was something with which he didn't have time to experiment.

Instead, he switched to *Water Stream* at Magnitude 7, which was slightly different in its Interval composition inside the *VREP* Fusion formation than the others – it was, in fact, a bit of the opposite. The reason for this was that *Water Stream* typically relied on a steady stream of water at a constant pressure against a target rather than individual projectiles; as a result, a Magnitude 1 *Water Stream* that turned on and off 20 times in a second wasn't as effective compared to if it was simply left active for longer. Therefore, the connection between Magnitude 1, the *Water Stream* Effect, and the Interval was actually the same as the Magnitude 8 Interval for the other Effects: 10 seconds. This essentially meant that it would be active for 10 seconds before deactivating, and then activating again almost immediately thereafter.

Obviously, at higher Magnitudes such as Mag 8, this would cause the *Water Stream* to activate 20 times a second, which might seem like it would have the opposite purpose behind regulating the amount of ambient Mana being pulled into the Fusion. However, Larek had discovered that with an Effect that was essentially being channeled over time, such as *Water Stream* and even something like *Healing Surge*, the amount of ambient Mana it used was entirely dependent on how long it was active, and it seemed to increase the ambient Mana draw the longer it kept channeling. During the initial activation, the draw was actually at its lowest and was nearly negligible, so activating a channeled Effect like Water Stream 20 times a second was approximately the equivalent of a *Flying Stone* at Magnitude 1.

At Magnitude 7, what the *Water Stream* Effect did was activate 10 times every second. This essentially created 10 individual, high-velocity streams of water that moved so fast that they nearly blended together from a visual perspective. Each strike by another segment of the *Stream* was like an additional punch into whatever it impacted, though it was much less precise and therefore made his usual method of cutting through flesh less reliable because they rarely hit in the same place as the one before unless one was *very* steady in holding the staff.

That didn't seem to matter against the Gators, however, as each impact by the powerful streams of water broke the sharp barbs and punched through to the flesh beneath the hide, leaving what were essentially finger-width craters over every area he targeted with the Effect. Seeing the effectiveness of Magnitude 7, he upped it to Mag 8 and saw the holes become smaller but penetrate further, even slightly cutting through bone when multiple streams impacted the same spot.

Unfortunately, the Gator moved so fast that hitting the same spot more than once was difficult if not impossible, and while he essentially chewed up the hide and flesh of his target, especially around the head where he aimed, it wasn't enough damage to do more than slow it down temporarily.

But it was enough of a delay that he was able to switch to the next, which was already halfway to his Air Skimmer, at about 25 feet away. Foregoing the barrage route, a Magnitude 8 *Flaming Ball* was shot at the next Gator, and while the barbed beast could move its body quickly, if not its feet, it was unable to avoid the 2-foot-wide ball of flames as it slammed into its head, just past its eyes. As it broke apart upon impact with the barbs, the flames spread over the entirety of its head and half of its upper body, effectively halting it in place.

With that Gator effectively halted, if not completely dead, he moved on and switched up his projectile to the *Icy Spike* yet again at Magnitude 8, as it had proven to be as effective as a *Flaming Ball*. The large chunk of ice that sprang out of the end of the staff practically crushed the head of the Gator he aimed at, prompting him to move on – which was when he realized he would quickly run out of time before at least a few dozen Gators arrived at his vessel. He realized that they were large enough that they could easily reach inside the Air Skimmer and attack him directly, and the last thing he wanted to do was fight where all his supplies were located. In addition, while it wasn't likely – given the strength of the materials it was made from – the potential for his vessel to be damaged in such a fight was greater than no chance at all.

Unfortunately, after launching a Mag 8 *Flaming Ball* and *Ice Spike* at two different Gators, they were both now on "Cooldown" because of the Fusion – so he couldn't use either projectile until 10 seconds had passed for each of them. Throwing himself out of the vessel, he hit the sand and nearly fell flat on his face as he realized that the ground was hard, as if he had landed on stone instead of small granules of sand. It seemed as though whatever the Gators had done to allow them to walk through the desert without them sinking into it had affected the whole area, and it was what had obviously kept his vessel trapped. Their appearance 50 feet away in a circle made a little more sense to him, as it was obviously used as a means of preventing his escape into the air.

Getting his feet under him, he slipped his axe out of the holder on his side and held it ready to attack while simultaneously firing his staff toward the Gator nearest to him, using a *Water Stream* at Mag 8 to completely ruin its face as it was filled with small-but-deep holes. That stopped that particular Gator, and he turned to blast another with water when he sensed that the *Flaming Ball* was ready to go once again. As it was closer to him now, a Mag 7 Flaming Ball impacted the nearest Gator at almost point-blank range, and he felt a wave of heat wash over him as his target was lit on fire.

He had the time to switch to an *Icy Spike* at Magnitude 8 and impale the head of the next-nearest Gator, and for once it actually went into and through the eye socket of his target, piercing through its brain, killing it instantly.

With the distance between him and danger running out, he quickly tossed the staff back into the Skimmer as he reached down to pull out a few things from his belt pouches. The first was a *Secure Hideaway*, which he activated and tossed into his vessel, protecting it from being harmed for a while; he was fairly certain that the Gators could break through the dome surrounding it given enough time, but it would hold them off for a little while.

Secondly, he tossed a total of 12 *Frozen Zone*, *Healing Shelter*, and *Binding Thorn* Fusions out toward the nearest Gators, hoping that they would take care of a few of them so that he wasn't overwhelmed, and then he threw a single *Weaken* stone at the furthest one, which was on the opposite side of the Skimmer and approximately 70 feet away. As it flew through the air, he activated the Effect and dropped to the ground, looking the other direction as it exploded.

Larek was sent tumbling from the force of the explosion, though he managed to keep a hold of his axe. When he got back to his feet, he immediately looked to see what had happened and saw that a large crater had formed in the hard sand, and at least 10 of the Gators had been caught close enough to the blast that they were blown apart. Unfortunately, there were also a few significant chunks of hardened sand stuck in the strengthened iron shell of the Air Skimmer, as the force of the blast had been such that not even his newly created vessel could survive it intact.

*That was too close. If it had hit the Fusion on the back....*

It appeared as though Larek would have to fight this the old-fashioned way, or else he risked damaging his airborne conveyance further. Thankfully, his offensive Fusions had done their job as they activated. Being flesh and blood beasts, the Gators were greatly affected by the cold and immediately froze, killing a half-dozen of them caught in his *Frozen Zones*; another half-dozen were killed as they were healed too much by his *Healing Shelters*; and another four were caught in roots that sprang up from underneath the hard sands and began to wrap them up and cut into them with their thorns. They didn't die right away, but they also didn't seem strong enough to break free.

Unfortunately, they wouldn't stay caught for too long, because Larek could already feel a lessening of the Mana density all around him. Mentally deactivating the *Frozen Zone* and *Healing Zone* Fusions to stop them from using too much of what was left, he left the *Binding Thorn* Fusions running while he moved toward the Gators he had incapacitated earlier. Using his best friend, he swiftly swung down at the head of one of the beasts he had originally burned badly with a *Flaming Ball*, and the blade of the axe passed into and through flesh and bone with relative ease.

As it fell to the sand shortly thereafter, he had to dive away and roll to avoid a second Gator snapping at his leg blindly, as Larek had drilled *Water Stream* holes into its eyes before he moved out of the Skimmer. Thankfully, his practice killing monsters in the Empire made moving away from the Gator fairly easy, because even though its attacking movements were quick, it couldn't walk quickly to get to him. As it attempted to snap at him again, he sheared through its descending upper jaw and took it clean off with another swing of his axe. Before he could finish it off, he had to dodge away again as he was nearly caught from behind.

Tapping into his Agility, he moved out of the encircling Gators by quickly cutting down yet another one of the previously wounded beasts and passing through the gap it made. Now out of immediate danger, he turned back toward the approaching Gators and held up his axe, practically inviting them to get closer so that he could chop them to pieces.

He had confidence he could do it, too… as long as he didn't get ripped to pieces in the process.

# Chapter 42

"Well, that was much harder than I expected."

Breathing hard for the first time in months, Larek finished healing his leg via a few small activations of his *Healing Surge* Fusion and slogged his way through the sand back to the Air Skimmer, leaving the blood that had pooled out of his lower extremities to soak into and slowly disappear into the desert. Putting his axe back on his belt, he climbed over the side of the vessel and practically collapsed inside, before picking up some food from his supplies and shoving his face full to replenish his energy. This was quickly followed by some water as he felt thirsty enough to drink an entire lake, and it was all due to the fact that the area around him had almost been completely depleted of ambient Mana. It was filling back up slowly, but even with the increased density that he'd seen, it would still be at least another hour or so before it was back to normal.

It turned out that despite not being able to pierce through his pants with their teeth, the Barbed Gators could still tear through his flesh from the pressure of their jaws against his leg and their head movements designed to rip their victims apart. He nearly had his left leg ripped completely off his body just a minute ago, and if he hadn't somehow decapitated the Gator that had his jaws locked around his knee, he would now be seeing if his healing Fusion was even good enough to reattach a missing limb of that size. He thought it might be, especially if the wound was fresh enough, but he had no desire to try it at the moment. Of course, that was all dependent upon whether he would've been able to survive without a second leg, which wasn't a guarantee.

A few seconds into the main axe-to-Gator fight, he'd had to deactivate the remaining Binding Thorns Fusions because at that point the ambient Mana was getting dangerously close to being used up completely. Another few seconds after tearing through one Gator after another, he was forced to deactivate his *Secure Hideaway* surrounding the Air Skimmer, mainly because he was beginning to feel the Fusions on his clothes and even his axe start to run into Mana supply problems.

If he suddenly lost all his boosts and his best friend wasn't as sharp as before, then he'd be in real trouble. Thankfully, by deactivating the *Secure Hideaway*, the Mana stabilized enough that it wasn't going away any faster than it was being used, so he didn't run into any problems with his closely held Fusions being unable to operate – but it was close.

What was more of a concern was the onslaught of just over 20 uninjured Barbed Gators swarming toward him with the intent to rip him limb from limb. At first, he was able to nimbly dodge out of the way of their relatively slow movements despite the fact that they could whip their heads (and the jaws attached to them) around with incredible speed, and he was able to kill a half-dozen of them with no issues. Unfortunately, the problems started as he killed more and more of them, as the sand underneath his feet began to lose its firmness, causing his boots to sink further into it with each death.

This inevitably led to Larek not being able to move quite as fast, but he adapted by continuing to put some distance between him and the Gators by backing up and leading them in a circle, striking out whenever one of them got close. With his axe being able to shear through their hide and bones without too much effort, he found that it was fairly easy to kill them – as long as he wasn't already surrounded.

Of course, once he was down to only 5 Gators left, his feet were essentially sinking down at least 20 inches with each step, and he was eventually forced to stand his ground and let the beasts surround him. With a coordination that appeared planned, they attacked simultaneously like a pack of wolves, and that was when one of them caught ahold of his left arm and nearly tore it off before Larek cut through both of its jaws in one slice just past his arm, which was torn open to the bone in just the second it had been enclosed in the mouth of the Gator. It was when he was distracted that the other Gator nearly ripped his leg off, but he managed to decapitate it with a return swing.

In mid-attack, he was forced to heal himself because it was too distracting for him to fight as wounded as he was – though it fortunately didn't hurt any after the initial attack thanks to *Pain Immunity* – and the healing depleted the ambient Mana even further than it was. He struggled to fight off the other Gators as they continued to move over the sand as if it was solid under their claws, feeling some of his Fusions stutter for a half-second or so before the ambient Mana density ticked up a little bit to keep them stable. Those distractions made the last 3 Barbed Gators much more difficult to kill than all the rest, and he nearly had his face bitten off when he bent down to kill one of them, only to jerk his head back in time to avoid the teeth that snapped in front of his face.

Now, as he laid himself down to recover from the ordeal on the floor of the Air Skimmer, he thought about the end of the battle and what he now knew about the beasts that attacked him. The first thing he discovered was that the Barbed Gators were indeed monsters, as they all expelled Corrupted Aetheric Force, which Larek absorbed and was still in the process of purifying into normal Aetheric Force for him to use for his Skill maximums.

Secondly, the Gators were much stronger and faster than what he remembered being taught in class; if he was to guess, then these were something he would expect to see out of a Category 3 or 4 Scission rather than Category 2 as he had been taught. Just a single one of them was a match for an entire Aperture's worth of monsters in the Empire, and their strength was largely able to withstand the downward force of his *Repelling Barrier* when it initiated during the battle – which was partly why he had been injured, because the expected "repelling" had only thrown off their aim instead of moving them away completely. Of course, if they hadn't been redirected, he likely would've been hurt even further, but the fact remained that his protective Fusion just wasn't able to hold up to a stronger monster's attacks the way it could with most others.

That, and when the ambient Mana density was so low, the *Repelling Barrier* didn't work nearly as well as it should've. The strong gusts that normally would've slammed them hard into the sand hadn't done more than shift them a little bit, and that was due to not being able to absorb enough Mana from the environment to create a Magnitude 10 gust in an instant.

The final thing that he learned *after* the fight and before he made his way back to the Air Skimmer was that these Gators had some sort of connection to the woman back in Day's End that he had been willing to try and free but had ended up killing, Serena Grovewhisperer. The reason he had a feeling they were connected was the way the first of the Gators he killed during the battle had started to dissipate into a dark-green and black smoke the same way that her body had after her death, and were, in fact still dissipating while he finished munching away at food. It was slightly disappointing because he had hoped to butcher a few of them to eat the meat they would've provided, but that hope evaporated as soon as he saw the first one disappearing.

Added up all together, with the facts that they were monsters with Corrupted Aetheric Force, were stronger than they should've been, had some sort of ability to manipulate sand so that it either acted like water or like a solid surface, and dissipated into essentially nothing after death, he wasn't sure what to make of the situation. Was it just coincidence that they were similar to the woman/monster he killed in Day's End? Or was it a sign of something more?

It was definitely a mystery that seemed to go right along with the whole desert shifting during the night thing, and any other time he might actually look into it if only for curiosity's sake. As it was, all he wanted to do was get out of the desert and back to the Kingdom. *It's not my problem, nor my responsibility.*

Once he was as recovered as fully as it was possible to be after the battle, something occurred to Larek as he finally felt as if his energy had come back. Standing up inside the Air Skimmer and looking out into the nearby sand, he absently noticed that there was now barely a trace that anything had happened. The Gator bodies and blood had disappeared entirely as it dissipated into smoke, the blood from *his* wounds was entirely gone as it seemed as though the desert had swallowed it all, and even his footsteps through the sand were almost entirely filled in or smoothed out. In the same fashion, the stones that he threw out with his offensive Fusions on them...

...had also disappeared.

Jumping back out of his vessel, he worked his way over to where he was fairly sure he had tossed them as he used his *Magical Detection* Skill to try and sense them nearby, hoping that they had simply fallen a few inches into the sand. He could usually detect Fusions – especially his own – at quite a distance, even through solid rock, but he found not even a *hint* of them within at least 100 feet below the surface, which meant that they were somehow further down than even that. *What is going on here?*

Frustrated and more than a bit angry at the loss of his Fusions, Larek made it back to his Air Skimmer and wondered if he could create some more before he left, as he was all out of them now that he had essentially thrown them all away. As he looked around the area with his *Magical Detection*, he estimated that it would be at least another 40 minutes until the Mana density had recovered enough to try something like that, because his natural Mana regeneration would affect the speed of its recovery, and he really wanted to be on his way. He wouldn't be able to use his vessel for at least another 10 or 15 minutes because of the draw of ambient Mana the gusts of air took in to operate. Once he was on the move, it wasn't that big of a deal because he'd be moving to areas with higher density, but it was getting there that would be the initial difficulty.

Therefore, he decided to wait until he stopped for the evening later that night, because he'd rather be gone as soon as possible than wait at the site of the recent attack, in case there were any more monsters out there. He had barely survived the first attack and wasn't sure if he would live through another before the Mana density recovered, especially since he was now out of all offensive Fusions except for the one on his staff. He still had his *Secure Hideaway*, of course, but it would only protect him so far; and he was fairly certain that if another group of Gators attacked him again, it wouldn't last long before they managed to get through.

As he sat there waiting for the density to improve before he took off again, he saw that he had a few notifications he'd received during combat with the Gators but had ignored.

**Throwing** *has reached Level 12!*

**Dodge** *has reached Level 20!*

**Axe Handling** *has reached Level 91!*

**Body Regeneration** *has reached Level 33!*

Most of them were Martial Skills, with only *Axe Handling* being a General Skill. Both Dodge and Body Regeneration had hit their maximum, along with his Mage Skills, so they wouldn't be increasing until he was able to raise their maximums. Speaking of which, he sensed that the Corrupted Aetheric Force had finished purifying for him to use, and he was surprised to see that each of the Barbed Gators had been worth 100 AF each, which gave him an additional 5,000 AF added to his previous total of 1,047 AF he had available. Not only that, but when he looked at his Status, he remembered that he had Advancement Points from recent personal Level increases, because he had apparently increased in Level at some point to Level 29.

**Larek Holsten**

**Combat Fusionist**
**Healer**
**Level 29**
**Advancement Points (AP): 3/22**
**Available AP to Distribute: 123**
**Available Aetheric Force (AF): 6047**

**Stama: 1500/1500**
**Mana: 2340/2340**

**Strength: 75 [150] (+)**
**Body: 75 [150] (+)**
**Agility: 75 [150] (+)**
**Intellect: 117 [234] (+)**

Acuity: 114 [228] (+)
Pneuma: 1,350 [2,700]
Pattern Cohesion: 27,000/27,000

**Mage Skills:**
Pattern Recognition Level 35/35 (350 AF)
Magical Detection Level 35/35 (350 AF)
Spellcasting Focus Level 35/35 (350 AF)
Multi-effect Fusion Focus Level 40/40 (400 AF)
Focused Division Level 45/45 (450 AF)
Mana Control Level 50/50 (500 AF)
Fusion Level 50/50 (500 AF)
Pattern Formation Level 50/50 (500 AF)

**Martial Skills:**
Stama Subjugation Level 1/20 (200 AF)
Blunt Weapon Expertise Level 1/20 (200 AF)
Bladed Weapon Expertise Level 2/20 (200 AF)
Unarmed Fighting Level 3/20 (200 AF)
Throwing Level 12/20 (200 AF)
Dodge Level 20/20 (200 AF)
Pain Immunity Level 20/20 (N/A)
Body Regeneration Level 33/33 (330 AF)

**General Skills:**
Cooking Level 8
Bargaining Level 9
Beast Control Level 9
Leadership Level 11
Writing Level 11
Saw Handling Level 15
Reading Level 17
Speaking Level 18
Long-Distance Running Level 20
Listening Level 43
Axe Handling Level 91

  Since he didn't have anything better to do while he waited, he figured he might as well spend some of his available resources to improve himself. The easiest to do was the Aetheric Force, because he'd been thinking about it for a while now. Previously, he'd spent most of his AF on his Mage Skills, but with all the combat he'd been participating in lately, and especially this last battle against the Gators, he was realizing more and more that he needed his Martial Skills to improve to stay alive. The two most useful Skills, *Dodge* and *Body Regeneration*, had both just hit their maximums, which he figured would happen at some point, and he wanted to be able to improve them in the future: one to avoid the hits that might hurt him and the other to fix him up when he couldn't avoid such an outcome.

Therefore, he bumped the maximum Level for *Dodge* to Level 30 and *Body Regeneration* to Level 40, spending 4,970 of his available 6,047 AF in the process. Leaving him with just over 1,000 AF, he spent all but 27 AF on raising *Pattern Recognition*, *Magical Detection*, and *Spellcasting Focus* one Level to 36; he eventually wanted to get every Mage Skill to at least 40 before adding more to his *Fusion* and *Pattern Formation* Skills, because he felt, like a few of his Skills, they were lagging behind and had already proved beneficial to keeping him alive.

His Advancement Points were a little bit tougher. Although he didn't think that he'd *completely* adjusted to his physical stats quite yet, especially while they were boosted, this last fight with the Gators had proven that he could probably benefit from being even stronger, sturdier, and faster. Of course, increases in his Strength, Body, and Agility didn't necessarily mean he would be a *better* fighter, considering that they didn't come with improvements in his techniques (such as they were) and ability to fight, but he was hoping that they would still give him at least a little advantage.

Therefore, over the next 10 minutes, he slowly added an AP to Strength, Body, and Agility one-by-one. He went slow so as not to overload his body from the sudden increase. Though he didn't think he'd had that kind of problem ever since he had his Martial side of things "unlocked", he was feeling somewhat vulnerable in the middle of a desert after just being attacked by monsters that were far harder to kill than what he was used to.

It was a bit of a jump, but Larek eventually decided to take all three stats all the way to 100. Once that was done, he stood up and jumped back outside the Air Skimmer to test out his new increases, which he immediately found to be disorienting as he got used to what felt like an entirely new body. He jerkily trudged through the sand as he fell a few times, his speed fluctuating as if his body felt as if it should be going faster but it wasn't used to the changes yet; thankfully, this was helped by the fact that he could now lift his feet out of the sand much faster because of his increased strength, making movement much smoother once he figured out how to regulate his speed.

Larek also noticed that he sunk at least another inch or two deeper than before, as if he weighed more than he did just a few minutes before. He figured that this might indeed be the case, as when he had been increasing his Body stat, it felt like his very bones were condensing and becoming that much stronger in the process; it was entirely possible that this had added some weight to him.

He ended up spending a little more time than he had originally planned testing out his new physical stats, but it was time well spent because he thought it would be better to work it out now rather than in the middle of a fight. By the end of approximately 30 minutes, he was feeling much better about his movements than he was when he started, though he thought it would take some time to get fully comfortable.

As for the rest of his AP, he debated keeping them until he found something for which he might need them; but eventually, he decided to put the rest into Intellect to increase his Mana pool, as that had proven to be useful while creating Fusions when the regeneration rate was so low due to ambient Mana density issues. Now at a base 165 in Intellect, he had a total of 3,300 Mana with his *Boost*, and looking at his Mage stats...

...Pneuma was all the way up to 3,600 because of boosts and the increase in his Body stat, with its multiplicative effect on Pneuma. Now with 36,000 Pattern Cohesion, he felt like he could make just about any Fusion he could think of and have plenty of Cohesion left over.

With nothing else to distribute, and having used more than an hour getting all of that done, the ambient Mana density had finally returned to normal. With a thought of how close he was getting to reaching home, he activated the *Multi-Thruster* on his Air Skimmer and lifted off from the sands. Soon enough, he was leaving the site of the Gator fight behind, with not a single trace that anything had even happened.

# Chapter 43

The seemingly endless desert that he passed over in his Air Skimmer was starting to get to Larek. It wasn't the monotonous sand dunes and lack of landmarks, or even the pervasive loneliness that was affecting him more than he thought it would considering that he had grown used to traveling by himself. Instead, it was the feeling that he wasn't making any progress with his journey, despite the fact that with his current speed he'd calculated that he'd gone at least 500 miles since he entered the desert. With his stops at night and the moving desert physically shifting his Skimmer, it was difficult to say how far he had actually traveled; but he figured that it wasn't any less than that, especially with how it had seemed to bring him further toward his destination.

Yet, there was nothing from what he could see to show that he had made *any* progress whatsoever. While traveling through the Empire, the landscape at least changed somewhat, from forests to plains to mountainous areas, with some sort of different environment visible on the horizon. Here, though, there was none of that, as it occasionally felt to Larek like the entire world had been enveloped by a desert and that it would never end, no matter how far he traveled through it.

Logically, he knew that it was only a matter of time before he passed through the entirety of it, but it was hard to keep that in mind when there wasn't anything visible by which to evaluate his progress.

Nevertheless, he pushed on, wary of another attack by Barbed Gators or anything else that might be under the sand of the desert. The night after the attack by the reptilian monsters, Larek nearly didn't stop to rest, wanting to put as much distance between him and the attack site as possible. However, only an hour after the sun dipped below the horizon, the strain of standing up all day after fighting in the morning, along with his need to sleep after the injuries he'd sustained, all caught up with him and he was forced to land. Paranoia about another attack tried to keep him awake, but he ended up fighting through it to finally get the rest that his body needed.

Unexpectedly, Larek wasn't attacked during the night *nor* in the morning as he got ready to leave. The next day was simply more of the same boring desert, the sand dunes all looking similar as he passed over them in his effort to speed his way east as quickly as possible. That night he stopped yet again, hoping that any threat to him had been left behind. By that point, the Combat Fusionist estimated that he'd passed the 700- to 800-mile mark, and he only had a day or two left before he was out of the desert. Again, there was no sign of him being attacked during the night or the morning, and he left in slightly better spirits knowing that his journey over the endless sand was coming to an end.

He didn't make it there on what was his sixth day in the desert, but he figured he was fairly close and would make it the next day. By the end of the seventh day, he was entirely confused because he *should've* reached the end of the desert at some point earlier that day, but the horizon still showed endless dunes and more of the same, without any sign of ending.

After coming to a rest and setting down on the sand after the eighth day with absolutely no progress visible in the landscape, he began to worry that his information on the size of the desert had been unreliable as to whether it was indeed about 1,000 miles from east to west. Even if that were the case, he doubted that it was *that* much bigger, and he should be seeing some results soon. At least, he hoped that was the case, because he only had about a week's worth of food left in his supplies inside the vessel. With what was lost overboard a few days before, along with how much he'd had to eat after being injured, Larek had depleted his food stores much faster than he expected. He was just thankful that he still had plenty of water thanks to his Fusions, because otherwise he would be in trouble if that were running out.

The only positive note in everything was that Larek was able to replace one of each of his offensive Fusions, using some wood from his pack that he'd been lugging around for what felt like forever. The wood he carved out of them into small flat squares wasn't as useful as the stones he had used before, but there weren't any stones in the desert to replace them with – only sand. Miles and miles and miles of sand.

By the end of day 9 with no end in sight, his frustration was so pronounced that when he set down for the night, he couldn't get to sleep; instead, he mumbled to himself about sand and deserts and how much he absolutely hated both of them with a passion that could be classified as murderous. A few hours after sundown and a couple of hours until midnight, Larek was startled in his plans to someday make a Fusion that turned the entire desert into some sort of humanoid figure that he could then strangle to death.

The desert began to move, taking him and the Air Skimmer along with it. This wasn't totally unexpected, of course, because he already knew that it did this, but it happening earlier than what he thought of as "normal" caught his attention. He was glad that it did, because he quickly found that instead of it pushing him further east, it was pushing him back to the west – the opposite of where he wanted to go. When he attempted to use the lifting gusts of air from below the Skimmer to extricate the vessel from the sand, he found that the entire Skimmer had been clutched tightly within the sand's embrace just as fully as what had happened against the Barbed Gators.

In other words, it wouldn't budge. When he attempted to push the vessel to its limit at Magnitude 6, he heard – and felt – portions of the wooden frame inside the Air Skimmer beginning to splinter and crack, so he stopped that immediately before he ripped the entire thing apart.

Helpless to stop it, Larek watched as his vessel was carried along back to the west, with the wind whipping at him as it moved; it wasn't a wind that naturally blew through the desert, but was instead a wind caused by moving at an incredibly fast speed. It was at least twice or three times as much horizontal wind as was generated by his own movement through the desert when he traveled during the day, meaning that he was likely losing most – or possibly all – of the progress he had made the day before.

Nevertheless, he was fairly sure he now knew why he hadn't hit the eastern edge of the desert yet – because it wasn't letting him leave.

Without any ability to stop what was happening, Larek went to sleep shortly thereafter, intending to get as much as possible for the next day. In order to get out of the endless sand dunes, he was going to have to keep moving through that night and possibly the next one in order to reach the edge of the desert.

With that plan in mind, Larek spent the next day traveling east, and instead of stopping for sleep, he simply took breaks every few hours to eat a little bit and stay hydrated while he flew through the dark. There was enough star and moonlight to at least see where he was going, and by keeping his course headed east without any use of his left or right gust adjustments used all night, he ensured that he stayed on the correct heading.

Except when the sun came up the next morning, it appeared on the horizon in the wrong direction.

"What? How is that possible?" He knew for a fact that he hadn't turned at all during the night, and while he might have been *slightly* off of heading due east, there was *no way* that he would've ended up heading due west at any point. However, unless the sun somehow teleported during the night and decided to rise in the west rather than the east, then he was going the wrong way.

"How long was I going west?" Unfortunately, he had no way of knowing since it wasn't like he could consult any landmarks, and without any way to know where he was in relation to the entire desert, he was at a loss for how much he had backtracked.

Tired from the sleepless night and frustrated that he had inadvertently got himself turned around, Larek fixed his direction and began heading east once again. Before it was completely dark that night, he set the Skimmer down and went to sleep earlier than usual. As a result, he woke up a few hours before dawn to find that the Skimmer was again moving to the west as the sands shifted – and it was moving faster than before.

"What is going on?" he mumbled to himself, completely at a loss for what to do now. Looking at his food stores, he thought he could hold out for another week if he was careful, but he had to figure out how to get out of the desert by that time or he'd starve to death. As it was now, it felt like he wasn't getting anywhere; the setbacks just kept adding up, and it felt like the very environment was working against him.

Another day of traveling followed by a second night where he continued through the night ended in disaster once again. He had deliberately made sure not to alter his course, like he had thought he might have done previously, and had even started trying to navigate by the stars above; while he didn't precisely know how to do it, there were a few constellations he recognized up in the night sky and he attempted to keep them in the same direction. Unfortunately, none of these worked, as he found himself traveling west when dawn broke over the horizon.

Setting down on the sand and shutting almost everything off, Larek sat down on a crate and deliberated what to do for the next hour as the world brightened up by the rising sun. *I can't tell if I'm actually getting anywhere near the border with the Kingdom, and it feels like something is messing with me when I attempt to travel at night. I **should** realistically be going east, but somehow I end up heading west – how does that happen? Actually, the better question might be **why** is this happening?*

From everything he could determine from when the sands used to carry his vessel east but now brought him west at night, he could only conclude that something was either deliberately keeping him in the desert... or was trying to bring him somewhere. What, or even who, was doing this wasn't something that he could determine at the time, but that it was happening was no longer in doubt in his mind.

With anger at being once again manipulated without his consent by outside forces, Larek made a decision.

He was going to find whatever was keeping him in the desert, figure out why it was doing it, and then make it stop – one way or another. He didn't have time to play games at this point, both because he was running out of food and because he needed to get back to the Kingdom, so he was going to put an end to this... whatever it was.

Just as he was about to get up off the crate and lift off from the sands, there was another rumbling underneath the Air Skimmer. At first, he was going to attempt to outrun the Barbed Gators that were inevitably about to appear by lifting off before they arrived, but his anger was still burning hot after he made his initial decision to stop whatever was keeping him in the desert. As a result, he waited for them to appear...

...which turned out to be a massive mistake.

Struck from below, the Air Skimmer tumbled through the air, arcing at least 30 feet high before coming back down on its roof with a slight crunch of wood as the frame took the brunt of the impact. Even with the strength added to the wood because of his *Strengthen Area* Fusion, it couldn't handle all of the abuse it underwent with being tossed into the air and landing on the mostly unyielding sand of the desert. None of the wooden frame supports completely broke, but a few of them were fractured to the point where they would indubitably shatter if they took another blow like that.

As for Larek, he only saw all of this because he was still inside the Skimmer as it tumbled through the air and landed upside down, with his food supplies landing all around him and spilling out into the nearby sand. The Combat Fusionist was able to twist himself enough that he didn't land on his head, but the impact of his left shoulder against the roof temporarily popped his arm out of his shoulder socket. Getting to his feet was a challenge as he was slightly disoriented by the sudden attack, but it cleared up quickly as he stood up, yanked on his left arm with his right, and then pulled his shoulder socket back into place with a hollow-sounding *\*pop\**. Relief at the uncomfortable feeling in his shoulder disappearing spread through him as he scrambled out of the flipped-over Air Skimmer, grabbing his staff that miraculously didn't tumble out of the vessel on the way out.

Expecting to see more Barbed Gators, he instead was presented with what had actually hit the Skimmer from below – and it was certainly not a Gator.

Stretching up to 50 feet tall at the apex of its tail, a giant scorpion, with deep-black-colored chitin comprising its exoskeleton, was staring right at him with its creepily beady eyes from where it had erupted out of the ground. Each of its sharp claws were larger than

Larek, and its legs were long enough that the width of the monster was at least 60 feet as it spread out over the sand. Unfortunately, a lot of that was something he ignored, as his main focus was on the stinger on the end of its curled tail, which glistened with what was likely a deadly poison on its tip, poised and ready to strike out at its intended victim. In this case, the intended victim was Larek, but he had no intention of dying that day.

Thankfully, the scorpion seemed to have the same sort of ability to manipulate the sand to make it firmer beneath his feet as did the Barbed Gators, so Larek was able to get traction as he ran away from his Air Skimmer, knowing that if he was going to get out of the desert without dying after he killed the giant scorpion, he needed the vessel as intact as possible.

The monster – which he had no doubt at this point that it was a monster, and not a natural beast of the desert – turned to face him as he ran to the side, displaying how nimble it was on its feet. Before he was even to the point where he wanted to turn and attack, the scorpion had apparently judged where he was going to run and charged forward, moving extremely quickly for such a large creature, and a claw came flying out at him with significant force behind it.

Diving forward to avoid being caught within its claw, his leg was clipped, and he was sent spinning away, landing hard on the sand and rolling a few times with a multitude of bruises all over his body. Nothing was broken or greatly injured, fortunately, and he found that the only reason his leg wasn't snapped by the impact with the scorpion's claw was the fact that it was deflected slightly away because of his *Repelling Barrier*. He instantly knew that if he was ever hit straight-on, he could be severely injured by it.

Jumping to his feet as the massive monster turned toward where he had rolled, and before it could charge at him again, Larek decided that there was enough room to start using his Fusions offensively. He first took out a *Weaken* Fusion that was designed to explode and flung it at the face of the turning Scorpion. It was an almost perfect throw, with it aimed to land near one of its eyes, but its left claw whipped around and batted at the fragile stone, causing it to explode.

Larek had already hit the ground as he was expecting it to blow up as the Fusion was shattered, releasing all the Mana, but he was still close enough to feel the blast as it washed over him and nearly lifted him off the hard sand and tossed him backwards. He was able to hold on just enough that he didn't move more than a foot as the force of the blast 60 feet away pushed at him, and the heat from the explosion singed his exposed skin slightly.

That was actually better than he expected, which was a bit worrying. Being in such proximity should've done a bit more damage to him, though not nearly as much as being at the center of the explosion, and he looked up to see what had happened.

The scorpion stood where it had been, seemingly stunned as it had its claw frozen in place in front of it like a shield, and a small chunk of chitin had been blown off from where the *Weaken* Stone had impacted it before exploding. That was it; a small, perhaps 1-foot-square piece of the durable chitin protecting its claw had been destroyed, from an explosion that was dangerous to Larek within 100 feet of the detonation. He immediately saw that the destruction caused by the exploding Fusion had been largely deflected upward because of the angle of the giant claw, thereby reducing the amount that Larek had been affected by it.

Getting to his feet quickly and pulling out yet another *Weaken* Fusion stone, he tossed it at the stunned Scorpion, hoping to take advantage of its incapacity, but he was disabused of that notion as it moved as soon as he released the stone, bringing its other claw up to block it similarly to the first. Even as Larek picked himself back up from where he had thrown himself to withstand the blast, he realized that the *Weaken* Fusions alone wouldn't do it, as instead of being stunned after the explosion, the only slightly damaged Scorpion was already moving toward him by the time he got to his feet.

*I guess this is going to be a lot harder than I thought.*

# Chapter 44

Larek dove away from another running charge by the scorpion, managing to avoid being smacked by a claw in the process, but his rolling dive was nearly interrupted when a stinger slammed down near his head. The strength behind the stabbing stinger was such that it actually pierced through and cracked the nearly solid state of the sand he was running around on, crumbling it into separate granules for a few seconds before it firmed up again.

After avoiding the last few charges, he was beginning to see that while the monster was fast in its speedy charges, it was slower in turning, though not by much. It was enough that he was able to rush away to gain some distance, which was what he did now as he brought his staff to bear on the giant scorpion and unleashed a barrage of Magnitude 2 *Icy Spikes* at its face as it turned toward him. As he expected, they were immediately blocked by a claw, and seemed to bounce off the exoskeleton of the monster, with the area blown up by the *Weaken* Fusions only allowing a tiny bit of penetration into the flesh beneath the removed chitin.

Before it could move against him, he altered the Magnitude to 8, aiming straight for the opening in the chitin, and he smiled grimly as the large icicle projectile pierced deeply into the claw, lodging at least a foot deep into it. The sand under his feet rumbled slightly as the scorpion seemed to stomp its feet in frustration at the sudden injury to its claw, and Larek's smile faded as it rushed at him again. This time, however, it moved so quickly that he was unable to dodge completely, and the uninjured claw caught him around the ankle.

Yanked away from his dive, he was pulled into the air as the claw tightened around his lower leg, trying to cut it in half with the pressure alone. While he felt his bones starting to grind together, he was thankful for his *Multi-Resistance* protected pants, which prevented his leg from being sliced through, though it didn't do anything to relieve the *squeezing* agony that paralyzed him at first before it was blocked by his *Pain Immunity* Skill.

Still clutching his staff and seeing the other claw coming for him out of the corner of his eye, which he definitely didn't want getting close to his head, he aimed for the eyes of the scorpion with the end of his staff while he dangled 10 feet off the ground. Changing his attack to his *Flaming Ball* projectiles at Magnitude 4, he began filling the monster's face with flames, and for the first time he heard it screech in pain as one of its larger eyes and 4 of its smaller ones – there were 12 of them in total, with a pair of larger sets of eyes in the center and 5 pairs on either side of those – were completely melted away by the fiery balls.

Before he could complete the total blindness, he was dropped as both claws came up to protect its face, landing heavily on the sand beneath him. Even as he was let go, he activated the *Healing Surge* Fusion on his clothing and his crushed leg began to heal. This healing was the only thing that saved him as he was able to push off with his semi-healed leg as he saw the stinger descend directly at his chest, and he was only clipped by the tip, which gouged out a chunk of his back as he rolled away. The missing skin and flesh was annoying, but he was glad that whatever substance was on the tip didn't penetrate his clothing, as it didn't actually pierce through; instead, it simply scraped him with such force that it ripped off a portion of his body.

Realizing that he had dropped his staff, Larek was forced to leave it where it was because it had rolled nearly underneath the still-burning scorpion. Getting unsteadily to one knee as his leg was still trying to heal completely, he pulled his axe out from the holder around his waist, and fumbled at his belt pouches. After only a second, he managed to grab one of the wood squares with his offensive Fusions on it, and he immediately tossed it toward the monster, where it landed directly under its body.

Unfortunately for Larek, it was his *Healing Shelter* Fusion that he had thrown, and it immediately went to work healing all the damage he had done to it. There was a small positive point, however, as when its eyes were repaired, the flames that still lingered around the area continued to burn them, inflicting even more pain on the monster as they were continually damaged and healed. That was a small consolation for effectively undoing all the damage he'd managed to do to the scorpion in the time he'd been fighting.

The *Healing Shelter* Fusion did more than just heal, as Larek could see that within seconds the interior of the scorpion's body began to shrink as it began to feed on its own flesh for energy, but it was quickly able to break out of the Fusion's range. Not by charging forward, however, but by somehow *jumping* up at an angle approximately 200 feet in the air. As he stumbled back as he finally was able to get to his feet after his leg was healed, Larek watched the descending monster that appeared ready to flatten him into a pile of goo and saw something that caught his attention. A slightly lighter color of chitin was stretched across the underside of the scorpion in a wide band, and it somehow looked *softer* than the rest of the creature's exoskeleton. Realizing that he could be making a mistake, he nevertheless stretched his arm back before launching his axe at the lighter-colored spot, knowing that it wouldn't just penetrate but *kill* the monster if he hit it in the right area.

    As it spun through the air, he took his eyes off it for a moment as he rushed forward in a dive, snatching up his dropped staff and deactivating his *Healing Shelter* Fusion at the same time rather than roll right into it. As he looked up at the falling scorpion after snatching up his staff, he witnessed the axe heading straight for where he had thrown it... only for the monster to somehow sense it coming and twist in the air. It didn't miss completely, fortunately, but it didn't hit its belly like he had hoped.

    Instead, the super-sharp axe head cut cleanly through one of its legs near the body before getting lodged in the thicker exoskeleton nearby.

    Another screech of pain hurt his ears as the leg was detached, and the landing that the scorpion was probably hoping to enact was foiled by the loss of one of its limbs. With his foe landing awkwardly on its remaining feet, Larek took advantage of its momentary instability to dive toward it, using his *Water Stream* projectile at Magnitude 8 to cut into the chitin as he rolled under its tail and toward its belly, where he had seen the lighter-colored area just a moment ago. Even Mag 8 wasn't enough to cut through more than an inch of chitin unless he held it on an area for long, but by the time he got to the area he was moving toward, he was piercing through the weaker chitin with ease. Black blood spilled out and nearly covered him in the disgustingly disturbing liquid, but he didn't let up as he changed from *Water Stream* to *Flying Stone* at Mag 2, and soon enough chunks of sharpened stone flew up and absolutely wrecked the scorpion's insides at a rapid pace.

    Larek was able to devastate its internals for all of 5 seconds before the scorpion stumbled away, moving faster than the Combat Fusionist could keep up with. Before it could move away completely, he shoved the staff inside the wound he had opened, lodging it inside even as he kept the barrage of stones going. As it walked over Larek, nearly impaling him with a heavy chitin-covered leg, he glimpsed his axe sticking out of its side where it had been stuck. Jumping with all the strength he had, he managed to reach the handle of the wood-cutting tool and yanked it out as he fell back to the ground, rolling upon impact with the sand. As he reached his full height, he pulled out another wooden square he'd taken from his belt pouch – this time knowing exactly what he grabbed – and tossed it at the stumbling, remaining trio of the scorpion's left legs.

*Frozen Zone* activated as it passed within its range, and Larek watched the legs, already weakened by his *Healing Shelter* Fusion, shatter as the blood inside them flash-froze. Collapsing on its side as it now had no left legs, the part of its body that fell into the *Frozen Zone* Fusion quickly started to freeze, but its claws and other legs pulled it out before too much more damage was done. Turning in a circle because of its lack of legs on one side, the scorpion's tail presented itself to Larek, and he immediately sprinted forward, aiming for the base of it just over his head. With a tremendous jump that brought him at least 12 feet in the air, the Combat Fusionist swung his axe at the extremely thick base of the tail, cutting through half of it in one swing, the edge of the axe cutting through the chitin with some resistance, though his strength proved to be enough to force it through.

Splattered by even more blood, Larek dropped after his attack and rolled, barely missing being swatted out of the air as the monster's tail attempted to hit him. With it only half-attached, the scorpion's unwise attack tore it even further, until it was hanging on by only a thick chunk of skin.

Breathing heavily at the exertion and the near-death experiences, Larek took his time cutting through the rest of the scorpion's legs as it attempted to ineffectually turn toward him, until all it could do was weakly turn itself with its claws. Even that ended quickly when Larek's staff finally punched through all of the scorpion's innards and *Flying Stones* began to emerge from its face, tearing through its eyes and mouth in an explosion of internal force, which finally made it collapse into death.

Sinking down into the sand as the hardening effect that the monster created faded, Larek knelt down in exhaustion as he looked at his notifications.

**Throwing** has reached Level 13!

**Dodge** has reached Level 21!
**Dodge** has reached Level 22!

**Body Regeneration** has reached Level 34!

Feeling the rest of his wounds disappearing as his *Body Regeneration* Skill finished off what he'd hastily healed earlier, Larek saw and then felt a significant amount of Corrupted Aetheric Force enter his body, even as the giant scorpion's corpse and detached body parts began to dissolve and disappear into a dark-greenish and black smoke-like substance – just as Serena and the Gators had. He quickly struggled through the sand to gather up the two wooden Fusions he'd thrown earlier before they disappeared, and then he grabbed his staff when it appeared after the corpse disappeared.

*Nice! I didn't lose anything this time. I'm practically starving now, of course, but I can eat when I get back to—the Air Skimmer!*

In horror, he looked toward his vessel, only to find that it had sunk halfway down into the sand and appeared to be sinking even further as he watched. "No! No! Stop it! Give it back!" he shouted to no one in particular, but hoping that the desert or something would listen. It was in vain as he rushed toward the sinking Air Skimmer, reaching it within seconds, before trying with all his strength to stop its descent. When the physical might didn't work, he attempted to use the Fusions on it to move it, but stopped after a few seconds as he found that he was doing nothing but ripping the entire thing apart. The gusts of air weren't meant to extricate the vessel if it was stuck upside down, after all.

Running out of time, he dove inside what opening there still was inside in order to grab a bag or two of food. Digging one of them out from under the sand that had started to cover them, he figured the others were lost and turned to leave, only to stumble as the Air Skimmer dropped a few feet all of a sudden, sinking even further down into the sand.

By the time he caught his balance and looked to escape, the sand was already covering all the openings and seemed to be moving faster to fill in any space there was inside the vessel. He attempted to dig himself out, but it was futile as whatever he moved was quickly replaced with twice as much, and soon enough, he was up to nearly his chest in sand. Looking upwards, the normally bottom portion of the vessel was the only thing that wasn't filled with sand, so he dragged himself upwards so that his chest and head were at least free, allowing him to breathe, but for how long that would last, he didn't know.

Eventually, the interior of the vessel stopped filling with sand, though after reaching down and grabbing one of his *Illumination* stones from one of his belt pouches, he could see that the sand was rushing by outside of the walls of the Skimmer, revealing that he was still descending at a rapid pace. As he stood there on the sand filling his upside-down vessel, unable to really move anywhere and the air slowly disappearing as he used it up, the only thing he could think of at that point was: *Wow. Now I know why anything that fell into the sand was lost to my detection so quickly.* It was a ridiculous thought, because he was probably going to die soon, but it was the only thing that came to mind since he had no idea how to get out of the current situation.

Larek wasn't sure how long he descended, but eventually he began to become lightheaded as the amount of air he could breathe disappeared. Right before he passed out completely, likely to never wake up again, there was a sudden lurch that made his mind focus a little bit more than it had been. Before he knew it, his body felt like it was in freefall for all of a second before it stopped abruptly, a few audible cracks in the wood framing of the vessel protesting at the sudden halt of their descent.

The next moment, the Air Skimmer tilted to the side and Larek went with it, the sand inside shifting as the bottom half of the vessel fell completely to the side and he held onto the side as the iron plates tilted at an angle and began to slide down what appeared to be a hill of sand. Within a few seconds, the vessel eventually stopped, allowing Larek to take a deep breath as blessedly cool, fresh air filled his lungs. When he stopped hyperventilating at the influx of glorious, clean air, he looked around for the first time since they came to a halt, and he was both confused and shocked at where he had ended up.

He had been expecting complete darkness, being so far underneath the desert, but instead he found himself in a large, circular, black stone tunnel with a flat bottom, and the very walls were filled with veins of a luminescent crystal that seemed to glow from some sort of internal source. It wasn't nearly as bright as full daylight inside the tunnel, but instead he would equate it to being as bright as dusk, just as the sun passed over the horizon. Still light enough to see most things, but not bright enough to hurt the eyes. The glowing crystal veins were strange, not because of their luminescence, but because they seemed to pulse gently in intensity, though it was hard to tell at first because the changes in illumination were very faint.

Looking up at the 100-foot-tall ceilings, he discovered that the apex of the tunnel was actually a strip of *sand*, hardened and solidified as well as what the Gators and the scorpion had done to the surface up above; right where he and his Air Skimmer had fallen through was a trickle of sand coming through a hole that seemed to be closing up, like a wound that had been healed by one of his Fusions. The vessel had apparently landed on a large hill of sand that had come through shortly beforehand, and after it landed on its top it tilted over and slid down the side of the sand hill, bringing him to where he was now.

Looking to either side of his location, the tunnel seemed to gradually turn after a few hundred feet in either direction, giving him no clear sense of where they led. Logically, he assumed that he had somehow fallen through the sand and all the way down into the tunnel system in which the Drekkin who lived below the desert lived, but exactly *how* that happened, along with *why* it happened in the first place, were things he wanted to find out. First, he wanted to know how to get out of there, as going back *up* seemed unlikely; second, he wanted to know why he was down in the tunnels in the first place, since it seemed like he had been deliberately dragged there.

Though, when he thought about it for a few seconds and really evaluated his surroundings, he thought the latter question about why he was there could be related to what he could suddenly sense at a distance.

For the first time since he'd entered the desert land of Lowenthal, he could feel an Aperture.

# Chapter 45

The only problem with what he was feeling was that it felt more like an extremely powerful Scission rather than an Aperture, because he'd never felt one like this before. Not only that, but if he had to guess at how far away it was, he would hazard to say that it was much farther away than any that he'd ever felt before. Normally, he could potentially detect them within a couple of miles at most, but this one felt as if it was somewhere between a dozen and a hundred miles away – which just felt like an impossibility to him.

Almost as if it was waiting for him to acknowledge the sense of an Aperture nearby, Larek received an unexpected notification.

*Beware, Guardian!*

*The local population underneath the far-ranging desert of Lowenthal have fallen victim to an ancient enemy! When the Corruption spread throughout the world and was subsequently unleashed upon this land, the **Umbral Demons** who inhabited the darkest corners of the Drekkin's underground civilization latched upon the physical manifestations of Corruption without hesitation. Having absolutely no defense against the soul replacement capabilities of the Umbral Demons, the physical manifestations succumbed to the onslaught almost as soon as they established their Apertures into this world.*

*On a positive note, with the physical manifestations compromised in this manner, the spread of individual Apertures has been halted because they were **permanently closed**. Unfortunately, the reason for this is due to a consolidation of all the Apertures within Lowenthal, feeding every single opening into the world of Corruption into a central location where the Umbral Demons have been organizing their army of soul-replaced minions to carry out their conquest of every single land. Previously restricted to the deepest and darkest places that could be found in this world, with their army of converted slaves, they can venture by proxy into the light, using the replacement capabilities of the Apertures to have an unending force that will be extremely difficult to defeat once it breaks free. By the time any of the nearby lands can react, they will have already seized the initiative and begun their subjugation and conversion of the world's population. At that point, the spread of Corruption will be a secondary threat to every form of life that currently exists in the world, as the outcome will be the same.*

*Everyone will, effectively, be dead – or will wish that they were.*

*The only obstacle to the advancement of their plans has been the Drekkin, who have been fighting a losing battle over the last few months against the onslaught of soul-replaced physical manifestations – along with those of their own kind that have been unfortunate to have fallen victim to the Umbral Demons' manipulation.*

*So, Guardian, you have a decision to make. Will you flee and warn the world of this threat, ensuring that they are ready to battle the forces that will inevitably be brought to bear against them? Or will you stay and add your great and powerful strength to the defenders already present and fighting for their very lives, with the intent of ending this threat once and for all, even if it is more than likely that you will die a painfully horrible death as your soul is converted to evil?*

*The choice is yours. Make the correct one, or all may be lost.*

"Uh, no thanks. I have no desire to get involved in any of this," Larek mumbled out loud as he read the notification in shock and exasperation. "Of course, if I *had* to choose, I'd rather leave and tell people about the threat, letting others worry about it… but I have no idea how to get out of here. But that doesn't mean I want to fight against all these 'Umbral Demons' and the monsters coming out of the Apertures at the same time. I mean, how would I even do that? Am I just supposed to find the gigantic conglomeration of Apertures and close it? Sure, sure, like that would—"

*You have made a choice. Fight well!*

"Huh? No! No, I didn't! I'm not going anywhere near that thing knowing what I now know about it—wait, did you just respond to me?" The shock of the previous notification had somewhat worn off at that point, but an even greater surprise rocked him back on his heels as it seemed to him that whatever had been giving him the notifications had directly responded to something he said out loud to himself. It, of course, didn't understand that he was being sarcastic at the thought of fighting against these "Demon" things it mentioned. Unfortunately, no matter what he said in opposition to that supposed decision, nothing else seemed to happen.

That didn't mean he couldn't flee anyways and tell people about the threat... did it? While he wasn't sure what was going on with this notification and how it had responded to him, he had the unwelcome feeling that if he tried to run and tell people, they would be disinclined to believe him even more than usual. Whereas if he had fully picked that decision from the start, he would've had some additional aid in convincing people that the threat was real.

Larek tried to evaluate where exactly these feelings were coming from, but just like with many things in the world he didn't understand, no comprehension flooded into him as he considered them. Still, it really didn't matter, because he wasn't planning on staying around and getting killed by something worse than a giant scorpion; as soon as he found a way out, he'd be taking it.

As Larek looked around the tunnel, figuring out where to go, he noticed a familiar crate sticking out of the sand pile he had landed on, and he spent the next hour excavating the entire pile, finding every single crate or bag that had been on his Air Skimmer when it had been flipped over – even the ones that had fallen off upon impact with the sand up above, which he thought might be lost forever.

So, at least he wasn't going to starve over the next week or so, but that still didn't help him escape the tunnels. Loading everything back onto his Air Skimmer, he spent another few minutes looking it over for damage, seeing that some of the wooden framing – especially that which was holding up the roof – was cracked, but it was still holding its shape well enough that he didn't think that it would begin to fall apart unless there was even more damage done to it. If it hadn't been for the *Strengthen Area* Fusion making all the iron and wood stronger, all the abuse that it had gone through likely would've destroyed it by that point.

Luckily, none of the Fusions were damaged in the slightest, including the *Multi-Thruster*, which worked just as well down in the tunnel as it did aboveground. In fact, once he was out of the area where the sand had piled up, it was actually better, because the stone floor had very little dust that was picked up. The loud roar of rushing air was a bit more pronounced in the relatively closed space than out in the open, but it didn't bother him too much. Of course, anything within a mile of the tunnel would likely be able to hear him coming, but there wasn't much he could do about that other than leave his vessel behind – and there was no way he was doing that.

Now, he just had to pick a direction and find a way out from the tunnels. As he stood in his Air Skimmer and looked down both directions of the tunnel, he realized that he had no idea which direction was which. He'd been so turned around during the fight with the scorpion, followed by his frantic attempts at keeping his vessel from sinking, that he had no idea which way was east by this point. Even the direction his flipped-over Skimmer had been facing at the time it started to sink was no help, as the landing upon the sand hill and sliding down it had turned everything around to the point where it was impossible to extrapolate where it had been facing.

With a shrug, Larek picked to go down the tunnel that his vessel just happened to be facing at that point, because there were no distinguishing characteristics between them that would make one way or the other the obvious choice. With the resolve to turn around if there was some indication that he was going the wrong way, his progress down the tunnel was swift – and largely unchanging. It wasn't nearly as bad as the skimming above the sand that he'd been doing over the last week, as at least the tunnels seemed to curve gently one way or the other seemingly at random, but the glowing crystal veins in the walls didn't really have very much variation to them. It got to the point where they were almost as indistinguishable from each other as the sand dunes on the surface had been, and after a few hours of travel, he began to think he was going in circles as there was no change.

Just when he was starting to doubt that he'd gone the right way and was contemplating turning around, something finally caught his attention. A large portion of the tunnel wall on his right had been destroyed by something, leaving rubble strewn over the floor, including what appeared to be crystal dust fragments that no longer had a glow about them. The opening was roughly ovoid in shape, and he estimated it to be nearly 20 feet tall and 15 feet wide at its widest, and when he stopped across from it, he couldn't see anything inside. Not because there was nothing to see, but because the darkness coming from whatever was through the opening seemed to smother the glowing light from the rest of the tunnel, like a wall of impenetrable shadows.

As much as he knew that he should probably keep going along the tunnel to find a way out, Larek was curious enough about this sudden change in the environment that he had to investigate. It was self-serving, though, because it was entirely possible that *this* hole in the wall could lead him to a way out of the mess he found himself in.

Taking out one of the simple *Illuminate +2* Fusions he had in his belt pouches, he activated it and tossed it into the opening. As soon as he saw it pass through the barrier of darkness, the brighter light illuminated what was inside briefly, which turned out to be a rough-hewn tunnel that led... somewhere. He couldn't see much past about 15 feet, unfortunately, because as soon as the stone he had placed the

*Illuminate* Fusion on had passed that distance, it seemed to be swallowed up by darkness once again. Or at least the wall of shadowy substance was strong enough that it smothered the light to the point where it couldn't reach outside the opening anymore.

Remembering his experience with the shadowy environment of the Shadow Rats back in the Empire, Larek set the Air Skimmer down near the rubble in the tunnel, jumped down and picked through the damaged stones strewn everywhere, and when he found a piece that was what he needed, he jumped back into his vessel. Activating his *Secure Hideaway*, Larek sat down and used his axe to carve the stone he had collected into a longer, roughly cylindrical shaped rod that he could easily hold in his hand. Once that was done, he spent the next 15 minutes creating a *Directional Illumination +8* Fusion on it, similar to the one he had used to defeat the Shadow Rats except slightly more powerful.

With that completed, he stood back up, left his Air Skimmer where it was with the *Secure Hideaway* protecting it, and then strode toward the opening on foot. While his vessel would've fit, he didn't know what was inside; if it was a monster more dangerous than simple Shadow Rats, he didn't want the Skimmer to take any unnecessary damage. The frame was already on the verge of breaking. Deliberately putting it into danger of being damaged further was a poor idea, especially since it would be relatively close-quarters inside the tunnel he had seen inside the opening.

Climbing over the rubble, he entered a tunnel that looked like something had literally ripped its way through solid rock. As opposed to the relatively smooth interior of the main tunnel he'd been traveling down, he could see what appeared to be deep scratch marks in the stone walls, and there were parts of the stone where the rock had been sheared off, as if it had been ripped out by physical force alone. Not wanting to meet up with something that could do that, Larek nearly turned around, but he pushed himself to go deeper into the tunnel. He was committed to finding a way out, and he wasn't going to let a little darkness stop him from gaining what he needed.

As he walked further into the tunnel, he quickly learned why it seemed as if his *Illuminate +2* stone had disappeared. The darkness seemed to thicken and become denser with each step, and soon enough he had to increase the Magnitude of his *Directional Illumination* up to 3, then 4 just to see a few feet ahead of him. By the time he found the stone he'd tossed inside, deactivated its Fusion, and slipped it back into his belt pouch, he was already at Mag 6; a few more steps and he was forced to use the nearly blinding light of Mag 7. As much as it strained his eyes, it was the only thing that helped to penetrate more than a few feet of the clinging shadows that surrounded him.

From what he could observe, the ripped-up tunnel he was in began to turn away from the main tunnel, which – when he looked back that way – was currently blocked by the darkness of his surroundings, even with the aid of his Fusion. Pushing on, he traveled nearly 200 feet with no significant change before something caught his attention just on the edge of the cone of illumination he was shining ahead of him.

Jerking the Fusion to look toward what caught his attention, his light touched briefly upon a shadowy figure that was at least 12 feet tall and vaguely humanoid in shape. There was no definition to the figure other than the fact that he could see that it had legs and a torso that was in proportion, but its arms were long enough that its hands appeared to drag upon the ground. Atop its shoulders was a perfectly round head with no neck to speak of, and two voids of blackness that were somehow *darker* than anything else he'd seen down in the tunnel stared back at him from where its eyes should be. In addition, there appeared to be 6 separate curved horns that sat on top of its head, all curved toward the front like a set of teeth.

It was shocking, to say the least, as Larek hadn't been expecting to find something quite like that. The screech of agony as wisps of shadow seemed to burn off the figure nearly made him drop the stone rod in an effort to cover his ears, but he somehow managed to hold on tight to it.

The amount of time that the light was upon the figure was no more than a second before it seemed to flit away, and Larek attempted to find it by flashing his *Directional Illumination* Fusion around, but it appeared to be gone. Calming himself and regulating his breathing from such a scare, Larek leveled the staff he was wielding in his left hand and prepared to unleash magical projectiles at the figure if he saw it again.

Unfortunately, Larek didn't have eyes on the back of his head, and the moment he took another step forward, he sensed something intangible hit him from behind. It began sinking into his body at a rapid pace, causing the Combat Fusionist to collapse to his knees, the stone Fusion and staff in his hands dropping as his fingers went numb. As he struggled to regain feeling in them and stay at least generally upright on his knees, he began to feel an intrusive presence that he immediately connected to the notification he had been given earlier.

An Umbral Demon had found him and was attempting to replace his soul.

# Chapter 46

    A sudden pressure against Larek's mind nearly knocked him unconscious as he struggled to keep from collapsing completely onto the floor of the extremely dark tunnel. Closing his eyes and feeling everything going on inside of his body, similar to how he felt for his Mana, he sensed that the Umbral Demon was attempting to seep into every facet of his flesh, muscles, and bones. The sensation was like a cold plunge into an icy lake, as he felt his body lethargically succumb to the numbness of the intrusion. Whatever the Demon was doing was beginning by essentially shutting down any physical resistance – and it was working.

    Larek didn't feel it when all of his struggles proved to be for naught as he lost control of his body and he collapsed on the floor, completely helpless against anything that might choose to attack him at that point. Fortunately, as well as unfortunately, the only dangerous threat inside the dark tunnel was the Demon that was even now concentrating on taking over his mind and then whatever constituted his soul, replacing it with its own.

    Unable to feel the pain directly, the Combat Fusionist nonetheless sensed the Demon working against his mind like a vise, surrounding his consciousness like a wet and heavy blanket on top of a fire in order to smother all the life inside of it. He did everything he could to fight back, but despite having high mental stats in Intellect and Acuity, it was like trying to fight against a Gergasi with his bare hands; in other words, he was completely defenseless against the assault.

    When his awareness of his surroundings faded as the information from his senses was snuffed out one-by-one, and his thoughts were reduced to repeatedly reproaching himself for being stupid enough to walk into a dark tunnel while *just recently* learning about the threats found within the deepest and darkest places in the world, Larek knew that this was the end. A tenuous connection to the mind of the Demon gave him glimpses into their methodology in replacing souls and how they planned to take over the world. Or more accurately, destroy every living thing within it.

    Just like the monsters he had fought, as well as what had happened to Serena, the cold darkness that suffused his entire body wasn't designed just to paralyze him temporarily, but would consume the flesh over a long period of time, replacing it with the solidified shadows of which the Demons were also composed. When the victim was killed afterward, their body would dissolve and disperse into the shadows from which it was made – which was exactly what happened when he killed Serena and the others, as they left no corpse behind. That was what would happen to Larek at some point, after his soul was essentially destroyed and replaced by the Demon's will.

After his consciousness was quarantined within his own mind, it would remain the only part of Larek that would remain *him*, giving the new possessor of his body access to all the information and even all the abilities that were available. It would essentially *become* him in nearly every way possible, and no one would even know it.

Except that the Drekkin could somehow detect when someone was taken over by an Umbral Demon, and they would bind them with a metal that possessed special properties that restricted the amount of information and abilities they could access. The understanding he received from the Demon's mind was that they absolutely hated even the thought of this special Enexro metal, and that was why they were now working to eliminate the Drekkin underneath the desert, so that knowledge of its creation was eradicated entirely. Once it was no longer a threat to the Demons, there would be nothing to stop them from killing everything in the world.

Why? Because there was no way to kill an Umbral Demon entirely, and killing a host too early would only unleash what was inside to wreak havoc on other unsuspecting victims. When a Demon took over a new host, they only left a portion of their natural forms inside of them like a seed, which grew as it consumed the flesh of the body over time; essentially, it was a way for them to reproduce. When the host died before the brand-new demon was fully formed, it would have a chance to escape and attack any other life form nearby. He could only assume that when Serena was found to have been taken over by a Demon, it was in its earliest stages, so that was why she was bound by the Enexro necklace and sent out of their lands – to make her someone else's problem.

With the sudden appearance of Corrupted monsters through Scissions and later Apertures, the Umbral Demons found something unprecedented – a living being without a soul. Because of this, once they took over their minds and replaced their flesh with solidified shadows at a highly accelerated rate, they didn't *need* to stay within their victims in order to control them; those victims became extensions of the Demons' wills after they replaced the controlling influence that the Corruption had over them. While the Corruption in them was still present, the Demons had effectively hijacked control with minimal effort.

What was even worse? With each monster they "consumed", they had a chance to reproduce, meaning that there were effectively *tens of thousands* of them down below the desert of Lowenthal, with more being produced every day. They were an unstoppable army of silent killers, and there would be very little defense against them once they eliminated the Drekkin and broke out into the world.

Not that Larek could do anything about it, because he was quickly becoming their latest victim.

There was a sudden detached feeling that suffused his consciousness, as he sensed that his connection with the Demon's mind had fully isolated what made Larek himself and took over completely. As much as he thought he should be frantically raving and mentally demanding that the Demon let his consciousness free, all he could do was docilely and detachedly experience his soul being essentially ripped out of his body and replaced with a foreign will.

At least, that was what the Umbral Demon desired to happen… but the result wasn't what either of them expected.

As soon as the invader moved on after fully subduing Larek's body and mind, touching the soul that it needed to destroy and replace with its own, the Demon was hit with a violent spiritual backlash. The Combat Fusionist sensed, rather than saw, the Pattern Cohesion that suffused his very being act like an impenetrable energetic shield that protected his soul, and the Umbral Demon's invasive tendrils weren't only repelled but utterly destroyed.

A mental screech of pain nearly ripped his own consciousness apart due to being connected with his attacker's mind, but the isolating barrier keeping it separate worked in his favor to keep it intact. It was the only thing that allowed him to concentrate on what happened next, as the enraged Demon apparently decided that it wasn't going to take no for an answer and counterattacked the defenses in place, throwing everything it had at what Larek pictured as a glowing barrier around the center of his being, where his soul supposedly resided.

That was the Demon's first and last mistake.

Rather than passively repelling the all-out attack by the Demon, Larek's Pattern Cohesion *moved* within him like it was alive and had a mind of its own. While it wasn't something visible, the sense he got was that the powerful Cohesion struck out at the attacking Demon and captured it in a blinding glow of unfathomable power. Reaching out with tendrils of energy, Larek's Pattern Cohesion began to rip apart the main core of the Demon and burned away the scraps, before doing something that sucked in every trace of its presence within his body. When it was all gathered together, it was smothered and ground into tiny motes of shadow like some herbs inside a mortar and pestle. Even those shadowy motes were quickly burned away by the intense energy inherent in his Pattern Cohesion, leaving not a single indication that the Umbral Demon had ever been there. Then, as if it was satisfied with a job well done, the sensation of his Cohesion faded away until he couldn't detect it any more than he normally did.

As soon as the last trace of the Demon was completely eradicated, Larek's consciousness was freed from the enveloping darkness that had isolated it within his own mind, and he was immediately disoriented by the influx of information streaming in from his senses all over his recovering body. Sucking in a deep breath as if he had been starved for air, he coughed at the scratchy feeling in his throat even as he tried to make sense of what had happened.

Opening his eyes, he had to close them quickly as he was nearly blinded by his *Directional Illumination* Fusion's cone of light bouncing off the nearby wall, which was more reflective than he expected. With a groan, he crawled over to the stone rod and used his senses of pinpointing Fusions to slip his hands around it, before turning the Magnitude down to 2, hoping that it would be enough to see by.

It definitely turned out to be enough, considering that the oppressive darkness of the tunnel had disappeared entirely. Sure, it was still dark, because there were no veins of glowing crystals like there were out in the main tunnel. Slowly getting to his knees as he looked around the tunnel he had entered what felt like hours ago, he was nearly knocked over again as he received some notifications.

**Pattern Manipulation** *Skill has been unlocked!*
**Pattern Manipulation** *Skill has reached Level 1!*
.....
**Pattern Manipulation** *Skill has reached Level 10!*

**Congratulations!**
*Due to your intensive study of spell patterns, Fusion formations, and your own internal Pattern Cohesion, you have unlocked the* **Patternal** *Specialization!*

Requirements:
**Pattern Manipulation** *Skill of* 10
**Pattern Formation** *Skill of* 10
**Pattern Recognition** *Skill of* 10
Intellect of at least 10
Acuity of at least 10

Pneuma of at least <u>20</u>

The **Patternal** Specialization also provides these benefits:

Ability to manipulate up to 10% of your Pattern Cohesion outside of spell patterns and Fusion formations
Ability to gradually manipulate your internal pattern
5% reduction in Pattern Cohesion requirements for all spells and Fusions

Do you wish to accept this Specialization? Yes / No

    As Larek tried to look over the notifications, his body spasmed slightly as he instantly gained 10 Levels in a brand-new Skill that he'd just unlocked: *Pattern Manipulation*. After a few moments he had recovered and was able to fully concentrate on what it all said.

    He had no idea what the new Skill was all about until he saw the new Specialization for something called Patternal, and it appeared to be an extremely basic Specialization considering its requirements. With only needing "Pattern"-related Skills at 10 and the highest stat at only 20, he suspected that this was something that most Mages should be able to acquire while at an Academy, if it wasn't for the fact that he hadn't heard of *Pattern Manipulation* before. He had a fairly good feeling that no one else knew of it, either; otherwise, he probably would've been told about it at some point.

    When he looked at the benefits for the Specialization, he began to understand what exactly this *Manipulation* Skill did when it came to his Cohesion. Thinking about what it had done against the Umbral Demon, he realized that his Pattern Cohesion could be manipulated in ways he had never considered before. While he knew it could be used in the creation of spell patterns and Fusion formations, because he was taught that was all it *could* do, in reality it was so much more. Even now, he could feel a portion of it waiting to be called upon to be used inside or *outside* of his body in different ways.

    As far as inside his body, creating protective shields around his soul was the obvious usage, but he thought that he might be able to move it around and use it to protect his mind from outside influences. For external purposes, he was fairly certain that he could pull it out and, instead of creating a pattern for a spell or a Fusion, he could change it in a way that would act as an external shield against attacks. It was a bit limited in application right now, as he thought he might be able to make a small circular plate of flattened Pattern Cohesion to help block an incoming blow, but as the Skill Level increased, he figured he might be able to do more – possibly even cover his entire body.

But it was more than just defense, as he could also use it to coat the blade edge of his axe, giving it the qualities of his own Pattern Cohesion, which seemed to have some sort of strength against the shadowy Umbral Demons. He wasn't sure what else it might be good for, but for now, that was enough for him.

The other benefit from this new Specialization, which said something about gradually manipulating his internal pattern, Larek was largely unsure of what that meant. He could only assume that it meant he could alter some things about his own pattern, but why would he want to do that? And what kind of side effects would that have if he decided, for some reason, to try it? Those were questions that he didn't try to answer at the moment, because that wasn't as important as getting out of the tunnel he was in.

Not because he was eager to leave, however. His opinion had changed on fleeing somewhat since an Umbral Demon had tried to not just kill him, but take over his body and pretend to *be* him. Most others might take their survival as a lucky break and get out of there before it happened again. While Larek was usually of that same mind, his experience of being entirely helpless and basically watching as his body was taken over bit by bit, knowing that he would essentially be a prisoner in his own mind for the rest of existence, was enough to convince him that he didn't want that to happen to another living person.

Whether they were someone from the Sealance Empire, one of these Drekkin he had heard about, people from his own Kingdom of Androthe, or any other land around the world, he knew he had to stop these things before they could spread from underneath the desert. The Drekkin might think it was impossible to kill the sneaky Umbral Demons, but Larek was fairly certain he had found the key to their demise. There were still a lot of unknowns, and there were apparently *a lot* of them down in the tunnels and near the Aperture according to what he picked up from the alien mind of the Demon that he had killed, but he was determined to stop them here and fight them with every bit of his abilities.

*Apparently that informational notification knew me better than I know myself. Fight well, indeed!*

# Chapter 47

The feeling of being strangely energized by his newfound determination to fight against the Umbral Demons lasted until he got back to his Air Skimmer and lifted it up, before trying to figure out what to do next. It was at that point that he recalled the information that he had gained from the mind of the Demon to which he'd been connected, and he shuddered at the recollection of helplessness that he felt at that point. Pushing past that, he worked on understanding exactly what it was he was up against, and he immediately felt overwhelmed.

The information was sadly incomplete and viewed from a perspective that was extremely foreign to Larek, but what he could pull from it matched what the original notification had told him about the situation under the desert. At one point, hundreds of Apertures had opened all around the underground world of Lowenthal, with the Drekkin who were changed into Mages and Martials working even faster than the people in the Empire had to understand their new status and abilities, as they immediately fought the monsters and temporarily closed Apertures within a day or two of everything happening.

It was at that point that the Umbral Demons discovered the monsters as well, locating an Aperture found in an out-of-the way area near the center of Lowenthal, and they immediately pounced upon their first victims. From the scattered information about these first monsters, they had apparently been some sort of burrowing worms he had never learned about which had an ability to pass through sand or dirt with ease, as well as being able to harden it with just as much ease.

Once the Demons captured every single monster from the Aperture, they turned their attention to the Aperture and did... *something* to it. Either the one he had killed hadn't been there, or the information was fragmented enough that he couldn't remember it clearly. Regardless of the reason, what the shadowy Demons did acted as some sort of anchor, so that when they ventured out with their converted monsters and attacked the next-nearest Aperture, they connected their original "anchored" Aperture to the newest one and it somehow *pulled* the newest one into the first. Again, it wasn't exactly clear how this had been done, but the end result was that the original Aperture with the burrowing worms absorbed the other Aperture and grew larger and stronger...

...as well as being able to additionally produce the absorbed Aperture's monsters. These newer monsters adapted some of the characteristics of the burrowing worms, most notably the ability to move through sand and dirt like it was water and to harden it just as easily. That explained why the Barbed Gators and the giant scorpion had been strangely able to do such things, which he had originally thought it to be impossible for two different monsters to do the same exact thing.

From there, they expanded their collection of Apertures, feeding them all into the original one, as they built their army. The Drekkin apparently fought them every step of the way as soon as they learned what was going on, going so far as to collapse the tunnels leading out of their domain, to keep the Demons trapped under the desert. At least, that was his understanding, because the impression he had received from the mind was that the Demons were extremely angry that this had been done, and he could only assume it had been done with that exact purpose in mind.

After that, the information became quite hazy, but one thing that he did understand about that Aperture that was under the control of the Umbral Demons was that it was *huge*. Not just in appearance, but in total territory; at that moment, the territory of the giant Aperture comprised around 90% of the entire desert of Lowenthal. Because almost all of the sand up above was inside the territory, which was based upon the environment the burrowing worms were accustomed to, they had the ability to manipulate the sand to a certain degree, though only at certain times of day. They used the sand to pull anything that might have been traveling over the desert toward their main Aperture so that they could capture and convert it to their cause, as they weren't quite able to break free yet of the underground tunnels because of the Drekkin.

That information explained a lot to Larek, as it solved the mystery of being transported at night, but at the same time he was left with the same question in his head. *Where do I go to stop them?*

Unfortunately, things such as directions and locations within the tunnels were either completely unknown to the Demon, or they were so foreign that they made no sense to his mind. For instance, instead of different places that could help him understand where he was in relation to where either the Drekkin or the Aperture was located, all he had received were impressions of areas with different darkness "flavors", for want of a better word. The tunnel he had just left was something he could only classify as, well, *tasting* new and expectant, like it had been recently created and was expected to accomplish something. What that was, he didn't know, and it didn't help that all the other impressions of different areas were associated with these odd flavors, where one was a taste of old, dusty stone and another had the coppery taste of blood.

Where those places actually were, he had absolutely no idea.

He thought he might be able to use the sense of the gigantic Aperture to find his way to it, but even though he acknowledged that he felt it, pinpointing exactly where it was located was impossible. He could only assume that it was so powerful, and its territory was so large, that the feeling of it suffused the very air around him rather than giving him a trackable location.

The only real solution by that point was to venture off, like he had been doing before he discovered the dark tunnel, and hope that, instead of finding a way out, he discovered a way to the Aperture and the Demons that he needed to destroy. *How* exactly he would do that was a bridge that he'd have to cross once he got there, as he wasn't sure how to go about handling so many of them.

Moving back down the main tunnel, it only took a half-hour before he found something. Or to be more accurate, *something* found *him*.

Larek slowed his Air Skimmer when he noticed dark shapes emerging from the sand above, a swarm of black-colored, fluttering forms that immediately swooped down toward his vessel. It took a moment to recognize the **Dusty Butterflies** that they were because instead of being in a riot of flamboyantly varied colors, these particular Butterflies were various shades of black that made them look like some sort of "death" Butterflies rather than the Dusty variety. What convinced him of their actual type was the cloud of pollen they left behind as they fluttered toward him, which was both an irritant and a poison that could kill someone who was unprepared for it.

As he brought the Skimmer to a stop, Larek brought his staff up and aimed it toward the descending swarm, noticing that they emerged from the sand above without a single granule falling through the opening, which told him that these were monsters created by the Aperture since they could manipulate the sand to a point that it was no longer an impediment to them.

So, he just started blasting.

Knowing that his *Flying Stones* wouldn't be as effective, now that he had some inside information on the abilities of the monsters he would be facing down below the desert, he instead switched to a barrage of *Flaming Balls* that rocketed out from the end of his staff toward the swarm of Dusty Butterflies; and at Magnitude 2, they were flying out at 10 per second. He needed to eliminate the pollen they were spreading, which had grown into an alarming cloud by that point, because there had to have been at least 150 Butterflies in the swarm.

With each of them with bodies that were a foot long and wingspans that topped 3 feet wide, his barrage of *Flaming Balls* easily found targets as they slammed into the front ranks of the flying insects. Each one that was hit was knocked backwards and lit on fire, quickly plummeting to the ground as their wings went up in flames. Killing nearly a dozen in them in less than a second, he was beginning to strafe his staff over the Butterflies to encompass as many as he could, when one of the *Flaming Balls* missed one of the leading monsters and passed behind it...

...right into the cloud of pollen. Unbeknownst to him, but probably should've been known if he had paid more attention in his classes, was that the poison pollen in large concentrations was flammable. When an entire ball of flames appeared in the middle of the deadly cloud, there was an audible *\*whump\** right before it ignited in a flash, enveloping all the nearby Butterflies in the radius of its effect. It didn't explode like one of his *Weaken* Fusions did, but instead produced an extremely hot conflagration that burned through the pollen and burned over 100 Butterflies simultaneously. Their delicate wings were destroyed to the point where they followed the previous ones that Larek had hit down to the ground.

Taken aback at the sudden destruction, the Combat Fusionist hesitated for a few moments, which allowed the remaining few dozen monsters to get close, but he managed to move his staff in the way of the incoming Butterflies to knock a few more out of the air. When the others were within 10 feet or so, he set his staff down and pulled out a Fusion he hadn't used lately because it was of less use against things like a Barbed Gator or a giant scorpion, and it also had a stone quality to it that he had recognized as not being beneficial.

However, even if the sharp slivers of stone being pushed around by his *Stone Shredder Dome +6* Fusion didn't hurt the Butterflies, the powerful gusts of wind inside the dome should handle them well enough.

So it proved to be, as he held the stone in front of him and directed the dome out in front of the Air Skimmer. As the monsters dove in to cover him in poisonous pollen, they smashed into the dome and were ripped apart by the air gusts inside it, along with the stones that weren't manipulated fast enough by the Butterflies to avoid being hurt. In a few seconds, the last of the attackers had disappeared into chunks on the floor, but even those quickly disappeared as the solidified shadows they were made from dissipated.

After absorbing the Corrupted Aetheric Force that they provided, he realized that he hadn't ever checked to see how much he had finally received from the scorpion up on the surface. He was surprised yet again when he saw that the powerful arachnid had provided him with *2,000 AF!* It was more than he expected, but it also made sense because it had been an extremely strong monster... which made him worry that there were more of them nearby, as he knew that they would be a challenge to defeat even now that he knew about them.

*What else is down here?*

As he let the Aetheric Force he accumulated from the Butterflies add to his available AF, which turned out to be 167 AF – or 1 AF per monster he had killed – Larek started to spend what he had to improve the maximums of his Skills once again. With an eventual 2,194 AF (once the Corrupted Aetheric Force was converted), he increased the maximum Level for *Pattern Recognition, Magical Detection*, and *Spellcasting Focus* to Level 38, leaving him with a whole 4 AF remaining. He was still planning on bringing them up to the same Levels as his Fusion-based Skills and was making good progress in that regard, though looking at his new *Pattern Manipulation* Skill with a maximum Level of 20, he knew that he would have to work on improving that just as much as the others – if not more.

He just had to figure out how to go about that, but he had some ideas that he thought might work.

Continuing to move down the tunnel after the relatively brief interruption, he was attacked yet again by another group of monsters, but this time they didn't come from the ceiling and the sand layer up there, but from below. He didn't recognize the half-dozen hulking monsters that were at least 6 feet tall even while they ran hunched over, but they closely resembled a cross between a horse and an ape. With a head that had the length of a horse but had their eyes on the front like a predator, accompanied by a pair of powerfully muscled arms on top of their torso, the monsters ran quickly at him as their four skinny-yet-strong legs cantered through the tunnel, their odd hooves striking up sparks as they went.

It didn't take much to identify them as monsters; having the same dark skin and hair covering them similar to the others he'd killed made it obvious, and he had to assume that the color change was a result of them being made of solidified shadows. Larek also hazarded to guess that Serena wasn't exactly the same as the monsters because she had a soul that allowed her to maintain her normal appearance.

Regardless of the reason, Larek once again used his staff on the galloping monsters headed his way, their intimidating hands squeezing together rhythmically as if they wanted to ring his neck – which he assumed they did. Instead of *Flaming Balls*, he filled them full of Magnitude 4 *Ice Spikes* before changing tactics after those didn't slow the charging horse-apes down at all. Despite the shards of ice stuck into their chests, they didn't seem to care or even be hurt by them all that much, so Larek switched to a Mag 6 *Water Stream*. Rather than aim for their easier-to-hit chest, he moved the line of powerfully cutting water downwards toward their legs.

He remembered a few years ago when one of their mules back home had broken its legs after it had fallen into a hole, and there had been no way to heal it completely; they'd had to put it down because of that, which he recalled being a sad time because he cared for all the mules they possessed. He nearly didn't want to do the same to these monsters because just thinking about it was depressing, but he hardened his heart and cut through and snapped the forelegs of the horse-apes mercilessly. One by one, they collapsed and rolled forward as their support was literally cut from underneath them – but that didn't mean they were any less dangerous. Leaning forward on their larger arms, the monsters continued running forward once they were able to pick themselves up off the floor of the tunnel.

Larek once again switched up his attacks and shot a Mag 5 *Flaming Ball* at two of them in quick succession, only for the horse-apes to reach up with their arms as the projectiles came close and literally *punch* the ball of fire apart. The flames washed over them, which singed patches of their hair as it surrounded them momentarily, but they appeared to be largely unhurt. Swapping back to *Ice Spikes* at a higher Magnitude than before resulted in nearly the same action as against the *Flaming Ball*, though this time the icy projectile shattered and flung shards of ice everywhere.

It was at this point that he noticed a dull shine reflecting off of the fingers of the monsters' hands, and he knew he might be in trouble. Whether they were coated in steel or some other strong metal, if they were able to punch magical projectiles out of the air, they would likely be able to wreck the thin plates of *Strengthened* iron that comprised the shell of his vessel.

With only a slight hesitation after seeing this, Larek jumped out of his Air Skimmer and rolled forward when he landed, bringing his staff to bear and pointing it toward the closest horse-ape. A split-second after he activated a *Water Stream* at Magnitude 8 and shot it toward the monster's face, the strange beast flexed its back legs, bending them in a way that looked unnatural, before it *jumped* a dozen feet in the air as it attempted to pounce on him. He was suddenly glad that he had vacated his Skimmer because it was obvious that these things could reach him even in the air.

Thankfully, the horse-ape that jumped had completed the maneuver slightly too late, as Larek's attack hit it in its face and in its *Icy Spike*-covered chest, and the rapid-fire water projectiles ripped through its head, neck, and chest, opening a massive hole as it pushed and then shattered the ice shards stuck in it. It died a second after jumping in the air toward him, and he moved quickly out of the way of its eventual landing.

**Dodge** *has reached Level 22!*

The instant Larek could target another of the monsters he did so, and he managed to score a wound in the upper chest of a second before a metal-covered fist came up and deflected the *Water Stream* he was aiming at it. Before he could try to maneuver around the blocking fist, it and the other horse-apes jumped at him, prompting Larek to toss his staff to the side, pull out his offensive Fusions and drop them at his feet after activating them, and then roll out of the way.

Jumping to his feet and out of range of his Fusions, Larek grabbed the axe off his belt and stood ready as the monsters landed right where he had been and then turned toward him. The Fusions still had a few seconds before they activated, so he moved to just outside of their range and raised his axe defensively as a fist came toward his chest. He grunted as he was pushed back, after blocking the hit with the haft of his axe, and he heard a worrying creak in the wood along with the impact. He also felt his *Repelling Barrier* Fusion activate, attempting to push the attack away, but all that happened was that the fist was pushed downward a fraction of an inch.

*I can't do that again—wait! My new Skill!*

Larek went on the offensive as another horse-ape attempted to flank him and completely destroy his ribs with a powerful punch, but he swung around and deflected its fist as the edge of his axe sliced through the fingers with a screech of protest and a few sparks to go along with the counterattack. He was happy to see that the fist was only *covered* in a thick coating of metal rather than being fully metal, as he wasn't sure if he'd have been able to cut through them all.

Even as he did that, he could sense another blow from the first horse-ape heading for his right hip, but he was already accessing what he knew about his new *Pattern Manipulation* Skill. Already being somewhat of an expert on directing his Pattern Cohesion outside of his body, he was only momentarily stymied as he figured out how to direct a bunch of it into a shape that he hoped would resemble a square piece of metal that floated approximately 6 inches away from his right hip. There was a drain on his Pattern Cohesion as he did this, and while he couldn't look to see how much had been used, he estimated it to be a few hundred.

Along his side, a faintly glowing square of *something* appeared, though it wasn't exactly how he pictured it. Instead of a solid piece of Pattern Cohesion, it was more of a grid-like net without any depth to it, almost like an odd Fusion formation that hadn't been filled in with any components.

Unable to do anything about it in the heat of battle, he turned his head enough to watch the blow from the horse-ape strike the square dead-on, and he silently cheered as it flexed inward with the punch. At least, he cheered until he saw that it was flexing *too* much, and the impact when it finally hit him snapped something in his hip as he was propelled away in an uncontrolled tumble.

Activating his *Healing Surge* Fusion before he even stopped tumbling away, he felt the fractured hip bone knit itself together even as the crushed flesh repaired itself. By the time he stopped rolling, he was able to stand back up on his legs without any debilitation, as the injury hadn't been *that* bad.

His attempt at stopping the blow hadn't worked entirely, but it *did* soften it somewhat. He wanted to stop and contemplate what he did wrong, but the horse-ape that had hit him was already leaping toward his location. As he looked back at the other monsters, he saw that his offensive Fusions had finally activated simultaneously, and the result was disturbing. Roots full of thorns shot out of the ground to quickly wrap around the hindquarters of the horse-apes, before they completely froze as the area was flash-frozen in an instant. The *Healing Shelter* then took effect and attempted to heal the freezing and cracking bodies of the monsters, only for them to freeze once they were healed, leaving them in a cycle of death and healing that was hard to look at.

Mentally deactivating the *Healing Shelter* and *Binding Thorns* from a distance, the others simply froze to death as they were already caught and couldn't escape.

Meanwhile, the last horse-ape nearly pounded Larek into the ground as it landed on him, distracted as he was by the Fusions dealing death to the others, and only his *Repelling Barrier* activating at just the right time shifted the blow that would've caved in his head. Instead, it smacked and then bounced off his shoulder as he felt his collarbone snap, but he pushed through the discomfort as he brought his axe around to lop off an arm.

The horse-ape roared in pain right into his face, and he was practically drenched in foul-smelling spittle, but he managed to throw himself backwards to avoid a retaliatory strike by the monster's other fist. As he landed backwards, his *Healing Surge* finishing up the repair of his clavicle, he realized that he wouldn't be able to avoid another blow that was coming to smash into his legs, so he attempted another block with his *Pattern Manipulation* Skill.

What formed as he pulled the Pattern Cohesion out of his body was thicker and less transparent than what he'd done before, but it was essentially still a grid-like net. As a result, as the horse-ape pounded down on it with its only remaining fist, it stretched nearly to the breaking point, hitting his leg and smashing into his flesh beneath his pants... but he didn't feel that his leg broke or even fractured, though it did seem to flex a little from the pressure of the horse-ape's fist.

**Pattern Manipulation** has reached Level 11!

**Body Regeneration** has reached Level 35!

Even in its anger at losing an arm, the monster looked at the square net that had essentially stopped its fist from crushing Larek's leg in confusion for an entire second. That was all the Combat Fusionist needed as he swung his axe while still on his back, detaching the other limb at the elbow. Before it could scream in pain and anger again, Larek sat up and sliced through the thick neck of the horse-ape with a Strength-enhanced slice of his axe, killing it instantly. Its body collapsed heavily on his lower legs, splashing blood from its open neck all over him, but he simply waited as it dissipated into the same dark greenish-black smoke that he was expecting, freeing him to get up and take stock of his situation.

The ambient Mana density was beginning to become a problem from the use of so many Mana-intensive Fusions, so he mentally deactivated the *Frozen Zone* Fusion and then brought his Air Skimmer back down to the floor. As he climbed aboard after collecting his staff and the wooden offensive Fusions, he grabbed something to eat while he let the Mana density climb back up to normal.

*This new Skill can be a great asset... as long as I figure it out. I think I'm going to have to practice with it a lot to make sure it does what I want, but I can definitely see the possibilities it has opened for me.*

Just as he was about to leave a short time later, he spotted yet another group of monsters heading his way from down the tunnel, the same direction that the horse-apes had come from.

*I guess that means I'm going the right way?*

That was the only conclusion he could come up with as he pulled out his staff once again and aimed it at what appeared to be a small horde of *Bog Goblins*, or at least whatever the equivalent ones were that were composed of all black and dark-grey skin and clothing.

*Regardless of whether this is the right way or not, it's at least a good way to gather Aetheric Force.*

With that thought in mind, he smiled as he released a barrage of Mag 1 *Flaming Balls* at the weak Bog Goblins heading his way.

# Chapter 48

A few hours later, Larek paused after absolutely obliterating a veritable horde of **Flojiggers**. Over 500 of the 2-foot-wide abominations had attempted to ambush him from above, descending from the sand stripe at the top of the tunnel he was traveling through, but his aim and significant amount of practice lately let him pick them off in the air. It helped that their stretched skin surrounding their spherical bodies was highly flammable, and the poisonous gas that they expelled when they burst apart exploded upon contact with a flame.

Watching them go up in flames in a chain reaction put a smile on the Combat Fusionist's face, as he particularly didn't like the dozens of tiny eyes that surrounded their bodies, looking every which way simultaneously, nor the 100 wavy, needle-like appendages that were used to inject their poisonous gas into a victim. When he added in their coloring, which was a mixture of black with a hint of dark-green at the tips of their slimy appendages, he could only shudder in revulsion at the thought of them trying to touch him; they were creepy to the extreme, and he was only glad that he didn't have to get near them.

Fortunately, the explosions followed by their complete dispersion into shadows meant that there were no remains left for him to look at after they were destroyed, and only his memories of their attempted ambush and the Corrupted Aetheric Force that was currently being purified were left over from the exchange. That latter thought forced Larek to realize that he hadn't allocated his AF in a while, as he had been inundated by one group of Umbral Demon-touched monsters after another without too much time to rest. The Combat Fusionist felt like he was swimming against a current as he traveled through the vast tunnel system, but he pushed on because he felt like he was getting close to something. This was compounded by the fact that the walls of the tunnel seemed to be changing, growing slightly wider in diameter, and the glowing crystal veins that illuminated the passageway had become slightly more structured and refined.

Taking a look at his Status, Larek was surprised to see that he had accumulated over 18,000 AF from all the fighting he had done, which was more than he expected, if he was being honest with himself. Almost all the monsters he encountered after the horse-apes had been what he was used to seeing in the Sealance Empire; in other words, they were relatively weak and easy to kill – even if they came in large numbers. Only one other fight had been challenging at all, and it wasn't even because the monsters he fought were powerful; rather, it was simply that they were a bit more resilient than the others.

Over 200 **Stone Chuckers** had rolled toward him, their 3-foot-wide cylindrical bodies looking like dark wooden logs rather than the stone that they were. At only 6 inches wide, they weren't very intimidating as it appeared as though anyone could just jump over them, but when they stopped rolling and somehow propped themselves on one of their flat ends, he discovered that they were relatively formidable as they stretched their stone bodies backwards... before snapping forwards quickly, chucking a small, jagged stone approximately 4 inches in diameter at Larek in his Air Skimmer.

They weren't particularly dangerous to *him*, as even if he was hit by a few of them, they wouldn't do much damage. His vessel, on the other hand, was a different story altogether. As one of the upright wooden frame pieces took a beating from at least a dozen stones pummeling it, cracking it just a slight bit more, Larek jumped out and landed on the tunnel floor, moving quickly forward to take the fight to the monsters rather than let them damage his Skimmer further. He first began to try to burn them with *Flaming Balls*, but after they appeared unharmed other than some scorch marks, he was forced to switch up his attack.

*Flying Stones* were out of the question, because not only were these things already made of stone, but they likely had that same manipulation ability as the other monsters he'd fought down in the bowels of Lowenthal. *Icy Spike* proved to be largely ineffective as well, as while the higher Magnitude variety of icicle projectiles could crack them apart upon impact, causing the Chuckers to crumble into death, anything less simply shattered against their stony exteriors.

Only *Water Stream* seemed to be effective at a distance, as he was able to sweep through the monsters and cut them apart – but he had to do it on a lower Magnitude. Only constant pressure, rather than the strong bursts of high-velocity water that the higher Magnitudes produced, was able to cut through them, and even then it required a few seconds to cut through one of them completely. After some quick trial-and-error as they continued to chuck stones at him, which he either dodged by rolling out of their path or let his *Repelling Barrier* deflect some of them, he discovered that a Mag 4 *Water Stream* was the most effective, though it still wasn't very fast.

After killing a quarter of the Stone Chuckers with his staff, he began to take some hits to his body. Where the barrage of projectiles had at first been coordinated and simultaneous, it had changed to be more sporadic and unpredictable, leading him to have to avoid a dozen different stones every second, coming from slightly different directions and angles. After one that he didn't see coming hit him in the face because his *Barrier* was already overworked by deflecting multiple projectiles simultaneously, he growled in anger and rushed forward, tossing his staff back up into the Air Skimmer. He wasn't necessarily hurt by the stone hitting his face, but the unexpected impact wasn't pleasant.

*Time to work on my Pattern Manipulation, I guess.*

Pulling out his axe, he moved quickly to the closest Chucker and used it to easily bisect the monster in half, but that was only a secondary concern for him. Pulling his Pattern Cohesion out of his body so that it could be manipulated, he created a flat, square grid-like net in front of his face as another barrage of about a dozen stones attempted to smash his head in. A few of the stones either flew around the square net made out of his Pattern or underneath it, with only a few making it through his Barrier to hit his *Multi-Resistance* protected clothing. The impacts were felt but didn't hurt him, though they did make it slightly harder to concentrate on what he was doing with his Pattern.

As for the other stones that hit his floating square net, he watched as it flexed a bit with each impact, but it held up remarkably well as the projectiles' momentum was entirely arrested. He had expected them to bounce off and possibly ricochet after hitting his Pattern, but it was almost as if they hit a super-soft pillow. He contrasted the last time he had used his Pattern in this way against the horse-apes, where his square net had barely slowed the blows from the apes down. The difference was obviously due to the force behind the impact with his Pattern, as the horse-apes were quite strong compared to the stone projectiles, but it also showed Larek something else.

His floating shield made out of Pattern was *weak*. Sure, it had blocked the stones easily enough, but they weren't really a threat all by themselves when pitted against his *Body* stat. The Stone Chuckers were relatively weak and weren't necessarily a problem for most Mages and Martials in the SIC because there wasn't a significant amount of strength behind the projectiles they threw at their victims, and they only had the one attack – unless someone were to stand in front of them and get rolled over when they moved. There were multiple ways he could think of for anyone who had graduated from an Academy or Fort to destroy them without too much effort; as a result, simply blocking their attacks with his defenses wasn't that much of a victory.

At that point, his Pattern was only slightly useful against weaker monsters, all because weaker monsters weren't really a threat to him even if they were able to attack him through his Repelling Barrier. If he wanted it to be worth using, it would have to be able to stand up to an attack by something stronger, such as the horse-apes or against a projectile that could actually do him serious harm. Thinking about his fight with the giant scorpion, what he could create now would've been almost entirely useless.

Therefore, it needed to be stronger. *But how am I supposed to do that?*

As he rolled to the side and sliced through another Stone Chucker with his axe, his Pattern net maintained its position in the air where he had left it. When he moved more than 10 feet away, it popped and disappeared like a soap bubble, and he felt that the Pattern Cohesion that he had invested into it had been lost to him. An extremely brief flash of his Status showed that his Pattern Cohesion was down approximately 10 points, which wasn't a significant amount – and less than he was expecting. It was already regenerating, of course, but he remembered that he had been able to reabsorb most, if not all of it, when he had been fighting the horse-apes.

Keeping all of that in mind, he rebuilt another Pattern net to block another round of stone projectiles, and this time he imagined pulling even more Pattern Cohesion out of his body to fill the square. For some reason, it was a struggle, something he'd never experienced before when working with his Cohesion outside of his body, either for Fusion purposes or for spellcasting – during the few failed times he had attempted the latter, of course. He thought he pulled out a little bit more, but it was as if there was a block on the amount of Pattern Cohesion he could extract for this method at one time.

He couldn't see much difference in the protective net shield he created when it blocked even more of the Stone Chuckers' projectiles, and he rolled away afterwards to cut through another monster and to quickly check his Status. This time, 15 Pattern Cohesion was lost when his net disappeared, which was still not much in the scheme of things – especially considering his 36,000 Pattern Cohesion.

*What am I missing?*

Another few experiments with trying to push more and more into the net had caused no discernable change other than an increase in his Skill to Level 12. After the Skill increased, he was able to push a little bit more out of his body, making the square net approximately 2 inches wider and taller, but it still didn't have the type of resilience he wanted.

Thinking about what made his Pattern Cohesion so strong in Fusions and – unfortunately – in spell patterns, he thought that perhaps it wasn't necessarily his Cohesion alone that made it strong, but that its strength was only fully represented when introduced to Mana.

However, just thinking about his Skill a little more made him fairly confident that this wasn't the case, as it seemed that he should be able to accomplish what he understood from it using Pattern Cohesion alone. Besides, he didn't want to add Mana to something that could become permanent, such as a spell pattern—

*Wait. That's it!*

It wasn't a spell pattern, nor a formation like a Fusion, nor even Mana that he was missing; instead, it was something similar to a spell pattern or Fusion formation, but entirely different. With spells and Fusions, what he created was essentially a list of instructions that was powered by the Mana that was pushed into it; they had a symbiotic relationship that meant that one was essentially useless without the other. However, that wasn't quite as true as it sounded, as Pattern Cohesion had a spiritual weight behind it that was different from pure Mana, something that he had certainly seen as it had counterattacked the Umbral Demon as it attempted to possess his soul. It also had a physicality that could be made manifest through the use of Fusions, though it was largely secondary in nature to its function in a formation.

And that word, function, was exactly what was missing in his attempts at manipulating his Pattern Cohesion for use as a protective shield. There was no specific function that the Cohesion he was pulling out was supposed to follow, meaning that it had no strength behind it. As it was, he was essentially just pulling it out and throwing it up in the air, with just a basic grid-like net as its form; it was likely that the only reason that it didn't get completely shredded whenever it stopped a projectile was the innate strength in his Pattern Cohesion. Since it looked like a net, that was how it acted, and as a net typically flexed when pushed against, that was exactly what it did. From what he could tell, this was its basic, default shape when he simply pushed it outside his body, a blank slate with no instructions of what function it was designed for.

Therefore, it needed an appropriate *form* to replace that blank slate in order for it to carry out the *function* he wanted it to perform. This wasn't the same as a formation in a Fusion, of course, but more of a flex of an intent or will to create what was needed, something that would take intense concentration and focus to hold in place while he fought.

Thankfully, being able to become hyper-focused was something of a specialty of his.

As he was battered by a few dozen more stones, Larek stood stock still as he focused on pulling his Pattern Cohesion back out and directing it in front of him. Rather than letting it do what it wanted, he instead focused on creating something else, using his actual *Pattern Manipulation* Skill to form a specific shape out of the Cohesion. In more time than he would've liked, especially as he was still being hit by chucked stones, he finally formed a large shield similar to the ones he'd seen some Martials wearing on their left arms for defense. It was approximately 3 feet tall and 2 feet wide, tapering down to a point on the bottom and slightly curved on top – or at least that was what he was aiming for.

In reality, it was only slightly more than a hunk of Pattern Cohesion in the general form of a steel shield, misshapen in a few areas and not very precise in its measurements or angles. What was more important, however, was that it was *solid* rather than being a net, though it was largely transparent. That only lasted for a second, though, as he knew how to fix that.

Pulling out even more Pattern Cohesion, he smiled grimly as another stone smacked him in the chin, nearly breaking his concentration; fortunately, the shield he had formed in the air filled in over the next few seconds with the influx of Cohesion, until it was completely opaque. When he focused on it further, he found that he could move the shield around with just a thought – though it required quite a bit of his concentration…

…but it was worth it.

**Pattern Manipulation** has reached Level 13!
**Pattern Manipulation** has reached Level 14!

It seemed he was doing something right, as he increased his Skill by two Levels within only a few seconds of each other. It wasn't just that he had succeeded in creating something with an actual form and function to it, but that it *worked*. As he moved it around him with a thought as he stood still, every stone projectile that it intercepted bounced off and ricocheted just as it would against a physical shield, though there was no sound of impact like it would have had if it had hit iron or steel. Instead, the only sound that was made was when the stone hit the ground after it bounced off, which was slightly eerie, but he didn't care overly much about the lack of sound.

It was the fact that his shield now had 10% of his maximum 36,000 Pattern Cohesion in it, a full 3,600, that made it extremely durable. From what he could tell, none of the attacks coming from the Stone Chuckers put so much as a scratch on his floating shield, and he was fairly certain that anything that hit it would have to be *incredibly* powerful to damage it in any way. It was possible that some of the

Gergasi could do it, as he didn't actually know how powerful they were other than what he'd seen his father and Chinli do, but he was unsure how that translated to sheer physical damage.

It wasn't perfect, either, or at least it wasn't perfect *yet*; while he could move the shield around with a thought, as soon as he tried to move, it was locked into place, as he had difficulty concentrating on two things at once. It shouldn't have been that much of a problem, because his Acuity was so high and his Skills aided in focusing on multiple things at once, but that didn't seem to matter to the shield made of Pattern Cohesion.

**Pattern Manipulation** *has reached Level 15!*

*You have reached Level 30 and have 22 available AP to distribute!*

**Pattern Manipulation** *has reached Level 16!*

As he increased his *Pattern Manipulation* Skill Level twice more over the next few minutes of deflecting stones that were chucked at him, as well as reaching a personal Level of 30, he found that his control over the shield improved slightly. It got to the point where he could move his arms and flex his fingers as he used his thoughts to direct the Pattern shield around, so he had some hope that it would improve as the Skill continued to increase.

After playing with it some more over the next hour, he was only able to increase the Skill one more time before nothing else he did with the shield seemed likely to bump it up anymore, so he relaxed his focus and let it dissipate, absorbing the Pattern Cohesion back into his body. Once it was gone, the bombardment continued unabated, but he was already on the move. Using the Skill to create an unfocused net like before, he kept it active as he went on a killing spree, rapidly cutting through the Chuckers with his axe. His net shield wasn't as effective nor as large as the one he had to focus on, and he was hit dozens of times by stones as he finished them off, but he was almost completely unhurt, other than a few bruises that healed themselves within seconds of them being inflicted.

Once they were all dead and he had continued on, he didn't really get a chance to practice with the Skill any further as the monsters continued to appear, one after another, as he moved down the tunnel. As they were all weak enough that he could kill them from inside his Air Skimmer with his staff, there was no need to use the Skill, though he had some thoughts on a few more experiments he'd like to try at some point. He felt that the Skill could be incredibly powerful once he mastered its use, though he was also aware that it wouldn't be as easy or quick to improve as had been his ability with Fusions.

But now that he had a bit of a breather, he had a chance to evaluate his Status and see where he could allocate the 18,075 Aetheric Force he had accumulated – as well as the AP that had come from his recent Level increase. He might even be able to play with his *Pattern Manipulation* Skill outside of combat and see what it could do.

As he leaned over on the Skimmer's handlebars, contemplating where to put everything, movement out of the corner of his eye caught his attention. With a sigh, he closed his Status and brought down the tip of his staff in anticipation of firing some more magical projectiles on some monsters, but he stopped and raised it again in confusion after a brief look at what awaited him in the tunnel.

Expecting a horde of monsters, he was presented with a relatively organized, armed and armored group of what he could only describe as 3-foot-tall, upright-walking lizard-people with long, thick tails positioned behind them on the ground. That wasn't what made him hesitate, because he'd killed armed and armored monsters before, such as the Bog Goblins, though they were rare. No, it was the fact that as he looked at them, he could sense a connection to them that could only be explained by the fact that around half of them had the feel of a Martial, while the others had the feel of a Mage.

*Those definitely aren't monsters. Drekkin, perhaps?*

He was about to say something to them when they suddenly burst into motion and attacked without a word.

# Chapter 49

"Are you sure you heard something outside of the perimeter?" Pyluxa asked him softly, slipping up against him and speaking at a low enough volume that only he could hear her. Silence and near-silence was a way of life nowadays down in the Lost Caverns, as any sort of noise could draw attention to the patrolling groups that were sent out from Draverdin to ensure that nothing suddenly snuck up on their fortifications.

This particular branch of the Lost Caverns would eventually lead toward the Kingdom of Androthe, their neighbor to the east, but all contact with all foreigners had necessarily been severed. It felt like it had been years since they'd started fighting the monsters cursed by the vicious hellspawn, the Umbral Demons, but in reality the fighting hadn't really started until approximately a month and a half ago. In that time, their smaller satellite cities along the trade route had been lost to them as they were overrun, prompting the majority of the Drekkin population to retreat toward the capital, Draverdin, in order to survive.

Thankfully, they had been able to provide for the refugees because their growth centers had been fiercely protected, allowing them to continue growing the food necessary to feed everyone – at least for now. With them losing contact with the last few satellite cities to the north and south, it was quite possible that the monster army would eventually turn its sights on Draverdin and the remaining Drekkin, keeping them trapped, contained within the underground tunnels of Lowenthal.

But they would be ready if that were to happen. Gharix, along with every other Drekkin blessed by whatever power gave them the capability to defend themselves using never-before-seen magics and abilities, had been improving himself day by day as a matter of survival. There hadn't been a day in the last month that Gharix hadn't killed at least a few monsters as he and his nest-brothers and nest-sisters ranged around the Lost Caverns, looking to thin their numbers. As he glanced at Pyluxa before responding, he couldn't help but notice how different she looked from his *real* nest-sisters, who had almost all perished within the first few weeks of fighting. He and the others in his current nest-group weren't actually siblings, unlike the groups they used to have before the catastrophe that befell them, but had come together through shared grief and a bond that was just as strong as family – or perhaps even stronger, as it had been forged through the heat of battle and was therefore tempered to last longer than anyone could have predicted.

But that was neither here nor there, as they needed to investigate the sound he had heard earlier. His hearing was marginally better than that of the others in his nest-group, and was only enhanced when he applied his Stama toward his newest Battle Art, *Heightened Senses*. It worked to enhance his hearing and eyesight for a limited time, which was why he was the primary scout for the group – as well as its nominal leader. As much as he wanted to play it off as his imagination, he seemed to have a preternatural sense of danger and had led them away from situations that would've otherwise killed them – and his nest-group appreciated that enough to put him in charge. Not that Gharix desired to be the leader of anything, but he was willing to wear the mantle if it helped to keep them alive.

Over the last few minutes, his sense of danger had been going crazy, which was what prompted him to use his Battle Art, but he had only barely been able to hear what sounded like constantly rushing air. The sound was obviously out of place, but it also didn't sound as if a monster was making the noise, so now they needed to investigate it so that they could warn the others back in Draverdin.

"Yes, I heard it coming from—"

He didn't get a chance to finish his low-volume response as a series of enormous explosions seemed to reverberate through the tunnel ahead of them, flashes of what appeared to be flames bouncing off the walls of the tunnel curvature. Even as the explosions continued, Gharix took off at a run, with his nest-group behind him.

"Why are we heading *toward* the dangerous explosions?" Pyluxa half-yelled at him as they ran, though her voice was barely audible over the detonations ahead and it wouldn't have mattered much if she had raised her voice.

Gharix just shook his head, not knowing how to answer the question. All he knew was that he needed to see what it was that caused the explosions; whether it was to stop whatever it was from moving any closer to Draverdin, or just to observe, was something he wasn't quite sure of at the moment. His senses weren't exactly precise in their nature, but he couldn't deny that they insisted he see for himself what the cause of the disturbance was.

They rounded the tunnel corridor at a sprint, just as the last of the explosions died away. From the remains floating in the air before they dissolved entirely due to their curse, he recognized a few scraps that could only be from what he learned were called Flojiggers – a strange name for a strange monster. He shuddered at the sight of the monsters and could only be appreciative that they were dead, because they were a horrid monster to fight. They weren't difficult to kill, of course, but rather *too* easy; the gas inside of them was flammable enough that it was common for them to explode upon death, which caused their needle-like appendages to impale and poison anyone who was nearby. They were best handled at range, but sometimes there was no choice but to take the hits to get the job done.

Someone had obviously killed them all by causing them to explode in a series of subsequent detonations, either uncaring or far enough away from them to risk the aftereffects. It was that "someone" that made him, and his nest-group, stop as soon as they rounded the corner to witness the destruction of so many monsters, and his sense of danger spiked as soon as he caught sight of what awaited them.

Floating above the ground and blowing powerful gusts of wind that seemed contained in an ovoid-shaped area beneath it, was what appeared to be a strange wood and iron contraption. It was around a dozen feet off the ground, and it appeared to be some sort of odd conveyance, because it contained a tall figure inside that immediately made the ridges along his backside rise in absolute horror.

While the person inside the contraption was tall like an Umbral Demon, though perhaps a bit smaller, they had the look of someone who came from the Kingdom of Androthe, even if they were wearing the clothing seen mostly on those from the Sealance Empire. He – because he was moderately sure it was a male – was holding a wooden stick in his hands, but Gharix could also see some sort of weapon attached to his belt.

It was none of those things that caused him to recoil slightly in horror, however. It was the strong taint of the shadow-touched that surrounded him.

Almost any Drekkin would be able to identify the taint that one who has been in close contact with an Umbral Demon possessed, which looked like a faint, dark aura around them. As the Demons possessed and replaced the soul of the individual, there was no other outward sign that they had been shadow-touched, but once it happened there was no reversing the process. It could be contained through the use of the blessed Enexro metal, which could slow down the assimilation of their body and restrict any inherent abilities they might possess, but they couldn't be saved.

At the point when their soul was lost, there was no choice other than to kill them – or exile them if they were from an outsider race such as those from the Kingdom or Empire. Unfortunately, executing the victims didn't necessarily harm the Demons inhabiting their bodies, as it was impossible to destroy their shadowy bodies, but it severely weakened them and made it so that it would be a long time until they were able to possess someone else. They had been a menace to the Drekkin living beneath the desert of Lowenthal since The Transition, when the land above was transformed from the lush, green environment it used to be to what it was now.

Stories that Gharix had heard from the elders purported that Lowenthal was merely an extension between the Sealance Empire and the Kingdom of Androthe at that time, which was why the two peoples were so similar, though they'd drifted apart after Lowenthal was devastated, which made passage between the two all but impossible other than through the underground tunnels the Drekkin built later. That was when the Umbral Demons started to terrorize the Drekkin as they emerged from the darkest corners of their underworld, but they hadn't been too much of a problem over the last few hundred years. That all changed recently as the Demons were somehow able to shadow-touch the monsters that emerged from the Apertures, which led to defenses being overrun and more and more people falling to the evil soul-snatching nightmares that were getting stronger by the day.

And this figure in front of them was most certainly one of those who had been possessed by an Umbral Demon. The aura wasn't as strong as around those he'd seen possessed before, which was strange, but he'd also never personally seen someone from outside of Lowenthal be shadow-touched, either. That being said, there was no mistaking the aura, faint as it was, and there was no defense against the Demons' touch once someone was caught by them.

This man had to die. Not only that, but they had to do it quickly, as they couldn't allow him to come any closer to Draverdin. Who knew what he had planned for when he got there? Gharix could only assume that it wasn't anything good for the city that was bursting at the seams with refugees from all over.

Thankfully, the man seemed slightly distracted, likely wondering how he had accidentally destroyed the Flojiggers; it was doubtful that he had done it intentionally, as they were on the same side as the Umbral Demons. Now was the time to attack before he could prepare—

The man suddenly looked up as if he could sense the stare of Gharix and his nest-group. Out of the corner of his eye, he noticed that Pyluxa's tail was swishing back and forth, a sure sign that she was angry, and it was likely this that had caught the shadow-touched man's attention. He didn't have to say anything to the others as they moved to attack, as they were smart enough to know that they couldn't let this individual live any longer and potentially threaten Draverdin.

Using his superior Agility of 50, Gharix shot ahead of the others as he loosely gripped the handles of his steel daggers, preparing to use them to stab the man before he could react to their presence. He had no idea of the shadow-touched man's capabilities, but they wouldn't matter if he could get to him before a defense could be prepared; his quickness had served them quite handily in battle against the other shadow-touched Drekkin they had fought over the last month or so, as well as the monsters that had been altered by the blasted Demons.

When he was approximately 50 feet away from the floating contraption, Gharix activated his *Power Jump* Battle Art, which funneled his Stama down to his tail. Using its flexibility and the extra strength that the Battle Art provided him, his tail slammed down on the floor of the tunnel and acted as a sort of spring. Launching himself at a run, he held out his daggers that were aimed for the heart and neck of the shadow-touched threat, a dual stab that would effectively cut the man's throat and pierce his heart simultaneously.

Even if he didn't succeed immediately, he knew that the others in his nest-group were prepared to finish the job if he failed. Pyluxa was likely already casting the *Fireblast* spell she was so proficient at, while Hakkin would be readying a quick cast of the *Ice Storm* spell he had just recently discovered how to create. Abarcen and the other pair of Martials in the group were more close-quarters fighters than Gharix and had been instrumental in their success as a front line, utilizing their high Body and Strength stats to prevent the more vulnerable Mages from being overrun during their battles against shadow-touched monsters. Even so, they had enough strength to jump up to the floating contraption, which he thought he heard them doing when he was only a dozen feet from his target—

—which suddenly dropped from the height it had been at, plummeting to the floor of the tunnel. Gharix sailed right over it, with shock paralyzing his body momentarily; he had no way to arrest his movement while mid-air, so all he could do was look back and see his other Martial nestmates also traveling through the air as their intended target delicately landed on the floor below.

"No!" he shouted, uncaring that he was being loud at that point, because now Pyluxa and Hakkin were completely undefended and separated from the rest. His intent to kill the shadow-touched man by throwing everything they had at him had completely back-fired, and now they might even lose some of their own because of his stupidity.

*Or maybe not.*

Even as he was touching down from his jump and had to roll to avoid being even slightly injured by his landing, he saw the two Mages launch their spells at the shadow-touched threat, and their aim was better than that of Gharix and the other Martials in the nest-group had been. The Drekkin nest-group leader watched as the man dove out of the front of his once-floating contraption, though it wasn't to avoid the magical attacks coming his way; instead, he seemed to be protecting it as he stood in front of it seemingly unconcerned.

Even as he was hit by the fiery projectile that exploded in a large blast of flames as soon as it made contact, and then by a barrage of icicles that were a foot long and 3 inches wide, Gharix was surprised to see the metal and wooden contraption suddenly disappear. *Where did it go?*

He dismissed the question as unimportant a moment later as he ran back to join the fight, pushing every point of his Agility into arriving to finish off the likely heavily injured shadow-touched man. Seeing the conflagration from the explosive *Fireblast* and the sound of icicles from the *Ice Storm* impacting something, he missed a step and nearly face-planted when he saw that the man was almost entirely unscathed from the attacks. Somehow, there was a floating shield suspended out in front of him which blocked the attacks, though a bit of the powerful attacks spilled over the edges to nip at the clothing of the shadow-touched – and didn't seem to do much to it. It certainly wasn't burning or impaled by icicles, as he had expected.

*No matter; he's distracted enough that I can finish him off from behind.*

Gharix raced toward his back, aiming to pass through where the metal and wood contraption had been. Before he was halfway there, he suddenly slammed into something invisible at full speed, and he felt his right leg, left arm, and the front of his face \*crack\* from the impact, as if he had suddenly hit the wall of the tunnel. He was barely cognizant of his body rebounding and collapsing into a heap as his vision swam from the pain. Attempting to get up, the nest-group leader was barely able to get to a knee before he became too dizzy to see straight, toppling over to lay on his side.

Already, he could feel his *Body Regeneration* at work trying to heal his injuries, but he'd never been this hurt before and wasn't sure how long it would take. He could only imagine that it would take hours or days to completely repair the damage that he had essentially done to himself – if he even lived that long.

He heard Abarcen and the others race past him, avoiding the area where Gharix had slammed into the invisible barrier, and his vision cleared just enough when he stopped trying to move to see them arrive and begin to surround the man with their spears, swords, and battleaxes ready to attack. The two Mages launched another pair of spells at him, and yet the man didn't move as the floating shield blocked the magical projectiles as if they were nothing more than simple rocks hurled in his direction.

"Stop! Why are you attacking me? I come in peace, I swear—"

The words he heard from the man were in the common tongue used by the people living in the Kingdom of Androthe and the Sealance Empire, which only confirmed that this person was originally from either one of those locations. Gharix understood and spoke it fluently, just like most of the other Drekkin living underneath the desert, as they interacted with the traders constantly traveling through their tunnels – or at least they used to, before access was cut off. Now that he had a moment to think about it since he couldn't really move much, he wondered how this man had found his way inside. *Is there a breach somewhere? If so, then the Umbral Demons and their shadow-touched monsters could be getting ready to head out. If that's the case, then that could also mean that they are preparing to make a final push to eliminate the last of my people. I have to warn everyone in Draverdin!*

Unfortunately, he wasn't going anywhere until his *Body Regeneration* fixed him up enough that he didn't collapse every time he tried to get up. He had a feeling that he might be well enough not to pass out in a few minutes, but those few minutes were a lifetime when in the middle of a fight like this against a powerful opponent. And it was obvious that this opponent was extremely powerful, given how easily he had defended himself against their attacks. He even watched the floating shield suddenly whip around the man when Abarcen attacked with his spear, thinking to gut him while he was distracted by blocking spells, but the *Piercing Strike*-enhanced blow simply deflected off the shield with no visible damage to it. It then rotated toward his back, where an axe wielded by Medrizz attempted to split him from sternum to crotch, with the Martial's arms glowing with Stama to reflect the enhanced strength in them. The axe head bounced off the shield and nearly smacked his nest-brother in the face, but he managed to prevent splitting his own head in twain.

Any other attacks sent the man's way did absolutely nothing, as they were quickly blocked by the floating shield as if it had a mind of its own. Meanwhile the man just stood there calmly and watched them all, calculating and observing. *Likely trying to figure out the best way to kill us all.*

Seeing that he was obviously toying with them, Gharix couldn't help but think it was only a matter of time before they were all killed. *I should've called for a retreat as soon as I slammed into this invisible barrier, and now they are all going to die because of my arrogance in thinking we could take down such a dangerous threat all by ourselves.*

*If I call it now, will the others be able to escape? I sure hope so.*

He was about to call out for the others to retreat and leave him to distract the shadow-touched man, but he was interrupted by their target speaking again in a measured, controlled voice.

# Chapter 50

Larek blocked yet another powerful *Fireblast* spell from one of the Drekkin using his Pattern shield, wondering how he could get out of this situation without killing these people. He was hesitant to simply eliminate them for a few reasons, one of them being the fact that he was *technically* invading their home and they likely saw him as an unknown threat; with them fighting against the monsters taken over by the Umbral Demons, it made sense that they would be a bit on edge. Another reason not to kill them was because he thought he might need their help to eventually get out of the underground tunnels – once he destroyed all of the Demons he could find, of course. The last reason was because they might be able to point him in the right direction toward the Aperture, as that was likely the best place to find those same demons.

*Oh, and they might have some food I can eat, too.* His supplies weren't depleted entirely yet, but they wouldn't last another few days at the rate he was going through them.

Standing still while he concentrated on moving his Pattern shield, he was pleased to find that his *Pattern Manipulation* Skill increased not just once but *twice* after he used it to block the spells that were aimed at him, along with the Battle Art-infused melee attacks trying to hit him from the sides and back.

**Pattern Manipulation** has reached Level 18!
**Pattern Manipulation** has reached Level 19!

It was only one Level away from its current maximum of 20, though he could vaguely feel that it wouldn't achieve that Level until he did something else with the Skill. Using it simply to block different attacks had gotten him pretty far, but there was a limit to how much it would improve by just doing that.

It also wasn't doing much to prevent the attacks being sent against him, and the Drekkin didn't seem to be letting up anytime soon. If anything, he was expecting to be attacked by something more powerful anytime now, and he had to find a way to stop it before things got out of hand.

As he wracked his mind trying to figure out what to do, he felt around for his *Secure Hideaway* Fusion to ensure it was still active, as he didn't want his Air Skimmer to be damaged by all the spells being flung about. That was the main reason he had let it descend and exited from inside its internal compartment, as being blasted by an explosive fireball would likely light it on fire. Thankfully, the protective Fusion both hid it and protected it with a dome of hardened air, which had also apparently triggered when one of the Drekkin slammed into it at full speed.

*Actually, that might be a way to get through to these people....*

He found it difficult to hold onto his concentration and his Pattern shield when he talked, but after a few seconds it became easier. His speech was a bit deliberately measured and monotone, but he thought that he at least got the point across.

"Please stop attacking me. I think there must be some sort of misunderstanding. I am simply passing through your tunnels. I want to kill all the Umbral Demons I come across, just as I killed the last one. Your friend might die if he is not healed sometime soon." Larek didn't know that last bit for sure, but he had definitely heard the Drekkin hit the protective dome hard enough to break at least a few bones.

Miraculously, his impromptu pleading seemed to have an effect, as the Drekkin paused in their attack. "What did you sssay?" one of the Mages suddenly asked, with a slight hiss to their speech. He thought it was a bit feminine-sounding, but he couldn't tell what gender they were by just looking at them; they all looked like lizards walking around on two legs to him. He was sure there was probably some way to tell, perhaps by their slightly varied coloring, but he was completely ignorant of those details.

Larek maintained his Pattern shield, wary of an abrupt attack from behind, but he answered with a little more feeling. "Uh, I said that your friend back there might die if he isn't healed—"

"No, you filthy ssshadow-touched, not that," the Drekkin said, sounding more feminine as *she* cut him off. "About the Umbral Demonsss. Why would a posssssesssssed one lie about killing that which cannot be killed?"

*Huh? Oh, right, they aren't able to kill the Demons. I guess I should've led with that. Wait... shadow-touched? Possessed one? Ah, they think I'm one of them.*

"I'm not possessed by one of those Demons, if that's what you're implying," he replied, slowly shaking his head so as to maintain his Pattern shield. "It tried, of course, but I fought back and killed it."

"Imposssssible! An Umbral Demon cannot be killed, and you are sssimply trying to buy time for reinforcementsss to arrive." She turned to the Mage next to her, before looking between the melee users behind and to the sides of Larek. "Kill him."

She began to form the pattern for another spell, but a voice coming from further behind the entire group spoke up. "Stop! I would hear more of this!"

Fortunately for the Drekkin, she hadn't even begun filling her pattern with Mana yet, so she was able to cancel her spell before it was cast. After having failed in his negotiation, he was already starting to pull out his offensive Fusions, which would've completely devastated the group that fought him in a matter of seconds.

Upon her halting her spell, there followed a tense exchange between the female Mage and the voice coming from behind him, which sounded as if it came from the Drekkin that had been gravely injured when he slammed into Larek's *Secure Hideaway*. Larek couldn't understand any of it because it was in a language that sounded like a bunch of hissing to him, which he assumed was their native tongue, but he could at least understand that the female Drekkin was not happy with whatever the injured one was saying.

In the end, however, it seemed as though the one who had stopped them was in charge, and the others put their weapons and hands down, reluctant as it seemed.

"I believe that our fearlesssss nest-group leader hit hisss head a little too hard, but I will obey his order," the female said with an annoyed hiss at the end, even as she shook her head. "I, for one, ssstill do not believe your claim to have killed one of the Umbral Demonsss."

Larek reabsorbed the Pattern Cohesion he had infused in his floating shield, knowing that he could bring it back up quickly if it was necessary. Along with his other defenses, such as his *Repelling Barrier*, he didn't think he was in *too* much danger at the moment, though that could change if he was overwhelmed.

"I would like to apologize for approaching your people so suddenly," Larek said, retroactively apologizing for his intrusion. It wasn't really something he could've prevented, because he had no idea where he was or where the Drekkin were in relation to his position, but he figured it might help to smooth over the tension that had developed between them. He'd prefer to have their help rather than be forced to kill them if they continued to be actively hostile.

"What are you doing here? How did you get into the Lost Cavernsss?" the female Mage asked, ignoring his apology.

"I'll try and explain in a moment, but wouldn't you rather that I heal your companion?" the Combat Fusionist asked.

"Don't you touch him! You've been ssshadow-touched and—"

"Pyluxa! Enough!" The leader of the Drekkin admonished the Mage in their other language, or at least that was what Larek thought was happening since he couldn't understand it. "You can heal?"

The sudden switch to something he could understand startled him after listening to them essentially hiss at each other for a minute or so, and he nodded. "Yes, I can." He didn't bother expanding upon that statement, as he didn't feel the need to describe Fusions and what they could and couldn't do at the moment.

"How long does it take? I have a leg and arm to be healed, and I think I cracked something in my skull."

"Not long. You'll be extremely hungry and exhausted after the healing, however."

The rest of the Drekkin watched him like a hawk as he moved around to the fallen leader, before kneeling next to him. He made sure that his pant leg was touching the skin of the lizard person before he activated the *Healing Surge +3* Fusion on it. He felt the healing Effect pass through him as well as the injured Martial Drekkin, and while he felt a drain on his energy, it wasn't nearly as bad as it would be if he had his own wounds that were being repaired. For the badly injured lizard person, however, the natural energy drain would be much worse.

When he screamed after the initial Effect hit him, Larek nearly had a spear shoved through his neck, but the group leader waved the one who was about to attack him off. It wouldn't have done too much to him because he still had his *Repelling Barrier* active, but it probably would've provoked additional attacks. It probably also helped that the damage to the Drekkin's face was being repaired at an astonishing and *visible* rate, much faster than a conventional healing spell would perform.

After approximately 30 seconds, Larek deactivated the *Healing Surge* as the almost entirely healed lizard wearily moved away from Larek and got to his feet. The Combat Fusionist would've kept going as he didn't think he was entirely fixed up yet, but it was apparently enough – and any more would've made him even weaker without rest and food.

"Thank you," he finally said when he was upright, his voice audibly exhausted. "That was... tiring. I feel like I could eat an entire grow field right now, but I can't deny that it worked." Looking around at the tense stance of the other Drekkin, he ordered them to stand down.

"But he's still a threat," the female Mage started, but apparently a tail swish from the leader was all that was needed to silence her from complaining any further.

"Again, thank you for the healing. That being said, we're going to need some answers. Who are you? Why are you here? And perhaps an even better question: *What* are you? I've heard about the Mages and Martials from the Kingdom of Androthe before the blessings were given unto our people, but I've never heard of anyone or anything like *you* before."

It was at that point that Larek realized that the leader spoke quite well in comparison to the female Mage, without any of the hissing that accompanied her normal speech. He took that as a good sign, especially when he mentioned knowing about the Kingdom of Androthe and the SIC there; he figured he might just be able to get the help he needed out of these people if he was able to handle the situation correctly.

"First, I'm Larek and I do indeed come from the Kingdom of Androthe," he replied, beginning his brief explanation of his origins and his reason for traveling over the desert. He didn't go into *how* he got to the Sealance Empire or about the time loss he had experienced, nor did he delve into his origins or mention the Gergasi at all. It seemed that they already knew about the shifting sands of the desert above and appeared skeptical that he had killed one of the giant scorpions by himself, but they didn't interrupt. The other Mage, which Larek assumed was a male from some of the mannerisms and a slightly darker set of scales around his eyes (he might be completely wrong on their gender, but until he had something else to go on, he was male in Larek's mind), appeared highly curious about his glossed-over explanation of the Fusions on his Air Skimmer, but he didn't speak up.

It didn't take him long to get to his exploration of the tunnels underneath the desert and his interest in finding an escape from them. It was only when he started to describe his encounter with the Umbral Demon that the female Mage finally switched from outright hostility to utter incredulity.

"You're a Mage? I find that hard to believe. Why can't I feel the ability in you like I do with other Magesss, then?"

Larek shrugged. "Yes, I'm a Mage, and no, I don't have any idea why you can't feel my ability for magic within me. I can feel it in *you*, as well as you," he replied, pointing toward the other Mage.

"That's not really a ssstretch if you're lying, sssince you sssaw usss casssting ssspellsss." The hissing accent was extremely thick as the female Drekkin got herself worked up. "Ssshow usss a ssspell—"

"Nest-sister, please stop," the leader said wearily, and it was obvious that his exhaustion was getting to him as he swayed slightly on his feet. Larek could only assume that the damage had been much more extensive than what was visible on the surface for him to still be so weary after the 15 minutes or so that Larek had been explaining where he came from.

"But—" A look was all that was needed to stop her complaint, and she hissed in what Larek assumed was an unsatisfied *hmph*.

"We already saw what he can do, as well as his floating contraption, so I don't think there's any need. Now, go on with what happened with the Demon. I'm anxious to hear how you survived intact... if indeed you are."

"Oh, I'm myself, don't worry about that," he assured them. "The internal fight against the Umbral Demon was harrowing, to put it mildly, but it didn't account for my Pattern Cohesion being strong enough to act as my defense."

"What do you mean by that?"

Larek hesitated for a moment, trying to figure out how to explain exactly what had happened. After a few seconds of thought, he finally answered with as good of a description as he could. "I was taught by my Professor at Copperleaf Academy that your Pattern Cohesion is more than just a resource to use while casting spells or creating Fusions – and he was right. It's more aligned with what one would consider the integral part of a person, their spiritual 'soul' if you will, and it can apparently act as a defense against the soul-replacing attacks of the Demons."

They all looked at him as if he had grown another head on his shoulders, disbelief evident even on their abnormal—to him—faces. The leader then turned to the female Mage and asked, "Is what he says about Pattern Cohesion true? Can you use yours to act as a defense against the insidious assaults by the Umbral Demons?"

She immediately shook her head. "Unlikely. There have been many new Magesss that have fallen to the predatory attacksss of the Demonsss."

"It has to be strong enough to make a difference," Larek interjected. "A new Mage would be similar to a toddler being given a small knife and told to defend against a battle-hardened Martial. They might be able to get in a lucky strike or two, but they wouldn't be able to hold on against something that powerful."

"And how strong, exactly, are you saying a Mage should be?" the leader asked. "I know for a fact that Pyluxa – as abrasive as she can be – is within the top 10 Mages among our people, so she should be able to wield her Pattern Cohesion as you say, correct?"

Larek shrugged, not really knowing the answer. "I honestly have no idea. I never had a reason to use my Pattern Cohesion in this way before coming here, so I can't tell you what the threshold would—or should—be. All I know is that I now have a way to completely defend myself against the Demons trying to take over my body, and I'm looking for revenge for what they almost succeeded in doing. Oh, and I guess that closing the Aperture that they've consolidated from all the others in Lowenthal would be beneficial, as their plan is to eventually kill or possess all of you before spreading their influence all over the world."

They were completely silent for a few seconds after that revelation. "How could you possibly know that? Didn't you say you just arrived here?"

Larek had to think about what he said before he responded to the Drekkin group leader. "Ah, yes, I *have* just arrived, but that knowledge came from the Demon trying to take over my body. The connection to my mind went both ways, and I was able to gain some information from it that it probably didn't think it would matter if it was shared, especially if it felt that it was going to take my body over."

"*See*, he's still being influenced by—"

"ENOUGH, Pyluxa!" The weary Martial lizard yelled, stopping the female Mage from continuing her accusation. "I believe him, at least in this. My sense of danger has receded now that I've gotten a chance to speak with him and understand where he came from. However," he said, turning back to Larek, "I would like to know how high your Pattern Cohesion is to have defended against the Umbral Demon. I'm not the best judge of age in those not of my people, but you appear quite young and likely haven't Leveled-up far enough to have excessive stats. I would like to know if this is something our Mages can use to fight against the Demons in the future."

"It's... abnormally high. Let's just say that it's probably a bit excessive, but I can see a Pattern Cohesion of at least 100 being enough to give some semblance of protection," he said cautiously.

"100? How am I supposed to reach that high? My Pneuma stat is only 25, and that is already considered excessively high by our people."

Larek shrugged again. "Again, I don't specifically know how much you need, but it's possible that 25 is enough—"

"*Hshhhhh...*" the group leader of the Drekkin suddenly cut him off, his hiss accompanied by a hand that was held up in warning.

As soon as silence descended upon the group, Larek heard it. Hundreds of feet padding against the floor, coming closer every second. From what he could tell, it was coming from behind him in the tunnel and not toward wherever the Drekkin group was defending, so he could only assume they were monsters.

He was proven correct a few seconds later as a veritable horde of black-furred **Jungle Panthers** raced toward them, their footfalls normally almost silent, but when there were over 200 of the 6-foot-long, 4-foot-tall, powerfully built cats running at the same time, they tended to make some noise. From what little he remembered of them from his classes, they weren't necessarily weak like a Category 1 monster, but they also weren't too much of a threat – at least in small numbers. As there were so many of them, he knew that they could be a problem unless he was able to thin them out.

"We have to retreat," the group leader said immediately. "I'm not in the best shape, and there's no way we can take all of them with just the 6 of us—sorry, 7 of us with Larek. We need to settle up behind some fortifications and—"

"Don't worry, I can handle this," Larek cut him off, before dashing forward and bringing his staff up with his left hand, pointing toward the approaching pack of Panthers. With his right hand, he reached into one of his belt pouches.

"Wait! You can't be serious—"

"Let him die if he wants to, but we should run."

Larek ignored all of that as he activated the *Flaming Balls* Effect on it at Magnitude 2, holding the staff against his side to stabilize it as he strafed the barrage of fiery balls against the left half of the horde. They were so closely packed together that almost every projectile he shot out – at 10 per second – hit one of them, and while they weren't the most powerful at Magnitude 2, they were still strong enough to deal some serious damage to them while knocking them down from the impact. When he saw them continue to move even after being hit by a *Flaming Ball*, he switched up the Effect to *Icy Spike* at Magnitude 2 to keep up the pressure and deal some actual damage. Soon enough, the ones he hit were killed or crippled as they took fast-moving ice projectiles to their bodies and legs, taking many of them out of the fight permanently or at least temporarily.

As for the right side of the horde, he pulled out a handful of *Weaken* stones and threw them as far as he could within the Panther pack, activating the Fusion on them at a distance. The explosions had a much greater effect in multiplicate than he was expecting, and Larek was rocked slightly backwards from the shockwave, but he managed to hold his feet steady and maintained his attack on the left-hand side of the horde. As for the right side, *dozens* of the monsters were killed within the point-blank range of the explosions immediately, but it also flung away many dozens more with such force that many of them hit walls and even the ceiling with bone-shattering impacts. More than a few even slammed into those among the left side of the horde, reducing their numbers even further.

With the right side largely taken care of other than some stragglers, he took the staff in both hands to better aim it and switched to a *Water Stream* at Magnitude 5 for more precise shots since there was now only a quarter of the original horde to contend with. He quickly aimed at anything moving toward him, using the powerful stream of water to easily cut through fur and flesh alike.

As for the Panthers, their greatest asset was their speed, which they used to avoid many of his secondary attacks, many of them dashing out of the way of his *Water Stream*. Unfortunately for them, they couldn't outrun the constant barrage of the focused cutting water as he swept it back and forth, quickly targeting his victims before they could move.

When the remnants of the horde closed in on him, an entire 10 of them making it through unscathed, Larek dropped his staff by his feet and pulled out his axe from his hip. Almost as one, they pounced on him from 15 feet away, likely hoping to overwhelm him with their bulk and deadly slashing claws, but he was ready. With a thought and a slight bit of effort, he created a Pattern shield using his Pattern Cohesion and used it to block one of the first to pounce, and he heard its neck snap as it collided with the immovable shield, falling dead to the floor afterwards. He was able to move his shield quickly to block and kill a second Panther, but he was forced to abandon it afterwards – losing the Pattern Cohesion in the process, as he wasn't able to concentrate on reabsorbing it – as he rolled away out of where the Panthers would've landed on him, dropping yet another Fusion from his belt pouch on the ground. He didn't move quite far enough, and two different monsters hit him hard – or they would have hit him hard, if they hadn't been violently pushed down into the floor by his *Repelling Barrier*. He still took a pair of blows as their weight was great enough that they weren't completely arrested by the Fusion's gusts of air, but it only made him stagger a slight bit.

**Dodge** *has reached Level 22!*

Larek moved quickly away from his location because he could feel that he was still in range of the *Frozen Zone* Fusion he had dropped earlier, slicing out at the nearest Panther that attempted to swipe at him, only to pull back a nub after he took its paw off. A second black-furred monster attempted to hit him from behind, but he frantically created a generic net-shield made out of his Pattern Cohesion, which blunted the swipe enough that the *Repelling Barrier* was able to direct it downwards.

It was at that time that the *Frozen Zone* Fusion activated, catching 5 of the Panthers in its deathly cold embrace, freezing them solid within seconds, but Larek still had a pair of monsters near enough to him to be a threat. Not a great threat, as they had trouble doing much more than battering him around through his *Barrier*, but still strong enough to hurt him if he didn't dispatch them quickly. Fortunately, they weren't as fast as he was, even as lithely as they moved, and he was able to retaliate with his axe to cut through their paws when they attacked, crippling them, and finally their very necks when they attempted to bite him.

Soon enough, it was over, and he watched the bodies of the slain Panthers dissolve while the Corrupted Aetheric Force they gave off was absorbed by his body. This was the main reason he wanted to kill them, as he had a feeling they were worth more than a single AF per monster, and he still needed to increase his maximum Skill Levels.

As he glanced back at the Drekkin to make sure they had survived unscathed, he saw their mouths opened wide in a universal sign of shock. Picking up his staff and putting away his axe on his belt, he rubbed the back of his neck in slight embarrassment, as he didn't particularly like being the center of attention.

Walking back to them, he tried to smile through their shock and asked, "Shall we go?"

They were silent for a moment before the leader finally broke out of it enough to respond. "Yes, uh, let's go." He sounded nervous, though Larek thought that it could've also been his exhaustion catching up with him.

"Want a ride?" he asked, smirking at their startlement as he deactivated his *Secure Hideaway* around his Air Skimmer, revealing it from where it had been hidden. He was fairly certain it could handle their weight, as they didn't appear to weigh too much, though it wouldn't ride as high. Balance would be key, but he was fairly certain that they'd handle it well enough.

"Isss it sssafe?" the female Mage asked skeptically.

Larek paused before saying, "Mostly? Just don't unbalance it, or we'll crash into a wall."

"I'll passsss." The others agreed, even the weary group leader, and Larek simply shrugged. "Alright then, as soon as I'm up, lead the way!" he said, jumping into the vessel before activating the gusts of air that would lift it up. The Drekkin shied away from the blowing air, but they were soon running back down the tunnel they had come from, with Larek following behind at a safe distance.

# Chapter 51

Larek's first sight of the Drekkin city the group led him to was awe-inspiring, as it was much bigger than he expected it to be. Based on what he'd seen of their height, the knowledge that they lived underground, and the fact that they had been essentially besieged by the monsters altered by the Umbral Demons, he had pictured something of a large town with small buildings, and perhaps a few thousand Drekkin spread throughout it.

In reality, as he approached the city after passing through the tunnel that grew increasingly wide and more ornate, with portions of the stone walls carved into intricate designs and even recognizable beasts and other forms of life, he was greeted by a massive cavern that sloped downward from the tunnel that stretched further than he could see in every direction other than the one he came from. With a ceiling that had to be at least 1,000 feet in height, the space felt like an impossibility, especially as there didn't seem to be any type of supporting columns or obvious signs of how it was kept from collapsing in on itself. Not only that, but that ceiling was made almost *entirely* out of the glowing crystal that he'd seen throughout the tunnel he had been traveling down, meaning that the whole city was bathed in a light bright enough to match a late afternoon day up on the surface.

As for the city itself, the buildings he could see seemed constructed of only stone, and the size of them boggled his mind, as a few of them appeared to be taller than even the walls surrounding Copperleaf. That was only the largest of the buildings he saw, of course, but there were a variety of different sizes and formations that demonstrated the sheer creativity of the builders, as each one was unique in some way.

That uniqueness was further enhanced by the fact that not a single building he saw was the same color as another, as while they were made from stone, they were constructed from an almost endless number of stone types, more than he realized even existed. If he wasn't mistaken, there was even one large building that seemed to be constructed of the glowing crystal like what was along the ceiling, though he wasn't sure how that was even possible. More than just different stones and the glowing crystal, many of the structures he saw had been painted over in a riot of different colors that should've clashed and hurt the eye, but somehow worked to be pleasing to the eye even with their marked contrast and varied hues.

The only thing that stood out like a sore thumb was the wall that surrounded the city, which was constructed entirely of the plain, dull stone that the tunnels had been carved through; while it appeared to be of relatively new construction, there was visible damage along a few parts that were in the process of being repaired. At only 30 feet tall around the majority of what he could see, it seemed woefully inadequate against the monsters he'd seen both down underground and up on the surface. He could tell that it was still being built up in areas, as if they were still trying to raise its height even further, but with such a stretch of wall it would take time. He could only assume that they either didn't have a wall at all before the Apertures appeared around Lowenthal, or it was so short that it had been demolished and this new, taller wall was constructed on top of its remains.

"Welcome to Draverdin, Larek," the Drekkin group leader called up to him. He'd learned along the way that his name was Gharix, which he might have heard during their initial meeting, but he hadn't really noted it at the time. "I would advise you to leave that... contraption out here before we enter."

Larek nodded, thinking that was probably for the best, especially since the small gate he saw along the wall barely looked large enough for himself to walk through. He set the Air Skimmer down after moving it along the wall, and then used his *Secure Hideaway* to camouflage its location and prevent anyone from messing with it. With enough force, especially by some of the stronger Mages and Martials, they could break through its defensive hardened air barrier, but he hoped it would stand up to any casual attempts.

It was only when Larek was walking along with the group surrounding him like some sort of guard detail – *either for an important personage... or a prisoner*, he thought – that he realized he hadn't activated his *Perceptive Misdirection* Fusion. He'd deactivated it after leaving the Empire, as it wasn't needed in the empty desert; the draw on ambient Mana, while comparatively small, was enough of a reason not to keep it active, especially when in combat against monsters. Just the thought of so many people looking at him as he entered this extremely foreign city filled with a race of people he had just recently met made him itch to activate it so that he wouldn't stand out as much, but he held off because he was fairly certain it would cause confusion among the group he had met, at the very least. He already had issues with gaining their trust up to this point, and suddenly changing his appearance within their perception would only give credence to their skepticism around his interaction with the Umbral Demon.

He couldn't really blame them, though, especially after learning firsthand how the Demons were able to replace a person's soul and *become* them almost imperceptibly. If any of them, or their stolen bodies, were to get inside the city, they could cause a lot of damage and potentially lead to even more possessions. Glancing up at the ceiling, the constant glowing light that illuminated everything with very little in the way of shadows made a lot more sense now, as he figured it was designed to give the entire area little access for the Demons to invade on their own.

Therefore, even though his skin seemed to itch from all the attention he was getting from the hundreds of Drekkin that watched him travel to the front gate, escorted by Gharix's group, he forced himself to simply be who he was and not hide behind the Fusion on his ring.

"Halt! Who is—? Gharix?"

On top of the wall, a Drekkin that appeared to be in charge of the defense around the small gate leading inside the city, called down for the group to stop as he looked them over. Around the area, more than one person outside the walls was already running away at the sight of Larek, even though he was surrounded by a group of Mages and Martials.

"Darden! Let us in, we have important news and need to see The Sire."

The guard looked closer at them before responding. "But that doesn't explain who *that* is, Gharix. You know the rules better than anyone, and by the look of him—hold! Back away, Gharix! He's been shadow-touched!"

But the group leader didn't move away from him, much to Larek's surprise. To his even greater shock, neither did any of the other members of the group, even the female Mage, Pyluxa. "No, Darden, he's not been shadow-touched; in fact, he's figured out how to—"

"Shadow-touched?"

"I see the aura around him—"

"Kill him before he gets into the city!"

Gharix held his empty hands out in front of him as he suddenly spoke in the Drekkin language in what Larek could only assume was some sort of placating and convincing tone, but it was clearly not working. From what the Combat Fusionist could tell, the guards on the wall were just normal guards and not Mages nor Martials; that changed as they responded in the same language with increasingly hostile-sounding words, and were quickly joined by dozens of Mages and Martials that seemed to sprout up from nowhere behind the wall.

*Uh-oh. This doesn't look good.*

Meanwhile, Gharix seemed to be getting desperate, and while Larek couldn't understand anything he said, the pleading tone was obvious enough to anyone listening. Suddenly, conversation stopped on both sides, and the silence that arose had a pressure to it that the Combat Fusionist didn't like the feeling of.

"Get ready to run. Larek, if you could help protect us with that shield?" Gharix said very softly, and Larek could just barely hear it.

*What's going on?* he thought. He wanted to ask, but he figured that the Drekkin group leader was speaking softly for a reason. Instead, he nodded almost imperceptibly and said, "I can only produce that type of shield if I'm stationary, but I'll do what I can."

His slightly louder speech was apparently all that was needed to set off a confrontation, because as soon as he finished, Gharix shouted, "Run!"

They turned around and took off just as spells were being cast upon the walls, and an arrow flew into Larek's back – only for it to be pushed down by his *Repelling Barrier*. A brief look backward showed that at least a dozen magical projectiles, ranging from weaker *Fireballs* to a massive boulder that was at least the size of one of the Drekkin, flying toward their running forms. Pyluxa and Hakkin were lagging behind, lacking the Agility that the Martials possessed, though Gharix and another of the Martials did their best to place themselves in front of the incoming attacks. Larek could tell that it wasn't going to be enough, so he ran next to the two Mages, created his Pattern shield, and used it to block the initial volley of magical projectiles.

Or at least he tried.

Moving it quickly enough, he was able to intercept most of the projectiles, but a *Fireball* and a small grouping of *Ice Spikes* made it through not only his shield but also Gharix and the other Martial, Abarcen, as they tried to defend their most vulnerable members. Cries of pain rang out as both Hakkin and Pyluxa were hit, Hakkin with a fireball to his back that knocked him down on his face, and the female Mage with an icicle through her left leg, sending her sprawling and unable to get up.

"Move! Run! I've got them," Larek said, even as three more arrows seemed to come out of nowhere to try to impale him while he was distracted. While one of them got through, it wasn't powered by any Stama or Battle Art, and his clothes did what they were supposed to do by stopping it from piercing through the cloth. The two Martials didn't move until he reached down and grabbed the two Mages, letting his Pattern shield dissipate and losing the Pattern Cohesion in the process, and he held them under each of his arms as he ran off with them.

It was just in time, too, as the Martials from the wall had jumped down and were closing in on them, even as another wave of spells was released by the Mages back on the wall. Larek took off running with every point of his Agility, only slowed down slightly from the surprisingly lightweight forms of the Drekkin he was carrying.

He was actually quite a bit faster than the others and quickly outpaced them, heading for where he felt his Air Skimmer was left behind. Larek was also forced to ignore the female Mage pounding at his back and her yelling for him to release her, as he knew that would be a poor idea if he were to let her go at the moment – and at the speed he was moving.

Regardless of her protestations, they made it back to his vessel as he deactivated the *Secure Hideaway* without being hit by anything along the way, and he deposited the two Drekkin Mages inside before scrambling aboard himself. He began the activation for liftoff and held it to just barely above the ground so that when Gharix and the others made it to him, they would be able to jump inside.

One of the Drekkin, who he thought was named Medrizz, tripped when he was clipped by another boulder, and was nearly set upon by the following Martials before Gharix managed to pick him up and drag him along with him. Larek guided the Air Skimmer forward, getting closer to the other members of the group, using his Pattern to extend a shield approximately 50 feet ahead of the vessel to help block the pursuing Drekkin. He felt the strain on his mind and body at projecting it such a distance, but he ignored it as he stood still in the middle of the Skimmer and used the shield to not only to knock away projectiles but also to shove back the Martials when they got too close.

Within a few seconds of this, he had to release the shield as the strain grew too great, and he sagged in exhaustion as the remaining members of the group reached them and clambered aboard, rocking the Skimmer so that it dragged along the ground for a moment before stabilizing. Without another moment to spare, he turned them around and shot out of the tunnel, activating *Secure Hideaway* at the same time. He normally wouldn't do that, as it consumed quite a bit of the ambient Mana in the area, which wasn't a very good idea even if he was traveling, because it would reduce the amount of Mana available for a fight if he was forced to stop, but at the moment he had no intention of stopping.

Just as they were passing the entrance of the massive cavern on their way out, a group of approximately 300 **Walking Skeletons** with dark-grey bones were apparently invading, but Larek didn't stop because he couldn't. The dome of hardened air around them seemed to shiver and shake as he barreled through the ranks of the weak undead monsters, scattering their bones as they were killed by the impact with the racing Skimmer, though "racing" was a bit of a stretch. They weren't going any faster than the vessel's normal top speed that it was capable of without destabilizing, but it was still fast enough to have an impact on the Skeletons.

As they left the disorganized horde of Skeletons behind, which were quickly set upon by the pursuing Martials, Larek was disappointed to find that he didn't receive any Aetheric Force from their deaths; a brief idea of simply running over any monsters in his path for easy advancement was quickly dashed.

Once they were far enough away from the city about 10 minutes later, he stopped the Skimmer and looked at the others inside, who were currently sitting around the perimeter of the inside compartment of the vessel, looking completely despondent and uncommunicative, their eyes cast down at their feet. As for the two Mages, they were doing their best to fight through the pain and used what appeared to be *Minor Mending* on themselves to alleviate the burn and the impaled leg, though it was slow-going. With such a weak healing spell, it would take a while for their wounds to be fully repaired – if they had the Mana to sustain the healing spell for that long, of course.

"Here, let me help," he said, quickly using his *Healing Surge* Fusion on the two Mages, healing them back to normal within seconds. It wasn't enough to knock them out, fortunately, but they were undoubtedly hungry after the healing. They didn't complain, however, but joined the others in looking down at their feet in obvious despondency.

Larek didn't say anything because he couldn't think of anything that might help. Their own people had apparently tried to kill them, and he didn't even know why.

"Thisss isss all *your* fault," Pyluxa hissed suddenly, raising her head to stare murderously at Larek. "If it wasssn't for you, all of thisss wouldn't have happened..." Her stare made him back up temporarily at the fire within it, but it quickly faded back into a blank expression. "But you also sssaved all of our livesss, ssso now I'm conflicted. While we wouldn't have been in that posssition if it wasssn't for your pressence, it wasss alssso our desssisssion to defend you."

385

Larek looked back at her and said, "I'm sorry they did that to you, but I also have no idea what just happened. I couldn't understand any of that after a while, so I'd appreciate an explanation."

They were silent for a moment as Pyluxa's once-defiant stare disappeared and she dropped her eyes to her feet, especially her healed foot, like the others. It was Gharix that finally answered after about 30 seconds of silence.

"They thought we had been possessed by the Umbral Demons as well, or at least that we were tainted by proximity to you." He sighed heavily before continuing. "We've been put on the kill-on-sight list as a result, as they don't want to take the chance of anyone under such a possession or shadow-touched in any way coming and making their way into the city.

"In effect, we can never go back to our people without being executed on sight. *That's* what happened."

Larek knew that a simple apology wouldn't cut it for something as serious as essentially being exiled from your own people, so he said nothing at first.

"Is there… any way they will let you come back?" he finally asked, feeling somewhat responsible for the situation. Granted, he had very little idea that such a thing could've happened at all, but he couldn't deny that he was the source of the contention. As much as he didn't want to get involved in their confrontation, given that he had another goal entirely, if it was something he might be capable of doing, he would like to try and rectify this horrible mistake.

Gharix chuckled, sounding almost hysterical. "Sure, sure. All we need to do is find some way to eliminate every single Umbral Demon, kill all the shadow-touched monsters threatening our people, and close this Aperture that no one still living has ever actually seen in person before, even if we know where it is."

*Huh. Seems simple enough – and it's what I wanted to do, anyway.*

"Well then, let's go do that, shall we?"

# Chapter 52

Attacking and killing everything in their way toward closing the Aperture was easier said than done. The first obstacle was convincing the Drekkin to go along with it, as they immediately dismissed his plan as foolish. In a way, they were correct; as they all were right now, they would likely be killed before they even got close.

"Fine. Is there somewhere we can go that is relatively safe and out of the way?" Larek asked, knowing that he – along with everyone else – needed some rest after the day they'd had. He had essentially been going at full-speed since the attack by the giant scorpion, and he needed some time to relax and finally spend his accumulated AP and AF since he kept being interrupted. That, and he had a plan to convince Gharix and the others to help him complete his objective.

The Drekkin looked at each other, silently communicating amongst themselves. After about a half a minute, Gharix sighed and said, "Perhaps. It was added to the roster of the Lost Caverns a week ago, but it's not well known and was supposed to be our fallback point if we ever got separated on a patrol." He hesitated for a moment before he added. "It's dangerous and is likely behind enemy lines by this point."

"Shouldn't be a problem," Larek assured him. "Tell me where it's located, and we'll get there as soon as possible."

Gharix got up from where he had been sitting in the Air Skimmer, and as Larek lifted back up, the Drekkin group leader started telling him where to go. He quickly learned that they had passed multiple side passages that he hadn't even noticed on their way to the Drekkin city, and he was instructed to take one of them that led what he *thought* was north, though it was still difficult to tell where he was underground. Regardless, the side passage was a lot narrower than the main tunnel, as well as less well-lit with glowing crystal along the walls scattered in a random pattern. Fortunately, he had Gharix to help light the way with the aid of his *Directional Illumination* stone piece he had stored in the vessel, which shocked all of the Drekkin to witness it working.

"How does it do this? We usually have to rely on chunks of Luxite to illuminate the darkness."

"Luxite? Is that the glowing crystal stuff all over?"

The group leader chuckled. "Glowing crystal stuff? I guess that's a good description, but yes. Now, about this… whatever it is?"

"Ah, it's a Fusion, like I described briefly before. I'll explain more once we get to wherever you're leading us."

Thankfully, neither Gharix nor any of the others pushed him for more information at that time, as most of them appeared to be on edge. The reason for that was evident shortly into their journey down the side passage, as they suddenly came upon a small group of monsters that flew toward them in a rush. "We have to land! We can't fight them like this!" the Drekkin group leader whispered as soon as the monsters were sighted, but Larek simply brought his staff tip forward and began aiming.

"They look like **Soiled Crowhogs**, and if that's the case, they shouldn't be a problem. I told you, I've got this," he answered as he began firing Magnitude 3 *Icy Spikes* out at the flapping figures.

Thankfully, Soiled Crowhogs were relatively slow, as their portly hog bodies weighed more than the average flying creature. They made up for this fact by having a 10-foot-wide wingspan, which they could retract into their bodies so that they could divebomb their victims on the ground. They were also dangerous if you got too close to them because they exuded a poisonous gas that would quickly restrict the breathing of anyone or anything that inhaled it. It was also flammable, though not as much as what came from the Flojiggers, but they were already close enough that any explosions would likely cause damage to the Air Skimmer and might even be dangerous to the narrow side passage. The last thing he wanted was to cause an accidental cave-in.

His aim had gotten much better from all the experience he'd had using his staff inside his vessel, and the Crowhogs stood no chance against the icy projectiles that they were unable to avoid. Sharp icicles traveling at high speed impaled many of them through their faces, not just once but multiple times, which was more than enough to bring them down. They fell to the floor of the side passage with loud *thumps*, killing most of them upon impact if they weren't already dead from his attacks. A few of them had their wings clipped when they attempted to dodge his projectiles, which still caused them to crash to the ground, and they were subsequently out of the fight.

Fortunately, there were only about 20 of them that attacked, which wasn't much of a threat, but he made sure to finish off the ones that crash-landed but didn't die, before moving on. He could feel the tension and... awe, perhaps, coming from the group of Drekkin as he quickly and easily dispatched the Crowhogs without any worry, but he ignored it.

"Where to? Keep going this way?" he asked, even as he finished absorbing the rest of the Aetheric Force that came from the Crowhogs.

"Uh, yes, this way," Gharix confirmed, pointing ahead.

They encountered a few other small groups of monsters, none of them any particular threat as they were quickly destroyed thanks to his staff, before they finally arrived at their destination. At first, he didn't even see it, but when he moved his Air Skimmer closer to the wall and off to the side where Gharix pointed, he could finally see a much smaller opening that blended in well enough that he probably would've passed by it countless times before he noticed it. It was just barely large enough to fit the Skimmer inside, thankfully, though he had to have the others get out so he could bring it down to just above the floor so he could gently guide it through.

Once they had passed through the opening and turned a corner that the vessel barely fit through, it opened up into an enclosed cave that was approximately 100 feet long and half that wide, with 20-foot ceilings. There was much more Luxite inside along the walls, illuminating the entire cave well enough that there were very few areas of darkness that would allow the Umbral Demons to hide, and those few areas were hardly larger than the palm of Larek's hand.

The light also allowed him to see the very sparse furniture made out of stone, including a small table with only two chairs seemingly carved out of the same material, as well as a small stockpile of what appeared to be thin stone crates, a few of which had been smashed at some point and some sort of leafy matter had spilled out all over the floor.

"Looks like something came in here and smashed a few things before deciding that it was empty, but there should still be at least a week's worth of food stored here," Gharix informed him. Larek thought that was a good thing, given that he barely had enough for himself for the next week; if he had to feed the others, then they would run out quite quickly.

"Settle down, then, and I'll set up my Fusion to block off the passageway. I'll know if anything tries to come through." The fact that none of the Drekkin protested gave evidence to how exhausted they all were, more so than Larek was if he was any judge. Despite that, they still made sure to check every inch of the room for any evidence that any threats still lingered, before they, one-by-one, settled down on the hard stone floor and passed out almost immediately, trusting Larek to keep watch.

It wasn't long until Larek joined them in their slumber, positioning himself closest to the *Secure Hideaway*, confident in his Fusion to keep them safe.

Unfortunately for them all, his dome of hardened air did absolutely nothing to prevent the Umbral Demons from somehow accessing their hidden refuge.

Larek suddenly woke up when the sound of a loud crack aroused him from his slumber, only to find the cavern they were in was almost entirely dark. At some point while they were all asleep, the glowing Luxite in the walls had dimmed until they no longer shone with light, and it was the final – and largest – crystal that had abruptly cracked with a loud report, and it was already dimming as if all the energy that caused it to glow was leaking away. As he shot to his feet, his staff in hand, he felt an overwhelming sense of pressure pushing at his entire body. Out of the corner of his eyes, he saw tall, shadowy shapes that were just barely visible along the perimeter of the cavern – and he knew exactly what they were as his rage spiked at their appearance.

He wasn't the only one who had seen them, as he heard Gharix shout, "Umbral Demons! Run out to the light!" In the rapidly dimming glow of the cracked Luxite, he saw that all the Drekkin had woken along with him and were on their feet, weapons at the ready. Unfortunately for them, it was now dark enough that the lingering light apparently didn't bother the Demons, and Larek watched helplessly as they almost seemed to fly across the space between them and their victims, slamming into the Drekkin and then disappearing *inside* their bodies. He knew exactly what was happening to them then as they fought against the invasive Demons attempting to remove all control they had over their bodies; they were just starting to grunt and strain against the force that was cutting off their physical bodies from their control, not giving in easily, when Larek felt something collide with his own back, staggering him for a moment.

*Oh, no you don't.*

Closing his eyes, he pictured the Pattern Cohesion suffusing his body and accessed his newest Skill, *Pattern Manipulation*. While he remembered what had happened during the first attack by a Demon and how his Cohesion had managed to kill the invader, he hadn't had a chance to practice trying to do that manually – and he didn't want to have to wait for the loss of control over his body for it to work automatically. Thankfully, now that he'd had some practice manipulating his Pattern outside of spells and Fusions, controlling it inside his body was almost simple in comparison to creating a Pattern shield, for instance.

Gathering up a significant chunk of his Cohesion from his body, he mentally gave it a form to perform a specific function; in this case, he created a ghostly, insubstantial axe that looked remarkably like his best friend at his hip. As for its function, it was now a weapon created from the pure strength of what one would say was his soul, and it was designed to kill one thing in particular: Umbral Demons.

With a slight grunt of discomfort as he felt more of his physical control leaving him, he mentally took hold of the shining, ghostly axe of his Pattern... and imagined it slicing his entire body in half, from the top of his head to his groin.

Larek staggered as an inaudible scream ripped through his body and the control over his body suddenly surged back, and he immediately knew that he had essentially ended up cutting entirely through the Demon inside of him. Not only that, but where his ghostly Pattern axe had touched the invader, its potency had acted like an open flame to a piece of paper, as the Demon was rapidly consumed as its touch spread through the rest of its form. In seconds, it had burned up completely, and he quickly *knew* that it had been entirely wiped out.

As he regained complete control and opened his eyes, he witnessed the last of the glow leaving the cracked Luxite, plunging them all into complete darkness. Just before all visible light was lost, however, he saw the shadowy figures around the perimeter of the wall stop moving as they likely became aware of what Larek had done. Rather than flee in the face of someone that could kill them, he was assaulted by an intense sensation of malice and retribution – and he caught a glimpse of at least a half-dozen of the Demons rushing toward him just as the darkness became complete – though he was confident there were many more than that.

"Ha! Bring it on!" he shouted, while at the same time forming the same sort of ghostly axe outside of his body like he would a Pattern shield, though it wasn't nearly as well-made as his best friend at his hip. It appeared in front of him, floating in the air, and while it had an internal glow to it, the oppressive darkness around it didn't allow it to illuminate more than a few inches around it. Without hesitation, he stood still as he directed it to cut through the Demons he had seen heading for him, and was satisfied to see three of them cut in half by his swipe as the glow from the Pattern weapon passed through them. They continued to disintegrate as the strength of his Pattern ate away at their shadowy bodies in a flash, and he started aiming for his next victims.

***Pattern Manipulation** has reached Level 20!*

Two things happened at once, and the combination of them made him lose his concentration for a moment, causing his Pattern axe to disappear. The first was the notification that he had increased his *Pattern Manipulation* Level, which wasn't enough to break his concentration, though in his eagerness to improve, he foolishly decided to pump 2,450 of his available AF into the Skill to raise its maximum to 30 – right in the middle of the fight. The sudden use of his AF was distracting, to be sure, especially with how it felt to be used all at once, but that still wasn't enough to break his focus.

It was when he was slammed into from behind by not just one Demon, but at least a dozen of them that caused him to fall flat on his face, the sudden loss of physical control causing his axe to disappear. Almost immediately, as soon as his physical sensations were cut off from him, he felt the assault on his mind, but Larek was already recovering from the abrupt attack and was marshaling his own response. He discovered that forming an internal Pattern axe was still *much* easier than one outside of his body, and he didn't hesitate to immediately chop and slash his way through his own body, destroying large portions of the Demons with every slice. The internal screaming nearly rendered him unconscious with its intensity, but he pushed through and eliminated every trace of the ones that had initially slammed into him, along with at least another dozen that had piled on the rest after he was taken down.

***Pattern Manipulation** has reached Level 21!*
***Pattern Manipulation** has reached Level 22!*

When the last Demon was destroyed, he regained control over his body in an instant, and he groaned from the abuse it had taken from being assaulted by two dozen Umbral Demons. Getting to his knees, he found himself breathing hard like he had just run at full speed for half a day, but what he was more worried about was whether any lingering trace of the invaders was inside of his body. He closed his eyes while he recovered on his hands and knees, finding no trace of a Demon left behind. Just to make sure, he passed his internal Pattern axe through every inch of his body again, and he thankfully didn't find anything at all.

*I did it. I killed them all—wait.*

Looking up as he opened his eyes, he realized that it was still completely dark inside the hidden cavern, and he could no longer hear anything. *The Drekkin!* Pushing through his exhaustion from the fight, which had taken a toll on his body, he got to his feet while he rummaged around in his belt pouches. Finding what he was looking for, he activated the stone rod that held his *Directional Illumination* on it and pointed it toward where he thought the Drekkin were located.

As soon as the light touched them, their still bodies writhed as if the Umbral Demons inside were made uncomfortable by it, but it didn't stop them from continuing their takeover of their victims.

When he created another Pattern axe and used its insubstantial form to chop through the Drekkin's bodies, however, that stopped them quickly enough.

It was another minute or so before the first of the Drekkin started to stir, but the others quickly followed within seconds of each other. "Y-You… you really killed them?"

Larek shrugged at Pyluxa's question. "I told you that I could, didn't I?"

"Yesss… but I ssstill had my doubtsss," she admitted, before taking a deep breath. "You sssaved my life. All of our livesss."

The Combat Fusionist simply shrugged again. "I couldn't let you all get possessed by Demons, now could I? We have a job to do, after all."

Instead of protesting like they had earlier, the group just stared at him with a look in their eyes that he thought looked remarkably like hope. "You really mean to do it? To kill all the Umbral Demons and close the Aperture?" Gharix asked softly.

"Yes, I do."

"Then… I guess we're with you." The others nodded, clearly agreeing with him.

**Leadership** *has reached Level 12!*

"Well then, I guess I better get working."

# Chapter 53

After Larek disbursed his very few available stones with *Illumination* Fusions on them to light the cavern, the Combat Fusionist used *Focused Division* to create another 25 of the Basic Fusions with some chunks of stone he carved from the wall. Despite the fact that he had killed the Umbral Demons that had attempted to take over their bodies, none of them wanted there to be any hint of darkness in the room; he couldn't really blame them for wanting more light, which his additional Fusions helped to accomplish.

"What exactly was that?" Hakkin asked after watching Larek create the Fusions.

"Like I've said before, these are Fusions," he explained as he handed them out to the Drekkin, instructing them in their use as they placed them all over the cavern. "They are like permanent spells on an object, though that is a bit simplistic."

"Can you teach me how to do that?" the Mage asked excitedly, only to be shot down a moment later when Larek answered.

"Yes, but I don't really have time to show how it's done," he said. "You can certainly watch while I work, and I'll try to answer any questions you have, but the ones I'll be making will be... a bit more *advanced* than you'll probably be able to understand." He felt slightly bad at not being able to teach the obviously eager Drekkin, but he wasn't there to teach them anything. He was there to gain a measure of revenge against the Demons for trying to possess his body, stop them from expanding out of the desert by closing their Aperture, and then escape the underground tunnels to get back to the Kingdom. As confident he was in his ability to protect himself from most weaker monsters, he was more than aware that he wouldn't be able to do all that on his own, especially finding a way out of the underground tunnels. He was still so turned around that even if he was able to find his way to the surface, he had no idea where he might end up.

"Fair enough. We will observe," Hakkin said, indicating himself and Pyluxa, who also seemed interested.

He nodded, before looking closer at the 6 Drekkin in the cavern. Three of the four Martials wore a heavy leather jerkin with bars of what appeared to be steel crossing it like a ribcage, as well as a pair of bracers that protected their forearms. With only the addition of a steel loop with two spikes attached near the tip of their tails, they weren't wearing anything else – which made him realize that they weren't wearing pants. Their scales appeared quite firm and durable, however, which was probably why they didn't have as much armor over the rest of their bodies, only their vitals.

As for the last Martial, Gharix, he also wore a leather jerkin without the steel bars on it, and while his scales seemed durable, they didn't appear as firm as the others. That went the same for the Mages, as they were wearing a simple leather jerkin as well, though they seemed to be more for an assortment of pouches than anything else. Neither of them had the ring and spikes on their tail similar to Gharix, but they *did* have weapons – a small shortsword that was easy enough for them to handle if they were unable to cast a spell in time, even if it wasn't with the skill and strength of a Martial.

It wasn't a lot to work with, but it would be enough.

Ever since Larek had appeared in the Sealance Empire, he had shied away from creating Fusions for anyone else, with the exception being the ferry boats – but that had ultimately been for the express purposes of getting him across the Swiftwater river and earning some spending money for supplies. Otherwise, he hadn't wanted to be bogged down by people wanting more and more from him due to their greed, which was similar to what happened back in the Kingdom with the SIC in Whittleton. He was slowly learning that his kindness and wanting to please everyone had been inadvertently getting him into trouble, and he had to put a stop to it. Of course, that didn't mean he was immune to the needs of other people, and he had no intention of deliberately turning a blind eye to things that he could realistically do something about, especially when he was at least partly at fault.

But he also wasn't intentionally planning on being the savior of everyone in the world by tackling the world's problems. That sounded a little contrary to his current goals, considering that he was going to try and close the massive Aperture nearby, but it was ultimately self-serving because he wanted revenge, more Aetheric Force, and a way out of the underground environment below the desert. That also meant that by using his knowledge of Fusions to make the group of Drekkin more powerful by outfitting them with powerful additions to their repertoire, he was ultimately helping *himself* achieve the ultimate goal of getting out of Lowenthal.

Besides, doing what he had planned would likely improve his Skills a bit, so really there was no downside here. Thinking about that, Larek opened his Status and looked to see what he could allocate and where to put it – the very thing he had been trying to do before the Drekkin had originally shown up and attacked him.

**Larek Holsten**

Combat Fusionist
Healer
Patternal
Level 30
Advancement Points (AP): 8/23
Available AP to Distribute: 22
Available Aetheric Force (AF): 18,129

Stama: 2000/2000
Mana: 3300/3300

Strength: 100 [200] (+)
Body: 100 [200] (+)
Agility: 100 [200] (+)
Intellect: 165 [330] (+)
Acuity: 114 [228] (+)
Pneuma: 1,800 [3,600]
Pattern Cohesion: 36,000/36,000

Mage Skills:
Pattern Manipulation Level 22/30 (300 AF)
Pattern Recognition Level 35/38 (380 AF)
Magical Detection Level 35/38 (380 AF)
Spellcasting Focus Level 35/38 (380 AF)
Multi-effect Fusion Focus Level 40/40 (400 AF)
Focused Division Level 45/45 (450 AF)
Mana Control Level 50/50 (500 AF)
Fusion Level 50/50 (500 AF)
Pattern Formation Level 50/50 (500 AF)

Martial Skills:
Stama Subjugation Level 1/20 (200 AF)
Blunt Weapon Expertise Level 1/20 (200 AF)
Bladed Weapon Expertise Level 2/20 (200 AF)
Unarmed Fighting Level 3/20 (200 AF)
Throwing Level 13/20 (200 AF)
Dodge Level 22/30 (300 AF)
Pain Immunity Level 20/20 (N/A)
Body Regeneration Level 35/40 (400 AF)

First to handle was the 22 Advancement Points he had available to distribute to his stats. As he was still getting comfortable with his relatively new Strength, Body, and Agility stats, Larek focused on his Mage stats for this round of improvements. Distributing half of it into Intellect and half into Acuity, he brought them up to 176 and 125, respectively. It had been a while since he'd increased his Acuity, and he wanted to see if it made any difference, especially since it seemed as though the relative Mana density in the area was much higher than in the Sealance Empire. He'd noticed a slight change already up above in the desert, but the closer they came to where he thought the Aperture might be located, the higher the density seemed to be. It wasn't a *huge* improvement, but if he had to put it on a scale of 1 to 10, with his original experience in the Sealance Empire before the Apertures arrived at 1 and the Kingdom of Androthe at 10, then the underground tunnels were currently at around a 4.

Whatever it might do as far as his regeneration went, his mind immediately felt clearer after all the Advancement Points were allocated, and he could vaguely tell that his speed of thought and ability to manage multiple focuses simultaneously had marginally improved. He resolved to look into increasing Acuity more in the future to see if that helped that even more, as he could always use the additional help.

As for his Aetheric Force, even after stupidly spending over 2,000 of it during the fight with the Umbral Demons which distracted him at a crucial time, he still had a total of 18,129 AF to spend on increasing the maximum Levels of his Skills. It took him a few minutes of deliberation, but he eventually decided to continue increasing his lesser-used Mage Skills to bring them more in line with his others, but since he was going to be making a lot of Fusions, he also increased the ones that were the most important for them. In the end, *every* Mage Skill got an upgrade to its maximum Level after spending 18,010 AF, which meant he had some ample opportunity for advancement.

**Mage Skills:**
**Pattern Manipulation Level 22/40 (400 AF)**
**Pattern Recognition Level 35/40 (400 AF)**
**Magical Detection Level 35/40 (400 AF)**
**Spellcasting Focus Level 35/40 (400 AF)**
**Multi-effect Fusion Focus Level 40/45 (450 AF)**
**Focused Division Level 45/50 (500 AF)**
**Mana Control Level 50/55 (550 AF)**
**Fusion Level 50/55 (550 AF)**
**Pattern Formation Level 50/55 (550 AF)**

With that all taken care of, he finally got down to business. "Can I see everyone's weapons? I want to add some Fusions to them to make them more powerful."

"Do you mean like your strange axe that can cut through stone?" Gharix asked.

"Yes, but also a little bit more than that. There are some things I want to try that will make you a bit more effective in combat, I believe."

There was a slight hesitation from the Drekkin as they understandably didn't want to give up their only weapons, but they finally gave in and placed their bladed implements in front of where Larek had sat down on the floor. In total, there were two knives from Gharix; a longsword (for a Drekkin, at least), a spear, and a battleaxe for the other Martials; and a pair of shortswords from the Mages.

The shortswords he did first because they were something for which he already had a Fusion. As Mages, they specialized in attacking from a distance with projectile spells, so the same one that he had on his own staff was perfect for them. There were a couple of things he changed about the Fusion while he was setting them up, however. The first, and most important in his opinion, was to ensure that the mental phrase activation only applied to the person in physical contact with the swords. The last thing he needed was the Fusion to detect the mental activation phrases from multiple people nearby, so this limited it to only the person holding the weapon. Fortunately, he had already set up his own staff with mental phrases that were keyed to himself, so this wouldn't be a problem with his own projectile weapon.

He also altered the timing slightly during the construction of the Fusion, so that the *Variable Repeating Elemental Projectile* Fusion didn't fire them quite as quickly, and he extended the time in between the more powerful projectiles. He didn't do that to make the Drekkin weaker, but to ensure that they didn't deplete the ambient Mana around them too quickly. There might be a higher Mana density in the area than what he'd been working with over the last few months, but if both of them and Larek activated the exact same Fusions simultaneously, that density would be depleted all the sooner. Still, it wasn't as if he had handicapped them by making the Fusions unusable, as he didn't think that 15 *Flaming Balls* per second at Magnitude 1 rather than 20 per second was that large of a difference.

He did them both at the same time using his *Focused Division*, to the astonishment of the two Mages. While the Martials could feel some of what he was doing, they couldn't exactly observe him funneling thousands of Mana into the Fusions he was creating, nor could they observe the entire process from start to finish.

**Focused Division** has reached Level 46!

**Multi-effect Fusion Focus** has reached Level 41!

"What—? How—? That was... *scary*." Hakkin had watched him closely at first, but had sat back after he saw Larek controlling so much Mana all at once.

That was a new one for the Combat Fusionist, as he usually got reactions that ranged from disbelief to astonishment. *Actually, now that I think about it, there* **were** *a few that reacted with horror that I would shatter the formation by pushing so much Mana into the Fusion all at once. I guess it is a little scary to those who don't know what I can do, isn't it?*

"It definitely can be," Larek agreed. "If you're not careful, you can overload a Fusion and it'll crack, potentially exploding and killing the Fusionist," he added absently, picking up one of the shortswords and inspecting it to try and see where the area of ambience was reaching without activating the new Fusion. After about 30 seconds of his focus on it, he finally saw a faint sphere around the Fusion's location which he thought indicated the largest area of ambience it would produce. With a satisfied smile, he was further pleased when he got a notification.

**Magical Detection** has reached Level 36!

According to the faint outline of the area of ambience he saw, there was still room on the hilts of the two shortswords for another Fusion. As much as he thought he could be fancy with it, there was only one thing that they needed, which was a simple *Strengthen* Fusion to ensure that they didn't break. He debated making them sharper, but decided against it, because if these Mages were anything like the ones he knew back home, they weren't exactly adept at using weapons like this, and the risk of them hurting themselves more than what the monsters could do to them was a distinct possibility.

Thankfully, he didn't have to wait long to put a pair of *Strengthen +10* Fusions on the swords, and he was only partly disappointed that he didn't receive another Skill Level increase. He supposed that such a Basic Fusion didn't really push him all that much, so the lack of increase made sense.

"I'll explain what I did for you later, once I finish these others, but they are done for now," he explained to the pair of Mages, who cautiously took the weapons back as if they might explode, and he worried for a moment that he had scared them a little too much with his talk of the Fusions potentially exploding. *Wait until they learn what my **Weaken** stones are.* Fortunately, after taking the weapons and seeing that they didn't seem on the verge of killing everyone in the cavern, they put them back in the sheathes attached to the belt at their waists without any further trepidation.

Next up were the melee weapons of the Martials, and he thought about what he'd added to some of them in the past. For his companions back in the Kingdom, *Strengthen and Sharpen Edge* was the common choice to make them deadlier, but he'd also added custom Fusions for each person, varying from a ranged projectile to being able to paralyze someone at a touch. While those would be useful to the Drekkin, he wanted something a little different for this set of weapons, as he considered all that he had learned over his time in the Empire and his unlocking of Advanced Fusions.

Having a ranged attack would certainly be useful but was unnecessary, as the two Mages would – along with Larek – have that covered. In addition, while *Paralytic Touch* was certainly useful, there were limitations on what the Fusion could affect and it didn't actually *kill* a monster, though it certainly helped. It was also limited in effective range, and all he had to do was think about one of the Drekkin going up against something like a giant scorpion to realize that paralyzing only a claw wouldn't do much when the other one claw cut them in half. Or, at least, *Paralytic Touch* wasn't as useful by *itself.*

Therefore, they needed a different way to enhance what they were already doing, beyond simply having a sharper edge to their weapons – which wasn't insignificant in and of itself, of course. After perusing his list of available Fusions and thinking about the advancements he'd made in his Fusion creation over the last few months, he finally settled on a combination of Effects that he thought they'd appreciate.

Cobbling together the formation as he picked portions of different Fusions and stuck them together, he evaluated his creation as it floated in front of him, looking for any flaws. It wasn't an overly complicated formation, but he also didn't want it to inadvertently backfire and kill the user. When he had finished looking at it for a few minutes, he saw a few lines here and there that needed some tweaking before he was satisfied, before he reabsorbed the Pattern Cohesion he had sent into the formation, ready to try it for real this time.

Carefully thickening it to the point where he could divide it into 5 separate Fusions using his *Focused Division* Skill, which he thought was pushing the boundary on how many of this particular Advanced Fusion he could create simultaneously, he started funneling Mana into the formation.  After only 45 minutes of adding Mana, as his Mana regeneration had improved substantially in the denser environment, he felt the strain as he divided up the Fusions and placed them delicately upon the different weapons.  As almost all of them were different in size and shape, it took him longer to get them individually placed than he expected, and he nearly lost control of them; fortunately, he was able to hold onto his focus long enough for him to hear the *\*click\** of their correct placement.

After they were in place, he smiled as he sagged from the loss of Pattern Cohesion, even as he was hit with a few notifications.

*New Fusion Learned!*
**Variable Elemental Gust Sphere +7**
*Activation Method(s): Activatable*
*Effect(s): Creates a contained sphere of rapidly moving gusts of air in an independent sphere shape a certain variable distance away from Fusion location*
*Effect(s): Forms icy chunks that are moved around by the rapidly moving gusts of air*
*Effect(s): Forms flaming balls that are moved around by the rapidly moving gusts of air*
*Effect(s): Forms sharp stones that are moved around by the rapidly moving gusts of air*
*Effect(s): Forms orbs of light that are moved around by the rapidly moving gusts of air*
*Effect(s): Using non-invasive mental manipulation, activates or deactivates Activatable Activation Method upon detection of mental phrasing by individual in direct contact with object*
*Variable(s): Mental phrasing of "Ice 1", "Ice 2", "Ice 3", "Ice 4", "Ice 5", "Ice 6", "Ice 7", "Fire 1", "Fire 2", "Fire 3", "Fire 4", "Fire 5", "Fire 6", "Fire 7", "Stone 1", "Stone 2", "Stone 3", "Stone 4", "Stone 5", "Stone 6", "Stone 7", "Light 1", "Light 2", "Light 3", "Light 4", "Light 5", "Light 6", "Light 7"*
*Input(s): Directional orientation, mental phrasing, physical touch*
*Interval(s): 1 second, 2 seconds, 3 seconds, 4 seconds, 5 seconds, 6 seconds, 7 seconds*
*Magnitude(s): 100% to 700% of base elemental strength, 5 to 35 inches in sphere diameter, 1 to 7 seconds of duration*

*Mana Cost: 660,000*
*Pattern Cohesion: 2,400*
*Fusion Time: 396 hours*

**Fusion** *has reached Level 51!*

**Pattern Formation** *has reached Level 51!*

**Mana Control** *has reached Level 51!*

**Focused Division** *has reached Level 47!*

**Multi-effect Fusion Focus** *has reached Level 42!*

Using the idea behind his *Stone Shredder Dome* that he had developed to help defend himself from attacks coming from above, Larek had the notion of weaponizing that idea for the Drekkin's melee weapons. Going even further with the ability to change Magnitudes using mental commands like he did with his staff and the *VREP* Fusion, he constructed the new *Variable Elemental Gust Sphere +7* Fusion with the idea that they would be able to customize the strength and type of elemental effect they wanted for each use.

And if it worked like he hoped it would, almost all of the different Effects would be quite effective.

After he rested for a moment and then added a *Strengthen and Sharpen Edge +6* Fusion to each of the weapons, he looked up at the expectant faces of the Martial members of the Drekkin group and smiled at them. Whatever they saw in his face made a few of them shrink backward slightly, but that quickly passed as he gestured to their weapons. "All done. Be careful – they are *extremely* sharp."

"What... what did you do?" Gharix asked as he only hesitated a few seconds before picking up his knives, inspecting them closely as if looking for any visible change. Other than the Fusion on them, which they couldn't actually make out as they were Martials and not Mages, there wasn't too much visibly different. He gently tested one of the edges against the scales of his arm, however, and discovered that Larek hadn't lied when he was able to cut through them with just the lightest of touches. Thankfully, he wasn't ignorant enough to go deep and didn't even draw any blood, but he did hiss in pleasure at how sharp it was.

As the others picked up their weapons, Larek paused for a moment before he realized that he had better be careful with them initially testing their newest Fusion, as he didn't want an accident. "I added something that can be highly dangerous, both to your target and to you if you aren't careful. With a specific phrase – which I will tell you in a moment, so that you don't activate it prematurely – you will be able to produce a sphere of rapidly gusting air that is filled with an elemental effect, either flames, chunks of ice, sharp stones, or even balls of light. I added the latter for use against Umbral Demons and to see if it might be useful against the monsters we'll be fighting, as they are created from solidified shadows, but we'll just have to wait and see.

"The sphere is produced a certain distance away from the *tip* of your weapons, or in the case of the battleaxe, from the center of the blade. What this essentially means is that it will form *inside* of your target, as long as there is room for movement; trying to form one inside of solid stone or something hard enough to prevent air movement entirely will likely not be quite as effective. In all other cases, however, it should be effective to essentially tear up their insides, so even if they have a tough exterior, you'll be able to penetrate it with this Fusion.

"There are different Magnitudes to the Effects, as well, ranging from 1 to 7, and the higher the Magnitude, the stronger and larger diameter sphere it produces. Before you ask why you would choose anything less than the strongest, there is what you could call a 'cooldown' between uses of the stronger Magnitude, up to 7 seconds, whereas at Magnitude 1 the cooldown is only a single second. In addition, the spheres will stay locked where they are formed, and will persist even if you move away, for up to 7 seconds for the lowest Magnitude, and only a single second for the highest.

"Why? It's all because of ambient Mana density. Just like *you* use Stama for your Battle Arts and it regenerates over time," he nodded toward the Martials, before waving around himself, "so too can the Mana density of the environment be used – and used up – before it can regenerate. Fusions tend to consume a larger amount of ambient Mana than normal, so it is necessary to balance out usage and availability so that it doesn't run out prematurely.

"Any questions before we test them out?"

There was a strained silence as they all stared at him. Finally, Gharix asked, "Test? You haven't used this... Fusion before?"

Larek shook his head. "No, I just created it right now by combining a few other Effects from other Fusions. Should be fine, though," he added, smiling innocently. He was fairly certain that they would work as intended, though it was always hard to say with something assembled together like what he had just created.

After a few seconds, Gharix took a step away from the others, as if to put some distance between them in case something went wrong, before nodding at Larek.

"Good. Alright, before I tell you this, I would advise everyone else to take your hands off your weapons for a moment, as they will only activate if you are in physical contact with them. I don't want you hearing this phrase and accidentally activating it by repeating it in your head when you aren't ready." As the others set their weapons on the floor and backed away as if they were snakes ready to bite them, Larek turned to the Drekkin group leader. "I just realized that you have the same Fusion on both knives, so if you're holding both, they will activate simultaneously. Keep that in mind so you don't hurt yourself. Ready?" At Gharix's now-nervous nod after sheathing his left knife, Larek said, "Ice 1".

A second after Larek said it, the Drekkin must have thought the phrase, because a swirling sphere of air and sharp ice chunks appeared 6 inches in front of the tip of his knife. The 5-inch-wide sphere hung in the air exactly where it had been created even when Gharix stumbled backward in shock, and it continued to violently swirl around even as a second one was created a moment later where the Drekkin group leader had moved to.

"Clear your mind of the phrase, so you don't activate it again accidentally – or drop the knife if you have to," Larek informed him when the Martial lizard seemed on the verge of panic. "Though make sure not to chop off your toes," he warned.

Rather than dropping his weapon, Gharix seemed to gather himself up as he watched the two swirling spheres of ice disappear after 7 seconds, and no other sphere appeared during that time. "Very good. Now, as you might be able to guess, the other mental phrases are 'Fire 1', 'Stone 1', and 'Light 1'. When you are fighting a monster, all you have to do is stab them – and your weapons should easily penetrate most defenses now – and think one of these phrases; if you do it right, then *that*," he said, waving toward where the spheres had been moments ago, "is what will appear *inside of* them. Does everyone understand?"

When they nodded, he added, "Excellent! I also mentioned that they go up in strength, all the way to 7, and they are easily created by changing something such as 'Light 1' to 'Light 3' or 'Light 5', all the way up to 'Light 7'. Why don't you practice with the 'Light' mental phrases, which should theoretically be a little safer?"

With visible hesitation, the other Martial members of the group picked their weapons up and started practicing. As flares of light orbs moving around like fireflies in the night filled the cavern, Larek was surprised at gaining another Skill increase.

**Leadership** *has reached Level 13!*

"What about usss?" Pyluxa asked.

Larek waved them over, before explaining how to use their own weapons. As they had seen his staff work before, they weren't anywhere as hesitant to use the shortswords as they aimed at one of the cavern walls and began launching projectiles.

He sat there watching them all and answering any questions they had, waiting for his Pattern Cohesion to fill back up after creating multiple Fusions. It only took about 15 minutes before the Martial members began to feel a little more comfortable with their new Fusions, and he even caught a few of them grinning, showing a large amount of sharp teeth inside their mouths in the process.

When he had largely refilled his Pattern Cohesion, Larek got everyone's attention and announced, "Alright, now I just need everyone to strip."

He somehow managed to keep the smile off his face as he watched them react to the sudden order.

# Chapter 54

With so little material to work with, considering that the Drekkin didn't wear pants, arranging the Fusions on the armor – which the group reluctantly removed from their persons – so that they all fit on them without overlapping was the hardest part. Thankfully, Larek was already planning on upgrading some of the boosting and defensive Fusions that he was working on getting placed on them, so in the end it just took some creative thinking to maneuver the areas of ambience to fit properly.

As he handed their armor back to each Drekkin, to their great thanks, the Combat Fusionist described what he had done. It wasn't anything revolutionary, at least as far as Larek was concerned, but it certainly was a step up from what he'd done before.

"First, every piece of your armor has been upgraded with a *Multi-Resistance* Fusion that makes the material – either leather or steel – much more durable, as it will resist being cut through better than ever before. Blunt force impacts can still hurt you, because this Fusion does nothing to stop the damage from something slamming into or trying to crush your body, but lessening the probability that you'll be cut in half if an attack hits your armor is at least something. For the Martials, your bracers have a little bit less resistance because I didn't have as much room as I wanted due to some other Fusions I added. Still, a Magnitude 3 *Multi-Resistance* is nothing to scoff at. In addition, all of it will provide a slight resistance to magical and natural effects such as flames and cold, but my best suggestion is to try and avoid them altogether.

"Moving on, you may notice when you put them on that you're going to feel a bit different almost immediately. That is due to the stat boosts I placed on your armor, which do exactly what they sound like: They boost your stats. In this case, they provide a 100% increase to your base stats, so they will effectively be doubled while you're wearing the leather jerkins over your torsos."

There were exclamations of shock and wonder as they experienced the sudden increase in their stats, and Larek grinned at their pleased expressions. He was just thankful that he was able to get the boosts on their armor at all, but he made it happen by combining all three of the Martial and three of the Mage stats into bundled Fusions instead of only having 1 or 2 boosts per Fusion.

*New Fusion Learned!*
**Martial Stat Boost Suite +10**

Activation Method: Permanent
Effect(s): Increases Strength
Effect(s): Increases Body
Effect(s): Increases Agility
Magnitude: 100% increase
Mana Cost: 275,000
Pattern Cohesion: 1,725
Fusion Time: 273 hours

New Fusion Learned!
**Mage Stat Boost Suite +10**
Activation Method: Permanent
Effect(s): Increases Intellect
Effect(s): Increases Acuity
Effect(s): Increases Pneuma
Magnitude: 100% increase
Mana Cost: 275,000
Pattern Cohesion: 1,725
Fusion Time: 273 hours

Theoretically, he could've made the boosts stronger, but after gauging how large each of the *Stat Boost Suites* were at Magnitude 10, their areas of ambience at a higher Magnitude would've exceeded what could fit on the armor. At the same time, he went ahead and altered his own *Boosts*, replacing them with a brand-new one that incorporated all 6 stats and freed up some room for additional Fusions on his clothes in the future.

New Fusion Learned!
**Omni Boost +10**
Activation Method: Permanent
Effect(s): Increases Strength
Effect(s): Increases Body
Effect(s): Increases Agility
Effect(s): Increases Intellect
Effect(s): Increases Acuity
Effect(s): Increases Pneuma
Magnitude: 100% increase
Mana Cost: 450,000
Pattern Cohesion: 2,875
Fusion Time: 342 hours

Again, he could've increased the Magnitude of the new *Omni Boost* Fusion on his own clothes past his accustomed 10, but he didn't want to have to adjust to yet another increase in his physical stats quite yet. He already had plans to increase the Magnitude in the future, but for now it worked for him.

"After those boosts to your stats and the increased resistance to damage, I added a way to recover in case you do end up getting hurt. For the Martials, you have a different Fusion called *Healing Surge* that is designed to work with your *Body Regeneration* Skill to increase your healing rate to incredible heights, similar to what I was able to heal some of you with earlier," he said, nodding especially toward Gharix, who had been the worst damaged upon their first meeting. "Keep in mind that while you might be healed, you'll be hungry and exhausted if the healing needed is extensive. For the Mages, you have something similar for healing, but in your case it relies on normal healing Effects that will temporarily paralyze the portion of your body that is injured while it is being healed. The *Graduated Parahealing* Fusion is also not quite as fast as the *Healing Surge* Fusion that the Martials have, and it is completely reactive to your injury, so it will automatically attempt to heal you as soon as you take damage, with a stronger healing and paralyzing effect with greater injuries. For the Martials, you'll have to activate the healing with just a simple mental activation, which I'll show you how to do in just a moment."

All of the Drekkin seemed thoroughly impressed at the existence of the healing Fusions, but Larek's hope was that they wouldn't have to use them all that much – especially with what he had next for them.

"That takes care of your stats, additional resistance to your armor, and healing, but I've also added in something for defense that is something new," he continued his explanation. "For a while now, I've been using a Fusion called *Repelling Barrier* that effectively creates a strong gust of air that blows downward at an angle when it detects anything moving past a certain speed around my body. It worked fairly well for a long time, but the more I've used it in fights against monsters, the more inadequate it has become. I won't list the faults that I've experienced in its application, as there were more than a few, but I think that I've corrected most of them with my new iteration of a defensive barrier to help prevent all of you from taking damage in the first place.

"Gharix, would you mind helping me with a demonstration?"

The group leader appeared confused, but he nodded after ensuring that he had his armor firmly settled around his body again.

Larek got up from where he had been sitting since he had started creating Fusions, shaking his legs out a few times to get the blood flowing through them properly again, and approached the diminutive Drekkin. He stood in front of Gharix for a few seconds while lifting his right arm up...

...before suddenly striking out with his fist, directly at the lizard man's face. He moved so quickly that Gharix didn't even get a chance to flinch before Larek's hand was stopped six inches away from the Drekkin's face as it cracked into something solid, which also pushed it back slightly. It wasn't a sudden gust of air that blew Larek's hand back, nor was there a wall of hardened air blocking his fist; instead, it was almost as if his hand had hit the stone wall nearby. That wasn't exactly what happened, though, because a second later a small block of ice shattered on the floor.

"Wha—? What are you doing?!" Gharix shouted as he scrambled backward, as if expecting Larek to continue hitting him. Larek did nothing of the sort, of course, as he stood there shaking his hand and seeing if he had actually hurt it.

"Don't worry, I only wanted to demonstrate the new defensive Fusion I put on your armor," Larek explained, dropping his fist to his side. "It uses some advancements in Fusion creation that I've learned over the last few months to detect anything attempting to strike you using your own perceptions – those that you actively use and those that are used subconsciously. There are some cons to this approach, as it will make blocking strikes that you can't detect *at all* pass through it, as well as ones that you may not consider a threat, but it is also a huge step up on capability and blocking strength from what my old *Repelling Barrier* is capable of.

"As you saw, when my fist came close to you, even though you could barely tell it was happening, your Fusion automatically detected the threat through the use of your perceptions, which saw it coming before you could fully comprehend it. Once it detected the threat, it reactively created an almost perfectly clear, square block of ice that acted as a barrier, but that block of ice was also projected forward by a brief, if powerful, gust of air that not only blocked my punch but pushed my arm back slightly. The Fusion also considers the speed at which the attack is approaching you and adjusts the gust of air to at least negate its forward momentum, if not push it back like it did here."

The Drekkin looked at Larek as if he was speaking nonsense. "That... seems impossible. If it was capable of that, then what's to stop someone from walking unscathed through a cavern full of monsters?"

Gharix asked, abruptly dismissing the fact that Larek had pretended to try and hit him.

"Ah, well, there are limitations, of course," Larek said, rubbing the back of his head in professional embarrassment. He hadn't been able to eliminate *all* of the drawbacks that the *Repelling Barrier* possessed, but he at least got rid of most of them; fewer limitations were left, but they still existed. "For one, it will rapidly use the ambient Mana in the area, just like many of the other Fusions I've created for you if used excessively, so being almost hit dozens of times within a minute or two would deplete the necessary Mana to keep this new *Automatic Ice Repulsion Field +12* Fusion running. The idea is to avoid getting hit in the first place, but when you have to take a hit, this will protect you.

"Secondly, it is still *ice*, and it doesn't have the same sort of defensive properties as, say, *stone*, so anything strong enough that attacks you will still be able to penetrate the ice and hurt you. That being said, the ice and air gust combination provides up to five times the protection when compared to *Repelling Barrier*, so it is definitely a step up in the right direction. Also, before you ask why I didn't just use stone… that would be because most of the monsters down here have an affinity for sand, dirt, and stone, meaning that using it as a protective device might have unintended consequences.

"Third, the Fusion—as you can see—produces ice blocks, which can be slightly hazardous underfoot. Their presence could be detrimental or advantageous depending on how they are approached, as they could be an obstacle that could either aid or hinder the monsters around you.

"Lastly, if for some reason you are assaulted by more than a dozen individual attacks within a certain time period, the Fusion will not be able to block them, as there is a Limiter on the number of consecutive blocks of ice that can be produced. In addition, there is a cooldown similar to your weapons on the Fusion. This is to reduce the stress on the Fusion's formation due to too many rapid infusions of Ambient Mana, adding to its longevity and usefulness.

"As for the cooldown time, it is dependent upon the Magnitude of the ice blocks and air gusts being used. For all intents and purposes, the stronger and more frequent the attacks that are blocked, the longer the cooldown time. For example, an attack by a half-dozen weak monsters would be the equivalent of being attacked by a single strong monster; whereas you might be able to handle blocking dozens of weaker attacks, only a handful of attacks by the solitary monster might trigger the cooldown.

"To be more specific, the threshold for a full 60-second cooldown is 100 within a five-minute period of time. What exactly does that mean? Well, for each attack blocked by a Magnitude 1 ice block and gust of air, the count toward the threshold is 1. For Mag 2, the count would be 2, and so on all the way up to 12. Therefore, you could block 99 weak Mag 1 attacks or 8 of the strongest Mag 12 attacks within a five-minute period before the next attack would trigger the 1-minute cooldown. Unfortunately, I have no means of displaying how close you may be to triggering the cooldown; again, this is meant to be an emergency defense against attacks that you have no way of dodging, so your first objective should be to *avoid* being hit in the first place."

**Speaking** has reached Level 19!

The increase in his *Speaking* Skill was a surprise, though with all the explanations and the intent listening being done by the Drekkin, it really shouldn't have been. It went along with his other Mage Skill increases that he'd gained while making the different Fusions, which certainly hadn't been insignificant in and of themselves, now that he took a moment to review them all.

**Pattern Recognition** has reached Level 36!
**Pattern Recognition** has reached Level 37!

**Magical Detection** has reached Level 36!

**Spellcasting Focus** has reached Level 36!

**Multi-effect Fusion Focus** has reached Level 43!
**Multi-effect Fusion Focus** has reached Level 44!

**Focused Division** has reached Level 48!
**Focused Division** has reached Level 49!

**Mana Control** has reached Level 52!
**Mana Control** has reached Level 53!

**Pattern Formation** has reached Level 52!
.....
**Pattern Formation** has reached Level 54!

**Fusion** has reached Level 52!

.....
***Fusion** has reached Level 54!*

     Larek had also reached a personal Level of 31 at some point during the Fusion creation process, giving him an additional 23 AP to spend on his stats. Still not wanting to add anything to his physical stats because he wasn't quite ready to tackle the adjustment – especially when he was just about to go into a fight against the Demons and their possessed monsters – he instead placed 15 points into Acuity, bringing it up to 140, and 8 into Intellect, bringing it to 184.
     All-in-all, it had been extremely beneficial for Larek to take some time out to create all these Fusions for his new companions – but he wasn't even done explaining what he'd created.
     "Now, in addition to all of these Fusions, because I was able to consolidate many of them into more comprehensive formations, it left me room to add something that I'd been wanting to create but never exactly had the chance or space to do so before. If you take a look at your Statuses, you'll be able to see what I'm talking about in your Mage or Martial Skill list."
     They dutifully all had that faraway look that indicated that they were looking at their Statuses, and the exclamations of shock were rewarding in and of themselves.
     "How—?"
     "Fusions, of course," Larek answered Hakkin with a grin. "I was able to make a relatively simple Advanced Fusion that boosted 6 of your Mage or Martial Skill Levels by a flat increase of 10; I wasn't exactly sure how expensive it would be as far as Mana Cost and Pattern Cohesion, but 10 felt about right. Any more than that, especially with Martial Skills, would likely throw you off until you were able to adjust to the changes."

**Martial Skill Hexa-Boost +10**
*Activation Method: Permanent*
*Effect(s): Increases Bladed Weapons Expertise Skill Level*
*Effect(s): Increases Unarmed Fighting Skill Level*
*Effect(s): Increases Pain Management Skill Level*
*Effect(s): Increases Throwing Skill Level*
*Effect(s): Increases Dodge Skill Level*
*Effect(s): Increases Body Regeneration Skill Level*
*Magnitude: +10 Skill Level increase*
*Mana Cost: 125,000*
*Pattern Cohesion: 1,725*

Fusion Time: 171 hours

**Mage Skill Hexa-Boost +10**
Activation Method: Permanent
Effect(s): Increases Pattern Recognition Skill Level
Effect(s): Increases Magical Detection Skill Level
Effect(s): Increases Spellcasting Focus Skill Level
Effect(s): Increases Mana Control Skill Level
Effect(s): Increases Pattern Formation Skill Level
Effect(s): Increases Fusion Skill Level
Magnitude: +10 Skill Level increase
Mana Cost: 125,000
Pattern Cohesion: 1,725
Fusion Time: 171 hours

    The Fusions weren't overly expensive when it came down to it, but he was sure they would help the Drekkin out significantly. Larek also was able to place them on his own clothing, adding to his own Skills in the Process, but he hadn't really *felt* a change in his Mage Skills once he had them. It probably had to do with the fact that they didn't seem to go past his maximum, despite the 10-Level boost to the skills, so they weren't exactly as beneficial to him as he would've hoped. However, he was interested to see what sort of difference his Martial Skills would have once he finally got a chance to test them in actual combat.

<u>Mage Skills:</u>
**Pattern Manipulation Level 22/40 (400 AF)**
**Pattern Recognition Level 37[40]/40 (400 AF)**
**Magical Detection Level 36[40]/40 (400 AF)**
**Spellcasting Focus Level 36[40]/40 (400 AF)**
**Multi-effect Fusion Focus Level 44/45 (450 AF)**
**Focused Division Level 49/50 (500 AF)**
**Mana Control Level 53[55]/55 (550 AF)**
**Fusion Level 54[55]/55 (550 AF)**
**Pattern Formation Level 54[55]/55 (550 AF)**

<u>Martial Skills:</u>
**Stama Subjugation Level 1/20 (200 AF)**
**Blunt Weapon Expertise Level 1/20 (200 AF)**
**Bladed Weapon Expertise Level 2[12]/20 (200 AF)**
**Unarmed Fighting Level 3[13]/20 (200 AF)**
**Throwing Level 13[20]/20 (200 AF)**

**Dodge Level 22[30]/30 (300 AF)**
**Pain Immunity Level 20/20 (N/A)**
**Body Regeneration Level 35[40]/40 (400 AF)**

    He had been slightly worried that having them maxed out would mean they wouldn't Level up naturally, but he did manage to gain one more Level in *Pattern Formation* after he had the *Mage Skill Hexa-Boost +10* on his clothing, so it didn't look like their development was hindered in any way.

    "And… no, that's it. What do you all think? Are you better prepared to face the unending armies of monsters created by the Aperture and Umbral Demons?"

    The clearly overwhelmed group of Drekkin looked at him in shock before what he could've sworn were smiles flashed over their faces.

    "Yesss…. Let'sss kill them all," Pyluxa suddenly said into the silence with a bloodthirsty-sounding hiss.

    Larek just nodded in response with his own smile, wondering if he was crazy to be looking forward to facing hordes of monsters and insubstantial shadow demons that could possess people. Regardless, he wasn't alone now, and his confidence in their success was high…

    …but then again, he had no clear idea of what they would be up against.

# Chapter 55

"...and then this tunnel leads to where it is believed this Aperture is located."

Larek looked down at the map that Gharix had meticulously and efficiently carved into the wall of their sanctuary, seeing the route that they would have to take to get to their destination. It was approximately 10 miles of tunnels that wound back and forth through the nearby area, filled with monsters and potentially Umbral Demons, the latter of which were something that Larek would have to take care of since he was the only one who could hurt them. The Combat Fusionist had mentioned his ability to manipulate his Pattern in such a way that it could be used offensively and defensively, but neither Pyluxa nor Hakkin had any talent in controlling their own Patterns in such a way. It was possible that they might be able to learn eventually, but for now, they would be relatively useless in that aspect of their fight.

After Larek created a couple of *Camouflage Spheres* for the Drekkin to use, Gharix and Abarcen had gone out of their little sanctuary to investigate their route, only coming back when they were forced to. With the *Spheres* active, they were able to slip by the monsters they encountered, but when they came to a section of tunnels that were completely dark, the two of them had to leave rather than risk being possessed by an Umbral Demon.

"It looks doable enough – but what did you encounter along the way?" Larek asked, wanting to know a little bit more of what they could expect to have to fight against.

The Combat Fusionist, of course, hadn't been idle while the two had been out scouting. He had spent the few hours they were gone creating additional *Weaken +10* Fusions upon some rocks he carved out of the wall, filling his belt pouches to nearly overflowing. They were accompanied by many, many *Adjustable Illumination +10* Fusions on other rocks (which essentially allowed the one touching them to dictate how bright they were when activated, up to Magnitude 10), as well as *Directional Illumination +10* stone rods that all of the Drekkin would be carrying.

He nearly started creating more of his other offensive Fusions, such as *Frozen Zone* and *Healing Shelter*, but decided against it; while they would undoubtedly be useful, the group would already be straining the ambient Mana density as it was. If he was to use them more often than in emergency situations, he could risk them all running out of ambient Mana even if they were on the move. They tended to use *a lot* of Mana, after all, and he'd rather have more options than less during any fights they engaged in.

"It's... bad," Gharix responded with a shake of his head. "We were barely able to avoid physically bumping into the hordes of monsters emerging from the darkened tunnel we located, even if we were rendered invisible by that *Camouflage Sphere* you allowed us to use.

"There are *thousands* of individual monsters – and those were just the ones we saw," he continued. "Once they get to this junction," he said as he pointed to a spot on the map he'd carved that split into five different directions, "they would divide and start moving down them. From what I can tell by the markings on the tunnels themselves, this junction leads to different hubs in our underground system, which typically held our biggest cities. Most—if not all—of them have fallen to the monster hordes, other than Draverdin, so what they are doing from this point I have no idea. We do know that this is why there is a constant but manageable flow of monsters that attack Draverdin, but that could change if all of the monster groups suddenly all flow toward the city instead of branching off."

Larek nodded along with the explanation, also wondering what the point of them branching off was when they could probably all swarm the Drekkin city and force their way in after a short while. He attempted to peruse the memories of the Demon mind that had connected to him for answers, but there didn't seem to be anything relevant to this situation within them. Or at least nothing he could comprehend fully, as many of those memories were strange because they came from a viewpoint completely foreign to him. It was like trying to understand the Drekkin as they spoke in their own language; he might be able to pick up a few things based on context, but other than the overall plan of the Demons and the few larger concepts he'd been able to pick out already, the rest of it was incomprehensible.

"How was the strength of the monsters? Did any of them seem particularly powerful?"

Gharix and Abarcen looked at each other for a moment before turning back to Larek. "Not particularly powerful, no. Some of them were what we've faced before, and while there were many more that were unfamiliar, none of their groups appeared to be more than what we could've handled even before we received these incredible Fusions you've gifted us with," the group leader answered with a thankful tone to his voice. Larek waved off the implied thanks, as he didn't feel like he deserved it all that much, considering that he was conscious that he was using them to accomplish *his* goal, even if they didn't see it that way.

"Then that must mean they have the stronger ones in reserve for some reason. I'm sure you've seen some powerful monsters over the last month or so, correct?"

"Oh, yes, we have; some of them required a much larger group of Mages and Martials to kill, and we were always forced to avoid them and warn those in charge of our defenses at home," Gharix responded wistfully, as he likely remembered that he no longer had a home to go back to at the moment. "We've even participated when the full might of our defenders in Draverdin were pitted against these monsters, but it was rare. As a result, we're more accustomed to fighting against the smaller, weaker monsters that infest the tunnels."

That made sense to Larek, based on what he knew about the group, which was more like a scouting group that would only fight when they had an overwhelming advantage. With only two Mages in the group, they were a bit more mobile than one with a larger complement, and there were technically no defenders like Bartholomew had been; in other words, none of them had a shield that would be necessary to fight against something a little more powerful. They were organized to use their overwhelming force to quickly destroy groups of weaker monsters and then flee before they were set upon by something that would give them trouble.

All of that meant they were perfectly poised to absolutely tear through the weaker monsters they would encounter on their way to the Aperture, but once they were there, they would be at a slight disadvantage after rarely ever fighting anything too strong for them. Fortunately, they now had quite a few advantages that they hadn't had before, which would hopefully be enough to get them through.

"Fair enough," Larek said in confirmation. "Do you need to rest before we leave?"

The two Drekkin who had scouted the pathway to the Aperture shook their heads. "No, but we should probably discuss how we're going to sneak in and close the Aperture. These *Camouflage Spheres* are powerful, but there are so many monsters that—"

The Combat Fusionist immediately interrupted the group leader. "We're not going to sneak in."

"—we won't be able to avoid—WHAT?! No, going in any other way is suicide!"

Larek shook his head even as the others agreed with Gharix. "Have you ever closed an Aperture before?" he asked after the protests died down somewhat.

They all looked at each other before the group leader responded. "No, but I've heard about it from some others who participated in the closing of the smaller Apertures before they all disappeared, and it seems pretty straightforward."

Sighing, Larek explained why they had to kill as many of the monsters on their way in as they could. "The reason they all disappeared from elsewhere is because this main one somehow absorbed them, due to the influence of the Umbral Demons – or at least that is the impression I get from the Demon's memories in my head. It's because they are all now tied together that we need to thin their numbers on the way in and not leave any behind us.

"If we don't, as soon as we even touch the Aperture, *every single monster* that has spewed forth from that portal into the world of Corruption will rush back to defend it. I don't know about you, but I don't particularly fancy fighting what are undoubtedly very strong monsters defending the Aperture while we are rushed by thousands of weaker monsters from behind."

Larek could see right away that they hadn't known this fact, and they once again looked around at each other in trepidation. Rather than let them reconsider and back out, he said as cheerily as he could, "Then it's settled! Let's get going and close this Aperture!"

Without waiting for them, he strode toward the entrance of their little sanctuary, mentally deactivated the *Secure Hideaway* that had been blocking off the passageway into the cave, and picked up the stone it was on as he walked past, sticking it in one of his belt pockets. His staff knocked against the floor as he used it as a walking stick, striding out of the entrance without fear – though he had to admit that he felt a little trepidation about what was to come. Running headlong into hordes of monsters was still as frightening as ever, even if he felt a desire to kill them and absorb their Aetheric Force, but he quickly tempered that fright with his need for revenge. The violation he had felt when that original Umbral Demon had attempted to take over his body, mind, and soul was still vivid in his every thought, and only by destroying every single one he could find down in the underworld would he be satisfied that they could never do such a thing to anyone else ever again. Of course, preventing them from overrunning the Drekkin and breaking out into the wider world in order to destroy every living being was also a goal of his, but it was secondary to ensuring that the Demons and their insidious ability to possess people were wiped out in their entirety.

He was slightly worried for a moment when he didn't hear anyone following him out of the sanctuary, but before he had gone more than two dozen steps from the entrance, he heard the soft scuff of scaly feet against the ground behind him. He looked back to see

Gharix and Abarcen handing the *Camouflage Sphere* Fusions to the pair of Mages, and he mentally nodded at seeing this. Even now, they were smart enough to protect the most vulnerable of them, though with their available defensive Fusions, they were a far cry from how vulnerable they were even just the day before.

As the smaller tunnel where their sanctuary had been located was only somewhat connected to the main thoroughfares where the monsters traveled out to the rest of the tunnels under the desert, it wasn't surprising that it took them about 10 minutes to encounter their first monsters. When Larek saw that it was a group of approximately 150 **Fanged Rabbits**, he thought that this was the perfect opportunity for the group to practice with their new Fusions.

The 3-foot-tall, dark-furred rabbits spotted them from approximately 250 feet away down the tunnel, and they screamed in fury at their appearance as they bared their teeth – including the 6-inch-long fangs for which they were named. The scream seemed to startle the Drekkin, who stopped immediately upon seeing the vast array of monsters that were now steadily eating up the distance between them.

"These are all yours – let me see what you can do now. Don't be afraid to practice with the Fusions you have, and spread out so that you don't hurt each other," Larek warned them. "I'll be by the Mages in case you need help, but I imagine you'll be fine." So saying, the Combat Fusionist retreated until he was nearby where he could sense both Pyluxa and Hakkin, who were both invisible underneath their Camouflage Spheres. Larek, of course, could sense them and the Fusion they were using, but they were effectively hidden for the moment.

At least until they unleashed a barrage of projectiles that spewed forth from the tips of their swords, spraying Magnitude 1 *Flaming Balls* and *Icy Spikes* at the incoming monsters that were bounding along the stone flooring. The Rabbits that were hit – and there were many of them – screamed yet again, this time in pain rather than fury, as they were burnt or stabbed by icicles from extreme range. Only a few of the Rabbits died immediately as a lucky projectile hit them in the eye or somewhere more vulnerable, such as their necks or chest, but more than half of them were at least slowed down after taking some noticeable damage.

Not to be undone, the Martial Drekkin finally reacted by spreading out and preparing themselves for the charge of the Fanged Rabbits, their weapons at the ready and their stances clearly ready for whatever was going to happen. Larek noticed only the slightest hesitation in their movements at the onset before they took their positions, aided by the fact that they were able to move twice as fast as they normally would because of their new Agility stats. Thankfully for them, they appeared to acclimate to the higher stats more readily than Larek had in the past, as it seemed as if it was simply normal for them.

When the front lines of the Rabbits arrived, they immediately focused on the four Martials out ahead of the two Mages, despite the fact that the barrages of projectiles continued to pour out of the invisible spheres that hid Pyluxa and Hakkin. Whatever it was that made them concentrate on the melee-focused Drekkin, the monsters mistakenly encountered an extremely stalwart resistance as Gharix and the other Martials absolutely tore into them.

Black-furred body parts went flying through the air as they were chopped, sliced, and stabbed in a flurry of attacks by the Drekkin. Here and there, Larek could see a few ice blocks suddenly appear out of nowhere when the crowd around one of them became too much, which sent the Rabbits that were much too close flying backwards with the crunch of a solid block of ice smashing against their faces. Gharix activated a Battle Art that somehow made him even faster, and he became a whirlwind of blades that absolutely chewed through his opposition, while the others used Battle Arts to aid in their movement, dodging the assaulting Rabbits with fancy footwork while they struck back.

When the first use of a *Variable Elemental Gust Sphere (VEGS)* was used by Abarcen, the resulting explosion of the Rabbit *from the inside* was powerful enough to trigger his *Automatic Ice Repulsion Field* to block the body parts from hitting him. The Fusion worked so well that the suspended sphere was powerful enough to shred another Rabbit that attempted to hop through it to get to the Drekkin, nearly showering him with the half of its face that was ripped off in the attempt.

Despite the screams of the dying Rabbits and the slightly disturbing sounds that accompanied the wholesale slaughter of the monsters, Larek heard Abarcen chuckle as that happened – and the other Martials took note of it as well. In the next few seconds, multiple usages of the *VEGS* were deployed by the others, and joyous laughter accompanied it from the entire group.

As disgusting as it was, they were obviously having fun. Their newfound strength and speed, along with the other Fusions they possessed, were enough to make the fight completely one-sided, which brought with it the knowledge that, unless they were really stupid, they were practically invulnerable against these particular monsters. It was a feeling that Larek had felt before when he had developed the *Repelling Barrier* originally, but now that feeling was amplified in the entire group.

The Mages hadn't stopped their barrage until nearly a minute went by, at which point they sheathed their shortswords and began casting their own spells. It wasn't technically needed because of the Fusion on their weapons, but Larek could tell that they wanted to contribute their own strength against the monsters, not wanting to rely on the Fusion despite it being as powerful as it was. He wasn't disappointed as he watched them deftly maneuver their spells around their groupmates to hit clumps of Rabbits, absolutely obliterating the monsters when they hit; it showed that they had a familiarity with working with each other to avoid friendly fire. Their teamwork was impressive, even though they were still getting used to their new stats and Fusions, and Larek was further confident of their future success.

In the end, it was a slaughter – as he figured it would be. As for the Drekkin, when the last Fanged Rabbit fell to a spear thrust through its head, nearly decapitating it in the process, they all froze on the field of battle as they looked around at the carnage – only for the remains of the Rabbits to quickly disperse into dark-green and black clouds of smoky shadows. It was only then that they all hissed loudly as they raised their weapons above their heads, the two Mages dropping their *Camouflage Spheres* to join in the celebration.

They had won, and won handily. Right now Larek knew they were feeling invincible, but he would have to temper that with the dangers they would be facing in the future. Right now, if they were only fighting these weaker monsters, they would have no problems; it was only when they were forced to fight something much stronger, such as a giant scorpion, that they would find that they were far from invulnerable. They would be protected quite well, at least, but he'd already told them that his Fusions were imperfect and had weaknesses that they would have to learn about through experience.

However, that was for a later time. The Combat Fusionist let them have their celebration against the Fanged Rabbits, because before too long, they would be facing one group of monsters after another… and he wondered if they would have the same feeling of exhilaration after hours of constant fighting.

# Chapter 56

"They're endless! Why are we doing this again?"

Larek looked at the shouting and complaining Drekkin group leader as he sliced through the neck of yet another **Night Wolf**, the familiar, black-furred monsters not looking too much different from the first time the Combat Fusionist had seen them back when he was traveling to Crystalview Academy. Even as the Wolf fell, Gharix spun and stabbed into the back of a second monster that was trying to sneak by to get to the Mages, activating the *VEGS* Fusions on his knives simultaneously. The Night Wolf suddenly exploded from the inside as whirling spheres of ice suddenly appeared within the inside of the monster's abdomen, killing it instantly.

Despite the adept attacks and execution of the two Wolves, Larek could see that the pace they had set as they entered the main tunnel leading toward the Aperture was starting to wear Gharix down. Not just him, but all the others were looking a little ragged, having fought near-constantly over the last few hours as they determinedly moved foot by foot down the passageway.

All except Larek, who was still in pretty good shape. It wasn't just because his Body stat was much higher than theirs, which it was, but because he hadn't needed to be anything but an additional long-range attacker for the most part. He had been physically attacked a few times over the course of their battles, but it was typically only by stragglers that managed to get through the front line of Drekkin and were easy enough to dispatch with his axe. It was those few times that he was able to use the *Variable Elemental Gust Sphere +7* he had added to his best friend, and was further pleased at how effective and *destructive* it was.

But to say that it had been a challenge, for Larek at least, would be a lie. Having the six Drekkin with him had taken the responsibility of killing every single monster off his shoulders, meaning that he was holding up much better than them as a result. An outsider might say that he was taking advantage of them or even using them as a shield against the hordes of monsters they fought... and they would be partially right. However, they would be discounting the fact that all of them, including the Mages who stayed out of any close-range combat, had gained something from the endeavor: Skill Levels.

In short, the constant fighting and use of their Skills, whether it was *Bladed Weapon Expertise*, *Dodge*, or even *Body Regeneration* when Abarcen had been temporarily overrun and suffered a number of bites to his lower legs by a cluster of **Rabid Beavers**, or *Spellcasting Focus* and *Mana Control* when the Mages cast their hard-hitting spells, they had all gained Skill Levels faster than they ever had before. At least, that was he deduced as they excitedly shouted it out whenever it happened. Larek knew that his own prevalence for rapidly increasing his own Skill Levels was highly abnormal, but the Drekkin were getting better at something approaching his own prodigious rate.

But what did Larek get out of it? Unfortunately, he hadn't increased any of his Skills since they had started fighting, as he was simply in the background using his staff to inflict long-range damage on the incoming groups of monsters. What he *did* get out of it was an absolutely disgusting amount of Aetheric Force – and that was only from the monsters he directly had a hand in damaging, if not killing outright.

Over 20,000 AF up to this point, and as the Drekkin group leader had stated, the monster hordes seemed endless; if they continued on for another few hours, he was sure he could double that amount, if not more. Unfortunately, his observations of their current exhausted state meant that the likelihood of them holding out was extremely low.

It was with good reason, of course, as their entry into the main tunnel had been fraught with one fight against relatively weak monsters after another. At first, the Drekkin had been almost excited to test themselves against their opponents, absolutely tearing through the **Thorny Tumbleweeds, Shambling Zombies, Acidic Slimes, Slowgres, Vampiric Bats**, and dozens of other monsters that were either ones that he'd seen elsewhere or were unfamiliar to him from his days at both Academies. Regardless of whether he knew what they were, they were all weak enough that even if the Drekkin hadn't received the upgrades in the form of the Fusions they were using, they would've been perfectly capable of defeating a half-dozen of these groups back-to-back. They would likely be injured and exhausted afterwards, but they could do it.

Now, though, they had already fought at least 150 different groups of monsters over the last few hours, and it was weighing upon them. They had made forward progress, at least, which was a good thing since they were using hefty amounts of ambient Mana to power all of their Fusions almost constantly, and only by staying on the move could they stay ahead of the drain on the local Mana density. The latter was going to be important soon, as Larek had already seen a few of the Martials falter, and their *Automatic Ice Repulsion Fields* were activating more and more frequently; any more frequently would mean that they would either start taking more wounds from the attacks, or they would drain the Mana density dry.

Long story short, they needed a break.

Sadly, it wasn't as if they could duck into a side passage and hole up somewhere for a few hours. For one, as he had told them before, the more monsters they killed now, the fewer would be able to rush back and defend the Aperture once they began to close it; halting their constant slaughter of the monsters heading down the tunnel would set them back significantly in that endeavor. Secondly, and more importantly, there weren't really any side passages to enter in the first place, and even if there were, it was unlikely they would be left alone for long.

All of that meant Larek would have to find a way to give them the break they needed. With that decision made, he finally responded to Gharix's question. "It's necessary so that we don't have to face them later!" he shouted at the Drekkin group leader. "But I agree, they feel like they're endless right now because you've been fighting nearly nonstop for almost five hours, and you need a break! Once the last of these Wolves fall, I'll take over!"

"What? No, you can't—"

"Don't worry, I'm more rested than any of you, so it isn't that much of a hassle." He figured he would be fine, especially since he hadn't used any of his special Fusions quite yet, as there hadn't been any need.

The fact that there wasn't more argument coming from any of the Drekkin only proved how tired they were, and as soon as the last Wolf was killed, they all practically collapsed in exhaustion where they stood. Meanwhile, the bodies of the shadow-formed Wolves disappeared, and the Aetheric Force that Larek gained from the fight filtered into his body. Looking ahead, he saw that the next group was approximately 2 minutes away from reaching them, which they'd found was around the standard distance in between monster hordes. It was also at this point where they would advance their progress in navigating their way down the tunnel, but for now the others had taken his advice and were getting some rest. They even began to pull out some food from some hidden pockets in their armor, quickly munching it down while they looked at Larek moving past them.

"What are you going to do?" Gharix asked.

Larek looked over his shoulder as he left the Drekkin sitting where they were. "I'm going to clear the way for an hour or so. Use that time to rest up and rejuvenate, because we still have a few miles to go."

"All by yourself—" Hakkin started to ask, but he cut himself off as Larek pulled an innocuous-looking stone from his belt pouch. "Never mind."

He knew what the *Weaken* Fusion was, after all, or at least had heard Larek's explanation of it.

The Combat Fusionist jogged forward approximately 100 feet before he stopped, prepared his staff to fire out of his left hand, and then slowly juggled the stone in his right. When he saw the approaching tightly packed horde of 300 Walking Skeletons – almost identical to the horde outside of Draverdin, which his Air Skimmer had bowled over – approach 200 feet away from his position, he threw the stone in his right hand. As it sailed in an arc away from him, he mentally activated the *Weaken* Fusion on it, making the stone extremely fragile.

**Throwing** *has reached Level 14!*

It wasn't a perfect throw, he thought, as it was slightly to the right of where he had planned it going, but the resulting explosion as the Mana was released from the broken Fusion was more than satisfactory. Landing just to the right of the middle of the horde, the force of the detonation ripped apart dozens of the relatively fragile skeletons and sent their dark-grey colored bones flying out in a spray of shrapnel that destroyed or crippled dozens more.

Before they could even figure out what had happened, a second explosion rocked the left side of the horde, a result of a second *Weaken* stone that he had pulled out from his belt pouch a second after throwing the first. Even more of the Skeletons were destroyed by the force of the explosion, killing many of the ones that had been damaged by the first as they were caught by the second. He couldn't tell exactly how many he had killed with the two Fusions, but he estimated it to be more than 100 of them, or just over a third of their total.

As much as he wanted to simply throw another *Weaken* stone, he limited himself to only two for the time being; if he was going to be killing these monsters for an hour, he was going to have to pace himself.

Running forward, he held his staff under his left arm as he used his left hand to aim it toward the disorganized Skeletons, and then he activated a Mag 2 *Flaming Ball* Effect from the *VREP* Fusion. As he strafed it back and forth along the left-hand side of the Skeleton horde, he pulled out a Binding Thorns Fusion and gently tossed it toward the right-hand side. As it landed just ahead of the first ranks of Skeletons, it activated and was ready to go. The first of the undead monsters passed through its area of effect and triggered the roots that immediately emerged from the solid stone underneath their feet, wrapping around their legs. The thorns that sprouted and tore into them didn't do too much as they didn't have any flesh to bite into, but that didn't matter; it was the strength with which they tightened around the fragile bones of the Skeletons that made all the difference as the first of the Skeletons had its legs shattered from the constriction of the roots. As it fell forward, the top half of the monster hit the ground, only to be crushed by the power of the additional roots that rose from the stone.

The best thing about it, however, was the fact that the walking undead were essentially mindless monsters, as none of them behind the first victim saw any reason to switch from their original heading, and so they passed through the deadly Fusion without any thought to their own safety.

With a portion of his flank taken care of by the offensive Fusion, Larek didn't stop as he waded into the depleted front ranks of the Walking Skeletons, maintaining a steady stream of balls of flame from his staff to his left while he pulled out his axe and treated the monsters ahead of him as a forest of trees that needed to be felled. Chopping left and right with his best friend held in his right hand, the Combat Fusionist cut them apart with great speed and very little actual combat technique, as it wasn't really needed. The Walking Skeletons were numerous, but they were actually rather fragile, so all it took was a single swipe of his axe to sever their spine, upon which they fell in pieces to the ground – but Larek didn't stop to finish them off. He kept wading through their reassembled ranks, destroying them as quickly as possible with a rapid stream of *Flaming Balls* and incessant strikes with his Logging tool.

Before he knew it, he found nothing else standing up to slice apart, and he turned around to see the devastation he had wrought behind him. With a little more than 100 dead in the original *Weaken* Fusion explosions, another two dozen were killed by his Binding Thorns, while at least another 100 were burnt to death or had suffered from a force impact by the *Flaming Balls*. That left another 60 or so he had personally chopped in half – and their upper halves were now doing their darnedest to crawl toward him with just their hands. Putting his axe away, he took the staff out from under his left arm and held it with both hands in order to aim a little better.

That's when he switched to a Mag 4 Water Stream and used it to drill through the heads of the crawling Skeleton torsos, which finished them off completely. Once they were dead, he jogged over to where *Binding Thorns* was located, turning it off from a distance, picked up the Fusion, and placed it back in his pouch. As he looked back at the astonished Drekkin, who had temporarily paused in their consumption of a snack, he realized that only a little over a minute had passed from the start of the battle to the end. That meant that he had some extra time to move forward, advancing further down the tunnel.

"Catch up to me when you've rested enough!" he shouted at them as the Aetheric Force from the slain Skeletons finished being absorbed by his body, before turning his sights on the next group of monsters. He could see them a distance down the passageway, and he jogged forward to get closer to them. Once he was close enough to identify them as **Pinchy Crabs**, which were 2-foot-tall, 4-foot-wide, black-shelled crabs with sharp and powerful claws, he pulled out another *Weaken* stone and threw it, followed quickly by a second. The Crabs weren't as clumped together as the Skeletons had been, but the explosions still killed at least two dozen of the Crabs – which wasn't too bad, considering that there were only about 50 of them in the first place.

From there, he had to experiment with his attacks, as *Flaming Balls* weren't as effective against their shells, nor were *Icy Spikes*. In the end, he used *Water Stream* at Magnitude 6 to effectively punch through their hard shells to damage their insides from a distance. Thankfully, a *Frozen Zone* Fusion was super effective against them as their insides froze and cracked their shells from the inside, making them practically burst in response to the freezing cold of the offensive Fusion's Effect.

It took an extra minute to finish off the Pinchy Crabs when compared to the previous Skeletons, but it was still fast enough to give him some time to move down the tunnel...

...before starting all over again with another set of monsters.

Larek had managed to progress a total of 2 miles down the tunnel by himself over the next hour when the Drekkin finally caught up, appearing refreshed and even chuckling amongst themselves when they saw how far the Combat Fusionist had gone. After watching him absolutely devastate the monsters he faced, most of the awe and disbelief had faded, leaving them to simply take it all in stride. Considering that they could now do many of the same things, Larek could tell that they now had something to prove as they ran ahead of him to engage the next group of monsters, leaving Larek behind for a moment as he caught his breath.

It wasn't so much that he was physically tired, as he barely felt like he had done much melee fighting when compared to the Drekkin Martials. But the constant battles, despite the satisfaction of receiving just as much AF fighting solo as he had gotten while in the group, were tiring on his mind.  He needed to stop for a few minutes and regroup his thoughts before joining them again.

Once he joined them, he jumped straight into his previous role as a long-range attacker, which helped to return his equilibrium after being so focused on large-scale combat for the last hour.  Eventually, he began throwing one of his *Weaken* stones into the groups of monsters to help thin their numbers before the others engaged, which was fairly accurate now that he had increased his base *Throwing* Skill up to Level 18 over the last hour.

**Throwing** *has reached Level 15!*

.....

**Throwing** *has reached Level 18!*

Over the next two hours, they fought and continued to progress down the tunnel, killing thousands of monsters in the process.  About an hour into the battles, Larek took a more active role to reduce the stress on the others, because he could tell that – despite their break – they were already starting to suffer from exhaustion.  It helped to spread the work around with him on the front lines, where he could use both his staff and his axe to great effect, though all of them were getting overly tired by the time they finished their latest monster group, only to look up and see... nothing.

It wasn't *nothing*, per se, but for once, they couldn't see another monster horde moving toward them.  Instead, distracted as they were by the progress they were making down the tunnel, they arrived in front of a completely dark tunnel, which had been marked earlier on Gharix's map as being unexplored, and which had been the source of the monsters as they streamed and attacked Larek and the Drekkin.  Now, though, there was only silence and not a sign of any others emerging.

"What'sss going on?" Pyluxa asked, the weariness in her voice as she spoke matching what everyone else was feeling at that point.

It only took the others a moment to realize what the stoppage of more monsters attacking them meant.

"They know we're here," Gharix said softly, but it was loud enough that the others easily heard the group leader, which prompted Larek to nod in agreement.  "And they're inviting us in."

"Well, we don't want to be rude, so let's go say hello, shall we?"

# Chapter 57

Pulling out one of his *Adjustable Illumination +10* stones out of his belt pouch, Larek warned the others to close their eyes as he activated it at Magnitude 5, as even at that brightness it could be uncomfortable to look at for long – especially for those who lived underground like the Drekkin. He had no such problem, as even though it was bright, he didn't look at it directly but instead tossed it into the yawning portal of darkness that awaited them.

The illuminated glow of the stone arced ahead of him and just barely pushed back the darkness as it landed approximately 15 feet inside the shadow-filled tunnel. Even at such a relatively short distance ahead, the formerly bright light was difficult to see clearly, as it was almost as if the darkness was trying to eat away at it like it had the Luxite in their sanctuary cave. Fortunately for Larek and the others, it seemed as though the Umbral Demons were unable to pull the light away from something made with a Fusion; otherwise, all the *Illumination* Fusions he had created for lighting in the cave would've been useless.

But that didn't mean they didn't try. A dark, fog-like barrier surrounded the glowing stone like a thick blanket over the next few seconds, only letting a small bit of the light it should be producing out to the people outside of the darkened tunnel. After another 20 seconds, it got to the point where it looked no brighter than a star in the night sky lightly covered up by clouds.

With another warning to the Drekkin, even Larek closed his eyes as he activated another *Adjustable Illumination* stone at Magnitude 10, and the shock of the bright light in his hand made him look away as it tried to push through his closed eyelids. With only that first flinch at the effectiveness of his Fusion, Larek threw the stone into the tunnel, probably a little farther than he intended, before opening his eyes to the sounds of pained exclamations coming from the Drekkin.

He could readily understand their issues, because when he went to open his eyes, his vision was distorted in strange wavy lines, like something had been burnt and these were heat lines. A quick pulse of his *Healing Surge* did the trick, and he could tell from the sudden use of ambient Mana by the others that they had done the same thing.

Fortunately, when he looked ahead at where he had thrown the stone, his vision wasn't affected again. That was because, even though he had thrown the Fusion approximately 40 feet into the tunnel, he could see it clearly – and could also hear what sounded like high-pitched screams of fury in response to its presence.

Larek could only smile as he looked at the Drekkin, who took a step back in either shock or fright. "Looks like we introduced ourselves properly. Let's go in. If there are any monsters, I'm going to need your help to kill them, while I deal with the Demons." He turned to the Mages specifically. "Continue throwing some of the stones I gave you throughout the tunnel to light it up; that," he said, pointing toward where his last stone had landed, "was a Magnitude 10 example, but I have a feeling while we're in there, a Mag 8 or 9 will work just as well."

At their nervous nodding, Larek stepped inside the first few feet of the darkened tunnel, which was still covered in shadows as it was out of the light being projected by the other stones. Upon his second step, he felt something intangible slam into his side, staggering him slightly, but he was ready. The half-formed thought of an axe made from his Pattern Cohesion crystallized into completion in no more than a second, and suddenly it floated out in front of him. With another thought as he stood still and felt the insidious presence of an Umbral Demon trying to wrest control of his body away from him, he mentally used the axe to cut completely through his body from his head to his groin. His own intangible implement of death sliced harmlessly through him, but the Umbral Demon that had entered his body was cut entirely in half, its screams of pain dying after a second as it dissipated into nothingness.

It was at that point that the rage that the Demons had exhibited at the presence of the glowing stone disappeared, leaving the slightly illuminated tunnel devoid of any sound at all.

For all of 5 seconds.

That was when the screams returned in greater numbers and intensity, and while he could sense that the Demons wanted to attack him en masse, they were prevented when a bright Fusion fell by his feet. Either Pyluxa or Hakkin had tossed one of them into the entrance, creating a "bridge" to the next glowing stone. Out of the corner of his eye, he thought he saw a few of the Umbral Demons with the additional light before they fled from the illumination; they were there and gone so quickly that those not expecting it might think it was a trick of the eye, but he had been watching and waiting for them to make an appearance the entire time.

"Thanks," he said without turning around. Even as he moved forward, he could feel the oppressive shadows around him attempting to smother the light that was just tossed in, but it was bright enough that it was able to withstand a good portion of the darkness closing in on it. Before long, he was passing through the first stone he had thrown in and approaching the extended range of his second, and while he still heard the screams of rage, nothing attacked him since he was in the light.

Larek's anger and yearning for revenge against the Demons for what they had attempted to do to him was burning hot in him, but he managed to refrain from flinging himself into the wall of darkness ahead of him so that he could start killing them. The reason he stopped himself from simply taking the expedient route was simple and terrifying at the same time: He wasn't sure how many of them there were. Every other time he had come across the Demons, he had felt a general sense of them out there in the darkness, even if he couldn't pinpoint them exactly and was only able to get a general count of them; here, though, he could sense them out there in the deep shadows, but there were also *so many* of them that it was impossible to put a number to them. He suddenly wondered if he was in a little bit over his head here, but he pushed that thought aside until he was able to better evaluate what he was really up against.

In addition, closing the Aperture was another of his goals, so it was possible that closing it would allow him a better shot of killing every Demon nearby, as they would be reeling from the sudden loss of monsters. That was the second reason he didn't simply jump headlong into the deep darkness ahead of him, because he was worried that there were monsters out of sight just waiting for him to do that. If he were to be attacked by Demons, there was the possibility that he would be incapacitated for a few seconds while he killed them, and that would give them plenty of opportunity to overwhelm his defenses – especially if there were stronger monsters just waiting for them to make a mistake.

Therefore, with that in mind, he took out another *Adjustable Illumination* Fusion to throw ahead of him, but Pyluxa beat him to it as one flashed by him to brightly illuminate the next 20 feet of tunnel ahead of him. As it passed through the darkness, Larek saw at least 20 dark, shadowy figures almost instantly disappear as they moved to avoid the light, seeming to teleport away with a screech of what sounded like pain. He was fairly sure that they weren't hurt overly much, especially considering how fast they escaped the range of the light, but what he actually saw was only a small fraction of the Demons he still sensed out there.

"I don't like this, Larek," Gharix whispered ahead to him. "This feels like a trap."

The Combat Fusionist initially dismissed the thought that this could possibly be a trap, but he stopped himself as he really thought about it. *These aren't mindless monsters, are they? They've been down here for centuries, hiding in the shadows, but there is an intelligence to them – I know that for a fact after unfortunately experiencing one of their minds. It might be almost entirely foreign intelligence, but that doesn't mean they're not capable of setting a trap. They somehow took control of all the Apertures, after all, and they have a plan to kill everything in the world, so why not have defenses in place in case someone came looking for them?*

He reluctantly acknowledged to himself that this might indeed be a trap... but what other choice did they have at this point in time? Turn around and go back, abandoning their goals? Retreat and continue to kill the endless monsters that streamed out of the Aperture? Look for a different way to get to their destination? How long would that take, if there even was an alternative route?

No, they had to keep pressing forward, even if this *was* a trap. The best solution wasn't always the smartest, after all, and all they could do was try.

Moving through the tunnel slowly, throwing out *Adjustable Illumination* Fusions like little islands of safety within the oppressive darkness, Larek felt slightly claustrophobic for the first time in his life. The shadows and the sense of the Umbral Demons just lurking out of sight seemed to press down on him like a weight, sapping his energy as it felt like he was suddenly trapped in the same void that had transported him halfway across the world a few months before. Looking back at the Drekkin, who were huddled together in the center of their illuminated pathway, he could tell that it was getting to them as well; frequent, wide-eyed glances out into the darkness and the twitching of their weapons as they listened to the screams of rage coming from the Demons were very obvious signs that they were starting to crack.

It was the combination of all these things that nearly led to their downfall as yet another glowing stone went out, and as Larek glanced back at them as he walked forward, he failed to notice that the light revealed something other than the bare stone floor that they had been passing over. The illumination reflected off of hundreds of pairs of eyes, all waiting for an opportunity to strike.

It was Abarcen's panicked, high-pitched scream that alerted him to the danger a second before it was too late, and Larek whipped around to see a huge mass of monsters of dozens of different kinds rushing at him from only 15 feet away. He saw many familiar ones of the same weaker varieties that they'd killed as they made their way down the outer tunnel, but there were new ones as well. Worse than that, however, was that there were stronger monsters included in the rushing horde, including the same Barbed Gators he had fought up on the surface, horse-apes, and even something he didn't know the name of, but had an immediate sense that they were stronger than the average monster that they had been fighting.

He barely caught a glimpse of it in the rushing crowd, but it looked like some sort of six-legged Frog, with wet, black skin that reflected the light of the glowing Fusion stone. Normally, that wouldn't have been that big of a deal, but this particular frog was also almost as tall as Larek and at least three times as big around. The reason he barely caught a glimpse of it was because it jumped almost straight up and into the darkness out of the range of the *Adjustable Illumination* stones as soon as he noticed it. While he couldn't see where it had gone, he had a feeling he knew where it was going to end up.

Therefore, with a cry of warning, he threw himself backwards, rolling in order to get back to his feet as soon as possible. Once he was sure of his footing, he began to unleash his staff's *VREP* Fusion upon the monsters ahead of him, joined a moment later by Pyluxa and Hakkin. The Drekkin Martials swiftly spread out in front of the two Mages while staying to the side of the line of fire, and they quickly engaged the wave of monsters that literally crashed into them, being pushed from behind as they did so.

*I guess this is the trap they were planning.*

The fact that he had identified it didn't make it any better, of course, but this was something they could handle. Or at least, he thought they could.

A moment later, the giant black frog made its reappearance, landing right where Larek had been a moment ago with a *\*thump\** that he could feel through his feet. Even as the Combat Fusionist pulled out a stone with a *Frozen Zone* Fusion on it and threw it further into the crowd of monsters still heading their way, the frog opened its mouth and a sticky-looking black and mottled grey tongue shot out, aiming for Gharix. The Drekkin flinched backwards from the sight of the tongue even as he sliced up a Fanged Rabbit that leapt at him, but it was blocked by his defenses as a block of ice appeared and pushed it back. The mouthy appendage was apparently either sticky or wet enough that the ice actually froze to it, and it was pulled back into the frog's mouth, only to be crunched apart by the rows of serrated teeth that the amphibian apparently possessed. After that, it jumped again, but this time *backwards* – or so he assumed, because he didn't see it again right away.

As much as they blunted the initial rush of monsters as they cut them down in large swathes of projectiles, melee attacks with *VEGS* activations, and the use of his *Frozen Zone*, they were quickly being overwhelmed. Without any choice other than running and attempting to escape, Larek pulled out his *Binding Thorns* and *Healing Shelter* Fusions and placed them in the never-ending horde of monsters that kept streaming into the light of the glowing stones. While they proved effective, it wasn't long before Larek pulled out his *Stone Shredder Dome* Fusion on a stone rod that he held out in front of him as he advanced into the mass of incoming creatures, completely ripping them apart upon contact with the rapidly moving stone chunks.

Meanwhile, even with all of their advantages, Larek and the Drekkin were being surrounded and attacked on all sides as portions of the horde swung around the darkened perimeter of the tunnel and assaulted them from the sides and behind, forcing them to all move together so that not a one of them was cut off from the others. Thankfully, after about a minute of frantic defense, it seemed to be working, as the tide of monsters seemed to slack off after *thousands* of the enemy had been slain in the hectic battle, though it was still dangerous enough that they couldn't take more than a second to breathe before the next wave assaulted them from almost all sides.

At the same time, the worst happened as Larek felt like something was wrong; his suspicion was confirmed when he used his Skill, which revealed that the ambient Mana density had fallen precipitously. He immediately canceled the three offensive Fusions that had been extremely useful in thinning the horde, and while they would've still been effective, they were also huge drains on the ambient Mana. He even put away his Stone Shredder Dome as it was also a detriment to the density of the area, and he switched to his axe as his primary means of attack.

"What happened?! We need those up!" Gharix shouted, seeing the offensive Fusions fail and let through a fresh wave of monsters derived from their location.

"We've drained too much of the ambient Mana!" Larek shouted, even as he waved about him with his axe, periodically using his staff to fire off a few projectiles when it got crowded around his location. "We either need to move back or move up! Otherwise, we're not going to be able to maintain—"

It was at that point that Larek felt a temporary stutter in the Fusion that boosted his stats, as the ambient Mana density dropped even further. The reason for that was the sight of Hakkin suddenly being piled on by a surge of Thorny Tumbleweeds that rolled into him from behind, triggering his *Automatic Ice Repulsion Field* multiple times within a period of a few seconds. Fortunately, Abarcen was nearby and was able to save him, slicing through the thorny, spherical bushes with his weapon, but the damage had already been done.

"Stop using any Fusions! We're just about to run out of ambient—" Larek shouted, but was cut off as he was hit from behind by something, causing him to stumble to a knee. Looking back, he saw a Slowgre, which looked like a 5-foot-tall bipedal pig with black and dark green skin covering its body, as well as a crude leather loincloth. It was a slow monster, unable to move quickly, but it also packed a punch if anything was foolish enough to stand still for it to hit. Unfortunately, that fool just happened to be Larek, as he was unable to move from his current position due to the press of monsters against him and had been a prime target.

At first, he thought that his perception must have missed the Slowgre attacking him, but he realized a moment later, when a Vampiric Bat swooped down and scraped at his upper arm, that it hadn't missed it; instead, it simply hadn't activated because it didn't have enough Mana.

*Uh, oh.*

Looking around for a solution that didn't end up with them all dying, he saw that without the offensive Fusions that Larek had deactivated, the influx of monsters had increased yet again. More than once, he watched the other Martial members of the Drekkin group suffer injuries as their defensive Fusions failed them, and they were getting just as overwhelmed as he was. Desperate, he began tossing out the last few *Weaken* stones he had in his belt pouches, but the resulting explosions only seemed to help minimally, reducing the incoming monsters while doing nothing about the ones already around them and in their faces.

Dropping his staff so that he could concentrate on destroying everything that came within reach of his axe, he tore through them using every bit of speed he could pull from his Agility stat, making large, sweeping attacks against the monsters around him. He abruptly staggered when a stone came out of the darkness, likely thrown at him by a Stone Chucker, and hit him in the back of the head, but he pushed through the abrupt disorientation to continue the fight for his life. He wasn't able to heal the small knot on the back of his skull because he didn't have enough ambient Mana around him, so he ignored it in favor of taking out as many of the monsters as he could.

A sudden cry of pain from one of the Drekkin distracted him as he looked up to see Pyluxa suddenly go down under a pile of monsters, with no one near to help her. Slightly saddened that she had fallen, he had already thought her dead when out of the corner of his eye he saw her unconscious and bleeding form being dragged from the light of the glowing stones to the darkness beyond by a group of monsters.

At first, he wasn't sure if he saw it correctly, but when Medrizz and then Hakkin fell a few seconds later, only to be dragged out of the light as well, he suddenly knew what was happening.

They weren't killing them; they were bringing them back to be possessed by the Umbral Demons.

As this realization hit him, he fought even harder, cutting his way toward the other Drekkin, who he noticed had all been separated at some point, but it was already too late. One by one over the next few seconds, with their defenses completely negated by the lack of ambient Mana, and even their stat boosts failing them (which was the same for Larek), the Drekkin fell under the onslaught, only to be dragged away into the darkness. Gharix was the last to fall; his knives were a whirlwind of destruction, but it wasn't enough.

Alone now, Larek felt some of the ambient Mana begin to come back as there wasn't as much of a draw upon it, and his stat boosts came back – for as much good as that did. Without another half-dozen targets to attack, the horde of monsters – which, to be fair, was already less dense than it had been before – didn't hesitate to throw themselves at Larek, and it was all he could do to keep moving, sweat pouring down his face from the exertion.

His *Repulsion Field* even came back temporarily before it was used so many times that it was on cooldown, which was precisely when the black frog that had been out of sight until then made itself known. From the darkness came a long, sticky tongue that suddenly wrapped around his waist from behind, and he could practically feel the acidic saliva through his clothing. Before he could react to its presence, he was suddenly pulled off his feet and sent flying through the air, yanked with such force that he was practically doubled over and touching his feet.

A brief memory of rows of serrated teeth at the other end of the tongue flashed through his head, prompting him to sweep the axe, which he somehow managed to maintain a grip on, behind him, severing the tongue pulling on him. He heard a pained croak a second later, but that wasn't important at that time, since he was still flying through the air backwards...

...and right into the darkness that pressed upon the small bastion of light provided by the *Adjustable Illumination* Fusion he left behind.

# Chapter 58

As the oppressive shadows enfolded him in their embrace, Larek was left unable to see anything as he quickly left behind any source of light around him. He wasn't sure if he should be thankful or not, but his eventual landing through the darkness was cushioned when he crushed something underneath him that yelped out in pain before it cut off suddenly. At the same time, the abrupt obstacle sent him flipping over and over, his arms and legs flailing as he quickly lost any sense of up and down, until he finally hit the ground on his left side, slightly injuring his arm from the impact. A quick activation of his *Healing Surge* Fusion helped to remove the injury, as well as apparently hundreds of smaller cuts and bites that he had endured from the monsters after his *Automatic Ice Repulsion Field* ran out of ambient Mana.

Fortunately, as he quickly got to his feet, a look at the current Mana density using his *Magical Detection* Skill showed that it was much more prevalent wherever he had landed, which made him wonder how far he had actually flown. It had to have been quite a ways since he could no longer see *any* hint of a glowing *Adjustable Illumination* stone nearby, which put him in a bad position if he was suddenly attacked by more monsters that he couldn't even see.

**Magical Detection** *has reached Level 37!*

Unfortunately, even though he could see the strands of energetic Mana around him, they did absolutely nothing to illuminate the area. He reached into his belt pocket to grab another stone—

*What? Empty? What happened?*

He frantically checked all of the other pockets on his belt for anything at all, only to find that they were all empty. Panicking, he looked around himself, and using his newly increased *Magical Detection* Skill, he was able to see something by his foot. He immediately identified it as one of his Fusions, one of his *Weaken* ones to be exact, and he suddenly realized that during his uncontrolled flailing in the air, all of his stones had fallen out since the pockets had all been partially opened for easier access.

As he bent to pick it up, he looked out and saw more stones further away, showing up to his senses like stars in the night sky. They were the only things that were visible nearby in the absolute void of nothingness, and helped to alleviate some of the panic that set in as he remembered being swallowed up by the attack of the Warped Void Hunters back in the Kingdom—

As his fingers brushed the top of the *Weaken* stone, he froze in place as he suddenly realized something.

It was completely quiet. He could literally hear the beating of his heart and the blood pumping through his head, it was so quiet. The last thing he had heard that wasn't himself was the yelp of pain when he hit something while he was flying through the air... followed by the sound of his Fusion stones impacting the floor, now that he thought about it. But now there was nothing at all.

*Where are the monsters? Better questions: What happened to the screams of rage coming from the Demons? Did they leave?*

As he stood back up after quickly snatching the *Weaken* stone into the palm of his hand, he quickly learned the answer to those latter questions.

They had never left. The Umbral Demons were just preparing to attack him with an overwhelming horde of shadowy forms similar to what they had just experienced with the physical monsters.

They had him trapped in the darkness and at their mercy, ready to be the next victim of their possession and soul replacement assaults. With their numbers, he stood no chance against them, and he should just give up now. There was no point in struggling, as it would only cause unnecessary pain and stress, so letting his new friends take and use his body was the ideal solution—

*NO! GET OUT OF MY HEAD!*

The insidious thoughts that pushed against him came from dozens, if not *hundreds* of different sources, and it was all he could do to keep his very sanity intact as he felt his knees crack on the floor. His physical strength had been sapped as soon as the mental assault had begun, the Umbral Demons staying out of range after having learned from his previous demonstration that he could hurt and kill them... somehow. The details of that were more than a little fuzzy to him at the moment, but it seemed as though the enemy wasn't taking any chances and were doing everything they could to wear him down until he had no more resistance to their soul-replacing attacks.

As he struggled against the mental pressure wearing at his mind, his left hand rolled the *Weaken* stone around and around with his fingers, the thought that he could simply end it all by activating it and crushing it like a clump of dirt played around in his mind. It would be the easy way out, after all, a different result than the Umbral Demons wanted, but it would completely mitigate the risk that they would take over his body and use it for their own ends.

But that wasn't who Larek was. As much as he might appreciate the easy way out of a problem, this "easy" solution wasn't something that he needed to contemplate for more than a second to realize that it would never happen. He hadn't come this far to give up now, and he wouldn't give the Demons the satisfaction of seeing him throw it all away without a fight.

That firm resolve was like a jolt to his mind as he very deliberately placed the stone back in one of his empty belt pockets, taking his hand away as he concentrated on fighting against the pressure threatening to snuff out his consciousness. Thinking was hard, however, as everything seemed to slow down around him, but the jolt of his mind was enough to push him into the same hyper-focused state he utilized when creating Fusions.

The instant his focused state snapped into place, his thoughts now seemingly segmented into a section outside of the Demons' influence, he understood what they were doing. Not only were they trying to snuff out his mind from a distance, their numbers amplifying the effects until he could barely think straight, but it also somehow suppressed his knowledge of how to fight against them. He had *completely* forgotten that he could use his Pattern to hurt them, as it was part of the very soul they were trying to replace for their own purposes; now that he could finally think clearer, he knew what he had to do.

An unbidden chuckle escaped from his mouth, which only prompted more laughter as he continued to struggle against the pressure rallied against him. By the time full-throated cackling emerged from the Combat Fusionist as the monstrous hilarity of the situation occurred to him, he could sense that the Umbral Demons were edging closer to him, bit by bit.

They likely thought his mind was finally cracking, succumbing to their attacks, but that wasn't it at all. Instead, Larek was laughing at the pure audacity and hubris that the Demons were displaying toward him, unsuspecting that their plan to force him to give up had been their undoing. They might be experts in dominating those people who couldn't resist them, whose souls were easy pickings because they didn't have any defenses, but the unique Combat Fusionist was certainly not one of those people. His Pattern Cohesion, and therefore his soul, was strong and powerful enough not only to resist their attempts, but also to fight back like nothing they had ever seen before.

The Umbral Demons had made a mistake.

They should have let the monsters kill him rather than try and trap him with their mental attacks with the intention of taking over his body. Their greed was their folly, and as he prepared his own response to their assault, he smiled grimly as he looked out into the complete darkness of the tunnel, letting his laughter subside.

The Demons were going to learn that *he* wasn't trapped by their insidious attacks, stuck in the darkness of the tunnel; rather, *they* were the ones trapped in the suffocating darkness with *him*.

Sending his mind within himself, he grasped his Pattern Cohesion and started to form it into the shape that he wanted. This time, it wasn't the form of a familiar axe; while that would've been ideal against a few Umbral Demons as they closed in on his position, he could now sense what had to be *thousands* of them all congregating around, amplifying their mental pressure against him to the point where any other person would've lost their mind almost immediately. No, an axe wouldn't cut it.

He had to think bigger, of a way that he could hurt them all simultaneously without having to hunt them down individually. He remembered what he had learned from the one that had temporarily shared his mind, and how the Demons abhorred the light, as it hurt them severely – but rarely ever permanently damaged or killed them. It just didn't have the strength behind it to do more than injure them, like Larek's skin would be burned if he stood too close to a fire.

But what if that light was created from his Pattern, his soul?

That was the question for which he wanted an answer. Thankfully, his understanding of his *Pattern Manipulation* Skill had improved enough that he was fairly sure he already knew the answer to that.

With a flex of his will, he directed 1% of his Pattern Cohesion – a total of 360 – to form an invisible bubble around his head, with the thought behind it designed to block out any form of mental intrusion. As soon as it snapped into place, every bit of pressure that had been pushing into his mind vanished, freeing up the rest of his consciousness to focus on what he did next. Even as he sensed the Demons suddenly stopping their advancement toward him, and even beginning to retreat at the sudden nullification of their mental attacks, Larek formed another 9% of his Pattern Cohesion into a ball that hovered outside of his body.

At first, it was simply just a glowing ball of largely transparent blue light, but it quickly changed as his focus on it transformed it into something that gave off light, heat, and life: a sun. As suddenly as if he had activated one of his *Adjustable Illumination* stones, the transparent blue light became substantial and overwhelmingly bright – for anyone but Larek. For him, it didn't affect him more than acknowledging it was there, because it was *his* Pattern; it couldn't hurt him unless he wanted it to, and that wasn't in its function.

That function was revealed a split-second later as it surged to life, sending out an incredibly bright and blinding blast of light into the tunnel, illuminating everything within sight. The shadowy darkness was instantly banished all around him, the light completely shredding it to pieces in less than a second, revealing a few things to him immediately. First, he could finally look back and see where the *Illumination* stones were, approximately 100 feet ahead of him; second, he could see thousands of monsters pushed back up the tunnel and around those stones, frozen completely still as if they were waiting for orders to attack.

Lastly, he could see the veritable legion of Umbral Demons surrounding him, packed so thick that he was barely able to look past them in places, and it was only when they moved in response to the sun that allowed him to look past a few of them to see his stones and the monsters nearby them.

Just as he could see them, *they* could see the miniature sun that he had created out of his Pattern. Instead of rays of light and heat being transferred from it, which the sun up in the sky did, it instead sent out rays of pure Pattern that passed through *everything*, as even solid material couldn't stop it from its function.

In order to accomplish this, Larek had to keep feeding his Pattern Cohesion into the sun he had created at a rate of 5% of his maximum per second, but it was worth it. Just like he would funnel his Mana into a Fusion, he funneled his Cohesion into the brightly glowing orb in front of him. Unlike when his Mana left his body, the depletion of his Pattern rapidly drained his strength. He was suddenly thankful that he had fallen to his knees earlier, as he didn't have the physical energy to get to his feet.

But the effort was worth it. As the rays of his Pattern flashed through the Umbral Demons, they began to get ripped apart piece by piece even as they attempted to flee. Unfortunately for them, their normal method of traveling quickly to escape such an attack was to slip into a nearby shadow, even if it was only a sliver of one, and use that shadow to teleport itself to another shadow; with the sun illuminating *everything* with nothing physical stopping its progress, there wasn't a single shadow to be seen within at least 500 feet of his location, if not farther.

Their screams as they were ripped apart as they attempted to flee, only for there to not be any refuge for them, created a cacophony that physically hurt Larek to the point where his ears started to bleed and his bubble protecting him from mental intrusion was stressed almost to the point of breaking. As they died by the dozens and then by the hundreds over the next few seconds, the screams faded away as their owners were completely shredded by his Pattern-based sun, wiped from existence as easily as they possessed the bodies of the unwilling.

Some of the strongest Demons lasted a little over a dozen seconds before they, too, were ripped apart by the overwhelming power of his Pattern, and only when the last of the screams faded and the shadowy forms of the Demons disappeared did Larek absorb the sun he had created, regaining the thousands of Pattern Cohesion he had infused into its creation. The additional Cohesion he had sent into the sun was lost, used by his creation to reach the farthest Demons and destroy them, but it was a necessary sacrifice.

**Pattern Manipulation** *has reached Level 23!*
.....
**Pattern Manipulation** *has reached Level 26!*

His body didn't think so, of course, as the loss of a little over 25,000 Pattern Cohesion over a short period of time made him want to collapse into a puddle on the floor of the tunnel. Thankfully, he managed to stay conscious and even used his *Healing Surge* briefly to heal his ears, while at the same time artificially bolstering his energy enough to stand up and look around. He felt extremely drained still, but there were still monsters—

A glance back at the monsters he had seen before, surrounding the glowing stones he and his group had placed, showed that they were still there... but they were still frozen in place. It was only when he looked around to see that the tunnel had lost its oppressive darkness that he considered what might have happened.

*Did I kill all the Demons? Are they going to wait there forever until something kills them or gives them an order?*

He didn't know, but he didn't want to waste any time finding out. He needed to get moving, even as exhausted as he was, because there were things he still had to do. The Aperture still needed to be closed, after all, but more importantly, nowhere in his view were there any signs of his Drekkin groupmates. They had obviously been dragged away somewhere after being knocked unconscious, but they were nowhere in view.

Looking back at the glowing stones, he spotted his dropped staff under the feet of a frozen horse-ape and debated retrieving it, but he didn't want to trigger another fight inadvertently.  At the moment, they were leaving him alone, but who knew how long that would last if he was right there in front of them?  With a resigned sigh, he elected to abandon it where it was, as over the next minute he quickly picked up as many of the nearby stones with his Fusions that he'd dropped earlier.  In the end, all he could find were a half-dozen stones with *Adjustable Illumination* on them, as well as an additional 9 *Weaken* Fusions that joined the one he already had in his belt pocket.  The offensive Fusions such as *Frozen Zone* and *Binding Thorns* were stuck in the middle of the monster horde somewhere, so he was forced to leave them behind as well.

With very little offensive firepower other than his *Weaken* stones and his axe with the *Variable Elemental Gust Sphere* Fusion on it, Larek left the site of the glowing stones and the monster horde behind, pushing himself further down the tunnel and to where he hoped to find his newest companions…

…and free them from whatever had them in thrall.

# Chapter 59

While the glow from the stones he had left behind him helped to illuminate the tunnel for a ways, a few of them extremely bright at Magnitude 10 that allowed the light to reach up to 500 feet away, as soon as the passageway he was traveling down began to curve to the right, Larek was forced to use more of the stones to light the way. He only dropped one of them before he decided to keep the rest, using it similarly to his *Directional Illumination* stone rods, though he kept the Magnitude to no higher than 3. It fortunately wasn't necessary, as there didn't seem to be any of the artificially thick darkness in the tunnel, so it was more than enough to light the way.

As he passed through the eerily empty passage, he looked at the walls and noticed that they were filled with Luxite, similar to the ones that comprised almost every other tunnel he'd seen down below the desert. Just as the Luxite in the sanctuary had had its glow sucked away, so too was the crystal here completely inert, as if all the energy keeping it going had been depleted. He made a mental note to ask Gharix what exactly Luxite was and what made it glow, but he was interrupted when, through the normal darkness of the underground tunnel, Larek saw that he was coming to an opening as the walls fell away to either side.

Stepping past the threshold, he entered into what he immediately identified as an enormous, roughly circular cavern, approximately 2,000 feet in diameter. It had an extremely tall ceiling to it, at least 700 feet above the floor if he estimated it properly, and the appearance of darkened Luxite continued along the walls and ceiling, though rather than simply looking "dead", most of it was cracked or damaged in some way.

The floor began to gradually dip down a few dozen feet from the tunnel's entrance where Larek was standing, and looking around the cavern he could see that the general shape was one of a flat-bottomed bowl, as the center was about 100 feet lower than the edges, forming a perfectly flat, circular stone floor that was about a quarter of the diameter of the entire cavern.

How was he able to see all this, given that everything else was extensively dark up until this point?

The answer to that was the immense Aperture floating 5 feet above the floor, located in the exact center of the cavern, as it stretched to a size larger than anything he'd seen before at 100 feet in diameter. It was a chaotic riot of hundreds of different colors all attempting to compete with each other as they swirled around inside the sphere-shaped Aperture, straining at its boundaries.

While it technically glowed from the chaotic mixture of colors, which was what gave the cavern enough illumination for him to see its full extent, the glow that it gave off was somehow tinged with a darkness, as if the light it gave off was tinted with shadows. It was like looking at the sun exuding its life-giving rays and seeing it altered in a way that it provided no heat and only provided light as an unwanted side effect.

It was uncomfortable to look at directly, as if it was a perversion of nature itself – which was a funny notion in and of itself, considering that the Apertures led to a world of Corruption. Regardless, the shadow-tinted glow was somehow even worse, and even if he hadn't already been planning on closing it, just the sight of it would prompt just about anyone to do the same.

The Aperture was such a draw to his eye that it momentarily distracted him from what filled the rest of the cavern. As he forced his attention away from the floating portal into another world, he immediately focused on the large number of monsters arrayed in front of and around the Aperture, waiting silently where they stood or hovered in the air.

Compared to the darkened tunnel and the hordes of monsters he and the Drekkin had fought, there weren't that many of them – only about 100. Unfortunately, what they lost in quantity they had gained in quality, as from his position he saw not just 1, but 5 giant scorpions identical to the one he fought up on the surface of the desert, along with small groupings of other large monsters, such as a dozen of the six-legged frogs, one of which had used its tongue to send Larek flying not that long ago; a dozen flying lizards, which reminded him of a miniature Cloud Dragon (like the one he had seen outside the walls of Peratin); hulking feathered beasts that looked like a mixture between a bear and an owl; and even a half-dozen coiled snakes that he judged were at least 70 feet long and 3 feet wide at their widest.

But that wasn't even the worst of them, as there was a single eyeless worm that sat essentially wrapped around the bottom of the Aperture, its girth so hefty that he judged it to be nearly 30 feet in diameter. It wasn't comparatively long given its width, only about 120 feet or so, but it exuded a palpable strength that Larek could sense even from more than a thousand feet away. The fact that it, and the rest of the monsters he saw, were colored in dark grey and black chitin, fur, feathers, or scales only enhanced the danger, because he knew that these monsters were all influenced and controlled by the Umbral

Demons. After the tunnel where he had used his Pattern sun to wipe out any trace of the Demons there, he thought that he might have killed them all, leaving the monsters he saw unable to move without orders. But now that he was inside the cavern with the Aperture, he was quickly disabused of that notion, as in random order down below in the bowl, there was a large group of *people* standing unnaturally still as they stared up at the entrance. While he was still far enough away that he couldn't see many of them clearly, he recognized that almost every single one of them were Drekkin, most with some sort of weapon or armor that they had equipped. A quick look over them with his *Magical Detection* revealed a half-dozen of them wearing or wielding weapons that had a familiar magical signature to them, which he quickly identified as his own Fusions. It didn't take long for him to realize that Gharix and the other members of his recent group had already been dragged down below and possessed, with each of their souls having been replaced by an Umbral Demon.

Anger and disappointment at himself warred within his mind as he looked at the Drekkin, as the ones that he had specifically told he would protect had fallen victim to the very enemy he had been so confident in being able to handle. The burning need to not only close the Aperture but also destroy the Demons actively controlling the figures down below flowed through his mind, but a sobering thought suddenly occurred to him.

*If I free them from the Demons, will they even survive the process?*

Knowing that the horrid shadow entities essentially replaced their souls, he had no idea whether simply getting rid of the Demons would bring his friends' souls back. Were they gone forever at this point? Or was there some hope that they might be able to recover?

Regardless of the answer, what he saw down below was enough evidence that he hadn't killed all the Umbral Demons yet, and that had been his ultimate goal after his own personal assault on his soul. Even if the Drekkin group that he had journeyed with were lost forever, that wouldn't stop him from destroying the Demons that were controlling their bodies.

Checking his Pattern Cohesion, he saw that it hadn't completely regenerated from his usage earlier, which had been a significant chunk of his maximum Cohesion at the time. Given another 5 minutes or so, he would be back to full, and then he would be able to create another Pattern sun to penetrate the bodies of the Demons' victims, destroying their shadowy parasites in the process. He would probably have to get a little closer, as he didn't think his sun's rays of soul energy could effectively reach from the edge of the cavern, but that shouldn't be too much of a—

Larek was interrupted mid-thought as the monsters down below began to move, their frozen states shattered by some inaudible order to attack. It seemed as though the Demons weren't going to allow him the time to prepare, showing that they were smarter than he gave them credit for. That was unfortunate, because with very little in the way of offensive capabilities right now, he wasn't in any way confident that he could survive the upcoming onslaught. The five giant scorpions alone were likely more than he could handle, considering that he had barely survived against one of them up above.

However, he did have one thing going for him that was a change from the usual.

The Mana density in the cavern was extremely thick. For the first time since he wound up in the Sealance Empire, he had the feeling that his Mana regeneration would be so fast that it would be indistinguishable from that of the Kingdom – because the Aperture practically pulsed with the energy he saw flowing rapidly out of it. Close proximity to such a source of Mana certainly had its benefits, though now he had to figure out how to take advantage of it.

The few things that would've benefitted from an abundance of ambient Mana were all left back in the tunnel, surrounded by a horde of monsters; he couldn't suddenly create any more of them because he would need at least a few minutes to create even one of them, and he had only a fraction of that before the first of the monsters arrived to try and kill him. After his destruction of the other Demons, he didn't for a second think that the ones controlling the people down below would risk keeping him alive to possess his body, so he could only assume that they were going to try and take him down for good.

So, what else could he do with abundant Mana? Casting unending spells would certainly be something that he'd *like* to be able to do, but that was also not possible. Creating spell patterns and making them act as Mana bombs similar to his *Weaken* Fusions was certainly possible, but it was also so physically draining that he would rather avoid that unless it was used as a last resort.

Quickly taking stock of his Fusions, looking for something that he might have missed, he was met with the same result as he expected: 5 *Adjustable Illumination* and 10 *Weaken* Fusions on stones, his clothing that held his boosts, protective, and healing Fusions, and his axe that was both sharp and had a *VEGS* Fusion that would certainly help against the stronger monsters. The latter Fusion was important because there really wouldn't be too much restriction to its use, as he could theoretically create as many of the destructive spheres as he wanted without having to worry about using too much ambient Mana. Unfortunately, it still had the Intervals on it that the Drekkin's weapons possessed, so it wouldn't be as effective as he might hope because it was designed not to completely deplete the nearby ambient Mana, as well as to reduce stress on the Fusion's formation through normal use.

*But I wonder….*

Larek was running out of time before he was suddenly attacked by nearly 100 strong monsters, but a thought had him looking closer at the *Variable Elemental Gust Sphere* on his axe. It was certainly an effective Fusion, that much had been proven already, but the Intervals made it less useful, especially when he wanted to use higher Magnitude spheres. If he wanted to use a Magnitude 7 sphere, for example, he would have to wait another 7 seconds before using it again. It made sense in a low ambient Mana environment, but at the current density in the cavern, draining the ambient Mana wouldn't be an issue.

Before he could think twice about what he was doing, Larek blocked out his surroundings as he turned his hyper-focused attention onto the *VEGS* Fusion on his axe. Finding what he was looking for, he tapped into his new *Pattern Manipulation* Skill and used it to alter the Pattern Cohesion infused into the Fusion's formation. There was a heavy resistance at first, as the strength of his Fusion was so great that it didn't want to be changed, but he persisted and bent all his concentration on altering just one little thing inside the Interval section he had targeted. Eventually, there was a sudden audible *\*snap\** as the 7-second Interval he was targeting began to break apart; it was a split second from catalyzing a cascading reaction that would've caused the entire Fusion to fall apart when Larek caught it with his focus and bent his Skill toward simply altering it, rather than trying to eliminate it like he thought might work at first.

With agonizingly slow and delicate manipulation of the Pattern already invested in the Fusion, he changed the 7-second Interval to one that was quite a bit faster: 0.1 seconds.

As he let it go, the new Interval slid into place like it had always been that way, and Larek pulled himself from the hyper-focused state he was in to see that he had succeeded. Or at least he hoped he had, though he was encouraged when he suddenly received some notifications.

**Pattern Manipulation** *has reached Level 27!*
......
**Pattern Manipulation** *has reached Level 29!*

The Combat Fusionist didn't have any more time than that, however, as by the time he looked up from his efforts, the first of the giant scorpions – which were extremely fast – was already closing with him. Rather than wait for himself to get surrounded, he ran toward the rapidly moving scorpion and leaped toward it, his axe ready to inflict some serious damage on it. As he flew through the air, the massive arachnid suddenly stopped and reached up with its right claw to snatch him out of the air, but Larek swung his axe at it and felt the edge bite deep into the chitin, stopping it in place as his momentum kept him moving forward. He activated the Magnitude 7 version of the *VEGS* Fusion with ice as the element, before activating it with fire, and then orbs of light – all in less than half a second.

The combination of all three together was enough to completely obliterate the scorpion's claw as he yanked his axe out on his way by. While the light orbs hadn't proven to be quite as effective as he originally thought they might, given that the monsters were made from solidified shadow, they certainly did have *some* effect on a monster's body. Unfortunately, it was more of a poison than directly damaging them as the others did, but just because it didn't kill something right away didn't mean it had no uses.

And when combined with both ice and fire, its efficacy seemed to increase substantially for some reason. Even as he brought his axe around to cleave through the disgusting face of the scorpion, he could see that the light orbs from his first attack had spread from the claw and to the right half of the monster's body, seeming to rapidly disintegrate the shadowy substance as it progressed. It wasn't enough to finish it off before the head of his axe buried itself into the scorpion's eyes and mouth, followed by another triple activation of the *VEGS*, however. He was sure if he had given it more time, then he wouldn't have had to bother killing it a different way.

As he stopped himself from crashing into the large arachnid by planting his feet against its upper body, he kicked off backwards just in time to avoid being speared by the dying scorpion's stinger. Landing in a crouch, he stood back up just in time to swat at one of the flying lizards he'd seen earlier in the air, but he was just barely out of reach.

Thankfully, that didn't matter as much as he triple activated his *VEGS* again, which appeared right in the middle of the flying monster's torso, ripping it apart in a spray of gore as it plummeted to the floor in death, splashing Larek's face in the process.

Quickly wiping the dark blood from out of his eyes, he braced himself for his next victim.

# Chapter 60

The wind rushed by Larek as he flew backwards, his chest stinging from where the massive snake had swung its tail at him like a whip, taking advantage of the cooldown on his *Automatic Ice Repulsion Field* to get a hit in. After blocking the other snake's lunging bite with an application of his Pattern shield, he hadn't been expecting to be slammed into by a portion of yet another snake that was half the size of his own body, and he was paying for it now. Hitting the ground with an "oomph", he rolled a few times before struggling to his feet, the exhaustion he had already been feeling only amplified as he continued to fight and heal himself from multiple wounds over and over. Nothing had seriously injured him yet, but it was only a matter of time before that happened.

Throwing yet another *Weaken* stone at the last of the giant scorpions approaching from his left side, he was hit from behind as a set of sharp claws raked his back, and he barely reacted in time to direct his axe up above his head as the flying lizard continued past him. His activation of the *VEGS* was enough to cause the scaled monster to essentially explode from the inside, taking it out of the fight, but it felt like a drop in the bucket when compared to what he still had to face.

Jumping back into the fray before he ran completely out of physical energy, he chopped at the snake that had sent him flying, activating his *VEGS* yet again to take a chunk out of its side, which only became a worse wound as the monster twitched and sent more of its body to pass through the lingering spheres of elemental destruction. He threw himself backwards as a black tongue zipped past him as it attempted to wrap itself around his body; he tried to cut at the tongue as it was retracted back into the mouth of one of the large frogs, but he stumbled and missed.

**Dodge** *has reached Level 23!*

The Combat Fusionist ignored the notification as he swung at yet another snake, finally managing to cut into its upper portion, and with another activation of the *VEGS* Fusion, the destruction of the monster was secured as he essentially decapitated it. Of course, the snake decided to take revenge upon him for its demise as it twitched uncontrollably in its death throes, which ended up slamming into him, nearly crushing his leg, though he managed to roll with the blow and saved himself from gaining a nasty injury.

It still hurt, however, even if it was temporary.

Out of the corner of his eye, he noticed what had to be the last of the flying lizards swooping down on him, so he paused in the middle of combat and created a Pattern shield, which he stuck right in its path. Its diving attack couldn't be redirected in time, and it smashed fully into the impenetrable and immovable barrier with tremendous force; but even as it fell to the floor, Larek was already moving it to block a horse-ape's swinging punch from his other side. Letting the shield go as soon as it prevented the blow from landing, he swung his axe at the monster and cut through its right arm, activating the Fusion just a moment too late to have any extra effect.

He wasn't able to plant himself well enough to concentrate on another Pattern shield in time to stop the next punch by the horse-ape's other arm, though he did manage to twist his axe so that an activation of the *VEGS* Fusion occurred right in its face. While it got chewed up by the elemental sphere, it did nothing to prevent the hit, and he felt a rib crack as he was sent flying *yet again*. As he healed himself, further exhausting his body from the frequent use of the *Healing Surge* Fusion, he finally landed and struggled to get to his feet... only to feel an overwhelming sense of danger from directly behind him.

Without thinking, he threw himself forward, but even with his high Agility, it wasn't fast enough to avoid being clipped by the mouth of the enormous worm that had finally entered the battle, having taken the longest to arrive. He felt his ankle break as the edge of the worm's horrendously scary, tooth-filled maw impacted his leg as he threw himself forward, but he was already activating the *Healing Surge* as he landed in a sprawl from his attempted dodge. The sound of stones rattling along the floor alerted him that his belt pocket had still been open from where he had grabbed one of the *Weaken* stones earlier, and he watched as his last three rolled past him.

With his ankle just now snapping back into place and healing from the damage, he wasn't able to easily get back to his feet, but he suddenly didn't care about waiting for it to heal as he looked behind him. The worm, which had been slow to arrive, was displaying a significant amount of speed now that it was there, and it raised itself up slightly and bunched the muscles in its body backwards, looking like it was going to spring forward – right at Larek. Its gaping mouth was wide enough to swallow him 10 times over, and he needed to *move*.

Scrambling away from the attacking worm, he felt his left hand close over one of his *Weaken* stones and he absently gripped it. The next second, his ankle healed enough to push off of it and he sprang forward, seeing another stone just ahead – and his exhausted mind and body decided that they had a plan. *If I can throw these stones inside the worm, it'll explode from within!*

He managed to grab the second stone on the run before spotting the third, just under the paw of a large bear with the head and feathers of an owl. Flinging himself forward with a cry, he smashed his axe down on the face of the strange hybrid monster, getting a claw smacking against his recently injured ribs as a parting gift even as he activated the Fusion on his best friend. As the monster was torn apart, Larek refrained from healing the new damage as he was already starting to push past his limits, and he picked up the *Weaken* stone at his feet instead.

He whipped around just in time to fling and activate all three of the stones at the open maw of the worm as it sprung forward in an attack designed to swallow him up. Already preparing to dive far out of the way of the incoming behemoth, he was flung sideways as the stones suddenly exploded in mid-air, halfway to their destination. At only about 30 feet away, the detonation of not just one, but *three* of the *Weaken* stones should've injured him severely if not killed him outright, but he belatedly realized that the cooldown on his *AIRF* defense had finally ended, which had created something that had essentially encased him in ice blocks. The pressure from the explosion was so great that even his powerful defenses couldn't stop it completely, and he was pushed back with enough force to send him nearly a hundred feet away.

Rolling to his knees with a groan, he looked back to see what had possibly happened, and it took him a moment to get his bearings. Once he did, he could see that the worm hadn't wiggled away from the detonation unscathed, as it had been close enough to mangle half of its mouth and a significant portion of its upper body, but it was still technically alive as it struggled to find its way toward him. The blast had also killed a few of the nearby monsters, but the collateral damage was surprisingly small considering that three of the stones had exploded next to each other. *But how did they explode prematurely?*

The answer wasn't long in coming, as he looked further afield, only to see that the Drekkin and other random people who had been possessed were on the move. An arrow shot toward him that he saw at the last moment nearly hit him in the chest as he moved to the side, a necessary dodge because he was fairly certain that his defensive *Repulsion Field* was back on cooldown after blocking most of the explosion. The arrow had come from a Drekkin holding a black wood bow at over 300 feet away, an accurate shot by any estimation, and he suddenly realized that the possessed person had *shot his Fusion stones out of the air.*

He shook his head at the unbelievability of that thought, but it was the only thing that made sense.

Dismissing the unfortunate interception, he looked around to see that not only were the remaining dozen or so monsters heading toward him to finish him off, but the rest of the possessed people were getting close, as well. He decided to try to eliminate the threat that the people posed to him, as they could interfere with his elimination of the last few monsters. Besides, it was about time to free his companions from the forced slavery that had overcome their bodies.

Beginning to create another Pattern "sun", despite not being completely full of Pattern Cohesion as of yet, he only barely formed it before another arrow out of the corner of his eye made him flinch away from it as he dodged its annoyingly accurate trajectory. Thankfully, he had been able to reabsorb the Pattern he was using rather than losing it, so he started again and—

A barrage of *Icy Spikes* flew toward him from the crowd, and it was all he could do to abandon his project and dive out of the way. He was forced to use his Pattern Cohesion to make a large shield that blocked the constant stream of projectiles, even as it was joined by a *different* barrage of *Flaming Balls*.

*They're using Pyluxa and Hakkin's Fusions? I forgot that they steal all of their memories, and that includes knowing how to use all their Fusions! This is going to get a whole lot harder.*

He couldn't drop his shield because the constant stream of magical projectiles wouldn't relent, but if he didn't do something soon, the monsters that were already running toward his location would likely kill him. The same issue arose when he thought about killing the remaining monsters first, because then the possessed people would have free rein to attack him with impunity.

*If the Demons have the same knowledge as their hosts, then they know that I can't move while I'm maintaining anything involving my Pattern. That means that they planned this sudden interruption in my battle against the monsters, waiting until I'm nearly on my last legs and unable to defend myself from multiple enemies. I'm not sure I'm getting out of here alive.*

He briefly looked over his Pattern shield as he continued to maintain it, just in time to see an arrow descending from above, completely bypassing his defense. He shifted agonizingly slowly to try to avoid it and succeeded for the most part, but it still struck his upper arm rather than his chest; it was only stopped from going through his arm by the sleeve of his shirt with the *Multi-Resistance* Fusion on it, but it still hit forcefully enough that he felt the bone inside creak as if it was on the verge of cracking.

Thankfully, he was able to maintain his floating Pattern shield, but he wasn't sure how long that would last. The closest of the monsters were only about 50 feet away by this point, so he had to make a decision of what to do soon. Indecision weighed on him as he considered whether he wanted to be eaten by a monster or to be killed by Demon-possessed Drekkin, but the decision was made for him when an impossibly long frog tongue stretched nearly 75 feet to wrap around his right leg while he wasn't paying attention. All of a sudden, Larek found himself yanked off his knees as he was pulled away, losing the Pattern Cohesion that he had used to fuel the shield as it dissipated behind him. As he was dragged toward the mouth of the frog, he managed to swing his axe and cut off the long appendage just past his knee, but his momentum made him roll right under the legs of a horse-ape, where he narrowly missed being trampled. In his uncontrolled roll, his axe managed to cut through one of the legs that had nearly stomped on him, severely wounding the monster, but that small victory was short-lived as he struggled to his feet to find himself surrounded by all the monsters but the wounded worm, which was still trying to move toward his location.

Panting from the injuries that he hadn't had a chance – or the energy – to heal yet, he held his axe loosely in his hands as the monsters paused in their attack around him as if awaiting the final order to kill. Beyond them, where he could make them out between the hulking form of a bear and owl hybrid and a massive snake coiled into a mound, appearing ready to strike, he could see the possessed people running as a group. Within seconds, the Martials he sensed within the group would be close enough to attack him directly, which only gave him additional proof that his time was just about up.

As they were closer, he could see both Pyluxa and Hakkin, their shortswords aiming straight for him even through the monsters, as if daring him to try something. Near them, he also saw Gharix, Abarcen, and the other two Martials that had recently become a part of his group, their weapons at the ready to be used against him. Beyond them, he could finally see the Drekkin who had been releasing arrows at him, and there was another projectile at the ready on his bow that radiated danger. He was sure that the Drekkin archer could draw and release the arrow in less than a second, and the closer it came to his position, the less likely Larek would be able to dodge it.

Besides the people he knew, or had at least been attacked by, he saw hundreds of other Drekkin, most of them giving him the feel of a

Mage or a Martial even from a distance. Most of them didn't seem particularly powerful, though he had an inkling that there were a few that were relatively strong – though they couldn't compare to Gharix and the others because of their Fusions.

There were also dozens of other Drekkin that appeared to be "normal", as in they didn't have the feel of having changed into a Martial or a Mage recently. Despite that, they all held weapons in their hands, from rusty-looking swords to steel-tipped spears; while they undoubtedly couldn't stand up to any decent Martial, their expressions showed that they were ready and willing to use them even if it killed them. As far as he knew, that was exactly what would happen if they were to assault someplace such as Draverdin – but he also didn't think that would bother them so much, as that would just free the Demon inhabiting their bodies to possess someone else.

Past them, behind the Drekkin that were the most prevalent, he saw about a dozen people he identified as coming from the Empire, a few from other lands that he knew about but couldn't match their appearance to their origin, and there were even a few people that looked so like the people from the Kingdom that they couldn't be from anywhere else. A Martial and a Mage, in fact, based on their armor and clothing, as well as the large shield and sword the woman was carrying and the staff the man held in his hands. Neither of them were familiar, of course, as the SIC was large and there were tens of thousands of members that he'd never met nor even heard of before, but just seeing them only seemed to increase his desire to return home.

*Not that I'm going to have much chance of that now, considering how close I am to dying here.*

He nearly dismissed all the possessed people as being of a secondary concern, believing the monsters surrounding him to be the bigger threat, given that they were closer and would be difficult to kill, considering that both his offense and defense were both limited for the moment. However, before he could completely put them out of his mind, something in the crowd of people caught his attention like an eagle spotting a small rodent on the ground, and he found that he couldn't look away. His first assumption of what he thought it might be was confirmed a few seconds later as he got a better look, and Larek felt his exhaustion completely melt away as it was replaced by an overwhelming anger that he couldn't prevent from taking over his mind and body, even if he wanted to – and in this case, he certainly didn't want to.

Feeling something familiar-yet-foreign stirring in his chest, Larek immediately recognized that it was his Stama reacting to his emotions, readying itself to be unleashed in a display of destructive force. The Combat Fusionist forced every shred of his consciousness that hadn't been swept away in absolute *rage* to try and influence the Stama now boiling through his entire body. It was about to blow, but he couldn't just allow himself to lose *complete* control, as he wasn't sure it would be conducive to staying alive. Instead, he managed to wrestle the tiniest portion of his leaking Stama toward his head, hoping that it would help to keep him just slightly more aware of what he was doing if his mind was connected to the volatile force that was about to take control.

It was a long shot, of course, but it turned out that miracles certainly did happen.

**Stama Subjugation** has reached Level 2!

New Battle Art Learned!
**Tactician Mind**
Effect: Boosts perception and awareness while in battle, applying 50% of Agility stat toward Intellect and Acuity
Duration: 60 seconds
Base Stama Cost: 800

More of his Stama was sucked up into his mind as a result of activating this brand-new Battle Art, just before he lost complete control of his body when the rest of his Stama seemed to take on a life of its own.

# Chapter 61

Unfortunately, as much as Larek wanted to have some sort of control over his body, *Tactician Mind* apparently only gave him a miniscule amount of influence over it. As soon as *Furious Rampage* and *Consuming Speed* activated, he found himself much stronger and moving at three times the speed he normally moved as his Agility was tripled, but this also aided in increasing his Intellect and Acuity, working together to allow his enraged self a clarity that he didn't have before when he'd lost control of his actions like this.

The increased perception and awareness due to his new Battle Art helped him to determine the ideal way to accomplish his goal, which at the moment was to break out of the monster encirclement. With blinding speed, he moved toward the massive, coiled snake, which began to move as soon as he took a step. While it normally struck so quickly that it was a blur to anyone else watching, the way it moved its fanged jaws toward where he *used* to be made it appear to be moving in slow motion. It didn't take long before Larek was close enough to jump, using his boosted Strength, and then cleanly chop off the snake's head with the aid of a single *VEGS* activation.

Even before the head was completely separated from its body, Larek twisted in mid-air to land feet first against its upraised neck, using it as a springboard to move toward the next monster in line, a heavily damaged giant scorpion that had taken the brunt of one of his *Weaken* stones' explosions but managed to keep one of its claws intact. He quickly landed on its back and chopped down, releasing another *VEGS* in the process of slicing through its upper back and causing its already-mangled face to explode from the inside. He crouched and then sprang off toward the next monster just in time to avoid the tail and stinger intending to stab him in the back that were already in motion.

Moving from one to another, he was so quick that none of them had a chance to even react more than moving a few feet one way or another by the time he arrived to absolutely demolish whatever defenses they had. Finishing off the last of them, one of the long-tongued frogs, he ran away and looked toward the possessed people, only to find that at some point, the massive worm had worked its way in between them and his current position.

The rage was still fueling his actions, and while his mind had been able to influence his body's angle and method of attack against the other monsters to make better use of positioning and momentum, his mind could do absolutely nothing to dissuade his body from tearing through the worm to get to its goal rather than jump over or run around it, which he would've been more than capable of at that point. Instead, he rushed forward and swung his axe into the side of the worm, biting deep, before releasing a trio of *VEGS* spheres, intending to start cutting his way through to get to the possessed people on the other side.

On the third activation of the powerful Fusion, the little portion of Larek's mind that was able to process the ever-changing information of the battlefield noticed something worrying. As his body automatically began to withdraw the axe to strike again, his *Tactical Mind* screamed at him, startling his reflexes so much that he ended up letting the handle of the axe go as he stumbled backwards. The reason for the scream came a split-second later as one of the concerns over Fusion misuse and stress on the *VEGS* formation was revealed, when his mind detected that the formation had cracked and was in the process of leaking Mana.

Despite the furious rage flowing through almost every fiber of his being, his instincts kicked in as he immediately turned around and fled, using all the Agility he could squeeze out of his body to run away. His muscles were screaming as he pushed them to the edge of what they could handle, but even his frantic run was just barely enough to escape being blown to bits as the Fusion on his best friend fractured completely, releasing all the Mana inside in a massive detonation that shattered the other Fusion on the tool, igniting a chain reaction that expanded outward with such intensity that Larek was lifted off his feet and sent flying – a common occurrence over the last few minutes.

As he tumbled through the air, unable to stop himself, the enraged Combat Fusionist was both extremely satisfied and absolutely devastated to look back and see the enormous worm being completely obliterated. The explosion was so great that it ended up bowling over every possessed person with the shockwave, though they were saved from the worst of the damage due to the detonation happening inside the worm.

Even as he landed from where he had been flung, the knowledge that his best friend, the same axe that he had acquired back in the Kingdom in Barrowford, had been irretrievably destroyed in the explosion ignited the rage to a whole new level. His *Tactician Mind* was barely able to hold onto what little control it had as his body ignored the numerous injuries that he'd sustained from the explosion, as it ran and limped toward the fallen possessed people, intending to kill them all with his bare hands if possible.

His plans were foiled when *Consuming Speed* wore off, dropping his Agility back down to normal levels, causing him to stumble and fall flat on his face from the abrupt change in his situation. The loss of speed also brought with it an overwhelming exhaustion as all the abuse his body had been put through hit him all at once, and it was all he could do to prevent himself from falling into unconsciousness.

As he dragged himself back to his feet, the anger still raging through every part of his existence, he noticed that the possessed ones were already up and looking straight at him. Before they could begin to attack him utilizing the very Fusions he had created for his companions to use, he began to create a Pattern sun to tear through the shadowy bodies inside their hosts.

However, Larek stopped before he had even begun as his *Tactician Mind* immediately identified a problem.

He didn't have enough Pattern Cohesion to create and keep the sun going. His Battle Arts, namely *Furious Rampage* and *Consuming Speed*, had drained his Body stat by 30% and 60% respectively, which was directly connected to his Pneuma. As a result, he had lost 90% of his Pattern Cohesion, and while it had gained 60% of the maximum back when *Consuming Speed* ended, it didn't replace what had been lost. It was currently regenerating, but he barely had a little over 3,600 Pattern Cohesion at the moment.

With a growl, his body got to its feet to enact its plan of ripping everyone apart, but his mind had other plans. Tapping into the desire to kill the Umbral Demons, he leveraged this desire into a new manipulation of his Pattern. Instead of a huge sun that sent his Demon-destroying soul *everywhere*, he realized he only needed it to go in a certain direction – right toward the possessed people ahead of him. With a thought on the form he wanted, 500 small icicle-like objects appeared in front of him, glowing with the same energy he saw in his Pattern shield and the sun. The use of almost all his Pattern Cohesion nearly made him collapse into unconsciousness yet again, but he managed to hold on by falling back to his knees, his vision going double as exhaustion dragged him down.

*I'm only going to get one shot at this....*

As the shortswords held by Pyluxa and Hakkin raised up to start filling him full of magical elemental projectiles, Larek infused the 500 floating icicles around him with the function he wanted them perform, and they shot off toward the upright possessed people so quickly that they were barely visible. They traveled in a flattened cone-like pattern, passing through each and every single one of them without any resistance; once they entered the bodies, they stopped... and then detonated in a shower of shadow-destroying light, shredding the Umbral Demons inside.

*Pattern Manipulation has reached Level 30!*

*You have reached Level 32 and have 23 available AP to distribute!*

*Congratulations—*

    Larek dismissed the rest of the notification as the unearthly sounds of every single Demon possessing the bodies screamed in pain as they were essentially erased from existence; it was enough to snap Larek out of the all-consuming anger that had overwhelmed him, while at the same time deactivating his *Furious Rampage*, making Larek feel weak as he slumped in place. Somehow, he managed to grasp at the fading edges of his consciousness as his body wanted to give up and either die or pass out, and he lifted his head as he heard the last of the Demon screams fade away as they, too, left the world.
    *\*CRACK\**
    The Combat Fusionist would've whipped his head up at the sound if he had been able to move that quickly, but the best he could do was turn slowly toward the Aperture in the distance as it began to make noise.
    *\*CRACK\* \*CRACK\**
    The entire cavern began to brighten as the shadowy energy that had seemed to envelop the massive Aperture unfurled from the portal to another world, dissipating like smoke as it released its grip. At the same time, enormous cracks ran through its surface like it was made of glass; it took his exhausted mind a few seconds to realize it was because the Aperture was beginning to expand, swelling in size until its normal exterior couldn't hold it all in. More and more cracks occurred around the Aperture, reverberating through the cavern with sharp reports, and all Larek could do was watch. He was distantly aware that he was probably in danger, as it seemed as though it was just about to explode, and after suffering from or causing quite a few explosions himself that day, he knew that if it had that same kind of energy released upon detonation, he wasn't going to survive. In fact, if its physical size was any indication of the size of the explosion, then it was possible that half the underworld tunnels under the desert would collapse. There was no running from it, and he had absolutely nothing left to give to try and prevent it from happening.
    If it was going to kill him, then there was nothing he could do.
    Growing larger and larger, straining at the invisible bonds that kept it all in one piece, the Aperture expanded until it was half again as

large as it started. Larek expected every moment to be his last, so when it finally happened with the sound of a million glass panes breaking simultaneously, he wasn't surprised.

What *was* surprising was that the expected explosion didn't kill him, nor did it seem to harm anything in the cavern. Instead, what was released wasn't the destructive energies he was used to in a *Weaken* stone detonation, but simply an explosion of bound Apertures finally released from their bondage. Just as the people possessed by the Umbral Demons had no choice over their enslavement, neither did the hundreds of Apertures that had originally been found around the underground world of the Lowenthal desert. When what was keeping them there had been broken, they exploded outward in a riot of different colors as they shot by him and out of the cavern, passing through the solid stone as if it wasn't there. It was as if they had been pulled toward this central Aperture originally by the Demons, but now that their influence was gone, they were snapping back to their original locations.

Best of all, they were all small enough that he was almost positive that they were all in their "closed" state – including the only remaining Aperture in the cavern, which was extremely small and therefore only gave off a little light in the otherwise completely dark space.

Breathing heavily with a shaky breath, Larek closed his eyes and started to drift away, the knowledge of having accomplished his goal relaxing him enough that consciousness just seemed like an unnecessary chore more than anything. However, the acute despair that pierced his mind at what that successful accomplishment had cost him woke him back up. *My... axe.... My best friend is gone.... Gharix... Abarcen... Pyluxa... all the others—*

At the thought of all the possessed people, his eyes flew open and he groaned as he began to move. Picking himself off the floor to get to his feet was too much for his body at the moment, so he was forced to essentially crawl toward the fallen and alarmingly still people who recently had their Demons exorcised so completely. He could barely even see them, because the glow that had lit the area had disappeared along with the massive Aperture; but he fortunately found one of his *Adjustable Illumination* stones approximately 50 feet away from his position, so once he had it in his possession, he used it to see where he was going.

When he finally arrived at the edge of the crowd, he spotted Gharix first, his dual knives seemingly unharmed by everything that had happened, and the Fusions on his armor appeared undamaged. As for the Drekkin himself, he appeared to be breathing, which was a very good sign, though the fact that neither he nor anyone else had woken up was a great concern. He didn't stop on his crawl as he passed by the group leader, next seeing the familiar faces of Abarcen and the other Martials, as well as the two Mages, Pyluxa and Hakkin. He also crawled around the Drekkin who was holding the bow that had nearly killed him multiple times, but he ignored them almost completely; he had a different goal and didn't want to be distracted.

    Dozens of others he managed to crawl by, though there were a few of them he had to crawl *over* to get to where he was heading. Like a ray of sunshine peeking out from behind the clouds, he was finally greeted by the sight that had sent him into a fury in the first place. The sprawled figure wasn't moving, just like all of the other fallen former possessed people he'd passed by, but that only worried him more.

    Dragging himself the rest of the distance to his destination, Larek knelt by the figure's side, before slipping his arm gently under their head, lifting them up so he could get a better look. Other than a few scratches on the face, which were minor and not that concerning to him, there didn't seem to be anything *physically* wrong with them. A gentle shake received no response at all, so it didn't appear as if they – and everyone else – were simply asleep.

    Instead, he was worried that the minds and souls of everyone here had been so irreparably damaged that they simply... didn't exist anymore. He wasn't planning on giving up, however, as his own experience with a Demon trying to take over his body and the information he gained from it led him to believe that neither the mind nor the body was destroyed – it was simply locked away. Now, he just had to figure out how to unlock whatever was keeping them locked up and free their minds and souls so that they could reestablish a connection with their bodies.

    Delicately taking a bit of his Pattern, which had regenerated to just over 250 by this point, he formed it into an insubstantial net and ran it through the small body he was holding in his hands, trying to see if there was any remnant of the Umbral Demon left behind. He figured that if it was some sort of shadow ability, similar to how the monsters had been reformed into solidified shadows, then his Pattern might be able to detect it or possibly even disrupt it. However, a thorough investigation with his Pattern revealed absolutely nothing wrong, no lingering actions by the Umbral Demon being evident no matter where he looked.

    Quickly trying everything he could think of to discover a means of waking the formerly possessed person up with their mind and soul intact, Larek was growing desperate. "No, no, no! This can't be happening!" he cried, clutching the small body to his chest as he rocked back and forth, unbidden tears tracking down his cheeks.

After a few minutes of wallowing in despair, an idea occurred to him of something he could try, but he almost immediately dismissed it. Not just because he had already told himself that he wouldn't try and use it again, but because its use was completely unreliable and he didn't know precisely how to activate it. Looking back down at the slack face in his arms, the practically empty shell of a person that would likely die for real if he didn't do anything, his resolve crumbled in the face of possibility.

With a deep breath to settle his nerves, he cradled the head of the woman in the crook of his right arm, the reddish-gold hair splayed out over his sleeve and the bare skin of his forearm. The next moment, he bent his head down to her ear and spoke, directing every iota of feeling and instruction into the words.

"Wake up, Nedira. Your body and mind are yours again; you just have to reach out and take them back."

There was a power completely unrelated to his Mana or Stama that seemed to flow out of his throat when he spoke, and he could almost see it settle upon the delicate woman's head like a sprinkling of summer rain. The Dominion magic disappeared into her skin, absorbed into her body, and at first nothing happened, leading Larek further into despair.

Just when he had given up hope, he felt a stir along his leg as her hand twitched slightly, rubbing against his knee, and a moment later Nedira's eyes fluttered open, staring up at the darkness above them before settling on his own eyes.

Smiling dreamily, the woman stared at him lethargically before her eyes opened wide in surprise. "Who—Larek?" she suddenly asked, as if she was just now realizing that she knew his name. "What are you doing here?"

He smiled down at her, completely overwhelmed with joy that she not only had recovered, but she also seemed to remember him as well.

"I was just about to ask you the same thing."

# Epilogue

Barrisha looked out over the castle wall, despair gripping her entire being as she looked at the monsters assembling outside of Draverdin's defenses. While the sight of monsters was a normal occurrence, especially over the last few weeks, it was the high *number* of monsters she saw that concerned her.

Just as it concerned everyone else along the wall.

"We're all going to die, aren't we?" Marfo asked from her side, his shortsword clasped tightly in his hands. Not that he'd be using it right away as a Mage, but she'd found since they'd undergone the change that her nestmate felt comfort in holding the weapon despite never having to use it in a fight. His spells were much more lethal, after all, though she supposed that any bit of comfort he could find was important to keep him from simply jumping off the walls inside the city and hiding.

Which was what Barrisha had to actively prevent herself from doing at least once every minute.

"N-No, we'll be just fine, Marfo," she stuttered out, the fear and despair gripping her for a moment before she got ahold of herself. Nervously adjusting the battleaxe in her hands, she glanced down the line of defenders along the wall, only to see that all of them appeared just as nervous as she did – which wasn't exactly the best sign, considering that many of them were stronger than she or Marfo were. Unfortunately, she was fairly certain that Marfo was correct and they were going to die, but she couldn't give in like that. Her fallen nestmates wouldn't ever let her live it down if she didn't give it her all at the end.

"But, Barr, you heard just as I did that—"

"I know what we heard," she said quickly, cutting him off before any of the others along the wall heard him. It wasn't exactly a secret, of course, but not everyone had overheard the scouting reports over the last day like she and her nestmate had, and now wasn't the time to spread the word to the defenders, sapping morale even further.

Thankfully, he snapped his jaws closed after her silent reprimand, not saying another word. It wouldn't be good for anyone to share that the scouts had noticed an increase in monster migration through the tunnels connecting to Draverdin over the last 24 hours. That alone wouldn't have been that big of a deal, as they'd been repelling monster attacks for weeks at that point, but this was different. All the other assaults had come from the main tunnel that connected to where they thought the Aperture that was causing all these problems was located, as they moved from the mysterious portal toward the city in a constant stream.

The other tunnels leading to Draverdin from different directions had been cut off because they still had small cities defending the passages, but they hadn't heard anything from them in days, if not weeks. As a result, those tunnels were undefended, as those remaining in Draverdin didn't have enough Martials and Mages to send out to secure them because of the constant attacks that hadn't let up.

In other words, the scouts reported that the inevitable usage of those tunnels had come, and the city was being assaulted from 6 different directions. As a result, the city's defenders, including Barrisha and her nestmate, were spread incredibly thin over the walls. And as if they had a plan of their own, instead of mindlessly throwing themselves against the walls as soon as they were in sight like they normally did, the monsters were amassing like giant armies of death, just waiting until their numbers swelled to the point where they would wash over the defenders on the walls like an unstoppable wave of destruction.

*No, I can't think like that. We **will** push them back because we **have to**.*

Sadly, the internal pep talk didn't really do much for her state of mind, as the despair continued to mount as more and more monsters arrived and their numbers ballooned to the point where the tunnel entrance was barely visible. The veritable wall of monsters was so thick in places that they seemed to be standing on top of each other in order to fit.

The worst part of it all was the silence. As many monsters as there were, they were almost entirely silent as they assembled themselves, and once they were in place they froze like they were statues – deadly, blood-thirsty statues. It was these last two elements of the monster army assembled in front of them that got to her the most, as the eerie feeling of being stared at by thousands of murderous eyes made her itch under her scales like they were looking at her very soul. Given that the monsters were reportedly controlled by the Umbral Demons and their shadow-touched, she wouldn't be surprised if this was the case.

Marfo stepped up to her and suddenly whispered, *"Should we try to run?"*

Even though she was slightly shocked at the question, she couldn't help but want to say yes. Knowing the futility of that idea, she responded with, *"Where would we even go? There's no place safe now."*

"Yes, but—"

Marfo cut his own words off as the monsters began to move, some silent command causing them to move as a comprehensive group. "Too late," she said to her nestmate, before she walked up to the edge of the wall, her heart beating so strongly in her chest that it felt like it was going to rip itself out.

Out of the corner of her eye, she watched as the other Martials also stepped up, knowing that they would be the first layer of defense once the monsters reached the walls and began to climb or fly, to swoop down on them from above. There was no running, no searching for another solution to the defense of Draverdin, and no more futile attempts to close the Aperture where these monsters came from; it was all down to what they would do here, this day, and if they succeeded, their entire people would live another day.

If not, they would likely be wiped out to the last man, woman, and nestling.

When they were halfway to the walls, the first magical spells and projectiles shot out, killing dozens of monsters in the process; they were so tightly packed together that it was virtually impossible to miss them, but that didn't seem to bother the invading horde. The losses vanished entirely over the next few seconds as holes in the assault wave were filled by monsters from behind, making the defenders' efforts to slow them down nearly futile.

That didn't mean that Marfo and the others with long-range attacks weren't going to try.

Volley after volley of spells and mundane projectiles enhanced by specific Battle Arts slammed into the incoming monsters, downing hundreds as they gave everything they could to their defense. Even when over a thousand monsters had perished under their assault, it was a bare drop in the bucket compared to what seemed like an endless wave of darkness given form.

"I'm out! I need to regenerate my Mana!" Marfo shouted from just behind her, which was repeated more than a few times by the others on the walls. Among those she knew were a higher Level, their Mana lasted longer, but when more than half of the Mages had run out of Mana after casting 10 to 15 spells, their efficacy was almost nil even when they managed to hit one monster after another without any possibility of missing.

It was just... too much. They couldn't survive something like this. No one could.

And this same thing was most likely happening all over the walls, from multiple different directions if she heard the sounds of spells and even the clash of battle from elsewhere along the city's perimeter correctly. Everyone was preparing to give their lives for the chance that the innocent civilians inside would have a chance to survive, and Barrisha knew that she would do her duty to the end. She wouldn't have run even if there was some place for them to go, as that just wasn't her; as much as Marfo sounded like he would run at the first opportunity, she knew that he was just the same.

It was time to put up one last defense and hope that trading their lives in defense of those inside the city was enough to turn the tide.

As the first of the monsters to reach the wall *leaped* from the stone floor with its extremely strong legs, she cursed the fact that the wall wasn't nearly as tall as it should've been. The rabbit-like monster easily cleared the top as it sprung toward Marfo, but Barrisha intercepted it with a swing of her axe, bisecting it cleanly with her significant Strength stat. The two halves fell to the top of the wall floor, and she immediately turned back to see another three dozen monsters leaping, diving, or even climbing the outer wall through the use of sticky appendages or simply digging into the stone for handholds.

Swiping through a black bird with a beak filled with dark fangs, she became unbalanced when a second one slammed into her from the side, though it was more like a shove rather than injuring her. Still, getting her feet underneath her, she swung wildly at another monster that was hurtling through the air at her...

...only for it to suddenly become nearly transparent in the middle of its leap. Before her axe could pass through it, the monster dissipated like they normally did when they were killed, evaporating into a dark-green and black smoke. Thinking that someone had destroyed it before she could attack and it disappeared quicker than normal, she managed to correct herself from her wild swing and looked for another monster to kill.

But when she looked around, all she saw were more monsters fading away into smoke before disappearing altogether. All along the wall, the same could be seen happening, and when she looked out at the seemingly endless horde that was getting ready to kill them all, what she saw shocked her.

It was almost entirely empty. The remnants of the smoke that came from the monsters' destruction dissipated over the next few seconds, until it was completely clear of any evidence that they existed in the first place.

Silence reigned over the wall as everyone attempted to process what had happened, as well as the fact that they were somehow still alive. This lasted for all of 10 seconds before someone shouted, "The Aperture... it's closed!"

Sure enough, when Barrisha tried to feel for the Aperture that had been a constant pressure upon her senses, it was nowhere to be found. What she *did* detect were three little pinpoints of pressure in different, yet definite, directions; she was reminded of when the Apertures first arrived and she could feel them and their general direction even from the inside of Draverdin. She couldn't be sure, but the locations in which she felt these new little pinpricks seemed to coincide with where she felt them what seemed like ages ago.

"Somebody closed the Aperture?" Marfo asked from her side, and she looked over to see him wide-eyed with his mouth open wide in amazement.

"I... guess so," she said, before celebratory shouts erupted all over the walls, the pent-up stress giving them a voice that echoed loudly through the massive cavern fit to shake the walls down. With a relieved smile, she joined in a moment later, along with her nestmate a split-second after she did.

*Whoever just closed the Aperture saved us. I wonder who it was?*

In the end, it didn't really matter. In the coming days, they would probably end up learning what this meant, especially when it came to their mortal enemies, the Umbral Demons, but for now, all Barrisha could process was the fact that she was alive to see another day.

\* \* \*

"Wake up, Gharix. Your body and mind are yours again; you just have to reach out and take them back."

The words reverberated in his head even though it had been hours since he'd heard them, and it only solidified the fact that he was now back in control of his body, his mind, and his soul – something he had thought was lost forever. He looked over at the powerful, yet strangely gentle, giant as he lifted the head of yet another former shadow-touched and brought them back to themselves with a few simple words.

Somehow, the miraculousness of the situation didn't seem to faze Larek, despite the fact that it was common knowledge that once someone was shadow-touched, their minds and souls were expected to be completely destroyed and replaced by a Demon. When he asked the giant about it, he was told that they weren't actually destroyed, just locked away with no hope of escape. Then he shrugged when Gharix asked him how it was possible that just a few simple words from him had been enough to unlock the cage their mind and soul were trapped inside.

When he wouldn't explain more about it, Gharix gave up asking and told the others to forget about it as well. Even though it was quickly revealed that no one else could simply speak and wake one of the shadow-touched, every one of them that had been revived had thought it better to simply count their blessings that they were alive and out of the nightmare in which they'd wound up due to the Umbral Demons.

Who were, apparently, completely wiped out – at least according to Larek. He wasn't sure if this was 100% accurate, but given the fact that the massive Aperture had not only closed, but had broken apart into hundreds of different Apertures that all returned to where they had been pulled from originally, he wasn't going to refute the explanation. Besides, the last thing he wanted to do now was to chase down any Demons that might be lingering around the underground tunnels; if he never saw or heard about another one in his life, he would be extremely grateful.

Physically shivering as he remembered what had happened to him, he was glad that he had been knocked unconscious during the process of becoming shadow-touched. While the memory of being overrun and knocked out was bad enough, remembering finally regaining consciousness only to find himself completely locked out of his body was somehow worse than death. He had only a rudimentary perception of what his body was doing after he lost control of it, and even the memories of his actions and the world around him were fading in the few hours since he had regained control.

He remembered the massive Aperture and how it was a conglomeration of many different Apertures that had been tainted by the shadowy abilities of the Demons, but how it got that way, or how it had been broken up, were not something he knew. Larek had mentioned that, when he had fought off the first Demon that had attacked him, he'd connected with its mind and had much of the knowledge the Demon possessed, but either it hadn't happened to Gharix the same way because he had been unconscious at the time, or it just didn't transfer over when he'd had to be revived. Regardless, most of what he did remember about the ordeal he was happy to let fade away over time, because most of it was simply too horrific to recall.

The only bright spot was that none of his nestmates had perished through all that they had been through, as Larek was able to bring them back. It was a slow process, however, as whatever secret way the giant possessed to wake them up was something that needed to be used slowly, or else he would, "Pass out from overuse," according to his own words. Still, within the first few hours, more than 40 of them had been brought back, though they were eventually coming to the point where it might be possible that no more would be revived.

Why? Because apparently Larek needed a name to go with a person, or else his words wouldn't connect properly with them. So far, they had been able to identify more than half of those who had been shadow-touched, but there were some that no one awake recognized. It was possible that once the rest were revived, those people might be able to identify the others, but it was also likely that they couldn't. If that was the case, they might end up dying from the fact that there was no consciousness in charge of their bodies, which would be a tragedy after having been saved from the Demons.

Unfortunately, there were also a handful of missing shadow-touched that had disappeared as soon as the Demons' influence had been removed. These were the ones that were possessed by the Umbral Demons the longest, and their bodies had turned to shadow similar to the monsters that they had slain on their way there; when the Demons were no longer controlling them, they simply dissipated into nothing as there wasn't anything holding them together anymore. Fortunately, it was a small number of those that had disappeared compared to those who were still in one piece.

Sitting with his nestmates, he smiled as Larek was successful in awakening yet another formerly shadow-touched Drekkin, someone that Pyluxa knew from a long time ago. As the newly awakened Martial was quickly taken away by some of the others to answer questions as best as they could, Larek seemed to slump in place, exhaustion wearing him down. After a brief recitation of what occurred after Gharix and his group were taken by the Demons, he could well understand why he was so tired.

*He probably could have done this all without us,* he thought, before mentally shaking his head. Seeing how exhausted he was, Gharix knew there was no way the giant would've been able to get to the point where he could kill all the Demons without their help; he would've fallen before the might of the monster hordes, despite his power.

In the end, even if Gharix and his nestmates had perished, their deaths would've been worth it after Larek accomplished what he did. Their people now had a chance to live, to fight back and take control of closing the Apertures that had returned to where they were before.

Wherever he had come from, and for whatever reason he claimed to be traveling through the desert above, the group leader could only be thankful that he had been there. They should *all* be thankful that he had come to save them, even though he was fairly certain that the giant didn't see it that way. From what he understood about the man, Larek had simply wanted revenge for what the Demons had attempted to do to him; even if it had ended up saving every Drekkin and freeing the shadow-touched from their possession, as well as returning the Apertures back to normal, it was just side effects of getting that revenge.

And now here he was, exhausted to the point where he could barely stand up without help, selflessly using whatever energy he had left to impossibly awaken people who should've been lost forever.

He was *a hero*. A strange one, that much was obvious, but a hero, nonetheless.

Gharix knew that Larek's help with getting his people back on their feet after everything that had happened would be invaluable, as even though the Apertures were back where they had started and were currently closed, his people weren't out of danger. However, he also knew that the man was planning on leaving as soon as possible, as he apparently had his own people to help save back in his own lands.

Sighing that such a powerful being with the ability to help them was leaving soon, but knowing that there was no way to stop him from departing, Gharix just hoped that the Kingdom of Androthe appreciated Larek the way that he, and the rest of the Drekkin, now did. He thought that was entirely possible, especially with the way the woman with the reddish-gold hair seemed to follow him around, as if he was someone important to the Kingdom.

*They must revere him like royalty there*, Gharix couldn't help thinking, a little jealous that another land would have access to his power and abilities. *They're lucky to have someone as selfless and remarkable as Larek looking out for them.*

*I bet they throw him a celebration when he returns.*

### The End

# Final Stats

Larek Holsten

Combat Fusionist
Healer
Patternal
Level 32
Advancement Points (AP): 2/24
Available AP to Distribute: 23
Available Aetheric Force (AF): 65,947

Stama: 2000/2000
Mana: 3680/3680

Strength: 100 [200] (+)
Body: 100 [200] (+)
Agility: 100 [200] (+)
Intellect: 184 [368] (+)
Acuity: 140 [280] (+)
Pneuma: 1,800 [3,600]
Pattern Cohesion: 36,000/36,000

**Mage Abilities:**
Spell – Bark Skin
Spell – Binding Roots
Spell – Fireball
Spell – Furrow
Spell – Ice Spike
Spell – Lesser Restoration
Spell – Light Bending
Spell – Light Orb
Spell – Localized Anesthesia
Spell – Minor Mending
Spell – Rapid Plant Growth
Spell – Repelling Gust
Spell – Static Illusion
Spell – Stone Fist
Spell – Wall of Thorns
Spell – Water Jet
Spell – Wind Barrier

- Fusion – Acuity Boost
- Fusion – Adjustable Illumination +8
- Fusion – Adjustable Illumination +10
- Fusion – Agility Boost
- Fusion – Area Chill
- Fusion – Automatic Ice Repulsion Field +8
- Fusion – Automatic Strong Temperature Adjustment +10
- Fusion – Binding Thorns +1
- Fusion – Binding Thorns +10
- Fusion – Body Boost
- Fusion – Camouflage Sphere
- Fusion – Directional Illumination +7
- Fusion – Directional Illumination +8
- Fusion – Extreme Heat
- Fusion – Flaming Ball
- Fusion – Flying Stone
- Fusion – Frozen Zone +1
- Fusion – Frozen Zone +10
- Fusion – Graduated Illumination Strong
- Fusion – Graduated Parahealing
- Fusion – Healing Shelter +1
- Fusion – Healing Shelter +8
- Fusion – Healing Surge
- Fusion – Icy Spike
- Fusion – Illuminate
- Fusion – Illusionary Image
- Fusion – Intellect Boost
- Fusion – Intellect and Acuity Boost
- Fusion – Left Gust of Air +4
- Fusion – Left Gust of Air +7
- Fusion – Mage Skill Hexa-Boost +10
- Fusion – Mage Stat Boost Suite +10
- Fusion – Martial Skill Hexa-Boost +10
- Fusion – Martial Stat Boost Suite +10
- Fusion – Muffle Sound
- Fusion – Muffling Air Deflection Barrier
- Fusion – Multi-Resistance
- Fusion – Multi-Thruster +6
- Fusion – Omni Boost +10
- Fusion – Paralytic Light
- Fusion – Paralytic Touch
- Fusion – Perceptive Misdirection +1

Fusion – Personal Air Deflection Barrier
Fusion – Pneuma Boost
Fusion – Red and White Illuminate
Fusion – Repelling Barrier
Fusion – Repelling Gust of Air
Fusion – Right Gust of Air +4
Fusion – Right Gust of Air +7
Fusion – Secure Hideaway +10
Fusion – Sharpen Edge
Fusion – Space Heater
Fusion – Spellcasting Focus Boost
Fusion – Stone Shredder Dome +1
Fusion – Stone Shredder Dome +6
Fusion – Strength Boost
Fusion – Strength and Body Boost
Fusion – Strengthen and Sharpen Edge
Fusion – Strengthen
Fusion – Strengthen Area +1
Fusion – Strengthen Area +10
Fusion – Temperature Regulator
Fusion – Tree Skin
Fusion – Variable Elemental Gust Sphere +7
Fusion – Variable Repeating Elemental Projectile +8
Fusion – Water Stream
Fusion – Weaken +10

**Martial Abilities:**
Battle Art – Furious Rampage
Battle Art – Consuming Speed
Battle Art – Tactician Mind

**Mage Skills:**
Pattern Manipulation Level 30/40 (400 AF)
Pattern Recognition Level 37[40]/40 (400 AF)
Magical Detection Level 36[40]/40 (400 AF)
Spellcasting Focus Level 36[40]/40 (400 AF)
Multi-effect Fusion Focus Level 44/45 (450 AF)
Focused Division Level 49/50 (500 AF)
Mana Control Level 53[55]/55 (550 AF)
Fusion Level 54[55]/55 (550 AF)
Pattern Formation Level 54[55]/55 (550 AF)

**Martial Skills:**
Blunt Weapon Expertise Level 1/20 (200 AF)
Stama Subjugation Level 2/20 (200 AF)
Bladed Weapon Expertise Level 2[12]/20 (200 AF)
Unarmed Fighting Level 3[13]/20 (200 AF)
Throwing Level 18[20]/20 (200 AF)
Dodge Level 23[30]/30 (300 AF)
Pain Immunity Level 20/20 (N/A)
Body Regeneration Level 36[40]/40 (400 AF)

**General Skills:**
Cooking Level 8
Bargaining Level 9
Beast Control Level 9
Leadership Level 13
Writing Level 11
Saw Handling Level 15
Reading Level 17
Speaking Level 19
Long-Distance Running Level 20
Listening Level 43
Axe Handling Level 92

# Author's Note

Thank you for reading Global DifFusion!

I want to thank all of my readers for the absolutely awesome response that this series has received, and I'm more excited to write more of this story than just about any other work I've done to date! I'm excited for when Larek gets back to the Kingdom!

There is a lot more of Larek's story to tell, so if you want to read more, you can visit the series page on Royal Road under **The Fusionist**, or subscribe to my [Patreon](#) and read advance chapters for as little as $2 a month!

Again, thank you for reading, and I implore you to consider leaving a review – I love 5-star ones! Reviews make it more likely that others will pick up a good book and read it!

If you enjoy dungeon core, dungeon corps, dungeon master, dungeon lord, dungeonlit, or any other type of dungeon-themed stories and content, check out the Dungeon Corps Facebook group, where you can find all sorts of dungeon content.

If you would like to learn more about the GameLit genre, please join the GameLit Society Facebook group.

LitRPG is a growing subgenre of GameLit – if you are fond of LitRPG, Fantasy, Space Opera, and the Cyberpunk styles of books, please join the LitRPG Books Facebook group.

For other great Facebook groups, visit LitRPG Rebels, LitRPG Forum, and LitRPG and GameLit Readers.

Also, on Amazon, check out the LitRPG storefront for a large selection of LitRPG, GameLit, and Dungeon Core books from the biggest authors in the genre!

If you would like to contact me with any questions, comments, or suggestions for future books you would like to see, you can reach me at jonathanbrooksauthor@gmail.com.

Visit my Patreon page at https://www.patreon.com/jonathanbrooksauthor and become a patron for as little as $2 a month! As a patron, you have access to my current Dungeon Core works-in-progress, as well as advance chapters of the stories I have running on Royal Road. So, if you can't wait to find out what happens next in one of my series, this is the place for you!

I will try to keep my blog updated with any new developments, which you can find on my Author Page on Amazon. In addition, you can check out and like my Facebook page at https://www.facebook.com/dungeoncorejonathanbrooks as well as these other social media sites:

TikTok: @dungeoncorebooks
Instagram: dungeoncorebooks
Reddit: r/dungeoncorebooks
Twitter/X: @DungeonCoreBook
Threads: dungeoncorebooks

To sign up for my mailing list, please visit:
http://eepurl.com/dl0bK5

To learn more about LitRPG, talk to authors including myself, and just have an awesome time, please join the LitRPG Group.

# Books by Jonathan Brooks

**Glendaria Awakens Trilogy**
Dungeon Player (Audiobook available)
Dungeon Crisis (Audiobook available)
Dungeon Guild (Audiobook available)
Glendaria Awakens Trilogy Compilation w/bonus material (Audiobook available)

**Uniworld Online Trilogy (2<sup>nd</sup> Edition)**
The Song Maiden (Audiobook available)
The Song Mistress (Audiobook available)
The Song Matron (Audiobook available)
Uniworld Online Trilogy Compilation (Audiobook available)

**Station Cores Series**
The Station Core (Audiobook available)
The Quizard Mountains (Audiobook available)
The Guardian Guild (Audiobook available)
The Kingdom Rises (Audiobook available)
The Other Core (Audiobook available)
Station Cores Compilation Complete: Books 1-5 (Audiobook available)

**Spirit Cores Series**
Core of Fear (Audiobook available)
Children of Fear (Audiobook available)
Carnival of Fear (Audiobook available)
Community of Fear
Caverns of Fear
Spirit Core Complete Series: Books 1-5

**Dungeon World Series**
Dungeon World (Audiobook available)
Dungeon World 2 (Audiobook available)
Dungeon World 3 (Audiobook available)
Dungeon World 4 (Audiobook available)
Dungeon World 5 (Audiobook available)
Dungeon World Box Set: Books 1-5 (Audiobook available)

**Dungeon Crafting Series**
The Crafter's Dungeon (Audiobook available)
The Crafter's Defense (Audiobook available)
The Crafter's Dilemma (Audiobook available)
The Crafter's Darkness (Audiobook available)
The Crafter's Dominion (Audiobook available)
The Crafter's Dynasty (Audiobook available)
Dungeon Crafting Series: Books 1 – 3 (Audiobook available)
Dungeon Crafting Series: Books 4 – 6 (Audiobook available)

**The Hapless Dungeon Fairy Series**
The Dungeon Fairy (Audiobook available)
The Dungeon Fairy: Two Choices (Audiobook available)
The Dungeon Fairy: Three Lives (Audiobook available)
The Dungeon Fairy: Four Days (Audiobook available)
The Dungeon Fairy: Box Set Books 1-4 (Audiobook available)

**Serious Probabilities Series**
Dungeon of Chance: Even Odds (Audiobook available)
Dungeon of Chance: Double or Nothing (Audiobook available)
Dungeon of Chance: All-in (Audiobook available)
Dungeon of Chance Complete Series: Books 1-3 (Audiobook available)

**The Body's Dungeon (with Jeffrey "Falcon" Logue)**
Bio Dungeon: Symbiote (Audiobook available)
Bio Dungeon: Parasyte (Audiobook available)
Bio Dungeon: Hemostasis (Audiobook available)
Bio Dungeon Omnibus (Audiobook available)

**Tales of Dungeons Anthology**
Tales of Dungeons Vol. 2
Tales of Dungeons Vol. 3
Tales of Dungeons All Hallows 2020

**Dimensional Dungeon Cores**
Core Establishment (Audiobook available)
Core Construction (Audiobook available)
Core Convergence (Audiobook available)
Core Retribution (Audiobook available)
Core Domination (Audiobook available)
Dimensional Dungeon Cores Complete Series

**Holiday Dungeon Core**
Christmas Core (Audiobook available)
Valentine Core (Audiobook available)
Easter Core (Audiobook available)
Independence Core (Audiobook available)
Halloween Core (Audiobook available)
Holiday Dungeon Core Complete Series (Audiobook available)

**Time Core**
Frozen Time (Audiobook available)
Corrupted Time (Audiobook available)
Poisoned Time (Audiobook available)
Scorched Time (Audiobook available)
Time Core Collection Books 1-4

**Magical Fusion**
The Fusionist (Audiobook available)
Academic ConFusion (Audiobook available)
Aetheric InFusion (Audiobook available)
Global DifFusion **(Audiobook coming soon)**
Martial TransFusion **(June 26, 2024)**

**Earthen Contenders**
Unexpected Healer **(Audiobook coming soon)**
Earthen Contenders Book 2 **(May 2024)**

Made in United States
Troutdale, OR
05/10/2024